Being an Introduction

Polarity Unbound

Michael Roth

Printed in the United States of America

First Printing, 2022
Cover Photo: The Three Graces (Aglaia, Euphrosyne and Thalia) by
Antonio Canova

Paperback ISBN: 978-1-7343428-3-3
Library of Congress Control Number: 2022946281

Lensgrinder, Ltd.
Kirkland, WA 98033

Questions, comments, concerns? mtroth@lensgrinder.com

Studies in Phenomenology & Social Philosophy

Lensgrinder, Ltd

Kirkland, WA

To you, dear reader

Being an Introduction

Act One

"...on the one side were people acting like lunatics and on the other people who promised me mere vanities."
— Aurelius Augustinus Hipponensis

The Sleeper Awakens

The Lawyer

"You are Lena F. Michaels?"

"Leh-na, not Lee-na."

"You are Lena F. Michaels?"

"Yes."

"Also known as Eleni Hajivassiliou?"

"Yes."

"I am to read this to you."

"Go on."

"If you try to make a thing, then it will never be right. No making ever turns out right, making isn't right. He said, 'Beware lest a statue slay you.'"

"What does that mean? I'm a scientist, I don't make..."

Her emotion was met with silence. The precise and narrow man did not look up. He continued reading: "He is not saying you shouldn't make things, only that when you do there will inevitably be something wrong with them. Thinghood is the bearer of our flaws. Sequences of the voice and the body, singing and dancing, are just ornate productions in the minds of an audience. Creative power lies in the act of going through it, of setting upon it, and letting whatever you find there happen and disappear. Experiences resonate in the heart. They beat like a heart. Nothing can contain you."

"My whole life... Everything I wanted... ...who is 'he'?"

The lawyer ignored her and continued reading: "I may have failed you, tried to convince you that you were less somehow. I didn't mean it. I could never mean that. Go see my friend. He has something for you."

"Making me feel like... ...telling me what to do..."

"What I always wanted to give you but couldn't without destroying it."

She shook her head and glared at the lawyer standing in front of her.

"I am to give you this," he said looking up and handing her a business card.

"Ben Thorne. The Writer?" she asked.

"You are to call the number on the card. He will take care of the rest."

"Is that everything?"

"Here is your copy. Thank you."

"Goodbye."

Mom

I came in through the garage and took off my shoes. I heard my mother come in from the backyard. She was carrying a leaf blower and set it down near the sliding door wall before coming back into the kitchen. She had been crying, but didn't pause to collect herself, moving furiously about, emptying the dishwasher, putting things away and taking things out. She was intensely focused and didn't notice me, standing just inside the mudroom off the breakfast nook next to the kitchen.

"What are you doing?"

She started and let out a whimper. "You scared me."

There was no way to avoid this. Whenever she was focused and working on something, anything that interrupted what she was doing would startle her.

"Sorry. What are you doing?"

"Making dinner."

"Where is Uncle Georgios?"

"He should be back any minute. How was the car?"

"It was fine."

"You should keep it. I can't drive it. Someone might as well."

"Why can't you drive it? Because it's a stick?"

"I can drive a stick, but something about that car. I don't know. I can't get the seat right. I can't push the clutch completely down to the floor."

"Weird. I was able to do it. Maybe we should try together."

"It's old fashioned. No autopilot. No GPS. Nothing. He insisted. The man never in his entire life owned a smart phone."

Her mind was made up. She didn't want that car. It had been my father's for a long time but had very few miles. He was the only one who ever drove it and he hardly went anywhere. Years ago, he started working from home and whenever they went anywhere together, they took her car. It was nicer and she could drive it, just in case.

"I don't want it," she continued. "It'd be too expensive to get it there. You should take it. He kept it in perfect condition."

"How will I get it back to school? You think it's safe to drive across country by myself?"

"Don't be silly. Your uncle will come with you."

"Doesn't he have to stay here? We can't leave you alone, there's too much to do."

"Your godmother is coming. He can take you and then come back."

I sat down at the table in the breakfast nook. My legs were weak, and I started wobbling. I was weeping. She was too focused to notice. The visions of the near future were overwhelming. I felt like I was breaking apart. Like nothing was reliable, like everything was about to shatter. She would sell this place, leave our home, and go back to Greece. So much was ending, too much was beginning. I couldn't imagine what it would be like not to have family in America, not to have anywhere nearby to call home. What would I be without this place?

I grew up in my mother's house. My father lived there with us, but it was her house. She taught me how to take care of things, all things: leaky faucets, chipping paint, unfinished wood moldings, dry plants, overgrown hedges, dirty dishes, cats and dogs, and dust. My father taught me that my mother took care of these things not because she was a woman and taking care of things was woman's work, but because she was Ermioni Hajivassiliou herself. The one and only. She was like this and so was her mother and her mother's mother and their mothers before them. He told me that she could not help but worry and that —try as any of us might— she could not be dissuaded. We would always try to help, but she was so very particular about how everything had to work and look. If you didn't do it right, she would take the clipper or the brush, the gloves or the paint, out of your hand and do it herself. She wouldn't say anything, she wouldn't be upset, she just wanted it done the way she wanted it done and she was going to make sure it got done that way no matter what.

With my father, she never had any patience. "Where is your book?" or "Don't you have work to do?" and then she would send him off to get him out of her way. With me, she made some effort to show me how to do it right, she would let me practice or watch. She might even describe what she was doing while she was doing it, explaining why it had to be done this way and what effect it would have. Maybe she did it because I was a girl and somewhere deep down she thought these things were women's work. Maybe those mothers before her taught her that without trying.

My dad justified it by saying she was born in Greece and came from a small town there, that things were very *traditional* in the years after she was born and that maybe she couldn't help but see things the way she did. He said we were like that. We couldn't help it. We weren't in control of what experiences we had and the impressions they left. The best we could do was try and understand how it happened and how it led us to where we were. Change was out of the question. He always told me that I could do anything I wanted, but that the most important thing was to figure out why I wanted to do it in the first place. Why *did* I want it? Where did the desire come from? Did it really serve my interests or was it something I was fooled into wanting for someone else?

I wanted my father's car.

This made me cry harder and I couldn't stifle the sounds of my labored breathing any longer. She stopped what she was doing and came over, leaned down, and put her arms around me.

"It was awful. I said horrible things about Dad in front of a stranger."

"You're upset. Whatever it was, you didn't mean it."

"I think I'm angry at him. I have no right, but..."

"What right? If you're angry, then you're angry. Right has nothing to do with it."

"I blamed Dad for things I didn't even know I felt."

"What things?"

"It doesn't matter. They just came out. I wasn't thinking. Why would he send me to that awful man? He was like a machine, discharging his duty. Why couldn't you come with me?"

"I don't know. It was what your father wanted. What happened?"

"I'm supposed to call some writer."

"What for? Do you know why?"

"Not a clue."

"Will you call him?"

"I guess, but how come you don't know anything about this? This doesn't seem like Dad. It was so creepy and weird. Did Dad know Ben Thorne?"

"Ben Thorne? I don't think so. He never mentioned it. That's something you would mention, isn't it? I think he has every one of his books in there. They're on the shelf behind the desk. Sometimes he would write to people after reading their books. Maybe they developed a friendship. He kept that to himself. He could be very secretive about his little projects."

The Minions

Fred Nozick and Carl Maxwell stood in the coffee shop waiting for their order. Ginna and Ben would both be waiting for them today.

"Collectivism is lovely in theory. It's possible to dress it up with poetic descriptions about the power of community. Because everyone has experienced little groups of friends or neighbors that work like that sometimes, we are seduced by those images, thinking these rare occurrences can be made into a social standard."

"They can be, if only we could get the greedy bastards, the pirates, out of our way. They suck everything good out of us for the sake of some sociopathic urge to produce more and more and more for the sake of nothing and to the benefit of no one."

"Yes, I'm familiar with how the poetics work, but that's a ruse. Mostly we suffocate each other. Friendship doesn't scale. Coercion isn't just the property of corporations and unruly governments, it emerges from the masses and constrains the individual. That works out well in most cases, because usually the individual is an idiot."

"The individual is whatever society makes it. If people suck, it's because this war of all against all that we call capitalism produces them that way."

"Them?" Fred asked flippantly.

They got their order and added some extras from the little table near the door. They knew what everyone wanted and how it needed to be finished off with sugar or cinnamon and some milk or non-dairy additive. They had reusable mugs and a reusable cupholder and left the napkins behind. Ginna wouldn't want it any other way, she was always the first one at the office and would do some writing of her own before anyone else arrived. This would be her second cup. Ben was always the last to come and their meeting, if Fred and Carl were required to attend, would start as soon as he got there. He always had decaf.

Their set of morning rituals were perfectly synchronized. Fred and Carl lived nearby and would meet in the coffee shop and then walk up the street to the office together. Carl usually arrived earlier after picking up the mugs and would study until Fred came in. It took him longer because he insisted on long circuitous walks through Williamsburg at the start of every day. He would talk to the shopkeepers and street workers that he would pass along the way. Some of them recognized him, but he would talk to them even if they didn't. Everyone was familiar to him. Carl mostly kept to himself and didn't make eye contact with anyone, keeping his nose buried in his book. Ginna lived a little farther out, but she would head directly to the office and get there first. Neither Fred nor Carl knew where Ben lived and he was always the first to leave in the afternoon, usually for a late lunch appointment, and then they wouldn't see him for the rest of the day.

Today was going to be a little different. They knew he would already be there and waiting for them. Last night it was clear that he wasn't going to leave. After he came back from lunch and locked himself in his office, the phone light in Collaborator was on almost constantly throughout the afternoon. He grumbled a barely audible goodbye through the door when Ginna announced they were leaving. Fred and Carl didn't say anything, and Ben Thorne didn't acknowledge their departure.

"Do you think he's okay?" Ginna asked as they locked the door on their way out.

"Why didn't you ask him," Fred responded sarcastically, making Ginna laugh.

"Was this guy more than just a work associate? Em. Were they related or something?" Carl asked. "He didn't keep any notes on him in the contact list. I thought he was just an editor. If they were such close friends or family, how come he didn't go to the funeral?"

They stepped out into the street and walked up a few doors to the bistro where they would go sometimes for a drink after work. They found a table by the wall near the window.

"He didn't need to put any notes on the contact. They would usually talk on his cell, he would forward me edited emails, strictly business, nothing personal. At least not that I ever saw."

"He was like that with women," Carl said. "He wouldn't talk about

them, but we knew who he was talking to, we always knew a little. We'd
have to get flowers or arrange a plane ticket or something. He didn't want
anyone to know about this guy. It seemed strictly professional. Never used
us for anything, did he?"

Fred and Ginna shook their heads.

"Still, we know he didn't go to the funeral. He couldn't hide that from
us. Why not?"

The conversation got them nowhere, they were stumped, they thought
they knew everything about him.

When Fred and Carl arrived at the office that morning, Ginna was
pacing back and forth between their desks in the bullpen. She took her
coffee from Carl and gestured with her head toward Ben's office.

"He's been in there the whole night."

"Doing what?"

"I don't know. He's not using Collaborator. I have no idea what he's up
to. He took a shower this morning. I heard the toilet flush and his phone."

She went to one of the desks and leaned over the keyboard, touching
the screen. "We're here when you're ready, Ben."

The three of them went into the conference room. Ginna sat just to the
right of Ben's seat at the head of the table and the guys were on the other
side with their backs to the window. She had her tablet and stylus, they just
listened and cradled their coffee mugs.

After a few minutes, Ben walked in looking distracted. He had changed
his clothes from the previous day but still looked disheveled. He was
moving a little slower than usual and didn't have any bounce in his step.
Whatever he did or went through last night didn't suit him.

"Change of plans," he said standing behind his chair. "I am expecting a
call. Her name is Lena. She has my cell number but if I do not answer it,
it will forward to the office. No matter what is going on, if you get this call,
you must find me and interrupt me. It is imperative that I take her call. If
for some reason, she does not call in the next few days, you will have to get
ahold of her."

"How do we do that?" Ginna asked curtly, causing Fred and Carl to
cringe and exchange a frightened look.

"She is a graduate student, for Christ's sake. How hard can it be?"

"Of course, but do you have her last name?"

"Michaels or Hajivassiliou. I do not know which she is using."

"Is that everything?"

He pulled out the chair and sat down, then stared off across the room
and out the window.

"My friend died a few days ago," he said. "A wretched robot of an
attorney is instructing his daughter this morning that she is to call me. She
likely has no idea who I am or why on Earth she should be doing it. I

cannot imagine what she is going through. What she thinks about this."

"Was there a funeral?" Ginna asked, the guys looked at her in awe, they wouldn't have been able to speak if their lives depended on it.

"No. He was cremated. There will be a ceremony later. Just for family and close friends. I do not have details. They do not know about me. His wife... widow, she has so much to do. I do not know... I wish I could..."

Ginna read him perfectly. "Should I look into that? There might be something we can do for her?"

"He did not leave any instructions. Only for the girl."

Carl looked across the table at Ginna, opened his eyes wide and nodded. She looked at him and nodded back. Then she followed with, "What about *Washington and Ashley*, should we keep on with those tasks? We've got quite a bit of research in motion."

"That does not matter. We can delay that. He was not convinced that was the right way to go anyway."

"The other appointments this week, should I cancel them? You're supposed to talk at the New School next week. Who wasn't convinced of what?"

He stood up and walked around the table to the window. There was a large platform ledge with room to sit. He leaned against it and pressed his head to the glass.

"I do not think she is going to call. He wanted that robot to tell her. It must have been awful. He wanted her to wonder who he was. He knew it would hurt her, but he needed to get her to think that maybe there was something she did not know about him. The cat is on the roof. He wanted to wake her up somehow. We will give her a few days, but I do not think she will call. Get ready. Find her. Then I will call her. Let us say Monday. No writing today."

He walked out of the conference room, back into his office, and closed the door.

Fred was the first to speak, "so no more work on *Washington and Ashley*, we're just supposed to stop what we're in the middle of?"

"You heard him," she said.

"Yes, but do the three of us really need to track down some girl who probably isn't trying very hard to stay hidden? Can't one of us just work on that and the others go back to what we were doing?" Ginna scowled at Fred as he was finishing his point.

"We'll find her first and then we can go back," Carl said.

"You guys are unbelievable," Ginna snarled. "Ben Thorne presents us with a few cryptic strands of an unbelievably odd private intrigue, gives us permission to dig into it, and you barely bat an eye. You complain that it'll sidetrack you from your important project of copy editing the master's work or finding out whether some restaurant still exists in the same place after thirty years. When have you ever seen that man get visibly emotional over someone he doesn't know well enough to be sure what last name she's using?"

"It's true," Fred said feeling properly scolded. "He said no writing today and he said *he* would call. This is just too weird."

Ginna was already up and out the door back to her desk to get started. Fred and Carl followed along shortly.

The Office

She walked in without knocking even though the door was closed. She assumed it would be empty and that her mother closed the door to avoid seeing inside. Her uncle Georgios was sitting at the desk. There was an unfamiliar decorative box just to his left.

He stood up when she walked in and went immediately to her. In the space he crossed to get there, she found herself many years ago and sitting on the floor, drawing and scribbling in her book with her pencils and pens. Her father at the desk, whispering something to himself while staring at the screens in front of him. Daddy, what are you saying? It's nothing sweetheart, I just need to hear it out loud to know if it sounds right. What is it though? You have your book there and I have mine here, that's it. Do you put pictures in your book too? More or less, it's like drawing with words. How come you draw with words? My hand isn't very steady so instead of drawing what I see, I describe it. If you practiced, you could draw better. You're right. Why don't you practice then? I am practicing, I'm practicing with the words. Don't you want to get better with your drawing? Very much.

"Lena mou," her uncle said when he got to her at the door. He wrapped his big arms around her and pulled her close to his barrel chest. She felt immediately calmer and lay her head against him. "Look at the dust, no one's been in here in months. Are you sure you want to come in? Your mother can't bear it. There are too many ghosts here."

"Yes, I have to. I am not afraid of them. I think they need me."

"That would not surprise me," he said, letting her go and lightly touching her cheek. "Shall I leave you?"

"What were you doing?"

"Bad things. Things that have to be done. Passwords and accounts, bills. The real terrors we leave behind."

"Mommy needs help. You'll help, won't you?"

"Of course, Lena mou. Ariti is coming too. We'll take care of everything. We'll make your mother let us. We might even be able to make her sit down."

She smiled. "Don't leave. It's better if someone is here. I'm looking for some books."

"There are plenty of those."

"Something specific. Behind the desk. Ben Thorne."

"What about him?"

"I'm supposed to call him. Apparently Dad knew him. Their books are on the same shelf."

She stood up close and saw a single copy of each of the three books her father had written over the years. She hadn't been able to finish reading any of them. One was just his dissertation published shortly after he got his degree. The other two he wrote after working for many years as an engineer. They were technical and not very interesting. She tried to read them a few years ago, but they didn't make much sense. He thought there was something that was taking over our personalities, something that was changing us, making us worse somehow, but she couldn't follow the details.

Her father had been very particular about where his books were placed on the shelves. Lena remembered weird arguments her parents would have. She wanted the books to be color coordinated to maximize visual impact and said they were like wall coverings and should be treated as décor. He thought it was sacrilegious to put some authors close to others and cruel to put others far away from people they should be close to. They were funny arguments full of laughter. It was mostly how she remembered them together, having arguments somewhere between disagreement and teasing.

Ben Thorne's books formed a long line on the same shelf. There were no other books there, whatever space was left was filled with a few trinkets and tchotchkes. The rest of the shelves were packed, and some were overflowing, but this shelf still had room to grow.

She looked at the spines and read them, one by one: *Fragmented. Fabrications. This Year's Harvest. The Middle American. Waymaking. The Lens Grinder's Shadow. The Temple on the Mountain. On Being Born. A Brief History of Thoroughly Requited Love. Time Between Summers. Princess Myshkin. Choreography. Artists of Despair.*

"He has all of them, I think. Cloth bound."

"He must've really liked his work."

"Must have," she said, still looking at the books but afraid to touch them. "I read *Princess Myshkin* when I was in high school. I loved that book."

"Everyone's read that book."

She nodded. "I had to read *The Lens Grinder's Shadow* in college, but I didn't understand it. It was for a class. The narration was impossible."

"Did you see the show they made from *Time Between Summers*?"

"Yes. I liked it, but I never read the book. I always meant to."

Finally, she took the copy of *Artists of Despair* off the shelf. She flipped it over and on the back of the dust cover saw a picture of the author. He wasn't smiling, looked rather severe, and had his arms folded. There was a blurb just above the picture. Usual stuff: list of awards, lives in Brooklyn, etc. Inside the front cover, there was some handwriting on the blank first page. "This one is yours," it said. Then "S.W." in big letters underneath.

"I'm going to take this one," she said.

"Take them all."

"Isn't Mom going to keep them? She shouldn't throw them away. Promise me."

"I can't promise what your mother will do. She'll keep your father's books, but I don't see why she should keep the others. If she wants to read them, she'll use her reader."

"Okay. I'll take them with me then. I think this one was a gift."

The Center

"May I speak with Dr. Holden, please? It's Lena."

"Hi Lena. One moment, I'll get her. Hold on."

"Hi Lena, I was just thinking about you. How are you..."

"I'm so stupid. I thought it would be easier. These last two days..."

"What happened?"

"I went to see that horrible lawyer. Some note Dad left in his will, he read something and then he gave me a business card. I'm supposed to call someone Dad might have known. It was surreal. To top it off, I went into his office and now, I don't know, it's overwhelming. I haven't cried this much in... ...ever."

"Oh Lena. I'm so sorry."

"You've heard of Ben Thorne?"

"Of course."

"I'm supposed to call him. He has something from Dad, or I think he does. The lawyer read something. It was weird because he would read a little and then I would blurt something out. I couldn't help it. He would pause and let me speak and then after I finished, he would just read some more as if I hadn't said anything. I interrupted a couple of times like that. The thing he was reading was from Dad, but the weird thing was that when he gave me a copy, there were like these little line breaks right where I said things."

"What?"

"Yeah. Like these little ellipses, as though he knew I would have something to say right then. It wasn't very long. Just something like how I can be creative or something, or I can know what it feels like to be an artist and that it has nothing to do with making things. 'Beware lest a statue slay you.'"

"That's non-sequitur."

"I know, it was a shock, and it seemed planned out. Like he wanted to shock me. Why would he do that?"

"He must be trying to..."

"The things I said. I didn't realize I was so angry."

"What did you say?"

"Just, I don't know, I was reacting to the message. It pissed me off. Emphasize the process over the result? The goal is the path? What the...?"

"I wonder why he said it. Why such clichés?"

"I don't know, but my reaction was intense. I resented him. Just for a minute, but it was strong. Like I blamed him for making me feel inadequate about accomplishing things."

"Well, you are the poster child. A classic over..."

"I get it, I know, so where did that come from? How did he know it was there? I mean, he must've known. He isn't going to feed me some ridiculous irrelevant platitude unless he knows it'll start just the right conversation, don't you think?"

"That was how things worked with him. Never giving out fatherly advice, he was always about questions and tangents."

"Yeah...."

"Socratic."

"Did that ever bother you?"

"I liked it. He wasn't a phony. He was never a day-to-day father to me. We figured that out long ago."

"I didn't..."

"It happened before you were born."

"Did you ever get angry?"

"Not really. Maybe a little. Teenager stuff. It was around that time when I started to notice how he talked about things, and it was always like that. He'd ask me a question and it might not have anything to do with anything, but somehow it got us going. After a while, it bent around and ended up somewhere important."

"Hmph."

"That was how his mind worked. He thought you had to come at it sideways. Straight on or from behind causes trouble."

"Do you think he's trying to teach me a lesson? As if sitting with my mother and holding his hand while he died wasn't enough. I mean, that'd be pretty cruel."

"He adored you. Whenever I asked him how he was doing, the most important things on his mind were always what you were up to. How you won some science fair or built some mobile app or whatever, learned to play some new song. There was always something. He was so proud of you."

"But that's just what he warned me about."

"Maybe that's why he said something."

"It *is* stressful, trying to be perfect all the time," she laughed, but Mia didn't.

"You think being perfect is about making sure whatever you do comes out perfectly. The perfect experiment, the perfect performance, the perfect test score. Daddy's perfect little girl."

"He knew how much I struggled with that. Why attack me right at the worst possible moment?"

"He wanted you to know there's another way."

"There are a million different ways to do that. Why have a creepy lawyer read some cryptic message in a sterile office where I was supposed to go by myself?"

"It's out of character."

"Yes, that's it exactly. It is out of character."

"It could be the beginning of one of those sideways conversations."

"Do you think I should follow through?"

"Absolutely. I think you have to. What are you supposed to do?"

"Call Ben Thorne and he'll take care of the rest."

"Well, do it."

"I will. Probably. When I get back to school. I'm taking his car. Uncle Georgios might come with me as far as Chicago. My godmother is coming too. And Eirini."

"That's a lot of commotion, are you sure you want to leave in the middle of it?"

"I have to get back. There are some things I need to take care of. I left quickly when he started to get worse. Not sure what my plan is right now. I have to sort that out."

"Can't you do that from out there?"

"I could. I don't know. I think my mom wants me out of the way while they settle some things. She thinks I'll be upset. She's going to pack up and sell everything."

"Doesn't she need your help?"

"I don't know. She's keeping her reasons to herself. Maybe she thinks I'll try to stop her."

"Would you?"

"Yes, and it's selfish. I know that. I want her to keep my childhood home intact. Who cares if she's by herself on the other side of the country, so long as my memories are preserved?"

"Guilt *and* anger. Maybe go a little easier on yourself. Don't you want to be a part of the decisions?"

"No, I'm okay with her taking care of it. They should be her decisions. Intellectually, I know that. Hopefully, my emotions will catch up. I wish she would say it plainly, but that's too much to ask. We're both going through something, but it's different. Losing your father and losing your husband aren't the same."

"I don't like the thought of you two being apart right now."

"We'll talk constantly. She likes it that way. On the phone, I mean. She can share more with me like that. There's something familiar about it to her. She's gotten used to it."

"Did you tell her about the lawyer?"

"Not really. You know how she is. She doesn't like that type of anger. She's way more threatened by women than Dad ever was. She thinks daughters should be dutiful. They never saw eye to eye."

"That's an understatement. He would always have to tell you everything you've overlooked. Tell you you're underselling it."

"Yeah, but he'd be sure to warn you that we've been complicit and needed to cut that shit out. 'No way men could pull that off without women's help. Patriarchy ruins men, and it ruins women by making them like it.'" She laughed after finishing her imitation.

"Geez," Mia said laughing. "Don't get me started, I have to get back to work. Listen Lena, I'd be happy to have you here if you're driving through. You're welcome to stay as long as you like, and Georgios can stay for a few days if he needs to."

"Thanks. Are you coming with me?"

"I'm still thinking about it."

"For the memorial."

"I know. I'm thinking about it."

"That would be great. You have to come."

"I have to go. Text me or call me every day from the road. I want to keep tabs on you guys."

"I will. Love you."

"Love you."

Keramoti

Ariti parked her car just north of the ferry launch and near the taverna where she was meeting her brother. She lived twenty minutes away, in Chrysoupoli, at her mother's house, with her husband and daughter. They lived together in the house where she grew up ever since her father died nearly ten years ago. Her brother, Nikos, lived in Keramoti with his wife and two children. His oldest, Eirini, was about the same age as Ariti's goddaughter in America. She was staying in Chrysoupoli at Ermioni's house but was coming with her father to arrange their departure to Seattle. It was very hot that day, but there was a nice breeze coming off the sea and the sky was perfectly clear when she looked out across the water to Thassos on the other side of the strait that the ferry boats traversed on short schedules during high tourist season.

Passing through the outdoor seating area, across the road and next to the water, she recognized some friends at one of the tables and stopped on her way inside to say hello. They had already heard the news worth hearing so they asked about Eleni and Ermioni and how they were doing. They wanted to know when they were coming home. She waved them off in that way she had by speaking generally about how much worse it was than they imagined. What could Greeks so far from Greece expect? "It's cold out there, people aren't as caring as they should be, they don't have community, they don't have true family. The children leave home when they're still teenagers. It's crazy. But don't worry," she told them, "I'll set things straight."

"Are you going alone?"

"No, I'm taking Ermioni's goddaughter with me."

"What? Renya is going with you? Why? It's so far. She's so young."

"She's twenty-six, and her English is perfect, like a native after her year in England. I never mastered it myself. I understand it, it's necessary, but I don't like to speak it. It makes me sound savage, not knowing the right way to put things."

"Of course. That'd be for the best. She's very clever. And he was her godfather, wasn't he? You shouldn't go alone. With everything that's been going on there. Is it safe?"

"They'll pick us up at the airport. Georgios is there."

"Oh good, good. That's very good. She shouldn't be alone. We must take care of her. Bring her home. You must bring her home."

Ariti left her friends and crossed over the little road running along the harbor. Inside the taverna, Nikos and Eirini were at a table near the front. They stood up and greeted her with kisses and hugs.

Once she was seated, the owner came by and said hello, bringing her a small glass of Retsina. They ordered a few small dishes for the table and Nikos asked her if she wanted some Tsipouro. Eirini was drinking beer.

They brought each other up to speed on family news and told each other about anything interesting from work that may have happened since the last time they saw each other. Since that was just the day before, there wasn't much new to say, but it's surprising how long they could draw that out while waiting for the food. The owner brought the horiatiki, beets, and brazed greens first so they could start eating while waiting for the grilled octopus and Gavros.

While preparing the ice and pouring the Tsipouro, Ariti instructed Nikos about what time they should leave for the airport. They were taking the early flight to get the connection to London from Athens. She'll stay at their house that night and her husband will come with Charlie to get the car later the next day. They could go directly to the airport from Nikos' house. He nodded in agreement.

"How long do we have in London?" Eirini asked.

"No time for you to go running around. Anywhere from 30 minutes to 6 hours."

"What do you mean?" Nikos asked.

"The connection will be tight. If the flight is late, we will have to wait for the next one. It's six hours later. If there's even room."

"It's a big airport, will you have time?"

"If the plane is on time, everything will be fine. It's going to be a long day. There isn't much time between the flight to Athens and the flight to London and then not much time before the flight to Seattle. If we make it the whole way without problems, it'll be a miracle."

"Or just proper airline logistics," Eirini said, teasing her auntie. "That's why they have schedules, not everyone is Greek."

Nikos laughed and put his arm around her, pulling her close. "You need to learn to appreciate what you have, Renya mou. You want to live in a place where people live like they are machines?"

"I'm just saying that British Airways isn't run by Greeks. There's at least a chance that we'll get where we need to be on time."

"That's right," Ariti said. "Organized, on schedule, and cold. That's what we can expect. Nothing like impersonal treatment and orderly queues to get you where you need to go at exactly the time they promised."

Nikos nodded emphatically and poured out the rest of the little bottle between his and his sister's glasses. "You have spoken to Ermioni, what does she say?"

"She is with Georgios and Eleni. They're sorting out a few things and will pick us up at the airport. We may be just in time for dinner."

"She better not be cooking. She should be taking it easy."

"Of course she's cooking. You think Europea's daughter isn't going to be taking care of everyone no matter the circumstances? There's no talking her out of it."

"Well, you must do what you can when you get there. She shouldn't bury her grief. She needs to go through this. What about Eleni? Is she staying?"

"I don't know. She's very American. She has to go back to the Michigan state right away for some reason. Something about school. She left very abruptly. Dropped everything. Ermioni says she has to go take care of some things. Today I found out that she is going to drive her father's car."

"That's across the whole country!" Eirini blurted out, visibly surprised and excited by the news. "Is she going alone?"

"No, Georgios is going with her to make sure she is safe. Then he will fly back."

"Will she come back to Seattle once she has taken care of things or come directly here?"

"I don't know, I'm not sure what her plans are."

"Could I go with them? Maybe that way Georgios wouldn't have to go?"

"Two kids driving across that country alone? It's too dangerous."

"We're not children."

"Niko, your daughter is trying to tell me she is not a child. Is it possible she hasn't learned what these words mean?"

"It might be okay for the two of them to travel together. It can't be that dangerous, can it? Has it really gotten so bad there?"

"Ermioni says everything is falling apart. Everyone hates everyone else. They want to hurt each other, they don't act like countrymen anymore. If you are a city person, you have to stay in the cities. If you are a country person, you have to stay in the country. They are at war with each other. She says it's why she wants to leave."

"Yes, but if Eleni is going to stay, how can Ermioni let that happen?"

"She doesn't want Eleni to stay, she wants her to come back with her, but I don't think they're talking about it. They aren't communicating."

"I could talk to her," Eirini said. "During the drive, I could tell her the great reasons to come here. I'll tell her how nice their house is. She might not remember. She hasn't come for a few years. Has she even seen it since it was completely finished?"

"She is studying at the university," Nikos reminded them. "She doesn't want to come live in a little town."

"I'm sure I could convince her."

"And if you fail, at least you got a nice drive across the country out of it. Shame on you Eirini. Her father just died. This is not the reason for our trip."

"But you said she's going to make that drive anyway. I should be with her to take care of her."

"She has a point, Ariti." Nikos said, eating the last little bit of fish directly from the plate at the edge of the table.

"If Ermioni and Eleni want it, I'll go along," she said while looking off out the window and shutting her eyes.

The man came over, cleared some of the empty plates by handing them to another man hovering nearby, and set a small bottle and glasses on the table.

"I'll message Lena to make sure it's okay."

"Mmhmm."

"Mestixa for the table," he said.

"Thank you, thank you, Mitso."

He poured, distributed, and then set the empty little bottle back on the table.

"Yamas."
"Yamas."
"Yamas."

Emission Analysis Feedback

> It was then in order to include the sleeper that Aristotle
> added the word "potential." (Diogenes Laertius, 1972, p.
> 481)

To include the sleeper? 1) The Greek ὑποπίπτη is a verb form and it is a non-trivial decision to translate it with a noun: the sleeper. 2) Does ὑποπίπτη mean it sleeps or is it more like it succumbs, it goes or falls under ...? 3) Why does the translator think Diogenes is referring to a word that was added? Is it the word that was added, or τὸ δυνάμει itself? 4) Why does the translator suggest Aristotle added it? The philosopher's name does not appear in the original sentence. Isn't this a huge leap? Is he assuming that Diogenes is just a biographer, and that biography has nothing to do with philosophy?

It may not be a sleeper at all. The one who goes under disappears from view and is no longer seen. The one who cannot be seen is the one who is not there, they are closed off and far away.

The hidden one must be included, of course, so there is potential. Including the hidden one may be the only reason why potential or δυναμει has to be added. Why would Aristotle have been so dedicated to the justice of giving each his due that he insisted on adding potential? Who is hypopipte, the one who has gone under, the one who must be included because they withdraw and withdrawing excludes them?

If something must be added to include the one who is not there, then not-being-there must, in fact, exclude. Does not being included mean that going under excludes?

Suppose there is an exclusive club. Anyone or anything that does not meet the criteria for membership will be excluded. The one who is not there does not meet the necessary criteria because being-there is required. Aristotle must add something to allow them to join the club. This is how ordinary grammar might have us understand Diogenes Laertius. Can I expect Diogenes to share our ordinary grammar seeing that he is not, in fact, one of us? Who are we and what relationship do we have to the one who is not there but has the potential to be there? Have I stumbled upon a set of exclusive clubs? If I am not a member or even a possible member, not there *with* them, and not capable of insight into their line of questioning, what hope is there that I will ever gain access to Aristotle's meaning? How will I open the matter for discussion and shed light on these questions? Is Aristotle's thinking exclusive?

I do not speak ancient Greek. Does anyone? I am not a Greek scholar, it is not my area of specialization, so perhaps I have no right to raise these issues and questions. If I cannot enter into ancient Greek philosophy, can I do philosophy? Is philosophy a genre with its roots in ancient Greece and the language spoken there? Is my inability to understand that world precisely the criteria which I lack? Can someone who is not there, who has gone under, do philosophy?

I here continue a project I began many times before by deconstructing exchange-based social systems and unfolding a distributed anti-order for the sake of... well, whatever. I will not, and have not, made plans to know the conclusion of that sentence until the conclusion of this inquiry. Does such a project require that I begin with Aristotle? How can I begin there if it is a locale to which I am denied entry? If I have control over my project's point of departure, why do I insist on beginning in a place where I cannot be, where I have no credentials, from which I have —in actuality— been excluded? Is it perhaps, ultimately, the meaning of exclusion and inclusion that orients this project? If so, perhaps there is no better point of departure. I will be included once potential has been added. Or am I deluded about what I can do? Does adding potential allow me to begin where I choose to begin? If I had the potential to begin there, to be there, it would not have been ridiculous to act as though I were there.

I should start simply. What is potential? It suggests "without which not," meaning that it describes both a possibility and a necessity. It is a required condition for a possible state. To realize that state, the potential must be present beforehand, but being present beforehand is insufficient. The state is not yet achieved and may, should the potential be squandered, never be achieved. Potential, therefore, incites the mystery of being over and against non-being. That which goes under *can* be something that it *is* not. When potential is added, it is included in something other than what it is already. This something other, this something more, stretches beyond not-being-there. Potential makes it more than it was, makes it possible to be-there despite not-being-there yet.

The one who is not there but who has potential can come to be there at any time. They may have gone under, but they have the potential to rise. That which hides is only hidden because it can be found. Going under entails the capacity to rise up. This capacity saturates the one who has gone under with power, the potential to be there yields the power to be there. It has been enabled. It is no longer merely silent but emerges with something to say.

Diogenes writes: "There are two senses of 'potential', one answering to a formed state and the other to its exercise in act. In the latter sense of the

term, he who is awake is said to have soul, in the former he who is asleep."
This power courses through the veins of the one who is there and the one
who is not there. It is the power of what is not there to be there, and it is
the power of what is there to act out. Potential haunts being like a ghost.
Going under excludes one from various things, those things that are part
and parcel of the life and breath of the ones who are there. We say that the
one who has gone under has the power to rise and we say that those who
have arisen have power too. We have the power to rise, and we have the
power, once arisen, to act. We rise up because we can rise up and, once
we do, there is so much more we can do. Rising up opens the ones who
rise to the powers and possibilities of what can be done.

These two senses of potential set the stage for understanding the
relationship between being-there and not-being-there. Potential sets them
off against each other as more than merely two unrelated but opposing
states, rather it puts them into a constant and intense relationship. In
Phaedo, Socrates —while presenting an argument about the immortality of
the soul, a soul that is there and never transformed into something that is
not-there— nonetheless concludes that "...all things which come to be...
...come to be... ...from their opposites if they have such." His purpose may
be to exclude the soul from this transformation that enables movement
from the one to the other, from not-being-there to being-there, from going
under to rising up. An immortal soul has no potential, it is always actual
and never comes to be nor ceases to be. The finite soul, the finite being, is
potential through and through. The one who has gone under and can die
may be transformed into the one who rises up, and the one who rises up
and can die may be transformed into anything, whatever its drive or
determination can make it be.

The act transforms the actor and can do so because it takes place out
in the open. The hidden one does not act and cannot be transformed.
What then does the one who goes under do? Is not-being-there nothing?
Potential enables a relationship between not-being and being. That is the
one sense. It also enables a relationship with action. That is the other sense.
Finding the relationship between these two senses is the inquiry into the
meaning of potential and why it has to be added.

There is the builder who is actually building and the builder who is not
building but who can build. Then there is the builder who is building and
the thing they build which is not yet complete. The one who can build but
who is not currently building has built before. They have completed what
they were building and have not yet begun to build again. They are between
projects, between the acts of their play. The one who has begun but has not
yet finished is there too, between the origin and the end.

There is a relationship of something that is there to something that is
not there, but which can be there. This pattern binds the state of going

under with the state of achievement. The one who goes under has the power to rise up and rising up is the power to make things that did not exist before. Rising and making are the power that lies in being-there. Being-there, out in the open, rising up above what is hidden, amounts to endless powers to make and build. Action repeats the pattern of going under and rising up. The pattern lies in the transformation from one state to another. It lies in the transformation at work in actions that manufacture something that *is* not-there, but which *will be* there, or which *was* not-there, but *is* there now.

Action makes something that wasn't there come to be. If anything goes wrong, that error is embodied in the outcome. It leaves a trace. If everything goes well, that too will be there. For the one who goes under, however, there is no right and wrong, there is no error or success, everything is pure potential, or it is nothing. It is power free of value and corruption, power not yet exposed to the light of that open clearing where action takes place.

Here and there is the world we are making. Not just things, but how it feels and how it seems. Mostly that.

If everything we do has been corrupted by the powers-that-be, what choice is left but to go under?

Only if we go under, can we rise up.

The Circle Begins to Move

Mom

When I came out of my room, my mother got up to greet me. She gave me a kiss and a hug, hiding her face by pulling me toward her. Then she quickly turned away and went to fix me a cup of coffee.

"What can I get you to eat? You want some fruit? Cereal?"

"Mom, why don't you sit down? I can get it. What can I get for you?"

"Don't be silly. The fruit is already cut."

"Then sit down and have some."

"None for me."

"Every day, you cut fruit for Dad. Why?"

"It was good for him."

"Then, wouldn't it be good for you too? Why don't you take care of yourself?"

"I can't eat fruit. It's hard on my stomach if I eat too much. I had some while I was cutting it."

The plate of cut summer fruit was on the table. There were Plums, Peaches, Apricots, Blueberries, and a few Cherries. Mom brought a carton of oat milk to the table and set it next to the box of cereal.

"What else can I get you?"

"Mom, this is fine. I usually just have coffee."

We sat together. I took a sip and cupped the mug with both hands, letting the heat warm my face.

"We could sit outside. It's a nice morning."

"This is fine."

"Okay. Today you should call the auto shop to have the car checked out. You need to make sure it's okay to drive across the country."

"That's a good idea."

"Here is the phone number. They know the car. Your father took it there many times. Ask for Manny."

"Too much information."

"I'm just saying. You'll need to call early to see if they can take care of it right away."

"Okay, I'll call."

"Ariti and Renya are coming tonight. We'll take my car to get them."

"I know, I heard from Eirini. Are we going to pick them up?"

"Of course."

"Will we fit? They'll have luggage."

"We'll fit."

"Eirini said she wants to come with me. Doesn't that make more sense? Uncle Georgios can stay, and you guys can stick with the original plan."

"Two girls alone. I don't like the sound of that."

"It's not a siteseeing tour. We'll be on the highway, we'll stop at properly lit places. It'll be fine."

"We'll see what your uncle thinks."

"Why is it up to him? It's up to us Mom, we can just decide."

"He might have a different idea about it."

I took another sip of coffee. I couldn't talk my mother out of this way of thinking.

"If we leave on Monday, we should be in Chicago by the end of the week. We're going to stay with Mia for a few days, probably through next weekend. Then next Monday I'll drive back to Ann Arbor and see if I can take care of school stuff next week."

"What stuff?"

"I have some tests that I need to move. I just have to make sure I can do that to free up time to come with you. Uncle Georgios can change Eirini's ticket and then she and I can travel together from Michigan."

"Let's wait until Georgios is here, then we can sort it out."

"Fine Mom. I didn't realize scheduling required a penis."

She pursed her lips and nodded. "You don't know everything, Lena," she said. "There may still be a thing or two you can learn." This was one of her favorite things to tell me.

"Like what? Like how to put myself second? To never take care of myself on my own, to always wait on other people and put their happiness before mine. Always trust their judgment and doubt my own."

"You think these are bad things? Relying on other people, putting other people before yourself, listening to their ideas."

"They aren't bad things, but it's bad when it's always women who are doing it and usually doing it for the men in their life."

She looked away and broke off. I tried to turn stony inside, certain she was trying to manipulate me, but I couldn't.

"I'm sorry Mom, but the first thought that occurs to you is to get rid of everything and move back to Greece. Why didn't you and dad move there long ago? If it was something you decided so quickly. Were you just staying here for him?"

"He wanted to go. For many years. I was always the one holding us back."

"Why do you want to move so quickly then? What's the rush?"

"What I want doesn't matter. Obviously. What I want is to get rid of this house, so I don't have to look at it ever again."

"Wait, why doesn't it matter what you want?"

"I can't have what I want. I'm not going to stay here by myself. I have no one here. There's no point."

"You could move to Pennsylvania. You could come live with me. There are other options."

"No. This makes the most sense. Your yiayia is getting old. I should've moved back before, like your father wanted. If it hadn't been for Renya's help, we would have had to."

"Yiayia is like you, she isn't going to let you help her."

"She will. We've talked about it."

"What?"

"She and I will move into our house. Ariti and Thimios will move into Yiayia's house with Despina. They'll have their privacy and it's closer to Nina's school."

"Doesn't that leave Stamatia by herself? That's not going to work. Did Uncle Georgios make up this plan? It's nonsense."

"Don't be smart. Renya will stay with her grandmother. Have some fruit." She moved the plate closer even though it was already easily within reach.

"You're still a young woman, Mom. How old is Yiayia? 87? You could live another thirty years. What do you want to do?"

"It's not about me. It's your time. I don't want to be alone. That's why I'm going back."

"Fine, but what will you do there?"

"There's a lot that needs taking care of. I'll have to take over everything Renya's been doing for us. She should have her own life. She doesn't need to be collecting rent and going to the market for someone else."

"But it's okay for you to do it? Why doesn't Nikos do this or Thimios?"

"I remember your father used to tell me a story about some great work of philosophy that he admired. He said there was a battle to the death that was going on between the master and the slave. Do you know about this?"

"Yes Mom, I know about Hegel's master-slave. I can't believe you know about it."

"Well, then you'll remember that history belongs to the slave, Lena. It's not that these things are woman's work. It's that the men are not capable of taking care of themselves. They don't pay attention to the right details, they don't know how to consider everyone's feelings and well-being."

"So you infantilize them even more by taking care of everything. Is that it? They'd figure it out if we made them do it themselves."

"But you're missing the point of the story. I may not have the education you and your father had, but isn't that the point of the story? The master can't do anything for themselves, their story is in the control of the slave and the slave knows how to do things and how to take care of things. That is why history belongs to them."

"In that story, women have the power only if they become conscious of it. That's the requirement for the slave to take over the narrative. They have to realize who they are. They have to get moving."

"I know. I remember," she said pretending she had already considered that. She smiled and reached out to touch my hair.

"When he would take me to karate class or the range, he would tell me stuff like that. Sometimes I didn't want to go, but he would say how important it was to have physical strength and be able to protect myself. 'Develop your core, Lena. Learn how to stop someone who is coming for you in a tight space.'" She smiled at my imitation.

"You agree with this because your father said it?" she said teasing me.

"No," I resisted. "It's just that... I'm remembering. I mean, he couldn't understand how half the world lived under the constant threat of violence from the other half of the world. Not just violence, but different kinds of harassment. I should say, he understood it, he just couldn't believe it. He told me we were stronger than we thought we were. Not emotionally, we knew about that, but physically stronger. United we're a force."

"Do you still keep up with the karate?"

"A little. Isshen-ryu. Mostly, I kick box. It's great for stress relief and reducing anxiety. My schedule's too crazy to go to a regular class, you can hit the bag anytime. But you're changing the subject. If that applies to me, then it applies to you too."

"I'm too old to change. That's for you now. If you two are going to drive across the country, maybe you should take the Derringer."

"Can I? I'd love to," she had finally succeeded at completely distracting me from the original point.

"Take them both, I'll just be getting rid of them if you don't. They're in the safe in our... my... room."

I stood up and wrapped my arms around her.

"But you should go to the range to practice if you're going to take them. Show Renya. Teach her how."

The Minions

"Freedom, if you can call it that, is just realizing the necessity of your historical position among the forces that are acting on you," Carl said.

"Don't be ridiculous, allocating this basic human spontaneous power to a socio-political structure. I will *is* the expression of power. But to you, we're always a moved mover, is that it? Freedom is more rudimentary than that, it's bound up with virtue and vice. It doesn't depend on what we are conscious of, only on what we are," Fred responded without missing a beat.

Before Carl could reply, Ginna interrupted. "Would you two please be quiet? I'm trying to get some work done."

"What should we be doing?" Carl asked.

"Why don't you go to the library, don't you have research to do?"

"He said to stop working on that."

"That was for me and him. We decided that you two aren't needed for this project. You can keep working on your assignments."

They got up and moved quickly toward the door. As it was closing behind them, she heard Carl say, "Your position depends on bourgeois notions of the person and action..."

She went back to her work and got in nearly an hour of uninterrupted concentration time before the door to the big inner office opened and Ben Thorne stepped out.

"Any luck?" he asked.

"Yes. Easy pickings really. She isn't trying to stay hidden."

"She is a graduate student in Ann Arbor."

"You knew that?"

"Of course I knew that."

"I wish you would've mentioned it yesterday. It would've saved me some time."

"I pay you for your time."

She huffed a heavy sigh and looked sideways at him. He smiled a little apologetically.

"Virginia, you are hardly in need of any help from me to do your job. I knew you could do it."

"Well, okay. She went to the lawyer's office on Thursday morning. We knew that. She's in Seattle and flew there about two weeks ago, just as they started home hospice. He died on Monday, just after noon. She was with him, I think. With her mom too."

"Good. What else?"

"Check. Is that it?" She snapped at him. "I don't think you've processed what that means. She probably saw him take his last breath. The funeral home picked him up more than an hour after he was pronounced dead. They were alone with his body. Don't you have any compassion?"

"I understand the point. That is why this is so urgent. I know what she is going through. Please. Go on."

"She lives in a rental house on the west side of town with three other graduate students. One is in Anthropology with her and the other two are in Sociology. I assume you know the back story."

"Probably. What?"

"She's mostly done with her coursework, and she is due to take her qualifying exams this fall. She doesn't seem terribly focused. The department has a bunch of sub-fields. I think they expect students to concentrate on one area, but she's all over the place. She studies in each of them: physical, cultural, even a little archaeology."

"Like her dad. The limits are artificial to her. What else?"

"She graduated Cum Laude in Computer Science from Stanford and then got a master's degree from there in biology. Had a lot of AP credits so she finished college in three years. Both the graduate schools are top of field programs, and she seems to be on the fellowship track. She's really racking them up. A new one every year just about."

"Probably does everything they want her to do."

"What's that supposed to mean? You know how hard it is for someone to do the things she's doing? Not everyone has the talent to quit a mediocre graduate school two years into a five-year program."

"Ouch. Okay, okay. Point taken. Her dad and I used to argue about that: having the pedigree, publishing in the right journals, being on the fellowship track. They figure out who to give them to from who has already won them. It is a racket. Once you get on the gravy train, it just gets better and better. But if you do not..."

"And you don't think it's because she's brilliant?"

"Of course, she is. I am reminiscing."

"Who is this guy? The one who died."

"Em."

"Your editor?" She sounded suspicious.

"The one and only."

"Why am I just finding out how important he was to you? All these years, you never said anything. You never even said he was your friend."

"What difference does it make? The tragedy is not about me."

She shook her head.

"Do you have anything else? I knew this," he said.

"Again, that would have been helpful yesterday. I got an email address. Might have a phone number, but it might not be current. I'll have to try it to find out."

"Can I see?"

She hands him the tablet.

"You know," she said while he was looking at it. "It's not just your work that's on hold, I was in the middle of something too. The least you could do is let me in on the secret."

"No secret. I am supposed to talk to her. I have been charged with a mission. I cannot talk about it. It is one of the conditions. Legal. You understand."

"Fine. She seems like a bad ass. The computer science gives her a huge edge. She's gotten her name on a bunch of good papers in good journals over the last couple of years. I think it's partly because of her mad programming skills. It's not simply new college grad stuff. She seems to know things. There's some pretty sophisticated modelling going on here."

"I am not surprised."

"It's a shame. This could derail her. I haven't even met her, and I'm worried about her."

"That is why I want to talk to her. I think she needs to hear what I know about her father."

"How long have you known him?"

"Forty-five years. We met our first day of graduate school. We had the same class together and both went outside to smoke afterward. I did the talking as I recall. He looked at me like I was full of shit."

"There it is. I thought so," she sounded as though she were accusing him, and he nodded as though caught. She went on more confidently. "He sounds like a wise man. It takes most people years."

"You joke, but it is true. Keep the ones who can see through you the closest. Remember that."

"Yes, Sensei." A barrier had been broken. She could see him more clearly. Her demeanor changed.

"I am serious," he protested as though sensing the change. "That is why his notes were always so good. He knew when to call me out and never hesitated to do it."

"You usually make people pay for that."

He laughed and went into the bullpen to get closer to the window. The view from there was the same as the one from the conference room next door. She followed him in and stood at the other end of the window as he looked up the street toward the crosswalk at the corner. There were always so many different kinds of people moving about.

"Most people," he went on, "do it because they are basically cruel, or they want to hurt you or take you down a notch. They are not to be trusted. Not him. He pointed to what he saw. It never felt like an accusation, you knew it was coming from the right place. He was the same with everyone."

She nodded, but didn't respond.

"You probably owe him your job."

"How so?"

"You are a lot like him. I saw it the first time we met. It is why I agreed to hire you."

"If I had known there was someone else to blame..."

"Ha, ha. Intellectual integrity is the most important thing, Ginna. Do not lose it. Besides, I think you have learned a thing or two. It cannot have been all bad. You would not have stayed if it were so bad, would you?"

"Of course. Don't go getting soft on me. Where else am I going to make money like this and still get plenty of time for my own work, and actually be encouraged to do it? I appreciate it, I do, and I've learned a lot from you. Your process, how you handle problems. How stories work."

"I have thought about your project a lot this week. The way the group of friends are mourning the one who died. It hits home. I like the stream of consciousness. You have a real knack for it. So non-linear." She searched her mind to recall whether he had ever complimented her work before. Yes, once or twice, but never this clearly. She couldn't respond and left a silent pause in place of where she was supposed to thank him. He went on: "I am glad you appreciate the situation. I appreciate everything you do around here."

"Yeah, yeah," she muttered awkwardly. "Okay, let's not do that. What's the plan?"

"I want to call her. I want to get her here, in person. Maybe we should send Tom and Jerry to go and escort her here. Just to take any guess work out of the equation."

"Carl and Fred."

"Do not be absurd. That cannot be their names. That has to be made up."

"But Tom and Jerry, that's not made up, that seems correct to you?"

"No matter. Where are they anyway?"

"I sent them to the library, they were driving me crazy. Today it was freedom."

"Another one of those vague concepts we use to let people fill in the blanks with their own meaning. Like God or Happiness. We can only be convinced to kill and die for those kinds of words."

"You never give them any credit. We vetted them. I would think you would appreciate that from your research interns."

"Whatever you say. What else have you got?"

"She has a house in Greece and is going there in a few weeks."

"Really? Her house, not her parents?"

"I did a little digging. It's normal there. The parents sign the house over to the kids while they're still alive. They built the house and then gave it to her when it was finished. It's probably still her mother's house. In practice. On paper, though, she owns it."

"Ah yes. Is it worth anything?"

"It's a small town in the north, not very desirable real estate, but still, it's worth something. There was an article about it."

"When?"

"In New Jersey, about five years ago. Apparently, they sent an electric heat pump over there and had a couple of New Jersey guys go and install it. The story is about the locals who did the installation. They don't usually use this type of heating and cooling system there, it's too expensive. They don't have residential gas either. People use oil to heat their houses, and even though it's really hot, they have these little wall units for air conditioning. So, they sent the heat pump to provide central air and heating. Then they put these solar panels on the roof to pay for it. The story was about how these guys were helping the homeowners with a sustainable energy solution."

"I heard about that when they were doing it."

"You talked with someone about heat pumps?"

"Whatever was on his mind. It would never just be about heat pumps, he would tell the story as though it were a world historical event culminating in this tiny action carried out in some out of the way corner of the world. That was history realizing itself in the mundane. The man could make connections like no one you have ever met."

"It would have to be something like that to keep your attention."

"Listen, book the tickets for Tom and Jerry. Send them to Seattle to make sure everything is okay. Kidding aside, are you sure we can trust them?"

"They're not morons, but shouldn't we check with her first? You can't just go off and interfere like that."

"Sure, of course. Try to contact her today, but we should be ready. Get them there ASAP."

"I thought we were going to give her some time to call first?"

"She is not going to call. She thinks this can wait. The more I think about it, the more I think it cannot. Verify that phone number and let me know."

The Boys

Nikos came in first and sat with the bartender until Charlie arrived. It was only just after six and still hot out, so the place was closed up with the air conditioner running. They talked about small matters until Horacio joined them. This was a place for younger people, but they met there out of habit just as they drank the local beer from the tap. Normally a boisterous bunch, they were somber at first. They raised their glasses.

"To Em," they said, and then they drank.

"I didn't come half away around the world to drink beer from Ireland and Whiskey from Kentucky," Charlie said. The others laughed, remembering. The bartender brought a plate of chips and olives.

"You expect us to drink without eating something, what are we savages," Horacio recited causing their laughter to continue.

"Guys," Nikos interrupted, "You are forgetting what Spinoza would say."

They roared with delight.

Then their laughter trailed off.

"What happened?" Charlie asked. "Do you have details?"

"Well," Nikos responded. "Of course, you knew he stopped treatment. There was no hope, they said, but he was okay for a while. Then a few weeks ago, something clicked. They're not sure. He just went downhill very fast and then, that was it."

"He died over the weekend?" Horacio asked.

"Early Monday afternoon."

"What about Ermioni? How is she doing?"

"I don't really know. We'll get more information once Ariti and Renya get there. They're on their way now. Georgios and Lena are already there."

"She's coming home though, isn't she?"

"Yes. She made up her mind immediately. Very determined to do it fast. I think she wants to get away from that house as quickly as she can."

They nodded.

"At least their house here is done."

They smiled at the thought.

"How many years did it take him to convince her to build that house and start living in it part time?"

"Many. She hated the heat in the summer and the cold in the winter. She said she was miserable and couldn't wait to leave. There was no way she was going to come back, but he was determined."

"That's why he went to so much trouble with the heating and cooling. What a fiasco."

"He was determined to build that house with local resources, but no one knew anything about those things. Who has a heat pump? No one knows anything about it."

"He had no choice."

"No one talked about anything else that whole month."

"I know. Everywhere I went, anyone who came into the shop, no matter what. What's happening with the heat pump?"

"We don't even have a word for it, so everyone is saying the English word. Heat pump heat pump heat pump. It was so funny."

"He was smart to share that with everyone. We learned about them. He knew maintenance was going to be the real problem. He wanted folks around here to learn about it, he thought maybe they might learn how to do repairs. Remember, he sent Ion to that course."

"Everyone thought he was touched."

"Is she going to live there by herself?"

"Europea might move in with her."

"But where would Renya go?" Horacio asked.

"I suppose she could move in with Stamatia if Thimios and Ariti move into Europea's house. Despina thinks she should be allowed to move in with them. She says she can keep her company."

"Ariti's Nina?" Charlie asked.

Nikos nodded. "We thought he was foolish, but that house really is the best place in the whole town on days like these, or in the dead of winter."

"True," they both agreed.

"I think Ermioni was pleased in the end. He only wanted to make her happy."

"I don't know if I'll ever be allowed in there again, she wasn't my biggest fan," Horacio said looking down into his glass.

"What about me, mate? Without Em, I don't think either of us will be invited over much."

"Well, she and I grew up together," Nikos responded. "So, she gave me a break, but I don't think she thought any of us were a good influence. When we would get together, when we would stay out the whole night, she thought we were to blame. She worried."

"If she only knew."

"Exactly. She thought he was so innocent. He just wants to be left alone with his book and his pen. She never knew how much of an instigator he was."

"She knew," Horacio said. "Of course she knew."

"Of course, she knew. He was a prankster. Subtle though. Not what I expected."

"Not what any of us expected," Horacio said.

"Did you guys ever hear his theories about women?" Nikos asked.

"What theories?"

"Not really theories, more like observations that he swore by and said were the key to survival when living with a woman."

"Oh, this is juicy. You have to enlighten us."

"First, every woman he'd ever known has some part of her body that she likes. It's true, she's critical of things, but there is always at least one thing she likes. And when she dresses up, she'll emphasize it. You got to pick up on that. It might not be something men care about: it might be her wrists or her neck or something, but it might be, it could be her butt or her breasts. He said you have to figure out what it is, and you have to keep it in mind, but don't let on that you know."

"For compliments?"

"For that," Nikos responded. "And also, to understand what makes her self-conscious and her heartbreak as she gets older. Which brings us to the second point. Every woman he'd ever known was unprepared to handle rejection. As girls, they don't learn it by practicing with the kids they like, boys I mean. When they don't learn to handle rejection as children, they have blind spots when they're adults. They come up with explanations whenever they face rejection. Sometimes the difference between a normal reaction and missing the point entirely depends on it."

"I get it," Horacio said. "Sometimes maybe it's because she's a woman, but sometimes it's because there's someone better. It could happen to anyone. My ex-wife couldn't tell the difference."

"I can't tell the difference either, mate," Charlie said. "Now the kids are the same way, none of them can handle rejection. If he'd been an official member of the ex-pats club, we would have learned this long ago, and it might've saved us a lot of grief."

"He really wanted to be one, a member of the club I mean."

"It's true," Nikos said getting more excited. "It brought them together. Both Ermioni and Em wanted to be ex-pats. Because they were from different countries, it was impossible."

They laughed.

"Did you guys ever hear the passport story?"

They shook their heads.

"They were in Kavala renewing her passport. They had to do this regularly, so he had been there with her before. Apparently, he didn't like the way the office was run. He brought a role of tickets, perforated and with a number on each one. He said they were very common in America. At the police station he handed them out to the people as they arrived to get in line. The entry area there would get very crowded, and no one knew who was next or who came before and who was after. Ermioni said the people loved it. Em pleaded with the clerks at the office. He said they should just get these and have people take a number. Track the number and call out the next one."

"They thought he was off his rocker."

"Sure, where can you get such things? We don't have orderly queues here."

"Mostly he appreciated things here. That was the only thing I remember him wanting to change. The bureaucracy is terrible. Even he couldn't pretend to like it."

"She must've grown used to America. It'll be hard to come back."

"I think so too. When they'd come, it was hard on her. She would complain. So many dogs and cats in the streets. They made her sad. She wanted to take care of them."

"Didn't Constantinos tell us Em had something to do with that whole thing about rounding them up and having them spayed and neutered?"

"That amnesty center, that's right. Everybody knew about that," Horacio said. "They were a tiny little organization. Just a few people. Em must've given them money or got them some from somewhere. Now they have an office and staff."

"They had donors," Nikos said. "But the problem is still bad, and you know Ermioni, she'll be feeding the cats and dogs on her street. More will come."

"Ermioni is just like Europea," Horacio added. "She'll be feeding everyone, not just the cats and dogs. If she's here the whole year, everyone will go to her house. Especially with that heat pump. It'll be the town center."

"Does she want that?" Charlie asked.

"It's hard to tell with her. She gets so focused on taking care of everything. She gets stressed making sure everyone has what they need. She doesn't look like she's having fun, but I don't know. I think she needs to be like that."

"What did Em say?"

"He said it isn't about fun and happiness. Sometimes people need to do things that put them in a certain state of mind. They need to be like that and everyone else lets them. They're focused, but it's not fun."

"Like with my work," Horacio said. "When I take photographs and am trying to figure out which are the best and how to present them to my customers. It isn't fun, it's delicate work and stresses me out, but I'm used to it. I don't know what I'd do without it."

"But I think..." Nikos started to say.

"Yes," Charlie jumped in. "Em said something about it to me too. He told me we do it to ourselves. He told me it goes back to Aristotle somehow."

They laughed.

"That's right," Nikos remembered. "Something about flourishing and the state of the soul. It isn't the same as fun and being jolly. It had to do with doing things you can do. Your virtues, but there are bad things too. Pathological things. He knew the ancient words. Doing things you could do and doing them well if you can, getting anxious if you can't."

"This is true for Ermioni, then?"

"I don't know," Nikos said. "Growing up, I remember Europea exactly the same way. They need to be in the thick of things like that: looking after everyone. Focused and anxious. It's not servitude. Not exactly. It's a skill and they constantly worry they're doing it wrong."

"She loved what he was doing for the cats and dogs."

"She worried. Everybody liked it, but she kept worrying. People saw them differently and she knew that."

"I'll miss that bloke," Charlie said. "It isn't often you meet someone who'll tell you a fart joke and then explain why it resonates with recent philosophy."

"To Em," they said. Then they drank.

The Center

"Mia, why are you even here? I thought you were going to take time off."

"I will. I will. My sister is coming next week. This one case needs my attention now though."

"Which one?"

"S. Taylor. Three children. Abusive boyfriend. She keeps going back to him. I don't know how to get through to her."

"She thinks he's going to change."

"No, I don't think so. She's not delusional. She gets away and then thinks she'll never get anything better, so she goes back. She thinks she has no other options, and she doesn't deserve better. Resignation to fate."

"It can't be a shock."

"Every time, it's still frustrating. Did the check come?"

"It did. I guess we can keep it together for another quarter."

"I keep thinking this magical benefactor is going to disappear."

"Shall we have a drink?"

Gwen swung the door closed and Mia took a bottle from the cabinet behind the desk. She poured a little into a couple of small glasses.

"The weekend."

They took a sip.

"He was your father then?"

"My biological father. He was never really my father. He and my mom were friends, and she wanted a kid. He was more like a donor. He didn't even know me until I was 7 or 8, I think. Once I found out about him, he took an interest right away. He would send me things, birthday presents and stuff. He wrote to me, called me now and then. Nothing too much really, but he was there. No rights or anything."

"You had a relationship? Your whole life?"

"Yeah. It developed as I got older. I went to Europe with him and his wife just before I started high school. That was before my half-sister was born. After that, I would call him sometimes. He was a good listener and didn't talk to me like a child. I would tell him things, and he would listen, ask me questions. Never judged or argued with me. Well, he argued with me. But he didn't judge. I remember he was one of the first people I talked to about misogyny. This was back in high school. He might've even been the one to teach me the word. Or maybe it was my mom. Still, he recommended books to read. Classics. Mary Daly, Judith Butler, Donna Haraway. MacKinnon, of course."

"Really?"

"Yeah. When I was in college, he would listen to me while I arrogantly explained everything to him. He was so encouraging. I mean, he was never a dad, but he was there. He had a lot of influence. It's a loss."

"Of course." She reached out and touched Mia's hand.

"When I was considering graduate schools and trying to figure out whether I should do the joint PhD Law degree, a lot of people I talked to thought it would be too much. He never did. He was sure I could do it. It made a difference."

"Your mom and dad must've been supportive."

"They were, but they worried. They thought I might be putting too much pressure on myself. Sure, you don't want to overdo it, Em said, but you're pretty damn tough."

"I'm so sorry."

"You know, his wife, my sister's mother, she was a stay-at-home mom. Very domestic. I said so many harsh things about her when I was in college. Even when I was in grad school. I accused him of hypocrisy and exploitation. He was so patient. He didn't get defensive."

"What did he do?"

"He would explain. Not everyone is the same. The whole point is for women to define womanhood for themselves. You have to allow people to have different perspectives. I thought he sounded like such a liberal."

They laughed.

"It sunk in though. I think of that every day. Every woman I work with has a different story. They need different things, want different things. You can't put them in the same category."

"So, you stopped thinking he was a hypocrite?"

"Well, we would still joke about it. He said it was a process, not a thing you could just turn off. He was probably the reason I came at women's studies through sociology. He was always explaining how institutions do so much of our thinking for us and how hard it is to use one against the other when trying to think for yourself."

"What do you mean?"

"Well, like he said that one of the purposes of feminism was to provide an alternative form of thinking to fall back on when trying to combat patriarchal attitudes in yourself. Patriarchal thinking was deep in his own education, and he read feminism to try and train himself to react and respond differently, with a different order in mind. He said this was true of women too, of me, and that I shouldn't be embarrassed about anything residual."

"Sounds pretty open-minded. When did you come out to him?"

"You know, it's funny, but in a way, I never really did. I remember coming out to my mom and dad. That was a very definite moment. Last year of high school. We sat down together and had this very formal talk. But with him, there was nothing like that. We would talk about who I liked or how I felt about stuff like that. Things I saw or was reacting to. I always told him the truth. He knew it as I started to know it."

"You were lucky to have someone like that. You don't think he's our benefactor, do you?"

"I don't think he had that kind of money. Plus, he had his own family to take care of."

"Yeah, of course, is your sister doing okay?"

"I don't know, I'm sure you can imagine. It's way harder on her. It's a lot to handle at her age, at any age really."

"How old is she?"

"Twenty-six."

"Oh, she's a lot younger than you."

"Yes, and she was very close to him. Ever since she moved away from home, he was texting every day. 'Good morning, extraordinary human.'"

"That's sweet."

"She was so funny about it. Pretending to laugh at him, but she loved it. I'm really dying for her to get here so I can put my arms around her. She's such a sweety. Just like her mom, and as brilliant a person as you will ever meet."

"She sounds amazing."

"Em always worried about her. He thought she got the focus and intensity from them and none of the silly fun-loving parts. He worried she was too serious."

"Is it true? Was he right to worry?"

"I think so. She's very serious. I think she feels guilty if she has too much fun, so she's always holding something back. Like if she ever really let loose, it would be just too damn much for anyone to handle. That was his take anyway."

"Well, I'm glad you two are going to get to see each other next week, and you really have to take some time off to grieve and let yourself heal. We'll take care of things around here, take as long as you need. Don't go thinking we can't manage without you. I mean, we'll miss you, but we can manage."

"I will, I know. Thanks for saying that, and thanks for stopping in. We should have dinner later. Why don't you come by?"

"Absolutely, that'd be great," she said. They stood up and hugged. Gwen opened the door and walked out as Mia started to collect her things.

Arrival

They walked out of the customs area and into the arrival terminal where they were greeted by the three of them, hopping and bouncing to draw their attention. It was sensory overload and they collapsed into a hugging machine that paired them off in sequences, repeating and permuting, bringing tears and laughter. Welcomers and travelers couldn't keep their histories straight and would sometimes pair off among themselves from the sheer joy of it. It had been too long and too much had happened. There was no calming them into conversation. When once they completed the circuit, they started it again with equal vigor and feeling. In the end, Georgios was left towing two suitcases while Ariti and Ermioni walked arm-in-arm. Eirini could not stop hugging Eleni and when they started toward the elevator up to the skyway to the parking garage, she kept both arms around her. She did not relax her grip, not when they came to the car and not after they climbed into the back seat.

Not a multi-tasker, Ermioni in the driver seat stayed focused on getting them out of the parking garage and onto the road. Ariti, in the passenger seat, immediately organized herself in preparation to provide whatever moral support was needed for navigation. She rattled through a list of questions to ensure that Ermioni's focus was where it was supposed to be, and that she had everything she needed to carry through on her assignment: parking ticket, glasses, wallet. Check. They fell right into the patterns they developed growing up together.

In the backseat, Eirini's two-armed walking hug transformed into a seated embrace with petting and nuzzling. Eleni, in the center seat, leaned against her sister-in-spirit and let her work her magical hospitality, never minding that she was the guest. One arm around her back and stroking her hair, the other across her chest and gripping her shoulder, neither showed any signs of letting go.

This left Georgios to take charge of the necessary conversation: how was the flight? Did you have any trouble making the connections? How was customs? Did the bloody English give you any troubles? Were the Americans their usual suspicious selves? Eleni took up too much space in Eirini's attention for her to process the questions, so once again the navigator was left to set everything right and follow through with the imposing order.

The time in Athens had been tight, they had to hurry across the airport to make the connection. Ariti made a mistake with the layover in London. The time difference had confused her. She thought the layover there was short, but when they arrived Eirini figured out that it was much longer. They had plenty of time in London and were able to get a nice English Breakfast in the airport while waiting for the flight to Seattle. The British had been fine, since they were just passing through, only the people who were staying got the third degree. Of course, the Americans were suspicious of anyone who didn't speak English but having a young translator along for the trip helped and the custom officers had seen it all before. They were exhausted, but mostly unharmed by the stress of inter-continental travel.

Eleni was leaning against Eirini and remembering how warm her Greek family was. She always forgot during the time away from them how much they show and how openly they feel. Her mother was not like them and that could be the reason she forgot. It explained so much. The way she fell into it so easily when they were reunited, and then went so easily back when they were gone. It's true, her grandmother is like her mother, but it's not common. The others reached out and took hold, they pulled her into their homes and their lives, they accepted her so quickly as family. Her mom and dad were only warm at a distance, on a call or in a text, but the Greeks were that way up close. How is it that they showed her more love and warmth than her own parents? She remembered thinking this way back during some of her early visits. How strange it was that these people who were not her blood relations would take hold of her and claim her for their sister or daughter. The hospitality they were famous for extended even to the quirks of character that made her own mother resist it. Ariti knew better than anyone what Ermioni was like, and it didn't put her off, it brought her closer, it's why she hugged her so many times, remembering her as she was throughout the years.

Eleni finally sat a little forward and came up for air. She tried to say something. She understood everything perfectly, but her speech was rusty. She gave it a go: "You are not travelers. You are not tourists. At these times, you must be visitors."

The whole car erupted in joy, Eirini kissed her on the top of her head. Georgios patted her on the knee and even her mother laughed at the adorable accent and awkward phrasing. "Have you been practicing?" Ariti asked.

"This is it," she said continuing her effort. "This is practice."

More laughter and more kisses. She laughed and leaned back again. She kept smiling while thinking how no one had said how sorry they were, no one had consoled them for their loss. It was so good to be with family like this. How have I gone so long without it, she wondered. She remembered the last time her parents went to Greece, and how they begged her to go with them, but she was too busy. She had so much to read and so much work to do for her courses and her studies. There was no time. Never any time. She shuddered at what she missed. The house at the edge of town with the chickens next door. The visits and the pastries. Watching her mother devour Bugatsa for breakfast, enjoying it so much she couldn't speak. Her father relaxed and taking a break from constant work. They were different people over there, and she was too busy to be there with them. She turned a little toward Eirini and wrapped her arms around her.

"I'm so glad you're here, Renya."

"Lena mou," she said.

After pulling into the garage, Georgios took the luggage inside. He put Eirini's bag in Eleni's room and Ariti's bag in Ermioni's. There was no discussion to decide this. Eleni took Eirini by the hand and led her into the house saying, "This is the car I told you about. We need to take it to the mechanic tomorrow to make sure everything is okay for the drive. You can see it then. Come inside now." She led her in and pulled her through the house showing her around. Ariti and Ermioni went right to the kitchen. Ermioni showed her what was cooking and they started getting things ready to eat. Eleni came running back out to the kitchen with a box of treats Eirini brought from the bakery in Xanthi.

"First we'll eat, then we can have that," Ermioni said. "Get the table ready."

Eleni put the box of sweets down on the kitchen counter and started getting the table ready. Eirini didn't follow her out after handing over the treasure. She stayed in the bedroom, fascinated with the decorations. Everything was still intact from when Eleni had lived there as a teenager. She was exhausted and laid down on the bed and looked around at the drawings and pictures, the books, and knickknacks. She smiled and stretched out pulling the pillow tight to her chest and letting her eyes wander over the walls and shelves. "So many books," she said when Eleni poked her head back in to see what was keeping her. She hopped up on the bed and looked down at Eirini. "Are you so tired? Do you want to come eat?"

"Of course, I wouldn't miss your mom's cooking for anything, but I am looking forward to sleeping too."

"Come on," she said, and they both jumped up and went back into the kitchen. Georgios and Ariti were sitting at the table where plates of food were already filling the space between them. Eirini joined them while Eleni went to her mother to see if she needed any more help.

"Go sit. Just making the dressing and then I'm coming."

The Office

The visitors went to sleep shortly after they finished eating. Lena did the dishes under Ermioni's watchful eye. That goes on the upper shelf of the dish washer. That needs to soak first. That sponge is only for the countertop, this is the one we use on dishes. When she was done, she hugged her mother and went into her dad's office leaving her mom with Georgios in the living room watching TV.

The box Georgios had on the desk when she caught him in there the other day was still there. She sat in front of it and looked straight at it. "This copy of the book," she said holding her hand up to show it to the box, "has never been read. I can tell."

She leaned back and put her feet up on the desk next to the box, then opened the book across her lap.

"Thinking. Doing. Being," she read aloud and then looked over at the box. She got up and put the book down, then turned to the shelf where the others stood side-by-side. She took them down and examined each of them in turn, looking at the spine and then opening the book to view the first page. Every single one of them had something written there with those same initials underneath. S.W. The writing didn't make sense. In one of the books, it said "Never anything else." Another said, "You're late." No discernible pattern, she was puzzled and sat back down again, getting into the same reading pose with the book in her lap. "Thinking. Doing. Being," she read aloud and looked up at the box.

"That's the table of contents. Part One: Thinking, subtitle Confidence. Part Two: Doing, subtitle Arrogance. Part Three: Being, subtitle Performance. That's what it says. Those are the main parts. Who is S.W. Dad? Why did he give you a copy of Ben Thorne's *Artists of Despair* and inscribe it with 'This one's yours'? If I ask Ben Thorne, will he know? Is that why you want me to call him?"

The table of contents looked like a work in philosophy. The chapters under each of the three parts talked about time and space, the categories of perception, a universal command for action, and the rules of associating the two. Then when she turned to the first few lines of the content, she saw that it wasn't philosophy, but a story about a fine artist forced to go to work for some giant mega corporation. He described his surrender to necessity as though it were death. The main character was giving up everything he cared about, everything that mattered to him. Whatever would be the object of his attention or the subject of his concentration, he was foregoing that to begin his life caring for and concerned about the projects and purposes of this giant corporation. Anxiety was pervasive.

She couldn't get into it. Not because there was anything wrong with the writing or the story, it was inviting, but what kept distracting her were the disconnects between these different pointers and cues. What was this book supposed to be? Obviously, it was polished, obviously it had been produced by someone skilled at writing stories to entertain, but what was going on? The painter was falling into something, or falling off of something. The new job gave him vertigo and dropped him off whatever high pedestal he stood on while painting.

It reminded her of how she felt that whole last month, how fragmented and disoriented she was. She recalled those pajamas he would never wear and his last breath, how she didn't know it was his last breath until an eternity afterward when he didn't take another. That shattered the fragments, that realization, that moment when she knew the last time had passed.

She shook her head and went back to the book. There was a fragmentary description of a painting on an easel in the artist's studio and then another of a print on the wall of the lobby in a corporate building. There was his arm at work moving the brush back and forth across the canvas, then there was his arm scanning a badge over a reader causing a door to click allowing him to pull it open and walk through.

The offsets were on the nose, but they were jarring, and reflected in the style. The voice of the narrator changed depending on which view it occupied. There was the corporate voice and the artist's voice. They seemed to be dueling, going back and forth, describing the one world over and against the other, describing the power of the one over and against the power of the other. This shocked her in ways she hadn't expected. Her initial impression was that she was following the artist's maneuvers in the middle of his death throes as he became a corporate robot. Those impressions were undermined when she realized that the other descriptions could destroy the corporate mindset too. The death knell resonated both ways. They kept going back and forth and it soon became clear that it was not yet determined which of the two voices would win the day.

This first section wasn't very long, but by the time she reached its end she felt confident she understood exactly what the whole book would be about. She was certain it would unfold as a battle between worldviews forced to live side by side but each capable of destroying the other and being destroyed by it. She couldn't predict which side would come out on top.

"Suppose I'm right," she said out loud looking up at the box again. "That just pits the life of the artist against the life of some corporate agent. What does philosophy have to do with any of that? Why does the table of contents make you think you are reading philosophy? Is that why you liked this writer, Dad? Did you think he understood something that you had been trying to figure out? Did he bring it together for you?"

She leaned back and looked up at the ceiling, letting the book sink down in her lap. "You were always so busy. I have so many memories of you working. Sometimes I was just dying for your attention. That was always magical. You liked it when I would explain things to you. Do you realize that you were never more attentive than when I was explaining the geometric proofs I learned in school? You made me write them on your white board. That precious space where only you were allowed to put things, but you erased everything and handed me the marker, 'Show me,' you said.

"I remember riding bikes together or going to the aquarium and the art museum all those times, but you were distracted, and Mom was the one doing the talking and leading. You were off somewhere on some flight of fancy, but you weren't distracted when I explained how cells worked, or when I showed you how to render data using a Single-Page-Application. I guess you weren't faking it, pretending to be interested in things you already knew or didn't care about, but you're supposed to do that with your kids, Dad. Everyone thinks you were so perfect and so enlightened. It wasn't easy being your daughter.

"You would answer every question I asked you and the more you knew about the subject, the longer you would talk. I figured that out early. I would ask you questions about things, and you would talk and talk and talk. One of the longest conversations we ever had when I was in college was when I told you one of my professors told us that 'Big Data' was bullshit and even though everyone says they know what it is, no one really does, and everyone who says they know how to do it is lying.

"Do you remember what you said? 'That is false,' and then you went on and on about how organizations know things, and how there are big companies building giant platforms for data movement and storage. Rivers and oceans of data coming from everywhere and constantly in motion, churning and circling around. You said you personally knew dozens of people who were experts, that the company you worked for employed some of the smartest people anyone could ever hope to meet, and they were devoted to it. 'But we're not theorists,' you warned me, as if that was the worst thing in the world. 'We're not trying to explain these systems to people, we're not trying to argue about their ethical significance or their relevance to social or political goals. No, we were just building them. Quietly. Your professor probably only listens to loud mouths.'

"That conversation went on for an entire semester. I kept bringing it up with you. It would keep us on the phone. I don't think I cared that much about it, my professor was just joking, and it wasn't a big part of the class, but you loved to go on about how important real skills are and how different they are from what these professors do in their lectures.

"Is that why this book mattered to you? Is that why your friend thought it was yours? Was it because that company you worked for was inside your brain, inside your body, your fingers, when you practiced those skills, when you did that work, when you were giving them so much of yourself?"

She shook her head and sat up in the chair. She tried to read a while longer, but was agitated and couldn't concentrate. She left the book on the desk and went back to her room where she slid under the covers and curled up close to Eirini. It was lovely to drift off in a warm bed listening to the rhythms of her soft breathing nearby.

Emission Analysis Feedback

It is a circuitous route. We start with the soul, and it becomes breath. Breathing becomes movement and movement becomes desire. Then desire shall become will and reason actualizing what was merely potential. The one who goes under finds herself inside a circle and the circle begins to move. Moving in a circle, she wants to get where she is going, she plots a path, and realizes it once she gets there.

Thomas Aquinas would say we are starting with *De Anima*. Aristotle would say *Peri Psychēs*. *On the Soul*. Aquinas, from the *Summa of Christian Teaching*, writes: "In other places Aristotle likewise speaks this way, as when he speaks of the first mover moving itself by understanding and willing and loving itself (*De Anima* 433b15)."

Aquinas refers to Aristotle's investigations on the nature of the soul. What is the soul? *Psyche*, from the verb *psychein* meaning to breathe. Breathing is made of two distinct parts: inhaling and exhaling. In and out. And then again. And again. And again. When we are excited, we breathe hard, with calm comes soft breath. The body speaks the soul's movement, perhaps even does its work when it strives to move, puts it to work in the body's breathing, and sets in motion actions appropriating nearby objects: the body has a mind of its own.

Movement includes its origin. It incites it. Moving by pushing and pulling, by being pushed or being pulled, both pushed and pulled. In and out. In the origin we find both the beginning of the movement and its end. The point at the center of the wheel is both the beginning and the end of the wheel's movement, the origin of breath is the fixed point between exhaling and inhaling. With it, we can move the world.

The body is the actualization of the soul. Remain calm. Just breathe. Desire will quicken the breath and fix upon what it wants, it points the being-complete this way or that way, it pushes it there and pulls what is there closer to it. The body, somebody, anybody, begins to move.

How can something be both a beginning and an end? The soul is more than just desire, it is also understanding or mind. *Nous.* They are interleaved, they work together to visualize and take hold. We are speaking of something that originates movement, of something that is specifically one. It plots a path and achieves an end that it already had in mind, that it already understood, that it already wanted. Even if it doesn't know, it understands. The principle of movement is that final cause which sets things in motion, which causes the movement to take place. It is the mark from which movement comes and that toward which it aims. The final cause is both an end and a beginning, it contains coincidentally both the origin of the movement and its end.

Let's back-up. Technically, the center of a circle is a logical point. To discover the geometric center of any given circle, one begins by drawing straight lines across its inside from the circumference. Straight lines must be drawn at a ninety-degree angle to the tangent line that intersects the circumference. At the very least, two lines must be drawn, and their point of intersection is the center.

Does the circle include the area enclosed by its circumference? If so, then the circle is more than just a line that has been drawn, it is a shape that already includes the area encircled. The geometric shape already delineates a space, and the circumference has its origin in the center. Rather than concluding that the center is the logical center derived by first drawing the circle, one might understand the circumference as essentially drawn from its relationship to the point at its center. Not an afterthought, the act of drawing the circle is more original than the circle drawn and from which its qualities can be derived. Imagine a compass with one end placed firmly at a point, then it is rotated to draw the line around that point at a distance specified by the angle between its legs. The logical first element of the circle is its center, second comes the radius, and finally its circumference is inscribed.

Such a circle has its origin in the center. In what way is such a point also the end of the circle? Don't we rather say that the circle is without end? The point at the center is the end of the circle only insofar as that point centers the act of drawing it. When that act begins, there is no circle, but when it ends, there it is right before our eyes. Drawing the circle is the origin of the circle's circularity, but only as an achieved result -after the fact— does the center become the actual center. What lies in the middle only comes to be in the middle once we have reached the end. We say that every point is potentially the center of a circle, and in the process of being drawn, every point wants to be the center of its very own circle. Once it has been drawn, it is.

Aristotle speaks of a wheel, not circles. So much the better, for the wheel has spokes connecting a hub to a rim. The center shines in countless radii toward its circumference. The movement of the circle, the wheel that spins, is the potentially endless revolution of the circumference around the center through the turning of the radius. As the wheel spins, the center does not move but the circumference races around it carried by the spokes.

Aquinas speaks of the first mover when describing circling movement. He attributes this same pattern to both the finite beings with soul and the infinite being that is the world-soul. His faith gets the better of him, he wants it to be so. He emphatically desires that his experience go on forever. Stay calm. Breathe.

What does such movement have to do with potential and actuality?

Some origins come from breathing things, others do not. The soul-body is actually what the body is only potentially. The origin is a power to actualize, a power to let something come out from inside itself, from its center, and become something that the origin already has present in itself. It is drawn out. Mind and body, potential and actuality, are closely interwoven and interleaved in being drawn. Something that seems twofold is, in fact, only one. Mind and body, actuality and potential, are themselves only one: the origin must be in the end.

Potential is the origin of a movement that draws a relation to something else, something that surrounds it like a circumference. The source of movement has the power to bring about change, a transition from being a point on its own to being a point at the circle's center.

The soul, the origin of movement, has a rational part actualizing its material accompanied by a formula. When an origin of some change is accompanied like that, it "is alike capable of contrary effects... ...the reason is that science is a rational formula...." (*Metaphysics* at and around 1046b5) Everything that can do something, but is not currently doing it, operates in a realm of potential and power, a realm of contingency driven to be this way or that way by the whims and deliberations of the soul. Stay calm. Breathe.

What distinguishes rational potential from the nonrational kind? There is an active synthesis at work in the rational formula. Let x = f(y) and thus let x be y through the power at work in the function that takes the value of y as an argument for producing x. The rational formula is present in soul and links x and y together. I link therefore I am.

In the context of the link, Aristotle integrates the notion of doing well, a normative claim about the nature of the act. With soul and with its deliberations, there comes the possibility of originating an outcome that matches the desired effect. A hierarchy of relations is disclosed: there is an order of rank in the values assigned. The soul begins to move, and that movement may be done well or badly. To do something well is to do it so that it actually corresponds with what it was potentially.

A stone flying through the air may be a material, efficient, or formal cause of movement, but it cannot be a final cause. It has no soul, it does not breathe. It does not move in a circle. Only what breathes can start where it ends. Actualization originates in capabilities that circle back in the realization of a final cause previously projected as the outcome of movement. Rational realization moves in a circle.

Now we understand why Aquinas thinks the prime mover moves by understanding, willing, and loving. The final cause present in breath and the origin of movement is the center of anything like understanding, will, and love. Understanding is an understanding of first and last things. Will is the movement between them. Love is where what was there in the beginning comes together with what is there in the end. Every soul moves as understanding, will, and love because love, will, and understanding are the actualization of potential.

Potential is already on its way toward actualization. The powers in the agent are potential only to the extent that they can be realized. The shape of realization is normative and determinate. Built within the capabilities of the soul, there is a limitation guiding movement. There is discipline and order. There is an organized process. The one with potential must act under the pressure of doing as well as they can: an artist who does not act is not liberated on that account, rather they are a bad artist. A doctor is supposed to heal the sick. A great doctor who stands idly by misses the mark just as much as the quack who does everything she can.

There is an understanding of power accompanied by a rational formula. Only because the potential is actualizable, is realizable, is it real potential.

The objective of action is either achieved well or badly. The outcome must be measured against the final cause, what lies at the origin. Things that exist by human agency either measure up or they do not. What is actual is saturated with value insofar as it relates to what resides in the soul as its originating power. Stay calm. Breathe.

The question concerning the meaning of being has been raised. I said it before, and I have not forgotten. What is-there comes from what is-not-there. If what is-there, is actual, how can something *be* merely potential? How *can* something *be*?

The actual is defined in relation to potential, the potential in relation to the actual. They are interleaved, they are the push and pull of a twofold that is one. The circularity of real capabilities actualizes itself in movement that is unity through duality, the rational formula pure and simple.

Movement drawn from an origin presents itself as a criterion for existence. Its beginning and its end are coincidental. The unmoved mover exists insofar as it moves. The final cause, the rational formula accompanying soul when originating movement, is already in movement. What can this mean? Movement is the unity that contains the twofold nature of the potential and the actual. Movement is the twofold nature telling us something about the soul which can move without being moved. Stay calm. Breathe.

The final cause is the end, and it is the beginning. In circularity, the unity of the twofold is articulated. The idea of Hermes may exist in a block of marble, and it is realized by an artist as they carve the figure. The duality in unity lies in the dual unity of movement, a process whereby the artist sets about crafting a statue of Hermes matching with their vision. Do you see it in her, can you see it? Or is it an illusion?

When something always already is, when it exists and is actual, there can be no point when it comes to be, no moment when it comes into existence. On the other hand, things that come to be are not yet existing things and only come to be through some movement. The always already and the not yet mark the basic distinction between actual and potential. The twofold movement derives from this moment of origin. Something that is marked by a limit, a not yet existing thing, is capable of coming to be and, eventually, coming to an end. It can exist potentially. Something that never comes to an end nor has a moment when it begins, such a thing actually exists and is never merely potential. Both relate to a limit saturated by movement. If we say that the end or limit accompanies the movement, we make a twofold distinction in the nature of accompanying. On the one hand, the limit accompanies the movement as an effect accompanies its cause. On the other hand, the limit is there whenever the movement takes place, it is already there, taking place throughout the movement. Stay calm. Breathe.

It is like the distinction between simultaneity and succession. The limit follows its cause, results from it, accompanies it by following it, coming after it, and marking its end. The limit that occurs simultaneously with its cause regardless of effect is already there in it. Movement and activity are different ways to accompany the limit.

The final cause is both an activity of thought and the origin of a movement toward an artifact that will guide action toward the end. At one and the same time, the final cause is both actual and potential, both an activity and a movement.

Here lies the origin of movement and the activity that is both its beginning and its end. We say that a builder is the origin of a building because they are capable of building it. The builder's talent is present in the builder insofar as they are a good builder. Human beings are not born builders, they must learn the craft. Some are more capable than others. The capacity to build rests on an actual talent for building which in turn comes from a capability to learn which in turn comes from actual understanding which in turn... And so on and so on. Stay calm. Breathe.

There is circularity at work. Potency and activity are in a constant circular round and round, pushing and pulling as the dynamic of soulful existence. The circular movement, breathing, acts as final cause. Only in and through the final cause does the circular relation of the potential and the actual take place.

I began with Aquinas and the unmoved mover of willing, thinking, and loving. Willing, thinking, and loving are ways of breathing according to a rational principle that may either miss its mark or hit it. The end that takes place in the origin is the end accompanying the endless movement of an actually existing center. Insofar as this endless movement accompanies an origin, it transforms itself into an end achieved.

If breathing's end is endlessly present in the soul's activity, why does it transform into potential for the sake of further movement? Transformation is necessary for anything like a world to be. In what does the endless activity of the world-soul find its finite reconciliation? Stay calm. Breathe.

The reconciliation of substance (Sein) with its finite realization beginning in an end (Dasein) repeats itself and is drawn out by the incorporation of soulful action coming from endless movement. It breathes. Whatever realizes the potential taking place in the actual can only be realized by something capable of action accompanied by a rational principle, a creature capable of acting on final causes, of moving in a circle, a creature that breathes life into its body with the power of deliberate action. Always already existing substance indicates reconciliation that is not yet accomplished: the patterns of the deliberating soul that thinks, wills, and loves. In other words, Ethics.

Ethical Reconciliation

The Market

They dropped off the car at the little auto shop on 124th Street and then went to the gun range in Bellevue. Eirini had never fired a gun before. Since they were going to have guns with them during the trip, Lena insisted that she learn the rules for firearm safety. It didn't take much persuasion. Eirini was excited at the prospect and eager to learn. Lena went through them before they took the guns out of the carrier. 1) Treat every gun as though it were loaded until you have personally verified that it is not. 2) Don't put your finger on the trigger unless you are going to pull the trigger. 3) Only point the gun at something you intend to destroy. 4) Know what you are pointing at, what is in front of it, and what is behind it. They went over them in English and in Greek, teaching each other the missing words. Eirini repeated them multiple times and reported them back to Lena. They bought ammunition for both guns: the little double-barreled Derringer and the larger Glock 17. Lena showed Eirini how to load and unload each of them, showed her how to put the safety on and off, and then had her feel the weight of each weapon when they were loaded and unloaded. Eirini was hesitant at first, but after firing for the first time, she became more confident.

"I was surprised how good it felt," she said afterward, as they were driving the electric SUV into the city. The car wouldn't be ready until late in the afternoon, so Lena decided to take her down to the public market to walk around and have some lunch. "Loud too. It was very powerful."

"I remember," Lena held back her desire to get into it more.

"Does everyone in America have a gun? That's what we hear back home."

"I think the data shows that some people have lots of guns, and the majority don't have any."

"Why do you have one?"

"In the last ten or fifteen years, there's been more violence."

"I looked at some statistics online before we came, and some say that there is less violence."

"I'd have to look more closely at those studies, because in the media they make it seem like people have been going crazy. Somehow, poor people killing each other must make someone a lot of money. My Dad hated guns, but he thought they had become necessary. Women more than anyone needed to know how to use them. He thought all women should be carrying."

"Why only women?"

"Women are in the most danger. Maybe that's what those statistics mean. Less violence between men, more violence against women. Domestic violence never counts as violence."

"That's chilling. Why is it worse now, though? The men my age in Greece, they're better than the older generations."

"Maybe. Here, our political troubles are openly misogynistic. Women are targeted more than men."

"On both sides?"

"The backlash goes both ways. They always make it seem political, but if you count the bodies..."

"So, men on one side attack women on the other?"

"Sometimes I think that's the whole point, they're just an excuse to express hatred for people we've always hated. Public catharsis of the ugliest feelings."

They parked behind the market and walked up the three or four flights of stairs to get to the main level. They strolled around and looked at the different stalls, the food, the flowers, and the knickknacks. Then they stopped at a little stall in the middle of the longest alley.

"Let's get some soup and a sandwich. This place is classic."

"Just this little stall with the counter?"

"Yes. People move in and out fast. A few places will free up if we just wait. This is a public market institution, It's been here ever since I can remember. My parents love this place. They took me here often."

"Not a big menu."

"No, not many choices. I usually have the grilled salmon sandwich and the chowder. The halibut is good too. This is one of the only places left where you can get this stuff. It's still wild caught. The fishermen are locals and usually work for themselves. It's sustainable, so I make an exception."

A few seats opened on one side of the counter, and they squeezed into them side-by-side. Lena ordered and Eirini said "the same" when the man behind the counter looked at her.

"In your studies," Eirini asked after the guy gave them their soup. "Are you studying the culture war?"

"It's not my focus. It would be interesting, but I think it's too big. We're more specialized. We look at teeny-tiny things. Once we know how to do that, then we can focus on broader subjects. Maybe when I get tenure," she laughed.

"So, what do you focus on then?" Eirini didn't get the joke.

"Mostly, I rely on my strengths and comfort zone: biology and computer science. The combination is good for modeling projects aimed at the role human biology plays in group formation and culture."

"That sounds relevant to the problems."

"It is, but to start talking about political positions or ideologies, that's way too complex. Our physiology is hard to link to something like that. You have to start with physical traits and their relationship to how we're organized, our migration patterns, alliances, stuff like that."

"Who does that help?"

"What do you mean?"

"Well, jobs are supposed to help people, aren't they? That's why we do them. How will your studies help people?"

"Acquiring knowledge about the species, about human behavior, how we are and why we are that way. That's helpful to everyone."

"How?"

"The more we know, the more we understand, the better we can address problems in a way that suits our nature."

"In my job, I help someone get what they need. Isn't there anything like that for you?"

"I don't think it's cut and dry like that."

"Why not?"

"We're animals. We're trying to increase our DNA on earth. We use ideas for that. People think they're arguing about which political ideas are better, but really they're just playing out a larger natural process."

"You believe this? Do you think it helps to know it?"

"I do. It's ironic that one side argues about freedom, and the other about justice. Each side uses their ideas to attack the other. Neither side is consistent, they make many logical errors."

"Then they're both wrong, is that what you're saying?"

"Not exactly. The logical errors show that the logic doesn't matter. It's not an argument about ideas, that's just a ruse to serve hidden causes."

"The culture war does this?"

"Something thinks so. It may be wrong, it's an experiment."

"Something thinks?"

"It's not any one person or group of people, but some order trying it out."

"Okay, but what exactly?"

"Human civilization relies on groups. That used to be purely geographic, but now it's based on attributes."

"Attributes?"

"Yes, we don't live in little villages anymore, or even if we do, they're connected to other villages, to many other villages, to towns and cities, to nations and people everywhere. We live in an enormous and organized society. Some groups contain hundreds of millions and even billions of people."

"Too many to only be connected to the people nearby."

"To live like that, we need special rules, alliances, and order. Behavior has to comply. The war is two competing ideas about order. We're trying out both strategies, experimenting with them while struggling against each other."

"Do you mean we're trying to do two things at once to see which is better, or we're trying out the battle between them?"

"I don't know, but that's the kind of thing you could study."

"Knowing this will convince people?"

"Uh well, I don't know if it will convince anyone, but it may change the order."

"How do you change an order without convincing people?"

They finished eating and paid at the antique cash register. In the little stall, it didn't seem out of place. They heard music coming from the street just outside the market, so they walked up to a nearby exit to see if they could find the buskers. It sounded pretty good, and Lena thought it would complete Eirini's experience.

"That's such a Dad question," Lena said as they stood a ways back from the crowd gathering around the two musicians playing in the street running alongside the market. "This whole conversation, in fact."

Eirini was half dancing to the music and didn't stop when responding: "I liked your dad very much. He was always so sensitive. I remember when I was little, no one else talked to me like he did."

"He thought kids had special insights."

"That's what I remember. He was a philosopher."

"Well, he wanted to be. He was an engineer really. You could always tell because when questions like 'how do you convince an organization' came up, he would ask whether it was philosophical or just an engineering problem."

Eirini smiled and nodded, continuing to move in rhythm with the guitar and the accompanying drummer.

"If you think it's only about persuading individuals with arguments, you run into those logical flaws we were talking about."

Eirini leaned against Lena and linked arms with her. She tried to pull her in rhythm with her, tried to get her to start dancing along to the music.

"Common sense tells you that ideas matter. You think of them and then you convince other people. Individuals make the rules. They convince other people that it's good for them. They get them to believe things and follow rules. But common sense is nonsense."

Eirini laughed and kissed Lena on the cheek. "You're not dancing," she said.

"No," she confirmed. "But organizations don't really work like that. They have a life of their own. My dad thought we had to examine how they apply rules and enforce behavior. We had to study how data was collected and used to shape people's desires and identities."

Eirini stopped briefly and looked at Lena seriously, "It's very abstract. I still don't see how it helps." She squeezed Lena's arm and started moving with the music again.

"By learning about the tools they use, we can use those same tools against them."

Eirini turned sideways. She took Lena's right hand in her left and put her right arm around Lena's waist. Lena put her left hand on Eirini's shoulder. They started to move together on the cobblestone. Others were dancing too. The pace of the music was increasing.

"He said big corporations control the social order. They manipulate the politics and the people."

Eirini kept them moving to the music. Lena laughed when Eirini tried to twirl her under her outstretched arm. She blushed when it went awry, and they had to let go of each other and reset their position.

"These companies, the law treats them like people. They have their privacy and other rights too. Corporate crimes justify spying on them."

The music was slowing down and coming toward the end, Eirini slowed them down too. She never broke eye contact.

"For really bad things, they should be incarcerated: make them work for the people, observe them closely, and discipline them. Rehabilitate them. Make them more socially conscious."

The song came to an end and Eirini slightly dipped Lena just as the music was trailing off.

"That's how you *convince* organizations," Lena said while giggling and looking up at Eirini, who was beaming a broad smile down at her. She let her back up and they hugged and applauded along with the rest of the crowd.

Passing in front of the musicians, they dropped a few dollars into a guitar case and made their way back into the market. Walking arm-in-arm through the stalls, they steered toward the elevator and rode it down to street level.

"He was more of an onlooker," Lena said as they crossed the street toward the parking lot.

"He wrote books though, didn't he? My dad said he tried to read them but couldn't understand very much."

"He did. He said he was learning about how corporations harvest data and used it to change behavior. He said he had a duty to report his findings."

"You've read his books?"

"I've tried. It's not really my area."

They got in the car and headed back toward the highway. It was late enough to go pick up the car. Eirini checked Lena's phone and found the message from the auto shop.

"The car's ready. Why do you have a text from Ben Thorne?"

"Did it just come? Read it to me."

"Hello Lena. I am writing on behalf of Ben Thorne. Please contact our office as soon as possible. Then there is a phone number to call, an email address to use, and a social handle. What's this about?"

They pulled into the parking lot by the auto shop. "I'll tell you later," she said. After getting out of the car, she turned back to Eirini and asked: "Do you remember how to get back to the house?"

"No."

"Okay, just wait and I'll come back around. You can follow me."

The Airport

They still had time before their flight, so they decided to have lunch. They went to one of the places where you could sit down, and a waiter would take your order. Very retro, it was styled as a sports bar. As soon as they sat down, the guy came over and they ordered veggie burgers and a beer.

"Take Thorne's approach as an example," Carl said. "He rejects the existence of any moral absolute baked into the universe, he even rejects any moral absolute baked into human being."

"Absolute, of course, but he doesn't reject the existence of norms and values," Fred responded.

"Of course, of course. There are norms and values, but they're contingent on specific historical developments and movements, and what's more, they apply to both the empowered and the disempowered."

"Arguably, that's their purpose. They maintain a status quo, they keep those in power in power, they justify the hierarchy."

"That doesn't mean that any attack on the order is a slave rebellion."

"It does when the order's version of the world is basically accepted as is and then inverted. That's what I'm calling a slave rebellion."

"The good people are the people who can do things, who have the power to do things, they are strong, smart, capable. These are the virtuous. The bad people, on your take, are the people who can't do anything, they're weak, not very clever, and they're incompetent."

"That's right, and they make their weakness and stupidity into virtues. They accept the order but invert the terms. They say that the bad people are really good, and those good people, well they're just evil."

The waiter set the beers down in front of them. Fred went on.

"The same table of values is in place, but they've been turned upside down. There isn't much difference between the Christian inversion of Roman virtues and this contemporary inversion."

"You don't see anything revolutionary in the arguments?"

"No. Marginalized people want to take over the mainstream. They don't reject the values of the mainstream. They just want to be the good ones according to its order."

"Can you elaborate?"

"They say there are groups of people who have the power, they say there are groups of people who make the decisions, have the high-paying jobs, make the policy, and so on."

"Yes, there are. It's a fact."

"And it has nothing to do with competence or competence is biased. They resent those groups and want to turn things upside down so that the people who have been on the outside make the decisions and have the good jobs. Doesn't matter if they're any good at it, that's their argument. Competence is a ruse."

"I see. Working people want to be the rich people, wealth is still the value. People of color, people with diverse sexual orientations, women, the groups that were traditionally marginalized, they want to occupy the power positions of that same social setting built by injustice."

"It may be that there are a few people here and there with a genuinely revolutionary point of view, but the majority who have jumped on the bandwagon, that's not what they want. They want to be rich and famous. They want to make the decisions. Desert doesn't matter."

"You think there's nothing moral going on here. It's just pure power, a struggle for power with no ethical basis."

"That's my position."

"I guess I agree that ethics is largely a fraud. Usually, it comes down to justifying a status quo. Wealth and power are split up and allocated to the ruling groups, then the ethics comes along to justify the division. Don't steal, don't take what isn't yours, don't rise up and murder your oppressors, that would be unethical."

The waiter set the burgers down in front of them and they started to eat.

Carl continued, "True revolution isn't going to be an ethical transformation of society. Instead, the revolution will be a radical change in the division of power and then a new ethics will follow."

"In your world, it doesn't make sense to make ethical arguments. The argument itself is just a surface tension that appears because of some deeper rumblings."

"That's right. The have-nots become aware of their condition. They might express that as resentment or anger. This is what you're calling the battle for power. It starts to surface in the different movements from the last decades."

"And backlash is just the defense of the old order."

"Yes, but antagonism is just a representation of the basic contradictions.

A civilization where only a few people have wealth and power is not sustainable. Divisions and tensions appear, trouble begins. The arguments are symptoms, they're unrelated to the underlying causes."

"The combatants may not know what they're doing. Is that your point? No thanks, we're okay."

"They're a parody or a representative farce. When they're in turmoil, the institutions start breaking down. The life they order loses its magic."

"For you then, there's some group of people who become self-conscious, it's a progressive process, they become aware of a relationship between these disputes and the underlying causes. That group spearheads revolutionary movement and educates people on both sides."

"More or less. The flaring tensions indicate crisis. People are learning. It's evolutionary *and* revolutionary."

"What guarantees that the movements that radicalize them will be truly revolutionary? It could be a downward spiral. Maybe the white supremacists are doing the exact same thing and just trying to get the word out."

"That happens sometimes, but ultimately it can't win the day. The underlying conditions are moving in a direction that will bring true change."

"Through a new social organization."

"Yes. Self-consciousness organizes the group."

"Well, my point is that this just gets you more of the same. You won't see a complete change in values or norms, you'll just shuffle the pawns to put a different group in charge. Organizations always require hierarchy. The aggregate always succumbs. The true believers will rule us."

"Not if the express purpose is to establish equality."

"That makes sense when there are 50 people but not when there are hundreds of millions or billions."

Carl was silent. He looked away. Fred continued.

"I think you have a hidden notion of human nature guided by universal principles. Whether it be equality or liberty, it's an absolute system of values. What does equality mean? You have to formalize nature to start building equations out of it and formalization is coercive. God is dead, my friend. Your equality is normative, pure invention."

"No, it's not a moral term, I'm using it to describe the underlying order of wealth and power."

"That just means your pushing some ideal down into the basic conditions of life. That's the exact problem Thorne opposes. You're addressing the problem of too many people and trying to come up with the right institutional order to support them. It's sociobiology."

"It's not moralizing, it's a fact. There are homeless people."

"People should have homes."

"Yes. It's barbaric to think otherwise."

"That's my point. You're moralizing, you have pushed the notion of equality and justice down into your basic conditions and insist that the social order reflect them. It's an ethically based position. That's what I'm saying."

"You reject equality as a material condition. You're calling me bourgeois. What's the alternative?"

"You're claiming the dignity of the person. We're each sacred, or the group of us is, or whatever, but to get that, you have to set some ethical notions into the fabric of existence, as if existence gave a crap about the individual human being or humans rather than saber-toothed cats."

"You don't have an alternative, then?"

"To have as many people as we do, we needed to universalize our value systems, apply it to everyone in the world. It isn't enough to say never kill a member of your tribe. Generalization is required. It's an engineering problem."

"You think ethics makes this possible."

"A new totem. Just like roads and mass transportation, mass farming techniques, high-tech requirements need to be in place. Universal rights and the Categorical Imperative or the Principle of Utility too."

"Not everyone agrees with your take on history, but I'll play along. What's the problem with that?"

"It frames the possibilities. It means there are changes you can't make. Your value system will always be focused on ordering and that means constructing behavior that is predictable and rational, that follows the rules, and obeys the principles of social well-being. Morality is an engineering problem to you. You'll never have a revolution in value under those conditions because organizational requirements prevent it."

"What's your alternative? I'm still not seeing anything other than complaining that we'll have to follow rules."

"The same rules we've always followed. Count on it. There will be winners and losers. Both will be equally domesticated."

"Again, not hearing any alternative."

"That's because I've given up on trying to convince anyone. I'm only interested in the rare individuals who under no circumstances will fall in line with the aggregate and have their behavior ordered in the optimal fashion for promoting the well-being of a social organism. I target the exception."

"The scavengers and vultures who would live off the productive fruit harvested by the rest of us. Is that who you're sticking up for?"

"Sure. That's what you would call them. I think of them as people who long for private moments."

"Privacy? Now who's grasping at the liberal social order?"

"I'm not talking about that bullshit where you worry about who knows what about whom. Keeping my data in a vault so that only people I want to access it can get in. That bullshit treats human beings in the aggregate just as much as your drive for basic equality. People complaining about privacy on giant social networks with millions of other people listening and watching, it's madness. I'm talking about a fierce and focused attunement to the moments you are living and experiencing."

"That's bullshit individualism."

"Then I'm explaining it badly because it's not about my individuality in the moment. It's about the fullness of being, the experience of time passing. It is the best that a human can be."

"Stop desiring, stop wanting something beyond the moment. Sounds like Buddhism."

"Who said anything about stopping? Desire is in the moment too. The swarming forces and relations are there, the whole world is too. Everything. Focused consciousness is the highest value ever achieved in the universe."

Carl put the credit card for their pay box on the table. "You dismiss humanity. You don't care if people live well, if they're supported and cared for."

"True, I don't think that's the most important thing. I see no reason why the universe is better off with human beings in it, just because we're human beings. Or put it this way, if the only way for us to survive as a species is if we are completely tamed and domesticated, then I don't see any advantage. There's no absolute good in having properly behaving human beings living well together for eternity. The greatest thing about human beings is the power expressed in those moments of attunement. If those moments don't happen, then there's no reason to preserve the species."

"People are easier to love en masse though, don't you think?"

"Not in the least. As a mass, we're brutal and detestable. Only in the singular are we lovable and extraordinary."

"Well, we should head toward the gate, but I take it that you're prepared to be called evil by those bad ones that I represent."

"That would be the expected response. The ordered masses with their predictable lives are likely to think singular outliers are evil. It proves that I'm right when they call me that. Is that what you think?"

"Of course not. I think it's just a sign of the times. One of the broken philosophies I would expect to see in an unjust and unequal world."

Carl took his card and the printed receipt and put them back in his pocket. They got up from the table and started down the concourse toward the gate, towing their carry-on luggage behind them. As they retreated into silence and traversed the long corridor, Fred mumbled: "It's not philosophy, it's the act of a highly specific being rejecting the anti-logic of aggregate attributes."

The Kitchen

Ariti and Ermioni sat at the table in the kitchen. They had apple cake and hot chocolate in front of them.

"What would you prefer?"

"Of the available options, this is what I have to do. This is what Em wanted, what he thought I wanted. It's settled."

"You agree? This is what you want?"

"Under no circumstances do I get what I want. He was such a jokester, I want to hear him laugh again. I want to keep the house where my daughter grew up, I want to stay here. What else am I supposed to do? It's settled."

"At least if you come back, you'll be with friends. Your mother. All of us. There are so many people who are looking forward to seeing you."

"I know. I appreciate that, but there are reasons I left, and they haven't changed. What about Lena? I'll be far away from her. When will I see her? We'll talk every weekend but when will I see her?"

"How often do you see her now?"

"This feels so much more final, and it's the worst time. She needs me more than ever. She doesn't realize how much. She thinks we're so far apart, that I'm so different from her. The only way to get through to her is to stay close."

"Don't you think she knows you need her?"

"She thinks I have my brother and you, she thinks I'm different. She doesn't think I know what she's going through."

"What does she think?"

"She thinks she's hiding something from me, but I know. Em was always backwards in the way he would put things. It was fine if you could talk to him and get him to explain, but a child can't do that. She thought he was judging her. Her whole life, everything she did, she was trying to make him happy, proud. Now he's gone, what's she supposed to do?"

"Why would she hide that?"

"She thinks I'm not the same as her."

"It's normal for kids to be like that. No one has ever gone through what they go through, no one has ever understood what they understand."

"We have fathers, we have husbands. It doesn't matter how they mean to be. We mean them to be like that. We make them The Father, we make them The Husband."

"What are you saying?"

"She thinks I can't understand how fathers and husbands are."

"How are they?"

"Em couldn't help it. There were things he liked and things he admired. He never got over his past, that he sold out. He never lost that feeling."

"From his school days?"

"He worked all the time. He had two jobs and never enough time for us. For her. What he loved was in those books and in those stories. She saw that and moved there so he could see her. He couldn't help what he loved, none of us can, and he couldn't help but pass that along to her. You see?"

"It was the same with my father. With yours too, I think."

"He didn't mean it, it's what it is to be a father, it's what it is to have a father. She felt what was in his eyes."

"You said fathers and husbands before. Was he like that with you too?"

"I saw his face, the way he looked at me. I knew what he didn't like, no matter what he said. I felt judged, less than the best, like I let him down."

"We learned this from our mother's. What else could we do? We take everything personally."

"Fathers and Husbands. Mother's and Wives, too. It's different, and we can't help what we do to each other. Even when we think we're doing the right thing. Our actions aren't our own, they're part of the world."

"You should just talk to her. Tell her you understand and that you're feeling the same things, and that it doesn't mean you hated him or that he hated you, it's how you come to terms with being a daughter or being a wife. Tell her."

"She doesn't think I can understand. It's connected."

"How?"

"She thinks I'm just a simple woman who never did those things Em loved, the things she so desperately wants, she thinks I don't measure up."

"She loves you, Ermioni, you're being ridiculous. You should talk to her. Don't let this eat away at you, don't let it poison your relationship with her. You have to talk to her."

"Whenever I think it's a good time, I see it in her eyes. She thinks there's so much distance between us. I lose my nerve."

Georgios came into the kitchen, and they stopped talking. He took a piece of cake and sat down.

"I spoke to the estate people. They'll come inventory everything. She said she'll call me back on Monday with the details. Have you thought about what you want to keep?"

"Yes, I've been making lists. Yesterday I called that company Em found. They'll bring a container to the house, we'll load it up, and then they'll move it to Greece."

"Good. The estate lady said she'll bring tags to put on the things we want to sell."

The Diner

"Tell me about E.M."

"Em."

"M.?"

"Just Em."

"He was always one of the first to read your stuff. Ever since I've been working with you. What's the story?"

"That started long ago, back when I was working on *Fragmented*. I started writing that book while he and I were living together. Well, not really living together, he was letting me stay with him. I was camped out on his couch."

"In Ann Arbor."

"Yes. He was writing about the same subject. Different genre. I do not think he ever finished it."

"*Fragmented* isn't exactly a traditional narrative..."

He interrupts her, "After I moved to New York, we would talk on the phone. I sent him drafts. He had a lot of *feedback*." He laughed. "I incorporated some of it."

"And you kept that up throughout the years?"

"He became an engineer, that is probably why he never finished that book. Always a good critic though. I will tell you more after we talk to the kid, but he was notorious for his connections."

"How do you mean? He knew a lot of people."

"Not those kinds of connections. Conceptual connections. He could find patterns everywhere. Boil things down and make comparisons. Like the three Graces. Beauty, Charm, and Fertility."

"The Charites? From Greek mythology?"

"Yes, but for him it was womanhood spun into a triangle, like scales. Musical scales."

"What?"

"Beauty, charm, and fertility are the paradigm of proper womanhood. Not eternally or according to some law of nature, but according to the ancient Greek understanding. C, E, and G."

"Women according to the ancient patriarchy."

"He was always doing things like that, identifying a mythology in the status quo, then pointing to something like the Hegelian dialectic. I am making this up, it is an illustration."

"What about the Hegelian dialectic? Didn't you talk about that in *The Temple on the Mountain* and *Brief History*?"

"Never mind that, it is hypothetical. He would draw out the mythology as a dialectical maneuver, like beauty is the simple presence of the thing, charm is its reflection back upon itself, its negation, then fertility would synthesize them. So, here he is describing the status quo on womanhood and then he goes and casts it into the dialectic."

"Got it, I think."

"Then he would talk about how the dialectical relationship between the three changes each of them into something else. Say, like beauty becomes bright light. Charm becomes justice or good judgment. Then fertility becomes tranquility or peace. How to explain?"

"It sounds familiar. Are you sure this isn't from *Brief History*?"

"The form of movement transforms the pattern. The change reveals coercion in the status quo. Those three things are not simple, but they are applied by power, they are part of an order. Beauty is just a way of coercing the object from its brilliance into something passive. Charm is flattering whereas judgment is truthful. Fertility -in the end– is not perpetual growth and increase, but fulfillment or peacefulness."

She pursed her lips and rubbed her chin. It was giving her a sense of déjà vu. She shrugged and looked off at the waitress who had been bussing the tables and was moving dishes from her tray to the basins at the dish station by the kitchen.

"I know," he went on. "The point is that there is a state in the way things are, then you attach a form of movement to set the story in motion. The characters on stage, they begin to move. Since they aim for something that motivated them in the first place, it is a circle. When the circle completes, it turns the original things into something else entirely."

"So, you identify a mythology. That's step one."

"Yes."

"Then you put it in motion by showing how the different parts connect. The way they connect causes everything to turn into something else. Wasn't there something about this in the *Harvest* book? It's alchemy."

"Right."

"And then what?"

"The something else turns out to be antagonistic to the original condition. Light, justice, and peace end up defining womanhood differently than the mythology of the Graces. That new definition disrupts the order behind the original mythology."

"How exactly?"

"Beauty was for the sake of the masters, for their enjoyment. When that changes into a shining and brilliant light it blinds the people who were looking at it."

"Is it a competing mythology?"

"It overturns the original form based on the movement. Beauty is visually pleasing, but the light is blinding. Charm flatters and pleases, whereas judgment makes the recipient uncomfortable, forces them to confront truth even if it is ugly."

"How does peace change fertility?"

"Fertility is constant striving, it is the never-ending pursuit of more. Perpetual increase made virtue. Peace breaks the chain. It stops the movement forward and attunes experiences to what is here and now. It is like the Buddhist affront to desire, where what is missing is replaced with an experience of what is not missing. What would desire be if you did not know what it was aiming at? If you could completely absorb yourself in that experience, it would be peaceful, a tranquil fullness lacking any irritation in the pursuit of more."

"But..."

"He could do it with anything. Point to some mythology, something I was taking for granted, some powerful and possessive trope that dominated the story, he would show me the motion associated with it, and then talk about its different forms of movement. That produced a transformed mythology."

"Dialectic isn't the only form..."

"It could be any form. When you list things, you might assume logic in the list. Tacitly."

"...of movement then?"

"Beauty, Charm, Fertility. It is just an ordered list, and I might mean it as a sequence. This and then this and then this. Three distinct things. That might be the original movement. Then he would apply a different logic, like dialectic or deconstructive, whatever, he would come up with different things. Simultaneity even. This logic changes the list, changes what it means. His point was that listing things depended on a type of movement assumed by the list builder. It is not just a bunch of things. There is an order to it. The status quo might assume sequential logic and that other forms of movement are capable of resisting it."

"Why do this? Was he trying to describe how a feminist might undermine a patriarchal definition of womanhood? *Princess Myshkin*."

"It is just an illustration. I think he wanted to prove that the movement form is the important part. It might be nuanced and complex. The purpose of any writing is to show the status quo, describe its transformation, and then elaborate the movement driving that, making it possible."

"The movement is the most important thing."

"The movement is the story, that is the yarn you are spinning. That was his aesthetic anyway. He thought story telling was movement transforming something given into something else. If you think of the mise-en-scene as the given and then you think of the outcome, the ultimate end, as the transformed state, the new mythology, then the story is just the movement from the one to the other."

"How did this affect your work?"

"He would frame his comments with it. Those notes. He would identify the original state and then the outcome. I might not even be aware of it so he would describe how the story advocated a logic that got us there. Once he showed me this, it changed how I thought about it, what it meant, and what twists and turns it needed."

"He did that for you with *Fragmented*?"

"*Fragmented* went through a huge metamorphosis."

"It reminds me of some of the stuff in *Fabrications* too. Every single one of the little demonstrations in that book shows how logical movements are transformations. As you put it."

"Exactly. In that book, movement always tacitly starts as desire. Not desire in the simple form of hunger or thirst or sex, but less distinct, more fantastic and aligned with feelings and sensations that we want to surround ourselves with."

"What the desires mean. What's in the background accompanying the drive for food, water, shelter, sex, and whatever else."

"Happiness."

"Happiness?"

"Yes, rather than seeing the chain of desire leading up to a state of bliss, this becomes a background behind everything else. It provides the environment for the rest of our lives. We do not want it, rather it is a logic against which our desires take place. It is no longer an end, but a form of movement, a conditioning power behind the scenes and transforming everything wc do."

"Why happiness though?"

"Do not think of it as a psychological state. Think of it like the Greeks did. A state of your soul, a condition saturating your actions. Saturated by them too."

"Happiness isn't pleasure or good feeling?"

"Do you think those associations hold with this new ethos, this new basis for movement?"

"How could they? It wouldn't necessarily be pleasant, would it?"

"It might be off-putting, it might make someone uncomfortable and even cause emotional pain. They might repeat it or be drawn to it despite that. Over and over again. Maybe even in some pathological way. That is not usually something we think of as happiness."

"This wasn't meant to be a theory, was it?"

"Rules for manufacturing things."

"Applying the logic spins a yarn. You might like the story, or you might not."

"Right."

"There will be stories you like and stories you don't like. They're made up just the same and they have a logic. That movement gets you from where it starts to where it ends. When you think about whether or not you like it, you won't just focus on where you started and where you finished, but on the whole movement it made and the logic in it."

"Em thought it was conceivable that a writer would tell story after story

and never use the same logical movement even if the upshot and the point
of origin were the same. You could repeatedly start in the same place and
end in the same place and tell infinitely many stories just by applying
different logic. On the other hand, you could tell the exact same story over
and over again using different starting points and outcomes so long as the
logic of the movement was the same. Like intervention..."

"Shit," she said interrupting him. "I have plans for tonight. I have to go.
Do you need anything else from me today?"

"No, no, go on. Have fun. I will see you tomorrow."

"Tomorrow is Sunday. I wasn't planning on coming in."

"That is fine. I will text you if I need anything."

"Don't text me. I'll see you Monday."

The Lincoln Park Brownstone

"Smile."

"Excuse me?"

"You should cheer up. It's a party."

"Ah, is it my turn to please you, I must've misread the schedule."

"Well, it can't hurt to use a little charm, I was told you're looking for
donations."

"Have we met? Who are you again?"

"Daniel Cohen. I'm a friend of Leo's. You're Miriam Holden, aren't
you?"

"Have we met?"

"No, but I've heard about you. Your work at the center. I was told
you're always looking for donations."

"Well, that's true, the county doesn't give us enough to meet our
obligations so we're always on the lookout."

"I run a software company, I think I have something that might be
useful to you."

"Money is very useful."

"I have something better."

"Let's hear it."

"You're still not smiling. You would be so much prettier if you would
just smile. No reason to be sour, I'm one of the good ones."

That made her smile.

"Alright, what've you got?"

"We're working on some models we think might help you identify
women at risk."

"Go on."

"It wasn't the original purpose of our collection, we were looking for
other factors, but we noticed a high degree of correlation between the things

we were looking for and the characteristics that typically apply to women in dire domestic situations."

"What were you looking for?"

"Shopping habits for household items, women who would be looking for new living accommodations, rentals that were good for children. Taking it together, we saw that many of the women we identified were living in domestic abuse situations."

Mia smirked and asked: "how does this help them?"

"What's your methodology now? You offer aid and assistance to people who call you or walk into your offices?"

"Pretty much."

"Wouldn't it be more effective if you could reach out to women who meet the criteria, who are likely in need of help? If you had access to data like that and could respond to it in a timely manner, wouldn't that be fantastic?"

"Depends how accurate it is. Does it also detect whether they are ready to reach out and get help?"

"Isn't that part of the problem? Their situation prevents them from being ready for help."

"Your plan then is to use data that these women are creating when they shop or when they browse various services looking for rentals and sheets or whatever and proactively contact them with an offer of assistance that they haven't yet asked for. Is that it?"

"Yes, and what we need to do to make it happen is a federal grant that's already out there and waiting for you."

"A grant for what exactly?"

"There are grants that are meant to help fund the use of technology in community-based social services."

"And where would the grant money go?"

"Well, it costs money to develop these models and acquire this data. The grant would fund that."

"You want me to acquire the grant so that I could give you the money to make it easier for us to invade the privacy of women who may or may not be in abusive living conditions. What else?"

"Well, nothing but if they're looking for living arrangements that are family friendly or household items, we have suppliers who can provide those things."

"You have customers that are looking for customers, is that it? So, this is advertising meant to look like sociological research and the application of social policy, is that it?"

"Technology can make people's lives better."

"Then why not do it without the grant and without the advertising advantage? You're suggesting this is an ethical imperative you are acting on and yet your plan is profit driven, isn't it?"

"That isn't a crime. I'm surprised at your reaction, frankly. I thought you'd be thrilled to get an offer like this. Privacy rights have been used to enable domestic abuse and yet you're still worried about protecting those rights and effectively helping those men."

"Does your data include biometrics? Wouldn't that help time the sales pitch? We go after them right when they're at their lowest point, we could determine that based on heart rate or blood pressure. What does the model say?"

"I can't tell if you're being serious, but that's not a bad idea. In fact, that would really make the grant proposal stand out."

"Excuse me, I see someone I need to talk to."

She made her away across the dining room where several people were standing around the table and helping themselves to the spread. She nodded at one of the women as she passed by toward the living room where Dina and Gwen were sitting on the couch and chatting over their half-filled wine glasses.

"I've just been assaulted by one of the good ones," she said as she came up to them.

"Daniel," Dina said in surprise. He must've followed her into the living room.

"There's no reason to be nasty," he said. "I was only trying to offer my help."

"This pogue," she said, looking calmly back at the two women on the couch, "wants to use a behavioral model to identify women living in at-risk situations, then reach out to them and try to sell them a new rental contract and household supplies. On a government boondoggle, no less."

"I had no idea that you were one of the bitter and resentful... ...feminists who..."

Her friends stood up and joined Mia in glaring at him as he searched for the words to finish his sentence.

"Yes?" Gwen asked.

"Look, I just meant that there is no reason to remain stuck with old methods and approaches. We can do a lot of good in the world with leading edge technologies. There's this wonderful grant program to bootstrap it. Isn't your focus supposed to be on helping women and not just feeding your ego?"

Mia looked back at the other two, "Dina, Gwen, do you know this guy? He says he's a friend of Leo's."

"There's no reason to be rude," he said and then went off in a huff back toward the kitchen.

"So emotional. Probably a rich liberal," Dina said after they watched him walk away.

"I think he went to school with Leo," Gwen said. "I don't know if they're still close. He's corporate. Runs a data science company or something."

"What do you think? Am I right? Isn't this idea horrifying? I mean, the experience he's targeting is complex and serious. Machine driven behavior modification doesn't seem well-suited to that."

"I don't know," Gwen said. "Maybe if he were doing it on his own it would be awful, but in partnership with the right organization, maybe it could be done well."

"Really, you think it's worth exploring?"

"I'm just saying, maybe the secrecy and emotion behind it helps the abusers."

"There should be targeted advertising for victims of domestic abuse? Like, hey we saw you were looking for a new place to live and researching the schools that are nearby, is everything okay? Reply all to this text or email and we'll send a representative over right away."

"You could add security services to the offerings," Dina said casually.

"Wait, you both think my reaction was knee-jerk? You think it's reasonable to explore this?"

"Using models for this is so common, it's everywhere. People are used to it. It might not be so bad. It might be a good antidote to the invisibility that women report when they've lived with it for so long. They think no one cares, no one is interested, they're on their own. Here comes a new service that finds them and exposes them. Not publicly in some grotesque way, but to concerned social workers who can offer them real help."

"I feel so old."

"If the model can identify someone who's suffering, there may be room for other models that help identify the perpetrators. You could target them in a different way, with different services. There might be cross-reference with other character traits that could teach you how to approach them and get them help for changing their behavior."

"An opportunity for selling goods and services, isn't that the proposal? These are companies that talk about helping people for a small fee. They dress themselves up as though they were doing the right thing, as though they were acting ethically, but they don't just give it away, they're looking for revenue streams and margins. I'll bet that guy has already put people on the task of researching the various grant requirements so that he could fast track it. They're the pork of government spending."

"Why do you care what his motives are if it gets us the funding we need?"

"Motives matter. When there are problems, solutions will be tinged by those motives. We're spending too much on services and not getting the right return on investment so we're going to cut the program. That's how they think. It'll pollute the whole process."

"Cross that bridge when we come to it," Gwen said. "That's not a new problem. We get that more often than you think. The county is always making us provide data to show that the investment is paying off."

"Yes, but that's an assessment in human terms, it isn't about profit, it's about effectively spending county funds. The desired outcome is helping people not maximizing profits."

"It couldn't hurt to look into it," Dina shrugged. "Even if they cut the program after the first year, that's still a year. That should be the measure, not whether this guy is an asshole or not."

She looked over her shoulder and around the room to see if she could find him. He was standing in the dining room next to Leo with a plate in his hand, laughing. This made him look even worse than on first impression. "Fine," she said, and then walked back that way, flashing a big smile as she approached him.

All the Places

In each of the places looking closely revealed all the places. At the dinner table where the five of them ate from the same dishes in the center of the table, at the hotel bar where those two men sat next to each other and talked out of the sides of their mouths, in the dining room where they stood opposite each other while she explained what is wrong with the profit motive and he ate from the plate he held in his hands. That was only the half of it, there were those two who sat in the booth opposite one another, bit into a sandwich, and saved the pickles for last. Then there was the father and his newly teenaged daughter who sat in the evening cool of the kitchen while the heat beat down on the coming night. They had guests, the brother-in-law and his wife who brought their son to share the weekend dining and lighten the load of the missing aunt and niece that left both families incomplete.

They were a bridge to the other worlds confronting their places and the time they passed there. They were always both less and more than their footprints allowed. Stacking them up into this group or that, finding the common ground as it would unplay in hypothesis and what drew near, made them look a little less human and a little more like furniture in a catalog meant to make the room more inviting or give the meal more flavor. Whatever could be said both reduced and excluded by assigning and attributing. These were lists we compiled to append, these were the brokered descriptions that revealed how we ought to feel and respond when hurt or pleased.

It's mesmerizing that none of this means anything to anybody. These hidden moments far away and out of sight, they were the one and the other alone and in pairs, nothing captured, nothing contained, and nothing that haunted their memories for years and years on end. This was just dinner, just an unremarkable moment, nothing to take note of or inscribe with an insignia.

We didn't enjoy the privacy we had, we cried about the privacy we lost. The more it poured out, the more blessed it was. As this rare thing...

Become subtle...

Everything changed when you considered it across different scales, small and large, Em and Am. People ate together, lived side by side, characterized by averages and norms, but this person here ate together with that person there, was that one and the same?

A list iterated using most programming languages was simple to achieve. When the list became enormous, however, you needed to build a complex mechanism to map and reduce operations through worker processes iterating as a distributed system: a properly built system scaled out infinitely.

Maybe the reason population size wasn't a worthwhile environmental problem was because we already built the complex mechanisms required to handle the population's needs. It was problematic to criticize that infrastructure without alternatives. Not just "how to grow and transport food without fossil fuels" but "how to maintain an international tribunal of nation-states," "how to gather and share knowledge," and "how to keep the billions of diverse people entertained."

Since nearly all of that came from large organizations, they needed to address the elephant in the room: "how to replace the self-serving and essentially status quo preserving large-scale organizations built solely for the sake of serving a large population."

Even if the problems were addressed in ten years or less, this last problem took more force of will and altruistic action than humans could muster. Only people willing to sacrifice could swing it.

What did such a sacrifice look like? Where would it come from? What lists were no longer enumerable once we took that alternate route?

One of them, the one who set so much in motion, was trying to discover something new and beyond the averages associated with women in their mid-twenties grieving at the loss of a parent while continuing to navigate life events. She was trying to discover him, become haunted by the life he hid from her when he was there to cushion the impact of its meaning.

What would she do and where would she confront what lurked behind her? It recalled the story of the young man looking to discover what happened to his wife after she was abducted from the gas station when they were driving through town years before. He discovered the truth alright, but not in some cold and distant fashion, by reading a description and learning the details from a chart or police report. Instead, he went through it. His discovery was pure and exacting, it recaptured the anxiety and the fear, it repeated in detail exactly what she knew then in what he knew later. In the end, the villain laughed at them both and called it justice.

Is that what remained for her? Was she searching for what he went through with that same hunger for an exact repetition and not the cold augury of facts and representations?

The data showed the wounds and highlighted the scenarios where opportunities were left on the table. Which of them was harassed at work, which mentally demeaned at home and in front of the children, which ones attacked by someone they knew, which ones engaged in high-risk antics exposing them to the cruelty of strangers? Places and spaces, times and events, made to look alike, modeled with the same sand and glass. Automated systems triggered events through monitoring principles that dispatched services, sent help, and alerted the proper authorities. Such an idyllic world where technology and the power of the market came to the rescue of an endangered group recast as a population segment ripe for positive outcomes.

Feedback was collected and routed back into the system to improve the model and increase the likelihood that future predictions were more crisp and more likely to avoid both false negatives and positives.

The point was to inhabit the logic of the movement, to occupy the places that stretched between origin and outcome. Doing so made more movements possible, increased the variety and diversity of the logic filling the world. Voices got their spotlight, performers had a chance to stand at center stage. The more we knew, the more options there were, the greater the meaning of our lives and the more we addressed problems before they got out of hand. It created a perfect world, that was obvious to everyone who suffered it. The result was a win-win situation where we were better off, living amid our like-minded fellows, and the economy was jump-started to create prosperity aiding those in the business of assisting the generic other in harm's way and in need of a helping hand.

Back to her, she winced at the thought, she dwelled in the details of her relationships. For her the model was a universalized vision and it captured events from descriptions that stood so far away. None of this satisfied her, she was devoted to the singularity of what he was and the singularity of what she could be. She did not know how to filter that down into properties and attributes, into a cross-section of traits that tended toward other traits, and which led toward specific behaviors appropriate for people like her feeling what she felt.

"How can it help us think their thoughts?" she wondered.

"It helped me discover his desolation," she said. "I feel it."

In the end they were both left wondering to what extent this repetition was the organizational goal and to what extent it was the revolutionary antagonism to it. When we had condensed our sense of the world into a singular track specific to people like us, we achieved the perfect integration of the particular and the universal. This overlapping life marked the individuation of the agent in its most perfect dialectical form.

The book she read told her a story about a personality that developed endlessly throughout time, in moment after moment of accumulated memory saturating the artist's body. The brush strokes and the mixing of color became limb and sinew. The cigarettes and the whiskey became blood and phlegm. The arguments, the slamming doors, the quiet brooding in the aftermath, these accumulations made for more accumulation. The personality formed while it expressed itself. In / as / through it. This construct, this undecidable string of prepositions, littered the story and told it. He perceived that in his poverty, his soul suffered. One day this may have been a passing thought, but day after day it remained and clouded the sky of experience only to dampen it. He did it to himself, the story suggested, he was the cause of it because we recorded his thoughts and made decisions from them. We observed his movement and projected his actions. They were his and he was free to do as he pleased, so who else would there be to blame for what happened and what followed? He decided to take the money, he decided to settle his path on an unanticipated route. Yet the decisions grew from his personality just the same as the whiskey and cigarettes, the brush strokes and color, all of it.

She paused and considered the upshot. His actions had to be his own, that's the notion captured in every moment of his life. He was at his liberty throughout, and yet these decisions came upon him like an alien mind occupying him, staying the night, and never leaving even when they muddle about in the back rooms and behind the scenes. She knew how one thing came from another. Once a starting point was established, the sequences followed of their own with a logic provided by social circumstance and the dynamics of desire and consequence. If there were no starting points, if the origin already happened, what then? If we already lived and dwelled in the given of a life that we did not choose, and this logic made us while being emitted by us, then where were we in that? How did she hope to find herself here in the place where she never thought she was lost? That night, was that what told her these tales? Or was it her body traversing the night? How did she name that movement with any of the well-known terms of the past and those who lived them? She was not there, how did whatever was there get here now with her in body and mind?

What she knew was that she was born as nearly nothing. Just pleasure, pain, and erratic movement, the simplest of things seeing only simple things. Before she knew it, she had grown. The logic of her movement, her supposed action, began before she was able to command. Who did that leave? Where did she come from? Where was she going? Were they right when they told her she only had to choose?

The last week was a lie, and she knew it. Mother and father were artificial stopping points along the way, she did not choose them. She did not and cannot. Contrary to popular ideas, the mother withdraws as much as the father. She circled upon her grief since the one next to her was no longer there. He was gone, and she was too. For a spell. Where did that leave her? What signs did she read in her memory and with it? This planted germ of a moment sought to yield an end, to emit something visible and visceral, more than just an endured past tense, but a frame of reference that took hold. It commented on her every deed and shined light on her every destination.

She paused with the book and set it aside. It was late and she wanted to go to bed. Not like this, she wanted laughter at the end of the day, but she could not find it. Then she recalled how silly he could be, acting the clown for the two of them. At the breakfast table, in the living room at night, for those brief moments on the weekend when he would emerge from his study and sing them songs without ever hitting two notes in a row from the same scale. The nonsense words spoken only for the sound they would make. The turnabout in language that allowed the joke to zig when everyone expected it to zag. She can't remember anything specific. What was wrong with her? No acts came to mind, there was just the duration of his playfulness and the resonance of his voice on the air. She heard him.

Emission Analysis Feedback

Aristotle's *Nicomachean Ethics* begins:

> Every art and every inquiry, and similarly every action and
> pursuit, is thought to aim at some good; and for this reason
> the good has rightly been declared to be that at which all
> things aim. But a certain difference is found among ends;
> some are activities, others are products apart from the
> activities that produce them.

Movement is made an ethical concern. The end is invested with value making it more than an end, something good. The ultimate end, the one and only end, is happiness and is desired for its own sake. As an activity, it has its end within itself and not as a product beyond its movement.

It cannot be a worthwhile end if human beings are not capable of achieving it. This activity of the soul is desired for its own sake by a creature that can be happy. Happiness aligns with the soul and is its appropriate function. What is a soul and what is it supposed to do? Happiness is the highest end because it best fulfills the full potential of the human soul. The soul is a happiness machine.

> For just as for a flute-player, a sculptor, or any artist, and, in
> general, for all things that have a function or activity, the
> good and the 'well' is thought to reside in the function, so
> would it seem to be for man, if he has a function. (I.vii)

A function is in the service of something. It serves to bring something
about, something that is both its origin and its end. Because the human
function embodies an origin and rational formula, those same metaphysical
elements discovered in substance and the world-soul, there is something
extraordinary at stake in ethical concerns. When human beings fulfill their
function by living well, we reconcile with the eternal circle of being initiated
by the prime mover. Happiness is not only a human end stemming from
the rational functioning of the soul, but the highest end. It is the
reconciliation of substance in a temporal being.

This makes ethics metaphysics in reverse where the object of inquiry is
not an origin more original than any other origin but an end more final
than any other end.

> Now if the function of man is an activity of soul which
> follows or implies a rational principle, and if we say 'a so-
> and-so' and 'a good so-and-so' have a function which is the
> same in kind, ...: if this is the case, ... human good turns out
> to be activity of soul in accordance with virtue, and if there
> are more than one virtue, in accordance with the best and
> most complete. (I.vii)

The soul as the origin of action is capable of realizing either of two
contrary outcomes: living well or not living well. This is its rational formula.
Living well is that activity expressing potential. It recalls the doctor who
heals her patient, who doctors well. A human soul is also capable of living
badly. There are quacks.

The twofold soul is wholly rational on the one hand and obedient to
reason on the other. Desire and thought are intimately related. This repeats
the work of substance and the world-soul. Desire in humans is not blindly
driven by its object, it can be disciplined. The person who desires may
effect a change in her desires through rational guidance. The rational soul
acts on the appetitive soul and causes change.

What makes something obedient to reason? That is, what does it take
for something to obey a command? It must be something upon which
something else can have an influence. Where reason is the influence, there
must be desires capable of listening to reason. Someone listens not just

because they have ears receiving frequencies from a speaker. Rather, they understand. If I do not understand Greek, I cannot listen to someone speaking it. If I occasionally pretend to listen to Greek speakers, it is a ruse. If desire listens to reason, is obedient to it, then desire must speak reason's language.

The relation between duality and unity repeats itself. Metaphorically, the rational part speaks and the obedient part listens. Reason and desire are the mouth and ear of the soul. The substrata, the soul, has two parts: one that is rational, and one that is not. Then there is an additional division between the properly rational and what is obedient to it.

We approach the logos from behind its divisions and folds. The logos both speaks and listens. These two belong together there in the soul. More so, logos both acts and is acted upon. It is the origin of rational activity, and it is the origin of that on which reason acts: mover and moved. The interplay of reason and desire in the practice of the soul reconciles with the origin of movement and the accompanying rational formula.

> It will also on this view be very generally shared; for all who are not maimed as regards their potentiality for virtue may win it by a certain kind of study and care. But if it is better to be happy thus than by chance, it is reasonable that the facts should be so, since everything that depends on the action of nature is by nature as good as it can be, and especially if it depends on the best of all causes. To entrust to chance what is greatest and most noble would be a very defective arrangement. (I.ix)

By study and care, ethics is a concern for living well. Not by chance, but deliberately as something learned and studied. Because we care, it is not left to chance. The fulfillment of the human function cannot be left to the whims of accident and contingency, to the autonomic nervous system.

Desire and reason are not only related through speaking and listening, but through potential and its actualization. The human being lives their life as a being that thinks and desires. Insofar as action is oriented toward the satisfaction of desires, it must be guided by reason, it must desire correctly. The ends of action, the objects of desire, must be honed and corrected. As a potential for action, twofold desire and reason are brought together in a chain repeating the relation between potency and actuality, but with something more added, something that supports reconciliation.

Desire must be tempered. It is wrong to trust what is best in us to the happenstance of contingency. We must deliberately strive for the good and bring it about in a calculated and reliable fashion. Without such calculations, we leave whatever is good in our lives to chance. As the ultimate end and highest good, happiness depends on the "best of all causes" and the best of all causes is the rational agent properly using reason interleaved with obedient desires. The link between desire and reason repeats the potency and actuality of the unmoved mover.

Books two and three of the *Nicomachean Ethics* further develop the repetition of first principles in the rational agent attempting to realize finite accomplishments. We have the capacity to be virtuous before we learn to be virtuous. He writes: "we are adapted by nature to receive them and are made perfect by habit." We actually are creatures capable of developing virtues that bestow us with the capacity to act virtuously. States of character are created by activities: habitual for virtues of character and taught for virtues of thought. These states of character are capabilities actualized by training.

States of character are present in an agent when the activity produced by that state is accompanied by the right rule. The rational rule accompanying virtuous action is the doctrine of the mean.

The resulting contraries are extremes, and the mean lies between them, where one side is excess and the other deficiency. The mean is not something absolute in the object but relative to the agent involved in determining right action under the circumstances. There is the athlete for whom 2 pounds of meat would not be enough and for whom 10 pounds would be too much. It does not follow that 6 pounds is just right. Rather, a trainer must account for the various factors: bone structure, the goals of the training, available nutrients, etc. The ultimate determination of the mean is relative to the athlete and their relevant purposes and conditions. Virtue indicates the proper balance and vice an improper one.

Deliberation is essential to ethical action because it must look at the world, the soul, and then decide on how best to act when trying to strike a balance between extremes. The agent must decide what to do. Decisions must grow out of an awareness of who we are and what we are capable of doing under the circumstances in which we find ourselves. Our possibilities are an interplay between ourselves and the world. Every potential already includes a relationship with whatever conditions it requires. Everyone needs goods and conditions to be virtuous, every virtuous act takes place in a context and relies on available goods.

We deliberate about means, not ends. Where do these ends come from? Happiness is the guiding light for the ends we set. Those ends which require the highest expression of virtue are the ends most desirable. Happiness is the greatest expression of virtuous activity. We hear the call of reason when our desires form in alignment with its ultimate end.

We are moving in a circle.

What makes something desirable is not its fulfillment, rather it is a link in a chain where happiness guides the way and forms the bond. Desire lies in a chain of relations made visible by potential and actual happiness. It contains the potential to be fulfilled, it is always intentional and at work in a circulating system: linked members of a chain guided by a principle. There is an actual state of desire referring to a potential state of affairs. Recursively, this can go on forever. Agency fulfills the desire, but does not end, rather it produces more links, it reinforces the chain of events. Realized desire always persists in some residual wanting.

If this sequence were not anchored at every step by something desirable for its own sake, then the agent would be constantly frustrated. The end in itself takes on a special significance, it grants the agent respite from her endless desire, permitting ultimate satisfaction. Some ends will not be justified. We say those desires are inappropriate, wrong, or bad. On the contrary, when the desired ends can be fulfilled, realized, or actualized in this chain bound by happiness, then they are appropriate desires. Happiness justifies each of the ends and is present at each point along the way. It is not enough for the virtuous to know what they are trying to achieve here and now. Rather, they must have the foresight to know whether the end promotes the highest good. The agent must know the ultimate end and have it in mind. It must be always already with them.

A virtuous person understands her ultimate end in happiness and is capable of deciding how best to achieve it. This end must be reachable even if it is not yet reached, the universe must be a place where creatures who want to be happy *can* be happy. Human virtues are part and parcel of the universe. They are not only contained in my personal being as an agent with desires and ends but are bound up with the causal relations of things themselves. Recall that Aquinas claims that substance moves through understanding, will, and love. If the prime mover moves through desire as well, then its ultimate end must be present as it begins to desire.

Does substance, the world-soul, want to be happy? Can it be happy?

Happiness is desirable for its own sake. Whatever the prime mover's ultimate end, it must fully and completely express its potential.

We are moving in a circle.

Reconciliation is the finite attainment of the infinite potential in the prime mover. The parallel between its ultimate end and the soul's ultimate end aligns something eternal with something temporal, something with an infinite potential and something with a finite potential. There is an interleave between the infinite achievement of the finite and the finite achievement of the infinite. The end of ethics is not only the reconciliation of the finite creature with the infinite through the former's happiness, but the infinite being —the prime mover— is itself reconciled in the finite creature's attainment of perfected finitude.

The life of study realizes this interleave, it is substantial organization intentionally realized as the soul's breath.

Understanding, realized in the life of study, is the supreme element of the soul, and it is that most divine of elements. In book six, the philosopher says that understanding is concerned essentially with origins. It is the attempt to come to know the origin of whatever is and the nature of those first principles guiding its movement. The ultimate first principle, the ultimate origin, is the prime mover or substance. The object of the life of study is inquiry into the nature of substance. Understanding is not only concerned with those origins that might be called first things, "[it] is also concerned with the last things, and in both directions. For there is understanding, not a rational account, about the first terms and the last." The best life, the life of study and care, is concerned with both metaphysics and ethics, the first and the last, as the origin and the end of what exists.

Understanding is the divine in/as/through human being, it is the life of the gods. It is also so very human, something all-too-human. The tension is the prime mover reconciling with itself, its eternal and infinite nature coming back to itself and realizing it through the life of study and care. When the soul becomes happy, the prime mover realizes itself as something that understands. There may remain a distance between them, the two only approximate each other, but the form of the union is there. Understanding is realized in the course of a human life, and it actualizes the essential nature of substance. As such, excellent understanding is both the prime mover's happiness and the soul's.

The distance that remains between the always already of the one and the not yet of the other plays itself out striving toward the infinite from the finite. Understanding incarnates the distance between the unlimited and a limit. Our happiness as humans lies in striving to understand the happiness of the world-soul, its function and circulating system. We cannot know a theoretical identity of the finite and the infinite, but we actualize the twofold relationship between them when we are happy.

We are moving in a circle.

Supposing that we have evoked the essential circulating dynamic of metaphysics and ethics, the reconciliation with substance in happiness, the details of this circulating system become visible as it approaches its zenith. The soul's logic stretches out in intentional relations to meaningful things. Since reconciliation lies in the ultimate end, the origin is preserved through continuous movement in a circle. The doctrine of virtue can be employed to manage its household in an intentional phenomenology aimed at preserving the origin in the ends idealized as perfect fulfillment.

Intentionality and the Circulating System

Excursus

Imagine a rich man who always does what he is and is what he does. Is it possible? Everything so transparent, there is no remainder, nothing left for the imagination. Yet that is how they would always have it. It is not a trivial coincidence that the monumental ethical positions in history have been integrally associated with monumental metaphysical lineages.

It was not chance that led Aristotle, Kant, and the utilitarian into their concern for the ethical. Ethics has always been about ends and the appropriate ends for human beings, the ends proper to the best of them. Metaphysics, likewise, has been about ends projected into the heart of nature. Through these deeply integrated insights, they hatched a plan for the ends of action, or what amounted to the same thing, the ends of nature. Religion has always been more honest than philosophy, even if it sacrificed truth to achieve it. The world religions did not veil the implicit design of their metaphysical hopes with their ethical agenda: god was the origin of what is *and* the origin of what ought to be.

The origin was present in desire, compelling it toward its end. What we are was essential to what we did. The end preserved its origin and realized it as the fullest potential of the functioning universe within the agent. The delights of virtue and the pitfalls of vice were once world historical in stories and imagination. The matter central to ethics involved the whole of existence in a struggle where human beings were the primary focus. It was difficult for humans to avoid thinking that the goodness of their agency was of universal concern, a riff played out in the music of the spheres. Nothing better spelled out the meaning of the word *god* and how it expressed the desire that the universe care what happens to us. It is irrelevant whether this implicated religion in an anthropomorphism of the deity or a deification of the human. Existential and ethical concerns were linked in the effort to realize a universal and exhaustive dynamic among actions at a human scale.

The end must preserve the origin. We inserted the deity into the agent, breathed the world-soul into the soul, and placed substance within the subject. The reconciliation of the ethical with the metaphysical turned a world of possibilities into human being-there present between them. This was a dream of elegant and auspicious individuality. The statue of Hermes stood on its pedestal. This tantalizing mythology seeped into every erotic thought and every visceral motion. Only the path remained, there was nothing beyond it. The Tao, the way, the logos drew us into a swarming black hole from which no light was emitted, analyzed, or fed back.

This circulating system, a delusion emitted by the mechanics of flowing blood and a faith in principle, welded together the chain of relations and brought the origin to its realization. The actualized end became the subject of investigation, the object guiding and governing questioning as its rudimentary urge and meaning. It became possible to find a political economy producing and reproducing human life through repetitions of patterns. For the time being, we remained focused on specific ways for life to embody achievement. The fantastic deity of lore and its projection into the hearts and minds of any and every one of us, linked us with others and with everything that is. The myth was a fabric, it was breathing, and it was being. It had been done well, and it had been done poorly.

Success was measured against fulfillment, posing as a realized content: willing it, loving it, and understanding it. It was already determined how we understood, loved, or willed, we just needed to realize it. Whatever god — or however we named the collective voice— understood, loved, or willed through us was at work in the findings of the philosophers, granting them their place. This dynamic was engineered to repeatedly encounter failure. The system always devolved into an economy. Fulfillment was based on an ideal that could never be realized. They wanted us to fail.

The incomplete middle was an interlude between the first and second act. Every difference in the world rested on whether you looked forward or backward. This middle space appeared metaphysical when looking backward and ethical when looking forward. Behind us lay knowledge, in front of us value. In the task of deconstructing metaphysics and ethics, interlude revealed itself, unconcealed itself, as a reconciling dynamic working through every movement interleaved between first and last things.

Morning

Who would take over now? There were so many details. How much did she know already and how much did I have to explain? These artists caught in the trap, they were the heroes, and they were the villains. The descent of order and its systematic processes yielded artistry both for and against, both here and there, they relieved the artist of whatever ache drove him forward from his humble beginning to his pathetic end. I thought that was what the story announced. This man, this poor man, was relieved of some burden by the corporate descent he suffered. Relief came in the form of goals replaced, supplemented by something coming from somewhere else, releasing him from his depictions and visions, from everything that tormented him with the right way to go and the right decision to make.

I would have to tell her about the money.

The goals flowed into his mind over the years. Build this, organize that, get this done, find out what they did, and so on. Those many little goals and projects meant nothing to him in the end. These little quivers that threw him here and there throughout the day, calling them, sending a note, gathering information, investigating the telemetry, everything for the sake of finding out what happened, where things went South, and what was the root cause. How long would it take before we got there? They would pay him for this, and he would be fulfilled when his breath and his blood received a purpose and were placed among his peers. No longer left to himself, this artist become mechanic experienced the wealth of movement through ideals that he could grab hold of and teach the language and symbolism of his god.

I thought this story, this long yarn about artists and despair, was ultimately about goals and where they came from. Whose goals were they and how did they come to speak in me as me when they made them mine? That was his journey and that was why they, not he, were the artists of despair. Goals, I thought, were manufactured. Fabricated. Their production came from a central dispatch, a source that described everyone who hovers around it, giving them what they needed and pointing them in a direction unknown. These imagined communities were the spring from which the tribes came. They were the source to which we returned when we could go on no longer. What made the hero/villain stand out in this tale was that, unlike the others, he had his own purposes, he assembled alongside a different tribe, and he imagined himself among ancestors who stood out like islands in the history of giants threatening to erase any memory that remained.

The company determined which things mattered. It determined which origins were realized and which failed. It told the history, and it inscribed the players in the game as it wished to see it played out. Intent was governed by the stories it permitted. What you wanted, what you loved, how you thought, it emerged from this order, these voices, and this set of ends that collected you in the realm of that deity who woke you, guided you, and laid you to rest come evening. God was the rule that guided the movement from beginning to end, from sunup to sundown. The deity was that active source that took shape as plans for action and ends idealized and set in motion.

Eirini groaned and rolled onto her left side. I couldn't help myself, some presence pulled me onto my right side to face her. We were close by, and her breathing created a pulse alongside my temple. Her eyes opened and I felt some ancient twist pull my lips and my tongue. There was nothing I could do to resist it. I was with her as she came out slowly from sleep. The draw of her eyes, the worlds opened in her mouth and nose, they streamed past me and I could not will myself beyond this measure of not being alone any more. She smiled and said, "Good morning."

"Good morning," I said without meaning to. Smile, I smiled without meaning to. I was with her in a way I had not been moments before when she slept, when I stared silently at the ceiling thinking about that artist and that corporate chain around his neck. My smile faded because I could see that even the draw of Eirini's breath and her eyes and her smile were chains around my neck, they pulled me into a connected whirlpool that I could not avoid, and that I was powerless to ignore. She was drawn into me too and knew that my smile abruptly departed because of some passing thought that disrupted our contact. She reached out and touched my face, calming me, and bringing me gently back to her and our common origin, our common tongue, and our common breath.

"Are you hungry?" I asked without meaning to.

"What were you thinking about?" She asked, ignoring my question, sensing that it was an attempt at pulling us both back into ordinary things and putting more distance between us and the alien pulse that comes and goes.

"That book I've been reading."

"What about it?"

"It's very sad."

"What's it about?"

"There's an artist and he goes to work for a company that fills his mind with nonsense. Slowly, that nonsense drowns out everything that used to fill it."

"Did he need the money?"

"He needed the money. But he is dying. In a way. Death is an end that destroys your other ends. Do you see what I mean?"

"I think so."

"Dying is anything that destroys your goals and dreams."

Eirini pursed her lips.

"It's hard not to think of my father when I read this. Some friend of his wrote in the front: 'This one is yours'. Maybe that friend thought my father was like the character in the story."

"Do you think he was?"

"Maybe. He worked so much, he spent so much time focused on things that weren't really his. They were his job. They were goals that were part of some company that made him spend his energy on their projects in exchange for money."

"It doesn't seem worth it."

"We give up so much for so little, don't we? All we get is old. We get the privilege of growing old without suffering the even worse fate of dying on the streets because we can't care for ourselves."

"What are you talking about?"

"It's not like we can just live as hunter gatherers and forage for food and shelter. The system of life, the economy, the social world, it requires that we adapt. We need money. We sell off every little bit of ourselves to continue living, because the suffering that comes from failure is abysmal and painful and threatens to turn us into dust."

She put her arms around me and pulled me close. She whispered, "I remember him happy. When he would come to Greece, he was always happy. He adored your mom and he loved you very much."

"He was a chameleon, I think."

She stroked my cheek.

"He would adapt to wherever he was. In Greece, he was different."

"You think his love was fake?"

"No, that's not what I mean. Either way, he wasn't there. The artist was dead in both places. The company wins or the family does."

"That's crazy talk. Your grief is blowing things out of proportion." She kissed my forehead and held me closer. No tears. I was determined not to cry. It would have been too much a luxury.

The doorbell rang and we heard commotion downstairs.

Outside

"There is nothing in the top few search results to explain why ableism is wrong."

"What are you talking about? All that says why it's wrong. It's discrimination and it assumes that there's some standard or norm against which value is measured. Whatever falls short is deemed less than or not able."

"That doesn't tell me why it's wrong though."

"Just unpack something from history then, there's plenty to tell you about equality and the role it plays."

"A lot of those pieces you're referring to were written by ableist thinkers. Equality is not your aim here, there's no equality. That's exactly the point. The rejection of ableism can't rely on an underlying claim of equality, it has to rely on some basically ableist notion of the being that is worthy because of some trait that it possesses."

"What is this now? More abhorrent ethics from you? Have you no decency?"

"None. At least nothing I can rely on. Nothing I can take for granted. So much the better. Good and evil are a hierarchy, the good want to be the elite. So many of your chums and bedfellows are always doing this, bullying everyone to get in line with their virtue signaling and dogmatic assertion of woke values. Most of which rely on some implicit conception of power that doesn't look much different from the historical edifice they oppose."

"Those are bots trying to pull the center apart to give the extremes more power. I'm not going to argue with you."

"Because you can't, you know I'm right. It's idealistic liberal bullshit. Vanity. Anti-racism for no reason other than the desire for more power, anti-misogyny for no reason other than the desire for more power, anti-ableist for no reason other than the desire for more power."

"These are *attacks* on power."

"And that's why they're nonsense. They attack the people with power only for the sake of getting some of it for themselves. They want to have more power than they currently have, they don't want to be exploited, they don't want to be discriminated against, or held in lower esteem, they want more power."

"You think that's unreasonable?"

"No, I think it's heroic and wonderful and extraordinary. But nonetheless it's an attack on power for the sake of it. There's no virtue in it, no drive toward a higher end. They cannot claim the moral high ground. They're animals struggling with other animals. As a group, they increase their power by forming alliances and attacking each other. They used to think that was bad."

"What's this now?"

"It would be a waste of time to attack the people who wildly disagree with them, so they attack people closer to them in the political spectrum. This is very clever. The progressive attacks the liberal, then once they get greater numbers and enjoy more power, the lot of them can go after the neo-liberals. Once they have them, they can keep inching to the right. All for the sake of increasing their power."

"I'm beginning to understand why you have so much time on your hands."

"I get it. That's what it's about though, isn't it? If you want to play nice with different kinds of people, you have to be amenable to their drive for power. You have to boost their egos, and you have to feed their fears and then give them an outlet. That's exactly why you can't batter the extreme opposite end of the spectrum with your politics. Those people don't give a crap about you and so nothing you say will reach them."

"You must have at least some shared ends to be able to persuade another person. That's not very original."

"I'm not trying to be original. I'm just pointing out that these ends in common are part of the communities we are in or want to be in. The moral power of accusing someone of racism or ableism or misogyny has to have teeth. It doesn't have any teeth if your opponent just says 'so what'."

"That's your politics then, 'so what'? You have no alliances, no empathy. You don't believe in anything? In education? In living well? In treating people well? You don't believe in freedom? Justice? Equality? Nothing?"

"Power. The exertion of force. That's it. What I want doesn't matter, only what I see. That's science. That's experience, free of any moralizing that injects desire into it. It is delusional, and based on those material relations you're obsessed with, fabrications that delude the creatures in the biosphere into playing along, joining up with others based on a wish. Joiners are wide-eyed and ready to give their life for something or other that they have no business giving a damn about."

They opened the doors and got in the car.

"Unless they wish to achieve a higher expression of power."

"That's the only thing they ever do, that's the mechanism itself, or the sophisticated mechanism of nature capable of adaptation. Organization is adaptation. It's power, the drive for it. To sustain, to maintain, to retain. Power through and through."

"Look, can you just say the address into the thing, for crying out loud. We need to get there already."

"That never works for me. One sec. Bop bop bop. Okay. Calculating route. Will you let the machine drive us there?"

"Why not?"

"Able and not-able alike can use the machine."

"Just press the damn button, would you?"

The car started moving out of the parking space and toward the entry of the covered garage. Carl sat in the emergency seat, Fred in the passenger seat. They entered the address Ginna gave them and once the car was on the road and headed in the right direction, Carl unlocked his phone and called her.

He looked away from Fred, trying to affect some semblance of privacy.

"We are," he said in response to her greeting.

"Hi Virginia," Fred said. "We're ready for our instructions now."

Carl looked nervously over at Fred and gestured for him to keep quiet.

"You're not on speaker. He's just a loudmouth. What are we supposed to do then?"

Carl nodded and listened, pressing the phone closer to his ear to prevent Fred from hearing the voice on the other end. He turned his shoulder as Fred showed his frustration. "What's she saying?" he whispered.

"What if she won't talk to us? Two strange men walking up to their door, they may not even answer. They'll think we're Jehovah's witnesses."

Fred mouthed the words, "let me talk to her," but Carl just turned his shoulder and then his head toward the window while he listened and muttered a few monosyllables in agreement.

"Okay, got it," he said. "We're pulling onto some residential side street. We must be getting close. I'll talk to you soon."

He set the phone down on the console next to him. The car stopped in front of the address and Carl put his hands on the steering wheel to take control of the last few yards.

"What are you doing?" Fred asked irritated.

"Habit. Don't get me started on my neo-Luddite father," Carl said. He pulled the car over to the side of the road, the two of them got out, and walked up the driveway to the front door. They could hear the car execute its shutdown sequence as they stepped up onto the porch. Carl rang the doorbell. Fred was standing behind him looking up the street. "This is the only house without an American flag," he said.

Far Away

He texted her early that morning to let her know he was going into the office even though it was Sunday. She didn't text back right away, so he sent her another letting her know that he wanted her to be there in case the boys called. He also had some questions on her notes for the piece he was going to be reading at that thing scheduled for next week. He walked into the office taking the usual side streets and stopped for coffee. People sometimes recognized him, but they usually left him alone. The coffee shop staff may have once said something or other to him when he came in, but the novelty wore off and now he was just an ordinary customer waiting for the usual. He ordered and paid just before getting there and went inside to stand off to the left and wait until they called out his initials. B.T.

When he arrived at the office, there was no one there. He checked his phone to make sure he didn't miss any messages, but there was nothing. He went into his office and sat down with his tablet rereading her notes. He sat alone like that for a few hours before he heard the outer door open and some rustling about before she appeared at the doorway to his office.

"What are these questions that are so urgent you need me to come in on a Sunday?"

"It is not about the questions, they can wait. It is the interns. Are they going over to her house this morning?"

"Yes, but they're going to call me on my cell. What value do you think you can add to this process?"

"Do you think she will want to talk to me?"

"You're probably right," she said to placate him. Then she went on: "So, these questions you have for me are just filler until we hear from them, is that it?"

"We need to work through them. It seems like you do not think this is the passage I should read."

"I have reservations."

"Go on."

"Isn't there a scene just like this in one of the earlier novels?"

"The intervention from *Time Between Summers.*"

"Yes. This feels like an intervention too. The characters have lured this guy out there and they're trying to stop him from doing what he's doing just like in the other one. It makes this story seem to overlap."

"That *is* what is happening."

"It's a little gimmicky, don't you think? This character is supposed to be that same character, is that the point? And now we learn this even though there hasn't been any other indication of it until now?"

"I think if you reread everything leading up to this scene you will see there are several clues."

"This is what you want? You want it to become clear now that all along this has been the same story, just coming from a slightly different perspective."

"Exactly."

"Is it possible this scene is too important to you? Have you considered that maybe this emphasis is because it should be the center of the book?"

"What makes you think it is not the center? Not only of this book, but of the other one too. The whole setup is in place. In the other book it happened right near the end, it might even be the climax. The main characters are crammed into a tiny geographical area."

"So, the exact same scene is the dramatic center of two different books with two different perspectives, is that it?"

"Yes. To be fair, it should be four different perspectives. Last time we got it from Eli's angle. Here it is from Stefan's point of view. We would also need Kai's and Marianne's. To be thorough. That is the plan for this book. It collects them together."

"I thought the last book was from Kai's viewpoint."

"What do you mean?"

"At the end, doesn't someone call her El Cide Hamete?"

"El Cide Hamete is fictional. He is the supposed writer of the tale, not the actual writer, remember? Cervantes wrote *Don Quixote*, it is farce to suppose that Benengeli was the true author."

"Eli is Cervantes? Or Don Quixote? I think you're making a mockery of that book. You've reduced it to absurdity. It's better when the author has only a vague notion of what's taking place. Leave the interpretation to your readers. By asserting your authority, you only risk making yourself ridiculous."

"The whole point of that book was to set up for this book and the whole point of both books is this exchange. If this notion is ridiculous then the two books are both nonsense through and through."

"That doesn't make the argument you think it makes. If you insist, then I think this book needs to replay the perspective of each of the four characters. Include Eli's point of view here. Include all four. Let this make the other book's scene indeterminate. It would become in retrospect yet another point of view that comes from some *unreliable* narrator just like you described it back then."

Her phone rang and she looked down. "It's Carl," she said.

"Are you guys on the way?" she asked as soon as she answered.

"Are they on the way?" Ben Thorne asked.

"Carl, take me off speaker," she said ignoring him.

She lifted her hand in his direction, left the office, and went over to the bullpen.

"Just go over there and talk to her," she said firmly. "Say that you want to talk to Lena. Tell her that you're there to be helpful. If she's willing, get her on a plane. He wants to see her in person. If there's something that prevents it, help her take care of whatever it is. The point is to get her here."

He came to the door and pressed against its frame as he leaned forward to watch her pace about with the phone close to her ear.

"We'll worry about that when the time comes if we have to. Have her call us. Give her your phone and tell her to hit redial. We'll try to talk her into it. Worse comes to worse, Ben can talk to her mother. That's our nuclear option."

"Absolutely," Ben Thorne said from the doorway. "She will know. Even if she does not, she will. She has to."

She turned away from him and said, "Okay. Good luck," then ended the call and turned back to face him.

"They're at the house."

"Is he worried they will not answer the door or talk to them? We should have let her know they were coming."

"In the last message I sent, I told her about it, but we don't know if she's getting those messages. She doesn't respond. We shouldn't be breathing down her neck like this. We should be giving her time. She's going through a lot right now, what is so urgent that we have to talk to her right this minute?"

"I want her to have the facts. I do not want her to make any rash decisions before she knows everything. Until I talk to her, until I tell her everything, she will not. I am concerned that she will do something she regrets."

"Fine. Let me ask you. Ten years ago when people were asking you about *Time Between Summers*, they kept asking whether the whole story was autobiographical. You said it was just a story and even though you borrowed the setup from your own experience, you're doing that constantly and it doesn't mean there's anything to it. The story was pure fabrication."

"Yes."

"Now, here you are coming back to it. Even if the story's made up, even if every story is made up. Is there something from this one scene that's real?"

"It is pure fantasy. Never happened. None of it. Not one word of it."

"Then why do you keep going back to it? Why do you think it's so important? Why does it merit such close attention from every angle? What is it about this scene?"

"Something is bending here. Time itself, I think. That is what fascinates me."

"How do you mean?"

"Eli and Kai, Stefan and Marianne. Something is bending or long since bent already. The whole engagement is about desire and the way it interleaves with time. There is the desire to tell the tale, but there is also the desire the tale has to be told."

"The story wants something?"

"Absolutely it does. Spinning a yarn is always a dialogue with the story that wants to be told."

The phone rang again.

"Hello. Ben Thorne's office," she said turning back toward the window. He remained at the doorway but watched her with keen interest as she turned her back to him.

"My name is Virginia Percival. I work for Ben Th..."

She waited.

"Yes. They work for him as well. They are graduate st..."

She stopped short and listened.

"Yes. He is here. We can book you on a flight to New York at your earliest convenience. We are very eager to speak with you about..."

Again, she was cut off. She stopped and listened, nodding her head.

"We understand that and are very sorry for your loss. I assure you we would not be..."

Same routine.

"He is right here. Would you like to speak with him?"

She listened for some time to the response. Ben Thorne said, "Does she want to speak to me? Give me the phone."

She shook her head and twisted away from him a little. She kept nodding with her ear glued to the phone.

"That's not a problem, we can book two for the flight if you..."

"I see. Okay. I understand."

"Goodbye."

She hung up and turned back to face him. She looked ashamed and a little frustrated. Ben Thorne picked up on it but urged her to pass along her findings.

"They don't want a flight, she doesn't want anything right now. She's with her family and is driving back home this week. She says she'll call you once she gets there, but that she doesn't have time for this now. They're going to Greece, and she doesn't think she'll have time until after that."

"She is driving back home. From Seattle? By herself?"

"She said we, but no other details."

"That is so foolish. Now is not the time for that. She cannot be serious."

"I'm pretty sure she's serious. She doesn't sound like someone who says things she doesn't mean."

"Have them go with her. They cannot leave her alone. They should go with her, make sure she gets there okay."

"You're serious? You want them to drive the rental car across the country to make sure she gets home alright? She doesn't want any help. She doesn't want anything from us."

"You did not offer this. Call them back. Tell them they have to follow her."

"Fine." She opened the contact and hit call. "It's me. Are you still there?"

"Okay. He wants you guys to drive back with her. We'll change the rental car and plane tickets for you. You guys just follow her and make sure she gets back okay."

"That's what he wants."

"Don't tell her by herself. Make sure her mother knows about it. She's probably worried too, so she'll help sell it. Let them know this is what you're planning. Let them know that Ben Thorne insists you do it."

"Okay. Let me know if you need anything."

"Are they going to do it?" He asked after she ended the call.

"Well, you heard. Let me call the rental company and make sure this can be done."

"Of course, it can be done. It is just money. Whatever it costs. Just get it done."

Inside

Georgios opened the door to two men standing near the door. They asked for Lena, and he paused to look them up and down.

"Who shall I say you are?"

"I'm Carl Maxwell and this is my associate Fred Nozick. We work for Ben Thorne. He was hoping to have her call him at her earliest convenience."

"Let me check. Wait here."

He left the door open and called up the stairs to Lena. Ariti and Ermioni came out from the kitchen to see what was going on. Lena and

Eirini came down together after a few uncomfortable minutes with Georgios silently staring at the two men while the older women stood in the background and asked each other what was going on.

"What's going on?" Lena asked when she got to the door, showing signs of just getting out of bed.

"Two men from Ben Thorne are here. They want to speak to you."

"What do they want?" Ermioni asked.

"They say they want her to call their boss."

"This is unacceptable," Lena said and then went briskly through the open door onto the porch causing Carl to abruptly take a step back off the edge and onto the pressed stone patio in front of it.

"What is this about," she said. It didn't sound like a question.

"Hello," he said just as friendly as the first time to Georgios. Friendlier even. "I'm Carl Maxwell and this is my associate Fred Nozick."

She nodded at Fred. "Your associate?"

"Yes. We work for Ben Thorne. We're research assistants. It's through our departments. We're graduate students."

She gave them the once over. Based on mere appearances, their story checked out.

"You came this far just to ask me to call him?"

"Yes," Carl said. "He very urgently wishes to speak with you. You can use my cell to call the office. Here." He handed her the cell phone. "Just hit redial."

"How do I know who I'm speaking with? You just want me to hit redial on your phone?"

"If you would. Please."

She paused a moment and looked over at Fred who had been carefully watching her since she stepped outside.

"What's your story?" she asked. "Are you studying literature or something?"

"Philosophy," he said.

She smiled. He detected some condescension in her eyes. He was about to say more, but she spoke first: "Why would a philosopher want to do research for Ben Thorne?"

"Are you familiar with his work?"

"A little."

"His narratives are all over the place. He plays with genre. No two books are the same, in fact. This has always been fascinating to me. I've been reading his stuff my whole life. My interests include the role genre plays in meaning."

"Are you learning a lot from him?"

"Not a thing," he responded with a grin. "He's a complete asshole. Never acknowledges my existence and has given me almost no insight into his work beyond what I got from reading it on my own."

Carl shot an uncomfortable look at Fred.

"So besides coming and bothering people who he wants to talk to, what else does he have you doing?"

"Research. He's working on something now and there are a lot of characters with different backstories. They're educated, and they know lots of things about different areas. I'm mostly focused on speech patterns and terminology common at the time. Making sure the dialogue is historically accurate."

"I see," she said as though she didn't see. "And you? What about you?"

"Political Science," Carl said. "We're at CUNY."

"Political Science? Why would a political scientist work for a novelist?"

"Ben Thorne is not just a novelist. What have you read?"

"I'm actually reading *Artists of Despair* at the moment."

"Then you know. That book is about social structures and how they inhabit the people who populate them. His work is totally relevant to political scientists. Philosophers too. Sociologists, anthropologists. Everyone's reading him."

"Do you agree with your *associate* then?" she emphasized the word as though she still didn't believe it.

"Oh yes. He's a colossal asshole. To us at least. I don't think it'd be fair to say he's always like that. He has an assistant. She's the one we usually get our assignments from. She seems to get on okay with him."

She looked down at the phone. The screen had gone black, so she handed it back to Carl who unlocked it and passed it back to her. She hit redial.

"Hello. Who am I speaking with?"

She waited for just a second to hear the answer and then got right to the point.

"There are two men here. They say they have come on Ben Thorne's request."

"Fine. Ben Thorne sent them. Is he there with you?"

She was becoming agitated. The more she put together the purpose of this visit, the more agitated she became.

"I don't have time to come to New York right now. We have a lot to deal with. It's very rude of you to barge in like this."

She paused to collect her thoughts. She didn't want to lose control.

"I don't understand what concern this is to Ben Thorne. Why is he trying to get involved? We're driving back to Michigan this week."

She paused.

"That's not the point. After we get back home, we'll be leaving for Greece straight away. There's no time for this."

"Goodbye."

She handed the phone back to Carl.

Ermioni had opened the door and stepped out on the porch, but she only caught the end of the exchange.

"Hello," she said smiling at the two of them. Both men nodded and mumbled something back.

"Would you two like some breakfast?"

"Mom," Lena said. "We don't have time..."

Her mother interrupted her. "There's always time for guests."

Carl and Fred exchanged looks, Carl said: "I'd love a little coffee if you don't mind." Fred nodded in agreement.

They went inside. While they were sitting at the table drinking their coffee and having a piece of apple cake, Georgios asked them about living in New York: their apartments, the cost of living, the nightlife. They were patient with him and Ermioni was listening and taking note. Carl's phone rang while they were talking.

"Hello." He looked down and spoke quietly.

"Yes. Still here." He listened.

"That's like 2000 miles?" His voice raised a little in disbelief.

"What should I say?" His voice deflated back to a whisper.

"Fine." Everyone else had stopped talking. They were waiting for him. He looked up and sensed they thought he was being rude.

"Will do." He ended the call.

"Problem?" Georgios asked.

Ariti and Ermioni were standing in the kitchen and waiting for an explanation. Lena and Eirini were sitting at the table where Lena hunched over a cup of coffee and Eirini hummed quietly while forking pieces of apple cake into her mouth.

"It was the office again," Carl said looking over at Ermioni. "They want us to drive back East with Lena to make sure she gets there okay."

"I don't need a chaperone," Lena snarled.

"We'll follow along in our own car," he said continuing to look at Ermioni who was still sizing them up.

"We'll need to discuss this. Give me your number," she said. "We'll call you after we've had a chance to discuss it."

Carl pulled out a business card and a ballpoint pen. He crossed out the office phone number and wrote his cell number just next to it. He left it on the table. They stood, thanked Ermioni for the coffee and cake, and then moved toward the door. Georgios was escorting them. "Thank you for your time," Carl said looking back at Lena, who hadn't moved from the table and didn't look up. Eirini waved and spoke for the first time, "Goodbye."

Evening

I didn't want to talk about it. It was an absurd idea. Later, my mother cornered me on the back deck.

"Do you think they are who they say they are?"

"Probably. Although it's possible that they're complete sociopaths who have figured out how to perfectly imitate a pair of socially awkward intellectuals with more knowledge than sense. Eh, what's the difference?"

"That's something your father would say."

"Mom. What's the point of talking about this? It's a ridiculous proposal."

"Why? If you think those boys are alright, It'll calm my worries."

"I'm sure it would. You trust men to take care of women. You're so naïve, Mom."

"You don't think they're good people? You don't think they can be trusted?"

"I don't know. Who knows? We only just met them."

"But you think they are who they say they are, don't you?"

"Yes, probably. We can look them up online to check."

"You spoke to Ben Thorne on the phone?"

"No. I spoke to a woman. Virginia Percival. She works for Ben Thorne too."

Mom picked up her cell and briefly looked down at it.

"She's written a book. A first novel. You think this is her?" She showed me her screen.

"I don't know, Mom. How am I supposed to know? Why are people just showing up on your doorstep thinking they can come with us on a cross country drive? Why are you so quick to let them?"

"It's not that strange, really. Your father wanted you to call him and he seems to be worried about you. You have to admit, in this day and age it's not safe for young women to drive across the country. Who knows what could happen?"

"I can take care of myself, Mother. Those two couldn't protect us from anything I can't already handle."

"Still, there's safety in numbers. Why do you want to handle things? Wouldn't you rather there's nothing to handle? With more people, it's more likely you'll avoid trouble. You don't really think they're dangerous, do you?"

"Those two? Hardly. They look pretty much like most of the men at school. They won't be dangerous until they get tenure."

"So, what's the harm? It'd make me feel better to know you had more protection. Don't forget, it's not just about you. Eirini will be with you. You don't want anything to happen to her, do you?"

"Of course not."

It was getting dark but still warm outside. A little muggy. The yard was quiet save for the sounds of birds rustling through the giant pine trees backed up against the fence from the neighbor's yard. It sounded like there were quite a few of them foraging around in there. Crows most likely.

"They're so opportunistic," I said.

"The boys?"

"No, the crows. Dad used to sit out here and talk about how he thought the whole lot of them were the devil incarnate. A murder of crows."

"Poor things."

"What do you mean? You feel sorry for them?"

"They can't help how they are. It's their nature. I don't like them either, but what are they supposed to do?"

"They have very complex forms of communication, you know. Those sounds, they're not just random. They're saying something to each other."

"What are they saying?"

"Relaying the facts, no doubt. Where's the food, what are the dangers and risks of coming here or going there."

"I've never gotten used to them. There are so many around here. They're afraid of the squirrels and bunnies though."

"I don't think so. Raptors could easily handle small rodents like that."

"You're the expert, but I know what I've seen. I saw one of those bunnies chase off a crow who was looking for food nearby."

"One on one? Okay maybe. In groups, they're vicious. I wouldn't be surprised if a group of them could stalk and kill a little rabbit."

"They're very opportunistic."

"And you feel sorry for them."

We sat and listened for a while. She was so calm and so alert to the sounds and rustling.

"Mom, that was something I never understood. When I was a kid, you used to always complain about the rabbits and how they would eat your plants. But you would put water out for them. Why?"

"They're living creatures, Lena. No living creature should be made to suffer when it's so easy to help them. I don't like the bunnies, but what am I supposed to do, they need water."

"I think you must be the only person who thinks like that anymore. Most people nowadays are perfectly happy to let others suffer."

"I know it. Your father thought cruelty had become a sport. Even the people who attacked other people for being cruel did it cruelly."

"I can't handle any political talk right now."

"It's not politics. I'm just remembering him. He always wanted to understand the people he didn't agree with. Did he ever tell you the story about the *Communist Manifesto*?"

"What story? I don't think so."

"When your father was in high school, he was like a parrot of what he heard his parents say. Like a parrot?" she said unsure of herself. I nodded, and she went on, "He hadn't really thought much about any of it, so he accepted what they believed. They were conservatives, but only about the economy. Reagan was president. You know about him, don't you?"

"Of course, Mom."

She smiled, recognizing the frustration in my voice. It was comforting. His ghost in me.

"The way your father told the story, he wanted to understand his enemy so much that he thought he had to read and learn as much as he could about them. He read the *Communist Manifesto* in high school, and he did it so that he could understand his enemy."

"Marx is not the enemy, Mom."

"Just listen to the story. Your father thought he was, that's the point. But he didn't close his mind. He wanted to understand what was behind it, he wanted to see what their grievance was and what motivated them. He read that book and he loved it."

"Alright Dad, good job."

"He said the poetry surprised him, and the passion. The love for human beings, the compassion for suffering and hardship. He said that's what drew him in."

"Hmmm. What if he read *Mein Kampf*?"

"Well, we need to have a moral compass, but I think your father thought we had to understand the Nazis too. If we didn't, we wouldn't know where the ideas came from and what motivated people to feel that way and do those things."

"Looking forward things are never as simple as they are looking backward."

"What does that mean?"

"Well, it's easy to know now that the Nazis were evil. If you rely on your moral compass, maybe when you're in the thick of it, while history is being made, you won't have the same bearings, you won't be able to see so clearly what's good and what's evil. Young men who look into white supremacy so that they can better understand it, they may not be able to rely on a proper moral education to find their way. They could be persuaded to turn against common decency for the sake of their family's values."

"I just wanted to tell you a story about your father. He and I were alike. In this way, at least. We both had a lot of sympathy for our enemies. You understand?"

"Sympathy can easily turn into aiding and abetting though. Those rabbits were getting strength from that water. Without it, they couldn't have eaten as much of your garden as they did. Who knows? They might have been forced to pick up and move off somewhere else if you hadn't been keeping them hydrated."

"Well, I can't describe it like he could. It's easy to turn things around and twist them. I'm just saying, where are we if we don't care for each other? I know that not everyone has good intentions. We shouldn't help people with evil in their hearts. I'm just saying that we have to understand each other if we're going to live in this world."

"Back to the issue at hand though. Are you going to call those guys and tell them they can follow us across the country?"

"It's okay? You don't mind?"

"Fine. Whatever. If it'll put you at ease, I'm okay with it."

Emission Analysis Feedback

Intentionality fulfills an act. The act fills with content. Potential is realized fully or partially when measured against contrary outcomes. In book theta of *Metaphysics*, Aristotle frames actualizing potential as the coming to its form of matter: "matter exists in a potential state, just because it may come to its form; and when it exists actually, then it is in its form." Rational formulas guide the way and give material a form. Matter forms through the activity of an embodied soul. Understanding is a practical philosophy, it weaves the soul together with its world.

When discussing how virtue fulfills the soul's function, some virtues are ranked above others. Understanding is the most divine. What relationship does intentionality have with virtue at its pinnacle? Virtues of character already display intentional relations and span the distance between parts of the soul: the rational part and the part obedient to it. The virtues of character evoke an intentional relation when they involve origins of movement residing in the materialized form of the understanding: the breathing body.

Among the virtues of character, justice ranks high. Friendship stands alongside it, providing good company. At the acme of virtue's order, friendship and love stand side-by-side with justice. These virtues are the all-important means to achieving happiness as the reconciliation of the origin with the highest end. In them, we unearth the intentionality of a circulating movement, we move in a circle. Specific virtues offer insight into the way reconciling movement, the circulating system, is lived as human being-in-the-world-with-others. We see what they see, and we hear what they hear.

In the circulating system's material, we expect to find the everyday existence of human beings together fulfilling their potential for happiness. The reconciliation of the origin with the end, the soul's exuberance, is achieved through community. As hypothesis, happiness reconciles in shared lives: the kingdom of ends is the fullest realization of the origin.

Friendship and justice involve the soul with others. We feel things together, we judge things together. Even the virtues of thought come from dialogue and the play enacted between teacher and student.

Justice concerns the "distributions of honor or money or the other things that fall to be divided among those who have a share in the constitution (for in these it is possible for one man to have a share either unequal or equal to that of another)." Sometimes there is a sense of justice in which it "plays a rectifying part in transactions between man and man." Justice spans the distribution of goods and restores balance in transactions. There is distributive justice and there is retaliatory justice.

Distribution can be done badly. Retaliation ensues. Both map and reduce to the transaction and any unjust form of it. Transactions submit to a judge who weighs and measures the equity of distribution and the equity of retribution. There must always be "proportionate requital" which is not the same as simple reciprocity. "[R]eciprocity in accordance with a proportion and not on the basis of precisely equal return" is the glue of social relations.

Justice sets in motion a circulating system of origins and ends. The principle of proportionate requital, applied by participant or observer, supplements exchange: "For it is by proportionate requital that the city holds together. Men seek to return either evil for evil —and if they cannot do so, think their position mere slavery— or good for good —and if they cannot do so there is no exchange, but it is by exchange that they hold together."

Human beings engage in just personal relations and give each other what they deserve in exchange for what they receive. The circulating system is just when it spans the distance between first and last things. Retaliation and distribution are both concerned with giving and getting one's due: the principle active at the origin and realized at the end structures and balances exchange within the circulating system.

Aristotle describes bargaining among equals where their equality results from proportion. Two doctors do not "associate for exchange, but a doctor and a farmer, or in general people who are different and unequal; but these must be equated. This is why things that are exchanged must be somehow comparable. It is for this end that money has been introduced, and it becomes in a sense an intermediate; for it measures all things, and therefore the excess and the defect—how many shoes are equal to a house or to a given amount of food." Money allows for trade of unequal things as the language of their comparison, the language accounting for justice. It introduces proportion into concrete relations. Money acts as though it were happiness, it is the principle that reconciles the circulating system where justice and friendship are at stake.

Need and demand lie beneath exchange and are even more essential to it. Money acts as a "representative of demand" "by convention." Because it can be used universally to buy things, every participant needs or demands it. Money has its place "because it exists not by nature but by law and it is in our power to change it and make it useless." Money interleaves with the exchange relations between actors, it introduces proportion and facilitates justice. It is instituted as a standard for measuring and ensures just relations, it enables proportionate requital, and judgments about them.

Demand is the fabric of human association. If people did not need anything from each other, they would not exchange things. Demand fluctuates at different times and the nature of these relations is unsteady. Money steadies and so "all goods must have a price set on them; for then there will always be exchange, and if so, association of man with man." Money stabilizes our communion where demand is volatile, and insofar as demand is channeled from the thing to the money that can buy it, demand itself is stabilized. Money can be used not only to steady the inequalities of worth between goods but as insurance for trade. There will always be a demand for money, so it holds people together, even if the particular goods in one's possession become temporarily or permanently useless to others.

Money realizes the need for proportionate requital and distribution, but it is not the whole of it. We must give honor to those who deserve it, we punish thieves and criminals without limiting that punishment to fines. Money is the representative of demand, but demand is at the root and has other representatives. Honor is due in proportion to the demand placed on the accomplishments. Demand is key and money is secondary, serving only as its surrogate. Likewise desire and happiness.

The circulating system set in motion by exchange is the circulation of just relations between people engaged in common ends. Where proportionate equality is the principle of justice and proportionately equal relations are the result of just acts, friendly exchange is the rational structure that mediates the coming to an end of a collective final cause guiding action, whether it be distributive or retaliatory.

There is friendship in such a collective. The philosopher says that "it is a virtue, or involves virtue" but in any case it "is most necessary for our life." It is next to justice at the acme of virtue's order. In fact, "friendship would seem to hold cities together, and legislators would to be more concerned about it than about justice. For concord would seem to be similar to friendship and they aim at concord above all, while they try above all to expel civil conflict, which is enmity." Demand holds cities together, but even more than demand, friendship does. It provides a strong *form* of justice: "if people are friends, they have no need of justice, but if they are just they need friendship in addition; and the justice that is most just seems to belong to friendship."

The young need friendship for guidance, the old need it for care and support, and those people "in their prime need it to do fine actions; for 'when two go together...', they are more capable of understanding and acting." Even where friendship involves the performance of virtuous deeds, it is still needed. In friendship, the capability of one's fine actions is increased, and with it understanding. We may do good alone, we may understand alone, but together we are still more capable.

Friendship is not only love for the other, but a reciprocal goodwill and awareness. This interleaves justice with friendship: to be just means to give each his due in proportion to what he deserves and only take what is due to oneself. Friendship, like justice, is a reciprocal relationship. Otherwise, one takes too much, claims what is not properly one's own, what one does not deserve: when someone relies on the other's friendship before it is reciprocated, they act as a thief.

The principle at work in friendship, making it a virtue, is one and the same throughout: awareness of reciprocal goodwill. Only in friendship does the other appear as both a rational agent engaged in potentially virtuous action and as an external good necessary for the practice of one's own virtues.

I can enter into just relations with the other without knowing much about them. If I know what I need, what I want, what the object in question is, and what it is worth to me, I can make a just trade for it. In friendship, I cannot be this way. Rather, it is precisely the other and not some object of exchange that I must know and who must know me. Reciprocal goodwill goes beyond mere means, it creates a commonwealth.

Complete friendship, friendship for each other because we are good people, involves other virtues. Not just virtues of thought that aim at truth, but virtues of character that make us loveable. Friendship based on virtue resembles an activity rather than a movement. The end is not external to the process (not useful or pleasant), goodness in the other is not good *for* something. Since human beings live among others, we need friendships of various kinds, but complete friendship is finer and more necessary to a good life because it involves virtuous people and completes their virtue. No one can be happy without friends.

"Concord, then, is apparently political friendship, as indeed it is said to be; for it is concerned with advantage and with what affects life [as a whole]." In concord, people agree and are willing to act on those beliefs. They make the same decisions and carry out the same actions. What is most important in concord is that distributive justice be its object. People will agree on what is proper for each to have and so will "have the same thing in mind for the same person." Concord interleaves demands and ends with justice.

Despite his focus on the circulating system of friendship in the political relations of human beings, their existence in a community at large and in public places governed by laws, the philosopher says the good life is best accomplished in friendship through understanding and knowledge. The ultimate end of human life, happiness, is best attained through friendship with the origin and its principle. Concord, goodwill, beneficence, self-love, etc., may be rethought insofar as they describe the friendship the thinker has with substance, that the soul has with the world-soul. One can only contemplate the origin by loving it for its own sake, for what it is, and not for pleasure or use. Soul and world-soul must have goodwill toward each other, be in concord with their purpose, seek to benefit each other, and so on. The philosopher understands what substance is and what it demands. In the life of the philosopher, the good life, the ends of substance become the object of inquiry, they become the matter at hand.

Substance realizes itself in friendship. It depends on something *external* to itself, on the contingent life of the philosopher. No human being is born a philosopher but becomes one, develops into one, and chooses that life. The reconciliation of substance with soul happens when the philosopher trains for and chooses to honor the necessary and infinite being of substance. Through specified contingency, the initial discord of substance's creation reconciles when it becomes capable of loving the necessity from which it came. Reconciliation takes place in the philosophical life of the virtuous attempting to befriend and understand substance's order. It is best that human beings do this together since no virtuous person could bear to see another go through it alone.

Substance —the world-soul— first appears as an external matter, as the generalized Other. Happiness involves understanding substance and marks its reconciliation with the philosopher. In the activity of happiness, the philosopher appropriates the external good of substance as the subject of inquiry into the conditions for happiness. It is a recursive maneuver. Happiness comes through understanding substance and not as pure activity, as prime and unmoved mover. When the origin is understood by its friend it returns to itself as purely intentional activity, fulfilling its potential and materializing its form, it becomes happy.

Potentiality for Being I

Excursus

Imagine a poor man who wanted to pull you close but who could only repel you. There was something wrong with his voice and words. They didn't fit with what you expected, they didn't draw you in. Instead of showing you how much he loved something, he butchered it as part of a suspicious agenda. His deepest sincerity appeared as cunning and detached rhetoric.

We don't know why he adopted this pretense, why he thought himself capable of moving in those circles. He described reconciliation with an origin, but his unfamiliar voice and strange stylings sucked the life out of a beautiful and living body. Looking forward, he claimed to pen criticism while looking backward.

Why did this happen? The history of philosophy presented for the sake of butchering it. This stinks of deconstruction. Parasitic and opportunistic, there was nothing noble there.

In that lineage, he feigned an absolute proximity between this so-called deconstruction and its metaphysics saying both that there was and was not anything to their opposition. They wrote, with one hand, that metaphysics was the attempt to establish the presence of the ground and, with the other, that establishing the presence of the ground was impossible. There never was any metaphysics. Don't we say this all the time? Appearances can be deceiving.

The irony was that to him the projects were about bridging distances. Theory set the world over and against us, it created a picture, and the viewer was reformed as part of it. To deconstruct was to demonstrate failure, to show how the distances dissolved and brought the viewers to life as part of everything that happened there.

There was meant to be a form of criticism that rejected the role of the spectator. It wreaked havoc on the language of theorists and showed how intimate its workings were and how deeply its meaning settled in their hearts and feelings. Little did they know that audiences loved being spectators.

There was always a narrator, even the great Aristotle was spinning a yarn, and he might mislead or be misled himself by the passion of the moment and the logic of the tale.

Is the unreliable narrator still a thing? Did contemporary fiction invoke observation as pure fact fashioned as aggregates from the raw data? Is that the new form of unreliability?

The notion was so immensely attractive, it infiltrated everything in his turn to dishonest genres. He found every narrator unreliable, and it drove him to distraction when philosophers acted as though there were no narrator involved. Backed by an ideal, they attempted to purify their writing. They would fashion a god. Theirs was the only character to unravel.

A Minor Literature was 1) filled with deterritorialized language, 2) political through and through, and 3) emitted in the collective without a singular voice.

It broke you, sitting on your throne and evaluating every word. It did not draw you in. The language was off-putting and jarring. Deconstruction practiced what it preached and shattered its readers, robbing them of their beloved schisms.

There was no place from where he could speak, there were no words to capture his intent with a friendly and familiar tone. He was absorbed by the theories he unravelled, his language drifted away from the earth, and his attempts at intimacy failed in producing an arrogant higher order for the twisted and the lost.

They shrugged and scratched their heads as if they were looking at hieroglyphics. He sang out in cuneiform, but no one heard a thing. "They lied to me," he said. "What broke the bonds, strengthened them."

Phone Home

Alexandros was away at school, so she only talked to her mom and dad. She told them about the two men who came from New York and were following them in a rented SUV. Eirini thought Lena was secretly relieved. She went on about the one man and his kind eyes who spoke calmly until he got excited and then it was as if he were dancing. The other man didn't talk as much and wasn't as nice, but he seemed clever and as if he had much to say even when he wasn't speaking. Her parents had so many questions, but they relaxed when they learned the men were students. Action, they presumed, would not be their strong suit.

It was still early, they had only just set out. While Eirini was talking, they came to the Columbia River and Lena pulled into a rest stop to stretch her legs and get a better look.

"Once you cross the mountains," Nikos said over the speaker phone. "Are you in the other America?"

"Yes," Lena responded patiently. "But it's not like what you're hearing on the news. There are no borders."

"There are many stories of trouble," Maria cautioned. "They will know from your car."

"The license plates don't say we're from the city, Mama." Eirini put the accent on the second syllable. "Across the mountains is still in the same state. It's not like it was before, they can't know just from looking."

"Where are these men who are with you?"

"Keeping their distance. They're just over there."

"Will you be stopping like this along the way? Maybe you shouldn't leave the road so much?"

"It's fine, Maria. There aren't any stickers or signs on the car. We'll be fine."

"Okay. Be sensible. How are you doing, Lena? Is it nice to have Eirini with you?"

"Very nice. Thank you so much for sending her. I'll take very good care of her. You don't need to worry."

They reassured Eirini's parents a few more times and then ended the call, letting them know they would call again tomorrow around the same time. They would make status checks with Eirini's parents in the morning and Lena's mom in the evening. In the afternoon they would call Mia. There would be a constant flood of reassurance.

"They are worried about you?" Fred asked when the two of them came a little closer after the call.

"Of course," Lena said. "Did you understand what we were saying?"

"Sorry," Fred said with a smile suggesting he wasn't really sorry. "I couldn't help overhearing. I mostly just know ancient Greek, but I could make out a little. I can't speak it."

"You study Greek philosophy?" Eirini asked.

"In a way," he said. "For modern purposes. I'm not a scholar."

"Democritus? He's from the North."

"Sure. The pre-Socratics. Plato. Aristotle. For modern purposes, like I said. It's common. We apply their ideas to contemporary issues. We're fed up with the Enlightenment paradigms and the harm they've caused. There are many who think we can go back to the Greeks and modernize their thinking."

"Always the Greeks," Lena said with disdain.

"You don't approve?" Carl asked.

"The European bias in philosophy is epic."

"And Anthro..." Carl started to say.

"Isn't philosophy in any other form just cultural appropriation?" Fred interrupted with a grin.

"What's this?" Lena asked, thinking she must've misheard.

"The Greeks invented scientifically informed philosophy. Anyone else who does something similar is appropriating essentially Greek notions and practices."

"And who exactly did that?"

"Contemporary East and South Asian philosophy. Contemporary African philosophy. Latin philosophy from the Roman empire. The

Scholastics, the Enlightenment. Should I go on? Basically everyone that wasn't Ancient Greek."

"You forgot to mention yourself, didn't you? With your *modern purposes.*"

"Yes, myself included," Fred said laughing.

"What's your point then, that traditional influence is appropriation?"

"Isn't it?"

"Perhaps appropriation isn't the best way to explain this," Carl said diplomatically. "Any globalizing theory contains exploitation and appropriation. Cultural, economic, domestic, and so on." They were falling into their rhythm, and it would escalate rapidly.

"The whole settler-colonial line is just plain lazy," Fred replied. "As if Homo Sapiens weren't the most vicious bastards that ever walked the planet, bringing death and destruction wherever we go. Human beings exterminate animals for survival and sport, we've been migrating and moving about for tens of thousands of years, destroying and stealing whatever is in our way without giving it a second thought."

"Your point is lost on me," Lena said. "It sounds like you're completely bought into settler colonial explanations of human migration, but you seem to be belittling them too."

"It's the way he talks," Carl said. "It takes some getting used to."

"It's because I include Homo Sapiens. The people who first came to North America, they murdered the large predatory animals that lived here. Some species were here for millions of years and were wiped out shortly after humans arrived. These were not innocents who were then colonized by another migrating group later on, they were apex predators who had their day and then were replaced. Just like the Neanderthals."

"Check your facts, but anyway you want to make it part of human nature. Is that it? Since we're all villains, none of us are."

"When I appropriate the Greek notion of Eudaimonia to understand human action, I don't care who I'm stealing from and how they were destroyed. I only care about advancing my understanding, telling a new story, spinning a new yarn, whatever it is that I'm doing, that's my only concern."

Eirini and Lena both laughed. "Ef-they-mo-ni-a," Eirini corrected him when he looked puzzled by what they found so funny.

"The point is," Fred went on a little less confidently. "That flourishing doesn't describe a state where we're keeping ourselves in check, suppressing or repressing our truest selves for the sake of some divine commandments, it's an expression of power, it's the realization of that power in excellence, in virtue."

"He and I have rehearsed this argument before," Carl said. "He thinks institutions domesticate human beings. We're wild beasts who're made tame by civilization and the constraints we place on each other."

"Deconstructing metaphysics just is deconstructing ethics," Fred interrupted. "Attacks on settler colonial history are assertions of power, there's nothing ethical there. Some introverted academics claim to be experts so they can condemn their colleagues. It's good for their careers. They have no true moral ground to stand on, they constructed a theory to gain leverage. Their theory exemplifies itself. It has resentment and a slave mentality written all over it."

"I don't understand," Eirini interrupted. "What is settler colonialism?"

"It's the theory," Lena answered, "that groups of people extend their reach across the world by migrating to new places and acquiring resources even if they have to enslave or murder the people already there. It mostly focuses on how Europeans settled and colonized the world as part of their Early Modern doctrine, and how that drives their support of Israel."

"The Greeks and the Egyptians, the Persians and the Mongols, the English, the Dutch. These people are the examples," Fred replied. "Unfortunately, it's harder to find counter examples. If our history started in Africa, then our migration to Europe counts too. We spread throughout the world and wiped out the competition."

"Competition?" Eirini asked.

"He means the Neanderthals and other human species," Lena said. "But that's false, the..."

"And large animal species too," Fred interrupted. "Human beings have never been good for the ecosystem."

"Is that supposed to excuse our behavior?"

"We don't need an excuse," Fred went on as though the question were a prop. "Domestic cats wreak havoc on bird populations in regions where the birds have no defenses against them. The cats won't apologize for that."

"The people who introduced them into those ecosystems are responsible, maybe they should apologize."

"The point is that species can't help but be what they are. Humans can't be something they're not."

Lena looked at him in disbelief. Always white guys, she thought. Why is that I wonder?

"We're causing a great extinction, we've changed the climate of the planet drastically, the Anthropocene is real, and the harm is identifiable and severe," Lena's tone was matter of fact, she was not trying to convince anyone. Her pulse remained at rest.

"It's nothing from the Earth's perspective," Fred responded with a similarly even tone. "A blip lasting just a few thousand years. What is that in the flow of billions? We're a failed experiment, soon the slate will be wiped clean. The Earth will move on, try something else."

"That's a great tragedy," Eirini whispered.

"Even Carl's idyllic end state of perfect justice and human excellence traverses a long road filled with tragedy. There's no getting around it."

"Any understanding of humans has to account for the presence and proliferation of tragedy. Of instigated suffering and cruelty," Carl said, having been infected and calmed by the collective tone.

"Patriarchal humanity," Lena interjected.

"Oh, you think it's just men?" Fred was speaking very slowly. "Women have been here the whole time, you're agents too. Human beings are powerful because of our social bonds, our ability to work together. Why haven't women risen up and overcome the patriarchy? Because they like the rewards, the comforts, the privileges, that's why. Who knows, maybe patriarchal values were sexually selected. Confidence has always been the best aphrodisiac."

"Oh god," Lena said. Eirini was confused, it seemed like things were escalating but the tones weren't changing. It seemed civil and hostile at the same time.

"There's no agreement among women anyway," Fred went on. "Most women are happy to support the powers-that-be, the ones who aren't, they just want a different form of power, they want to appropriate what's been built with that instinct for cruelty and they want to put it to their own use. There's no divine justice to fall back on."

"Well this has been pleasant," Lena said simply while pulling back. "I'm going to the restroom and then we can get back on the road. For whatever it's worth, that's the Columbia River over there."

She went off toward the buildings nearby. Eirini went with her. Carl said, "I better go too. Way to pour on the charm, Fred."

The Estate Agent

"The White Party," Georgios said to Ariti, "is leading a disinformation campaign. On the dark web, they say the White Party has the power. They manipulate politics, but they live in the shadows. They are the puppet masters." They were sitting on the couch while Ermioni hovered over the estate agent who was touring the house and putting stickers on everything to be carted away and sold. "Make no mistake," he clarified. "They are not called white for their race, it's just that, well, you know, red, white, and blue."

"This is a conspiracy theory, isn't it?"

"It's a theory about a conspiracy," he conceded. "The White Party has invented many of the more ridiculous conspiracy theories and worked hard to spread them so that people will dismiss conspiracy theories including the one that says there is a White Party. It's like 9/11 when the US government leaked those ridiculous theories about the controlled demolition of the towers, that was to hide the fact that they used fighter jets to shoot down that passenger plane in Pennsylvania."

Ariti pursed her lips, then asked, "Are they like centrists?"

"Not exactly. Their purpose is to destroy the center. To pull it apart because it used to have the power."

"If they are in the shadows, how do they have power?"

"They pay for *all* the politicians. They pay them to be extreme and to be rigid and uncompromising, to be enemies of the center. The conflict between extremes prevents opposition to their agenda."

"How do they benefit from the violence? Those women from Chicago killed in Missouri state last week, how do they benefit from that?"

"Directly? Well, media outlets reported that story for days. That means viewers, clicks, and likes. That's money, those are transactions. Terrified and anxious people are a good audience for anything that stimulates fear and anxiety."

"It stimulates the economy. All this just to get rich?"

"Well, the media are huge consumers of network resources. They store video in the cloud and stream it on the internet for viewers."

"It's collusion."

"What's good for the media is good for the tech companies. Those companies make billions. They stimulate everything around them."

"Ordinary people have to benefit at some point. Otherwise why would they go along?"

"Look at this place, Ermioni's house. It's worth about two million dollars."

"This house?"

"Yes, it's shocking. This same house back in my neighborhood would be less than half that. The big tech companies are here. They pay their employees well. This doesn't just impact a few people. The plumbers and the electricians charge more. They can afford to live in these same houses."

"But the people don't seem rich."

"Of course they're not rich, a modest house costs two million dollars. Poor people, truly poor people, have to live in different neighborhoods or they're homeless. That's how America works. Segregation is everywhere, in every city. It's the American standard of living."

"I still don't see how these companies benefit?"

"It's like in video games. There are game items that are really hard to get. That creates a pecking order. The people who don't have the rare items envy the people who do."

"So the cities are segregated into rich and poor."

"Yes, you live with people like yourself and that's it. If you want to live better, you have to move, and in order to move, you need a lot of money. Rich people are made into icons, and everyone wants to be like them.

Their lifestyle is entertainment."

"But where is the benefit?"

"The media again, its whole payment model depends on people drooling over that kind of stuff. Clicks and likes and views."

"If you know this, how come everyone doesn't?"

"Everyone does know this. We can't help it. It's because of aggregates."

"Aggregates?"

"Groups are just aggregates of data. Tuples made into linear equations. We identify with one of them and that makes us vulnerable to algorithms and their models. Every trait you think is part of your true self, is really part of a pattern that includes others and makes you conform with them. But traits are weird. Sometimes what they make into one thing is really a million things. Like being a woman. Most people think that's just one thing, but really it's millions of things."

Ariti nodded.

"It's obvious. Problems occur when people reduce it to one single thing. There are arguments about who are the real women."

"With the transsexuals, you mean?"

"With them, but not just them. There are many ways to be a woman. Different colors, different styles, ages, different cultures, different kinds of women."

"Ermioni is different from living in America for so long."

"She's like our mother, but different. You two are different. Lena and Renya. And so on. Look at how Ermioni is following the agent around and keeping such a close eye on everything. Who does that remind you of?"

They laughed.

"So woman is an aggregate?"

"Yes, and made to look like one thing. A single checkbox on a form."

"Man too."

"It's just an example. In the end, the best way to get people to have crazy passionate arguments is to create an aggregate that seems like one thing but is really a million things."

"The aggregates cause the arguments?"

"It pulls the people apart, makes everyone rigid."

"Every topic turns into one thing against one other thing. That's what everyone thinks."

"It makes it easier to form people's opinions. Especially online."

"Everything is online."

"Even things that aren't online can be part of a model. Like with facial recognition. Your movements are captured and tracked."

"That should make us more alike."

"Some of us. Depends on the aggregates and what audience you're in."

Ariti was nodding, but looked hesitant. It was a lot to take in. Georgios, unsure of how much of it he believed, went on as though trying to convince them both.

"It's about manipulating people. If too many of us are in the center, we'll be too powerful. The extreme positions are marginalized. They needed to pull the center apart and make the extremes more powerful."

He paused and nodded. He seemed to want to stop but couldn't help it. He went on.

"No one thinks about anything anymore, they just line up with their side. Thinking is dangerous. The aggregates and the opposition, they make everything predictable, controllable."

"Well, I won't say I understand everything."

"No one does. It isn't something for individuals to understand. So long as we think like individuals we'll be tricked and fooled. The White Party is counting on that. When we think like individuals, we're at the mercy of the aggregates and those who manufacture them."

"So how should we..."

Ermioni and the estate agent finished their walk through and came to the front door. They were discussing the logistics for the pickup later in the week. Georgios got up and went over to listen in and see if he could help. Ariti followed closely behind him.

Skyway Café

They had to leave the highway for a bit to get there, but it was worth it. The retro airfield diner was decorated with propellors and pictures of airplanes. They made it just in time for the lunch rush, but you could still order off the breakfast menu. They waited a bit before getting a table.

"You're awfully quiet," Lena said to Fred who was sitting across from her.

"He's sulking," Carl responded when Fred hesitated.

"If it's about this morning," Lena said. "Forget about it. Let's just move on."

"Move on, sure," Fred adjusted in his seat. "But you'll never forget what I said. The cretin. The neanderthal."

"Over what?" she said. "What is it you think you said that was so monumentally offensive?"

"Nothing. I don't think that. It's just, I know how people are these days. No forgiveness, everything is so amplified."

"Look, the only reason I was so abrupt this morning is because you got into some topics that I don't consider part of any argument. I know how it can be, people think they're arguing for something, that they're producing theories about this or that and then they're trying to persuade each other of the truth. That's not how I see it."

"How do you see it?" he asked sounding genuinely curious.

"Language and conversation, there's so much power and potential there. They give structure to our world. I'm thinking of some of the great Anthropologists. Everything in the world that can happen, happens through meaningful connections and associations. Language isn't a set of references meant to describe the world, it evokes meaning in things and is the world. Prayers, incantations, blessings, threats, promises, commands. It's ceremony and ritual."

"Significance, I get it. You don't have to dumb it down for me."

"That right there. See. That's what I'm talking about. That doesn't just communicate information, tone is expressed, feeling conveyed. I've injured you, you think I was talking down to you, so you make a remark like that to defend yourself. The meaning is rich and carries so many possibilities, that's what's going on right now at this table in this restaurant along this road and so on."

"I don't see how that changes the fact that you've been insulted by what I said this morning."

"I'm getting to that."

"Are you guys ready to order?"

They looked at each other and generally nodded. Lena went first and Eirini said she would have the same. The waitress didn't write any of it down, she just listened as they each gave their order.

Once the waitress left, Lena went on. "My dad and I used to have conversations about this. Sometimes they would go on for days. This was when things were getting really bad. The attribute politics, the backlash on the right, the attention economy, the people trying to make a name for themselves by being more shocking than anyone else. Everyone was developing their brand."

Carl and Fred were nodding somberly. Eirini was fixed on Lena. She put her hand on her shoulder and lightly rubbed her arm.

"He used to tell me to imagine that the only thing you could hear was tone and not the words. He thought it didn't matter nearly as much what they were saying as how they were saying it. Some people were saying things that were really supportive, but they were saying it in a way that made it seem angry and hostile. Sometimes criticism and backlash came out that way too. It didn't matter whether people were saying supportive or critical things. What mattered was whether their tone was caring or hateful. What world were they making? That's what mattered."

"Sure. I think lots of people were talking about that back then. And now," Carl said trying to be supportive.

"Yeah, he didn't think he was being original or anything. We were commiserating. It wasn't a theory. We were together having a discussion. Long conversations were how we spent time together."

They looked at her sympathetically.

"He said that even when we had arguments, we weren't just arguing. There was so much more going on. The emotion and feeling from so many different things in our lives. Anyway, this morning, when you said that. About women and how we've been complicit. I could tell how angry you were, and I didn't think of it as a theory. I just didn't want to deal with your anger just then. You can be angry, but you have to understand that you don't get to just throw that at me like it's my responsibility. We barely know each other. You have to work through it and until you do, I'm just not sure you can have an intelligent conversation about it."

"Okay," Fred said. He was lighter. Not sulking anymore and even feeling a little relieved. "You're right, I think. Because people can be angry in common but for different reasons. Maybe you didn't want to make any assumptions?"

"Never," she said smiling. "And it's not my job to fix you or force you through something you're not ready to go through."

"Some men might say the same thing I did because they think they're losing their privilege. Like their masculinity is at stake, or their control. Like women are trying to take something from them."

"That's right," she said calmly. "That's usually the case."

"Because we are," Eirini said laughing.

Fred shrugged and smiled at her. The sound of her laughter made him want to give her whatever she wanted. He turned back to Lena and went on, "But not all men, and I can see that my anger, even if it has a different source, well, the optics are terrible because it puts me in the same group as those others. Who knows? Maybe I start to think like them."

"Why are you so angry?" Eirini asked simply.

"If you're a nice guy," he said hesitantly. "The girls don't find that attractive. Many young men aren't desirable to the young women they like because they don't have more traditionally masculine traits."

"Back to sexual selection," Lena responded.

"What is that?" Eirini asked.

"Well, Darwin separated Natural Selection from Sexual Selection. Natural Selection is survival in the environment, fitness relative to the terrain you live on, the predators that might live in the same area, or whatever, anything that would make specimens with one trait more capable of surviving than those with other traits. Sexual Selection is about what prospective mates prefer, what traits are desirable for sex and procreation."

They were nodding.

"He talks about a Green Woodpecker somewhere. He says you might think that its color is the result of some naturally selected trait, like maybe it kept them hidden in the trees better than other colors of birds who were eaten by predators. But it might just be a preference that female woodpeckers have when they select their mate."

"I see," Eirini said. "Fred is angry because he thinks women have made men how they are by being attracted to the worst traits."

Fred smiled and blushed a little.

"Fred," Eirini had moved her chair closer to Lena during the conversation and was now leaning across the table. She drew them in together to hear her point. "Girls are different. They grow up. Things little girls like, teenagers don't like. We change. We're different in one place than we are in another. The girls you knew in school here are different than the girls in Greece or in Kenya or Indonesia."

"That's true," Lena offered support. "People aren't in control of what they want, not always. You make it seem like these girls you're talking about had perfect insight over what they wanted and who they wanted. They were under the influence of so many things. So were you."

Eirini took over: "Maybe there was one particular girl who hurt you because she liked a more confident boy. But why were you so focused on her? Weren't there other little girls? Is it possible one of them was feeling rejected by you because you never noticed her?"

Lena interrupted again: "She wasn't thin enough or blonde enough or whatever it was that was the big attraction where you were from."

"Do you think even in our Sexual Selection, we might be constrained by Natural Selection?" Carl asked turning from Fred to Lena.

"Well, I wouldn't want to socialize this stuff too much. Evolution is about how species come to be, not about variation within them. Sociobiology may be overreach. But in the origins, yes, I think Sexual Selection and the varieties of it are probably the result of Natural Selection. Desires and attention are traits in that general way Darwin understood them. Remember he didn't have access to everything we've come to know since about genes and DNA. His theory was extremely coarse."

The food came while Lena was talking and the waitress, after putting the dishes in front of them, said, "I heard Sexual Selection and my ears perked right up. You don't hear that every day."

Lena laughed and the others smiled. They thanked the waitress and she said, "I'll be right back with your sides."

They sat quietly waiting. They started eating only after she returned with the rest of the food.

"Classic psychoanalysis, isn't it?" Fred was the first to break into the clanging of flatware and smacking of lips that passed for silence. "My anger is really just my resentment at not getting the girl I wanted and that's ultimately my fault for not being open to the other girls but having my heart set on just this one or that one. Then, to make matters worse, I turn it around and blame women for encouraging patriarchy through their behavior, but I ignore my role in it by focusing on just those women who patriarchal men set in high esteem."

"To emphasize fault," Carl said. "You have to attribute the agents involved with wills and rational decision making. Lena's point is more nuanced than that."

"Sure, sure, sure. I get it," Fred said. "We're at the mercy of this underlying power that's coming to play on our actions and words. These forces of nature and civilization and whatever else. I get it."

"But..." Lena said with a smile and no intention of continuing.

"The method still has an argumentative form, doesn't it? You're trying to say I'm being uncritical. If I were more critical, I'd see these factors at play and my anger wouldn't be misdirected. I might still be angry, but I wouldn't start casting blame on you or women generally or whatever it was you think I was doing. But what if that's just an emotional expression of your interest in getting the better of me, it's a tactic you're employing to win the interaction, to control me or discipline my behavior, convince me of the right course of action, or the appropriate way to respond, just for the sake of serving your purpose. There's still too much theory and persuasion in your approach. If it's just pure force and the expression of it, if there really aren't any arguments, then even this way of calming me down is nothing more than that, it's coercion."

"Doesn't that make it easier for you to enjoy your lunch?" Eirini asked squinting her eyes and smiling at him. Fred smiled but looked quickly back at Lena who had visibly become sad.

"What is it?" Fred asked gently. "What did I say?"

"Nothing," she waved her hand. "It's just that engineers call it recursion, that thing you're talking about. It blows up our conversations in the end, my dad would say 'you have to understand recursion in order to understand recursion.'"

They laughed at her imitation.

"Like every attempt at sorting things out falls victim to forces trying to sort things out. Unless, of course, you know when to stop."

Fred nodded. Eirini touched Lena's arm again.

Carl asked, "Lena, I hope you don't mind me asking, but your dad was Jewish, wasn't he? How come you aren't sitting Shiva?"

"My parents didn't know that many people. They weren't really part of a community or anything. So who would come? And then my mom really wanted to get everything settled so she could leave. There's too much to do."

"What's the rush?" Carl asked.

"That's just Mom for you. She's like that. My dad didn't die suddenly. I mean, he was sick for a while. They prepared. There's a plan. He didn't want her to be alone. Neither of them wanted that. So..."

"Can I get you anything else?" The waitress asked putting the bill on the table. They shook their heads. "Where are you guys headed? You just passing through?"

"Is it that obvious?" Carl asked.

"Well, you get a sense for these things."

"We're driving through to Chicago," Lena responded.

"My that's a long way, you be safe now. I'll take that when you're ready. That's how we still do it here." She refilled the coffee mugs and then was off. They sat a little longer, paid, and then used the restroom before leaving. Fred chattered about the heat and humidity the whole way back to the car.

Now Entering Montana

"Hi Hi, Mia. You're on speaker. Eirini's here too. We've just crossed the border into Montana."

"Hi Eirini, I'm so glad you came. I can't wait to see you. The scenery must be so lovely."

"The mountains are beautiful," Eirini said. "But it's drier than I thought. The trees don't look so good."

"How is the weather? Is everything okay? Lena are you actually driving that car?"

"Yes, it's ancient," she laughed. "It's like a time machine. The car and the places it's passing through. Everything is fine though. Couldn't be better. Not too hot now that we're a little higher up."

"You must've left pretty early if you're already in Montana."

"Yeah, it must've been about 8 or so. We got a good start. Mom had a lot to do today, she was anxious to get rid of us."

"She can't help herself. Did she stuff you full of food?"

"So much food," Eirini said.

"Listen," Lena said getting a little more excited. "You're not going to believe this. These guys from New York, they're actually driving back with us."

"In the car with you?"

"No, no, they have their own car, they're following behind us. Put on video." The video came up and they waved to each other. Eirini turned and pointed the phone out the back window toward the SUV following along behind them.

"Do you see that car back there? That's them. Can you believe it?"

"That's wild. How did it happen?"

"Ben Thorne sent them to my mom's house yesterday. They wanted me to fly to New York."

"They came to the house?"

"Yes, and he's very pushy. When I said I didn't have time for that and that we were taking the car back East, he insisted they come with us."

"You spoke with him."

"Not exactly. His assistant. Virginia Percival."

"Virgina Percival is Ben Thorne's assistant?"

"Have you heard of her?"

"Yeah. She wrote a novel. I read a review of it. It was a really good review, so I read the book. Just beautiful."

"Weird. Why would she be his personal assistant?"

"Hang on a second."

The video went on pause. Mia came back after a little bit.

"I thought I read something about it. She's not his personal assistant, she's like his personal editor or something. I mean, her role is literary. She doesn't pick up his dry cleaning or anything. She's involved."

"Why would she be answering the phone and talking to me then?"

"I don't know, her publicist probably wrote the article. It's trez strange, that's for sure. What are the guys like?"

Eirini looked over. She was curious to hear how Lena would answer the question.

"They're interns in his office. Graduate students. They're the ones who get the dry cleaning. One's a political scientist. He seems reserved and cautious. Then there's a philosophy student, he seems pretty intense and maybe a bit wild."

"Figures."

Lena laughed. "Not bad company so far. We'll see how it goes. They paid for lunch, or Ben Thorne did."

"You have to get to the bottom of this."

"I will, I will. But there is just too much to deal with now. I can't handle one more thing. What's going on with you? Are you working this week?"

"No, I'm at home. I've actually been looking at some old case files. You know those women who were killed in Missouri last week?"

"At the music festival?"

"Yes. We found out this weekend that they were clients of ours. They used the career services."

"Oh that's horrible. Do you remember them?"

"That's why I'm looking at the files. To see if anything jogs my memory. It's been a while. Nothing yet."

"Do you know what happened? I don't remember any details from the news."

"It's not 100% clear. The festival was mostly white people. They were women of color, a Latina and an African American. Witnesses said that some men were harassing them. They exchanged words but there weren't a lot of details. You can imagine. The women didn't back down. One of the men had a gun and one of the women reacted. She must've done something to him because they said he was injured. Anyway, he fired a shot.

It didn't hit anyone, but it set everyone off. Many of them hit the women. Just horrible. They were beaten to death."

"Oh my god," Eirini said and put her hand up to her mouth.

"Wait a minute. There's a picture in the file. I think I remember them. They were a couple. Yes, yes, I remember. A very cute couple. They had just gotten married and needed some help with immigration paperwork, they didn't really know anybody. She was from Guatemala. They were so nice and so patient. Oh god. I remember them. This is so horrible, such a tragedy. What is wrong with people?" She was choking up. Lena's voice went soft.

"Do you think the reports are accurate?"

"Not clear. I don't know. The testimony sounds the same. It's like people are learning what they have to say to justify their actions. Fucking culture war."

"It seems like anything anyone can do to get us out of it, only gets us deeper into it."

"They don't want to get us out of it, and they don't give a damn who gets hurt. We're expendable to them. No one is legitimate anymore, there's no one to be trusted, there are no independent parties. There's no one to shed good judgment, peace, or light on anything. Be careful. That's what's left. Watch out for yourself. It's the war of all against all." She paused and wiped her cheek with her hand. She shook her head and went on, "Montana is a long state. What's your itinerary? How far will you go today?"

"We'll try to get about halfway across the state if we can. I was thinking we would stop in Butte. Not the most scenic option, I guess, but it's the right distance if we want to make it to Chicago by Thursday or Friday."

"Well, be careful."

"We will be. We'll talk again tomorrow. Are you going to be okay?"

"Yes. I'll be fine. It's just... Eh, I hate this. It makes me so fucking angry, but don't worry. I'll call some friends. We'll talk tomorrow. Goodbye, my darlings."

Fred was in the emergency seat and Carl called Ginna to give the latest update.

"Hey Ginna. How's it going?"

"Hi Carl. What's happening? Where are you guys?"

"We're on the road, just crossed into Montana. Been a long time since we saw this much space."

She laughed.

"Maybe that explains it? People who live around lots of buildings might just be wired differently from people who live in the middle of this open space."

"I wouldn't be surprised. How are things with Lena and Eirini?"

"We had lunch together. It's okay. They're really nice. Great, in fact."

"Yeah. You're getting to know them?"

"Her and Fred, you should see them. They've already gotten into it a couple of times."

"I hope you're on your best behavior, Fred," she hollers but he can't hear her.

"He isn't. He's just like he always is, but she can take care of herself. She's dusting the floor with him."

"Oh, that's precious. I wish I were there to see it."

"Yeah, you should. I think he's in love."

Fred looked over. "Hey, what are you guys talking about? Put her on speaker."

"Fred, are you in love?" she said after Carl put the phone into the cradle on the dashboard.

"Don't be daft," he said.

"He went from being angry to sulking to googally and giggly," Carl explained.

Fred grimaced, but didn't say anything. There was a little extra color in his cheeks and neck. Carl was enjoying the reaction.

"Seriously Ginna. It's not just that she's clever. I mean, she's wicked clever. But it's more than that. She sees a lot."

"She doesn't see a lot," Fred said simply. "She is the light that makes seeing possible."

"See?" Carl said.

"Oh my. He's got it bad."

"What about Eirini? What's she like?"

"Oh she's just the sweetest. So caring. She keeps us honest. It's nice. It's fun."

"Well good. I'm glad you guys are getting along. Ben would like to see that turn into coaxing them to come to New York on their way to Greece. Try to talk them into it. Don't push too hard, we don't want to force them. He said he'd be willing to go to Ann Arbor to meet her there if you can't get her to stop here."

"So what's the story? Why is he bending over backwards? Doesn't he have to get ready for the keynote?"

"Yeah, we're doing it. We're getting ready, but he's totally distracted. I think it's morphing into something else."

"He's not going to read that passage you sent us about the intervention, is he?"

"It's changing. The intervention is changing. I'm convinced that this guy Em, Lena's father, he's the guy from the intervention."

"What?"

"I think so. The scene calls attention to a part of his life and how important it was for what came after. The two intervening characters are trying to save him from something. There's so much more emotion in the scene than there was when we started. I think he's feeling a lot of grief, and he's putting it into the work."

"Wasn't there an exchange just like it in one of the earlier books?" Fred asked.

"Look, I'm just saying that this same event –whatever it was– is based on something that happened and two of the people involved were this guy Em and Ben Thorne."

"Hmmm," Carl responded. "Well, let us know if you figure it out or if he enlightens you. We'll check in again tomorrow."

"Alright, Thanks guys. Talk to you soon."

"Bye."

Butte

They were very hungry when they checked into the little motel just outside Butte. The man at the desk said they might like the place just up the road, it was a restaurant on one side and a bar on the other.

The way Fred remembered it, he said it was like a cheesy thriller movie. The four of them took Lena's car up the road and when they parked in the lot out front, they were shocked when she opened the trunk and removed a small, holstered firearm from a safe bolted to the ceiling at the back of the boot.

"Open carry," she said. "I won't be the only one in a place like this. Besides, it's small, people who know will know, people who don't won't."

They appeared apprehensive but none of them objected. Inside, their apprehension disappeared. Now that they knew what to look for, they noticed several customers had similar bulges on their hips. For reasons that Fred was never able to explain, this calmed him.

After eating dinner, they decided to go to the little bar. They sat at a table and talked about the scenery and how tired they were from driving the whole day. Carl went to the bar to get another round for himself and Fred.

There was a group of three men and a woman sitting on nearby barstools. They were comfortable in the place, had clearly been there before, and knew some of the others who sat at tables or worked there. Fred noticed that one of the men spoke to Carl and that whatever he said made Carl tense. He pointed this out to Eirini and Lena, but before he could stand up to go over and see what was going on, Lena jumped up and walked over to lean against Carl. Fred followed behind her.

Whatever the man said to Carl, and whatever the others were looking at between them, they stopped when Lena got to the bar. The four of them looked her up and down just like they did Carl when he first got there.

Fred saw that the man who spoke to Carl flashed a snide smile at Lena and heard him say: "Do you even know how to use that thing?" While hearing the man speak, Fred noticed that the man had a holster under his left arm with a much bigger handgun snapped in place.

Lena met his smile with a smile of her own and said sweet as honey, "Look where it is. While you're sweeping that whole side of the bar, I'll be out quick and right on you. You'd probably end up shooting the bartender and causing a big ole mess."

Eirini came up and stood by Fred as the three friends howled with excitement. The woman said, "Daryl, she just met you and already knows you're all flash and no function." Daryl initially seemed wounded, but when he saw Eirini's face, he relaxed his shoulders and smiled at the joke.

"What are you guys drinking?" Lena asked.

"Just beers," Daryl said.

"Bartender, four more beers."

"And two more for us," Carl added.

The bar tender pulled out 6 bottles from the fridge and popped them open before placing them up on the bar. Carl paid the man.

"What brings you guys this way?" the woman asked.

"My dad just died last week," Lena said looking down. "We're driving his car back home."

"Well, I'm very sorry to hear that," she said. The men nodded. They raised their beers and she said, "To your dad."

"Thank you," she said.

"My mom died last spring," one of the other men said after they finished drinking. "How'd your dad die?"

"Cancer. Lung."

"Mine too. Breast."

"It's a fucker for sure," the woman said.

"What's your name?" Fred asked.

"I'm Leon."

"Hi. I'm Julie and this is Bob. You met Daryl. He's real special." They laughed.

"Let's drink to your mom, Leon."

They raised their bottles.

"You guys come from the city somewhere?" Daryl asked.

"Fred and I, I'm Carl, we're from New York."

"I'm Lena, from Seattle, but I live in Ann Arbor. I'm going to school there. This is my cousin, she's visiting from Greece." She put her arm around Eirini and pulled her into the circle.

"How come you two aren't drinking?" Leon asked.

"I'm the designated driver."

"Old school. I like it. Where you guys staying?"

"Just up the street at the motel."

"Aw hell, you can walk back and leave your car here. It'll be okay. Folks from the motel do it all the time."

The bartender got two more and opened a tab now that they seemed to be settling in.

"I knew y'all were blues," Daryl said after a bit.

Carl shook his head, worried about where that might lead. He might still have been shaken by what Daryl said before they came to his rescue.

"Daryl don't go starting with that," Julie scolded him.

"I'm just saying, we don't get too many in here, and when we do see 'em, they're usually not armed."

"I know my rights," Lena said. "All my rights."

They laughed and raised their bottles again drinking to their rights. Daryl, feeling like he needed to explain what started them talking, began to say. "Maybe you came to stand by your friend because of what I said. When he, when Carl, come up to the bar, I was asking him if he was white. I mean, he don't look white. I didn't mean nothing by it. I'm just saying. It's a fact ain't it? Look at his skin. Am I supposed to not see that? Blues are always sayin' I'm not supposed to see that."

"You can see whatever you see," Carl said. "But you know people aren't always going to take that question the way you mean it."

"Ah, I see," Fred said. "You meant white in color. I thought you meant White Party. I thought you were asking him if he's in the White Party."

"You know about that?" Daryl said. The others looked a little surprised too.

"I sure do," Fred responded. "The way I heard it, though, not everybody who's in the White Party knows they are. You know, a guy could call you up at work and ask you to do something. They pay you just like usual. You do what they want because maybe it's normal for your job. You don't know what you're doing or why you're doing it. Turns out, later you find out that the guy was working for the White Party and what they asked you to do was for them. And so, even though you didn't know it, you were acting for the White Party yourself."

"I heard that too," Bob said. "They say whenever you're doing something that isn't exactly your idea, you might be doing it for the White Party."

"I've never heard of the White Party, what is it?" Eirini asked.

"It's in the government," Leon said.

"The idea," Carl said. "Is that it's somewhere between the parties. They're in the center somewhere and the only thing they care about is profits and money. Supposedly taxes are just a way to siphon money away from average working people to give it to the White Party."

"Like the Jews," Daryl said.

"Now we're back to the beginning," Carl replied defensively. "When you asked me if I was white, what I said just before Lena came up was, 'Do Jews count as white?'"

"Well, they may not be properly white," Daryl said. "But they're still behind the White Party."

"Wait a minute," Lena jumped in. "The companies that are getting the government money, they're mostly run by Christians. Some by Hindus even. Why blame Jews? Carl and I are Jewish, and we don't have anything do with the White Party."

"You both are?" Leon asked. "But you don't look alike."

"Have you met a lot of Jews," Carl asked.

"I don't think so. On social."

"Well, I'm not the White Party type of Jew," Carl said. "I'm more the socialist kind. The complete opposite. That's how stereotypes work. Maybe they're wrong. If you're not meeting Jews face-to-face, how would you know?"

"You know what you grow up with," Julie said.

"You know about socialism, then?" Leon asked.

"Yes." Carl said.

"Socialists want to take away our rights, and you were saying before how you're in favor of all our rights."

"I *am* in favor of our rights. Socialism is economics. Like when you make something at work and your boss goes off and sells it, how come he gets so much more of the money than you do when you're the one who did the work? That's socialism, it's for workers."

"But without jobs, there are no workers. These companies provide jobs and if you go after them, the jobs disappear."

"It isn't about going after them, it's about making sure we still have rights at work and making sure they pay for everything they get from us. Why do only our taxes pay for police and fire departments, roads and sewers? That stuff is good for business, but they make deals with the city to avoid paying."

"You know," Lena said. "Most people have an idea of what it means to live well. And it might mean fishing a little bit here and there, hunting every now and again. Having a cookout with your friends, talking with them about what's going on in your town or your state."

"Sure," they nodded.

"Some socialists think the purpose of the economy is to make sure we can live like that."

"But they want to do that by taking my money and giving it to people who don't work. Who don't want to work."

"Like the White Party that takes the tax money without paying any taxes, is that who you mean?"

"Well, I was thinking about people on welfare."

"Bob, for every dollar we spend on taxes, only a few cents go to people on welfare. Even Medicaid money ends up in the hands of private healthcare, so most of the money goes to corporations with cushy contracts or subsidies. Isn't it convenient that we don't have any oversight to make sure we're getting our money's worth from them?"

"I don't want to argue with you about it. Especially not when you're buying the beer." Daryl raised his bottle. "But I just don't think we'll ever see eye to eye."

"We don't need to," Fred said. "America is supposed to be a place where you can live differently in different parts. The people in New York City may be different than the people of Montana. There shouldn't be any problem with that. We should have a government that looks out for both."

"That's not how it seems," Julie said. "It seems like when the blues are in control, they only care about folks in New York City."

"And when the other party is in control, they only care about folks in Montana. Is that it?" Lena asked.

"I don't see it that way," she said. "I think we're looking out for everyone even if they don't know it."

"Everyone thinks like that," Eirini said speaking for the first time. Her voice cracked a little. She sounded nervous, speaking English in front of a larger and unfamiliar group. "In Greece we think the same way. And we have completely different parties. They think they're looking out for the good of everyone. They disagree, but they agree that they're trying to do what's best."

"Are you from a big city or a small town?" Leon asked her.

"I'm from a village on the coast. There's a small town nearby where I went to high school. Then I went to university in the big city a few hours away. After that I moved back home to the village and went to work in the town. I work for the, well, you would call it the county."

"After you finished school you moved back home to the village?"

"Yes. Back with my parents."

"So, you live back with your parents in a little village, and you work for the county? You sound like you're one of us."

"Things are different there so I don't know if you can say that. Immigration is a big problem and people are divided about how to deal with it, but people who are strict on immigration might be more socialist in their economic views."

"So people can be a mixture like that?"

"Yeah," she said cheerfully. "It's different from here, and they think they're looking out for the good of the country. But people don't agree. That's true in politics everywhere. It's hard for me to get too passionate about it. Maybe that's cowardly."

They were shaking their heads and trying to be supportive.

"I mean it," Eirini went on. "I just don't know much about it. I don't know what every person is going through. It must be hard for them, and I can't imagine what troubles they have. Immigrants are going through so much when they lose their homes and have nowhere safe to send their children. Or the people who are worried they'll lose their jobs when too many people come, and the new people want to work too and are willing to do it for less money. Everyone has a different story and I only know a few people so I can't know what's happening to everyone. Maybe they're right, they have it hard and need more help. When I hear people talk about politics, I always get scared to say anything. I don't know enough, there's too much to know, too many different people and different lives. How can I say what's right for everyone?"

"That's real nice," Leon said. "Everyone thinks they know what's best."

"Alright, come on, one more drink, but then we have to go. We got to get on the road early tomorrow."

"Bartender," Carl said holding up his hand.

During the walk back to the motel, Fred kept repeating. "While you're sweeping the bar..." and then he would roar with laughter. He would narrate the events leading up to it and then repeat: "While you're sweeping the bar..."

Carl eventually interrupted him and said, "What does that even mean?" He was just as drunk as Fred.

Lena ignored the question but eventually blurted out: "I have no idea where that came from and never in a million years would I have thought it would come out of me."

Emission Analysis Feedback

> Dasein is an entity for which, in its Being, that Being is an issue. The phrase 'is an issue' has been made plain in the state-of-Being of understanding—of understanding as self-projective Being towards its ownmost potentiality-for-Being. This potentiality is that for the sake of which any Dasein is as it is. (H.191)

If I hated you, I would let this begin a detailed reading of *Being and Time*. Only such a reading could unpack its nuances, let alone explain the untranslated German word: Dasein. Being-there. It's not an exotic word. In German, it just means existence. That's it. Of course, we already know what that means.

Dasein is the hero of the book. It's a who not a what. The whole book is an attempt to define it. Not so much define it, as analyze it. Not even that. Put it this way. You exist, I mean, I think you do. Don't you? Well, I do, at least. What does that mean? Am I like a pencil or a star or gravity? Do I exist just like they do? The book doesn't assume you know who Dasein is, rather it is an attempt to figure that out. In order to figure out what something is, you have to already know what to look at when you do the figuring. *Being and Time* starts by making the point that we don't know what existence is, that despite its being so commonly used, it is not commonly understood. We are so full of prejudice when it comes to existence that we don't even ask about it anymore. What do we mean by the word Being? We don't even ask that. But we can. That is how the book begins.

Assume you don't know what Dasein is, you don't know what it means, you only know that it is the hero of a book trying to figure out what it is. The first time the word appears, the philosopher uses it to *terminologically fasten* "[an] entity which each of us is himself and which includes inquiring as one of the possibilities of its Being." (H.7) If you think this is nonsense, you are not alone.

The theme of the book is set by the question that we don't ask, and that the author wants to start asking again. There is a question that we take for granted and he proposes we stop doing that. That is Dasein: both the stopping and the proposing. Heidegger speaks directly to his audience to convey this. He says, "each of us" (*wir selbst je sind*). Each of us, insofar as we follow along in this uncommon effort to raise the question, questions. Questioning exists. It is a way of being. We don't yet know everything about Dasein, but we know this for sure: it asks a question.

Don't race ahead. Just hold on to this one thing. It questions. Eighty pages later, we are reading about world. Don't ask me how we got there or what it is. I don't hate you and I don't want to get into that. The philosopher distinguishes between "towards-this" and "for-the-sake-of-which" and "in-order-to," ordinary phrases that sound weird when he puts them like that, with dashes and no objects on either end.

Whatever he is going on about while relating these to each other, he introduces the notion of "potentiality-for-Being." Again with the hyphens to show that where English uses a few words, German only uses one. "In understanding a context of relations such as we have mentioned, Dasein has assigned itself to an "in-order-to" and it has done so in terms of a potentiality-for-Being for the sake of which it itself is..." (H.86) This is as easy as taking a deep breath under water.

I jumped here because these are the first rumblings of the central motifs in the passage mentioned at the start. We know that Dasein questions, it makes an issue out of things. There have been additions in those eighty pages. Forget that. Whatever it is, let's just lump it together and call it Dasein. It questions, etc. etc. Leave it be and bear with me. In the passage where he introduces us to "for-the-sake-of-which" and "potentiality-for-Being," he tries to set something up, a circulating system, characterized by an intentionality flowing backward and forward between first and last things.

The voices and tones deterritorialize, they break from what's familiar.

> In the *act of understanding*... the relations indicated above must have been previously disclosed; the act of understanding holds them in this disclosedness... The relational character which these relationships of assigning possess, we take as one of *signifying*. ...it gives itself both its Being and its potentiality-for-Being as something which it is to understand... The 'for-the-sake-of-which' signifies an 'in-order-to'; this in turn, a 'towards-this'; the latter, an 'in-which' of letting something be involved; and that in turn, the 'with-which' of an involvement. ...a primordial totality... ...*as* this signifying in which Dasein gives itself... ...as something to be understood. The relational totality of this signifying we call 'significance'. (H.87)

That should remind you of something. It's not just that Aristotle uses the word "potential" and Heidegger is using the phrase "potentiality-for-Being" to suggest a connection between them, it is a shared pattern. As the origin moves in the direction of the end so does the for-the-sake-of-which move alongside the towards-this. The ultimate end plays along with them and moves in its direction, an in-order-to that sets the order. All in, there is understanding, and the relations are ordered and meaningful. Dasein is involved in a world. It breathes, reconciles, and cares.

Questioning marks an involvement with whatever the questioning is about. You cannot question without getting involved. I'm paraphrasing and splicing it together, but you can look this up. H.86 and 87. Read the whole page. I'm ignoring everything between 7 and 86. It doesn't matter. Questioning is enough. Questioning is already involved. Involvement suggests relationships: "in-which" and "with-which." You are involved *in* something and *with* something. There is the "towards-this" of the involvement. It's heading that way. There is the "for-the-sake-of-which" of the involvement, what or who you are doing it for. Then there is the "in-order-to." We head toward the answer for the sake of something in order to do something else. It's a recognizable pattern. There is the origin and guiding principle (the for-the-sake-of-which) and there is the end (the towards-this), then there is the highest end (the in-order-to). Questioning questions something for the sake of something in order to get something else. Dasein not only fastens questioning but questioning as involvement strives toward something in order for something and for the sake of something. In and with, world is disclosed in this matrix of relationships.

Potentiality-for-Being is that for the sake of which Dasein is involved. Heidegger may have broadened the scope of Dasein beyond questioning in those eighty pages we skipped, but it doesn't matter. Questioning entails involvement in things. You cannot question if you are not involved. Questioning grasps that it does not understand, but that a pathway exists to get *there*. Involvement indicates a set of relations that hold between the questioner and the things they are involved with in their questioning. There is a pathway. This whole action context, this pattern of movement, is what he is calling potentiality-for-Being and significance circulates within it.

I mean to force you to see that this is an elaboration of Aristotle's pattern. Aristotle reconciles the soul with the world-soul through movement addressing first and last things. Likewise, Dasein demonstrates this same way. The origin comes along in the movement that aims at the end for the sake of the soul, the breathing body, in order to make it happy, in order for it to flourish and be excellent. If you are thinking these terms beyond the pattern, then you supplement them beyond my message. Forget everything that happened between its breathing body and its repetition as Dasein (so many pages between Aristotle and Heidegger, 80 to the power of 80). Focus on the pattern.

Questioners live in the world. They breathe its air. They ask about this or that because they have some reason to understand these things. If I am helping my father retile a bathroom, I may ask someone how to do various pieces of the work. My questions elaborate involvement. I ask about tile in order to complete my project and my project is for the sake of having a bathroom my family can use. I reveal my world when I ask questions. You learn about my father's house and its bathroom in need of retiling. There is a cluster of things and relations in that world, all of which you come to know by paying attention to the questions I ask.

Questioning and investigating are actions, and those actions revolve around a target that is for the sake of questioning. Why do I ask, what drives me, what am I ultimately trying to take care of with this activity? The potentiality-for-Being is a name for why I do this, but then again, it isn't really something other than this. It's a name for this whole dynamic, this whole pattern of movement. The origin that accompanies action in a rational principle aiming at the end for the sake of the well-being of the soul, that also fastens Dasein. Forget the kingdoms built on these terms, the fiefdoms and other economic systems. *Seinkönnen.*

The dynamic that reconciles was instigated through the uncommon questioning concerning what we mean by existence. Questioning always moves in a circle: what we want to understand at the end drives what we set out to understand in the beginning. This is a circulating system where the origin accompanies the movement toward the end. This accompaniment, this guiding light, is potentiality-for-Being. Dasein is for the sake of what it can be. The movement, the turning and circling, there is so much of it, and it is for the sake of the questioner, the one who studies, cares, and makes their way toward the end in the company of the origin.

Dasein is involved with first and last things. They are its world. They are the backward and the forward along which it moves as it questions, actualizing its potential. Never fully actual, it is always already actualizing. Its very own potential is this course of movement. We don't need to have the entire picture before us at the same time. It is enough to say, when asked, that Dasein questions, and that when it does, it is involved *with* things, and *in* things for the sake of that potential that it realizes. Anything anywhere that realizes potential by questioning fastens Dasein. We don't have a finished product. We haven't identified it with anything else. Dasein may or may not ride a horse, it may or may not count to 27, and it may or may not have made a profit last fiscal year. What it does do, is question and it questions for the sake of realizing potential, articulating its potentiality-for-Being.

Dasein realizes potential so long as it is Dasein. Wherever Dasein is, potential is realized. Were Dasein to stop being Dasein, this would cease. No more Dasein is a possibility for Dasein. We learn later, much later and I won't test you with the details, that Dasein can die. When it does, there is no more Dasein and no more potential to be realized. The realization of potential is what Dasein starts doing when it is born and only stops doing when it dies. This further repeats the pattern. The reconciliation of infinite substance and finite soul is repeated in the reconciliation of Dasein with Being and its finite potential to realize it. Potentiality-for-Being is always already underway and not yet complete so long as Dasein lives and breathes.

> The house has its sunny side and its shady side; the way it is divided up into 'rooms' is oriented towards these, and so is the 'arrangement' within them, according to their character as equipment. Churches and graves, for instance, are laid out according to the rising and setting of the sun—the regions of life and death, which are determinative for Dasein itself with regard to its ownmost possibilities of Being in the world. Dasein, in its very Being, has this Being as an issue; and its concern discovers beforehand those regions in which some involvement is decisive. (H.103-104)

Potentiality for Being II

The Recap

Early the next morning, Fred and Lena met outside the motel to walk up the road to get the car. When they first met, he was nearly speechless, tongue-tied. She picked up on it immediately.

"What's wrong with you?" she asked.

He mumbled something and flushed red. She knew the signs.

"Come on Fred, get it together. Don't wimp out on me."

He gathered some composure and said, "Great, emasculate me for it, why don't you? I can't help it. You shouldn't beat me up for it."

"Shouldn't? Oh, you and your 'what does not destroy me'. You don't know what strength is."

He grimaced, and then decided to change the subject.

"What did you think of that stuff last night?"

"Not much really. It didn't get us anywhere, did it?"

"For a second there, it seemed like maybe hatred of the White Party united us. No such luck," he chuckled.

"Minority rule in what's supposed to be a democracy isn't good for morale."

"Did you ever read Ben Thorne's *The Middle American*?"

"It's on my list."

"Well, *The Middle American* reminds me a little of what might be going on. The one character, Stephen Wolfe, he's like a complete outsider. He's travelling around, he belongs to nothing, he's connected to no one."

"Stephen Wolfe? Steppenwolf?"

"Yeah, I know. Kinda cheesy. But that's the point he's trying to make. There are these communities that tell him he's an insider. You know, he comes from a good family, not too rich, not too poor. He's moderately well educated, of average intelligence, not bad looking, not good looking. Completely mediocre in every way."

"A middle American."

"That's right. And these other people, they accuse him of that, of being the norm, of being average. The standard. The world was made for people like him, people of his height, his weight, his abilities. There's lots to entertain him, movies for his demographic, music for his tastes, books for his enjoyment. Everything targets him, everything is there for him."

"Interesting."

"Yeah. But wait, I haven't got to it yet. The story's written in that

existentialist vein. Like *The Stranger* or *Notes from Underground.*
Nausea."

"*Steppenwolf.* A book by a white man, about a white man, and for white
men."

"Exactly. This guy has been warped. Like I said, he's a loner, he's an
outsider. No real friends, no deep connections. Yeah, there's this stuff
made to suit him perfectly, but he doesn't want it. He can't connect with it.
He's alienated."

"The white man's disease," she said.

"Right. There are these others who criticize him. They're people who
don't have it so easily, they don't have the luxury of being average, of having
their tastes met. They're the wrong size, the wrong shape, or whatever."

"But they have each other."

"They have each other. They have communities, they connect easily.
Their condition gives them instant connections."

"Whereas he's the consummate outsider. Boohoo. Poor man."

"He's using it to explain backlash. Don't people generally reduce the
impact of everyone else's suffering? They complain about injustices, and
maybe they're right. There's tons of evidence. Accusations of privilege,
plenty to support that too. But his experience rejects the evidence, it
doesn't fit. The crap that supposedly meets his tastes, he rejects it. He's
alienated by exactly those things that were made for him. Do you get it?"

"Sure. This has been done to death. So what? Why should everyone
else give up their grievances just because the spoiled child is bored with
what the world offers him?"

"Is that what you think it means? That's not my take. I don't think the
idea is people should abandon their grievances, I think Thorne's point is
that they should study him. He's their prognosis, their future. If only people
were interested in the truth."

"What truth? That the privileged are just as caged as everyone else?"

"Who are *you* to disagree? You've got quite the pedigree yourself.
Objectively speaking. Aren't you on the gravy train? As soon as you get
your degree, you'll have departments tripping over themselves to hire you.
Before you get it. Your research will always get grants."

"I've worked my ass off..."

"No one is denying that. Forget about merit. Whether you've earned it
in some interpretation of merit or not, you still have it. So, you're perfectly
actualized by it, aren't you? You feel totally on top of things, it's your world.
You are at the top school in the country, you have exactly the right
background to get what you want, you must be so at ease and so at peace
with your opportunities."

"What do you know about it?"

They arrived at the little bar/restaurant and decided to go inside and get some proper coffee. When they came back out, Lena went to the trunk and returned the sidearm in its holster to the safe. They stood next to the car for a few minutes before getting in.

"My point is that you should be on top of the world, but I'm guessing that -like most people- you don't feel it. There's something about these advantages that still doesn't gel with you. Am I right?"

"Well, sometimes there's a lot of pressure to do things that aren't exactly what I'd prefer."

"Sometimes?"

"I get your point." She paused and took a sip of coffee. "My dad used to talk about this. It would actually make me feel pretty shitty. I resented him for it. Fuck, why does this keep coming up?"

"What? What did he say?"

"It's like that painter in *Artists of Despair*. You know, he's successful, but it doesn't feel right. He's got this weird sense that he's a ventriloquist's dummy."

"Right. Like someone else is talking through him. Like he's in there somewhere but he can't find it because of whatever it is that's taking over."

"Impostor syndrome," Lena said, rolling her eyes.

"It's not impostor syndrome, it's not about desert. Having impostor syndrome is proof that you don't have it. Smart people with high standards have doubts. That's normal. The point Thorne is exploring, he keeps going back to it, is that even the winners are fucked."

"But see, when my dad said these things, they didn't have the intended effect. They made me experience it. For a moment, I was happy that my name was on some paper or that I received some grant for something or got into the school I wanted or whatever."

"He would shit on that."

"Yes. But no, not really. It wasn't like that. He'd be really happy for me. But later, he'd say something in a totally different context, and it'd remind me. Get me thinking. I questioned whether the paper was really what I wanted to say, or whether the research was something I really cared about. Maybe I was only interested because it got me ahead. Maybe my interests were formed by the expectations of success. That made me feel horrible. Like I was selling out or something. Like I was a phony."

"It's like this character, Stephen Wolfe. Sorry I keep going back to that."

"It's okay, go on."

"In so many ways, he's so genuine. He's sensitive and he listens, but he's alienated because he keeps thinking that he's being corralled into experiences that were made for him, that he's supposed to have to further some agenda. If we can dismiss his suffering as privileged malaise, then we can dismiss yours too. In fact, you do it often. Isn't that what you mean by feeling shitty? You don't think you have a right to question your success. It's what everyone thinks you should want, it's what everyone thinks you should be trying to achieve."

"Maybe the characters shouldn't have been white men."

"He says no matter what he makes them, they'll be white men. To some extent, that's because he's a white man and every one of the characters are him. Even if he bases them on people he met once, no one is fooled."

"So, he writes what he's comfortable with."

"He's not trying to fool anyone. We're under the same spell. Black or Brown, we want to be successful white men. It's about backlash and how it comes from a wound denied and simultaneously revered. If you can't see it when the light shines on the prototype, then you'll never see it until it slaps you in the face."

"The painter in *Artists*, the traveler in *The Middle American*, they have to be white men."

"There's a lot of criticism. The people who attack him –professors at elite universities– miss the whole point, and will never make any progress because they fail to see how paradigms work, how archetypes are constructed in their own experience, and how power is baked into every civilized organization. Becoming delusional about your potential is how power inhabits you. Becoming disillusioned and resentful too."

"Hmm. Well, it's on my list. We should get back."

"Listen, Lena. We don't know each other very well, but I know that Ben Thorne and your father must've been close. Good friends. That man never gave a crap about anything anyone ever said about his work. Only Ginna and your dad. That's it. That's what I've seen."

"What's that supposed to mean?"

"Just that... I mean... I don't think your dad was trying to tear you down when he said that. I think he was trying to warn you about something."

"What's the difference?"

The House

They came for the books that morning and now the shelves were empty. Ermioni kept a few of them, the art books, the Jane Austen and George Eliot, but that didn't amount to much in comparison to the shelves and shelves that were carted off. It was the only thing he ever bought for himself. He didn't like gadgets or gizmos. They didn't have a lot of fancy TVs or devices, the house wasn't filled with smart appliances or wired components. No digital assistant. They didn't have a special doorbell that wrote video to the cloud, they didn't have picture frames that cycled through digital photographs or visualized the extinct rain forests or Arctic ice. The refrigerator wasn't keeping track of their consumption and the washer and dryer didn't automatically order fabric softener when supplies were low. But there were a lot of books. Not electronic books hidden away on an e-reader or available through its WIFI connection. She would often read those, she preferred them, but not Em. He almost always worked with tangible objects, books that had a smell and cover art. Books where you knew how many pages it had just from looking at it, where you knew how far into it you were from the weight on the right-side counter-balanced with the left-side. Some of the books were cloth bound, most were paperback.

Initially, the book collector thought it was unlikely he would be interested, but he said he would come around anyway to take a look. When he saw the collection, mostly philosophy and sociology, some rare, some extremely common, he changed his mind. She told him it was all or nothing and he didn't hesitate before saying he would take them all. He praised Em's taste and was excited that morning when he came by with his crew to pick up the cargo.

Now she was left with empty shelves. The estate agent hadn't sent their people for the furniture yet, but that was scheduled for Friday. The small pod was in front of the house and would be picked up around the same time. Ermioni sat on the couch and stared at the shelves in disbelief. She was crying softly. Georgios was outside cleaning up the yard. Ariti was in the other room doing laundry before packing. The plan was to get it done by the time the real estate agent came by later that afternoon.

Ariti saw Ermioni go into the other room after the book collector left and now the silence gave her cause to worry. She went in to see how things were going. Ermioni looked up.

"We planned to build these shelves as soon as we moved in. It was his only requirement. I had a long list of things, but he just had the one."

Ariti sat down and put her arm around Ermioni.

"Those were our biggest arguments." She chuckled through the tears. "He was always moving them around, sorting and shuffling. Trying to make more room. I would complain that the shelves were packed too tight. Then I would rearrange things to make the colors more balanced."

Ariti pulled her closer and swung her other arm around her.

"He would sneak a book into some place that I didn't think there should be any, or he would insist that the Husserl had to be next to each other, and I would complain that one was too big, and it would be more symmetrical if a few unrelated books were next to each other in the middle with the bigger one on the end. Those were our fights."

"Those aren't fights."

"I made him keep track of his reading every year. We argued about why he had books that he hadn't read yet but was still buying new ones. Why couldn't he just read the ones he had? He said it didn't work like that. He kept track because we agreed that no matter what, he had to read more than he bought. I thought that was the only way to control the numbers."

"It doesn't seem like you did a very good job."

"Over the years, he would get rid of some every now and then, but it was agonizing. He would pull a book off the shelves and set it on one of the tables in the other room. He would talk through it with me. 'I'll probably never read it again, but I may need to reference it. I can't decide.' It was so funny. Why was he so attached? I told him, 'you know, if you need to look at it again someday maybe you could just buy a new copy or get it from the library. Maybe,' I would say, 'you could even get an electronic version of it.' He would nod. He knew it was reasonable, but he couldn't bring himself to do it."

"What do you think they meant to him? They couldn't just have been books. It wouldn't have been so hard if they were just books."

"There was a story he used to tell. He would repeat it every few years whenever the subject came up. He said that when he was little his parents were frugal when it came to toys and things. Just because he wanted something, didn't mean he could get it. He might have to save up his allowance or do more chores or something, but they wouldn't just buy him whatever he wanted. One time he was in the bookstore with his mom. He was holding two different books. He must've been about 8 or 9. He shyly asked her if he could get them and she immediately said 'sure, of course.' He asked her why it was so easy, and she said, 'books don't count, you can have any book you want.' That story was very important to him. He used to say the same thing to Lena when she was little."

"That's lovely."

"I think that was part of it, what they meant to him. There was more. This is going to sound weird. I've never told anyone this before, but no one ever knew that his whole life he felt like a failure."

"What? How?"

"He had this perfect job, and he was so good at it. Many people would kill for that. He was respected by his colleagues and well rewarded by his company. None of that mattered to him. None of that was his gauge for success. Don't get me wrong, he wasn't oblivious, he loved us and was proud of our family. He was happy in our life together. Professionally though, he felt like a failure. He wanted to be a philosopher, being a great software engineer meant nothing to him."

"I can't believe it. It's so sad."

"I think the books had something to do with it. He held on to them, it was his way of holding onto what he lost. So long as he didn't give up, he couldn't fail. Having these books reminded him. He talked to philosophers online. He thought that would make things better."

"Did it?"

"No. He'd complain about it, then he doubted his complaints. They only paid attention if you had the right credentials. They never broke ranks and didn't pay attention to anything he said because he wasn't one of them. He wasn't like any of the other software engineers, and he wasn't like any of the other philosophers."

Ariti nodded patiently and continued her slow petting of Ermioni's hair and shoulders.

"He knew he wasn't part of their clique. It was painful to him. He doubted his own taste."

"What do mean, doubted his own taste?"

"He liked what he was working on, what he was thinking about, he found it so compelling, but no one else did. That made him think he didn't know the good from the bad, that his taste was no good."

"He wrote though, didn't he? The books Lena took?"

"Yes, that's what I mean. No one cared about any of that. He was so grand when he talked about it. He always used to say he would quit if he could, but he couldn't, so he had to keep doing it. I think it was the only way he could stomach the fact that he was going to work every day and doing things that didn't matter to him."

"That's such a shame."

"Some days he'd say the work was evil, that he was doing bad things. Every day he helped make the world worse. The only saving grace, the only thing that offered any redemption, was that he felt like he understood it in ways that others couldn't. He could write it down, go into the darkness to learn the truth about evil. But no one cared, it wasn't good enough, incoherent, no one paid any attention. It was for nothing. A rationalization."

"Why didn't you ever talk about this? Why didn't you tell me?"

"It's just because I'm focusing on it right now. It wasn't like that. He was happy and funny. He could make me laugh even when I was angry or miserable. It wasn't always like that. Even when we talked about it, even when he went off into some very dark places, it didn't seem to get him down. He was like a stoic."

"You are too, I think."

"We were well suited. He used to say that he knew he was going to fall in love with me because one day, when we were first dating, we were together at his house in the city, the one he had when we first met. It was afternoon, and a beautiful day. The sun was coming in and we were lying in each other's arms. I described the scene and said, 'everything is so perfect, it's so depressing.' We both laughed so hard. I didn't have to explain, he knew exactly what I meant. He was like that too."

"Everyone could tell that you two were perfect together."

"We knew it too and felt it. These thoughts, those empty shelves, they aren't the whole story. The engineer. It was heartbreaking that it was for nothing, but it wasn't his whole life. He appreciated what he had and dismissed his delusions as a hobby."

"Delusions?"

"Yes, in the end, he figured he was probably wrong about everything. People want the evil. His taste and his judgment were no good."

Ariti squeezed Ermioni's shoulder and then touched her lightly across her back. "Alright, alright," she said. "That's enough. We can't go on like this all day. There's work to do. I have to finish the ironing. What else do we need to get done before the appointment?"

"Let me get my list." She reached over and took up a small tablet from the table at the side of the couch.

"Books, we can cross that off. The guns are gone now too, so we can cross that off."

"Lena took them?"

"Yes, that's good. She knows them, she'll take care of them. She took a few of the books from the office too. And Em's laptop."

"Okay good. What else?"

"We're going to have the estate agent take the rest of the furniture, so that's done. We'll have the real estate agent do the staging. We'll tell her this afternoon. Whatever she thinks we need."

"Is there anything else then?"

"Not for today. If you can finish the ironing, I'll talk to Georgios about what we need to do in the sheds. I think we'll have to make a few trips to the dump, but we can leave some of that stuff behind."

Carl

For the first leg of the morning's journey through Montana, Fred and Lena were set to drive. Carl asked if he could go with Lena. Eirini lit up at the suggestion and said she was happy to go with Fred. Once they were on the road, Lena asked about his work.

"We usually think that abilities are inside a person. Like a thing in a container. But potential has so much to do with opportunity and that has everything to do with what kinds of things there are in the world: in your civilization, in your community. Being good at science or research or anything like that requires that society has facilities for it. The people who become scientists depend on their society having infrastructure for scientific investigation, otherwise they end up as alchemists or astrologers."

"That's what you're working on then? Potential."

"Not exactly. It's background. There's the whole structural aspect that describes how these institutions enable reproduction of the means of production. It's not just about making things."

"You're an historical materialist then?"

"That's a given. I consider it non-controversial. Dialectical materialism, that's another story."

"How so?"

"Well, it's a conclusion about a higher order logic at work in history. It's risky. There's a threat of idealism in it. Fred's always reminding me. God is dead, you know."

"Traces of idealism are forbidden."

"It might even apply to aims and goals. They might be part of that idealist invasion. The hypothesis, in essence, is just a rule used to describe correlations in the data. To attribute ends to those correlations, analogies enabling us to posit goals and intentions, that's already a step toward idealism and ideology."

"Dialectic introduces ends and that's controversial, according to you, so you want to stick with the mechanism absent any ideals."

"Not sure yet. Let's set it aside. Getting back to the hard foundation. Reproduction. Research institutions like universities reproduce the means of production. The system of grants, the educational hierarchy, the journals and the peer review, it's there to reproduce the capitalist system."

"Including your own university and the system that backs your research and -eventually–your doctorate."

"Yes, exactly. These two points are connected with individual action that we usually think of as talent or capability, as human potential expressing what is inside the container in terms that reproduce the dominant system."

"So, the whole 'what are you going to be when you grow up' game that we play with children is to get them used to the idea of imagining themselves part of the economy. You're at the intersection of reproduction and the individual's experience."

"Yes, that's my area."

"Can I ask again, how does a novelist fit into that?"

"Ben Thorne? His work's always moving around this point. I think of him more like a philosopher than a novelist. A social philosopher. His characters are almost always dealing with tension and the forces at work in this point of intersection, they are expressions of the connection, they are interleaved."

"Like the painter from *Artists of Despair*."

"That's probably the most sophisticated example. The structure for what it means to be a painter, this immensely creative calling that exists on the fringe of the economy, is nonetheless spelled out in detail. Colors. Brush strokes. Historical styles. He lays it out, and then he sets it off against the professional stooge who works for the mega corporation."

"Sure, he slams the reader over the head with it."

"In a way, the ability to fulfill the role has so much more to do with abilities beyond the techniques of painting. To be a great painter, you need specific technical skills, but you also need taste and vision and something like a unique perspective. That's how the story goes."

"The genius."

"Exactly. Those qualities are related to others, they're social skills. But there's so much more to it than that. There's navigating the art world and the perils of mass consumption, the difficulty in getting the attention of an audience, marketing your skills and artifacts to brokers. The business side of it, that's part of being an artist."

"But the character is a failure. He's a great painter, but he doesn't know how to present it, or spin it, he can't take it to the marketplace."

"He's missing some skills. But that's okay, there's a fallback and the system provides it. You can hand over your taste and skill to others who have that marketing ability and their hand on the pulse of a target audience."

"The designer."

"The designer draws the painter into the machine that will slot his skills into something bigger. Something that augments the skills. Organization."

"I see, but how can a Political Scientist use a novelist's work for theory like that? Don't you need data?"

"That's the beauty of the project. It's an example of itself. I use political theorists to perform the reading. That puts the interpretation in context. That's pretty standard, but I can also talk about the artist himself as the author of these novels. It isn't just about the work of Ben Thorne, I'm incorporating analysis of Ben Thorne himself."

"What about him specifically?"

"Well, he's reached the top of his profession. He's won these awards, and yes, to some extent, it's because he has talents that earn him status. But he's a master of charm too. He sold himself correctly to literary agents, he worked his way up the ladder. He knew what that meant, he was farming specific skills to lock into connections and networks. The goal ultimately was to get into a publishing machine that included the right publicists and the right connections to award committees."

"He's got a talent for sniffing out what he needs to do to become a well-respected author. It involved becoming part of a structure that goes way beyond what he can do alone."

"He doesn't just write about this, he does it. His office is a part of it. He's accumulated even more skills over the years, and he passes them on to his assistants. Some of his past assistants have become highly regarded authors. And he helped make that possible by teaching them the industry."

"They get the right connections and learn to excel in that world."

"There's that, and it forms their voice too. They learn how to tweak and correct their work to meet the standards. They know what goes over well with the agents and publishers and what won't. What draws them in. That's the experience. The writers change their behavior, they learn the discipline so they can meet the requirements. They're shaped."

"It's a common thesis. You could explain the same thing from a biological perspective. Humans are not extraordinary as solitary creatures. We've talked about this. There are plenty of animals that can easily kill us. As social creatures, we're formidable because we have an unparalleled ability to coordinate. A lot of what you're describing is just a sophisticated form of it."

"Do you have something specific in mind?"

"Language. The complexity of human language makes it possible to coordinate activity in an extremely detailed fashion. The existence of artists which, like you said, is an institution, a set of traditions, is also an extremely sophisticated form of communication and coordination. Hundreds and thousands of people separated by space and time learning from each other, influencing each other, and coordinating their actions. They make a history. These social abilities are wired into us, we've been cultivated for them. Even the innovator learns the traditions before they innovate. That's a sophisticated form of coordination."

"So is there a biological capability beneath the social influences?"

"Definitely. And an ancient historical process that predates human beings and provides the conditions. You could say that Natural Selection honed these social skills in our ancestors. The better we're able to coordinate and cultivate roles and social positions, the more fit we are for survival among large mammals that eat creatures like us."

"We're a social species."

"Yes, but we also have this ability to individuate ourselves. It's implicit in the sophistication of language and augments coordination. I think that's a key part of what you're describing. It isn't just that there are social opportunities allowing us to explore our potential, the pattern of doing that, of individuating ourselves, that's part of it too."

"The social side is like bees or ants. The hive mind where each of us fulfills the role we were supposed to have, but we're more than bees and ants because we can individuate, add style to the role."

"They might do it too. The dancing bees and heroic ants. But basically yes. A lot of the tension you're describing is related to styles of individuation. Some forms click with the rest. They're like role models. When we collectively approve of an individual, their potential is applauded. Others fail to get our approval. They're not individuating themselves in a way that captures our attention, it doesn't resonate."

"That's a nice point," he said. "You could say that the social functions are a corrective. Awkward attempts at standing out get immediate feedback, this tells the agent they should change what they're doing, reorient themselves, aim for different forms."

"Like the painter in *Artists of Despair*."

"Going to work for the corporation as a designer is an adjustment based on information gathered from feedback he received as a painter."

"This changes his voice. The writer changes what they write. That's how civilization changes the individual to make it fit better with its goals."

Carl was getting excited. He pulled out his phone while Lena was talking and typed a few notes.

"This fits with what I'm trying to do in my research. One example I play with is the rise of attribute politics on the left. Feminism, gender studies, and critical race theories were formal defenses of specific kinds of individuation. They revealed a sickness. You have a civilization that historically rejected persons with specific traits, and this leads people to respond, to organize, to do something to change things so that people with those traits have more power."

"Okay," she said hesitantly.

"You wouldn't have feminism, for example, if anthropology or political science or whatever weren't already excluding women's experience and history. Its existence already indicates a problem."

"What does that mean?"

"The goal has to be its own dissolution. Anthropology, for example"

"If Anthropology, as a discipline, ceased to be patriarchal, you think the need for feminism would go away?"

"It raises a lot of questions at least. Is that a state or an ongoing process, what guarantees that feminism is effective for that, for its own dissolution? This is just an example."

"I get it. Go on."

"What guarantees feminism can change those institutions or understand them once they've changed? It has to be transformed by its success."

"Transformed or deconstructed?"

"That's the question. Attributes ultimately rest on socially determined possibilities, potential that is baked into our lives. Even if we notice something doesn't feel right, something doesn't suit us, we don't fit the boxes, the analysis comes from the same discussions and traditions. The ways of individuation are predetermined and communally described. Genre. It's about genre. And what are their legitimate forms. It's something Fred and I agree on."

"Well, it's fascinating. Where are you in the program?"

"Dissertation. Trying to get the research done. I have a committee assembled and a prospectus. So, in theory, I'm supposed to be making progress."

"How come you're driving across Montana then? Shouldn't you be working?"

"It's an outlier. He doesn't usually give us assignments like this. Not exactly what they thought I'd be doing when they approved the internship."

"Is that why you know so much about me? I was talking to Fred, and it seemed like you guys have a dossier. It felt pretty creepy."

"Yeah, that's Ben Thorne. He has access to so much information, but I don't think we had to dig that deep. People are pretty easy to investigate when you have several points of intersection, places they've lived, institutions they're associated with. A woman living in Ann Arbor and affiliated with the University of Michigan is an open book. The university doesn't have your back."

"Just on the internet, publicly?"

"Well. Actually, your dad might be to blame. He was a data guru, wasn't he? I think he got Thorne access to the data systems that Ginna used."

"Ginna's the puppet master."

"Oh definitely. She runs that office. If you come to New York, you'll meet her. She's incredible. The latest of those authors that Ben Thorne is grooming."

"I don't think I'll have time for that. I still think this whole thing is too random. Why does he want to talk to me?"

"I don't know much more than you do. I just know he really wants to, and it has something to do with your dad. That's it. I'd tell you if I knew more."

"Hmmm. Well, he's definitely persistent."

"To say the least."

They drove quietly for a bit, then Carl cleared his throat and shyly asked: "Would you have shot that guy last night? I mean, was that for real?"

"I only saw your reaction. You looked frightened. I didn't hear what he said. None of us did. But once I went over there, I thought they were pretty harmless."

"I'm sure you're right, but you know you hear so many things. When a guy with a gun asks you in a threatening voice 'Are you white?' horrible things run through your mind." He paused. "It's actually funny, because I've asked myself that same question, but I never thought of it as threatening."

"You've wondered whether you're white? How does that work?"

"Well, it's not like concepts of race are so clear. He wasn't really asking me about melanin content, was he? It wasn't just about skin color. There was a lot behind that question, and I've always thought that with Jews it depends on who you ask. Most people would be like 'yeah sure, he's white', but not the antisemitic white supremacist, he doesn't think Jews are white."

"Okay, but maybe you were reading too much into it. I mean, he's a young man. Looking at you, I could imagine someone asking the question innocently. Imagine there wasn't some big stigma around skin color, and we recognized that genes are prevalent in people we don't necessarily expect to have them. Maybe you have an African great grandparent. It's possible. It's also possible he was just asking like 'hey, are you white or is perhaps there a little African in you as well?'"

"Is that what you think he was doing?"

"I don't know what he was doing. I'm just saying. When I came over, it wasn't like they were these evil horrible people. They almost immediately started laughing and joking around with us."

"Don't you think that had anything to do with your show of force?"

"Maybe. Look, there are people in America who love the tradition of rugged individualism and wild west liberty. That's a version of America that isn't very safe. Shootouts at the OK corral. Gunfighters and border wars. For some people, that's America. That liberty, according to those people, can't be guaranteed by government decree. The people have to own it. It's the whole theory behind the right to bear arms. Individuals are supposed to be able to protect themselves so that they don't have to rely on the government. It also protects them from the government."

"Oh my. You sound like one of them."

"I'm not trying to assert a universal moral truth, Carl. I'm telling you about a long and significant part of American history. There are people who identify with that."

"Racists and xenophobes."

"I get that people think that way, but what can I tell you? Deep down I'm an anthropologist, I'm trying to understand a way of life and point of view. It's not like it's some fringe. Every side of the equation agrees that this was a long-standing part of American history. What service are you performing when you deny it? You think you can just educate people out of the things they've grown up loving and learning? What were we just talking about? Only social forces and conflicts will change forms of individuation, but that is way more difficult when there are long-lived institutions behind them."

"There are values in the facts. That's the tyranny of the White Party or whatever. It makes discourse chaotic and violent, banishing reason from public view. What do you suggest we do?"

"I don't pretend to have the answers, but I suspect it's like how the missionaries proselytized Christianity among so-called animists. The idea was to study the local religion, find points of connection, and infiltrate them to convince the village or the tribe, whoever, that they could hear their stories in the Christian tradition. When those people pray to the virgin Mary, they're thinking of a spirit ancestor."

"That falls into Fred's trap and makes your point about deconstruction versus transformation. The perils of intellectual settler colonialism."

"Right."

"But you haven't really answered my question. Would you have shot him?"

"I don't know. It's out there. What I can say is that I'm trained to use a handgun for personal protection. My parents made sure of that. The training just kicks in, so I can only assume that I would have done whatever I needed to do to protect you."

"So, you really do know how to use it?"

"Yes. He insisted."

"Sorry to put it so crassly, but even though you're a girl?"

"Especially because of that. My father was horrified that women weren't safe. Having a daughter motivated him. He thought the only solution was to take matters into our own hands, it's delusional to start a fight without knowing how to defend yourself. Remember that the next time you try to strike up a conversation with a woman reading by herself somewhere."

They laughed. Then she went on, "Seriously, it's part of that wild west tradition. You can't wait for the government to protect you. You can't expect them to coerce people into treating you right. You have to stand up for yourself, you have to learn to keep yourself safe, and -if freedom matters to you—you might have to risk your life to do it."

Fred

In the other car, Eirini paired her phone and was playing some old Greek pop music through the car's sound system. Fred said he liked it as she lightly bounced in her seat to the rhythm. He struggled to figure out what to say to her.

"So, what do you do?" he finally managed, settling on the mundane.

"What do you mean?"

"For a living?"

"For money? Oh. I work for the region. Dimou, uh, county? I don't know. For the administrative offices."

"Oh right. You said something about that last night. What does that mean? What do you do for the county?"

"Handle complaints. Public relations. Sometimes I process paperwork for permits, I take a lot of notes, lots of different things. Whatever the people need."

"Is it interesting?"

"It doesn't matter. It's necessary. People need these services."

"You aren't like Lena, not ambitious?"

"We're different. I think Greece is different. We work so we can help each other. In the North, I mean. I don't know about Athens. Sometimes, I tutor. Younger people. English. Science. People do what needs to be done to keep everyone going. It's work. It's not what we really care about."

"What do you care about?"

"Our family, our friends. It's normal. Our lives."

"I see. You said Lena is your cousin?"

"We say that, but not really. It's easier. My grandmother and her grandmother were best friends. They still are. Our mothers grew up together, we grew up together. We're family, but we're not related."

"It's a small town?"

"Yes, a small town. We stay close to each other. We try to buy from each other. Not at the supermarket. You know? Here, everything you buy was made by a stranger."

"You can live like that?"

"Not everything, but many things. Food. Services. When you have to buy an appliance, no one in the town makes refrigerators, but someone sells them. Maybe you could get a better deal if you went to Kavala, but it's better to pay a little more and buy it from your neighbor."

"That sounds nice."

"What about your family? Do you have brothers and sisters? Are you close?"

"I have a sister. We're not really close. We're very different."

"You grew up together."

"True, but we want different things. We've spread out, we don't live nearby."

"Your parents. What about them?"

"They're different too. Spread out. None of us are that close, not geographically, not at all. Put it this way, if I were to get sick they'd take care of me, but I'm not sure I'd be happy about it."

"No extended family? Childhood friends, cousins, nothing like that?"

"Not really, no. I get on with my colleagues at school. Carl's probably my closest friend, but we've only known each other a few years and we mostly argue."

"You still study."

"I'm going for my doctorate. In philosophy."

"And who will you help with that? How?"

"Whoever wants to learn, I guess. I don't know, it's not like that."

"You don't want to work to help your town or the people around you?"

"Well, I'd like to, but I can't control whether they want to be helped by the stuff I'm doing. I think everyone could benefit from learning to think critically. That's how I would help if I could."

She pursed her lips and flipped through her phone to see what music to play next.

"I guess the institution will determine whether I'm really very helpful to anyone. The university. I don't know. You can't really control what you're interested in and what motivates you, can you? I mean. I don't like people that much. I don't really like spending time around people. I'm not trying to be insulting."

"I'm not insulted," she said simply. "I think it's sad."

"Hmm. There's a joke I heard once. A guy says, 'I need a leaf blower, except for people'. You know, something that'll keep the people away. The other guy says, 'I think that's called a fart'."

She laughed.

"Philosophy is like a really big fart. It's great for keeping people away."

She smiled and looked over at him. He looked over briefly. He was beginning to notice how extraordinary she was. Whenever she was with Lena, he only saw Lena, but he saw something in her eyes just then. He didn't know what it was, but it made him shiver. Pleasantly.

"I can't believe I just told you a fart joke," he said. "I'm supposed to be educated."

"It was a good joke," she said trying to sound encouraging.

"You won't think less of me for it then? Tell them to take away my credentials."

"No, I won't think less of you." She smiled broadly and squinted her eyes at him. He shrugged and squeezed his eyes closed.

"What about your family, you must be close with them."

"Very close. I live with them. Well, I was. I'm staying at Ermioni's house now. Sometimes. My brother is away at school, but he might come back when he's done. Most people live with their parents until they get married."

"You only have one brother?"

"Yes, but many cousins. In that way. The kids I grew up with, kids from the villages."

"Do you have a boyfriend?"

"Oh yes, boyfriends, girlfriends. Many."

"No, I mean is there one special person?"

"Ah yes, sorry. No, I don't have a boyfriend."

"Or a girlfriend?"

"No."

"That must be a problem living in a village and spending your life in the town. There aren't a lot of people to choose from and you've known everyone since you were kids."

"It's true, but people change, you get to know them better. I might already know a man who I'll marry one day, but maybe we just don't know each other like that yet."

"You plan on getting married? Having kids? That whole thing."

"I don't plan on it, but it may happen. It happens to many people. What about you?"

"No, that doesn't fit with my whole keeping people away strategy."

"You really don't like people. You like Carl though?"

"I guess. I like people one-on-one, I just don't like them in large groups or even when they group think alone."

"What does it mean, group think?"

"It's when they think just like everyone else. If I talk to someone about philosophy, for example, they might stumble onto something interesting. The more educated they are, the less likely that is. They probably can't do philosophy well, they'll spout half-baked ideas that fit with someone else's way of thinking, someone else's system, or some traditional way of dealing with the problem."

"Why are you studying it then? Won't it ruin you?"

"I think it already has. People who don't study it have raw charm. You know? Like, they have no guile. Nine-year-old kids are the best. They don't have any preconceptions, they just put it however they can. The more education someone has, the less raw they are, the more nonsense they'll spout."

"So, you are ruined already."

"There are two types that do it well, the raw and uninitiated who stumble into brilliant ideas, and then there are the absolute geniuses who manage to rise to the top of the system. They're extremely rare, and you can't always recognize them when they're right in front of you. It takes time, the fashions may need to change, and you have to see what lasts beyond that."

"It sounds like there's little chance of success."

"There isn't. So, I'm too educated to be raw and then I'm not talented enough to be one of the great ones. So, what does that leave me? Basically, I'm just amusing myself."

She was looking over at him so simply. No judgment, she was just listening. He grew increasingly self-conscious as he became more aware of her eyes fastened on him.

"Maybe you would be happier with a job working for the county? You could try to become raw again."

"You make a good point, but honestly, I'm full of shit. I have prejudices and values that I have no justification for."

"Like what?"

"Like that the unexamined life is not worth living. There's an aspect of human culture that is better, that people who live that way are better. That it's better to know more, to understand more, to think more."

"How do you mean better? You'll be happier?"

"No, happiness doesn't matter."

"You'll live better?"

"No, not necessarily. But you'll get the jokes, you'll be in on it. Does that make sense?"

"No. It doesn't. How are you better off if it doesn't make you happier, if it doesn't help you live better?"

"Because it's true, because it's an insight into how things really are."

"You're sure about that? Maybe that's your education tricking you, like you were saying before."

"It's not... It's different..."

"How?"

"Huh. You know, it's interesting. I'm always talking about the revaluation of all values. It's meant to be a radical challenge to the things you think matter, turning everything upside down."

"Like the cave?"

"The cave? Oh yeah, the cave, yes. Like that. The people only see the shadows and the philosophers turn everything upside down by seeing what's casting the light on the wall to make those shadows."

"Seeing that light ruins their eyes, according to the people in the cave."

"Yes. That's right. Even the philosophers were foolish to focus so much on that perfectly intelligible world outside. The philosopher said god is dead and when he said that he meant the things that rely on it, they're gone too. The revaluation of *all* values. It's a bias to put so much faith in understanding and cleverness, wit and insight."

"Always getting the joke, you said. Even fart jokes."

Fred laughed and looked over at her with her knees pulled up close to her chin. Something in her gaze relaxed him. For once he didn't feel the desperate urge to make his point absolutely clear so that there would be no misunderstanding. He didn't feel the need to head off every possible counter argument so that it would withstand every criticism. He just felt peaceful, and he smiled, listened to the music, and relaxed in his seat speeding down the road behind the familiar car where he could just barely make out Carl and Lena talking in the front seat.

"It must be nice, where you're from," he wondered aloud.

"You should come see," she said turning back to look straight ahead. "It's paradise."

Interleaving and Intervening

"Hello, Ben Thorne's office."

"Hi Ginna, Gail. I wanted to make sure you are set for tomorrow."

"Yes. I think we are good. I have the email, I looked it over. I think you have covered everything we need."

"Great. Glad to hear it. By the way, I was wondering. Can you send me the copy for the reading? As I mentioned in the email, we like to get that in advance so that we have it on our file shares. We make it available for the listening impaired. So that everyone can follow along."

"I have not seen the final text yet. Can you hold while I check?"

"Sure. Thank you, Ginna."

She clicked the hold button on the phone software and took her headphones off, setting them down on the desk. She walked over to the inner office door, tapped lightly, and then swung it open.

"They want a copy of the text," she said, poking her head in.

"It is not ready. I am still working on it."

"It's tomorrow. I can't tell her that."

"Tell her we will bring it with us."

"Fine." She closed the door and went back to her desk.

"He is not available at the moment. Can we bring it with us tomorrow?"

"We like to have it in advance."

"I understand, but I do not have the final copy and I cannot get ahold of him just now. He has his rituals. We will have it tomorrow. Thank you so much for taking care of things, Gail. We are really looking forward to it. We will try and come early. I think it is going to be wonderful."

"But we really..."

"I understand, I understand. We will see you tomorrow. Very much looking forward to it. Thanks so much for checking in. Goodbye."

"Goodbye."

She got up and went back to the office.

"She must know I was stalling."

"So what? Who the hell is she? I am still working on it."

"I thought it was settled, you were going to read the new intervention, juxtapose it with the intervention from *Time Between Summers,* and then talk about that. How time works on memory, how time bends in the event, that sort of thing."

"No, no. I do not think so. It is more complicated than that."

"That's not what I want to hear the day before the talk."

There were pages on the desk, and they were disheveled in a way suggesting he had been shuffling through them. She walked farther into the office and picked up the top page.

"What is this?"

"Em had this whole thing about interleaving."

"Okay," she said hesitantly.

"Well, I was remembering this one time, way back, when he was telling me about a very specific instance of interleaving that he was working through. He was reading Popper, *Conjectures and Refutations,* I think. And he was interleaving that with Habermas' *Communicative Action Theory,* volume I or II."

"Okay." She reluctantly put the page back on the desk, still skimming it, still distracted by it.

"He told me that it was more than an interleaving of the two, it was something of an intervention."

"Who was intervening upon whom?"

"Not sure. Habermas on Popper, I think. Em said that Popper missed his chance for a true communicative theory of science, he missed out on seeing the voice of others inhabiting the practices of the scientist as they worked. The community of scientists was already there in the method. His bourgeois individualism and hatred of dialectic blinded him."

"I don't see..."

"The point is that Em was claiming intervention as a form of interleaving, you see? Interleave is the potential, intervention actualizes it. In its purest form, void of coercion and co-optation, but that purity never lasts."

"Okay. But this stuff is truly strange. There are no characters. I hope you're not planning on reading something without characters tomorrow. The conference is about storytelling and they're celebrating your use of characters to tell stories."

"Why do stories need to have characters? The ideas are characters."

"I'm just not sure this is the right audience for exploring that."

"I get it. Em and I used to argue about this story I wrote. He thought the names in the story referred to people, he thought of the women as goddesses. I never agreed with him. There was no dialogue, there were no physical descriptions. They had names, but they did not do anything or say anything. The men in the story. There were a couple of them. They would ride their bike or walk through parks, do things, say things to other people. They were clearly human beings. But the others, they just had names. The narrator did the speaking. I never even said they were women, he just assumed they were. Because of the names. Goddesses. A muse."

"This seems really interesting, but I don't see why you want to disrupt the plan for tomorrow and go down this path. What is so urgent?"

"Wait, wait." He stood up and started moving around the room while he continued to talk. "Em was interleaving Parmenides into my story way back then. He was also interleaving the muses and that whole mythology. That interleaving was an intervention. Even though I never agreed with him on that, it forced me to think about the story in a different way. I might have even rewritten it a little, revised it surely."

"How does this come back around to what you're trying to do for tomorrow. Tomorrow." She repeated the word, drawing it out syllable by syllable.

"Look at the café scene in *Time*, those are not men and women, they are just characters. Characters are not men and women. Do you see? They are only projection and shadow play. They are not real. That is what it means to be a character, it means you are not real."

"Men and woman, don't you mean?"

"No. I do not mean woman, I mean women. The librarian is in that scene too. Remember at the beginning, the typesetter goes into the bar and meets the librarian for the first time."

"Right. Of course. Men and women."

"But they are not men and women. They are characters. They are shadows in time, from a light cast years ago. Just ventriloquism. The author is enacting them, speaking them, or letting them speak through him. Time is bending. That is not just an accidental outcome of interleaving and intervention, it is the substance of it. When we experience interleaving, in the books we read, or in our lives, we are experiencing intervention. And that means something from outside of time has been injected into the time of something else."

"Outside of time?"

"Well, I mean, outside of the frame of reference. So, you have two distinct systems at work. Say Popper and Habermas, or *Time* and *W&A*. These are frames of reference. We do not just lay one over the top of the other, we inject the one into the other, and vice versa. Intervention is a name for this injection."

"Okay. What does that mean? Practically speaking. For tomorrow."

"It means there is never just one intervention, never just one interleaving. I cannot just take the one scene from the book written so many years ago and place it next to another scene written now. Doing that, even doing it once, causes everything to multiply. The permutations of characters and dialogue, of interpretation and meaning, they multiply. The one intervention becomes many interventions. Intervention repeats itself again and again."

"So, what are you saying? This gibberish here is just another way of framing the intervention, one of the many ways that automatically emerges from the two once you set them side by side?"

"Yes. Exactly. *Washington and Ashley* is not a story with a single intervention scene. It is the multiplication of interventions, it is many interventions. One may be made up of a professor, a typesetter, a librarian, and a Wolfe. Another might be made up of these characters from *W&A*. Then another might be a parrot and a group of cats."

"Cats?"

"Yes. The one cat intervenes while the other cat stalks the parrot."

"Is that what this is supposed to be?"

"No, that bit there, that's water interleaving with weeds. That's rain falling on a pond. An intervention. How can I make this clear?"

She shrugged and bit her lip.

"Characters are an accident. Can there be dialogue between the rain and the pond?" he asked. "That would be very hard to do. I agree, so you don't write it as dialogue. The reader would find that cheap. But that's how prose and description work. A dialogue between rain drops and the surface of the pond. Then there are drops of dew and weeds."

"Oh, there are weeds alright."

"Look, I have not thrown anything away. I have the versions. I am still working this out, trying to remember those times. The way he would talk. He invented this. Can you see that? These were his ideas, I just turned them into stories and people, gave them my voice because his was too jagged and disruptive. As a conversationalist... ...he would talk about ideas like they were in the room with us. They would come alive. That is how he could inspire me, that is why I needed to talk to him about my work. No one could intervene like Em."

"But... wasn't he the one you were trying to change in that conversation between...? On Washington near Ashley."

"Most definitely."

"And you failed, didn't you? You fell short, you couldn't reach him."

"No. I could not reach him. From that day forward... It was like he turned to secret codes and it was my job to decode it."

"An ongoing interleave. A continual intervention."

"Multiple."

"And this is what you want to say tomorrow. This is what you want to tell them."

"Yes. I want them to know. All these years, these many interventions and interleaves. That whole interlude stretching between that day on the street in the café and the day he died. It was a farce, but his meddle has been tested by ridicule."

"That's from Fred's research on Lord Shaftesbury, isn't it? Do you really think this is the right audience for that?"

"Absolutely not, but it is the right event. The talk will be recorded, it will be remembered. There will be a form for capturing the material. The keynote address for this conference, every year, is captured and stored. The focused author or topic, it is catalogued. No one knows. People have to know. Even if the *critics* in the audience are not the right people, the mechanisms are there. It is a memory machine and there is an addition."

"Okay. Do you need help? What would you like me to do?"

Minerva's

"I wish we could eat standing up," Eirini said.

The others grunted in agreement.

"We would be on the other side of Europe by now, if we drove this far in just two days."

"Not really, it's like Athens to Vienna, what we've covered so far."

"I would never drive from Athens to Vienna," she said.

The waitress brought their food. It was a nice place. In Rapid City and not far from the hotel where they were staying.

"Glad to see you still have your protection," Fred said.

"Open carry. We can complain if we want, but there are a lot of people in America who live like this. You can't just sweep it aside and still say you want to defend democracy."

"The minority shouldn't dictate," Carl said.

"What laws have they broken? You can't just say everything you don't like is bad. There is nuance."

"Last night was a perfect example," Fred said. "Those people melted in your arms, Lena. You showed strength and they loved it."

She shrugged.

"It's true," Carl said. "The civil war, or whatever you want to call it, it's between those who love autocrats and those who love oligarchs. Either way, the people love strength. Political power or economic power, whatever it is. They're mesmerized by it."

"Only one side is armed," Fred chimed in. "They will do whatever it takes to rule, the other side will do whatever it takes to avoid it. Don't listen to what people say, pay attention to what they actually want. They love power. However they conceive it, and they do conceive it differently, they love it the same even if they would do something different with it."

"This might be something we agree on," Carl said looking over at Fred. "I would think this would be terribly interesting to an anthropologist," he went on, looking back at Lena.

"How do you mean?"

"Back to Sexual Selection. View the different sides of the war from the point of view of women's preferences for partners."

"Holy shit," Fred said. "You've come over to the dark side."

Carl chuckled. "It's not the dark side. I think anthropology is a powerful tool for ideology critique. Isolating a demographic reveals wonders."

"Hello sweety, what's your name?" Eirini said to a little girl who was shyly pausing in front of their table as she walked by. She stared at Eirini, ignoring the others. "Are you here with your family?" she asked.

"Can you finish your thought?" Lena asked. "I'm still not caught up."

A man came by and apologized as he took the little girl's hand and started to lead her back to their table.

"We have a private language," Fred said. "It's a very long and ongoing conversation."

"What's her name?" Eirini asked the man before he could get away.

"It's a point Fred has made many times," Carl said.

"Chumani. Sometimes we call her akita mani yo. Say hi, Mani," he said as she buried her face behind his leg.

"There are women who love warriors," Carl went on. "There are women who love poets."

"She's so adorable. Bye Mani," Eirini waved and kept looking as the two walked off. Chumani looked back and almost fell over trying to get another glimpse.

"Imagine the civil war from that point of view," Carl continued, "and not from the point of view of the media discourse or the political ideology or whatever else we're force fed."

"The hard man who is allied with the traditional values of patriarchy," Fred said.

"Yes, but spun in its most seductive fashion. Not bogged down by self-consciousness and indecision."

"Not Hamlet," Fred said.

"That's right. A man of decisive action. A man you can slap, and he won't curl up into a little ball."

"Those days are gone."

"They're not," Carl said firmly. "I mean they are, and they aren't. That's the point. Half the straight women in this country still prefer that man. Even if the others want Hamlet."

"Hamlet on a journey of resolution and recovery."

"Well, Hamlet with throwdown, but who is still in touch with his feelings and the divisions in his soul."

"Well, you two have clearly had a lot of time to work this out."

"In Greece, the line is not so clear," Eirini said.

"I bet," Carl responded. "It's an American phenomenon. At least it's a huge part of our culture war. It might be the main cause. Those men don't want to be domesticated. Those women don't want that either. The division is huge, and what's more, the other side is made up of lots of rough hard men who are ready and willing to fight for what they believe in."

"So they say," Lena said sarcastically.

"Our side, the side with the gentle men, like me and Fred, we're not fighters. That's why things are so out of control. It's a fight without two sides that can fight."

The waitress came by and cleared away some of the dishes.

"It's like Kolokotronis," Eirini said.

"Kolokotronis?" Fred asked.

"The general in the war of independence. Greece could never have won without him. He was a great hero in the war with the Ottoman Empire."

"Of course, and he was not a sensitive man in touch with his feelings, I bet," Carl interjected.

"Oh no. He was hardened in prison. An archetype. I always think of the Kazentzakis' character, Captain Mihalis."

"What book is that from?" Fred asked gently.

"I don't know how it's called in English. In Greek it is *O Capitan*

Mihalis. He is a fighter for independence from the Turks. He is a very hard man, everyone is afraid of him. He has a sword, and he cuts down his enemies. He's very fierce. Without him, we don't stand a chance."

"Very interesting," Carl said. "Yes, maybe he isn't the man you want to marry and have children with, maybe you don't want him for your father, or as a colleague at work, but if there's a war, he's the man you need."

"Of course," Lena said. "Once you start following the rules of patriarchy, you need a patriarch. This is the principle behind your precious White Party, isn't it? They use autocracy to foster oligarchy and oligarchy to foster autocracy. Each rising to the occasion of fighting off the other. Ultimately, the White Party gets richer while the warring factions fight."

"Yes," Carl responded. "But you understand it in the light of the real political circumstances. The early days of the division created great disparity. Some people were clearly driven by the interests of the alienated white man. Angry and isolated, these men were becoming dangerous, and there were women who loved these men and stood by them."

"It's women's fault? We wanted to castrate these men and that started it, is that what you're saying?"

"It's not about fault. It's not about blame, it's about understanding historical causes. Like you were saying today. Yes, women had a lot of responsibility here. The backlash from that movement is a central part of the culture war. Even if women are right, they have to recognize the role those demands have in shaping history, even when that means the creation of counter-revolutionary movements."

"Alright, suppose you're right. What then?"

"The point is," Carl went on. "You create a situation that you have to be ready to address. That means someone has to step up, and that someone might have to be like Kolokotronis. But there aren't any men left who are like that on your side. So, what are you going to do? How will you fill the vacuum? You can't talk them out of it, that's the whole point. And they aren't going to accept the terms of your moral condemnation because they don't share the same morality. So, what are you going to do?"

"When you're a catalyzing agent, something might snap back at you," Fred said. "Women lack the cold-blooded determination necessary to take on a real adversary."

"The movement has been extremely effective at persuading those who were already predisposed toward those values," Carl went on. "The college educated, the white collar, the cosmopolitan men. They are already properly domesticated fathers and husbands. They were easy to win over and -in a sense—subdue. But these other guys, how are you going to handle them? What's the plan?"

Eirini was looking over at Lena, waiting for her answer. She worried it was too much.

"Reason won't work, is that your point?" Lena finally asked. "That's where the talk of reeducation, incarceration, and rehabilitation comes from."

"Exactly," Carl said. "That's what they have -ultimately—for their bitterest of holdout enemies. They assert that even these hard men have it in themselves to become softer, but the women don't want to stoop to violence. Yet, the act of reeducation is violent, rehabilitation is violent. There is coercion involved. It's a proclamation of oligarchy. The liberal ideals are its content. Long live the panopticon."

"There really hasn't been any extraordinary revaluation of values in this." Fred took up Carl's point. "The whole push in the last twenty years has been based on the liberal ideal of tolerance and equality. Balancing the scales. But they ain't buying it. So, what then? What comes next? Violence and coercion. So much for your liberal ideals, now we're back to the oligarchy. Even if it's promoting the good guys."

"Rational autonomy is a myth," Carl said. "All ethics derived from it too. All politics. Everything. The disempowered want power. It's a power grab. Those who are losing their way of life will fight back. What then? What is your plan, what will we do?"

"Extermination?" Fred asked.

"That's enough..." Lena said.

"Back to my initial point," Carl was responding to Fred and didn't seem to hear Lena. "You could spin this as an anthropological study from women's point of view. And maybe the conclusion is your little friend on your hip there. Knowing how to use it. Displaying skills for the traditional forms of power that used to be the exclusive right of men. You learn to kick ass, to carry a big stick, to threaten those who would betray the new ethos, to take a punch for the cause. Literally."

"But then you have to release your holier than thou attitude toward the patriarchy," Fred said. "You will have succumbed to its same methods. You will no longer be the purified upstarts cleansed by their history of oppression."

"Enough. Fuck. It's like an argument automaton. I'm taking issue with your whole way of setting this up," Lena said after pushing her plate out of the way to make room for her elbows. She barely touched her food. "It's a false dichotomy, either women are the charming mirrors for the hard man, his supporter and servant, or we're the warrior. The sword of justice. But what if there's an alterna..."

"The sword of justice made room for the alternative," Fred interrupted. "You're only able to get to that point because of the sword of justice. How will you know when to stop? How will you know when it becomes the new oppression and that the coerced victims are now the villains?"

"The purpose of the movement in the last twenty years has been to shine a light on bad behavior..."

"But what if they don't agree that it's bad behavior? The women on their side support them. They agree, they're attracted to that, they want to raise their boys the same way. Ain't they women too?"

Lena pursed her lips but didn't speak. She just looked back and forth between Fred and Carl.

"Your hesitation speaks volumes," Fred said.

"Oh? What does it say?" she asked, breathing evenly and looking directly at him.

"You are powerful. You are a light in the darkness. Those men yesterday. They were afraid and attracted and in awe of you. They were so happy to drink with you. They didn't give a crap about Fred and me. You were the one that broke the ice and made it possible for us to hang out together. Even the woman with them, even she was drawn to it."

"That's right," Fred jumped in rapidly. "But you're afraid to be that. Afraid of the contradiction. Because deep down, despite what you said, you still think like an autonomous agent who has to prove something and persuade everyone that it's true. Our whole concept of democracy is based on that, and yet it's based on a metaphysics and an ethics that make no sense anymore. God is dead, Lena."

She shook her head slowly, never breaking eye contact.

"If you're going to remake the world in your image," Carl said more calmly. "You have to be confident. You have to have a little bit of Kolokotronis in you. He didn't shy away from his own power, and he didn't try to persuade the Ottomans. He was the general. Once he was involved, it had already gone beyond that."

"Right." Eirini said looking back and forth between Fred and Carl, but tracking Lena closely out of the corner of her eye. "But you're not seeing... Confidence can be... It's different..." She trailed off.

"I'd like to walk a bit," Lena said, abruptly putting an end to the conversation. "We've been sitting too much today. Can we take a little walk? I'll see if I can put together a prospectus with my response. Maybe it'll be my dissertation."

Carl got the attention of the waitress and asked for the bill. "Why is everything manual here?" he asked in frustration to no one in particular while the waitress stopped at the cash station to total up their order.

They paid and got up to leave. Lena was quiet, still trying to think of a response, torn between anger and self-doubt. What if they were right, but wrong to make her feel this way? Or was she angry at them for failing to play their proper parts, confirming that she believed there were proper parts? What's next, she wondered, what's the answer?

They walked up the big avenue in front of the restaurant. Their hotel wasn't too far off.

Carl paired off with Lena, "Sorry if that was unfair. If we were being belligerent."

"It doesn't matter," she said. "That's the one thing I agreed with. Words don't matter so much."

"See, that's what I mean. That already separates you. I think maybe you understand that if you start something, you have to be prepared to follow through."

"Yes, but I don't advocate violence."

"Of course not, but you're not in control. Once you break the chains, the rules are gone, and you never know what's going to happen. You have to be prepared."

"I know that."

"I believe you, but I'm not so sure everyone does."

"My sister told me today that she's going to work for the families of those women who died in Missouri. She's following up on some reports that the police helped the killers."

"That's a national story. How did it happen?"

"She started looking into the rumors out of curiosity, but they told her she couldn't get some of the information she wanted because she wasn't working on the case. Formally. So, she contacted the families. They didn't have anyone looking out for them, so they agreed."

"That didn't even occur to me. To do that, I mean."

"Well, that's just it. She's a lawyer, she thinks about these things in those terms. Very concretely. We have to use the law; and be civilized. It might take years, but we need the same patience they had. It might be true that constitutional democracy is an invention of European hegemony, but what else is there? If we want to avoid savagery, it's the best option we have."

"Remaining civilized might be a bias, it might best serve the White Party's interests. Are you ready to confront that?"

Behind them, Eirini and Fred were walking side by side.

"Do you think American men are really that way?" she asked him.

"What way?"

"Either the poet or the warrior? Like you were saying."

"Those are archetypes, rosiest possible picture. Some might say the reality is more like cretins and wimps. Philanderers and cuckolds."

"Cretins?" she laughed, but Fred didn't seem to get the joke. "Which are you?"

"I suppose I'm a little bit of both. Actually, the worst mixture of the two."

"And Carl?"

"Him too, a mixture. Weak because we defer to others, but cretins in that we say things like that."

"Like what?"

"Like someone who says that a wimp is someone who defers to the virtues of attribute politics and evangelical correctness."

"I don't understand."

"I'm trying to be funny. I mean, we're wimps because we aren't aggressive and tough like Kolokotronis, but we're cretins because we resent our domestication and say witty things about how women are to blame for castrating us."

"Ah, I see. Do you believe it?"

"It doesn't matter if I believe it."

"What matters then?"

"It's like we were saying before. What matters is that you're attractive. Carl put it more scientifically, of course, like we should do a study to see what character traits women are encouraging through their partnering preferences. I would put it more crassly."

"How?"

"People want to f... ... get with each other, they try to make that happen."

"Wouldn't it be better to just act the way you act and then fuck people who like you for who you are?"

Fred blushed a little but didn't pause. "That was part of the point. There is no 'who you are.' That's the myth of rational autonomy. 'All we are' is a set of compliances to norms that must be followed to realize our desires. We don't even see the ways we change ourselves to get what we want."

"But what you want is already who you are, isn't it?"

"The desires and the behavior, they come together as one big package while we're growing up and learning from our friends and neighbors."

"Do men who are wimpy cretins always talk like you two?"

"Pretty much. Aren't you glad you came to visit? You're getting to see the real America."

She laughed.

They got back to the hotel, said goodnight, and went off to their rooms. Effortlessly and smoothly, Eirini kissed both Fred and Carl on their cheeks while Lena waved and let a very slight, somewhat forced, smile cross her lips.

Emission Analysis Feedback

Dasein is an entity for which, in its Being, that Being is an issue. The phrase 'is an issue' has been made plain in the state-of-Being of understanding—of understanding as self-projective Being towards its ownmost potentiality-for-Being. This potentiality is that for the sake of which any Dasein is as it is. (H.191)

Relations, the for-the-sake-of, the towards-this and the in-order-to, each of these semes are ordered through an ideal union with the final cause indicating something that exists prior to any attempt to realize it. Such is the rule that lies beneath the act and steers it as it comes to fruition. This elaborates potential as a rational principle, as a guiding rule directing movement toward an end. More than just a chain of causes and effects, it is anchored by the highest end.

Dasein is not an ideal being, however, a soul breathing in the ether. It is in the world. The system of relations is anchored and comprehended by this primary "for-the-sake-of" underlying every involvement. The "'for-the-sake-of' always pertains to the Being of Dasein, for which, in its Being, that very Being is essentially an issue." (H.84) Dasein's existence is that for the sake of which involvements happen. It builds things, does things, makes things happen. Why? To make other things happen. It's for the sake of Dasein: the origin of movement moves things that move other things. Questioning existence moves within a circulating system, it moves in a circle.

Dasein reconciles itself in its movement setting out to realize its origins. It is the comprehensive conclusion not as an end or a goal, but as something that it is for-the-sake-of. "Towards this," "in order to," "with...in...," etc., are elements. Significance and meaning underly means and ends. The "for-the-sake-of" is set in order. It doesn't mark the process with an end where movement ceases, Dasein comprehends movement as its circumference and center.

The origin, like the end, is not a mark that places an exterior limit. The economy of relations begins when Dasein guides and acts through its involvements, through whatever it takes issue with. No boundaries are marked, they are a beginning and an end, and they inhabit activity, they carry its origin and end within as the most comprehensive trait.

Dasein is the entity that asks the question, asks the meaning of the question, makes questioning a matter for questioning as a manner of being. It attempts to comprehend itself as the creature that comprehends, it attempts to understand its activity as the activity of understanding. There is nothing deeper than questioning that keeps circulation going and avoids letting it be marked by a boundary that separates it from an exterior as though its life were a product, something fabricated.

Dasein's self-understanding is not a thing, but related significance delimited as a circulating system, a conscious being. Traditionally, proximally and for the most part, it closes off to itself, its edges are marked by a world in space and thus its movement is without residual. The end inhabits and saturates it, guides it as both origin and end.

Imagine a creator with a driving need to create something that expresses its original state. Would it be a realistic tale if it reached its end and then stopped? They had their need, they expressed it, and it was satisfied. The end. Is that how it goes? Or does the need repeat itself? In and out, in and out, it could go on like that forever. We do not name an end with desire, we name an ongoing activity, a recurrent event, emitting in intervals.

The impossibility of producing anything becomes essential to activity. Because the activity is an activity for the sake of Dasein's self-understanding, and because that self-understanding is marked by the attempt to comprehend itself fully, to realize itself, Dasein cannot come to an end. Rather the only end that guides Dasein's movement is its own annihilation. Because that end is itself an impossibility, something that cannot be realized, it is an end that is always there along with them, but never actual. When Dasein is, its end is not.

An impossible end that guides the movement and never allows it to suffer a moment of completion, this is the greatest weight, what is most difficult. The impossibility of the end is the impossibility of movement pure and simple, of ideal movement. Dasein's incompleteness guides and preserves its movement as a circulating system. No doubt its systematic nature is called into question, it becomes an issue.

The origin wears away in the process, loses its distinction, and ceases to be comprehended. The end too wears away and ceases to be understood. The closure of the system that circulates as the reconciliatory movement of a finite activity comes to terms with and fastens its own incompleteness. There is still a semblance of the systematic here, but the boundaries are worn away. Without beginning or end there has been a transformation. The boundaries that marked the finite origin and end cease to set the process off against something else. Rather, the boundaries have been incorporated. Without beginning they are always already. Without end they are not yet.

Possibility and impossibility are in relation to an end projecting into the future, thrown by the past. Like the beginning, the end is always already there. Like the end, the beginning is not yet there. Possibility and impossibility are transformed into something other than a simple relation to a predictable outcome. "Potentiality-for-Being" is what Dasein already is. The circle is unending, but it is finite and comprehends a center contained by a circumference. It has a form, a body, and it breathes.

This finite circulation cannot be understood as a linear function with an origin and an end. Rather it is a set of relations, a system of relations where the end and origin function as their form. The origin and end are incorporated into the circulating system and intensify its movement, charge it with greater force. This hermeneutic phenomenology transforms the traditional project and resets philosophical thinking. One can no longer speak coherently of subdisciplines like ethics and metaphysics. This fundamental ontology doesn't unify the science, it threatens its order.

What am I capable of even if I am not currently doing it? The circulating system suggests activity is already there. Possibility or impossibility are not deliberations or results of deliberation actualizing a potential. What do they point toward? Yet more possibilities. Actualization becomes suspicious. This circulating system is incarnated as a system of possibilities that are an issue for Dasein.

But it is not so simple. It is saturated by the impossibility of coming to an end, of achieving itself, of realizing and actualizing itself as a system. It is incomplete and sputters under that weight. Dasein's potentiality-for-Being is an impotence that Dasein *must* be. Being marked by impotence makes it turbulent. Turbulence presents Dasein as an entity already in motion, swarming, fragile, on the verge of collapse and dissemination: itself but always at risk of not being itself. This uncertainty is an issue.

This turbulence marks a conflict. Potentially reoriented and involved in impotent potential, Dasein can do both because Dasein is both. The to and fro motion is nothing other than Dasein at issue with itself. It overcomes its impotence by overcoming its finitude. This lures Dasein into dismantling or consuming its potential, making it even more impotent. Everywhere you look, Dasein exhausts itself in its impotence. Every *one* knows this.

This is one attempt at mastery. Dasein asserts itself as infinite, as unending and omnipotent, but cannot do it, cannot actually achieve it. The circulating system is modified. It no longer belongs to itself, it does not hear itself, but only what it wants to hear.

Transformation relates to the limit, attempts to transcend it, to move beyond it. Such a limit is imposed on finitude as an impotent capacity. What is retrieved or repeated in the circulating system is the meaning of the attempt, of the effort to overcome powerlessness as the primordial power of the actor.

This repetition is Dasein's deconstruction, it is the deconstruction of metaphysics where Dasein is the ultimate entity in any metaphysical system, it's guiding principle and subject. As such, it is something it does to itself to be no longer. What can Dasein do to itself to become no longer Dasein? It can die. Dasein dies and dying is something it does to itself. Not voluntarily or with any effort but in fact and despite its efforts. Suicide is neither an example nor a counterexample. Dasein can try to kill itself: pull the trigger, swallow the pills, drag the razor, leap from the edge, but these efforts are not the same as the effort to die. Dying is not a behavior. In dying, ends evaporate. Pulling the trigger may or may not kill Dasein. A suicide attempt may be unsuccessful.

Heidegger names this impossibility, this self-destructive attempt at overcoming, *transcendence*. Dasein does not transcend itself by overcoming itself for the sake of something but already is this transcendence. Dasein comprehends itself as transcendence through its movement in a circle. This can only be a circulating economy for it has lost the rigorous closedness, the guiding principle, that provided its systematic form. This self-imposed retrieval, this repetition that does not present Dasein in an alternative matter or manner of existence, allows it to come forward as an issue for itself, an introduction to itself.

Dasein comprehends itself this way. It is already this economy. The change that takes place occurs in a mode of understanding. It understands itself as finite and impotent to change that. Dasein already understands what it can come to understand. It is inhabited by the power to understand what it has already understood. In short, it moves in a circle and repeats itself when it discovers that repeating itself is what it is and has always been.

The Transcendence of Dasein

The Porch

Eirini's mother answered the phone, "Yes." Then immediately there was commotion in the background: "Maria, who is it?" It was her father's voice. There was more talk in the background, it sounded like Thimios and Despina were there too.

"Who is there?" Eirini asked. "Where are you?"

"We're at Ermioni's," Maria said. "Thimios is not taking care of things. He isn't opening the house in the morning, he isn't sweeping the porch. It's very hot, but he just sits in the air conditioning, running it all day. He thinks the electricity is free."

"It's on the solar," Lena said seriously. "It is free."

"Is that Eleni? Hello Lena, where are you? What is going on?"

"We're in South Dakota. Heading toward Minnesota today."

"Alright. Good. Renya, your father is going to sweep. Let's see how that turns out."

"Let him sweep, Mama, you sit and talk to us. What is going on there?"

"Nothing, it's the same. Very hot. There are a lot of jellyfish this year. East. West is not so bad. We went swimming. Alexandros came home yesterday. He and his friend spent the night. Today, they've been sleeping the day away."

"He didn't come with you?"

"No, they're going to Thassos. His friend has a car."

"Mama, what are you doing?"

"It's very dirty, I have to clean this up. I'll put down a sheet in the kitchen. Thimios needs to stay on the sheet."

"Make Thimios clean it, Maria," Lena called out from the driver's seat. "He knows how to clean a kitchen. Someone must be cooking for Despina."

"Someone? Of course someone is. I am. Stamatia and Europea. We are. She would starve if we didn't. Thimios would starve too."

"Have you heard from Aunt Ariti, Mama?"

"Yes, yes. They are very busy. Cleaning out the house, getting rid of those things. They aren't bringing very much back with them. A small container. They're selling the house. I never heard of such a thing."

"That's how they do it here," Lena said.

"They should give it to you, Lena mou. That's the way it's supposed to be. If she doesn't want it, she should give it to you. I told her. I've told her many times."

"I don't want it, Maria. We discussed it. Once my mother leaves Seattle, I won't have any reason to go back. I don't want to worry about a house on the other side of the country."

"Maybe you should worry about a house on the other side of the country. Maybe you should have a reason to go back. It's not right. Families with children don't sell their house. It's not right."

"It's different here. They don't keep everything forever like that."

"Well, it's not right. That's why they have those troubles. That's the real shame with the immigrants. They should be learning from them, not trying to throw them out. They've lost their way."

"What are you talking about?" Eirini asked trying to stifle her laughter. She mouthed the words to Lena: "She's triggered." They both laughed.

"It's out of control, we hear stories every day on the news. America is broken. I hope you two are staying safe. Are those boys nice? Are they behaving themselves?"

"Yes Mama, they're very nice. It's good to have them around. They've been fighting off the bad guys."

"Bah. You shouldn't tease me. It's serious. I hope they can fight off the bad guys, but you shouldn't joke."

"They aren't like that, Mama."

"What does that mean?"

"They can't protect anyone. They're good at talking. They'll find out why someone is bothering us, but they can't do anything about it."

Lena was shaking her head, laughing.

"Mama, we have to go. We'll talk again tomorrow."

"Bye bye darlings. Kisses."

"Bye Maria."

"Goodbye Mama."

Maria hung up the phone and went to find a sheet for the kitchen floor. She was dead serious about laying something down to prevent Thimios from messing up the place. She overheard him and Nikos talking, "How long have you been running it?" Nikos was asking.

"I leave it on the automatic setting at 23. It comes on throughout the day. It goes off when the temperature is right. Em told me that's how it's supposed to work."

Maria jumped in, "It doesn't matter how it's supposed to work. You need to air out the house every day. You need to open the windows every morning, and you should be opening things up at night too. The air in here is stifling. What have you been doing? I knew we should have been coming by with the food instead of letting you pick it up."

"I told him," Despina said from somewhere farther away and out of sight. Maria came farther into the room and looked through the door wall to see Despina sweeping the porch.

"I thought I told you to get Thimios to sweep the porch," she said to Nikos.

"I did. He told Despina."

She shook her head in disgust at the two men sitting on the couch and watching the girl sweep the porch. Maria walked through the room to the glass door and looked out. "Good job, sweetheart," she said. "Has your baba done anything to take care of you since your mother left for America?"

"We went to the Taverna last night. It was yummy. Is Alexandros home? Did I hear you tell Eirini he came home last night?"

"Yes, he's home, but they've gone to Thassos. You can see him this weekend. We'll have a cookout."

"Thimios, how can you..."

"Maria, what did she say? How is our daughter?"

"Who knows. She doesn't say. She's with Eleni. They sound fine. The boys are talkers, not fighters. That's what they say."

"Where are they?"

"They are driving through South Dakota."

"There are many native Americans there," Thimios said.

"Yes. Sioux, Lakota. There was a program not too long ago. There was once a giant city. By the Mississippi. Is South Dakota by the Mississippi?"

"No," Thimios said. "It's farther west. It's where they took that land and made the big statue."

"What big statue?" Maria asked. She went to a closet in the hall to look for a sheet.

Thimios stood up so he could see her bending into the closet. "They carved the heads of some American Presidents into a mountain. It was once a sacred burial site. They did it to demoralize the people."

"That's why they don't want immigrants," Nikos said. "They're afraid they will act the same way they acted when they were the immigrants."

"What? You think we're so open and friendly with immigrants," Thimios warned. "Every country struggles with this."

Nikos nodded. "We think being Greek means having family that came here during the Catastrophe, or who lived in Thrace for generations. We treat Africans and Albanians as foreigners even when they've been here for generations."

"That's because being Greek isn't just citizenship, we're a race of people."

"Don't be ridiculous," Maria said from outside the room.

"It's not ridiculous," Thimios insisted. "Maybe it's not the right word, but we're not like the Americans. We've been here for thousands of years. We've endured so much, 500 years of occupation, Smyrna, Cyprus. So much. A few people show up in the last fifty years and they think that makes them Greek."

"When did you show up?" Maria said. She found what she was looking for and went back to the kitchen, leaving them with a shake of her head. "Worthless," she muttered. "If you're going to have such foul opinions, you could at least clean up."

"What was that Maria?"

He shrugged and sat back down on the couch. Despina moved off around the corner of the porch that wrapped the house. They could still hear her sweeping, but they couldn't see her.

"America has no traditions," Thimios went on. "They need immigrants to keep them grounded. We don't need that. We're grounded. We invented being grounded."

"Things have changed, Thimio," Nikos pointed out casually. "You sound like a barbarian when you talk like that. Like those fools who march in Athens and demand that the immigrants leave."

"Who says they should leave? I didn't say that. People need a place to live. I'm just saying we're not a melting pot. If you immigrate to America, that's one thing, you bring your country with you and put it with the others. That's how America works. In Greece, it's different. If you come here, you have to be Greek, you have to become Greek."

"Maybe Greek needs to change. Be more international."

"You mean like in Athens? Bah. That's Chinese capital buying up everything. That's no good for anybody. Here we should maintain the Northern ways. We live well, do you want to see that ruined? Do you want to be living in big housing tenements like they do in Athens? No thank you."

"I don't think there are going to be millions of people pouring into Chrysoupoli, Thimio."

"Even still, There's Thessalonki. Doesn't anything from our past matter anymore? How can we hold on to our history if the population changes so much? We don't want globalization here. Who's to say how long that will last? If many immigrants come, everything will change. Kavala, this has already happened."

"You mean because there's a Chinese restaurant now?"

"No, that's not what I mean. There are more international stores. People aren't spending their money in their neighbors' shops anymore. This will cause problems."

"Maybe. But we have to be hospitable, don't we? If we lost that, wouldn't it be worse? Wouldn't it be exactly what you're worried about? It's what got us through the Catastrophe, don't forget that. We were all refugees once."

Thimios waved his hand and stepped outside to check on Despina.

Nikos took advantage of the opportunity to get up and go into the kitchen to see if Maria was almost done. It was getting late, and he wanted to go to the Kafenio.

South Dakota

"I love talking to your mom," Lena said. "She's changed a lot since I was a kid."

"You think so?"

"Yeah, she was such a hippy back then, wasn't she? The way she would dress, the way she talked."

"You think she's changed? I think she's still like that."

"Well, maybe we just caught her at a bad time. She was pretty frantic."

"Thimios and my dad were probably winding her up. She doesn't want to let Aunt Ariti down. The things she has to put up with."

"Which one?"

"Both of them."

They laughed.

"I wanted to ask you," Eirini said. "At the stop back there. I couldn't follow everything. I think I missed something at the beginning and couldn't catch up. Then, with everyone talking at once, it was hard to decipher everything."

"I know. And they talk fast."

"Did you feel like they were ganging up on you again?"

"A little, but I'm used to it. It happens all the time at school."

"That doesn't sound nice," Eirini said scrunching her nose.

"It's the way it is, you get used to it unfortunately. It's part of the training."

Eirini shuddered and paused for a moment. "Were you arguing about freedom?" she asked.

"Yes," Lena exhaled a soft chuckle. "Freedom. They think about it differently."

"How?"

"Normally we say that either you have to be free to be moral or moral to be free. Only if you can choose, can you be praised or blamed for your choice. Only rational action is moral and free. One or the other."

"Okay."

"Choice and reason are complicated though. Conscience plays a part. Where does it come from? That voice in your head. Fred thinks it limits your freedom. It's meant to constrain people's drives and what they express, usually for the sake of someone else's interests. The herd, he was calling it, wants you to play nice with everyone. Be pliable. Your conscience is like their values applied to everything you do."

"And Carl?"

"He thinks freedom comes when you understand your class interests and align with them."

"How does morality fit?"

"Morality comes from class interests and fools you into promoting someone else's. Freedom means a different morality based on your own class interests."

"What do you think?"

"I think they both have problems that the other can fix. That's what I was trying to explain. Fred underestimates the liberating power of social consciousness, it's only oppressive to him. Those forces, they're not just raw nature, they're people and history, like Carl was saying. Whatever is in us trying to get out was probably put there by other people. The good and the bad."

"What's Carl's problem then?"

"He didn't say much about the individual. The examples he gave were really idyllic and simple. Maybe he thinks life needs to be simpler. I don't know."

"Simpler how?"

"Well, limit the things that require lots of skill and experience."

"Why? What's an example?"

"Health care. I don't think you can casually be an oncologist. You know, hunting in the morning, oncology in the afternoon, critique after dinner."

They laughed.

"Seriously, some areas of expertise take a lot of effort and require complex social structures to support them. It seems like complexity breeds more complexity."

"Fred wasn't saying enough about the good things in society. Carl wasn't saying enough about the good things in individuals. Is that it?"

"That's the gist. We need to merge them together. Not simplify life so much. On either side."

"Like what?"

"Expertise is important. The individual is created by society and its divisions. It doesn't stand alone. It can't. But once it's created, it really exists, and has desires and needs. Society imprints itself, but the recipient isn't passive. There's a physical body. It can do things."

"Biology."

"Exactly. Science that starts from the individual and science that starts from society. Immune systems, for example, aren't isolated. They've evolved to protect the population, not just the organism. Some cells are sacrificed to protect the organ, that's common. It's not the only way though. An immune system might destroy the organism to protect the population."

"How?"

"Like the way it reacts to a virus. Sometimes the host is killed by the immune system fighting off the virus. In those cases, the genes might've formed the immune system to protect the pool of genes in the population. We mourn this, but we don't call it morally wrong. It's just nature."

"But we can prevent it, we're different from genes. We can change things."

"Like build health care systems. People focus, they study and become experts. The group may promote bad qualities, but the group can also struggle against them. We build infrastructure to intervene against nature."

"It's like you're trying to steer between the two of them and whenever you run into a problem with one you turn back to the other."

"Like you're shuffling the pages from their work together into one thing."

"Americans are so divided, but everyone says they're defending true freedom and being patriotic."

"People aren't always honest. They don't listen to reason, and they have ulterior motives. Politicians say things they don't believe, and ordinary people don't bother to prove everything. They'll get behind a politician just because they make them feel better. Doesn't matter what they do."

"We should be suspicious when they talk about morals and freedom."

"The cell isn't free. It doesn't self-destruct because it thinks that's good or bad, it just does it because that's the way it works."

"Not just cells. Stars and planets."

"Electrons and molecules."

"Everything. Only breathing things. Why are people so special? Why do we get to have freedom and morals?"

"It's taboo to reduce it to evolution and biology. We're supposed to let the philosophers answer that question."

"Are philosophers the ones who know about morality?"

"They certainly think so. If biologists try to answer, they'll accuse us of Social Darwinism."

"Weren't the philosophers the ones who came up with the lies? They have interests. They get paid. They work for rich people or the state. Maybe they work for the White Party."

Lena smiled and rolled her eyes. "It's the philosophers who invented slave moralities in the first place. They're behind every battle. We're free, no we're free, no we're free. We're the good ones, you're bad. Everyone has their philosopher."

"They pander to people to get them to listen."

"When they put morality and freedom everywhere, they made sure it was no longer anywhere. There's just fighting between people convinced they're right. Everything is so amplified. It's a battle to the death. We need to know about anthropology and biology, and to value understanding for its own sake. Now, everyone is part of the ruling order. Maybe they always were."

"It makes more sense now," Eirini said after grabbing a bag of grapes from the back seat and putting one in Lena's mouth. "Why were you guys talking about oral sex?"

Lena laughed and choked a little.

"Fred had many colorful examples to illustrate his point. I think he was talking about power when he brought that up. The person who's getting it thinks they have the power, and the person giving it thinks they do. The action is the same, but they think about it differently."

"I still don't get it. What does power have to do with it?"

"Well, maybe it's cultural, but if you're giving a guy head, you think you're in control, you can get him more excited if you want. Slow it down if you want. He responds to everything."

"Yeah. Okay. Sure."

"So, you feel powerful. But that may not be how he sees it. In his mind, he's in control. It's for his pleasure. You see what I mean? It's fantasy and it works both ways. That's what he was saying. When a guy goes down on you, you think you have him right where you want him." She laughed. Eirini smiled. "In his mind, it's completely different. He thinks he has the power."

"I don't know if that's always true."

"It has to be good oral sex. For both parties. That's what he was saying." She tilted her head and half nodded. "I can see it."

Eirini shook her head. They both laughed.

"I thought it was clever. The fantasy of freedom. It made sense in the end. Same with what he said about academia and being flattered vs flattering."

"Academia is like oral sex?"

They laughed and ate more grapes.

"I think that's what he was saying. Everyone acts like there isn't any going on. Flattery, I mean. Oral sex too, I guess. Point is, you're either getting someone off or someone is getting you off, either way you feel like you're the one in power. Even your complaints about being mistreated are just resentful expressions of power. Your friends flatter you when you do it. It's a counterbalance. You're above it, you criticize it from a distance. It's an unjust exception. Always deferring the payoff. When I get tenure, I'll be different."

"That's twisted."

"Don't get me started. I know people in cliques who flatter each other, stand up against anyone who doesn't belong. They run around accusing everyone else: racist, misogynist, homophobic, colonialist, ableist."

"Ableist?"

"Like when certain things are treated as normal and everything else is beneath that. You say, 'that's crazy' as a way of normalizing mental health and putting down people who struggle."

"Hmmm."

"Right, so you have someone who attends one of the most elite graduate schools in the country criticizing their colleagues for being ableist. The entrance requirements are totally ableist. The whole conversation is full of contradictions. Other cliques form to oppose them. They use their contradictions against them but come off as cruel and unsympathetic. They contradict themselves. The whole fiasco is nonsense. Like with oral sex. Everyone interprets it to suit themselves. Pure fantasy. They shame. They don't teach. They don't think. The status quo wins. The herd."

"So is that what they meant when they said slaves and masters agree on at least one thing, that everything is about mastery and slavery? It's about power, fighting for freedom and morality where ideas are weapons."

"It only makes sense if there is an ultimate purpose. Empowerment is what everyone wants, dressing it up as morality, securing liberty and justice. All to achieve the best possible world. We're stuck.

Eirini looked over. "It's sad. The whole world is paying for it."

"The big debate was that I think even talking about it is part of the problem. It's recursive, you have to know when to stop." She paused a moment. Eirini was looking off into the distance through the passenger side window.

Long Distance

Mia hung up the phone then got up and went down the hall. She tapped on the door, and Gwen waved her in.

"What did you hear?" she asked.

"We'll have to make a separate motion. They're holding back the body cam footage."

"Did they give a reason?"

"Ongoing investigation."

"Okay, if you write it, I'll take it from there. When is your sister coming?"

"She said Friday, but today she said they might be here tomorrow."

"They've been making good time."

"Yes, and I gather Eirini isn't very happy about it."

"Oh?"

"Yeah, she wanted to stop at Yellowstone, and she wanted to see Mt. Rushmore. Crazy Horse monument. Everything from the guidebook."

"Lena's not into it. Has she seen it before?"

"I don't think so, she's just not in the mood. She seems distracted. She's depressed. Maybe a little detached. She just isn't herself. I can't wait to put my arms around her."

"How are you doing?"

"I'm fine. I was prepared. It was a long time coming. It's not the same for me."

"Okay, but don't worry. I've got this covered. I just need you to write it up. Don't bother polishing it. I'll take it from there. You go off and take care of your sister. We just need to get things started, and Bert is going to help in Missouri. Are we going to be able to cover his expenses?"

"The estate lawyer said I can't use any of the money for work, and the Center's budget is pretty tight."

"There's a stipulation on the inheritance?"

"Yes, the old bastard. He knows me, I guess. It's set up so that it would be easy enough to get around it, the lawyer pretty much told me that there's no micro-management, no one is going to audit me or anything, but he made his intentions clear."

"Well, I think it's a good thing. Use it for yourself, do something for yourself. We should be able to get funding for Bert's expenses. There are a lot of people who are interested in this case."

"I agree. I'll have one of the volunteers put something out there to raise the money. Not just for Bert, but for anything else that comes along. Let's try and keep the Center out of it. It's enough that we'll both be on the case."

"Agreed. How sure are you?"

"About what? That we have a winner, not in the least."

"No, I mean, how sure are you that the reports are true."

"They're either sociopaths or it's true."

"The police aided and abetted in a public lynching."

"Yes, I think that's what happened. A group of people decided that their lives were not worth anything and that they had to be punished for being somewhere they didn't belong. It's possible those people would have only scared them if left to themselves, but with police support, the attack escalated. That's the case, and the body cam footage will prove it."

"We've been down this road before. And lost."

"I know. I started to twitch when I heard their reasoning. They're stonewalling."

"How are the parents?"

"They're terrific. Under the circumstances. Of course, they're devastated, but they don't want to compound the loss by letting them get away with it. They're fighters."

"Good, and you've told them it'll be a long fight with lots of setbacks."

"Most definitely."

Mia stood up and was about to open the door to leave the office. "I was just thinking. My biological father, the law was always so philosophical to him. He would talk about how it was just a set of rules to institutionalize inequality, the usual lefty armchair rhetoric."

"Could be worse," Gwen said looking up at Mia who was paused at the door.

"Sure, but I recall once I really blew up at him about it, told him it wasn't just theory, it wasn't some remote abstraction, but that the law was realized every day in people's lives. It could either make things easier or harder. Laws and getting around them or having them arbitrarily enforced are some of the most rudimentary experiences of our lives. They impact how we understand everything, we can't separate them from our experience, you can't take a step back, it's a real part of what things mean to us. If injustice is in our blood, then we see everything that way."

"Sounds like a passionate plea."

"I was so frustrated. I remember thinking he just didn't get it. How real it was. I don't know why I thought he was responsible."

"What did he say?"

"Of course, you're absolutely right."

"No argument."

"None. He wasn't in the trenches. It's such a luxury to have an opinion sometimes. He knew how it worked, but it wasn't his business so... I was too hard on him."

"I'm sure he understood."

"Once we were arguing about free speech. I was in grad school. Very idealistic. Absolutely in favor of it: the most fundamental liberal notion."

"Sure."

"He talked about performative speech. It drove me crazy. Blah blah blah, yelling fire in a crowded theatre. But he didn't let it go, he wondered whether speech was performative, whether experience was flavored by others' speech. If there were a bunch of people spouting nasty brutish notions about greed and vicious antagonism, then the rest of us are forced to live in their greedy vicious antagonistic world."

"Tough one."

"Yeah, and it occurs to me that maybe he really did agree with me. Was I just being terribly ignorant? Was he letting me know that free speech was beyond my oversimplified liberal ideals?"

"Words are how the law is expressed."

"The body of a law is not speech even though it has its material in language. It is performative."

"Do you think that was his point?"

"He was just trying to let me know that things are more complicated than they seem. I thought he was saying something about logical possibility, making a scholarly argument that dismissed practical reality."

"This was a long-standing discussion you two were having."

Mia laughed. "Years. The first amendment is cowardly. It's only talking about legislation. But that's so esoteric and theoretical. We know the reality of it. It's irrelevant to nearly every part of our lives. It doesn't apply at work or at the grocery store. It doesn't matter online. It actually protects coercion."

She shook her head, and paused. She seemed to be weighing whether it was worth going on. Then she did. Very deliberately.

"You have free speech on the steps of the post-office or the library, if your town even has either of those, otherwise, the security bot can pretty much tell you to shut up or bar you from access if you don't follow the service agreement or terms of use."

She paused again. Looked away from Gwen who was patiently waiting.

"It's part of people's behavior now," Mia continued. "They talk about free speech, but their body knows better, they're inert, knowing they spend most of their lives in places where constitutional protections are irrelevant. It's just loud."

She stopped again. Shifted weight from one foot to the other and played with the handle.

"He may have had a more realistic view than I did. Bad word choices maybe. I misunderstood."

Gwen nodded and looked softly at Mia who smiled and said: "Okay, back to it."

The 26th

"Shooby do op, shooby dooby do op, shooby dooby do, shooby dooby wah. Na jah. What's up Speusippus?"

"Happy 26th."

"Happy 26th, agape mou."

She put her arms around his neck, he wrapped his around her waist. They kissed and held each other, swaying lightly.

"I miss you so much," she said. He pulled her tighter. "Do you miss me?"

"Technically, I miss everything," he said.

"Even that? You even joke about that."

"That's the part they don't prepare you for. It's hilarious."

"What do you mean?"

"There is nothing and it turns out nothing is ridiculous."

"Or everything is."

"Akrivos."

"There is so much to do. I don't know how I'm going to get through this."

"It's ready. You just need to call the people on the list. Let them do their jobs."

"I'm doing that. That's not what I mean. What am I supposed to do now? That's the hard part."

"You're so much stronger than you think. Everyone is, really. Living takes strength. It's such a mistake when the kids say that strength is really weakness. They don't know what they're talking about. How can they? If you think you're weak and would make a virtue of it, condemn strength as an illness, how can you possibly know? You're lacking exactly that which you judge. Of course, the strong needn't correct them since they're strong and don't care if they're understood by the weak. But the weak should know that they're wrong, that they're not weak. They should know that living takes so much strength and that they can find it in places and ways they didn't realize."

"Is this your newfound wisdom? Is this what nothing has to teach us?"

"No, it's you. You're teaching yourself. All these years we quietly agreed. Never talked about it, but we both knew. There is an aristocracy. Not based on blood or birth, success, or riches, but on character and devotion. The good and the bad. Living is not for the meek and no political movement will change that. You've always known this."

"But you would scold me when I said it."

"And you knew I was right because deep down you agreed with me. Strength of character means you know that you cannot legislate these qualities and force them onto others. You must bear the resistance of those who do not yet believe they have it."

"You contradict yourself, sir."

"That's right."

"Well which is it? Is there weakness or not?"

"Exactly. There are many who don't know what they are. They think they're weak and so they're weak. The scales are not in their favor. They grab onto foolish things, they distract themselves, they scream and dictate their weakness to everyone else. That's their weakness speaking. But it speaks with great strength. They dictate, they command, they strive to make an order that everyone must follow. There is nothing more dangerous than strength that thinks itself weak."

"But you're saying people who believe they are strong must support them."

"Yes, absolutely. And people who feel that strength in every breath, they are strong enough for that."

"Can I ask you something?"

"Anything, agape mou. Go on."

"Is that why you were silent throughout the years? Is that why you never said a word about any of it, about those Monday mornings, about those awful weeks where your time was not your own?"

"No one's time is their own. Being strong doesn't mean things aren't hard sometimes."

"But you didn't complain. You just got up every day and did the work. You didn't brag, which you always said was like a complaint. You didn't let on that it was hard. Is that why? Because you thought that was what you had to bear, that was what your strength demanded."

"Look who's talking."

"I'm serious."

"I don't know. Like I said, I disagree with those kids. I didn't see it that way, but I wasn't going to argue with them. Who am I, after all? It would be the worst contradiction. Sometimes, the hardest thing in the world is to remain silent when you have something to say. I practiced that."

"On Mondays?"

"Mondays were the worst of it. But they're a sign of success too."

"How?"

"Well, the transition made me buckle. I was going from one to the other, and switching gears was always painful. It was silly to organize things so that every single week repeated the same drama, but what choice did I have?"

"How is that a sign of success?"

"I was doing it. If that makes sense. My mind was where it needed to be. It's why I felt the conflict."

"I think maybe this is my Monday morning."

"It's far more than I ever had to endure. Mondays are small and repeated. It's rationed so you only have to suffer a little bit at a time. This is a big one, all at once."

"You're forgetting what you went through."

"I'm not forgetting."

"Last month you told me you didn't want to die."

"I didn't."

"Last week you told me you were ready."

"I was."

"I can't stop thinking about what you must have gone through to get there. You had to go through that."

"It doesn't matter now. I'm sorry for breaking my promise."

"You promised to try, you didn't break that promise."

"Maybe that's how it is with promises. We always over-promise. We want to promise to do things even when we can only promise to try."

She shook her head deliberately back and forth with her eyes shut tight. "You're a walking contradiction. Flitting about. There are strong people. Resentment is a sign of weakness. Then you go on about injustice and how it's a duty to help the weak even if they scream bloody murder while they're being helped... blah blah blah. Then sometimes you call that a collar around their neck." She stopped and stepped back a little. She gave him a stern look with a shake of her head. "Hey, you're being naughty. Don't try to distract me. The fact is that you left me and leaving is leaving. I didn't expect to be angry with you. I expected to be sad, I expected to be lonely. I didn't expect to be angry."

"I know."

"Who can I tell? Ariti knows. I don't have to say it. We talk but there's no relief. What I really want, I really want to tell Lena. She's angry too. But I don't know how to talk to her. These last few years...."

"She is yours and you are hers. The difficulty will go. Just talk."

"I'm afraid. She thinks I'm nothing, she thinks I've done nothing. The more she does, the farther away she gets."

"She got the worst of both of us, didn't she? My stubborn drive and insensitive determination, and your loving doubts and caring worries. She's angry with both of us."

"Why?"

"Because we are her destiny. Because we made her, and this is how that bends back to where it came from and where it's going. She's our laughter and our trouble, she's our silence and our chattering nonsense. Between us."

"You may be overthinking it. She's an accomplished young woman. She compares herself to me, she sees me... She doesn't..."

"Shhhh, shhhh. Don't think like that. I spent nearly my entire life striving to say that one pure thing that binds you to what is in front of you. It struck me as the most magical of things."

"You? Do you mean me? What are you saying?"

"People always get lost and distracted. They're dazzled by riches or by fame, by things. The attachment of the conscious mind to its deed, the moment of experience, the presence of the being in its act. These are the most extraordinary human events."

"You saw this?"

"Absolutely. You couldn't help yourself. You're like no one I've ever met. You cared about every detail in the world your daughter woke up in. All of it, you were more present in your acts than anyone I've ever seen or known. I did everything I could to grasp it, to write it down. Phenomenology. Pffft. What connects you to your act, puts you in the presence of... You taught me about distractions, interventions from somewhere else: injected and alien, coercing attention and devotion."

"How will I make it, though? Who will be my witness now? Who will see that if you don't? If there's no one to see it, maybe I won't be it anymore."

"I wish I could tell you it was going to be okay. That's exactly what's in front of you. It isn't about me, about losing me. It's about holding onto the part of yourself that only I knew. If you had to give a name to your grief, that would be it."

"That's the answer then?"

"Keep taking care of things, keep worrying about things. Keep being present to what is in front of you. From the perspective of eternity, a street cleaner and an evolutionary biologist aren't much different. Their hearts beat, they breathe. Feel that in each act. That's the answer. I'll be there with you."

"Is that what was behind your... What did you call it? ... stubborn drive and insensitive determination?"

"Yes, and now it's yours because there is no one else who would have it. No one else who would even care to remember it."

"That writer might."

"No. Only you. But we have to go now, there's a lot to do."

"I'm not ready."

"Yes you are."

The Key Note

Being an introduction, the conference organizer had nothing but nice things to say before bringing Ben Thorne to the podium. He grimaced as he made his way into the light and in front of the large audience.

"Thank you for having me," he began, and was immediately interrupted by scattered laughter. He smiled, nodding.

"Thank you for those kind words, Dr. Lessing, and thank you for allowing me to speak on the topic of my own choosing. I must, however, apologize. Despite my promise that I would be reading to you today from my latest work, I find that I am unable to proceed.

"Like much of what I have written throughout my life, my latest work – if I can even call it that– aims at bending time as though it were a tree being shaken free of its fruit.

"Nearly forty years ago I sat outside a little café on Washington Street with my friends Em and Kai. Kai and I were trying to convince Em that he was making a horrible mistake and needed to immediately cease his pursuits and try something else. Whether or not we were successful is a question that I am still struggling with so many years later.

"There was an alley halfway between Main and Ashley. A small garbage dumpster parked in it. A stream of filthy water would gather behind it during heavy rainfall, it would run down to the street over the sidewalk. There was a glass door between the café and the alley. Two young women would come and go. There was an apartment upstairs. She opened and closed the door five times before stepping outside. She swung the kitchen garbage bag three times before bringing it to rest in the dumpster. Then she opened and closed the door five times before going back in.

"You may recognize the setting from this story as the intervention scene and you may wonder why I would, yet again, go back to it. If I were to keep my promise and read from my latest work, if it is my latest work, I fear you would only become more puzzled. You see, I continue to focus on that same scene. Not once, as an event that sits at the beginning, middle, or end of something else, but over and over again. The story from this angle and that angle, with these events and those, with this outcome and still another. It is the constant reawakening of a what-if or some other such imagining that I invoke to bend those forty years back and reach out to touch those two friends of mine.

"In that fugitive time, I evoke the potential that lies inside it as it moves forward. The bending back is that power to evoke, the conjuring of that potential, and I swear to you that I would show it to you as if it were here with us in the room if that were possible. But it is not. Bending time to reveal the potential that lies in it, actualizes the moment in that same act and so dashes its efforts in failure. That actualization is coercive, and it inhabits whatever occupies its time, whatever power and potential we may have found there. Duration, some might say, evaporates into space when we try to demonstrate its presence. The clock is ticking. It has hands and each moment is a discrete movement. One time becomes many times, the multiplicity of time. Never resting, never anywhere, this hobgoblin casts its seed over us and we sink further into its fertile flow. While this train plows forward, Emit Flesti hides.

"Beware the bitterness of your hardship. Stronger does not mean colder and harder. It means being able to feel more, and bear a greater burden. It means more passion. Do not curl up. You will never carry anything that way. Beware of confusing your image with your soul. Your image is not real, and it cannot feel anything. It does not carry anything. It has no passion. It is a fabrication. Let your experience make you still more real, give you more flesh and blood.

"Have I lost you? Surely, I must have. It is my lot, to lose and to be lost. If you think back to those stories, the tales and yarns, you will admit that in every single one of them there was a philosopher. Sometimes he or she is off to the side, sometimes front and center. The story will dictate their role in its midst. There is no formula for that. Rather, the formula lies in being lost, in the losing, and in the lot that agonizes over it.

"My friend Em is the one who told me long ago that there was always a philosopher. He was not talking about books or writing. He was talking about something he called interlude. That intervention we were performing was an intervention into his interlude and with that, where that takes place, there was always a philosopher nearby. Not some serious old bloke with white hair and a long beard, or a stylish woman with a Bowie cut and beautiful lines carved into her face. No, this philosopher was a freak and a fool.

"He would emphasize the two facets of any true philosopher: fear and ridicule, and they were aligned. Do you recall that bit from Wittgenstein somewhere? Something like: a friend and I were sitting in a garden, and we were saying 'I know that is a tree, I know that is a tree.' Someone came along and heard us. 'No,' we said, 'we are not insane, we are doing philosophy.' Wittgenstein showed us in that moment that he was afraid and that what he was most afraid of was being ridiculed by a passerby in the garden.

"So, there is always a philosopher nearby, and that philosopher is always a harbinger of the fear and the ridicule that threatens every story and the events and persons in it. Forty years ago, Kai and I were trying to convince our friend, convince Em, that he should be the philosopher nearby, that he should feel more and forget about his image. For whatever reason, he refused. He wanted to be a professor, he wanted to be an engineer, he wanted to be a boyfriend, or a husband, a father, or a friend. He wanted to be so many things, but the one thing he did not want was to be the philosopher nearby.

"And this did not make any sense because it was the only thing he ever talked about. His actions and projects, his tasks and his schedule, everything bent toward being the philosopher in every story, alongside it, exposing the fear and the ridicule nearby, just up the street, in the alley, or around the corner.

"How could this be? What does it mean for someone to completely dedicate and devote themselves to a task that they do not want to perform? Is that a strike against freedom in favor of determinism? Is it morality? Is that the owl of Minerva taking flight?

"If I knew, I would write it down and show it to you. I am not holding something back for the finale, something that will only become clear at the crescendo. No, I cannot tell you because I do not know. What I do know is that there is always a philosopher, and that the philosopher speaks endlessly about fear and ridicule.

"There is a mythology that you may have heard. It is very popular and has grown quite old by now. The story goes that the gods created a perfectly autonomous individual, granted it rationality and liberty, and then turned it loose upon the planet, hoping for the best, but expecting the worst. This golem walked the earth in search of what was true and good, knowing it by sight and directing measured judgment toward it according to a correct order while following a proper method.

"We hear this story growing up and come to love it as children. As with any good story, we imagine ourselves the hero and fantasize about the adventures we might have if we were on the pathway they are forging. Does this *Waymaking* remind you of something? The road from Bregenz to Innsbruck perhaps?

"Philosophy, as it turns out, always speaks through the autonomous individual, or pretends to, aspires to it, proclaims it even when denying it. Tales with multiple points of view, diverse genre, and voices, these are the approaches that shatter the mythology and take on the mindset of the wolfpack. That is what you will find if you venture inside bending time and find these fabrications there.

"Bear with me. If I have not lost you forever, my friends. Out there. So far away. So silent. Waiting and following along. Adjusting your position in your seat. I can hear you breathing.

"The philosopher nearby, they are always talking about their precious transcendence. None of us have any idea what it is and yet there we are. In it, as it, through it. Transcending away, but not used to the word and stumbling over its complexity and power. What comes between you and each act? There is always a philosopher nearby. And their precious transcendence.

"Well suppose that it was one of us. Not a golem like we have come to imagine ourselves, but as we are, among each other, bent backward and forward, coming and going. What happened? What comes next? Do you recognize yourselves? What if... what if... it was one of us, here in our midst? Suppose it were a character. Give it some character. That is what you do, that is what you are. You bend it just like I do, here and there. Together. Be careful what gets between you.

"In its idealized form, a form that it never has when anyone is looking, it rests purified. It is more than just clay. That is what I meant by potential. That which cannot be touched or licked, smelled or heard. As it begins to move, and you must now see that it absolutely must move, there is corruption. It came out of itself and is littered by trash and debris. That is your tomorrow, your yesterday, and your today.

"Em died last week. While the pseudo thinkers among us ask why there is anything at all and not rather nothing, I scream at the nothing and demand to know what it has done with my friend. It does not speak but I know what it would say if it could. He has gone back to where he came from, back to the mythological source, individuated by that power within him, lost to it. For you see, like you, I have lost him.

"And this makes me wonder whether I ever had him to begin with. Do we have each other? Are we there together? Is that what the nearby philosopher says while cooing over this precious, unfamiliar character? Does its alien form lie, most essentially, in this being-with? Or are we rather plucked from our idealized mythology and lured into an endless movement of the one who occupies us here in our bodies and our lives?

"What carries such a capability? What bears it? What is it that can do that to us? It comes from somewhere and draws us into it, makes us this and that, adds properties and principles, attributes and associations, we become just like each other, and like ourselves over time from one day to the next. We become predictable and manageable. Not alone, but together, alike and in the aggregate piled high between the act and its content. It corrects myopia at the cost of sight.

"*Their* sequences have been transformed into aggregates. The freedom of the organized group hinges on the collective order of human beings within and without. Internal and external relationships stretch over its surface. It is how a group's consciousness realizes itself. It is done for the sake of an existential effort to persist despite its failure to be an organism in the strict sense. The group function, the indefinite article, realizes social being in the concrete. Such an unfamiliar character. That is what brings the child in you out into responsible adulthood. That is how you become who you are.

"Perhaps we are lost while we live, perhaps life itself is that loss, where we are pulled from the mythology and breathed alive into each other to be alike, to carry our character, to align with this group or that organization, this institution or that tribe. We fall into our roles and learn our lines, make them up and improvise when we forget. It does not matter. The role is the pure form and that is what guides us. It is when we leave this form behind that we rediscover our freedom. The good, as well.

"My friend who is no more, he can be whatever I want him to be now. He is no longer held by this Earth and these reins. He does not owe us anything. We have lost him."

He paused and took a sip of water. He looked around the auditorium. It was silent.

"You see, the philosopher is always nearby. Fear and ridicule. Remember that. Treat it like a baseline, like a drumbeat. *Bah* bah bah, *bah* bah bah, *bah* bah, *bah* bah, *bah* bah. That philosopher nearby, that is the lens grinder's shadow. I have told you about this. Really, it is not polite to make me go over it again. You know this. If you are here, then you must already have it in mind.

"I know I picked this trope up from somewhere else, but I cannot recall where. At noon, there is no shadow. Perhaps there is only glare in the bright light of such a perfect midday. Most importantly, at this hour, there are no shadows. Let us call that *sub specie aeternitatis*. That is the moment without shadow. Then let us offset that, place it over against the great shadows of the daylight. Not against the night, leave that be for now, but against the other hours of the day. The lens grinder's shadow fills whatever in the daytime is not high noon.

"The lens grinder himself has fooled us. He told us that the goal of the philosopher, the highest ambition, is the view from eternity, the view where there is no shadow. Where there is no character. We strive for that, and worse. I have known some who would kill for it. Here is the perfect moment. No, here it is. *Incipit tragedia*, the tragedy begins as the two perfectionists wage war against each other, deny each other's shadow, and stab at the bright light that bathes their every moment and glance.

"I am calling this a ruse. I am saying it is saturated through and through with fear and ridicule. The bird flies past. I apologize for the theft, but that is how it goes. You feel sorry for yourself, you are alone, you live in your mythology and the loneliness it brings. 'What do I matter?' So much self-pity in that. Then, only then, the bird flies past. 'What do you matter, what do you matter?' That bird is chirping at the sunlight, that bird is calling you into the shadows, that bird is reminding us of our friends, the friends that have died, the ones that are no more, the limits of our time, the shortness of our lives.

"I am trying to tell you about shadows, and I am trying to tell you about a philosopher who does not have a white beard or stylish haircut. This is not the philosopher who tells you which way to turn to find the truth, but the one who tells you how to persevere without it.

"Jealousy lives in a jealous world. Greed lives in a greedy world. They aim at the sunlight and the complete possession of all and sundry from eternity's point of view. No one is jealous of the shadows. No one wants to possess them.

"There are many of you here. I am told it is over a thousand. So quiet, this room." A light laughter fanned across the auditorium. "Thank you for coming, but I must now reveal my true motives. This is an intervention, and you are the subject. You see, I want you to leave off with your pursuits and I want you to become philosophers. Not with beards or stylish haircuts. See there, nearby, that is the lens grinder's shadow. Thank you."

Rochester, MN

"It may be true that civilization is collapsing around us, but it's a miracle that it ever existed in the first place. That an organism in this universe would ascend to such complexity and not spend all day every day in a free-for-all war of all against all is truly exceptional. With the billions of years stretched out, how can it possibly be now that we are? What are the odds?"

"How can it possibly be now that we are?"

"Yeah. Just now. There are billions of years. The Earth is billions of years old and to come. Even if there were another planet like this one somewhere, maybe there is no way to get to it because to get to it at the right time you'd have to go backward, or forward. Our Earth hasn't always been like this. Even a planet that can sustain life may not sustain it now. Potential, that's the key."

"And complexity suggests chaos to you?"

"It sure doesn't suggest order. I'm just saying that it's a miracle that any of us manage to live through a single day. There's such a huge universe with so much randomness, so much destruction. The odds must be astronomical."

Fred took a sip of his beer. The waitress came by to see if Carl wanted anything. After taking his order, she asked, "Is that your SUV out there? The one with the Washington plates."

"Yes."

"Did you guys drive here from Washington?"

"We sure did," Fred said enthusiastically.

"Did anything happen? Did you see the militia?"

Fred smiled and shrugged, then started to answer. Carl jumped in: "Sometimes I think the news exaggerates the problems to get people to pay attention."

"You're saying it was perfectly fine?" She said in disbelief.

"I'm saying it was a simple drive. No one seemed to pay much attention to us, and we didn't pay much attention to anyone else. It was routine."

"What have you heard?" Fred asked her in a whisper.

"I heard they drag people out of their cars. It's not safe."

"They're hearing the same things about driving through Minnesota."

"That's ridiculous. We're Christians here. They started this mess, and they're the ones escalating it."

"We heard the same thing in Montana," Carl said.

"Who was saying that?"

"No, I mean, they're saying the other side started it. Everyone points a finger."

"Well of course they say that. That's how it works. They can't just destroy democracy now, can they? That wouldn't fit with their philosophy. They've always wanted to destroy the government. Spend it into debt so we can't keep funding it. They've always said that. Now they want to make sure no one has any faith in it. They have to say they're doing it because of what we're doing. We're the ones who're really causing the problems and they're just reacting. They have to say that."

"But you think they really did start it?"

"Of course they did. Everyone knows that. They hate democracy and they hate government. A democratic government is still a government. We the people. They don't think it's fair if the majority rules."

She turned and went off to get Carl's drink and put in the food order. He wanted Hummus and Pita bread. It was a staple and he missed it the last few days.

"In this republic, the minority has always ruled. She doesn't see it that way. It's a perfectly self-sustained and well contained logical bubble," Carl said turning toward Fred.

"Well, you know my take. There are active agents involved, they benefit. The politicians are phonies and getting rich from the lies they tell. The rules don't apply to them. The White Party is real."

"I know, I know. But you sound like one of those dark web conspiracists when you talk like that."

"Sure. A lot of this started with that big terrorist attack."

"Which one? In Kansas a few years back? The one at Leavenworth?"

"No. I mean way back. To 9/11. Before we were even born, but we still keep hearing the whispers. The weird thing is that no one ever denied that it was a conspiracy. The only question was who was in on it. Was it just Bin Ladin's group? Or was it the Saudis or was there a controlled demolition? Fact: it was a conspiracy. Question: who was involved?"

"What does that have to do with anything?"

"Everything. They won, they destroyed us. That was when the laws were written, the laws that made it possible to hide and the laws that made it possible not to hide."

"What?"

"The laws to protect us from terrorism gave secrecy to government agencies and took it away from people. Only corporations and the government have any privacy anymore. We lost contact with our own experience. That's what it means to lose privacy. Your connection to the world is broken. But they're still connected, they still have their privacy."

"The cabal. The White Party. It's the biggest conspiracy going. Is that what you're saying?"

The waitress brought the beer and hummus. She had overheard the last line.

"What do you know about them? Did you see them while you were crossing? What aren't you guys telling me?"

"Nothing like that," Carl said. "He's cooking up a theory about how it began."

"It's true," Fred said looking at the waitress. "After 9/11 they built an information compliance platform. They instituted rules and laws, they created organizations and agencies. The production of information slowly became ubiquitous and the control over its flow fell into very few hands. An oligarchy."

"Private companies did a lot of that," Carl responded, sounding irritated. "This is counter-productive."

"No, it's true," she said. "They're always using private companies to take care of this stuff. Didn't private companies fight the wars in Iraq and Afghanistan? They sub-contract everything. Their budget is enormous."

"That's right," Fred said. "The internet was built by the federal government of the United States in research labs at universities and the department of defense. It was a joint operation, but once it passed the proof-of-concept phase, it had to find its way into private hands to mature."

"That's how it works," she said. "That's how our whole government works now."

"These are contrary..."

"Exactly," Fred interrupted him calmly and quietly. "The flow of information became an interest the minute they decided they could gather it from everybody. The information systems weren't just meant for gathering and analysis, they assist in production too. It's everywhere because it comes from everywhere and gathering it is built into production."

"I knew it," she said. Carl stared at her in disbelief.

"And these same organizations have an interest in hiding. Government leaks started most of the theories, I've told you this a million times Carl. They manufacture conspiracy theories and instigate their spread just so they can hide behind the biggest conspiracy of them all."

"And what is that?" Carl asked.

"That the White Party, a coalition of conservative, neo-liberal, and corporate bodies, has an interest in control and coercion."

"Control and coercion of what?" Carl asked.

"Of information," the waitress responded. "The more we produce, the more they gather, the more they use it to make us do things."

"And what are they making us do?" Carl asked rhetorically. "Look, I agree that the majority of the country has come under the control of capital interests. I don't even disagree that they're colluding with exactly those government agencies you're describing. My only reservation is that I don't think collusion has to be intentional or conscious. I think it can be baked into the system itself."

"What's the fucking difference?" Fred asked. "What you don't realize is that you're agreeing with us. The government is tasked with building the government, aren't they?"

"What do you mean?"

"I mean, the government spends money. Some of it they give to private enterprises to do things on behalf of the people, don't they?"

"Sure"

"Some of it they use to build government agencies and organizations to deliver those functions. Government is organization building."

"We've had this discussion. You know I agree with that."

"Then why don't you see that their actions can be intentional? They build systems to facilitate projects that further their interests and goals. If they're aiming at a more pliable population, wouldn't they build structures and systems to make it that way?"

"Of course, but calling it the White Party makes it seem so seedy and exotic," Carl said. "It makes it irrational. What you're really saying is that there's a highly rational mechanism to foster private investment to increase data flow and recovery. It stimulates analytics and then cultivates intelligence from it to be filtered back into policy. Thought control. Getting between the mind and its object."

The bar manager said something to the waitress, and she ran off to take care of other customers.

"Collaboration is the key, isn't it?"

"Yes," Carl responded.

"You think I'm collaborating if I do anything to further a way of life or a system of controls even if I'm not actively communicating with others who are doing the same thing. Even if I don't know I'm doing it."

"That's right. Political parties can take this role..."

"And when they do, isn't that like an intentional form of collaboration."

Eirini and Lena came into the bar with a bag of supplies they had just bought at the grocery store next door. Eirini sat down next to Carl and asked, "What are you guys talking about?"

"The White Party." Fred said. "The waitress got us started. She thought there were armed militia patrolling the roads across Montana. She can't believe we drove here."

"What's your take, Lena? Can this be settled via some sequence in the Genome?"

She laughed. "I don't know about that, but it's certainly become clearer over the last fifty years or so that we're seriously unstable as a species."

"That's what I said," Fred leaned forward on the table. Lena picked up a piece of bread and scooped up some Hummus with it. "It's a miracle we've had any peace at all. We should be killing each other all day everyday everywhere we suck air."

"I wouldn't say that," she said covering her mouth while she spoke. "But we are hostile toward everything around us. Our sophisticated social capabilities make us a threat to the planet. We can collaborate at an enormous scale, unlike any other species on record."

"It would make sense then," Fred said. "That those same social abilities are so powerful and so unpredictable and unharnessed that they could easily lead to our own demise."

Carl wanted to respond, but he kept his eyes fixed on Lena. He was still feeling guilty about the previous day.

"I tend to agree," she said. "The myth of the autonomous individual and the pristine place in our lives of atomic consciousness. It is so obviously false and yet the stories persist, the grant money keeps flowing. We conceptualize our solutions in terms of a world populated by homunculi, little atomic beings running around making decisions. Careerism is a form of it. Theory too."

"That's funny," Fred said. "Evil and apish kobolds."

"Shhhh," Carl cut him off.

"It's a distraction. It prevents us taking a critical approach to what guides and directs us. Arguments about the validity of science have been raging for decades. What people mean by science is usually Biochemistry or maybe Physics. Never Sociology or Anthropology, and those are the crucial ones. We're babies in those areas, by comparison. It's hard to make a compelling case. Our science isn't very good."

"But our engineering sure is."

"What does that mean?" Eirini said leaning into the conversation. She was very much on the edge of her seat. It was the tone.

"Everything we learn comes through experiments, and they often require enormous feats of engineering. Like with modern physics and the role of ballistics. We wanted to shoot cannon balls better, that got us studying and learning. Sociology and Anthropology are front and center nowadays. That's my point. We're pouring money into social engineering, and it's stimulating increased study and research, experimentation. We don't call it that, but it's changing the sciences."

Lena paused and took another bite.

"Experimentation on how people behave given certain stimuli," Lena went on, still holding her hand over her mouth. "A / B testing is huge in the dataverse. So many of the PaaS companies are innovating this way, making it easy for low knowledge customers to easily perform social experiments. They build this functionality into their platforms and then sell it."

"What's PaaS?" Carl asked.

"Platform as a service. The cloud. Companies sell a platform with lots of different generic functions. They do the heavy lifting. Privacy compliance, that's a feature they supply. The platform doesn't keep or violate your privacy, they don't sell or gather data. They just provide tools that their customers want. When government policy evaluates their actions, they aren't doing anything wrong because they aren't gathering or using data, they're just building a platform for others to do it. The customers are the ones who actually do it, but they're following the platform. This gives the appearance of regulation, while creating an ecosystem that is effectively the wild west."

"Is this relevant to your work?" Carl asked.

"The genome sequencing and analytics. It's highly sensitive data. You can make predictions about people. Maybe medical at first, but that's just the tip of the iceberg. The programming I do is heavily constrained by these requirements. I use common platforms to stay compliant with the regulations. Doing that, I saw the holes. The safeguards distribute responsibility and create gaps. No one is responsible for them. The big tech companies, their customers. No one. A / B testing itself isn't called into question. It's scientific dogma, everyone knows you have to do it whether you're looking at atoms or human behavior."

"Fred," Carl said. "I think my take is that we can apply Ockham's razor here. We don't need some White Party to explain this. They're implicit in the micro-techniques of structural capitalism. Even the government must succumb to the market."

The waitress came back and took more food and drink orders.

"My boss chewed me out for spending so much time over here," she said. "I get so carried away with that stuff." She went back off toward the bar before anyone could respond.

"The information system is just an extension of that. Of her life. Being bossed around. Better employees, more efficient work, cheaper labor, reduce costs and increase profits. This whole way of thinking unleashes everyone into independent actions that comply with the same principles. That's collusion without intent, it's just baked into the rules. We don't need some White Party to explain it. We already have everything we need."

"How can we change things?" Eirini asked. She would've gotten up from the table and started if they just told her what to do.

"You have to take on basic material conditions and change their organization," Carl said.

"But how?"

"How is the right question," Fred responded before Carl could. "Those same conditions have built mechanisms to make it so difficult to undo what's been done, to change any of the basic structures. Protecting the status quo is built into everything. Even our entertainment."

"Especially our entertainment," Carl said. "They're the narcotic that keeps everything in order. They're the primary system."

"Bread and circuses," Fred said with a big grin spreading across his face.

"So there is nothing we can do?" Eirini repeated her question. She leaned forward even farther, her arm pressed against Carl's.

The waitress came back with more drinks and a few more small plates for them to share. "My boss is really giving me the stink eye whenever I come round," she said and then she was off.

"If the same principles and rules that were created to control the population were exercised on the corporations controlling our lives, maybe that would have an impact."

"How do you mean?"

"They call it advertising, but the purpose of this information was to gather intelligence, intelligence that could be used to control behavior. And not just behavior. Feelings and emotions. Our whole sense of right and wrong. If that works on humans maybe it could work on groups and organizations. Institutions. If we could gather information on them, maybe we could generate intelligence from that information and use it to get a better grip on the system. Control its behavior."

"But how?" Eirini insisted.

"Especially if the population is narcotized," Lena added while forking some beets from the small plate at the center of the table.

"I know this sounds lame," Carl said, "but it may be that the law is the way to go. It's difficult for the powers-that-be to control how the law is interpreted in every context. They would like to, and they do their best to make it happen, but it gets away from them sometimes. The last twenty years there have been a lot of decisions that make it clear that corporations are people. This punches an invisible hole in their logic. It might be possible to use these legal precedents to change the way we think about incarceration, tax codes, and citizenship. Maybe that makes it possible to regulate corporate privacy."

"Lena said the same thing," Eirini said.

"From my dad," Lena responded, shrugging and pursing her lips.

"It's Ben Thorne. No offense, Lena, but this *really* sounds like wacko dark web stuff," Fred said sarcastically. "I thought rational people wanted to repeal those precedents."

"Good luck with that," Carl said. "Why? Maybe the solution is to double down. Subsume don't subvert. Imagine if corporations were incarcerated for committing felonies instead of just being fined, making it part of the cost of doing business."

"How can you put a corporation in jail?" Eirini asked. She turned to look at Lena, "Is it the same?"

"I guess. Loss of privacy, loss of liberty, enslavement. For 3 to 5 years. For life. It depends on the crime and the penalty," Lena responded.

"It doesn't seem very likely," Fred said.

"It isn't," Carl replied. "But that's not the question. It isn't very likely, but it may be the only hope. Everything else we could try would be blocked by those same corporations or the government acting on their behalf. I think it's fine if you want to call that the White Party, but I think it plays into their hands. They want to be thought of as a wacky conspiracy theory, it makes it easier to do what they need to do to keep making use of us and keep applying the narcotics that prevent us from doing anything about it."

"Don't forget armed insurrection," Fred said.

"That's where the real power of the culture war comes in," Carl responded. "Its whole purpose is to prevent that from happening. We might kill each other, but we would never band together to attack the real powers-that-be. Insurrection is only desirable if you do it for one party at the expense of the other."

Emission Analysis Feedback

Dasein has projects. Without boundaries to be crossed, it is inhabited by a limit which cannot be escaped. Everyone dies and their projects end. Trapped in their own circulating system, they cannot come to an end because they are inflicted through and through by that ultimate end. More and more projects unfold, will this be the last one? Recursion never crosses that boundary, marked by an unending temptation to do so.

The response to endless temptation is either authentic or inauthentic.

Facing temptation, Dasein takes issue with itself. Without the possibility of fulfillment, no single act can become fully actual. There is nothing more, no capability to become more, than a potentiality-for-Being. Incapable of pushing beyond its limit, it cannot be fully actualized.

The change that takes place in the move from system to economy is no change at all. The power of the question resonates: will this remain unfinished?

The *meaning of Being* is at stake here. As either system or economy, raising the question offers the inquirer the potential to transform its significance into something more appropriate.

Dasein wonders whether it can be without *ground* or rational principle. The difference between this groundlessness and its ground is the first condition of existence. The difference lies at the origin, and it lies at the end. It is already this difference. This split inflicts both origin and end conditioning every possibility. There is no origin and no end, they are fabrications. The circulating movement is nothing other than the difference between system and economy: nothing other than the deconstruction of metaphysics, a transcendence that transcends nothing.

Edmund Husserl, Heidegger's teacher and foil, said that "every possible content of judgment is thinkable as the content of a question." Does that mean the content of a judgment is one and the same as the content of a question, or does thinking change when it casts the one into the other? Heidegger raises the question concerning the meaning of Being. Does the change that is not a change, the difference that is not a difference, does it boil down to rethinking a judgment as a question?

"Our aim in the following treatise is to work out the question concerning the meaning of Being and to do so concretely." (H.1) And: "By considering these prejudices, however, we have made plain not only that the question of Being lacks an answer, but that the question itself is obscure and without direction." (H.4) Being becomes questionable. To the extent that Husserl thinks questions aim at resolving multiple possibilities into a single judgment, Heidegger isn't questioning. He isn't bringing questioning to an end in a judgment, rather he reveals the multiplicity questioning discloses and reconciles memory with fact by recalling what has been forgotten.

"This question has today been forgotten." (H.2)

He writes:

> Looking at something, understanding and conceiving it,
> choosing, access to it—all these ways of behaving are
> constitutive for our inquiry, and therefore are modes of
> Being for those particular entities which we, the inquirers,
> are ourselves. Thus to work out the question of Being
> adequately, we must make an entity—the inquirer—
> transparent in his own Being. The very asking of this
> question is an entity's mode of Being; and as such it gets its
> essential character from what is inquired about—namely,
> Being. This entity which each of us is himself and which
> includes inquiring as one of the possibilities of its Being, we
> shall [terminologically fasten as] 'Dasein'. (H.7)

Being and Time is not a book. It's an abomination. Not because it is so difficult to understand, but because it is difficult to read. Books require a decision on the part of any reader, a decision on how to read them. There is a presupposed sense of what one is to get out of it. The author might make this decision for the reader and explain it in an introduction or prefatory remark. Or they may choose a traditional genre and let it do the work. Such mechanics might fail in their purpose and make the work an abomination. It could be unfinished, or it could reinvent grammar and fail to align with tradition.

Heidegger writes:

> When tradition thus becomes master, it does so in such a
> way that what it 'transmits' is made inaccessible, proximally
> and for the most part, that it rather becomes concealed.
> Tradition takes what has come down to us and delivers it
> over to self-evidence; it blocks our access to those
> primordial 'sources' from which the categories and concepts
> handed down to us have been in part genuinely drawn.
> Indeed it makes us forget that they have had such an origin,
> and makes us suppose that the necessity of going back to
> these sources is something which we need not even
> understand. Dasein has had its historicality so thoroughly
> uprooted by tradition that it confines its interest to the
> multiformity of possible types, directions, and standpoints
> of philosophical activity in the most exotic and alien of
> cultures; and by this very interest it seeks to veil the fact that

> it has no ground of its own to stand on. Consequently,
> despite all its historiological interests and all its zeal for an
> Interpretation which is philologically 'objective', Dasein no
> longer understands the most elementary conditions which
> would alone enable it to go back to the past in a positive
> manner and make it productively its own. (H.43)

These remarks on tradition indicate that covering up of the question is itself a historical way of Being. It introduces his claims that destroying the tradition is not a specific annihilating act, but rather that the movement of destruction is a program for analysis that allows what has been covered over to come forward. We might call this deconstruction.

In the first paragraphs of the section on destruction, he writes: "Its own past—and this always means the past of its 'generation'—is not something which follows along after Dasein, but something which already goes ahead of it." (H.41) Thinking of the past, of the generations, of genre, and of gender, are not something that I am done with, something gone and forgotten. They spread the world out in front of me, before me, as a text to be read. I may see that world and its genres and not think about what is given there. To do so would be to ignore Heidegger's charge, his charge to deconstruct. For although deconstruction points backwards to texts long since written, it also points forward into the future, a future that is already there as possibilities projected in questioning.

Reading *Being and Time* means that its genre cannot be taken for granted. The manner of meaning, of coherence, the voice or voices of being and time open up in reading as questioning. This has been easy for some, for those who without trying —as though it were happening behind their backs, read it as a literary work. Dasein is a character in a novel. Not what, but who is Dasein?

This is a question and by no means the answer to one. Characters are at home in novels and aren't constrained by just one genre, but many of them, multiple genres interspersed, multiplying genres: letters, dialogue, prose of different kinds. The novel is disruptive of genre. This does not solve the problem. It only deepens it. Horizons, not limits, open before us.

So then:

"Our task is not to prove that an 'external world' is present-at-hand or show how it is present-at-hand, but to point out why Dasein, as Being-in-the-world, has the tendency to bury the 'external world' in nullity 'epistemologically' before going on to prove it." (H.250) This demonstrates a tendency to posit origins and ends for the sake of crossing over boundaries and limits. As such, this question is no different in scope than questioning why Dasein has the tendency to understand itself as the subject and origin of the difference between itself and what it perceives.

The problem of transcendence was always about truth: how does one know that what is in here, the idea or belief, is adequately representative of what is really out there, the entity in the external world extended in space and time? Responses have been rigorous descriptions of how we know our mental acts are (or are not) really in contact with existing entities. The goal of this analysis is to inject something between the act and its object, to inject a justification and methodology that orders experience.

Dasein's transcendence is transformed by movement from system to economy. It is transformed as judgment is transformed into a question or as the origin and guiding principle becomes a for-the-sake-of at work in every potentiality-for-Being.

The meaning of Dasein's Being is transcendence.

In the 1928 lecture course on *The Metaphysical Foundations of Logic*, Heidegger says:

> The peculiar neutrality of the term "Dasein" is essential, because the interpretation of this being must be carried out prior to every factual concretion. This neutrality also indicates that Dasein is neither of the two sexes. But here sexlessness is not the indifference of an empty void, the weak negativity of an indifferent ontic nothing. In its neutrality Dasein is not the indifferent nobody and everybody, but the primordial positivity and potency of the essence. (MFL 136-7)

Neutrality is a misleading translation: the word is *Geschlechtlosigkeit*. The withoutness-of-*Geschlecht*, of-gender, of-genus, of-genre.

How can Dasein be *without* such things?

> ...Dasein harbors the intrinsic possibility for being factically dispersed into bodiliness and thus into sexuality. The metaphysical neutrality of the human being, inmost isolated as Dasein, is not an empty abstraction from the ontic, a neither-nor; it is rather the authentic concreteness of the origin, the not-yet of factical dispersion [Zerstreutheit]. As factical, Dasein is, among other things, in each case disunited in particular sexuality. "Dispersion", "disunity" sound negative at first, (as does "destruction"), and negative concepts such as these, taken ontically, are associated with negative evaluations. But here we are dealing with something else, with a description of the multiplication (not "multiplicity") which is present in every factically individuated Dasein as such. We are not dealing with the notion of a large primal being in its simplicity becoming

ontically split into many individuals, but with the clarification of the intrinsic possibility of multiplication which, as we shall see more precisely, is present in every Dasein and for which embodiment presents an organizing factor. Nor is the multiplicity, however, a mere formal plurality of determinations, but multiplicity belongs to being itself. In other words, in its metaphysically neutral concept, Dasein's essence already contains a primordial bestrewal [Streuung], which is in a quite definite respect a dissemination [Zerstreuung]. And here a rough indication is in place. As existing, Dasein never relates only to one particular object; if it relates solely to one object, it does so only in the mode of turning away from other beings that are beforehand and at the same time appearing along with the object. This multiplicity does not occur because there are several objects, but conversely. This also holds good for comportment toward oneself and occurs according to the structure of historicity in the broadest sense, insofar as Dasein occurs as stretching along in time. (MFL 137-8)

Only fabricated justifications deny multiplication. The origin, Dasein as transcendence, is multiplying —many folds unfolding. There is an original multiplying that comes to be as Dasein in each of its various and many ways of engaging entities for use and abuse, for theory and blindness. Dasein is a writing without genre, but not absolutely or by constitution. Rather, Dasein is the possibility of concrete instances of genre. It is because Dasein is without that we live in the midst of genre.

There is never a moment in time without *Geschlecht*. Without *Geschlecht*, Dasein comes to be in the manner of each and many *Geschlechts*. Dasein's transcendence is its immanent ongoing dispersal through spacetime, and this dispersal takes on the ambivalent ambiguity of the occasional *Geschlecht*.

This thrown dissemination into a multiplicity is to be understood metaphysically. It is the presupposition, for example, for Dasein to let itself in each case factically be governed by beings which it is not; Dasein, however, identifies with those beings on account of its dissemination. (MFL 138)

Dasein, without *Geschlecht*, seeps into every nook and cranny of the world, uncovering everything everywhere in search of multiplying varieties. This endless search for self-constitution, for self-realization, covers Dasein's essential *Geschlechtlosigkeit* so that it no longer considers it questionable. Deconstruction renews the questionability of the without, of multiplying, of a non-indifferent potent essence that comes to the fore in reconciliation with what has been forgotten. This is done for the sake of what we wish to expect: the claim made on us to be without genre, the claim made on us to be without tradition, to be without refusing to retrace our steps. This multiplication of/at the origin is Dasein's dispersal. Both its possibility of transcending itself and its transcendence, the end is multiplied. Death waits for it everywhere in everything.

Genre is a question that has been forgotten. Posing the question grounds transcendence. Because Dasein is its transcendence, it questions. Questioning, there is transcendence. Dasein, the null basis of a nullity, free and without determination, is its without as questioning. Dasein lives its questioning in many ways: as desire, intellect, will, feeling, and so on. Even love.

Dasein is at its limit and attempting to transcend it. It multiplies as the difference between them locked in a constantly threatened and entangled difference *between* these possibilities, an interlude of sorts. It emerges at odds with itself, as the difference between itself and what is at issue. Between acts, Dasein emerges as the deconstruction of metaphysics, as both self discovery and self-disclosure.

The terminology of the movement must change. The origin no longer functions as a point of departure or rational principle. It is difference at work in a struggle between opponents. Thrownness and facticity bring out the tendency of the origin to be already beyond itself, already in the midst of a dynamic unfolding, already at work in its moment of incision and struggle. Projection and anticipation are employed for an end that is neither a resolution nor an achievement. It is not the goal within the act, rather it is a manner of dispersing. Such an end is unfulfillable. It is nothing other than possibilities projected in/as/through orientation. It may project the limit, or it may project transcendence. It does both, it projects both, it is both. Horizons, not limits, open before us.

The whole economy of the potentiality-for-Being involves constant dismantling of the self. When we work toward realizing potential, when we develop a talent, we repeat a training activity to destroy old habits for the sake of improving. The same work that was once called talent is exactly what must be denied and dismantled when developing that talent. Should we stagnate in what we can do, we squander potential and make a principle from bad habits.

Because Dasein's movement is a dance of development and stagnation, of squandering and growth, it always comes to itself both appropriately and inappropriately, authentically and inauthentically. The effort must be handled carefully. It isn't that authentic Dasein is truly disclosed while inauthentic Dasein transcends that as though crossing a boundary. We are not deconstructing the old gods for the sake of some new god. Dasein's self-transcendence, the dynamic by which it comes to itself in transcending itself, in unfolding, is already both authentic and inauthentic. Transcendence is either: 1) the attempt to move toward something that lies beyond a limit, or 2) the attempt to inhabit that limit.

This introduces a turn toward temporality, toward movement unfolding. The difference inhabits it. There are not two forms of time deliberately chosen by free Dasein, rather temporality unfolds as the difference between... It is not reducible to a thing. It is not a thing.

The difference between authentic and inauthentic Dasein (the deconstruction of metaphysics) rests in the manner by which Dasein comes to itself, its genre. To come to itself, it must both not be itself and be capable of becoming itself. Coming to itself speaks of what has been and what will be. Being introduced, guilt shows itself as the incarnation of temporality's difference. Horizons, not limits, open before us.

Being-Guilty and Temporality

The Beginning and the End

"What was Lena saying?" Despina asked.

"She was talking about the ancient people in America, about how little we know about them," Maria tucked the phone back into her beach bag and handed it to Thimios who set it next to him on the sand.

"What does that have to do with now though? She was saying something about that."

"She studies this at school, but there's politics. The scientists take sides. It interferes with her work. People give her money to study something but if she says the wrong thing, they'll take the money away from her."

"I never understood that," Thimios said. "We're supposed to believe these ancient humans walked thousands of miles across mountains and forests. Why would they do that?"

"It's not like that," Nikos said. "Maybe they moved a mile a year over a thousand years. Or twenty miles every generation."

"I'm going swimming," Despina said. "Baba, will you come with me?"

"Let's go," he said running off with her toward the water.

"We need to get them out of there," Maria said to Nikos once they were alone. "The news is so terrifying. So much hatred. Everyone claims to defend morality."

"That program was really terrifying. The guns. They make more. They buy more. The only thing they agree on is that they should spend their money on guns. Those intelligent drones. Everyone has them now."

"We have to get them out of there. All of them. Lena, Ermioni, and Georgios. They have to come home."

"They'll be here soon enough, but will they stay?"

"We'll get Lena to stay. We'll talk to her. We'll show her."

"But her studies."

"You heard her. She isn't happy. She doesn't like the fighting. What did she say?"

"You mean, 'we could have built anything we wanted, this is what we chose.'"

"Yes. That's haunting."

"They don't realize their fight effects the whole world. They only see their own side, only what they want to see."

"They hate their enemies and would rather see them miserable and defeated."

"I've never heard of such a thing," he said. "People who don't want their own children to be able to go to the doctor. They don't want their own parents to get the care they need. Things we take for granted. Just because they don't want their enemies to have it."

"It's like the stories they tell us as children, about the people throwing stones at the sinner. They claim they are the moral ones."

"And that's the air their children breathe."

"The whole world is suffering. Keramoti will be under water, and it doesn't matter what we do here to stop it. This beach and the little chapel. All of it washed away while they fight and fight and fight."

"Lena was reminding me of Em," Nikos said.

"What did she say?" she poured water from a thermos into a glass and handed it to him. Then poured some for herself.

"Something about Ethics. With a capital E. She said that and it reminded me. People have their commandments and their principles. They don't consider the world they make when defending those beliefs or forcing them on others."

"They aren't mindful."

"They say their enemies are evil and that justifies everything. 'You can't tolerate Nazis. You can't let them destroy your way of life.'"

"It's like the Terror."

"The Terror?"

"Yes, isn't that what they called it in France? During the revolution. Everyone justified murder by accusing their enemies of treason. Everything was treason."

"Counter revolutionaries. Anyone who disagreed. They're accused and persecuted. Same as Russia, China, Germany of course."

"No one is immune. The people in power protect themselves. They can't feel their power. It's constant anxiety. They worry about losing it. It's like a person, when someone is very stressed, they act even more frantic to get control."

"They should be doing yoga," he said laughing, sensing she might be headed that way.

"They should. Or meditate, or something to quiet themselves and focus their attention. You shouldn't make fun. It can be like that for whole countries."

"That's what Eirini was saying. I think she was agreeing with you. In a way. She was saying people needed to find peace."

"In their minds? An entire nation?"

"They're riling each other up. Constantly chattering and bragging in front of each other. Competing for attention and status. Too many useless conversations. She said that. They need to quiet down and be with their thoughts, focus on what is nearby, the people around them."

"Do you remember that time when they just finished the kitchen at their house and Ermioni was making filo? Em was standing right next to her and talking about her."

"That was so funny," he said. "She was concentrating so hard. She had no idea what he was saying."

"He was telling us about how she retreats into a trance."

"It's hard to make filo. It's a lot of work. Why doesn't she just buy it?"

"In America you can't so she got used to making it. But that wasn't the point. He was saying she was in a trance, and it made her forget English."

They watched Despina as she climbed up on Thimios' shoulders, balanced precariously for a moment, and then dove off into the water.

"You'll hurt yourself, Thimio. Be careful," Maria shouted.

He waved back at them, both dismissing their concern and letting them know he was fine.

"That filo was very good," Nikos said after a moment. "I think it was better than the grocer's. She blocked out everything."

"In this world, you have to pay attention to what's happening everywhere, you can't block it out," she said in a strict tone as if to scold him.

"Why? I know why, of course. We have to worry about each other, we have to think about the impact of things from far away, but maybe we worry too much. Em was always so calm during discussions. He knew his limits. Ethics was just a theory for strangers, for what's happening far away. It riles your emotions and helps others convince you, that's what he would say. Lena reminded me of that. She said we need Ethics for a worldwide society. We don't need it for our friends."

"He was not ideal. I think he was too closed off. You two were closer, I know, but I thought he was too focused, it was like an obsession. He was too protective of his privacy. That's too far in the other direction. We have to find the right balance."

"Maybe so, but he was always well-informed. Realistic. He didn't think getting upset was helpful. We're upset about what's going on over there. What good is it doing us?"

"If we plan to do things, if it motivates us, gets us to take action, then it's doing a lot of good."

"Absolutely. But maybe we need to know when they're motivating us and when they're just whipping us into a frenzy. Do you know what Em told me once?"

"What?" she asked.

"He said he believed that deep down he had seen evil."

"Evil?"

"Yes, that's how he put it. He said there was a monster, and he knew what it looked like and how it worked."

"How did he know? Everyone thinks like that. What were we just saying?"

"I know, I know. He knew that. He said he saw it because he was a part of it. He was doing evil and was aware of it."

"But he kept doing it?"

"This was late one night. We were out together, the boys, and we were walking back to the car from Attalos."

"What did he say?"

"He said that evil wasn't some ugly thing that appeared in front of you. It wasn't even a person. It worked through you and never showed itself as evil, it just took over. It hid in you while you did its work."

"Couldn't he stop it? This sounds ridiculous. The church fathers talked like this."

"He knew it. I don't think he would say this out loud. But we were alone and a little drunk. He said that the nature of evil made it so you couldn't recognize it unless it was in you, guiding you. He said as soon as he saw it, he felt a duty to describe it."

"If he never said it out loud, who was he going to describe it to?"

"That was part of it. Because of how it worked. You can't just say it."

"Nonsense," she said. She was growing increasingly disturbed.

"He said it was in our communication. It was complicated. The conditions had to be just right. He had to figure out how to whisper it directly into each person's ear."

"Why?" She was openly agitated. "It sounds ridiculous."

"He thought so."

"He thought it sounded ridiculous?"

"He said that was how it worked. It's the only way. If he said it publicly, differently, talking to audiences, it would be corrupted. The evil he was describing would change the message, make it unrecognizable. To describe it, the form mattered. He had to concentrate and focus on something nearby, like a whisper."

"Hmmm. I don't know. It sounds off to me."

"It was something about genre. He never figured it out."

She thought about it a little less harshly. "Still, it's no excuse for doing evil," she said finally.

"He knew that. He worried it was a complete waste of time. Just an excuse. Then he'd flip flop and say it's how he was made. His only option. His experience was magical, it controlled and contorted him. Whispering was the only cure."

"What's past is past. We can forgive him. We have to focus on Lena and Ermioni now."

The Rental Car

"They'll be in Thessaloniki on Sunday," he said. "They came for the container this morning. Listen, we'll have six big suitcases. Will it fit?"

"Uh, we can tie them to the roof, maybe."

"Or you can leave some at the airport and go back. There's no hurry."

"Sure. It's not a problem," Thimios said. "What's the flight number?"

"I don't know. I'll text you. There's only one Sunday afternoon flight from Gatwick. There shouldn't be any confusion. It arrives around 3, I think."

"How is Ermioni?"

"She's quiet. She doesn't want to be a bother. It's good Ariti is here. They sit together a lot. The chores keep her focused."

"Did she get rid of everything?"

"Nearly. I didn't think she could, but she just keeps going to the next thing."

"We talked to Eirini when we were at the beach earlier. They're arriving in Chicago today."

"Good. No troubles?"

"Eh not sure. Maybe their spirits are down, but no problems."

"It must still be sinking in," Thimios was quiet, so Georgios changed the subject. "I'm taking the car to the dealer. They'll take me to get a rental car. We'll drive that to the airport. I hired a car service to take the luggage."

"When will you come?"

"Soon, I think. I have some things to do back home first."

"You haven't been back in a while, aren't you curious?"

"I'll come soon. Just need a week or two."

"It's a shame. There are so many people who want to see you."

"It's been this long. What's the hurry?"

"I'll tell you," Nikos jumped in. "Your mother wants to see you. Don't you have time to come see your mother?"

"I talk to my mother all the time, thank you very much. Niko, what are you doing lurking there?"

"We're at Europea's. Spanakopita."

"What a day for you? And not even Friday yet. You were at the beach and now you're having a feast. No work today?"

"I was up at dawn my friend. That means I finish early. It's late here. Europea is not too happy about moving. She insists on packing everything herself. I think she'd carry the boxes if she could."

"What moving? Where is she?"

"Down in the cellar. She's been at it since this morning."

"Get her, I want to talk to her."

"Thimio, go get Europea, tell her Georgios is on the phone."

"She has to stop this. That is not the plan. That's why I'm coming. We're going to get everyone settled. Why does she insist on doing this herself before she knows what to do? Nothing is decided yet."

"We told her that a hundred times. We can't be trusted, you and me."

"She's 87 years old, she's going to give herself a heart attack."

"Try telling her that."

"She won't come," Thimios said in the background.

"What do you mean, she won't come?" Georgios responded, drawing Thimios closer to the phone.

"She's busy and says you don't know what you're doing."

"Niko, do something. Tell her you want more food."

"Good idea," Thimios says. "I'll ask her where the marmalade is. That'll drive her crazy. She'll storm up here to see what we're up to."

"You see what we're up against."

"It's like a time machine. Where's Stamatia? Is she helping?"

"No, she left. She was trying to get Europea to wait too, but she won't listen to anyone."

"What are you two up to here? What do you need marmalade for?"

Georgios heard her in the background and then heard some cabinets opening.

"Don't eat that, I have some nice cake instead. Sit."

"Mama," Georgios called out. "What are you doing? Can't you wait? We'll get everything settled, we'll do exactly what you tell us to do, but please wait for us."

"It's very inconvenient. This whole arrangement. You can't make these decisions and not expect people to do things."

"What's she doing?" Georgios asked.

"She's sitting. Here she is."

"Georgios. What is it, what do you want?"

"Mama, it's just a few days. Have you done the shopping for Ermioni's house? She's counting on you?"

"I have the whole day tomorrow. What do you think I'm doing? You think I'm relaxing? There's a lot to do. I've lived in this house a long time."

"The house isn't going anywhere, Mama. Ermioni needs us. We have to take care of her."

"What do you think I'm doing? Don't be smart. She's coming through Thessaloniki. Why? Isn't it faster to go to Athens? Ermioni and Em always used to come through Athens."

"Ermioni wanted it this way."

"Okay, okay. You'll stay as long as it takes, no?"

"Of course. Ariti and Ermioni will be there."

"What about you? Georgio, you can't stay with your family? Why don't..."

"Let's not get into that. I'll be there soon enough, and we can talk it through. Don't worry. Just please wait, okay? There's no hurry. Everything will be taken care of just the way you want it."

"Fi. Don't think I don't know what you're doing. I've almost finished with the cellar. I'll just be a little longer. I'll see you Sunday, Georgio. Kisses. Bye bye."

"Mama," he said urgently.

"She's gone," Nikos said. "Cake sliced, a little white wine. Poof."

"Can you go down there and help?"

"Of course, Thimios went with her. Don't worry. She goes on like this every day. She's the same woman who raised you. What do you think?"

"You think the whole plan makes sense, don't you? I mean, it makes sense to move her in with Ermioni, doesn't it?"

"Of course, stop worrying. Everything is fine."

"Not everything. What will Eirini do?"

"She could move in with Stamatia or back with us."

"She needs to stay in town for work, doesn't she?"

"I suppose so. She didn't put up a fuss when I mentioned it."

"She wouldn't though, would she?"

"What are you saying, it's settled. Stop worrying."

"But it'd be better if Stamatia and Ariti's family stay together in Stamatia's house. My mother could stay in her own house with Eirini."

"Then Ermioni is alone."

"She won't be alone. Eleni will be with her."

"Lena will be with her for how long?"

"We'll see. She's still in shock. Once she gets there, she'll remember, and maybe she'll want to stay. While they're driving, every day she gets a little closer."

"Has she said something?"

"She has doubts. That's what I'm saying."

"Doubts about what?"

"About what she's doing, about what she wants to do. About who she is. This is what happens when you lose people close to you, you have to grieve for them. You have to learn who you are without them."

"When are they coming?"

"Next week. End of next week, I think. She keeps saying there are things she needs to do at school. I think she's going to take a leave of absence."

"Can she do that?"

"I think so. She has to decide now because the new year starts soon. But with her there, Eirini can stay with Europea."

"She doesn't want that."

"That's what I'm saying, I think she does."

"That's news to me. I'm surprised she didn't say anything."

"She's that way. You should know this. She was very happy when we discussed it the other day."

"She didn't mention it. What do I know? This is the problem with raising girls."

"For you raising this girl."

"Oh, you think it's just me? You think I'm the only man with a daughter who doesn't tell him the truth about what she wants?"

"No, I'm sure you're not the only one. Ermioni says the same about Lena. Maybe it's something."

"She tells me what she thinks I want to hear. What am I supposed to do?"

"Well, maybe more than just say 'are you sure?'" Georgios responded hesitantly. "Ask what she wants before telling her what you want."

"Is that how you found out she wants to stay in town?"

"Well, I kept asking her. But not saying, what do you want or are you sure? That doesn't get anywhere. I said, 'I'm not sure what to do. Europea doesn't want to move out of her house.' If I say it like that, then she has suggestions, Lena has suggestions. Then they're happy to speak up because they think I'm asking for help. They love to be helpful."

"Okay, I need to go. There's a commotion down there. I'll try to get her to stop. I'll let her know that we have to wait for you because there are still many things to discuss."

"Good. Don't say too much, but she needs to stop trying to do everything herself."

"Weren't you paying attention, Europea is just a daughter who has grown old. Why would you expect anything different?"

Q&A

"That was Carl," Ginna said coming back to the table.

"What is the status?"

"They're just arriving in Chicago now. They'll be in Ann Arbor tomorrow or Saturday. He said they weren't sure. It depends on the sister. She's coming with them. Something about a cat."

"They need not stay with them any longer, they can just come back."

"Fred and Carl want to stay with them. They're devoted."

"Who? Okay, fine. So, make the arrangements. We will go tomorrow."

She picked up her phone and got to work. While she was tapping and typing, he went on to something else.

"About last night, was I wrong?"

She was distracted, but played along, "No, you weren't wrong. The conference is devoted to your work. That's why everyone came."

"Exactly. I think it was damn nice of me to let them go on and on with whatever it was they were saying. I let them share my platform. That was the fucking keynote. No one stopped them from talking."

"No one stopped them."

"What were they saying? I tuned it out."

"Nothing you haven't heard before. There was something that you weren't talking about that you should be talking about, something you were taking for granted that clearly indicates your privilege."

"Why must everyone have an opinion? We are wrong if we lecture, and we are wrong if we remain silent."

"It's a privilege to remain silent," she said without looking up.

"I do not accept that. Why people think they need to form an opinion about everything that goes on in the world is beyond me. Why they feel compelled to broadcast it too. The desire to comment. The other in me, me in the other, the world-voice I speak and the I-voice the world speaks."

"You think it's enough to cede time at the keynote."

"I do."

"But isn't there a question of justice? Of fighting for justice for everyone?"

"Justice is a higher order concept. Why are they so keen to toss out the mischief and arson of the Enlightenment, but not its love of higher order concepts?"

"You're denying the claim for justice?"

"You cannot have your cake and eat it too. The science and the philosophy, the ethics, those mechanisms of power and knowledge, that has European origins too. How can you appropriate that? Pick and choose, is that it? We will take Newtonian Physics, but reject its application? Keep the construct of justice but throw out the colonization."

"So, you're the victim now?" She asked as she looked up at him briefly.

"You are just trying to goad me. Talking like they do. It is kettle logic, and opportunistic."

"So not the victim, you just blame the victim."

"I do not see them as victims. Like I said, I yielded time."

"If there's injustice and you're aware of it, you're obligated to act."

"By the moral imperative. Another European fabrication. Genetically and biologically, we are empathic creatures, but the values are derivative. We are wired to make communities so if our fellows are racist misogynist homophobes, then we are going to empathize with that. What helps us survive is sticking together, it does not matter why or how."

"Biology trumps ideology?" She paused with her phone and looked at him. "We're wired for concepts too, aren't we?"

"We have basic cooperative impulses, but we cooperate to wipe out others. Other animals, other tribes. We absolutely must be cooperative. This makes us vulnerable to social manipulation best served by malleable minds capable of concepts and ideas. That does not determine how it turns out. How does it turn out? What is the good? The highest good?"

"Ideas go through their own evolutionary process. They're selected. The strongest ideas are the ones that lead to the longest lasting civilizations. Is that your point?" She said and then looked back down at her phone. The up and down of it gave her a safe distance. It increased her control over the exchange. She was only casually granting him her attention.

"Yes, and what is more, we are just as well-served by the drive to stick together when opposing those we hate. In fact, it is helpful motivation. Falling back on morality. Hah, as if it were somewhere beneath us, as if it were not a tool to reinforce the status quo. Hatred of evil is good."

"The reservations are set. We leave tomorrow afternoon."

"Great. We must both have an opinion and enforce it. They attack people for their silence. Why are they silent? Because they do not agree and do not want to suffer the consequences of voicing disagreement. Theories are not facts. Political points of view are not facts. If someone is beaten or killed. If a rich man commits fraud and gets aways with it. I have an opinion about that, but what must I decry in general? Must I have a general rule in place that aligns with the proper codes and order? Well, I disagree. It is coercion."

She was shaking her head, still looking down and doing something with her phone.

"The generalized notion is a form of the telemetric."

"The what?" She looked up.

"From one of those unreadable books Em wrote years ago."

"Ah," she nodded and went back to her phone.

"I cannot say I ever really understood any of it, but he thought there was a relationship between coercion of personality and manipulation of behavior on the one hand and a distanced form of experience on the other. We are most malleable when our behavior is linked to remote events. His model was big computer systems."

"What type of big computer systems? Like social?"

"No, those are applications, he was working on the infrastructure they required. Giant distributed systems with hundreds of thousands of computers. Storage and compute. That is what he always used to say. AI and something called telemetry worked together. That is what they call it when the system emits descriptions of what it does for forensic purposes. If something goes wrong, these events are useful for diagnosing and analyzing the root cause."

"And that's related to behavior, how exactly?" She typed something while talking.

"It was a muddle. In my brain, or in his work, I am not sure which. But it was something like the AI learned patterns and could steer events. Since the events were generated by users, steering events was the same as steering user behavior. Distance was significant. People stirred up by things not directly in front of them."

"Is it something like it's much harder to convince someone of something if they're looking right at it?."

"The purpose of these computer systems was to insert morsels here and there and then cull them out later. You are constantly primed for things that will only become clear later."

"And this is related to justice?" She went back to scrolling the list of unanswered texts.

"An abstract notion of justice facilitates manipulation. It can be poked and twisted over the course of weeks and months so that when some specific things occur, people will be lured to the desired conclusions. It is a tool for adapting the mind. Absurdities will follow."

"Like what?" She was typing again.

"Believing poor people are to blame for your poverty. Believing that people with common characteristics are to blame for your more uncommon qualities, that women have penises or men vaginas."

"Oh god. Keep your voice down."

"The very notions of characteristics and qualities are derived from this distanced perspective. Aggregates. Playing one attribute off against another depends on ordering. It makes it easier to manipulate people."

"And this is relevant to last night somehow?" she said continuing to scroll. "Sounds like you're managing to have some opinions."

"Those people had their say. No one disagrees. But that is not enough, they want to stir up trouble, they must stir up trouble, they have learned that stirring up trouble is how to get attention. Did you see how many people were filming the exchange? They wanted a clash, something that would go viral and get them followers."

"And you ruined their plans by not having an opinion," she briefly looked up and smiled, then looked back down at her phone.

"That becomes the outrage, the reason for the viral moment. Here is a group of people with no power over policy, with no legislative or executive authority, they are generally sympathetic to the remarks, but the keynote speaker does not respond. How dare you not have any characters from this or that group? What do you have to say for yourself? Nothing. That enrages them."

"I saw. Are you saying their rage is manufactured? That they aren't passionate about it? That they don't really mean it? It's theatre?" She set her phone down on the table.

"They *are* passionate, they *do* really mean it. It is real *and* it is theatre. It is manufactured *and* it is real. Some of these little idiots run around talking about how this or that is socially constructed, gender is socially constructed, it is a false binary. What does that even mean? Cars are manufactured, cars are socially constructed. There are fucking cars. Get out of the street."

Ginna rolled her eyes. "Socially constructed things are real. I think they know that. That's exactly the point. These things must be resisted," she said.

"Yes, yes, because gender is non-binary."

"Absolutely."

"Well, then what exactly are trans-gendered people? Are they people who have been warped by the binary system? They do not seem to break it, if anything they seem to reinforce it."

"Well, I'm glad you didn't say that last night."

"They spout nonsense, kettle logic, contradictions. They belligerently defend themselves and they cut critical discussion short because they know the contradictions and problems would come out if they were seriously discussed by people with diverse perspectives. This is between us, you see."

Ginna nodded.

"This is the natural and normal response to have. Where did I pick it up? How did I come to have this response? I do not need to have an opinion about this, nothing in my immediate experience forces me to think about it or understand it in any way. I am at a distance from it. If you force me to have an opinion, I am going to fall back on whatever has been crammed into me by my experience, by the people I associate with, by my history, by whatever was shaped and formed by forces, those same ones that construct gender norms."

"Then you're saying your own position is nonsense too. It's biased and privileged."

"Definitely. I do not trust my own reactions. I do not trust my thought process when it comes from a distance. I cannot be a reliable contributor."

"And that's why you should be allowed to remain silent? Silence means that those who aren't silent will have their way."

"Not all silence is the same. It can be hard to distinguish. Being silent last night in response to some question during the Q&A of a keynote, that is not the same thing as the people who lived down the street from Dachau."

"So, there are some issues that would get you to open your mouth?"

"If they are concrete and clear. Police are using deadly force on people of color more than they use it on white people. That is a concrete thing. Homophobes and Transphobes beat a person to death in an alley somewhere. That is a concrete thing. It is the generalized notion that I reject. I think campaigns in favor of the generalized notion are misguided and play into the hands of those who seek to distract us."

"Oh my god," she whispered. "Does the great Ben Thorne side with the White Party conspiracy theorists? You sure sound like them right now."

"The White Party conspiracy theory is simply that there is a reason we are misguided. That our political notions, formulated at a distance and applied universally, are what makes it possible to turn us around and focus on the wrong things. Morality is the outcome, not the input. They rely on that. Those evil lunatic politicians. They do not give a damn about their constituents. But none of it is new. Conservatism has always been cold-blooded. Liberalism has always been too tolerant. These political mantras have been around for as long as I can remember. People should learn their history. We lose focus so easily. We never do anything effectively. We never criticize the right thing."

"What's the right thing?"

"Shutting down the money machine."

"How do you do that?"

"Stop buying anything, stop making anything. Organize and insist that it shut down before you buy and sell yourself ever again."

"People would starve, they'd be thrown into the streets. The poorest would be hurt the most."

"Indeed. It would be painful."

"You sound like such a crack pot. Can you tell me then, what is the plan? Do you think they'll just surrender? What would that suffering be for? Be concrete. What would a general strike accomplish?"

"The power of the White Party is based on the power of the corporation. That is the message in *Artists of Despair*. We must remove the yoke."

"What does that look like?"

"One penal code, one tax code, one set of laws for immigration and work. If a person murders someone, that person should be punished. Same punishment no matter what. Life in prison."

"Concrete actions and concrete responses, that's what matters."

"Fraud. Libel. Slander. These crimes are bound by a new sense of intent that includes machines and mechanisms, various forms of chemistry. Organisms and organizations built to get results, they are responsible, and accountable. The situation is the same."

"And you think this would make a radical change?"

"Afterward, discussion would be possible again. We would stand a chance of forging agreements. Absent manipulation, we could see through the mess and develop common goals and hopes, sort out what is not common. The commonwealth is the conscience of the people. A great civilization must express it."

"And the christofascists who have never listened to reason ever, what about them?"

"Take away their megaphones and they will be revealed as the inconsequential sect that they are. It will be a hard lesson to learn: the minority cannot dictate."

Ginna shook her head and tried to wrap things up. "And the full circle?"

"Of this conversation? The full circle is that they will not care if my books have characters with whatever traits they are defending. They will not care because it will not matter, there will not be any machine grinding them against each other, forcing them to compete for attention. In fact, it will be good that I do not have an opinion, because who the hell cares what some old cis het pass-for-white guy thinks about it anyway?"

"Over lunch, at least, I have to," she said getting up. "Alright, let's go. I have a lot to do if we're going to leave the city tomorrow."

The Full Circle

"It was almost twenty-five years ago when I first held you two in my arms." Joy came first. "There was a singing voice in my head. It was Christmas. Or almost. Your dad and Ermioni brought me with them to help. And for the experience. Everyone was so pleased to see you two together. And the three of us."

"What did it say?" Eirini asked.

"The voice?" Mia responded. "That you were mine. That I was yours. I didn't know anything back then. But I knew that."

They stood like that, the three of them together, for what must have been only a few minutes, although it felt much longer.

"And it was singing?" Eirini asked, breaking the silence sealing them.

"It was. Your little heartbeats were the song. I had never held a baby before, much less two at the same time. It brought us so much closer. Everyone who was there. In Ariti's house. Stamatia's house. I can still remember the way it smelled. She was always baking. They all were, it seemed. It made a huge impression. I'm so glad you guys are here."

They were crying. Just a few tears at first, through the silence. Then Lena was sobbing quietly. Mia pulled her closer. Eirini kissed her head and stroked her hair. That's how the sadness came and how they chose to greet it.

"I wish my house smelled like that. For you. My house. But it never smells like that, not when I was growing up, not now."

"It doesn't matter," Eirini said. "We're welcome and that's what matters. Hotels are not nice for very long."

It was relief now. Lena was calmer. Eirini's voice. Mia's voice. They soothed and balanced her. Mia took the bags from the front stoop and carried them into the house, directing Eirini and Lena up the stairs. She left the suitcases on the ground floor. "The guest room and bathroom are down here," she said. "It's ready for you guys. The kitchen and living room are upstairs. My bedroom is on the top floor. Where are these boys you've been telling me about?" They walked into the kitchen out of habit. Mia gets them water. "Are you ready for some wine?"

"Yes please," Eirini said. "What to eat though?"

"Eat? Are you hungry? I have some spring rolls."

"Don't you remember?" Lena said as she climbed up onto one of the stools next to the kitchen island.

"Of course, how silly of me."

Mia took the spring rolls from the freezer and turned on the oven. "It takes longer, but they're crispier this way," she said. Eirini climbed up onto the stool next to Lena. Mia poured the wine while the oven heated up. "Does it have to be synchronized? Can we start drinking the wine now?" she asked. "The food is coming."

Eirini laughed. "I didn't mean..."

"It's one of the advantages of being from an old civilization," Lena was becoming more animated. "You grow up naturally more civilized. I always thought that was one of the best customs. And the baked goods."

"I remember," Mia said. "When we went to Ariti's house that day, we brought this beautiful chocolate cake that I was dying to try. But we brought it and then never touched it. Stamatia served something else. Something very good, but it wasn't the cake we brought."

"You wouldn't serve the same thing right away."

"But then, on another day, we were there again, and she served it to us. We brought something else, but she made sure to serve the other one. I think she knew I was dying to try it."

"If you told her how good it looked... There's something about the patisserie and baking. Whether you buy it or make it... Ariti must have noticed."

"She's sensitive like that, our Auntie. You should put out the things we brought," Eirini said.

They laughed. Mia took the box from the Northside bakery and opened it. She put a few of them on a plate and set it between them. "Not sure it goes with spring rolls but take whatever you like."

They laughed again. It came so easily now. Mia went on: "Yeah, it seemed so orderly. Part of a ritual. The drinks are an important part of it. People would ask you what you wanted but they had something in mind. Maybe a traditional pairing, so you were better off not saying anything and letting them offer you whatever they wanted to serve."

"That's true," Eirini said. "There are many rules. We naturally follow them. We forget that they aren't obvious to everyone. Lena, you must know them though. Your mother in her house. She's just like that."

"Oh, I know the rules alright. When friends came over, I was always so embarrassed. My mother planned what to serve. She wanted to know how many people were coming and how long they were staying. We would quarrel if I showed up unannounced with friends."

"You were embarrassed by that?" Mia asked. "Such a little brat." She took the spring rolls out of the oven, put them on a plate, and then placed it next to the pastries. She raised her glass. "Welcome, you are both so welcome here" she said. "I am so glad to have you." They drank.

"I was a brat. It's funny because my friends would love to come over. Their mothers were nothing like mine. They loved the snacks and the way my mother would talk to them, ask them questions. They thought she was so friendly and warm. Everyone would say, 'Lena, your mother is soooooo adorable.' I was humiliated."

"Your mother is adorable," Eirini said.

"Hence the brat assignation," Mia said sipping her wine.

"Isn't everyone embarrassed by their parents?"

"I'm not," Eirini said.

"It's an American thing," Mia responded. "Not that every American mother is embarrassing, it's that American teenagers are embarrassed by their parents. Their existence makes them uncomfortable. They're so busy trying to emulate adults, the existence of parents destroys the illusion."

Lena and Mia laughed.

"Really?" Eirini asked.

"It has to be," Lena said. "I can't believe how I felt back then. In high school. My parents would never embarrass me for real. I mean, my mom wouldn't talk nonsense around my friends. Not like their mothers would. No stories about bed wetting or childhood moments, pictures of me in braces. Nothing like that. My parents. Especially my mother. They would never dream of that. I really don't know why I was so sensitive."

Eirini rubbed Lena's back. "Silly things. Children. I remember believing so much nonsense. About people in the town. So open to gossip."

"What's my excuse?" Lena asked. "Gossip is how the department..."

"Wait," Mia interrupted. "What about those boys? Where are they?"

"They're staying at a hotel. We'll text them in a bit. I was thinking maybe they could come by later tonight after we're settled."

"That'd be great. What's the status? First impressions still holding?"

"They're nice," Eirini said.

"Graduate students," Lena rolled her eyes. "Everything that's wrong with academia. We're so very lucky to have time with them, as knowledgeable as they are. They are full of information. The best route to take to get back to the highway, the best places to eat based on the distribution of good and bad reviews."

"Excluding the fake ones," Eirini reminded her.

"Ah yes, of course, excluding the fake ones. You have to exclude the fake ones when programming the DA."

"Memories," Mia looked off into the distance, feigning wistfulness.

"But they don't know the best place to eat or the way back to the highway," Eirini said. "They are so articulate and sound so confident, but really, they don't know anything. They're very cute. Like puppies. So excited to lead the way, but they don't know where they're going."

Mia and Lena laughed.

"Eirini likes Fred."

"I like both of them," she said taking a bite out of a spring roll.

"No, I mean you *like* Fred."

"Don't be silly, he gets a crush on every woman who talks to him. He's not reliable. I just like to flirt sometimes. I flirt with both of them. Don't you ever just need to flirt?"

"I get it," Mia said. "But maybe it's best not to flirt with a man who gets a crush on every woman who talks to him."

"He's harmless."

"I agree with that," Lena said. "And Carl's very nice. He has a very steep personality, not naturally charming or anything. Not like Fred. But he seems to know it and compensates. I think it ends up making him come off better."

"True," Eirini said, "but he isn't as cute as Fred."

"Is that true?" Mia asked, looking at Lena.

"I suppose so," Lena responded. "But what difference does it make? The whole thing is so weird."

"Alright, let me get this straight. Ben Thorne sends these guys to Seattle to escort you across the country. Is that it?"

"No, that's not it. Ben Thorne sent them to get me to call him. That was the big plan. They came to the house and put me on the phone with the assistant."

"Yes, you told me. Virginia Percival."

"Yes, Ginna. I don't even talk to Ben Thorne. I talk to her. She wanted to get me to meet with him. He doesn't want to talk on the phone, he wants a face-to-face meeting. So aggressive. He wants me to come to New York. Like I have time for that now."

"So you said, but I still don't get it. You tell her you're going to drive across the country and don't have time for him right now and then they tell you that they're going to drive across the country with you. Ostensibly, to make sure nothing happens on the way."

"Exactly. And these are not the guys for that job. If anything, we kept them out of trouble," Eirini said. "But they were a good distraction."

"That's true," Lena confirmed. "They were good at that."

"What distractions?"

"Oh, nothing interesting," Lena said. "Fred has this tendency... I was constantly trying to discover whether he was an asshole, or just socially inept."

"What's the difference?" Mia asked. "So okay, why does Ben Thorne care if you get back to Michigan alright?"

"It's surreal, isn't it?"

"He's very famous, isn't he?" Eirini asked.

"Yeah," Lena said. "He won the Nobel Prize."

"He's horrible," Mia said. "Backlash. He's a cretin."

Eirini giggled and scrunched her nose.

"I've been reading *Artists of Despair*, it's not so bad. I mean, sometimes I see it. But his version of masculism isn't the toxic kind."

"What was that book from a few years ago? *On Being Born*, I think it was called."

"I haven't read it," Lena said.

"What's it about?" Eirini asked.

"There are these thirty-two main characters. Hundreds of supporting characters. It's chaos really. Each of the main characters has a full life, so there are many different names and places. Just chaos. The narrator is the great-great-great grandchild of these thirty-two people."

"That sounds interesting," Eirini said.

"It's conceptually very interesting. The idea is that the narrator's existence hinges on these chaotic and random events that bring the thirty-two people together into sixteen pairs. Then sixteen of their children become eight pairs, and so on."

"It makes me dizzy. Everyone's life has these stories."

"It's clever. I'll give him that much. But the setting is a long time ago, so everything is really traditional. It's thinly veiled, like a throwback to simpler times when men were men and women were obedient. There's a lot in the story that drives the point."

"It's true though, isn't it?" Eirini asked. "Things were like that then. Does it take place in America?"

"No, in Europe mostly, a small part in America, in Africa too. Over a century ago. But that seems like an excuse. His idea is that we have that baked into us. These histories and these stories. We don't really know them, but we couldn't be who we are without them. It's very retro. The olden days. Hierarchy. That kind of thing. So, we're dependent on that way of life. We come from that."

"Is it nostalgic?" Lena asked.

"Not so much nostalgic as... It reminded me of that novel by Bashevis Singer, the one about the family over a few generations. Not exactly nostalgic, but definitely tragic. It's mourning the impending loss of something."

"He wants us to appreciate where we come from."

"That's the problem. He thinks we should appreciate where we come from even if we come from murderous patriarchal dictators."

"But we wouldn't be who we are without them. Like Kolokotronis."

"Oh god, don't go there."

"What is this?" Mia asked.

"One of the many distractions along the way. When the turks invade, you need a real bastard to fight them off. That's where Kolokotronis comes in."

"Kolokotronis wasn't a bastard," Eirini said. "He loved his country and wanted to defend it."

"I've heard other versions of this before," Mia said. "The virtues required to staff the military, or the fire and police departments. The idealized protector. Only necessary because of the traditional love of piracy and brutal violence."

"But fires..." Eirini started to say.

"Let's not get distracted," Mia went on. "They're so good at that. I know what you mean. I'm talking about this Ben Thorne character. He doesn't hate those drives. *On Being Born* is a tribute to them, really. He says that so much of our lives rest on these qualities, we can't remove them completely without changing who we are and jeopardizing our existence. Many feminists wrote critiques of that book."

"Why not just ignore it?" Lena asked rhetorically.

"It was too popular to ignore. There had to be competing narratives."

"I guess I see some of that in *Artists of Despair*. Half the population and all that. He thinks bravado is an important evolutionary trait and he makes the case for it in efforts at surviving the horrors of modern capitalism. He says it's why we resist oppression, and that women learned everything we know about struggling for equality from men who struggled for it. Marx could only be a man and modern-day feminism couldn't exist without him."

"And you don't think that's foul?"

"It can be foul and true. Many pointed out that women were allowed to work when economic conditions required it. Not working was a bourgeois problem, only rich white ladies were complaining about it. It took a Marxist critique of 19th century feminism to correct that."

"You mean because poor women always worked?" Eirini asked.

"Yes, so the right to work was already an issue forged by a very specific type of woman. Marxist critique was used to broaden the scope."

"Why is Marx necessarily a man?" Mia asked.

"That's not the way he puts it. Rejection of the status quo despite overwhelmingly popular acceptance requires masculine bravado. Refusal to submit to the current order is arrogant. Traditional femininity, he argues, trained women to keep the fires burning, to uphold and tend to the status quo. Only a belligerent over-confident person could reject it in favor of a vision that isn't widely held by others."

"They only let us sweep up after them and then they say the only thing we're good for is sweeping up. There's a reason witches ride brooms, you know."

"But that becomes real," Lena said. "Oppression has real effects. He doesn't say women are incapable of resistance, he says feminine ideals don't include it."

"Does his version allow women to have masculine traits?"

"That's my reading. I haven't read the one you're talking about, but I seem to remember *Princess Myshkin* was like that too. The main character is learning to unmake herself. She does it using traditional virtues that aren't usually associated with her sex. In that book, you get the distinct impression that gender roles are how the power dynamic is replicated."

"I've seen that reading too. Many of the virtues that are presented over and against toxic masculinity, according to that line anyway, are the more traditionally feminine values. Communication, community, caring. The traits typically allocated to women."

"Traits good for keeping things stable. I'm not defending him, but I don't think he's trying to reinforce traditional patterns so much as show us what they are and how they continue to be affective. It may not be the best theory going, but I wouldn't call it evil either. If this view were the only backlash we ever had to deal with, it wouldn't be the worst thing."

"They're just stories," Eirini said. "We don't really know this man or what he's like. He writes stories. Does he believe them? Do you have to believe a story to write it?"

"Lots of people read those stories," Mia said. "He's accountable for the atmosphere they create."

"Who's reading them though? Is it popular fiction?" Eirini asked.

"They're best sellers. A lot of people are reading these books," Mia responded.

"What people?" Lena asked. "You think the men who read these books are anti-feminist? It seemed to me like he was more of a writer for the New York literary crowd, for English lit professors. I don't think the average Joe is reading this stuff."

"There aren't any English lit professors anymore. The ideas get around. There were television shows."

"I remember the women in that show being really strong and the men weren't that bad."

"Why are you two defending this guy?"

"I wasn't defending him," Eirini said. "I just meant we don't really know him. We shouldn't judge. I think Lena should talk to him."

"Oh, I definitely think Lena should talk to him, but that's a different question. I suppose it's possible that he, the man himself, might not be a cretin even if his stories make him out to be one."

Eirini giggled again, but no one noticed.

"I suppose I *am* defending him," Lena responded. "Because I'm not even sure that his stories make him out to be one. Fred was saying something like this to me. What was it?"

"About Ben Thorne?" Eirini asked.

"Not exactly. He was talking about that whole Diotima thing in philosophy, 'you say you are going to woman, bring thy whip.'"

"Oh god, you mean *that* Fred."

"No, this one. He was saying there was another way to read it. That it shows he knew women were being coerced. That it took great effort to make us the way we are. It's proof against essentialism. That women really are this way or that way. The whip signifies training and discipline. It shows that these ideas were in our heads and colored our experience. They were forced upon us and then they were real. It takes a lot of work to change."

"Like what?" Eirini asked.

"I guess I'm feeling sorry for myself. Maybe I'm reading too much into it. We've talked about this before. When my father would say 'follow your passion,' I heard disappointment. Like he thought I wasn't following it. He didn't say it right, but it could've been my fault. Maybe a son would have heard it differently."

"You've mentioned that a few times this week. Why do you think... I don't know. Never mind, just don't leave me alone with this Fred," Mia interrupted herself, trying to change the mood. "I can't promise I won't kill him."

They laughed, but it was a little forced.

"Do you want anything else? Can I get you something?"

"Can we just settle in a bit?"

"Sure, there's fresh towels in the bathroom. The bed's made up and ready. Whatever you guys want. There's a TV in there. Stream whatever you like."

"Great. I'll text the guys and tell them to come over. They can bring food. They're very good at that. Following orders."

The House

"I always hated this house. Even on the day we decided to buy it. It's what I thought I deserved. Em thought he failed me. He apologized many times. Especially this last year. Can you imagine?"

"He thought he failed you?"

"It was the one thing I wanted. He felt like he never gave it to me. The house in Greece was supposed to make up for everything."

"It's a lovely place."

"It's perfect. My dream house."

"You don't sound convinced."

"It wasn't supposed to be in Greece, and I wasn't supposed to live in it alone."

"Why did you buy this place if you didn't like it?"

"Oh, it was impossible. Real estate. Our luck was horrible. There were other houses, but many people were buying and few were selling. The prices were going up from week to week. There were investment people buying houses with cash. It was a nightmare. We were at our wit's end."

"It's a cute house. It's where Lena grew up."

"I should be grateful, but it just wasn't what I expected. Now I'm leaving it and I'm terrified it's going to devastate me."

"What do you mean?"

"Today I'm happy to be getting away from it, but what'll it be like tomorrow and the next day? I'm afraid I'll start thinking these were the good times."

"What's wrong with that?"

"Maybe I only know the good times after they're gone."

"Was your life here happy? That's what matters."

"I suppose. When we first moved in, there was a cat that would come by. Every day. We didn't feed it or anything, but it still came to see us. It followed me around and loved to perch on Em's chest while he was reading. We thought it was used to coming here from the last people, but they had a dog."

"Do you know who it belonged to? Was it wild?"

"No, it had a collar. We knew where it lived, but it didn't like those people. There were two teenagers and one day they chased it into our yard and rang the bell to ask for help getting it. They wanted to bring it home. I tried to help, but not very hard. The cat was afraid of them and didn't want to go."

"It preferred you to them."

"It preferred Em, that's for sure. Em gave him his name."

"What was it?"

"Throck. The name on the collar said Bentley, but Em would call him Throck or Throcky or Throckalocky or even Throckmorton."

Ariti laughs. "It sounds funny."

"It is funny, but the cat liked it. The cat would come from very far away when Em or I would say that name. The cat chose it. And us."

"What happened to him?"

"That's what I was getting to. Eventually some other lady in the neighborhood, this was after three years of the cat coming to see us every day and even sleeping here most nights. This other lady took the cat in and turned him into an indoor cat."

"That's awful. You never saw him again? How did you find out?"

"Well, we hadn't seen him in a few days and were starting to get worried. Em was taking the trash out one night and happened to run into the man from that house where the cat lived. He told him the story. The cat had a cut on his head. We noticed it. I cleaned it, in fact, but this lady, she fed the cat sometimes, and she noticed the cut and demanded the people take better care of it. She said there was a coyote around and that the cat was lucky to be alive. They gave it to her. They said he hardly ever came around their house anymore. They had another one anyway."

"Why didn't they give the cat to you?"

"They didn't know about us. No one knew the cat stayed with us. They thought he was living outside."

"You never saw it again?"

"We did. We left a note on the lady's door and then went to visit. The cat was a mess. It was awful. He was crazy. She said he wasn't sleeping. She had him trapped inside. That cat didn't like being inside during the day. He must've been miserable."

"That must've been painful."

"It was. I thought it was a mistake. I worried that by going over there Throcky thought we were giving him to that lady. That it was our fault."

"Awful."

"Em felt horrible too. He thought it was his fault. He thought he should have gone over and talked to that family long ago. He said he would have given them money for that cat."

"Very sad story."

"Yes, the point was about happiness though. I mean it was sad, but it was an experience. Like even this really sad thing was a part of our life. That's what makes it a home."

"Maybe in that way you were happy here. There must be lots of stories like that."

"Many. When you add them up, it amounts to something. There was one time. We were eating dinner. Em was going on about something. The way he would. Lena must've been eleven or twelve. She would listen very closely to him when he would talk."

"Oh, she must've adored her baba."

"She did. And he had that way of talking. It was about something he was reading. Some book. They were so alive to him."

"That must be where she gets it."

"I don't remember what he was talking about, I don't remember how he got off on the topic, but somehow, he started telling us about how he wouldn't read some book that someone recommended because the author was still alive, and he preferred to read books where the authors were dead. Lena was fascinated and started asking questions."

"At eleven or twelve, she was interested in this?"

"She loved to read too. Even as a child. But I don't think she ever gave much thought to the writers. As people, I mean. She never thought about whether they were alive or dead. This was new to her. She was curious."

"What was she asking?"

"Well, she wanted to know why he preferred books like that. What difference did it make?"

"What did he say?"

"He talked to her just like she was anyone else. No sugar coating or simplifying. He was like that with everyone. He said writers are annoying when they promote their work, when they advertise or analyze it. He said that wasn't what reading and writing books was about. Reading and writing were humans at their best, advertising and analyzing were humans at their worst."

"Forget about the drone attacks, there's marketing..." Ariti laughed. "What effect did it have on her?"

"She was fascinated. She couldn't have understood it completely. She was excited anyway, but she took it in a dark direction."

"How do you mean?"

"She asked whether he would ever read anything she wrote? For school or for fun. She liked to write things. She kept them to herself, but what if she wanted him to read it."

"Was she upset?"

"Not upset, more like worried. Or maybe I was the one who was worried."

"What impression did you get?"

"I was paying very close attention. Maybe we were both worried about what he would say."

"What did he say?"

"Of course, he would read anything she wrote if she wanted him to. He was honest, and I don't know if I agreed with what he was doing, but he said it would be different. It wouldn't be like what writing and reading normally are. He couldn't read his daughter's work properly. He emphasized the word and said his love for her would make it hard to read critically."

"How did she react?"

"I think she liked what he was saying in a way. She wanted to hear more, to understand what he thought proper reading was. He talked about being alone when you write and being alone when you read and about how the experience is very personal and direct. He said that's why he thought the writer had to be dead. Because living writers got in the way. If the writer talks about it, that ruins everything."

"Did she understand?"

"I think she understood better than I did. She liked to read when it was completely quiet."

"Was that often?"

"Yes, very often. It was a quiet house. Em and Lena would sit in the office. They'd both be reading there. She liked it. It was one of her favorite things."

"Happy moments."

"Maybe. Later I was talking to Lena about what her father said, trying to find out what she was feeling. I think it had a bad effect. Something was wrong with her if she couldn't write something he could read properly."

"Poor thing."

"She kept a journal. She wrote different things. Never showed it to me, but I couldn't help it, I read it. Just to see."

"She's your daughter."

"It was nice. She was comfortable writing her thoughts. I was jealous. She wasn't self-conscious in the least. It was her own private place."

"That's lovely."

"Yes, but after that conversation with Em, I don't think she felt the same way. She didn't write things down anymore. She kept reading and she would ask if the writer of the book was alive and where they lived."

"Those writers, the dead ones, they were alive when they wrote."

"We're talking about a child. She didn't put it together like that. When she was in college, she would complain about her writing classes. She wanted to do science and math. She didn't care about writing. I thought it came from that one conversation."

"You think it made such an impression? One conversation can't change someone's whole life."

"It can. She's like that. Very sensitive, very intelligent, and very intense about things in her mind. She remembers everything. She was so keen on everything that was going on around her. She could pick up on how we felt about things and how we reacted. Even if Em never said anything about it, I think she would've come to think of it that way. It's how she was with everything."

"What do you mean? What else?"

"It's nothing, it's just her decisions, everything she wants. I think she's trying to be what Em admired and avoid being like me."

"You're her mother."

"Still, she picked up on what he admired. She knew how he spent his time. I still think her focus in school is because when she was in high school Em had a project with that at the center. She absorbed that. And that I was so far from it. She asked me questions. Why don't you work, Mama, why aren't you reading when Baba is reading? She repeated them. Her respect for him was inflated at the cost of respecting me."

"That's nonsense. Children don't judge their parents like that."

"Here they do. It's common. I still feel it when we're together. It seems worse now. She seems far away. She'd talk to him on the phone. I mean, we would talk, but it was always 'are you eating', 'are you taking care of yourself', and stuff like that. She would talk to him about her projects and passions, about the things she really cared about. Now, what will she do, will she even talk to me about it?"

"You're her mother. Of course, she'll talk to you. You'll figure out new ways, you need to get to know each other over again. She's still your daughter."

"I'm sure you're right, but it's part of it isn't it? These experiences, they make us miserable or sad. It's possible, in the end, that they're what makes us happy, that they're what life is about."

Ariti wrapped her arms around Ermioni and pulled her close. They were leaning into each other. Ariti whispered, "It's almost time to go, let's get ready."

Chinese Food

"We're aristocratic about some things, but it's taboo for others."

"Such as?" Mia asked dubiously. She had been suspicious of Fred since he arrived. It came out whenever she said anything to him. Even 'can you hand me a spoon' had a little bit of nastiness in it.

"Expertise is emphasized all the time, but if you call it out in political decision-making, people get defensive. Oh no, democracy is the way to go. It takes extraordinary humans to build a great civilization."

"We've seen what oligarchy can do and we know what it thinks a great civilization is."

"Aristocracy is not oligarchy. The White Party, they're oligarchs, they want people anesthetized and infantilized. Always at the circus with their entertainment. What can I stream this weekend? What should I binge next? Anything to keep them from participating and claiming their due."

"The White Party again," Mia hmphed.

"Yes, they aren't aristocrats. The purpose of the aristocracy should be to virtuously ensure the well-being of the commonwealth. What makes them truly aristocratic, in fact, is that they know this. They sense where the people are and know how to get them to where they need to be. Those are great statesmen and women, they are experts. They have vision."

"Okay, I see what you mean," Carl said. "How do you make sure?"

"Well, there's Plato's point. No great leader would ever want to lead. The desire to be a political leader disqualifies them. Only people who are good at it and need to be compelled should be in that position."

"How do you ensure that?" Eirini asked.

"It's a good question. It has to be built into education. We discover aptitude in children, and we encourage attitude based on it. Maybe you have to cultivate your leaders, and what we're doing now cultivates people like we get: people greedy for power and control who use it to feed their egos and their wallets."

"The call," Carl said. Lena laughed.

"Yes," Fred replied petulantly. "It's like a call. They're called upon to promote the general welfare, the commonwealth, the collective conscience. It takes a big organization to govern and guide a large-scale population into an extraordinary civilization. The organizers must be called to it. That's how it works best. The White Party is devoted to making sure that never happens."

"I've heard this before," Mia said. "You need organization to build organization. Recursive problem. It's nonsense and you sound like you actually believe it. Neat trick. Usually, contradictions like that are ideal for uniting people in some heinous crime."

"I've often thought a lottery is best. I see the bootstrapping problem, but is the idea sound?" Carl asked.

"It's misleading," Mia responded. "It relies on a false equivalency with a single underlying principle: leadership is flawed. You can't lump them together. People follow leaders for different reasons. Different myths with different effects. Mythologies are tailored to segments of the population, creating distinct pathologies. No single revolutionary movement can unite them."

"You don't think that ultimately people share the same class interests and can unite over them?" Carl asked. "It's implicit in Fred's point. We're equally fooled. New leaders can teach us to see what we have in common."

"The avant guarde? It's too late for that," Mia responded. "The creation of the groups, of the opposing parties, isn't an accident. The party is not an expression of class interests anymore. The middle was split into extremes. No one can hear the call. There's too much noise."

"The White Party," Fred said urgently.

"The White Party is an invention of the conspiracy theorists. It's a tool to consolidate power, not form a revolutionary opposition to it."

"Not how I'm describing it," Fred looked as if he was just getting started, but Mia cut him off.

"Yes, exactly the way you're describing it," she explained. "The crisis itself is fodder for more manipulation. This is classic. The White Party is a bogeyman invented to increase control. Political interests want a consistent and reliable block of people behind them. These myths ensure that."

"You think the White Party myth is meant to unite the people while actually driving them further apart?" Carl asked.

"That's exactly how it works. We've been arguing over these same things for decades. Facts are clear and they don't change anything. It's bullshit to think disinterested observers and reluctant participants would have a different effect. Randomly selected or not."

"Police are victims too. So are politicians and oligarchs. We're under the spell," Fred responded matter of factly without noticing that it made Mia wince and had little effect on advancing his case.

"Data doesn't lie, that's my point. We have to hold people accountable for their actions. That's how you break the cycle of seduction and manipulation. The institutions aren't perfect, but we can't start over. We must rebuild the ship while we're at sea."

"The data does lie," Lena said quietly.

"What do you mean?" Mia asked.

"There are no theory independent facts. How you ask the question, how you measure the response, who you ask, how you ask them, where you get it from, under what conditions it's gathered. Peer reviewed science with good methodology would never be wrong if the data was good, but we constantly discover problems. New analysis discredits old analysis and almost always suggests that the old theory had data that was lying. In a way. Metaphorically, I guess. It was a biased picture, or it was built on an anomaly or any of a million reasons why some measuring device didn't gather the data properly. There's no disinterested data collection."

"Alright, data gathering is a process, but scientific methodologies are meant to sort that out over time. We may be fooled for a while, but the methods will prevail. We'll see the error eventually if our process is correct. Data gathering improves when we look at how our institutions treat people, who they help and who they hurt."

"I don't disagree with you," Lena looked at her sister sadly. "It's just that, well, it's always going to be far away from the real matter."

"The real matter?" Mia asked.

"Yeah, the people. Up close. What they need, who they are. It's so theoretical when we talk about it."

"It's not purely theoretical, but you're absolutely right," Carl said trying to be agreeable. "Analysis is a social process. It has to be dialectical. These days, one side is vicious and mean and thinks others are taking and stealing from them, and the other side wants to broaden the net of inclusion so long as corporations can profit by it. One side wants to make it harder for people to vote, the other side wants to make it easier. These are simple policy matters. I agree with Mia. The data is clear."

"People just define their groups differently. We augment our observations with values and moral judgments. The people who want to be more inclusive villainize anyone who doesn't fit with their ideals. Their analysis is moralistic," Fred said. "A great human sees a scared animal and wants to comfort it, not condemn it. Only a weak human would play off that fear and attack it, calling it justice."

"Only one side is selling fear," Mia responded simply, smiling wryly at him.

"Fear comes in many flavors," Fred fired back.

"Enough," Lena said. "This is too analytical, it's abstract. Dialectical or not, it's just talk. Everyone's an analyst now and no one sees that *this* might be the problem. Haven't you ever thought that this shouldn't be an argument? Not like this, at least. Mia, when you do your job, you do what I'm saying, but when you try to generalize from your experience of doing your job and turn it into a theory, everything gets messed up."

"The law *is* analytical, but it's both attached to and detached from the particular case," Mia responded, seeing that Lena was getting increasingly upset as she spoke. She tried to calm her tone. "We focus on the specific case to establish precedent which only then works like a generalization."

"It's problem solving," Fred said, defending himself and nodding in Mia's direction. "You don't want to solve every single problem differently. They can be grouped together, like goes with like, the same solution applies."

"Like goes with like. Isn't that the same problem? I'm not sure I know the answer," Lena said. "Differently, though. It needs to work differently."

Eirini put down the cat and went to sit on the arm of the couch next to Lena. She draped her arm around her. The cat followed her and mewed until Eirini made room for her.

"When I was a kid," Lena went on. "My dad said something. I think about it a lot. I talked to him about it later, we used to talk about it a lot."

"What?" Eirini asked.

"He told me, well he wasn't really talking to me, more like around me, that's how he was. But he said something about how he couldn't read some book because the author was still alive."

Fred slapped his hand against his leg. "That's fantastic. What did he mean?"

"That changed over the years," Lena said, smiling. "But I think he was a bit of a misanthrope. He didn't always think that talking brought out the best in people. He loved people when they were doing things they cared about, but he didn't like them much when they were talking."

Eirini and Mia both laughed. Eirini nodded rapidly in agreement. Mia looked over at her and said, "He got that right."

Lena went on: "Living people write a book and then want to talk about it. Everyone has so much to say. The interpretive framework here and the conditions of investigation there, the methodology this and the methodology that."

Carl was smiling. Fred was nearly howling with delight.

"It's not funny. Not really," Lena said. "They're learning. But what are they learning? He thought reading was like meditating. Someone sat down and quietly framed their ideas, presenting them to a reader. The reader would sit quietly and let those ideas and words pass through their mind, maybe repeating them with an inner voice. It was like whispering in their ear. It's a very intimate experience, the writer's words in the reader's mind."

"Very intimate," Eirini said.

Lena's eyes were visibly moist. She touched her hand to her eye to prevent a tear from falling onto her cheek. "What's unclear was what dead means. There was something about that intimacy that he equated with death, with the writer being dead. Maybe it was like deconstruction says, that intention is gone, and intention is the mark of the living. Reading is a type of mourning or whatever they were saying. But the interpretations, the act of reading and finding meaning in it, that had to be more like storytelling than psychoanalysis. I think that had something to do with what he meant. You can't psychoanalyze the dead."

"You can," Fred said. "They always do it."

"They're doing it wrong," Lena snapped back at him. "It's a talking cure. Without the patient, it cannot happen, it's unethical. To psychoanalyze a patient that you have not met is wrong."

"They use their written work," Fred responded.

"That presupposes intention, that it's something more than storytelling. Fabrications."

"You can ask why these fabrications and not others, can't you?" Fred asked.

"That means you think you already know what story is being told. Reading tells the story, not writing. That's why he preferred dead writers. He thought only dead writers could be properly read. It's because reading is where real storytelling happens. If the writer is alive, they will try to spin and turn the story around, make it something different. Make it more relevant, more popular. Only a dead writer releases the story to readers."

Her hand was no longer keeping up with the tears.

"That seems just as subjective as the other way around," Fred said.

Eirini cut him off, "Aren't you looking at what is right in front of you, Fred? Why are you so insensitive? Can't you see anything? And this is her point, it's exactly what she's saying."

"But I..." he started to say.

"But you what?" Eirini responded. "The partisan electors this and the gerrymandering that. Is that it? Is that what you want to say?"

"What?" Fred was confused.

"This talk, it's too far away. It can't measure anything that's really happening. Lovely pictures, but completely false."

"For the reader to be *with* the writer," Mia said softly. "The writer must be dead. Unable to speak, unable to say anything more than what they said already. The reader's experience is paramount. Not theory, it's a real experience of an unfolding story."

Fred nodded somberly but was aching to point out that everyone can't live in their own reality. Carl looked over at him, using his eyes to caution him to remain silent. Mia moved closer to Lena on the couch.

"It makes me wonder," Lena went on. "Whether he thought the reader had to be dead too. Otherwise, it would just be delusion."

"What do you mean?" Eirini asked.

"I don't know. I guess the reader can't be dead, not in the same way, but maybe proper writing has to think of the reader that way. Not yet alive or something. However you'd say it. To really write, you have to write for the dead. Otherwise, that chatter and talk gets into your head. You'll write what you think the audience wants, or what will sell books or get people to cite you. If you write for the dead, none of that matters. Maybe that's what he meant." She turned toward Eirini. "Do you think so?" Eirini didn't respond, she put her arms around Lena. They sat in silence.

Mia, looking over at Fred, said, "Analytical communication can be hostile. Hell, who knows, maybe the structuralists were right and we just moved on because academic fashion always requires the next big thing."

Carl nodded. Fred pursed his lips.

"Analysis is the problem," Lena said. "Analysis isolates six genetic factors and calls that race."

"Analysis has to be a moment in a dialectical process," Carl said gently.

"Analysis expresses power in the gathering and application of the analyzed conditions," Fred said, matching Carl's tone.

Eirini shook her head at both of them. Lena forcefully exhaled a large breath and rolled her eyes.

"Read the room guys. The ladies are in the 'you don't get to have an opinion about this' mood," Mia said. Philosophy probably has a lot to learn from biology and anthropology, she thought. Lena was sitting up straight and staring quietly into space. Mia's mind was racing. The structuralists were right. We just don't understand how to map that social structure back onto biology through consciousness. And while the philosophers have pushed us down the path of 'I think therefore I am,' the politicians and mathematicians have understood that 'everyone is the other and no one is themselves.' Ordinary people killed those girls in Missouri. Ordinary people whose minds were filled with hate and who fed off each other like a pack of wolves. Simple, in a sense, but fermented over decades in the math. We've been calling it ad business, but it's social engineering. It's math and statistics made practical and applied. A new Copernican Revolution, recast as a dialectic of enlightenment. This is our new and enhanced version of distributed power. Not the colonization of foreign lands, but of bodies, families, and communities. Whatever populates our experience, that's where you'll find the math. Call it the White Party if you want, but it isn't sitting in some room somewhere, it's in our heads seeing with our eyes and speaking with our mouths. "Theory won't change anything for the better," she said finally.

"Maybe storytelling can do it." Eirini said.

"Written by the dead for the dead," Lena whispered.

Emission Analysis Feedback

Being-guilty is Dasein's way of Being whole despite the constant threat of death that defers completion. This suggests that in Being-guilty Dasein comprehends its multiplication and difference, both between authenticity and inauthenticity and between the subject and its multiplying issues. Temporality only comes forward as a theme for inquiry after wholeness has been rendered by guilt and the conscience that attests to it.

When Dasein comes to itself inauthentically, there is already more going on than it can see: there is a residual interpretation. It thinks of itself transcending a limit, but only comes back to itself. In the defining moment of its return, something is left out of the equation, something exceeds the boundary. This excess, this something more or residual, resonates. As a residual, as something more than the result of a process, this something else remains at work and effective, it continues to incite the difference. For everyday Dasein, on the other hand, coming to itself inauthentically, this residual can only be conceptualized as a quality attributed to a thing. This is the meaning of its resonance, it is "the call of conscience."

The call appears other to Dasein, alien and uncanny as it resonates. It gives something to be understood, calls out to it. It does not bring anything to an end, it forbids accomplishment. The call of conscience comes from Dasein's potential to disclose and reaches it in its average everyday existence. As such, conscience is the way transcendence resonates. The condition for the possibility of limits —of origins and ends, is in a fierce and intense relationship with the attempt to cross over. Dasein wants to have a conscience because it already understands that it is the entity which can be more. It has a conscience because it understands that it can only assign a quality to itself because it is an entity capable of assigning qualities. It can comprehend itself as an issue, it can question, and it can care.

Conscience is a call. It comes from somewhere and goes somewhere. Like Dasein who is coming to itself, conscience comes to itself. More than just a qualitative state, the residual is left over, and resonates when calling back to what was left behind in excess of the accomplishment. Dasein always hears this call. It haunts it and summons it to its own wholeness.

Being-guilty names the split in Dasein's being. It is the way Dasein comes to live its difference in that call. As guilty, Dasein both hears the call and lives with what it is, has been, and will be. Because guilt is difference embodied, it is already two ways of hearing, it speaks and listens among things, and it speaks and listens as more than a thing. Dasein hears the guilt of conscience as a negation, as a negative that rejects the way potential is fulfilled. In medias res, Dasein hears that it has not fully been everything that it can be. Insofar as it calls out to itself, summons itself, it realizes that it is more than just a thing. It is its guilt as the disclosive power to be otherwise than a thing. Guilt cannot come to an end, cannot cease. It negates the state of things and presents itself as the comprehensive Being of Dasein at issue for itself. As long as there is Dasein, it is in the middle of things. As long as there is Dasein, there is something more than being in the middle of things. It lives this difference as itself divided, as guilty.

Call it resoluteness. It is not the result of a deliberation. It is not a decision to opt for one approach over another. Rather it is the resolution to remain divided. Ordinarily, Dasein is not resolved, but it can become so. Resolution is anticipatory resoluteness. It is already a relation Dasein takes to its possibility of coming back to itself. Anticipation holds open the division, does not try to close it, maintains its openness, and the difference between concern for things and their residual. It unravels the expectations that guide everyday being when achieving ends.

It is a question of remaining open and of closing off. The difference is in the moment when the one lies near the other, it's the moment when the contraries collide and unravel. Anticipatory resoluteness is already a way of holding open potential, indeterminateness, the absence of definition, and the absence of genre. We say that Dasein is already both the potential to be resolved and unresolved. Both are at work without end in an ongoing existence. On the one hand, Dasein lives its guilt as an attribute, on the other, it lives it as the disclosive power of the residual.

Dasein's individuation embodies the character of guilt. Guilt sets Dasein apart through the shame of not being otherwise. It makes itself known in a constant and forceful way and appears as the experience of a proper personality. It lives this by attempting to transcend it, and by making it an essential possibility that can be achieved. Individuated Dasein cares, however, and so unwinds, is unwound. It is in virtue of caring that it projects self-overcoming. Individuation is experienced as something that can only be maintained by continuing to project, continuing to overcome.

Even the most banal discourse on individuality includes becoming. The individual is not static but overcomes itself. It wrenches free from its individuation through a pattern of projection that dismantles stable structures. It grows.

What Dasein projects to maintain its individuality is something other than what it has been. Projection has the character of something with a foundation, a base. It comes from a past that has not been chosen and in which it finds itself. This facticity burdens Dasein with character and a trajectory to be otherwise.

Everyday Dasein can only project itself into possibilities that are part of past and current conditions. Thrownness presents Dasein with a double burden. It is not only the source of projection, but also guides and guards the direction of that projection. Dasein's individuation escapes it, becomes something it cannot control. Attempts to gain control are thwarted and this marks it with great anguish. Guilt appears there.

Dasein's despair at losing control is the joy of thrown projection. This anguish that is also joy, that is the very difference between anguish and joy, hinges on whether Dasein's residual is heard as the voice of a friend or the voice of a fiend. It is a ghost either way.

Dasein usually comprehends itself in the present. It understands its past as something presently burdening it with an imperative to overcome. It understands its future as a present possibility that overcomes actuality. The temporality of the present is a never-ending anguish. The future made present quickly fades into a state to be overcome. That event repeats itself. Dasein is restless, unable to escape this cycle of recurrence. From individuated Dasein's point of view, it makes progress toward its goal by making real progress structurally impossible. The future is just another moment like the present.

If the future takes focus, however, then what comes fades. Dasein no longer expects some thing that comes, but rather resolves itself perpetually. The joy of the circle replaces the anguish of the cycle.

Nothing changes when anguish systematically dismantles everydayness.

Dasein makes history through this constant coming and going. History is always the history of the difference, the history of Dasein's self-deconstruction, the history of the deconstruction of metaphysics. In Dasein's history, there is nowhere to go, there is no clearly and distinctly posited goal. Nothing is more comforting. Nothing ends the anguish of history better than an ultimate goal. Not only Kant and Hegel, but Aristotle, they are implicated in an eschatology. Dasein's history is rooted in a capability to deconstruct, to systematically dismantle its current state in something already at work (the origin) achieving what has been at work since the beginning (the end). Since positing is rooted in care, the circulating economy, the impossibility of coming to an end is implicit at the beginning.

We can think coherently about an authentically historical being only if we think the end of attempts to come to an end, only insofar as the pattern emerges in the anguish of its everyday failure. This suggests Dasein's being as transcendence, as the difference between its being a thing and its being at issue. Transcendence is not only temporal, but historical insofar as

Dasein carries the difference along with it in a global facticity. The transcendence at work is a circulating economy emitting itself historically, temporally, and structurally in everyday events. Dasein dwells in the difference as its history, it remains a being that questions and comes to itself when transcending itself without positing a goal, and as the power to exceed its boundaries in practice every step of the way.

What a beautifully tragic creature Dasein is! Its tragedy is its beauty. It can try to do things that it cannot do, and this displays its overwhelming power, the incredible force that makes it so extraordinary. Deconstruction, in order to be the systematic dismantling of metaphysics, must incorporate the inner need and drive *of* metaphysics. Suppose the highest ideal is posited as a god, the origin and creator of everything. Suppose that such an origin implies the end of history when god's being reconciles with conditions on earth. Whereas deconstruction points to this desire as the root of metaphysics and shows the flaws and problems in its systematic structure, it is rarely emphasized that this is a beautifully tragic goal. Only when deconstruction fully incorporates the goal's tragedy and beauty does it emerge as the deconstruction of metaphysics.

Heidegger, somewhere, refers to emergence (issuance) as the awakening of a sleeper. Inauthentic Dasein awakens to the impossibility of its thinghood. It wakes up and asks why there are entities at all and not rather nothing. Woke, it asks a revolutionary question in the wake of being the entity that it is. The emergence of the difference is a sleeper waking up. The potentiality-for-Being is added to include the sleeper. Not added later as something contributed after the initial work was done, but added right from the start as the onset of the difference between the sleeper and the one who is awake. The sleeper wakes up and comes into its own. Potentiality-for-Being is added at the beginning as something to be achieved, but which is never achieved.

Potentiality-for-Being is Heidegger's way of naming transcendence at work in the difference, as the difference, through the difference, between entities and existence. It is the play between, it is an origin, and it is not. It is a source open to itself and circulating endlessly there. It does not lead anywhere, it does not have results, it does not have a place to get to that will mark it as something more than it once was. A ridiculous farce, it is Don Quixote going nowhere. It is a circulating economy, and already lies in efforts to make things come out right, transcending what came before. It is an economy of exchange where growth and development happen, but which does not grow and develop.

What resonates throughout the process of exchange is the ability to grow, to extend beyond limits. The transcendence of Dasein resides in Dasein's efforts to overcome itself.

When exchange becomes the circulating system for an economy of growth and increase, the tension reaches crisis. Dasein is preoccupied with hiding the impossibility of its projections. Such an economy accentuates the deconstruction of metaphysics. It is the epoch in which metaphysics emerges as its own deconstruction, while forcing it into oblivion. The question is forgotten. The goal is impossible and yet drives Dasein onward. The pleasure and joy of the goal conflicts with the anguish and pain of its impossibility. Dasein becomes expert at hiding from itself, becomes expert at covering over the schism where it lives.

Through radical individuation, Dasein hides the crisis at the origin, presenting itself as an individual without residual, signaling the impotence of growth and development. The power of individuation to cover the crisis at the origin works the same way as that ideology which covers up crises. Covering up is an existential facet of intentional acts and is emblematic of judgment.

Insofar as ideology is a product, it reveals an entity that fails to find ideas in experience precisely because they drive it. The production of an idea is comprehended by a produced intentional act. This capacity must already be effective in Dasein's economy of movement.

Dasein's tendency to individuate allows it to be moved by something that has been produced. This is part and parcel of careful orientation. The belief-product is a projection that marks Dasein with its thrownness. Such thrown projection can be an operative element in orientation only because Dasein can be moved by belief-products. Every employment of a belief for-the-sake-of carrying out some action or practice embeds Dasein in an exchange relation that resonates, that both makes exchange possible and forbids fulfillment.

It is equally possible to deconstruct metaphysics in material relations and ideology. Both are textiles. Neither maintain a grip on transcendence seamlessly. In the ideology and material of individuation that saturates intentional acts, guilt and unravelling resonate. Such ideology, such material, reveals Dasein's tendency to transcend for-the-sake-of a residual.

[exeunt all]

Interlude

"The sorest misfortune is when your views are in advance of your work."

— Leonoardo da Vinci

Emission

Because she operated a car within the last year, Virginia Percival got the job of chauffeur in the parking lot of the rental car company at the Detroit airport. It was a field promotion. She accepted it with a heavy sigh resigning to yet another responsibility undeclared in her job description. Ben Thorne rode in the backseat with a laptop computer on a fold out table. He complained that the car's WIFI was spotty. Carl Maxwell let them know Lena Michaels' travel plans but the timing of their arrival was a little off. Ginna and Ben Thorne arrived the night before the women were due, but Ben could not wait, and insisted they press on. He was anxious to see the place. He hadn't been back in years and wanted to know if any of his old haunts were still there. He was busy searching the internet to discover what remained.

"The Fleetwood is right where it is supposed to be," he said.

Ginna shook her head and rolled her eyes. The navigation vocalized its operations in a pseudo-female voice. She sat in the emergency seat and was comforted, just like she was supposed to be. Nothing for her to do, but the law required it so she couldn't sit in the spacious backseat with her boss. She hated these assignments. They reminded her that she worked for him, that their relationship was professional, and that she depended on his good favor for her livelihood. When she first started working for Ben Torne, she was an intern. Jerry Porter was the assistant. G. B. Porter. She thought about him sometimes and remembered the ill will she felt. Now, of course, she understood how misdirected it was. Carl probably thought about her like that. She adored Ben Thorne when she was his intern. *Princess Myshkin* had come out the year before and was just announced as the recipient of the Pulitzer Prize for Literature. She had been mesmerized by that book. The opportunity to work for Ben Thorne was surreal. He was such an established and highly regarded author with such a broad and deep sphere of influence. How exciting. She shook her head and grimaced at how naïve she was. Looking in the rear-view mirror, mounted in the usual spot to meet safety regulations in case of manual intervention, she could only see him as petulant and affected.

Truly, she had no idea what they were doing. It seemed like a farce, and she wondered if she had become Sancho Panza. She recalled the epigraph from Ben Thorne's own Quixotic novel and grumbled something about being responsible for this nonsense. What exactly was he hoping to accomplish? He was about to force himself upon a young woman just to redeem himself with her father. All these years she knew of Em's existence but never met him. He never came to New York and, to her knowledge, Ben never went to visit him. She wondered what must have happened in their common past to make him so beholden, what made him think he needed to redeem himself this way. Ben Thorne was more adamant about achieving this than anything she had ever seen.

Of course, the men exchanged many emails and called each other frequently. Clearly there was a connection, but she thought it was strictly professional. The conversations she overheard were all business, they focused on whatever book Ben was writing. She first came to learn of Em through an email she was asked to print and go over with Jerry and Ben in a staff meeting. The email contained extensive notes on the work in progress, *Choreography*. She was so fascinated by the process. She knew that Ben Thorne was composing regularly throughout the weeks and months during her internship, but nothing would cause more activity than these missives, and this one in particular. At the time she didn't think much of it, but the email contained an attachment that she opened and started to read. She asked Jerry if she was supposed to print it too and he told her to ignore it. "You don't need to read that," he said.

She read it anyway. "Choreography is deliberate repetition in space. Angles for our refinement, they play in the light, the shadows offer and receive our senses. Those dancers know the motion of tears and their semblance is like vapor leaving traces behind as they move, making their way, and delivering others in awe. Assembled enchantment was our first song." She still remembered that passage, the whole document. It was the first time she ever saw raw composition from someone so accomplished. Later she wondered whether it was really so raw. Ostensibly, Em provided his reaction, but why attach the source to the response? Em provided edits and rewrites. It didn't occur to her then, but after *Choreography* was published, she wondered. Ben Thorne was always applauded by his publishers for his editing, but perhaps he was a thief. Now he was off and in search of something left behind, something left undone or that he owed that editor, involving his adult daughter. Whatever it was, it was so urgent that he needed to act on it before she had time to recover or reset her bearings.

The timing seemed awful. She couldn't imagine anything more insensitive and unfeeling. At the moment he was trying to redeem himself, he would add an injury to the tally. This was the very essence of a farce where efforts to make something better only made them worse.

"The Del Rio is long gone," Ben Thorne said as they pulled up into the carport at the hotel where she booked the only two-bedroom suite for the next couple days. "The building is still there, but it is a restaurant now, or an extension of one."

She checked in with her phone and downloaded the keys. She

forwarded one to Ben Thorne who put his laptop computer into a bag and switched to his phone. As they got out of the car and handed it off to the valet, the only interest he showed in his surroundings was when he asked how to use the key to connect to the hotel WIFI. "The key will connect for you. Just touch it," the agent said. The valet programmed the car, the bellhop put the bags on the bot, and the two of them went to the room. While they were settling in, she called Carl. They had arrived earlier than planned.

"The sister," he said. "The lawyer."

"Mia Holden."

"Yes, Mia. She was ready to go sooner than expected. What Mia wants Mia gets."

This made Ginna laugh: the sheepish way showed how demur he must have felt in her presence. He told her how Mia really had it in for Fred. Both of them really. It got to the point where they didn't want to say anything. They would wait until they were alone before they made their observations or mentioned the points of interest from the conversation.

"Fred became absolutely silent. He stopped saying anything at some point. She's quick-witted and well-informed. And she doesn't take any shit. None of them do, really. But she seems scarier somehow."

Ginna was smiling broadly. "Sounds like someone I would like."

"Well, you will meet her if you're planning on going to Lena's place tomorrow. The three of them are staying there."

"I have a room for you two here," she said. "Forwarding the key."

"Should we say goodbye to them then? Is this it for us? Now that you guys are here?"

"Probably. I'm not sure of the itinerary yet. Your flight isn't until Monday, but Ben won't like it if you're around tomorrow, so best say your goodbyes now."

"Got it," he said. "She's really great. The way she looks at things, at people. She's so present, cuts right to the point. I like her. Fred does too. Everybody. Eirini, from Greece, she's like a sister to her and can't keep her hands off her. She dotes on her every move. Mia watches her so closely. If anything happened to hurt Lena, she'd take care of it. They're so different. It's hard to believe they're sisters."

"They must get it from their mothers."

Carl mumbled something. Then more clearly, "The more I know her, the more shocking the thing in Montana is."

"What thing in Montana?"

"She asked me not to mention it. Some locals were giving me a hard time in the bar after dinner, and she stepped in."

"Brave."

"Yes, and she can handle herself. She was carrying a little pistol and there was this whole thing, and it was so easy and fluid. She cooled the situation off. She's tough."

Ginna had lots of follow up questions, but Ben Thorne was ready to go to the hotel restaurant and was standing out in the living area between the two bedrooms. She told Carl she would talk to him later and to text her when they got to the hotel.

The next day was Sunday and shortly after 1 PM they took the car across town and parked on the road next to the little house where Lena lived with her three roommates. Ben waited in the backseat while Ginna walked up the driveway and rang the bell. It was a two-story house located just North of downtown in a convenient location for students who didn't want to be too close to campus but didn't want to be too far away either. A man in his mid-twenties answered the door casually, both in dress and demeanor.

"Hey," he said.

"Hello, I'm looking for Lena Michaels. Is she home?"

"Uh yeah, just one second. And you are?" he asked only after giving it a second thought.

"Virginia Percival."

He closed the door and went off. She turned and looked back at the car. Ben Thorne was leaning forward in his seat and staring out the window. He looked like he was set to pounce and jump out of the car instantly once things developed. The door opened causing Ginna to turn abruptly back toward it. The woman in the doorway, who was looking at her sternly, must have been in her early forties. This wasn't Lena. Her gaze made Ginna uncomfortable and despite not having much faith in Carl's perception, she thought he might've been on to something when describing Mia.

"You must be Mia," she said sticking out her hand.

"Mmhm," she said without shaking. "What's this about? What do you want?"

Ginna was taken aback. Mia was shorter than she expected but had an amazing face with character and incredible eyes. She was prepared for the possibility that Mia wouldn't receive her well but not for her alarming good looks.

"This is awkward," she said. "And I know how inappropriate it is, but my boss is over there in the car, and he wants to speak with Ms. Michaels. Is there any way that could happen at some point today?"

"Who is your boss?" she said looking over at the car suspiciously. Their eyes met. It was clear that she already knew the answer but was going to make Ginna say it anyway.

"Ben Thorne," she said submissively. "He was a friend of Lena's father. Your father, I think."

"My father lives in Illinois. Listen, you seem like a reasonable person, you must know how very unreasonable this is. Lena is grieving and busy getting ready for a trip. There isn't time to talk to some stranger with an inflated ego who thinks he has a right to barge in and demand an audience."

Ginna smiled and said, "I didn't realize you already knew Ben Thorne." This made Mia smile. Ginna took the opportunity to continue: "Of course, you're right, but he does have something to discuss that he believes is of significance to her. It is directly related to her father's death. He hasn't shared the details with me so I can't be more forthcoming, but I believe he has a genuine and timely need to speak with her."

Mia closed the door without a word, leaving Ginna confused. She turned back to the car and saw that Ben was still paying very close attention. He shrugged as if to ask, "what is going on" and she shrugged in response. She had no idea. She waited.

The door opened again after a minute or so and this time Mia told her to come in. "Just you. Tell your boss to wait." Ginna turned and raised her index finger to the car. Ben Thorne nodded and Ginna went inside past Mia who closed the door behind her. Inside the house there was a small entranceway and then a living room just to the right. There was a long couch and a chair around a coffee table, and then a TV in the corner. On the other side of the room, there was a little dining area with some bookshelves on the left-hand wall and a dining table on the right side. Two young women were sitting there. They stood up as soon as Ginna came in. Ginna recognized the woman on the left. Lena looked just like she did in her college graduation photo. Ginna crossed the living room and they met at the threshold.

"Hi Lena, I'm Virginia Percival. We spoke on the phone." They shook hands and Lena introduced Eirini. Ginna had been anxious up to that point, the sight of Lena had shaken her further, but shaking hands with Eirini calmed her. Her smile was delightful. There was something in her look, something about her. "Nice to meet you," she said with a thick accent making the words sound more beautiful than Ginna ever thought they could.

"I'm sorry to disturb you at a time like this, and I'm so sorry for your loss."

"But?" Lena said. Mia followed Ginna into the room and was standing off to the side, effectively between her and Lena.

"I am sorry, but my boss is very persistent. He wants to talk to you, and he believes it concerns a matter that will be of great interest to you."

She used the word boss very deliberately. She relied on it in circumstances like these, knowing it had an effect, that it conveyed that she was not to blame for her actions, that they were beyond her control, that some alien force was driving her, and she had no choice but to comply. It worked like magic, it smoothed over so many awkward situations, but today it didn't have any effect. The women weren't relieved to learn that such an inconvenience was brought upon them by managerial forces of nature.

"Is he here?" Lena asked after Ginna finished. Her tone was simple. She didn't sound irritated or annoyed. Even her previous remark, knowing that a "but" was coming, didn't have any sign of emotion. She was even keeled. Prepared. Ginna's take was that she was curious.

"Yes," she said. "He's in the car."

"Okay. Let him come in then."

Ginna retraced her steps, walked out to the car, and opened the door. "Come on," she said. "She's agreed to see you."

"Alone?"

"I got you in the door. What happens now is up to you."

He got out of the car, and they walked back to the door. Mia must have followed along behind her as she went out because she was waiting on the porch when they arrived.

"So, you're Ben Thorne," she said as the two of them came up the steps. There was a touch of sarcasm in her voice.

"And you are?" he asked, unfazed.

"Mia Holden," she said sternly.

"Ah Dr. Holden. I have heard so much about you," he said calmly. There was no sound of alarm in his voice, nothing in her tone had put him off. He was not easily swayed by other people's demeanors, he preferred to set the tone. "The Women's Center, I believe it is called. You do good work. But what are you doing in Ann Arbor Michigan? Should you be in St. Louis?" Then he hummed the little tune from that old movie and said, barely audibly, "St. Louey, Louey."

She ignored it and let him pass by her. He didn't wait for an answer, knew she wasn't going to give him one. He was in the lead, Ginna close behind, and then Mia closing the door and following. Lena and Eirini hadn't moved from the spot where they first met Ginna. They stared in wonder as the older man came through the living room. He was dressed well, with a lightweight sport coat and slacks, a casual shirt and nice brown leather shoes. It had something of a shocking effect, they knew him to be about seventy years old, but he didn't look it. With the stylish clothing and the way he carried himself, he seemed like he could've been Mia's age. He wasn't what they were expecting. The photographs online always made him look so distinguished. They weren't prepared for this, for his presence.

He went right to Lena without hesitation and, nodding deliberately, said, "Hello Ms. Michaels, Ben Thorne. I would know you anywhere. I have seen pictures of you your whole life. I feel like I have watched you grow up."

She nodded but didn't respond. She introduced Eirini.

"So lovely to meet you, Ms. Kallistidou. Ben Thorne." He got the pronunciation exactly right and Eirini blushed while shaking hands with him. She was charmed. All of them were, though only Eirini was willing to show it.

"So, what did you have to talk to me about? What is so urgent that you had to come so far?"

"And send Carl and Fred," Eirini reminded her.

"And send Carl and Fred," Lena repeated.

"Yes, yes, of course, I understand how very unusual this must be. But perhaps we might speak in private." He looked around and tried to convey to the others that there was no disrespect in his request.

"These are my sisters," Lena said.

"Yes, yes," he said interrupting her. "Of course, anything I have to say to you I could say to them. Your father knew you would have this response. He told me that if you refused to talk to me in private I was to say this to you."

"Go on," she tried not to show that mentioning her father caused any distress. She didn't want him to know it.

"Just this. Speusippus," he pronounced the word deliberately with a hard f and a long u.

"What did you say?" Mia had made her way up alongside the two of them. She recognized the word too, and it made her mad to hear him say it. It shook Lena. Tears filled her eyes. Eirini, always ready with a tissue, helped her wipe them away.

"She knows what I said," he said quietly.

"Okay, fine," Lena responded. "We can go in the office here." Next to the bookshelves there was a closed door which Ginna thought was a closet. When Lena opened it, she saw a room with two desks and two chairs. There were old-school desktop computers under each of the desks and a small closet without a door. There were books stacked up in the nook on the upper shelves and on top of a file cabinet that was jammed in against the back wall. Lena let Ben Thorne walk past her and into the room and then, before closing the door, told Eirini and Mia that it would be okay and that she would holler if she needed anything. She closed the door.

Once it was closed, Eirini looked at Mia and said, "What does it mean? The Greek philosopher. Plato's nephew, I think."

"Technically," Mia responded. "But that's not what it means. Lena's dad used to say it. As a term of affection. It was nonsense. I don't know. It was when he was being very sweet."

Eirini turned to Ginna. "Would you like something to drink? Tea or something."

"Yes please. That would be great. Can I help?"

...

In the little office, Lena gestured for Ben Thorne to sit on one of the desk chairs. She was about to sit in the other one, but that would put them very close to each other, so she thought it better to stand back a little. He sat down and saw that she wasn't going to do the same. "Won't you join me?" he said gesturing toward the other chair. "Please."

She moved to the chair and pushed it back a little while swiveling on it, effectively moving it a foot or so farther from him as she sat down.

"So," she said making it sound like a question.

"Eirini is adorable," he said. She nodded.

"You two are not really sisters, are you?"

"No, I don't know the word for what we are," she said. She looked down then away. She was awkward and didn't know where to look.

"Friend," he pronounced the word deliberately. "Please do not be nervous. It is so strange to meet you. I feel like I know you, but of course I do not. It is common really. You hear so much about a person, and you know everything they have ever done, but you never spoke with them, never shared anything with them. You only know about them."

"I suppose I only know about you too then. Only I didn't know you were friends with my father. The lawyer had to tell me that."

"The lawyer has no idea, but I cannot imagine why your father never mentioned it."

"Nor can I. I wish he had."

"But why? It cannot be of any significance to you. What do a father's friends matter to a young woman?"

"Still, I wouldn't have been so shocked. It was bad. Being called in like that. On such a day. If I had known, it might've been easier."

"I doubt that. But let us forgive him anyway. Now that he is gone, I can repay him what I owe and finally he is powerless to resist. Since we did not get to bury him..."

She pursed her lips and continued looking at him. She was more afraid to look away than to keep looking. She didn't speak and refused to reveal any discomfort in the brief silence that passed.

"Em was extremely sensitive to influence. I suppose that is one way to put it. Influence on him and his influence on others. He must have thought it would influence you badly. He would have had his reasons."

"You make him sound like that character from your book."

"Very likely. Which one?"

"I've just been reading *Artists of Despair*," she said almost shyly. She didn't want to come across as star struck. Her resistances were still rather high, and she didn't want him to get the wrong impression. Or the right one either.

"Yes," he said. "I know the passage you must mean. I think that one is definitely your father. He told me so much about it. The way he would come to distrust his own thoughts and desires, his instincts even."

"What do you mean, distrust?"

"Em's job was demanding. He had to be innovative and creative, focused and smart. The problems he was solving, technical problems, organizational problems, they were complicated. There was a lot at stake. He worked with capable people in a highly collaborative environment."

"That sounds like the corporation in your book."

"It is. He described his work in such detail. He talked about how his projects were not his projects, his interests were not his interests. He talked about the experience of really wanting to get something done in a specific way and how that conflicted with the fact that none of it belonged to him, was not his, but belonged to the company. This meant that the thoughts in his head, the actions he performed, none of it was his own. His experience of that alienation was so deep and articulate... He understood it very well."

"You make him sound possessed."

"I suppose so. That is how he would describe it. An external force internalized, and now a part of him. He called it distributed consciousness."

"That sounds familiar, is it in the book? Or maybe he talked about it."

"Both perhaps. When you have hundreds or thousands of people acting this way, bound together by the organization they serve, you achieve a structured consciousness unfamiliar to any of the individual actors. He thought that even though it seemed like he knew exactly what he was doing, in truth he did not have a clue, because the meaning of his actions was part of this larger organization and there was information he did not possess, and which gave his work purpose. Only other members of the organization had it. And vice-versa. No one had the whole picture. That is how bureaucratic structures work."

"Is this what you came to tell me?"

"In a way, yes. But okay. I will get to it." He paused and looked around the room as though he were trying to find something. "What I am going to tell you, I am obligated to tell only you. It is information that I am not allowed to share with anyone else. Having said that, once you know, you can tell anyone you like. This is why we had to speak in private. It is because I have to keep this a secret. You do not. Do you understand?"

"Yes. But why? That's a strange condition."

"It is." He smiled. She got the distinct impression that he was buying time, trying to work out the best way to say whatever it was that he had to say. "I am not Ben Thorne." He paused and saw that she looked puzzled. "Rather, Ben Thorne is a corporation. Ben Thorne, Ltd. Technically. Everybody knows this. It is not a secret really. But it is not obvious to everyone what it means. It is common enough for an individual in my position to create a corporation to cover the liability of their professional work. Everyone assumes Ben Thorne the corporation is owned by Ben

Thorne the writer. I never even had to explain it. Everyone assumed the shell companies were a legal tax dodge. But the truth is that I am not Ben Thorne, that is not my name, and in fact that name was invented by your father many years ago. We have been running the company together since... Well, since we published the first book long ago under the pseudonym Ben Thorne."

He paused, looking at her, waiting for what questions would come.

"Why tell me?" she said, feeling certain that she already knew the answer.

"Because he has left his share to you. You and I are now Ben Thorne."

"So many questions." She looked down. She didn't know what to think or what to ask first. She started carving out the space and the issues, breaking everything down into bits and pieces. Divide and conquer, she repeated to herself.

"He made you keep this a secret?"

"Yes, it was part of the legal documentation establishing our relationship. I had to act as the front man and was never allowed to reveal the nature of the agreement."

"But he could say whatever he wanted?"

"It was left out. I did not care at the time and did not bother to make it a condition. Since we defined the relationship based on his concerns, he was not worried about betraying the secret, so it was not included in the bylaws. I reminded him of this when he told me you would inherit his interest, but he did not seem concerned. He said you would do the right thing."

"And what did he think the right thing was?" she asked simply.

"He did not say, but he was convinced that you would know."

"So, what does it mean? You two own a company."

"We two," he corrected her.

"We two. Are you saying he wrote that? You two were partners? Who wrote those books?"

"We were partners, yes. Your father had certain gifts. He had some stories, he had some insights. He did not have a voice. He did not know how to speak or say what he imagined. That was my gift. But he could edit. He had a nose for bullshit like no one else. He would ask me, do you know this? Are you truthful here, do you know what you are talking about? Never, never, never lie to your reader. He would say that so forcefully. It was an ethical imperative. Never bullshit. Always be as truthful as you can."

"So how did it work exactly? You would write and he would edit."

"Not like that, not really. That is not how these kinds of stories come about. Hmm. How to describe it? We would riff. Do you know this term? Riff."

"Like in music. I know it. I think I recall seeing something about that somewhere among his things."

"Yes. That big, awful book he wrote by himself. That monster of self-ridicule. Yes, that is it. Riffing. We would riff together about something made up. Some poor soul or group of souls. We would turn them into facades and aspects, we would pivot them. He knew how to turn an idea into a person and then split it into three people and then move them around. Not stories. Conceptually, I mean. He was flexible like that."

She smiled. "That reminds me of these little ditties he would tell me. They weren't stories exactly, they were more like fairy tales or fantasies. When I was little. He would take a word or a sentence and turn it into people. Like each word was two people and then the whole sentence was a crowd. 'Misery loves Company, but it is unrequited' or 'Love and Death were walking by the river.' They would struggle or play and dance, whatever. It would depend on what we were doing that day. But that play or that dance, that riff, that would be the meaning of the story or the sentence or whatever. Misery and Company were trolls that lived under the floating bridges."

"Yes, yes. That is what we would do. And as you must know, it was mesmerizing. He and I would talk for hours. *Fragmented.* That first book we wrote. That is what it is about. It is about people being born out of sentences. And not just born, but borne, and broken apart, and turned into many people. Packs of people. Unpacking each other. Packing together. Bouncing off each other and meaning things."

"When was that written?"

"I wrote most of the first very rough draft here in Ann Arbor while sleeping on his couch. In a way, it was the best year of my life, and the worst. I thought I knew everything. That has the makings of a tragedy."

"Is your name Stephen Wolfe?"

He laughed loudly at the timid way she asked it, it was the first outward sense that she gave of not being completely sure of herself. "I hardly remember any more. No one in my life today knows me by that name." He looked down and nodded assertively. "But yes, I am Stephen Wolfe."

"That's one of the character's names in *Time Between Summers.* In fact, isn't that the only character there who actually has a name?"

"Do not get me started on that horrible beast of a thing. Making that damn TV show was absolutely the most ridiculous thing I have ever done."

"I loved that show."

"Well, I am glad. Your father made me do it and I hated it. That character was not me, not in the least. You have to understand. That is how it worked. There was so much of him in that book. He insisted that one of the characters had to be named Wolfe because that was the splinter from the sentence that launched the story. Something about a wolfpack and then using the name you never use. It was not me, it was me through him but splintered off."

"I don't understand what that means."

"Sometimes when an author writes something, people read it and ask something like 'which one is you?' meaning that one of the characters must surely be the author. I seem to recall having to do some press back then and some critic may have even asked me that question. I said exactly what Em prepared me to say. He said, 'they are all you, you are the writer, they are all your characters. Everything they say, you are saying, everything they think, you are thinking. They all have your name in one way or another. In you they are incorporated.' The way I thought of it, it was like that sentence we riffed, whenever something fragmented, that was our term for it, they would become that fragmenting, their self would be in the shards and pieces of it. That is the self. And breaking apart like that is how you become yourself, how you are yourself. That means you are yourself through people, through the people you know and the way you know them, how you understand them and how you understand yourself through them. Does that make it any clearer?"

"Was the wolfpack supposed to be you or him?"

He smiled and said, "somewhere in that book, during the intervention, it comes out that Wolfe thinks the typesetter is El Cide Hamete Benengeli."

"From Don Quixote."

"There is a layer in that book where it comes out that someone has taken the story of the knight errant and packaged it for publication, written the exploits of our poor hero. Is that the book we are reading? In our tale, El Cide was the typesetter. The one who sets the type. It seemed so very clever at the time. Overly literary. These are just the kinds of gimmicks he liked. These curios that would reside in between the lines of the work and appeal to the overeducated reader. He left them morsels and made fun of them at the same time. But in a nice way, where everyone is in on the joke."

"Well, I'm not sure I understand it."

"I can commiserate. That was so long ago. I cannot swear that I have left it behind though. In my latest work... well... I find myself going back there again and again. I must be trying to sort something out."

"What?"

"The character in *Artists*, he is not just in touch with how his ideas and actions are possessed by the corporation. He feels desire too. He wants his projects to succeed, he is passionate about them. These desires yield pleasure when they are satisfied and displeasure when they are not. They are alien desires. In them, the character experiences what he wants as something separate from himself. His most personal desires are not his own. They came from somewhere else and were implanted in him."

"I can identify with that. You want something so badly and then you get it, and it doesn't seem like it was ever really yours. None of it does."

"He wanted to show how farcical it was. But a lot of that tied back to the intervention. It was not just one conversation on a particular day in a particular place. It was the whole year, our time together. He succumbed to a strong desire, something that would make him forever ridiculous. I think he was angry at himself for satisfying it. Like it was a betrayal."

"A betrayal?"

"Through that desire and its achievement, he betrayed himself and what he always wanted. He had a name for this, a name for the betrayal, he called it interlude. It was a centripetal force that pulled him into something that he absolutely had to get out of. That he must get out of. The result was that his energy was spent finding a way out at cross purposes to himself."

"The desire that inhabits you."

"For him, it was romantic. But only superficially so. It was a metaphysical presence."

"Is that why you had to make it look like you did the writing? Because he was lost in this interlude or whatever it was and helping you was the only way he could get out of it. It was the only thing left."

"He was a complicated man. He did not share everything with me. If you read the books with Ben Thorne's name on them and if you knew the details of everything that I did to make those books and everything he did, then you would know. Only in those details, in those sentences fragmented and broken apart, could you find answers. But who knows that? I have tried to piece it together..."

She nodded. A slight sense of relief came over her. She felt something leave the room and something else enter. This was what she needed. The judgments, the failed expectations, and trying to make him happy, his presence throughout her life, it wasn't gone, but it was breathing again. The pain that started when he stopped breathing gave way to signs of relief. He may have been incapable of comforting her when they were in this world together, but something in this mess that he left behind was set in motion. He was out of control most of the time. He didn't have a choice. The inheritance was as much as to say I know what I've done, and I understand it, but this is life, this is how people fragment each other, this is how we make each other's worlds and then live there with them. It's what it means to be together and to belong together *with* each other.

"So what happens now?" she asked finally. "What do I do?"

"Well, you are half owner of a company that has assets. That lawyer you talked to is a member of a firm we use. They are the only ones who know the details about the company. They are your lawyers. They will not cheat you. If you want to liquidate your share or sell it or whatever. They will help you do it. But you do own exactly half, so you still have me to deal with so long as we are partners. I am just a writer, and I do not care much what people think or what happens next so long as I can keep working. When you are ready, when you have time, you can contact that lawyer in Seattle, or I can give you the name of his partners in New York. Whatever you like. It is yours. You have my phone number. You can call me any time. I would love it if you returned that offer to me, but that is for you to decide."

"The thing you've been working on, will you publish that as Ben Thorne?"

"That was my intention."

"What if I don't want you to? What if I have a different idea about what comes next?"

"Then we will have to come to an agreement. We cannot do much without the other's permission. We have to collaborate."

She nodded. Then, as they got up to leave the room, Ben Thorne or Wolfe said, as if casually only just remembering it, "Do you have his computer?"

"Yes," she said opening the door.

"Was he in the middle of anything?"

They were now back out in the dining room. Mia, Eirini, and Ginna were sitting in the living room, but abruptly stopped talking and stood up as the two of them came out.

"I didn't really find anything on the computer."

"Remember that he had those weird software engineering habits. He insisted on keeping everything in online code repositories."

"Really?"

"Oh yes. He was a freak about it. Managing differences and versions. I am reasonably sure he had his own source depot somewhere. Look for something like that."

"I will. I most definitely will."

The three women joined them in the dining area. Ben Thorne or Wolfe looked at the group and said, "Now, who is hungry? You simply must let me take you to lunch. I am dying to go to that place that has taken over the old Del Rio."

Mia hesitated and looked at Lena who was visibly changed after coming out of the room. If Lena was amicably disposed, she was too. They both nodded in agreement.

"I'm starving," Eirini said. "Can we get Carl and Fred to join?"

"Carl and Fred?" Ben Thorne or Wolfe asked with some confusion.

"Your interns," Ginna said, rolling her eyes and smiling at Mia. They appeared to have become fast friends while waiting in the living room.

"No, that cannot be their names," he said. "You must be mistaken."

"I'm quite sure," she said dryly, knowing that there was something in this back and forth that was a private joke to him and that he wasn't going to let go of it anytime soon. "I'll text them and let them know where we're going if you can give me the name and street. We can take our car, it's big enough to fit everyone."

"The Grizzly Peak," Ben Thorne or Wolfe said with an ironic flair. "Tell them it's on Washington and Ashley."

Analysis

Ginna managed to secure a table in a private dining area. A young couple recognized Ben Thorne at the hostess station. This was a common occurrence, and usually led to photo requests or feedback on some unacceptable aspect of some published work. The requests and attacks happened more often than you might think. Ginna learned to take precautions.

As they filed into the little section near the back of the restaurant, Ben Thorne insisted that Mia sit at the head of the table. He put Ginna on her right and he sat to her left. Lena was next to him and then Eirini next to her at the end of that side of the table. Fred sat across from her, and Carl was between him and Ginna. After he assigned the seating and while they were getting in place, Lena leaned closer and asked him what she should call him. He noticed that the others had heard the aside and so loudly proclaimed that there was no need to stand on ceremony and that everyone should just call him Ben. He then turned it around and asked if he could do the same. He doted on their affirmative responses and showed great pleasure at their increased familiarity. He went around and said each of their first names. Mia. Eirini. Lena. His voice filled the room.

Despite putting Mia in the position of honor, he took the initiative to lead the discussion and, through eye contact, leaned forward and looked side to side to ensure that everyone was included. This gave the appearance of inclusiveness and empathy, but in fact was a controlling effort to ensure that people didn't go off into their own little silos of conversation. He was expert at holding the attention of everyone in the room and didn't hesitate to do it. He ordered wine for the table, both red and white, and acted as an intermediary between the guests and the wait staff to see if anyone wanted anything else to drink. He ordered one of each item from the appetizer menu and then made sure everyone knew they could share and get additional plates of anything that was more popular.

As the waiters were pouring the wine, Ben Thorne went on at length about the time he had spent on this street, repeating much of what he had said to Lena when they were alone. He described the scene from the earlier book and explained how it had been oversimplified in the TV version. He talked about interlude and how it was an intervention that disrupted power. Things that pull you into them, he said as though lecturing and advising, benefit from the ways in which you scheme your escape. The truly powerful centripetal force is one that knows how to consume and manipulate efforts at evasion. Interlude was a dynamic of power universal to relationships of force and resistance. He referred to Nietzsche's notion of the will-to-power and described interlude as its unstated central pattern. Without waiting for or receiving any encouragement from his audience, he explained how this pattern was the essence of intervention into the history of a particular body tossed about in life.

Nietzsche, he explained without anyone asking, got the solution to this great riddle backwards. The three metamorphoses were inside out. Rather than going under for the sake of learning proper forms of resistance allowing you to overcome the pattern with a newly born childlike innocence (a view he uncritically attributed to the philosopher), we must make ourselves innocent for the sake of resisting the powers that possess us. Ultimately, we must learn to go under. Going under was not a precondition for achieving innocence, rather going under was the end. Going under, he argued, was the way in which the great beast emerges in its extraordinary splendor. This led him into a substantial diversion where he indicated that egalitarianism and the love of equality falls powerless on the immediate and the extraordinary right in front of us. Being in the presence of an extraordinary human, he warned, shows you in the most immediate way that not every human is equal, that some burn brighter and more passionately. That is not to say that this should be attributed to any mundane economic sense, he was not saying that the businessman has changed the world through some consumable gewgaw. No, his point was that the sheer force of will in some human beings could be an immediate object of experience and that when ordinary people found themselves in its presence, they were humbled —and seduced— by it.

This was more than Mia could take. She had begun drinking her wine as soon as it came and hoped it would take some of the sting out of his speech. But it became too much, and she couldn't hold it in any longer. "Why are you the only person talking?" she asked. "Don't you have any self-awareness? How did you write those books without any clue of what's going on around you? I've heard you say that your form of masculism is less misogynistic than any male writer has ever yet managed, and I can see that so much of your work checks those boxes, but you pontificate. Your work sucks the air out of the room just like you're doing now. What you say and what you do are not aligned. That might have flown with your generation, but it isn't cutting it now."

He apologized, explaining that he was just so excited to be out with them. No doubt it was getting the better of him and he must calm down and let someone else talk. "Young people today may be different. That is true, but you should not act like they are in agreement. There are different kinds of people, even among the young. The people in and around Chicago do not line up with the young people growing up in rural California or central Pennsylvania. So please, by all means, I would love to hear your take on this and how the Center is a radical new approach to social problems. Tell us about the work you are doing. I would love to hear about this high-profile case of yours. How is it going? What is the prognosis, any facts you can share? That would be fascinating. Please, let us know how you are spending Ben Thorne's money."

"Excuse me?" she said, obviously irritated. "What does that mean?"

"Ah, my mistake. I did not mean to let the cat out of the bag so abruptly. But, of course, you must know that we are your anonymous donor. That big check we send you every three months. The little donation we made the other day to your fundraiser. I am sure you are putting it to good use. I would so like to hear how. You have my undivided attention."

Mia was agitated by the revelation and even more so because he had used it as a conversational weapon. She could not hide her emotions from her tone. "Is this supposed to be a threat? Someone stands up to you and you can't take it, so you have to flex your muscle? How insecure does someone have to be to use their money and fame to protect themselves from criticism? What were you just saying? You don't even listen to yourself. You'll cut off funds if I don't defer to your wisdom, is that it?"

"Oh, absolutely not," his tone remained polite. "That is not my purpose. In fact, the funding for your Center is so legally bound that I do not think I could cut it off if I wanted to. It is not up to me anymore. The lawyers have made sure of that. You can thank your father, or whatever you call him, for that. You do not have to be nice to me, Mia. You do not have to like me, and there is absolutely nothing I can do about it."

Mia was confused, but Ginna stepped in before she could form a question. She lightly touched Mia's arm and told her that she could confirm this, that she had seen the paperwork establishing the trust but didn't realize how it was connected. There was money in a financial account controlled by lawyers and a signed agreement stating its purpose. It declares that the capital gains must be sent to the Women's Center.

"Minus some withholding for the taxes of course," Ben Thorne added once Ginna finished explaining. He went on still very calmly. "Does that irritate you, Mia? Why? Because it makes my personality more convoluted? I speak out against a cause and then contribute money toward advancing it. You say I fill the room with an overbearing personality that lectures on how wrong it is to be overbearing. I write a book with misogynistic undertones that even the author is not aware of, and then I go and sell it to woke Hollywood. Such contradictions aggravate you. The contradictions in people's lives, those are their seams, those are the places where different powers possessing them come in conflict."

Lena matter of factly pointed out that she thought *Artists of Despair* was an attempt to show exactly how those conflicts appear as experience and how social factors and institutions are driven by them. It's the point of tension between the individual and the institution. The three parts, like the parallel three critiques, she argued, were supposed to show how nothing matters until it is committed to the world through deeds.

"No," Mia responded firmly. "This can't become yet another interpretative maneuver in our reading of the great author's oeuvre. He must be held accountable."

"Accountability?" Ben asked. "You use the justice system and call it corrupt. It is theocratic, white supremacist, and patriarchal and damnit you will file the paperwork to prove it. You see? You accept what contains you. You have no alternative. You preach the dignity of every individual life, buying into the politics of attributes. And that same politics gives us the snowflake and it gives us the neo-Nazi. They are both rabid adherents of personal identity and depend on the assignment of qualities to establish it, for use and abuse by marketeers and profit mongers. Your identity has a price tag."

"There are alternatives."

"There is no such thing. Habeus Corpus, councilor, community-based collaboration is an Enlightenment ideal, the rational kingdom where everyone works to satisfy the collective good. It was uncovered by a scientific worldview that developed its methodology from the intersection of science and engineering at the foundations of the Enlightenment itself, right amid its slave trade and colonial rule. The paradigm of proper science is ballistics. Never forget that the new science and its rigorous methodology had its origins in canon ball trajectories. Never forget that the Chinese invented gun powder and then used it to shoot off fireworks while the Europeans took it to hurl projectiles at rapid speeds and cause massive harm to bodies."

Lena's mouth dropped open. The ideas lost their familiarity, she couldn't understand how the same words could come out of someone else like that with such a different meaning. She wanted to interrupt and understand the origins, but Mia was too fast.

"Science and morality are the property of the Enlightenment, is that your argument? Ethics and epistemology are essentially patriarchal, is that it?"

"And integral to white supremacism, Christian Nationalism, and election denial. There are some attributes for you. That is the ugly truth of interlude. That the demons were able to bear fruit. That there is beauty in ugliness, that there is salvation in coercion. War is peace. The family is a corporation. That is the ugly fact. We can only overcome power by organizing against it and that organization is submission to the most powerful thing there is. Worse, it is the secret to our success. We are incapable of outrunning those structures that have us in their grip."

Mia insisted that he was just uninformed and wasn't familiar with the extraordinary work being done to provide alternatives to European paradigms. But Ben Thorne was not impressed or intimidated, he rattled off a list of marginal thinkers, dismissed them as stooges for the corporatized university, and described how their work had a thesis and followed forms of genre and voice, made arguments, used data, and tried to establish their case over the competitors and alternatives that history provided. These forms of presentation are historically determined. Women have not made any progress in overturning anything, he said, they have only managed to get a seat at the table. This is the pattern he has been raging against his entire life. It is why they accuse him of these small-minded attitudes. They cannot fathom his breadth. He said this so firmly and then tried to make eye contact with Eirini and Lena to make the point personal. Eirini, however, wasn't looking at him, she was leaning across the table and talking to Fred who was leaning across the table and listening closely. Ben Thorne paused and shot a venomous glance at the intern, causing both Lena and Carl to fidget in their seats while Ginna shook her head thinking she was likely to be scolded for this impertinence. "I am not an enemy to women," he said regaining his composure. "I do, however, hold you accountable. You are half this world. Nothing has been done to you. The single man is weaker than the single tiger, but one hundred men can organize and destroy one hundred tigers with traps and projectiles, poisons and complex tactics. Women could have done the same. In fact, I wish you would. I would love to see the world you would make."

"What makes you think you'd be allowed to see it?" Mia responded as the entrees were served and the wait staff kept their wine glasses full. Ben Thorne had ordered each of the entrees on the menu just as he had done with the appetizers. He urged everyone to help themselves to whichever dish they wanted and to speak up if they needed more of anything. All this in bits and pieces during Mia's response. "You don't believe it anyway. You make the grand gesture, but don't worry that it will come true. You know the power in place will prevent it from ever happening and that serves your interests while you appear to be on the right side of history. You're just like any corporation, you can afford to pander because the system serves your interests and continues to do so regardless of what you say."

"That is interlude's pattern. It is powerful and I have pointed to its ubiquity. When I call on women to radically revolutionize the world, I am looking to see that pattern broken. But you are not going to break it by repeating it. That is the farce. Interlude. Where there is no getting out. You are just one more distributed node in a system of actions and epiphenomenal insights meant to obfuscate actions caught in the grips of power. To truly break it, you must begin by accepting that you are just as responsible as those you would accuse. You must accept that mothers have been raising their daughters and their sons in this world for as long as there has been this world. We, every one of us, are sexual beings," he went on. "And every being's great weakness lies in that. A woman will transform herself into what she believes a man wants. A man will do the same. We spend our whole lives this way. We have exactly the world we want. We have exactly the world that men *and* women desire."

"Not everyone wants a man," Mia said.

"That does not matter. We are driven by these aboriginal desires," he responded. "Lesbians are not exempt. You grew up making yourself into what you thought would be desirable. This is how civilization works. These are not opinions. Biology and Anthropology mature as we speak."

Lena didn't take the bait. Instead, she indicated that it was more complicated than that. There's still work being done to sort out the connections. She insisted that Freudian biological anthropology was not the dominant view and that there were many who were dismissive. If men have been selected by women to be the way they are, and vice versa, there is yet to be consensus on how that works and where it comes from. Ben Thorne pressed the point, however, claiming that humans —as they become socialized— become acclimated to behaviors they believe will make them desirable. Being pleasing to each other is at the root of that orientation which we thoughtlessly call empathy.

Ginna responded that empathy isn't the only driving factor. Stirring up people's desire is one thing, stirring up their hate and loathing is another. "There's a lot of hate-fucking going on," she said to general approval and laughter. She suggested that Ben Thorne crafted his position for this latter purpose, to irritate a specific audience. This was where his success came from, she said. Arguably, people's attention came easier when they were angry and scared. Isn't this conversation an example? She urged him to turn his critical eye toward his own behavior and how he pitted himself against others for the sake of getting everyone's eyes and ears on him. Mia touched her hand while she was speaking, and everyone at the table noticed. Ben Thorne noticed. It consolidated the point and added force.

"That makes sense," Lena said in response, ignoring Ben's protests and cutting him off before he could voice them. "And it fits with everything you've been saying, Ben. You can't help it that you've been constructed this way. Your personality has been fashioned, your insights are not original or innovative, they're exactly what we would expect from someone of your age and background."

Ben Thorne leapt to his feet with his wine glass in hand. He raised it and scanned the length of the table even making eye contact with Fred and Carl. "To a truly wonderful and lively afternoon. Friends. I couldn't be happier. Mia, you will always have a place at my table. Lena, Eirini, you are always invited. You need not stand on formality. To each of you. The three graces. How lovely and extraordinary you are. Thank you so much for joining us and letting us share in your lives during these trying times."

Eirini laughed and raised her glass up high, leaning across Lena and clinking Ben's glass. "Chin, chin. To everyone, together we at least stand a chance" she said, and they eased into the moment and took part. Touching glasses and looking each other in the eyes, they drank and laughed. Looking into the bright light shining in Lena's eyes as she raised her glass along with the rest, Mia melted. She knew deep down that struggle offered a way to get closer, to understand better, even when it seemed like that struggle was lost. Her opinion of Ben didn't improve much in the course of lunch, but his approach had been respectful, showed that he wanted her to understand his point of view, and wanted to understand hers. Whatever else he might believe, this sustained their connection and helped them break the pattern of the interlude otherwise preventing their exit.

In the car after lunch with Ginna and Ben, Lena wanted to speak to them alone. Does she know? That's what she wanted to discuss and Ginna, in the emergency seat, wanted to know what she meant after Ben said no. It didn't take long for the car to navigate the roads home and this small exchange of "Does she know," "no," and "do I know what" already took most of the time. The few phrases expanded during the ride and filled the interior when they came to a stop on the street in front of the house. Carl was in the emergency seat of the other car with Eirini next to him teasing him about the bad music he was playing. Fred and Mia were in the back seat together, but they weren't talking or even looking at each other. The car pulled into the driveway and Lena gestured through the window that she would meet them inside.

These cars that drive themselves, the new models, they self-park and the legislation limited their unattended operation to that alone. Well, that and follow mode which was only just approved. The point was that no one knew their way around anymore, the cars do the navigating. The inhabitants could talk and barely pay attention, they could even watch a video or take a nap. The requirement for a person to sit in the emergency seat was increasingly absurd as drivers became more and more detached from operations. Ginna was so distracted during the three-line exchange that she would have been useless had the car malfunctioned and required human intervention. Even if she hadn't been distracted, she didn't know her way around and wouldn't be as quick to steer as the other vehicles driving past.

Tell me. She wanted to know what she didn't know, what this young woman from out of nowhere thought she should know. I can't tell you, Ben Thorne said. He gestured toward Lena. I am serious, I cannot break the agreement, but you can. What Lena heard and what Ginna heard may vary, their emotions may have changed the meaning or made it insidious or manipulative in retrospect, but the words themselves were what they were even if no one could say any longer exactly how they were spoken, with what tone, and what gestures and body language.

He told me before lunch, she said slowly, deliberately, that Ben Thorne is a corporation owned and fully operated by this man here, and – previously—my father. Now, me. It wasn't polished and perfect. She didn't plan how to say it but got it out and made it clear.

Is this true, Ginna wanted to know. Yes, he said, because it was, and his face told Lena that he wanted to tell her for a very long time. His face didn't tell Ginna this because she wasn't looking and was too puzzled and focused elsewhere to see it in his eyes. She was looking at Lena when she asked whether it was true. Lena confirmed.

What is your real name then? she muttered when finally looking at him. In many ways Ben Thorne. It has been almost forty years. Technically though, it is not, then he whispered Stephen Wolfe while looking down and away and anywhere he could that wasn't Ginna's eyes. Feeling whatever it was that she was feeling, she didn't know yet what that was, she tried to have a reaction, tried to figure out what it meant. This was a betrayal, and she was supposed to be angry. But it explained so much, and she knew it already. Didn't she? She didn't feel betrayed. Why not? She thought she knew someone and then found out there was something she didn't know. Something important he hid from her. Where can she look for cues and signals for the right way to feel? Who could tell her?

Ben Thorne or Wolfe tried to say that he did not think it mattered since it was just a name, but Ginna wanted to know more, wanted to know whose work it was, and Ben Thorne insisted that Ben Thorne did it all. But from whose head does it come? She insisted, again trying to trace the subject of everything she knew. She was of the opinion for these last years that Ben Thorne was a great writer and a wise man even if he were sometimes crass and rude and mean-spirited. She knew him to be passionate and provocative and that turning these things into craft could be visionary and extraordinary. Now she couldn't see him anymore. She wanted him to explain her broken expectations and her misconceptions. She wanted him to explain why she needed them.

Ben Thorne or Wolfe obliged not because he was wise, pulling brilliant explanations and insights from the ether, but because his colleague of many years instigated a response through the person of his daughter, the spitting image of her mother, sitting there before him in the front seat, without guile and without malice, wanting everything to be out in the open among the people who mattered. Lena suspected that Ginna needed to know this, that her affection demanded it.

Em was awful in a way. Brilliant in others. Ben Thorne wanted very much to make that clear to both of them, but he only looked at Ginna while he spoke. No affectations, no squirming. He was ready to face the consequences. He channeled his colleague and friend and went on about how awful his work had been, how horrible and unreadable it was. He just couldn't say it. The smallest things grew large in the telling. Somehow, he knew how to weave meaning and event into perfect sketches. He knew how, but he couldn't do it. He had the techne, but could not fulfill the project, he lacked the voice, he lacked the genre, he could not give flesh to characters, that was what was beautifully and seamlessly delivered in the earliest draft of *Fragmented*. The literary agent loved something about that book, something that made her take it on, but she couldn't bring herself to accept it as is or to describe exactly how it needed to be fixed. Only Em saw it. The flaws and the ways story needed to come. How the voice should find its content. Wolfe sent him the manuscript and he worked it over. The impact was enormous, and the literary agent none the wiser. When she learned that the young author wanted to use a pseudonym, she didn't resist and didn't question. The only one who knew, she took the secret to her grave before the author achieved notoriety.

How did I not see this? Ginna wondered aloud without expecting an answer. You could not see it because we hid it, he responded. He knew she would find something lacking in herself for not coming along the right way, for not being on top of everything, and for giving so much of herself to these projects. He tried to tell her that it did not matter, that Em wanted it this way. He wanted to remain unseen. Some people want to be in front, and some in back. Attention would rob him, get inside his head and tell him how to feel and think. He spent his life striving for a purity that was, by his own admission, unattainable.

Ginna still did not know how to feel, but feeling was everywhere and on the verge of overwhelming her. Ben Thorne or Wolfe told her he did not think she should cry, that it was not worth crying about. She was not going to cry, she said looking firmly at him. If anything, she was struggling to prevent herself from tearing his eyes out.

Mia must have known something was going on. She hadn't gone into the house. She stood by the front window and stared out looking into the car. Lena was hyper alert. This was visible from a distance. Ben Thorne was hyper alert. Anyone would have been able to see it. Ginna was at the center of a storm. There was quiet there too, but a storm all around. If you asked her, she wouldn't have been able to tell you why she felt responsible, but she did. Mia couldn't resist the draw. She couldn't look away or pay attention to anything else. She went out onto the front porch without an agenda but wanted to get closer thinking maybe she could see things differently from there. Mia knew not to trust her angle of vision absolutely, but hedged with twists and turns, with an open door and a view from the porch with her hands on her hips.

In the car, Lena wanted to know if Ginna was okay, but Ginna didn't know if she was okay. Ginna just didn't know. That's where she was. Didn't know anything, she thought. There was a knock on the window next to Lena. The passenger side window. Mia ever coming closer came right up to the side of the car. Lena put down the window. Is everything okay, are you okay, Ginna? Mia asked bringing everyone's question out into the open. They wanted to know. I don't know, she said, I didn't know. I don't know. May I go inside, she asked. I need time.

Mia pulled open the door and took Ginna out of the car. No one objected. Ben Thorne or Wolfe got out and watched Ginna walk with Mia back to the house. Lena was still sitting in the front seat when he got into the emergency side door and sat next to her. I hope I didn't, she started to explain, and he said I am glad you did before she could finish. I really did want to tell her all this time. I wanted her to know. I am glad you did. I was hoping you would. She is the closest I have ever come to having a family, and I wanted to be able to share this with her. Why don't you tell her that? Lena said, not needing an answer but thinking it was good advice. I should, I will, he said knowing that she was right, happy that she was there to say it, and there when he repeated it back to her.

He did not think he could explain. People are different, they have strengths and different abilities. Sometimes it takes more than one of us to make something. Em was unique, for better or worse, he was unique. In fact, he was quite sure it was mostly for the worse. How do you mean? she wanted to know. Being successful in this world, he tried to say simply, involves meeting with the demands of your contemporaries. You see? No one is this or that, we are what we are through those around us. To be unique, is to be nothing. It is to matter to no one. As a father and as a husband, there were billions like him. As an engineer, millions. But as a man, I was never sure. He seemed lonely to me. I met lots of people in my life. As the spokesman, I was privileged to meet Kings and Queens of the different worlds we inhabit. I never met anyone like him.

You're giving him more credit than before. Before, it seemed like you were the writer, and he was just an editor. But now it seems like he was a storyteller, and you were just voice and genre. Nothing more. I think you're saying something different now. No, I am saying what I have always said. Ben Thorne is a writer, Ben Thorne is an author, Ben Thorne is the prize winner and the laureate. That is what I said before and that is what I meant. That unreadable book. And the commentary he provided. That is what he could do by himself. He knew it was ridiculous. You never saw what I could do by myself because there was nothing. I could not even do that. But together we could do this, everything we have done. Ben Thorne wrote those books. Ben Thorne wrote those lectures. If you could read that huge monstrosity, that awful and terrific tome, you would see he spells it out. The way it speaks and writes, the way it surfaces into individual people. He wrote it down. He took responsibility for every word, but he did not want his face out there.

Lena, who thought she understood the message delivered earlier that day, was now beginning to wonder whether she knew anything. What should she feel, what emotions should she have and who could she turn to for advice? She was breaking apart. Every sentence in her head was like running water. Ginna went into the house, but her frame of mind remained behind and occupied Lena's body. It was a hobgoblin that moved about the car, not knowing what to feel and feeling it anyway, feeling it creep up on you and turn your head or open your mouth and point you this way or that. The hobgoblin incorporated and brought outcomes and results, fodder for analysis and data for computation: actionable content demanding purpose and decision.

Did he ever tell stories from his teaching days? Ben Thorne or Wolfe asked simply. There was a young woman, a college student, twenty or so years old. She came to him before or after class, he did not remember which, and explained why she missed so many sessions and was unable to turn in her assignments. She had been diagnosed with ovarian cancer and had been struggling with treatment options and recovery throughout the semester. Em cut her off and told her she did not need to explain or give details, that it was okay and that his class should be the least of her concerns. Hand in what you can when you can, come when you can, let me know what I can do, if I can do anything. That is what he said, but when recounting the tale, he was angry. He did not like that this young woman had to say so much to a stranger. He could see the pain in her face and that no small part of it was coming from having to tell him about this personal experience that she had not fully digested herself. He was angry at what forced her to it. What conditions must exist, he thought, to make her think she has to go into such detail? The institution caused the lying, and the lying forced the policy and the policy forced her to tell a stranger.

For better or worse, he was unique. He wanted to experiment with being unregarded. Not disregarded. Never regarded. His notion, he wrote it down in that huge, horrible book, was that this young woman's desire was built around the social urge and was its most dangerous form. Desire that shaped minds and behavior. It's what made us bent and broken by the schemes in our history. This was what was wrong with the world. She was forced to tell him things, and he was forced to wonder whether perhaps she was sick or whether she had merely acquired sociopathic abilities to spin any tale to achieve an end. The thoughts were an abomination, the actions cruel and impossible. What type of system permits this to become routine?

Emerging personality coerced by excavation repurposing the individual for itself. Ben Thorne was guilty. We were guilty. The corporate body holds that guilt and its sting. That sociopathic question that corrupted every outpouring, it was questionable. Deposited long before, it is what drew it out of her in the end. The anti-social social being led us to reveal what it is inappropriate to reveal, to portray what it is wrong to portray. On the other hand, the extraordinary freedom of human beings, distributed in personality, is vulnerable to coercion. The story of the Professor/student was the wasp/orchid assemblage that the philosopher described. The distributed moment was itself the focus and the specimen, it was the person made real. Our judgment must be harsh and clear-eyed with steely vision in claiming the way we orient ourselves and the way we capitalize, the way we share and the way our meaning seeps out of us. Subject and object were mythology for the sake of storytelling. He knew that. He sought out the higher organism for the sake of it. His idea bubbled over for years before finding an opportunity to come forward. *Fragmented* was his excuse, it was his vehicle. He conjured it with the intention of making it real. The notion of the collective was conjoined. Ben Thorne.

His was a persistent reverie on the subject/object dichotomy. Originating in Ann Arbor, he replaced it with the one and the many of a distributed model. The real question, as it turned out over the many years required to realize it, was not the boundary between the one and the many, but why did we ever think it was a problem in the first place? Why did we ever think there was only one and from it many? Not, how is the self constructed by the other, but why did we ever think they were separated in the first place?

She listened to the pearls and the drops, to the ways and the whats of it. His voice was calming. This is why Ginna departed when Mia poked her head in. She did not want the calm, she wanted the storm, but could not find it because she couldn't recognize anything anymore. There was no one there to tell the tale since Ben Thorne was no longer whole. Lena could complete the circuit if she knew it was now hers to complete, but she sat in silence. Lifted and dropped by that same homunculus, that evil apish kobold that threatened to jump onto our back at every moment where we looked each other in the eye and wondered what was having its way with us through us in us around us and toward us.

There was that terrible book he was writing back in those days. Something about Heidegger and Aristotle. Ben Thorne or Wolfe was lost in an effort to explain it, not to Lena and certainly not to the empty space Ginna left behind, but to himself. He was trying to explain it to himself because even he was forgetting what to feel and what emotions were right, what reactions were proper and what expectations in order. He sent that idiotic manuscript off to someone for some reason, something he cooked up no doubt. They said this is not the kind of thing we are interested in publishing. This twisted him somehow. Not broken but bent. This thing that came out of him was the only thing that could come out of him. He was quite sure of that, and they were not interested in it. They represented everyone, and he knew they were right. He was not even sure what it was, but he knew they were right even if being right made it impossible for him to know any longer what to feel, what emotions were expected, and what he should produce and deliver now. Where were his obligations and what were his alliances? That was where the whole notion, in those stories, that is where the essence of the matter came from. The unattended, the drive to become nothing, a non-subject, a non-object, a thing not seen, a thing not having ever been.

In that link that came to him, he thought he discovered the meaning of true evil and wanted to document it. Not the faux monologue of an enlightened subject, but a truly evil and horrifying sample. The beast or the god that Nietzsche wrote about, it was pure evil. Or pure good. Without the shadows of others, it was impossible to tell. He completed an experiment indicating corruption, and he wanted to document it, to confess everything, to let everyone know that this is where the pattern led, but also to show that the alternative was fraught with peril. Inauthentic or authentic. That is the choice, and you will regret both. He knew this better than anyone. He was alone in knowing it because no others knew how to hear it or how to gather meaning from it. This was what it meant to be unique. It meant you utter cries that fall nowhere and leave no impression, they were the unattended words of no one.

Nietzsche said you have to go under so that you can go over. Camel Lion Child. In the unattended work, there was a reversal. Individuality was an achievement, and the child its nemesis, born to a world ready to attend to its every need and care for it, nurture it. There was no value judgment here. In fact, the forensics of value judgment were strictly left behind. Rather, this individual, this camel, made its own value. And the only way to know is to go under, to achieve that state specific to creation where no one else could share it. Complex and contradictory, since such a beast was both anti-social and criminal, but also fit with some paradigms of the great artist, this was another facet of the farce called interlude. The effort to escape the pull was a becoming felonious that seduced us into following through on the mythology. The dome of stars. The feeling in one's soul. The hypocrisy of sleeping through one's life with no sense for what transpires along the way.

Unique.

Or the appearance of it. The mythology of it. So many stories and so many parables. Cautionary tales and yet the draw cannot be evaded. You are lucky, he used to say to me. When you think of him, you think of a bug. When I think of him, I think of a throat closing and a man gasping for air. Not remotely and hypothetically, but in full possession of the imaginative force in a story happening around him, luring him into it, and making him account for every feeling and every effect.

Lena pulled back. She could not engage. Every step would have been unstable, every response, unknown. She could not give him anything to hold him up while he struggled to make sense of what they did and what it meant now that the secret was out. He fell back on reliable sources. She shuddered as she remembered his last breath.

Ben Thorne or Wolfe explained that Em did not like Gargamel, he thought its take on radical individualism was ontologically naïve and socially ridiculous. But he didn't like the Smurfs either. He thought their take on community was ontologically ridiculous and socially naïve. The bottom line was that it was a fabrication, a myth to keep it going: the glue that kept it together. It was the origin of feeling and knowing, of how to orient in the midst of confusion. It was responsible for expectations and its grip on our lives amounted to production and distribution along proper demographic lines. He desperately wanted an alternative, but the only thing he could fall back on was the endless potential of human beings: our capacities to love and feel, think and act. He adored them but thought them corrupted, and was heartbroken when their products were consumed by his peers. Potential displayed as the delusions of a crackpot made ridiculous by his aspirations. To be unique, for better or worse, was to fail, to never become real, to never find a place. The cost was unrecoverable and made life uncomfortable. The true story, the one he told over and over again, was how this farce made it possible to let each other down, fail each other by not realizing ourselves in perfect union with expectations coming from somewhere else, somewhere we could not control nor even describe if our lives depended on it. And they did.

Only if we constrained the order adversely integrating us with others could we even begin to understand connections and their meaning. Was this due to their sovereignty, was it how sovereignty worked? The commonwealth, by nature, superimposed itself upon everything. Only by constraining it were we subjected to it. The sovereign must be visible. Surveillance tactics worked best when directed at its power.

He muttered such nonsense endlessly, thinking it meaningful. It was underneath every story and played a role in every conversation. He had no choice but to fabricate Ben Thorne. You must understand that. He thought it was the only way to tell people the things that mattered without hurting them. Otherwise, the delicate wings would break off or splinter. He would weep and speak of you like that. His dear girl, splintering around him trying not to be alone, but he did not know if he could say it. He could not give you what he wanted you to feel. He thought maybe if the mechanism produced a work, that work could lead you through it.

She wanted to go inside and didn't want him to come with her. She was leaving and he should go. She would talk to Ginna and explain. They might be able to figure something out together, some way that might help them both to understand. It might let them learn what to expect and what to feel. After she got out, something stopped her on the walkway, and she came back around to the driver's side door. He put down the window.

She told him that *Princess Myshkin* inspired her in ways she thought her parents didn't understand, but that somehow some stranger captured it in such perfect form, in such a perfect story with such a friendly voice and tone. He nodded and smiled gently. Ben Thorne or Wolfe told her to check the dedication, and reminded her that he never had any children. It said: to my daughter, wherever she might be.

Inside the house, the chaos of not knowing had begun to spread. Carl was at the dining table with a book, but he couldn't concentrate. Eirini and Fred were in the little office, leaning over one of the screens and looking at something together. JP's room at the back of the kitchen was empty now, he must've cleared out when the commotion began. Mia's suitcase was pushed up against the window on the far side. He would be sleeping at a friend's house so she could have his bed. Up the stairs, there was the bathroom that the three women shared. Zoe's room was at the top of the stairs and Beth's was next to the bathroom. Lena's room was at the front of the house, furthest from the top of the stairs. They were small rooms, but at least they each had their own. The door to Lena's room was closed. She approached slowly and knocked. After a few seconds she went in and found Mia and Ginna sitting quietly on the bed. They looked up at her, but no one spoke. Lena sat down on the chair next to the closet. She had to move some clothes around to make room. The floor was crowded with the two suitcases. She hadn't unpacked, and Eirini's lay next to it taking up the floor space between the bed and the window.

It was clear that Ginna hadn't said anything. Not because she said so, but Lena felt it. The non-knowledge was there. They were just sitting, and it surrounded them. Lena spoke it, put it into the clearest possible terms and then asked if they could at least agree that this is not information for the public. She said he wanted Ginna to keep calling him Ben. He is Ben. It has been nearly forty years. He said she is his family. He couldn't tell her. He wanted to, but he couldn't.

Ginna nodded. She knew that. It nagged at her even if it never found the words. He never seemed autonomous, there was always so much in his process that came from somewhere else. She should have known. She had the pieces in front of her. His personality cast a shadow.

Mia was attentive, but she didn't want to interrupt. She went off to make tea while Lena and Ginna remained and wondered how things would change, how he would finish the work in progress. Lena explained that he was interested in knowing what was on the laptop. They nodded to signal everything came together. There wasn't much to say. Ginna didn't ask Lena how she should feel but she read her to learn how she did feel and took cues from it. They had different strengths. They could be a team. They could collaborate. They might have already begun. How had they been fooled?

I wanted to believe in the mythology, Ginna said. Even with my education and study, I bought into that whole lie of the independent artist who creates something out of nothing.

It makes sense, Lena explained. Ben's actions make sense. He loves the attention. He wants to give readings and go to conferences, he wants to publicize his genius and socialize with an adoring readership. Ginna nodded in full agreement. She saw it first-hand, and knew how easy and guilt-free he was. He was playing a part, an assigned role. He had a clear conscience because Em gave him permission. They wanted things just as they were. Lena said that was the part that was so mystifying. It wasn't Ben's actions, they fit with everything she saw in just these last few hours. The thing she couldn't wrap her brain around was her father's role. Demanding absolute secrecy, wanting complete seclusion. Hiding it from his wife and daughter. In an attention-driven world, it was as if he wanted to be nothing, non-existent and invisible. This thought came to her in waves. It kept pulsing.

Ginna pointed out that so much of the work, the stories, many of them, involved characters with similar qualities. One that was flashy and outgoing, another that was more private and hidden. Nature before you and nature that loves to hide. The light and the dark. She could see, and always had, that the books were a constant conflict between them. They had disagreements. She remembered some, but thought they were just standard editorial jitters. Often, she didn't see the before and the after, she didn't see the full body of their debate. Now, she recalled the language in their disputes and the wording of their compromises. There was never a winner. Instead, they would work it out so that both approaches found their way into the work. The dispute would become dialogue. She said that there were many critics who called this out and hailed it as a major innovation in narrative form.

Was it a fraud? they both wondered. Is it less masterful if two authors are involved? Are dialogues less magical when they are true, did that simplify what the critics thought was a master class in altering perspective?

Mia returned while they were ruminating. This proves my point, she said. He's a misogynist, and he isn't. I knew it. This explains everything.

You can't tell anyone. That's a shame. It'd make it so much more notable. The patriarchy doubles, it turns on itself. It splits and starts telling its story. Think of the rereading this would trigger. All the work reread as a battle. I know, I know, Ginna said. She saw the popular readings impacted by it. So much hung on the idea of the lone artist and his creative muse. Now, everything would change.

Not just backwards, but forwards, Lena reminded them. What about this thing he's working on now? Can he finish it alone? No, I don't think he can, Ginna said. She saw maps unfold before. Everything is so familiar. The voice and the tone covered everything, and it came from everywhere: Ben Thorne's style. There was no doubt, but the story and the material, the order, the way characters represented this or that and how they muddled everything by struggling. Other worldly. *Washington & Ashley* had none of that. Ben Thorne was locked in a vision, and no one man could get there. She never understood where it came from, how someone like him could do it. Now, she saw.

In the end, Ginna said she didn't feel betrayed or manipulated. Going over these last years, they spent too much time together for him to be false. There were things he kept from her, but there were things he didn't. He never lied about the facts. He needed to get that feedback, he couldn't do it until Em wrote back, he would say that, be very clear about it. She knew how important his contributions were, she chose to emphasize the singular creator and the myth of the autonomous thinker. Even knowing it was a lie, she chose to believe it. She wasn't angry, but that didn't mean she felt the same way anymore. He was different now, more vulnerable, less ethereal.

She could not take her eyes off Lena. That was where the mystery lay. She wondered how much of his mind worked in hers. How many generations does it take to produce the right mixture of qualities? They agreed to keep this between them, but they couldn't stop the wondering. There was nothing left to say. They thought aloud but didn't make progress. There were no reinforcements or support, and they hesitated to leave the room.

Lena left before Mia and Ginna were ready. They needed more time, she felt, and so she took her tea and stood up and left them there. She went downstairs and sat down next to Carl at the dining room table. He looked up at her and asked what was wrong.

Nothing, it's just been a long day. So many strange things. So many.

He pursed his lips and nodded but had no idea what she was talking about. Eirini and Fred were laughing in the office next door. She called to ask what was so funny. She hadn't heard Fred laugh like that, it was so carefree and absent any cynicism. Eirini came to the door and described the video she was making Fred watch. There were many scenes of animals, dogs and cats mostly, doing silly things. Falling over each other, running around terrified at something ridiculous. Fred followed her out and moved into the living room where he sat down on the couch. Lena followed him and said she never had him figured for a pet videos guy. Eirini moved past her and plopped down next to Fred. I'm trying to loosen him up, she said.

Not everything is so serious. They agreed.

Carl moved past her too and sat down on the other end of the couch next to Eirini. He explained the role that distraction is supposed to play. Fred fell into a dispute with him. Carl thought distraction was meant to draw attention away from the class struggle and focus it on more culturally insignificant things. Fred said that class was just a way to spin power, there were those who have it and those who don't. We were reified into collective subjects and even the owner of the means of production was a slave. There were haves and have nots, Carl countered, the point was always to make sure that the have nots remained obedient, and this required distraction.

Eirini watched them like she was at a tennis match. She applauded the back and forth, it was fun to her, something she had grown used to. Fred and Carl were just realizing their friendship as they had been trained to do. Eirini was entertained. Mia and Ginna were not there. These were the positions. This was where and how everyone was at that moment when Lena loses her calm and cool demeanor. Her rapidly increasing intensity shocks them.

Fred and Carl start down the road of trying to figure out how race fits in their dispute, but they never get very far. Lena's voice overtakes the room, it is a shout, and it is a howl. She orders silence and demands peace. Eirini exchanges looks with both Fred and Carl, and they stop talking. She stands up and goes over to Lena who is now standing at the seam between the dining room and the living room. Eirini puts her hands on Lena's shoulders and tries to get her to look her in the eyes, but she isn't responding. She doesn't want any more and makes it very clear.

It is not entertainment. What is it you think you're doing? It is a stream of words, accusations. Eirini tries to get her to face her, but she won't do it. She is there and she is not there. You aren't creating anything, your argument isn't getting you anywhere. She isn't talking to anyone in particular, but she is talking about them, and they know it. They don't know what to say. They are trying to apologize, but she can't hear them. She goes on. She talks so loudly, almost screaming. You are deliberating about nothing. When you go back and forth over something that isn't there, something that is off somewhere, you're talking nonsense. How everything aligns, what substances are real, and which are fictional. It's bullshit.

Mia and Ginna come down the stairs. Mia wants to know what is going on. Eirini looks at her. Only Lena's voice is in the air. A look of fear and desperation fills Eirini's eyes. Mia moves to them both and puts her arms around Lena from behind. The three of them together like that. She quiets down but continues through the lull.

Who cares what we think?

Institutions and discourse. Framing a study. It follows fashion, otherwise chaos. Unfiltered and coarse, what are they missing and why?

One begets another and another, we excavate and supplement, add our two cents, and then more and more and more. It goes on like that forever. We will never get to the end, we will never shut up.

The lunatic fringe teaches us. There are nut jobs, there are innovators, and there are defenders of tradition. Actions and words. What's real? Behavior speaks louder, doesn't it? She doesn't look around, she isn't connecting, there is no one else there. She is alone. Eirini and Mia are holding on so dearly, they won't let go. They want her back. Who cares what nonsense Ben Thorne spouts? You see. We are so lost, so very lost. It has us and we can't argue our way out of it. Words do not escape.

There are tears in her eyes and running down her cheeks. She is not crying, but there are tears. She says the masters of forensics should go fuck themselves. She yells that Fred is right and he is wrong when he says it. She screams that Carl is right and wrong when he says it. Sometimes, she says, when it happens it's gone and when it hasn't happened yet, it is very much there and with you. Mia has her from behind, Eirini in front. Mia's head on her left shoulder, Eirini's on the right.

We must let the things that are silent speak. She is so forceful. The tears keep coming but her voice doesn't crack, her gaze does not waver. She is so certain. You have to understand this, she is not crying. There are tears. She is not crying.

Feedback

For me, the interludes are always Nietzsche's. Between play. That is the way I laugh Nietzsche to myself: the one about whom I am reluctant to say.

To actively not say is to renounce, and the hypothetical need of the systematic dismantling demands Zarathustra's services. Who better? Who else? A gift. The greatest gift. The one who excels at the gift-giving virtue. But I renounce Zarathustra, perhaps he has betrayed me, I must beware...

Rather, for reasons that I also renounce and actively do not say, there is the metric of Human, all-too-human. There is a struggle greater than I can know going on in this book that, until the last few weeks, I never thought much of. Why now? I renounce the reasons. That does not prevent anything, and perhaps only assumes the guise of preventing something from being said, prevents it only for those who have long since given up on hearing, those terrible deaf ones who never hear what you want even when the desire comes as a howl. But this should be clear, it is the howl that has deafened them. It should not have been so piercing.

> Art makes the thinker's heart heavy.—How strong the metaphysical need is, and how hard nature makes it to bid it a final farewell, can be seen from the fact that even when the free spirit has divested himself of everything metaphysical the highest effects of art can easily set the metaphysical strings, which have long been silent or indeed snapped apart, vibrating in sympathy; so it can happen, for example, that a passage in Beethoven's Ninth Symphony will make him feel he is hovering above the earth in a dome of stars with the dream of immortality in his heart: all the stars seem to glitter around him and the earth seems to sink farther and farther away.—If he becomes aware of being in this condition he feels a profound stab in the heart and sighs for the man who will lead him back to his lost love, whether she be called religion or metaphysics. It is in such moments that his intellectual probity is put to the test.

Ouch. I thought I remembered reading somewhere that Nietzsche thought one had to be mortally wounded by every phrase in this work to have been its proper audience. I imagine Nietzsche a giant, with millions of pinholes burned into him. And each has a name. Art makes the thinker's heart heavy. A name.

Deconstruction —it must be said— is not without its art. The dismantling of system has its impetus in the drive to make an art of it. This is the self-dismantling of the metaphysical even so far as it is dressed up as self-dismantling. The horror of the metaphysical imposition placed on the predicament of the deconstructor is beyond redemption. Making art of the metaphysical, its becoming techne through a technique called writing —the writing of metaphysics— already says it as a drive to reconcile, to recuperate what lies at its origin.

Do I show my age when I say the best critical response one could possibly have to Nietzsche is, "fuck off"?

Would then deconstruction be nothing other than metaphysics' own wondering about itself, wondering -endlessly— about the meaning of its death, the nature of its death, the imminent not to be outstripped coming of its death? And more, it's wandering toward it, not merely a wandering, but a fleeing, flying even, right into the face of it. So much so, that its uncanny impossibility becomes the be all and end all of metaphysics' deconstruction. Such is to be hoped. But only on the ground of a never yet recurrent reconciliation with the very meaning of the metaphysical in human being. What ground is a never yet, a not-yet? The entire movement of the death of god is the origin of existence in the not-yet, in the wondering/wandering of death, and —with it (wandering/wondering)— the artist's sublimation (making sublime) of the movement back to itself in the unreconcilable ground of the art. It is practiced as yearning, as wanting-to-be. Wanting to be what? Doesn't matter, something, anything at all, for metaphysics, even if only its deconstruction. Whatever this means in essence, at the very least it means that deconstruction and the systematic dismantling will have had something to say about it, will have had a part in it, will have hung on to it, loved it, and been bathed in the pleasure of its highest glory. And this, a moment of symphony —or does he make it sound rather like sympathy? But for whom? For the free spirit itself.

How beautiful it would be if there were indeed gods. Nietzsche doesn't deny this, does everything he can to do quite the opposite. The reconciliation of the thinker with this beauty, what should that be called? With matters of beauty, with the manners of beauty, the only techne left is art, and fine arts at that: the only practitioners capable of earning the name artists. What a yearning there is in the name. The culture, the history of our kind, has always said "artist" with a longing, with a meaning that raises any lovers of beauty above themselves. What are these fateful voices? What is the language they speak and why should they be the highest representation of an aspiration coveted by any and all inspiration to be more, to exceed oneself, to extend finally and at last beyond oneself? The artist has always been prone to exuberant self-description. Occasionally, even in the case of those artists who have come to be known as extraordinary, art is nothing other than this longing. The artist's art amounts to little more than an interest in becoming an artist: not from a lack of content, not from a need for subject matter or material setting them apart. Something so superficial and useful is never enough to bear the artistic — i.e., parasitic— spirit. Instead, the artist finds the longing that humanity holds dear (even today when art seems so commercial, the Hollywood movie star continues to derive a strange pleasure from being called an artist even when they are selling you a car). The artist aspires to become herself, to inhabit the form in the same artistic longing that has become the object of longing. As such, the drive to art is nothing other than the drive to metaphysics, to reconciliation ('to become what one is'). There is little more to such an art than patterns of practice —void of content, meaning even— and approaches to longing and yearning. It is not for nothing that Nietzsche envisioned the artist in its highest form as an experiment, a hypothesis produced by the origins of will-to-power to organize and pattern themselves. It is a preferred —ha!— pattern and the reconciliation of an aboriginal dynamic.

In matters of systematic dismantling, of deconstruction, of metaphysics' longing for itself, we must take care even with such seemingly dismissive approaches. The experimental nature of the artist, the artist as an economy of effort aiming at realizing a true self within her, is also an attempt at incarnating that same sea of forces in waves that acutely recur: the artist, pure and simple, is Zarathustra. He is the one who provides the message of the eternal recurrence, the one whose method and matter of prophesy are one and the same: Zarathustra too, greatest of artists, marks the moment of reconciliation between the origin and the end, between the play of this and that, the moment of reconciliation even as interlude.

As such, there is something pristine about Nietzsche's inversion of the philosophical spirit. He —more than anyone else in the history of philosophy— stands Aristotle on his head for the first time. For reconciliation is not an activity with an activity —as one might read Aristotle, but potential with potential. The origin as unending dynamic (and because it is unending, it is a moved unmover) comes to a full stop through a variety of instantiations that experiment and hypothesize their way up a ladder or chain of being, building more, until -ultimately— Zarathustra emerges as the teacher of the end, the end of the end, of the eternal recurrence. Thus, Zarathustra speaks of an unending potential that can be achieved (sic). Achieved? But truthfully, fairly, ha, there is no such talk of achievement. It is precisely because Zarathustra speaks of something that ultimately cannot be achieved that he is Zarathustra. If once he suffers himself the thought that he has some purpose, some goal to achieve, it will fill him with a great and crippling nausea. And, of course, it does. In the very moment when Zarathustra realizes his own end, he becomes sick. Vomiting out the recurrent thought that provides him his realized end is not his finally coming to think it, to understand it, to realize himself as the one who can clearly and loudly proclaim the message as though preaching it. Rather, Zarathustra's recovery from the nausea of the eternal recurrence and his understanding of himself as its teacher is ultimately his having done with it, his no longer having anything to say about it.

This is what marks Zarathustra as a convalescent, what forces him to reconcile with the necessity of recovery. And recovery is the recovery of that from which one has become sick. Note the economy of movement. The sickness is not a fall from grace, not the result of something external or alien inhabiting and dismantling the essential health of the prophet. Rather, Zarathustra —the teacher of the eternal recurrence— is made sick by the thought that he is a teacher of. He is sick of his health, sick from his health, it is precisely his health that makes him sick. Of what does he suffer? His health. The cause and the symptoms, the disease and its cure, are one and the same for Zarathustra, they are his health. The eternal recurrence makes Zarathustra sick, and Zarathustra is the teacher of the eternal recurrence. So it is with teachers and their teachings.

The recovery then, what will that amount to if anything? In Nietzsche's rendition, the recovery amounts to the coming to an end of teaching. Zarathustra continues to wander but he seems oddly silent, as though unable to bear the burden of his own task, of his own aim. Perhaps he has surrendered it? But for the sake of what? What does Zarathustra become, if anything, in the aftermath of his illness? Well, he seems to be an endless victim of temptation. One after another. So many monkeys, so many fools, so many distractions and ill tidings. Zarathustra does not look away or run from such things as he did when he was the teacher, but rather invites them into his home, extends his hand to them, does everything in his power to make the temptations as tempting, as familiar, as overwhelming, as possible. What then is it that tempts him? Is it the particular personalities of those he meets in the forest? Is it rather temptation itself? Are these two different possibilities?

Personality is the higher man, and it may tempt more than anything. The temptation of personality is the temptation to be anything at all. I am such and such, this is me, etc. Doesn't he say in *Ecce Homo* something about how attributing himself with such and such a nature is a violent rage against the pride of his instincts? How odd. What type of person is he? One that rejects the seductive tendency to say, "I am this type of person or that type." Is it unfair to use Nietzsche's autobiography to demonstrate the meaning of Zarathustra?

Zarathustra strives to be tempted by personality. He is tempted by types, by kinds, by ways of Being, by patterns of will-to-power. He does whatever he can to resist. But here temptation comes to mean anything but the absence of will-to-power. It is the most intense and fullest expression of the attempt to resist being anything at all. This is a reconciliation with will-to-power because as much as the striving of world reaches out to organize itself into this or that for this or that end, it also resists this organization. Resists it because of its definiteness, the limitation it offers to the swirling dynamic of power. What an odd form of metaphysical reconciliation this provides. The human being attempts to be nothing human and so instantiates will-to-power as a particularity that rejects its particularity. And why? Because that is already to reconcile oneself with the unending potential that dynamically persists as the be all and end all of Being. This is an inversion of Aristotle, no doubt. And in such a fantastic way as to suggest the very impossibility of the inversion in terms set down by the philosopher himself. Suggest here meaning accept. The dynamic of inversion accepts the principles of that which it inverts —and perhaps is attempting a reductio, but to no avail— and inverts even them. Thus, what becomes clear is the impossibility of the principles to be inverted. Opposite lies the pattern and the pattern of thinking at work in the inversion reveals the pattern at work in what is being inverted. That pattern is ultimately one and the same. The drive for an unending reconciliation with something that resists coming to an end and from an origin. Only in the impossibility of the inversion can the possibility of the initial position emerge. In this case the origin emits a possibility and is already its inversion —meaning, for Aristotle, the origin is much much more than merely possible.

If I'm not careful in this line of thinking, I might suggest something that is absurd from about every point of view imaginable. That is, I might suggest that Nietzsche is the crowning achievement of metaphysics, that will-to-power is the complete inversion of substance from activity to potency. This is absurd because, in making that move, I will enact the highest moment of metaphysics by systematically inscribing it into a historical movement that has a crowning achievement, where what has been achieved is its own inversion. It is also absurd from the point of view of nearly every page of the writings signed with Nietzsche's name. Nietzsche the one who tells thinkers ready to listen to beware of system, kinds, categories, and types; and yet the one who insists on presenting his view as a view about systems, kinds, categories, and types. This contradictory reading would be absurd only if Nietzsche is right (and hence wrong). How could that be? In a swordfight over a matter of honor, does it follow that the one capable of the most fatal blows is right? And the one mortally wounded wrong? And what if the deconstructor is both the one who makes the fatal blow and the one most mortally wounded by it? What did Nietzsche say, I think, directly to this point? Again, something human, all too human: "The life of one's enemy.—He who lives for the sake of combating an enemy has an interest in seeing that his enemy stays alive."

Why does deconstruction need to say, "metaphysics is..."? Why have the practitioners always felt it their lot to say, "metaphysics from Plato to Nietzsche, from Plato to Husserl, and so on"? What system are they trying to build in this quintessential moment of deconstruction? Perhaps it is not the psychoanalysis of philosophy, but its torture. Like that frequently used example when teaching utilitarian ethics, deconstruction has heroically kept metaphysics alive, saved it from drowning perhaps, only to torture it. In this torture, it concerns itself with the health and well-being of the victim so that the victim will stay alive, will recover the strength torn from it in the torture, and permit it to continue. What if deconstruction is not easily reducible to anthropomorphic images of torturer and tortured? That is, perhaps I am right, and deconstruction is something that metaphysics already has implicit in itself, is already a relation that metaphysics takes to itself to keep itself working and alive. It does this only for the sake of torturing itself. The life of metaphysics becomes unbearable, the tortured life of a thing that keeps itself alive only so that it may continue to inflict pain upon itself. Why unbearable? The metaphysician does not experience it this way. Aristotle, for whatever reason, thought the life of the metaphysician —the philosopher— was the best and happiest. Mill thought it was better to be an unhappy philosopher than a happy fool.

Now this is good and dandy, full of romantic and artistic vision. It reveals a drive to make something beautiful out of metaphysics' self-torture. Sometimes biography inflates the value of art, and what the artist went through comes to inhabit the work. Then, as a form of self-torture the artist cannot quit, as an addiction without sympathy from contemporaries, the work becomes a symptom of something deeper and more insidious. Sympathy can only come from appreciation by an adoring audience, but that never truly fulfills the need. Adulation does not pay off. It never does although both artists and audience might return to its trough again and again in hopes that perhaps this time it might. Rather, sympathy only comes for them if its origins lie in kindred spirits: their work makes a rhizome. This is not pity, but commiseration.

The connection appears in the guise of reconciliation as though it were compensation. Someone worthy understands. Well then, that makes it worthwhile, the debt is repaid. This is hollow and there is always the risk that the deferred payoff will never come. But suppose the thought of it is food for artists, keeps them going, keeps them alive, and enables them to continue torturing themselves for the sake of those who come later, for the sake of their heirs. Compensation comes in the moment. The act of torture is itself an exchange of value. Suffering for the sake of such sympathy is nourishment —just the thing to keep the enemy alive.

In that case, artists either create a massive debt or bestow a lavish gift.

If they suffer for the sake of their heirs and create a debt so large that the whole economy is a bankruptcy, those heirs will come to the work as debtors. Get to work, dear reader. You owe me.

If the heirs are recipients of a gift, it is a gift no balanced person should wish to receive. It comes in the form of an anguish parading as a link in a chain. The heir can refuse the offer and go on their merry way. If it is a matter of choice, then choose not to. Only necessity forces the hand.

All of this as interlude. Nietzsche the between play, playing between Aristotle and me, taunting us both. Speaking out of turn and taunting the end and origin from the middle. From him, nothing but contradiction and irony. Nietzsche offers an impossible project that it doesn't make any sense to lay hold of, to accept. Philosophy is a disease that has come to inhabit me against my will. It fills me with a cruelty toward myself, with a yearning to torture, and a lust for making that torture seem beautiful.

Why not just stop? Stop! That's insane. How? What else is there? What would ceasing even amount to? We are not talking about a leisurely walk down the street by your house, but about the history of our kind made particular. What does that mean, stop? The circulating nature makes stopping an impossibility. Even the system that marks circulation by coming to an end isn't the same as ceasing, as stopping. Rather, it's a way of managing movement in a patterned and orderly fashion. The circulating system does not permit alternatives, does not permit the possibility of stopping. As such, it is itself the place where I am and the time which demands its own ongoing existence. It self-dismantles and self-deconstructs. There is no stopping, no getting out, no way to do it, no way to even try, no way other than the effort which I've shown again and again is nothing other than remaining in it, as it, and through it. What is it that remains? What is the residual and resonance? This is not a questioning that even attempts to get out, but still it —proximally and for the most part— reaches for a deeper grasp, a firmer hold. It moves into the circulating system, tries to discover its manner of being at work, and finds there the impossibility of getting out. It finds what remains in the impotence for any and every getting out, and that is the residual of any transcendence, the resonance of any attempt.

The most interesting section of *Human, all-too-Human* is a journey like this, a wandering down into the depths of this impossibility to avoid trying any longer to get out of it, to escape it. It is a wandering into the depths of impossibility to discover the possibilities that remain. I'm thinking of the last section called "Man alone with himself". An explosion of self-torture, of wandering, this section routes, it roots its way into the residual not to take possession over it as though it were a nugget dug out of the earth, but to open it up, to tear its sheath, as though it were a deep wound needing to be picked at to assuage a temporary pain with a much more enduring one, an endless pain. Perhaps Nietzsche isn't digging for gold nuggets so much as iron, because this rooting around for resonance is the route of his irony:

What is dangerous in independent opinions.—Occasional
indulgence in independent opinions is stimulating, like a
kind of itch; if we proceed further in them we begin to
scratch the spot; until in the end we produce an open
wound, that is to say until our independent opinions begin
to disturb and harass us in our situation in life and our
human relationships.

Our whole circulating relation throughout the world is disturbed and
harassed by this open wound which bleeds out as the individual's
separation from a circulating system. Independent suggests a move away
from other people. Yet this move to the center retreats from the
extremities, inflicts a disturbance, a harassing turbulence, on those same
limbs. Man alone is thus an ultimate irony. Man alone with himself is the
one who scratches the itch of his independent opinions and in so doing
opens disturbing relations with the rest of humankind. Man is therefore not
alone with himself. Rather, he tortures himself to be with others. Even if
turbulent and harassing, it is still a manner of *being-with* them. This whole
section of human, all-too-human is laden with this strange irony, this pattern
by which psychological observations take on sociological implications.

Technically, this terminology is correct. It is right and proper to refer
to man's journey inward as psychology and also the relations with others as
sociological. Yet, when one whittles it down to a pattern of thinking, it
ceases to be either psychology or sociology. Instead, it becomes an
economy of the residual: a way of uncovering the hidden center to expose
the circulating system. The irony is in the dynamic, the way in which man
finds the world in himself, finds the social economy on a psychological
journey. The turbulence is no doubt caused by a tremor residual to that
journey. Yet the inward is only inward because it is away from the outside.
Its independence is its negation of the primordial dependence, it shuns the
circulating economy for the sake of rediscovering it in the opposite
direction to provide everything involved with a greater turbulence: an open
wound, and a becoming harassed.

From such ordinary discourse, it is apparent that there is residual in
both directions, in many directions. The journey is driven by residual and
in search of self-discovered resonance. The journeyer seeks a residence by
wandering away from it. Independence (as the privative state of addictive
dependency on the circulating system and its guiding principle) retains a
relation to what it flees, is haunted by its independence. All the more so,
the more it scratches at the itch. There is residual in the itching, the wound
itself resonates there. So loudly that ultimately the circulating system
returns with a vengeance as a renewed source of grief and torture, a place

of immanent harassment. Rather than trying to rank order these resonances, these residuals in the double movement appearing as a dialectic of understanding, it is more fitting to ask how such a symmetrical binary permits a residual and where it is if it isn't one or the other? What then is the exchange of the thinker capturing and what prevents him doing so? What resonates and drives him away and what remains to drive him back again?

What?!? You want a name for this?

I am attempting to discover a pattern, one I have long since been aware of and one that -perhaps, because it is a pattern already at work in any attempt to find it- constantly remains. It is the very thing at work in the searching, in the temptation to find, and in the attempt itself. Questioning. This residual, that by its nature eludes identification, is both the mark of something beautiful and extraordinary and of something terrible, haunting, and vicious. It is the sublime and beautiful instantiation of self-torture to even attempt to find it, it is the will to justify the world and the will to destroy it, the will to understand it and the will to impose oneself upon it. The deconstruction of metaphysics.

But why Nietzsche? Why Heidegger? Where are they going? What are they doing? What's the answer goddamnit? It must mean something, there has to be some result, otherwise, what is the point?

Ah, just a hint. "It must mean something." The homunculus laughs: "Iron necessity.—Iron necessity is a thing which in the course of history men come to see as neither iron nor necessary."

Its absent necessity is not its contingency, but its potential to be necessary. It must mean something because it can. If I work at it, strive for it, give everything to it, it will mean something. Bah! The circle rages on, another attempt, another striving, another exchange of debts. A circulating system that systematically dismantles itself, that economizes its movement out of self-torture and the longing for beauty. A fucking wound, I tell you.

And I tell it you. The same moment, the same retreat to independence —only supposed— the same ruinous social relations, self-destructing in a torturous death throe, the same longing for art, for meaning, for artifact and product and the whole "must have been meaningful." I don't just do it, I am it, it inhabits me. And you too. Admit it.

> In the fire of contempt.—It is a new step towards independence when first we venture to express views regarded as disgraceful in him who harbors them; even our friends and acquaintances then begin to worry. The gifted nature must pass through this fire too; after it has done so it will belong much more to itself.

Comforting at first, but ultimately irony and only that. We come to perform this ugly self-torture to remain alive and worry ourselves in the process. To no avail. The process —albeit a gifted one— lands us just where we began, at that point of origin residual to fleeing and thus called independent. But belonging, belonging much more, to itself even. There is a system of relations unreconcilable as the middle way between end and origin. The absence of reconciliation here marks its perpetual potential and is nothing other than this economy of movement implicating even the most noble of natures in some trap they cannot escape, some impossible condition requiring what is ugly to be beautiful and failing to reconcile its movement toward some other end. It just doesn't make any sense.

One has to be humble even in the face of one's vanity. Whatever stupidity or ridicule I open myself up to by such a public display of sophomoric nature, it is nothing when compared with that stupidity and public display of sophomoric existence that is the history of humanity. I will not be humiliated into backing off, I will not say it clearly so that you will have an easy to read and entertaining story in front of you. Look at yourself in my mirror, do it now and often. What do you see looking back at you, you greedy origin of want, you tempestuous source of temptation and attempts to know and understand and manipulate —to create and to destroy a world that is so massive and extraordinary in the light of you? Do you want a name for this? A light to show it to you? Idiot. How dare you laugh when you are the source of just such laughter yourself. I am a reluctant comedian, but a comedian, nonetheless. I am not afraid of you or your laughter.

> Chimera of fear.—The chimera of fear is that evil, apish
> kobold who leaps onto the back of man at precisely the
> moment he is already bearing the heaviest burden.

The best I can do in saying this, decrying this interlude (that which I renounce as I say it), is that there never was any metaphysics and deconstruction is a fantasy, rather there is nothing other than the deconstruction of metaphysics. I renounce this immediately because it is quite obviously false, it self-contradicts when written, it tortures itself in persisting to lay out a meaning that annuls and destroys something that cannot come to an end. The phrase berates itself with its own impossibility as a sentence in English. Oh, how clever you are. I am cornered.

Throughout the first part of this treatise, I try to emphasize the greatness of the deconstruction of metaphysics, why it is beautiful, why it is extraordinary, why it is so understandable that we would desire it as a history and as a people. Now, in/as/through Nietzsche, I try to show how just that which is beautiful in metaphysics is also ugly and tortured, violent and base: a self-destructive tendency that overwhelms humanity not just periodically, but every moment in every life through every thought and act. I spare nothing and refuse to exclude myself. I make use of myself to explore it, to see it, each beautiful and ugly facet. I write both from a deep sense that I am both. What is more, if I do exclude myself, there is nothing left to speak of. There is nothing to write, at least nothing I —the excluded one— can write.

The situation seems hopeless. The situation cannot be hopeless. Contained in the hopelessness of the dynamic, is the hopefulness of the dynamic. It is both, it cannot be one at the expense of the other. In the play between hope and loss of hope lies the residual, a residual that can only emerge as an exchange signaling play between. It is an interlude, nothing serious, just folly. Only a farce between the acts, devoted to that kobold fear, that homunculus Nietzsche, that ape on our backs: in short, laughter.

Why make a deal with the devil? He is after all proof for the existence of god. Deal making is always with the devil. God makes no deals. That is why it is useless to pray. "Oh god, please alter the laws of the universe for my convenience." Or perhaps for another, a stranger even? I imagine god has learned to tune out the cries of those who beg for themselves. We certainly have. So much so that even those who have good reason, true sufferings of injustice, are only listened to as though they were begging for themselves. We cease, like god would have long ago, to hear any of the cries. Truly god is dead and no longer hears our cry. As Aquinas tells us, god's death is the death of a friend that moves the world. My friend's death moves the world. In my friend's death the world moves. It is a haunting and my friend's ghost persists as memory and time. What is left in this loneliness, this world without my friend and my friend's love, is mourning.

My friend is dead.

I think I know what that means.

But I look away from that death to see that which is a part of myself that dies with my friend. Selfish maybe? But wait. For my friend, I am something that I have never been before. With my friend, in their presence, in the eyes of others with whom they speak, in my mind when they look at me. I am something to them. And with their death, I will never be that again for anyone else, ever.

Unless I mourn.

Let my friend's memory be a blessing to me. Be what they see me as and be it despite their death, be it to spite their death. In mourning I keep the dead alive and allow myself a haunting in the memory of what passes. My friend is a ghost, true enough, I am that ghost. I live as the haunted memory of what they make me be.

Now I tell you that every death is to be mourned. Even the death of a beast, of a fool, of a hollow shell that will not be missed. Every death is to be mourned. In the wake of interlude, every story is a ghost story.

I learn this as I study the death of philosophy that deconstruction seems to callously await as if for a triumph. What triumph can there be in the death of something so old and essential to telling the story of our kind? For that reason, I -with a mignon of others- will mourn the death of philosophy. The meaning of it lies in Nietzsche's bold claim, a storm warning really, a proclamation describing the history of the next 200 years: "God is dead." Nietzsche knew, in a way that no one has yet seemed to understand, that this is a death to be mourned. The work of the last human beings is mourning, mourning god's death. Only then can mourning pass into the great afternoon.

> It is the stillest words that bring on the storm. Thoughts that come on doves' feet guide the world.
> The figs are falling from the trees; they are good and sweet; and, as they fall, their red skin bursts. I am a north wind to ripe figs.
> Thus, like figs, these teachings fall to you, my friends: now consume their juice and their sweet meat. It is fall around us, and pure sky and afternoon.

I am your friend.
[Signature]

Act Two

"I contradict myself. I am large. I contain multiples."

—Walt Whitman

The Curtain Rising[1]

A Digital Library

"Thou art a scholar. Speak to it, Horatio."[2]

Shakespeare's Hamlet mediated by Joyce. It's always like that. Never just one thing, but two things on top of each other.

We three are asleep, everyone else is in the library.[3] Sovereignty is divided. Or stripped away. They are having an argument. Someone must win. Someone must've won. Stephen? Oh yes, please let it be Stephen.

Once I know what to look for, I find it. Everything.[4] If he is using source control, then he's probably using text only formatting to manage changes and versions. A standardized format. Once I start looking for markdown documents, I find everything. The repositories and their diffs. There is a separate one for each of Ben Thorne's books, and more. There are repositories for Dad's books and for things I never heard of before.[5]

There is cloud storage too. Digital notebooks are kept there. They are massive with endless tabs and pages filled with notes and half-baked ideas. Some of them are crossed out, some underlined, some bold. Some just italicized and some both underlined and italicized. There is usually a

---

[1] Notes provided by the custodians of the Ben Thorne archive who graciously approve their publication along with Lena Michaels' commentary on EM's notebooks in this revised and expanded second edition of *Being an Introduction*.

[2] From Shakespeare's *Hamlet*, Act One, Scene One.

[3] The reference is to chapter nine of *Ulysses* commonly known as Scylla and Charybdis. The scene takes place in the National Library of Ireland and includes an argument about the role of the ghost in Shakespeare's *Hamlet*.

[4] Lena Michaels is referring to her father's (EM) collected notes and rough drafts. She discovers the collection on his laptop computer. Based on a reconstruction of the first act's relationship to the second, she is referring to remarks made by Ben Thorne reminding her to treat her father's work as though it were written by a software engineer. When they (Lena Michaels or Virginia Percival) write (or edit) the *Interlude*, paralleling EM's *Interlude* from forty years before, they dramatize Lena's discovery and attribute the warning to Ben Thorne after she learns he is Stephen Wolfe.

[5] Lena Michaels is referring to the original work in philosophy *Being an Introduction* as well as the uncategorizable and unpublished fragments from *Further Investigations of a Dog*.

notebook for each of the document repositories. I am overwhelmed. There is too much to go through. My first reaction is to give everything to Ben Thorne or whatever his name is, but I get over that and go through it myself.

I start with *Being an Introduction*. There is an outline, and whole chapters. There is the interlude. That's it. It trails off. It just ends. I don't have enough time before we leave, I figure out where to begin. It's a long flight and I get started. I have to pace myself. There is too much for a brief survey. This will take months. And that's just this one project. There are dozens of them.

In these last days, everything is so frantic. The not-knowing of Sunday turns into sex. It's everywhere. Well, not everywhere. Mia and Ginna make no secret of it. They don't even try to hide what they're doing. She never goes back to the hotel. It makes sense for her. Not knowing is a terrible place to be. She has nothing secure, nothing to hold on to. Sex gives her that. She knows how to feel that. Her body tells her. I can relate. Not Mia though. It's not like her, so irresponsible. She has people, obligations. How can she let herself go like that? And why? She isn't in the same place. She doesn't have the bumpy nights of nothing to come for her, she doesn't have the not-knowing how to feel. Why should she take such a risk and act so immaturely? She tells me not to worry.

The other case is funnier, more clandestine. Maybe because it doesn't happen in the house and leaves me unclear about details. Eirini, quiet Eirini, gentle Eirini, sleeping in the seat next to me. She goes off. Whatever she is up to, she isn't up to it nearby. She leaves with Carl and Fred. At the last minute, they decide to stay until we leave for Greece. I'm not sure what's happening, but they're a funny trio. All those books and she still leads them around. She comes back every day, is helpful with everything, but we don't talk about what's going on.[6] She doesn't tell me what she's doing or who she's doing it with. Whatever it is, it's having the same impact it's having on Mia and Ginna. The only clue she gives is when she asks if it's okay to spend the night out. She wants permission. I'm fine with it. I've grown used to having her in the same bed, but I can manage. Whatever. That's what I say. She doesn't want to read too much into it, I suppose. I assume she's going with Fred, but when they come around, it's both Fred and Carl she flirts with and looks at now and again with secret glances and private smiles. I can't tell what's going on and don't ask. I don't really want to know.

At night I read. The time alone. I don't know what cosmic force causes it, but what I find fits with where I am. There are notes about sex. At first,

---

[6] This is the time period when Lena Michaels is writing a petition for a leave of absence from her graduate department without suffering a penalty against her financial aid eligibility.

I feel scolded or guilty, like I'm doing something wrong, but they're easy to absorb. They're observations. Matters of fact. Great sex, it says somewhere, isn't inside a single person, it's between people. It's what happens when they find one another at just the right time. He says some are more likely to have it than others, but it always requires the right pairing.

The most important thing is enthusiasm. It depends on many factors. True, there are people prone to it, but their partner can deflate it by doing or saying the wrong thing. It's possible for marginally enthusiastic people to become much more so with the right encouragement. There's a lot of detail in the descriptions. What it boils down to is genuine and authentic enjoyment of what they're doing and being moved by the response it gets. And vice-versa. Vice versa is extremely important. It's both italicized and underlined.

There's a bit. It's fragmentary, the way one note follows another, sometimes completely unrelated. But the first page stays focused, and there's one bit about the thrust versus the slow circling. When I begin reading the little paragraph, I have no idea what it means. It seems disconnected from the previous blurb on enthusiasm. But then the images become clear, and it makes me blush. The feeling that I should not be reading this is overwhelming, but I can't stop. It's absorbing.

The thrust and its relationship to friction. The way forward and backward movement work against the skin, how the skin forms and evolves to be sensitive to these motions. That's on one side of the table. It isn't an actual table, but the paragraph has a columnar layout. The other side is about circling momentum. Skin being circled, friction coming from circular pressure. His description essentializes the movements and promotes them as two distinct forms pleasure can take. Each elicits excitement differently. He calls it the domain of the erotic and asserts that orgasm is bound to it. Underlined. It's an elaborate theory. Images, scents, and feelings contribute to the sensations, strangely at odds with each other creating tension. One of the italicized sentences underneath the two columns says something like "the central problem of heterosexuality lies in fostering these disparate domains in one and the same action context." It makes me laugh, it's out of place and abrupt.

He goes on to say that the chief factors of patriarchy and its presence in heterosexual congress (he uses that phrase *heterosexual congress*) is that men ignore this difference, and its management is left to women. A woman, however, is not-well suited to sort it out on her own. He doesn't mean she's incapable, just that no one coming from either angle can observe the distinction, conceptualize it, and bridge the gap in real time with an oblivious partner. In many cases the partner is incentivized to be oblivious. There is a long paragraph on something irrelevant. It includes a quotation from some book.[7] I don't recognize the passage and can't decipher the reference. After that, he comes back to the dichotomy of thrusting and circling. He writes that he's learned very early on that attention to this dichotomy is advantageous for encouraging enthusiastic interludes. It's underlined.

I look back at the passage with the quotation. It's about the circling nature of language. About how circling is an endless and ongoing dynamic promoting an eruption of meaning. Sense is explosive, a conflagration, and it comes through circular momentum. There is a lot to unpack, and there's a parenthesis at the end. In it, it just says "Jouissance? Barthes? Lacan?" with question marks. It isn't an irrelevant tangent. It's related. He's trying to tell a story, but it's so cryptic and fragmentary.

Then back to the next paragraph. More on the erotic domain. The act of seduction, where a man plays the aggressor realizing the thrust and making pursuit a contributor to mood. A man's arousal is triggered by it. That alone is sufficient foreplay, and this makes for a precarious balance since the recipient needs more. She requires circling: language, around and around, innuendo, deferral, and endlessness proposed even if only temporarily. This frustrates him but is erotic to her.

> If you want to drive her wild don't bring her to orgasm, bring her near it, next to it, close by. And then stay close. Keep moving around it, this plays with the movement of the circle, it instigates an unparalleled enthusiasm. Give her room, wait for her, but let her finish. That is her affair.

It is so explicit. He describes what he calls *phenomenological* pointers, the experience of pleasure in each pattern. The short burst of the thrust is intense but short lived. The undulating flow in the circular is long and broad. It covers more ground with less depth. The thrust marks its end. It comes to an end, ironically, in pleasure, but the circle is just getting started. It is an escalation, an arising, a movement upward and outward. Any man who hopes for enthusiasm must hold to the principle of ladies first. Consequentialism is masculism. Bold and underlined.

Eh, I cannot get the right distance. Sometimes I forget because the language is detached, but something like this, a cliché that works like a slap, it breaks the spell. I blanch and hold my eyes closed tight in shame. I remember the feeling from high school when he tells me I can ask him anything and he'll do his best to answer. He means well, but it is so embarrassing. Daaaaaaaaad, I say. Or something to that effect. This is why people should not keep notebooks.

---

[7] The quotation comes from EM's doctoral dissertation.

These notes are on the second part of *Being an Introduction*. I can't get a sense of what year or time frame it covers, but on another page, I see that he's in Ann Arbor and living with Wolfe. There are word documents attached to the notebook.[8] They must have been written long before they were attached, and he must've moved some of the older notes to the newer format. It's chaotic, but he says that after writing interlude, he becomes enamored with a woman who is out of reach. This stimulates both his urge to thrust and her urge to circle. He stresses that the mood of this interplay is exacerbated by the intermission fulfilled by interlude.

Sex, he says, is an interruption. He uses the word intervention underlined and italicized. This recalls two things. 1) Something Fred or Carl said during the road trip. It was a delightful little theory about how oral sex works.[9] There is too much in common between that description and these notes. It is very curious. Perhaps Fred, or maybe it was Carl, was parroting something they read in one of Ben Thorne's books. Of course, this could be the original source. Maybe Fred or Carl put the wrong emphasis on the story, maybe its incarnation in Ben Thorne's writing is a different angle. This is a literary goldmine. It's like a dump of anything and everything useful. 2) Something Ben said at lunch that day, something about the intervention. He said it happened just outside. He said it was a paramount event, that the entire story leading up to it is completely transformed by it. What is the relationship between intervention and interlude and how does it suggest the sexually charged interruption, the logic playing out in the universe and causing an abrupt end or intermission? The interlude, the intermission, the intervention.

Based on the software installed on the laptop, I think the attached documents are the same format, so I try opening them and it works. The connections are clearer. *Being an Introduction* is a scholarly project. It's an analysis of Heidegger's *Being and Time*, or some central themes in it, and their relationship to Aristotle. The interlude is a momentary tangent to explore a Nietzschean interpretation of deconstruction. That's big in the nineties, he's probably trying to lock into some fad or trend. Very standard stuff, no doubt. This is likely a continuation of themes from his dissertation,

---

[8] The notes in question are from the period between 1995 and 1996 when EM writes the better part of *Being an Introduction*. Further forensics indicate that EM uses word documents and brings them forward into digital notebooks sometime after 2015 when his fragments exclusively appear in that format. Lena Michaels does not explain this in what follows, but we see later that she pieces it together. The text-only format she refers to is the so-called markdown formatting supported by many word processing software applications.

[9] Cf. Act One, Chapter 7.

something he's doing for purely professional reasons. He's trying to find a job. Then the interlude jumps off the page. It's emerging and turning into an erotic ensemble. He can't help it. That's underlined. Even back then he decorates his ideas with these same markers. The underline. Italics. Bold face.

There is mourning in the language. He never passes the interlude. Not exactly. He goes a little way, but there's only a trickle. The full flow never returns. The blurbs and false starts in the later chapters, the impossibility of continuing under the influence of that slow circling. So much noise, so little signal.

> She draws me away. She leans and lures. I'm coming to know her ways of moving. She is language unfolding, she is the circling of saying. It disrupts any introduction to being, it forever loses it in interlude, an evil apish kobold. A homunculus. A daimon/demon monkey who dances and disrupts, who chatters and chitters drawing your attention away from its focus. Do you think that's significant? You signify. I will never know the end of it because the act's thrust is lost in an endless circling. The work lies in tatters. She cums and cums.

There are things a girl should never know. Mia and Eirini are both asleep. Enough, I'll be a basket case if I don't join them.

Schiphol (AMS)[10]

Of course, I never talked to my father about sex. It would have killed us both, I'm sure. But I did talk to him about boys. And, surprisingly, he wasn't completely useless. He told me that we change ourselves so that people we like will like us. This is at a time when I'm trying to sort a lot out. How to dress, how to wear my hair, how to look when leaving the house. He tells me so much of this is broadcast by the boys I like. Because I like them, I want to know what they like, and I want to become that. He says this as though it is an inevitability, something I will do no matter what, something everyone does, that we can't avoid doing. But it can be up to me how I handle it. If I'm aware of what's happening I can make deliberate choices. Alternatively, I can be oblivious and let those choices be made for me. The former will probably make me unhappy. You can try to be in

---

[10] The international airport outside Amsterdam in the Netherlands. Lena Michaels writes this section of the commentary in the airport while waiting with Miriam Holden and Eirini Kallistidou for their connecting flight to Thessaloniki.

control of your life and be miserable or you can go with the flow and be blissful. This isn't true of everything, but when it comes to making yourself desirable to the people you desire, those are the options.

I ask him if the fact that we're discussing it changes things. He nods and gravely says something like "I see." He doesn't realize he's setting me up, I suppose. It doesn't occur to him that making me aware makes the decision for me.

It must've been my first year of high school. What type of girl am I going to be? The question already occurs to me, he doesn't put it in my head. I don't think the boys I like are the answer. What type of feminism is this? Is this how men who want the best for their daughters teach them? He says boys do it too. Everybody. It doesn't matter what their preferences are, they get to know themselves through the things they like. Peers. Wanting to be liked by the other girls. Which girls? Wanting to be liked by the other boys. Which boys? These are the questions. He says it's not sexist. The boys are figuring it out too, the girls. We are animals. It's silly to think sex is irrelevant. Of course, it matters. When you're little, nothing matters more than figuring out how to get what you want. You learn strategies. You play with your friends, you act out mini dramas, you explore possibilities, doing it just to figure out which type of person you are.

Totalizing.[11] That's what he calls it. I remember. Fourteen? Fifteen? How old am I? My silly father using the word totalizing in a conversation, trying to explain that it's what I'm doing, that I'm in search of an attribute, trying to bring some fragments together, trying to make something, to fabricate it. Those many words and weird sayings. He always does that. It's odd, it always makes me laugh. He riffs on words and plays with their sounds, it's mostly timing and rhythm. He can be so funny. He makes my mom laugh and laugh and then he dances her around the room, as if going in for the capper after the set up. Nothing Ben Thorne writes is even remotely funny. How does that work? How can someone so driven by humor, how can his writing be so serious?

It's a digression. But it isn't. When he tells me about how I make myself into what I think those boys want while they're making themselves into what they think I want, when he says that, he's making jokes. He's playing, so playful, with the words. It's funny. I am worried about asking him questions. So shy bringing it up. And before I know it, I'm laughing, he's joking about what I'm doing and wanting to do, what I shouldn't be doing, and shouldn't even be thinking about doing. He knows how to talk. It's like

---

[11] This is a reference to Deleuze and Guattari, *A Thousand Plateaus*. It might also be a transitive reference to the later work of Jean-Paul Sartre, i.e., *The Critique of Dialectical Reason*.

riding on a merry go round.

He's right though. It isn't just about hair or clothes, it's about who else is wearing their hair like that and who else is wearing clothes like that. Which boys are interested in the girls like that, and which boys are interested in the other girls? There are the smart girls, and they don't seem to care one way or the other. They are my friends from middle school, and they don't have time for that. They aren't learning how to straighten their hair or curl it. They aren't practicing with eyeliner and lipstick. They aren't watching the videos and the influencers. At least not with me. Then there are the girls who do it for the wildest effects. They buzz one side of their head and grow the other side out. They wear bright colors and go to vintage stores. They're artsy and creative. The boys who like them are like that too. I see the pairings. I can't help it. It's what I see. The shallow boys who talk about sports, they go after the shallow girls who talk about boys. I see the pairings. It's like I am learning a secret code.

How am I supposed to decipher it? He says it's to be expected. Knowing it's a path makes walking it more difficult. Self-consciousness is ideal for penetrating the mysteries of a being, but it's not the key to happiness. He repeats that. It's the flip side of a philosophy: it's better to be Socrates dissatisfied than a fool satisfied. Self-awareness comes with dissatisfaction and unhappiness. Socrates is unhappy even if he's better off. That's what he says. The fact that I'm confused, that I feel lost in a decision I don't know how to make, is proof of how extraordinary I am. That's what he tries to teach me. I don't focus on it, don't want to learn it. How can I? How can that make any sense to me? All I know is that I have to decide and having to decide, it seems impossible. The girls I know, every girl at school, makes this decision, but here I am unable to decide and paralyzed by the fear of getting it wrong. One false step will cost me my whole life.

My father senses this in me and says one day that not deciding amounts to a decision. What? Well, every day you get up and go to school. What are you wearing? How's your hair done? What are you telling the others? Who are your friends? These are facts, these are things that happen, are already happening. You think you get to decide, but what everyone sees is that you've already decided.

I resist. He has to be wrong. Truth be told, I am wearing the clothes my mother is buying. My mother cuts my hair. She makes these decisions. I don't stop her. I don't have an alternative. That leaves me with her choices and her taste. My father points this out and tells me that I shouldn't blame her for it. Of course, I don't listen and even as I register it, I am already blaming her. I can't help it. Just as she can't help getting me dressed and ready for school.

Decide, he says. She'll accept it. She wants you to be your own person. We're that type of parents. You must have friends like that? Don't you?

Stop taking it out on her.

Once again, it's my fault. Both parents against me. That's where I find my adolescence. Music is the instigator. I don't think about it, I don't pay attention. I listen to the music my mom likes. It's there. What the other girls are listening to is awful. I don't give it any thought. I just like what I like. The Smiths. Radiohead. David Bowie. Portishead and Cat Power. Mazzy Star and the Cardigans. She develops her musical taste growing up in Greece. That's what she listens to. Since my father only ever listens to guitar music, it's my mother's taste I acquire. Our yearly trips to Europe reinforce my choice. I don't need to think about it. While I agonize over clothes and shoes and hair and boys, music seeps in and takes hold. At school, I judge people. That girl has awful taste in music. She only listens to the best stuff. That's the boy who's always blasting something hideous from his car. He's always got that rain music. Does anyone call it that? Rain music.[12] It rains my whole childhood. It isn't a choice.

My father never explains that everything is mediated by sex. It never occurs to him to explain this to his fourteen-year-old daughter. Even if that is what he means to say with his talk about desire and the desire to be desired making choices for us. Even if that is what he means, he won't say it. Sex is thinned out and dispersed into these things that aren't sex. He talks about them, and he knows that's what we're talking about, but he never says it. Probably for the best. It would have completely screwed me up if he'd connected the dots. He does enough. Hair and clothes. But not music, that doesn't occur to us. It connects with the rhythms of my senses and my soul. That's personal. That's it, that's his point. This is personal. It is held close and part of me. Learning things and drawing the ones that matter closer, you make yourself, you decide how to be, and you make these decisions. You come across people who make the same decisions, who make the same choices, and because of that you bring them closer. That's why we make friends so easily when we're young. These decisions align, and we're drawn to those who make them. The boundaries are not strict, they're not set. We're still elastic and made anew from day to day, the decisions change, every day you'll change your mind.

While I fumble with the decision, music –behind my back—makes it for me. The girls who like what I like become my friends. Where they shop, what they wear, what they talk about, that's where I shop, what I wear, and what I talk about. The boys who are interested in girls like that become interesting to me. They're cuter than the other boys. I notice them. They notice me once I get the right outfits and go to the right parts of the school

---

[12] There is no reference in popular music from the teens and twenties to a genre known as Rain music. It may be her invention, as she suggests.

and eat lunch in the right part of the cafeteria. Everything comes together. It's okay to be clever, it's okay to be creative, and you don't have to think about things the way the other kids think about them.

My father explains it to me. We don't put it into some big theory. I don't even let him know I'm going through something and can feel my way to the other side. I just let him know that my friends are coming over and when they do, I want him to meet them. That's it. He meets them, and he's funny. They laugh. Dad dorky funny. In a good way. They like him. He says he likes them too because they seem smart and sensitive, and he likes that. I like it too: that he likes them and that he sees what I like.

He explains it to me. He can't help himself. He says this is how dialectic works.[13] You are creating things while they create you. There is an interchange at work, an actual exchange of energy and emotion, of blood and existence. You choose them, they choose you, you align, you organize your world around theirs and they organize their world around yours. An order is created. That's how it works. You think you choose, but you've been chosen. Choosing is being chosen, deciding is being decided. Even when confronted, even when your jokester of a father explains it to you, the deliberations and the choices happen behind your back. When I let him know it's about music, he says he isn't surprised. It could've been music or movies, it could've been books or food. It could've been anything that moves me one way rather than another, that orients me like this rather than that. What's important is that I understand that this dialectic, this logic, part thrust and part circle, goes on and on forever and ever. It'll always be happening behind my back, and I'll be made and remade as time passes. First comes one phase and then another and another. There's no telling where my life will lead as it meanders through these routes and the people who populate them.

Eirini and I draw close. Around that time, we make our regular trip to Greece.[14] We have always been friends, but it's different when you're kids. As teenagers, there's a risk we'll grow apart. We don't and it's because of music. I play it for her, and she loves it. She plays things for me, and I love them. That seals our friendship. Many of the kids are listening to rap. In Greece and in the US. If I brought her rap music, we might not be close.

---

[13] It is this reference to dialectic that leads many to believe the earlier reference to totalization is to Sartre's work and not just Deleuze and Guattari's. Given what we know of EM's work, he may be opportunistically inserting himself somewhere between the two different approaches. Of course, we must allow for the possibility that Lena Michaels' memory or understanding are skewed.

[14] The reference is to a trip they make around Christmas of 2022.

It's okay, but she doesn't love it. In the US, they're listening to it. For everything to line up, so many details have to fit together just perfectly. Where would I be without her?

The explanation is spot on, so correct. I see evidence everywhere. How did my father figure it out? Cutting through race and class, the popular attributes in vogue, cutting past education and culture, in the desire to be desired he predicts the primary alliances of my life. He predicts which boys I'll like and which girls. He sees that Eirini and I will draw close, and he sees how it will happen. It's a pathway opening up in front of me and his insight is both thrilling and irritating. He sees how my life comes together, and I want to resist being seen.

This is for the best, because I'm so used to twisting things from Mom and Dad into bad things, into things I do wrong or don't do right. The decisions my mom makes for me, I resent them. Then I resent how easily she lets go when I make them for myself. This is in the music. Maybe it's decided for me, then and now. How am I to know? What I know for sure is that no one ever does anything right. That's the pattern I fall into, and it comes from the music. My mother is inadequate, my father too. He shouldn't tell me that. It comes out right in the end despite, not because of, him. My mother shouldn't let go so easily. How dare she tell me how to cut my hair? How dare she stop telling me? She doesn't care about me, about the real me.

The real me. That's what it's about. He tells me too much, he tells me just enough. The real me is always a debate, a repeated thrust and an endless circling. I hear him telling me what to do and resent it. I hear him approve and resent that too. No one wins.

That's why Socrates is unhappy. He understands this and knows whichever way he turns he won't be getting out but only going deeper in. Knowing that you're making a choice while choices are being made for you behind your back, knowing that you're a human being and this is what that means, that and the hormones of a fourteen-year-old. No one stands a chance of coming out of it without resentment and trauma. Especially when resentment and trauma are what the other kids require to fit in. Even the sages. Those loving pairs, even they can't navigate the landmines of adolescence. Imagine how I manage? How any of us do?

They are calling for boarding now. Mia is too exhausted to notice how distracted I am. Eirini just smiles and reassures. She's watching me even now. So much love in her eyes.

Facticity

I need to take a step back and try to remember. I meet two professors after entering the anthropology department who very publicly proclaim that they each have a book they read every year. It is a ritual for them. You cannot meet these men without learning this fact, without seeing signs of it. In the one case, it's *Don Quixote*, in the other, *Middlemarch*, and both professors keep signs of their affectation around their office: a little statuette of Sancho and the Don, a painting of George. Their colleagues identify them with these works. Two random white men born in the latter part of the twentieth century manage to appropriate the historical power and notoriety of two major figures. Their colleagues are happy to concede this to them. If *Don Quixote* comes up, we better defer to Al.[15] If *Middlemarch* is mentioned in passing, we better tell Larry[16] and see what he has to say about it. To be clear, none of it has anything to do with anything. These are professors of anthropology. Under no stretch of the imagination is there a scholarly link. Yet, the link is assigned. It is a ridiculous affectation, and their colleagues help them support it in a collective delusion. It bothers me even if I can't explain why.

Over the last three years, it becomes a rule rather than an exception. The gimmick economy forces everyone to find their niche, and these bizarre academic foibles are a reliable means. This isn't what I want to talk about. It's not what I'm trying to remember.

When I think back, not sure when it was, I'm formulating this gimmick phenomenon throughout high school and college, and it comes together when I meet Al and Larry. Why? As a caveat, I should say that I have never read Heidegger's *Being and Time*. Never. Not once. There are four copies on my father's bookshelf, and I notice long ago and wonder why he needs so many copies of the same book.[17] I never ask anybody about this. I don't need to. What dawns on me when I learn of this whole *Middlemarch* and *Don Quixote* fiasco, is that my father is likely just as big a poser as these two guys. He reads this book once a year and tries to eek out a scholarly identity from it: an inadequate attempt at an article here, a failed review there. When I realize it, I see that I'm hunting for reasons to accuse him of fraud. I know deep down that he's one of them and I just need to collect the evidence. Realizing the purpose *Being and Time* plays in his life gives

---

[15] Professor Alan Cooper.

[16] Professor Lawrence Settler.

[17] The records of the King County Library describe the content of EM's library. There is a copy of *Sein und Zeit*, published by Vittorio Klustermann. There is also both a clothbound and paperback edition of the Macquarrie Robinson translation, both published by Harper & Row. The fourth volume is the Stambaugh translation from SUNY press. Although the library disposed of most of the books from the collection, the records remain available for public access.

me the opportunity.

Reverie works against condemnation, and I wonder whether they aren't trumped up charges. He never talks about it like they do. He never says, "well, you know I do read *Being and Time* once a year, to continue exploring its many depths." No, he never says anything like that, and no one ever seeks him out for his opinion either. He doesn't even read it every year. He reads it often. He repeats it. But it isn't like November comes around and there he goes with *Being and Time* again. Thinking back, I remember seeing it on his desk every now and again. Enough for a teenager to notice. In college, he mentions it twice and there might be a third time because I see it on the table when I come home for Christmas break.

For three years, I think this is evidence of his fraud and today, or yesterday, it gets so confusing, I wonder. Maybe I'm getting it wrong. Maybe he isn't like Al and Larry. I'm sure it's not a coincidence that these are exactly the type of creeps you never want to find yourself alone with. They are disgusting. I hear stories. Why group Dad with them? I can't even think of it now. But wait, that's still not the point I'm trying to dredge up.[18]

He talks about it, he says things. They don't mean what he thinks they mean. Like he's trying to give me some insight into the meaning of the universe and what I hear is something terrifying and horrible.

We are going to do it, we are born racing toward it. That's one thing he says. As soon as the heart starts beating, the possibility of stopping it begins. He explains this and probably thinks it'll help me put my life in order or make things more important somehow. What I hear is that I'm small, that I'll have to work hard to make something of myself, and that there's limited time to do it. He's trying to teach me, but it gets twisted around. That's what Heidegger means to me. I know he's explaining the book and that it's something he thinks is full of wisdom and insight, but what I get is condemnation. The *they*. I remember him saying it so many times. They do this. They think that. Whatever. It means no one but everyone, it's everywhere and nowhere. It's shorthand for mindless chatter or oversimplified thinking and coming to conclusions just because they're the conclusions everyone else comes to. I'm just like everyone else. Simple like the rest. This is comforting, but it makes me feel horrible too.

Every decision I make tries to correct that fundamental flaw in my character that makes me just like everyone else. Just as thoughtless, just as

---

[18] Whatever allegations Lena Michaels is making here, nothing is ever proven and there are no official records of misconduct on file involving either of the professors at the University of Michigan. For the relationship between the charges and EM, see Elizabeth Menke's classic study *The Daughter's Father: A Patriarchal Colonization of Personality*.

simple minded.

It still makes me angry, thinking of it.

That's still not what I want to remember.

The thrust or the circling orients you, it underlies your enthusiasm and draws you toward these clothes and these shoes and these boys, that's yours. Your facticity.[19] That's what he calls it. Well, not yours so much as mine. It's important to say it like that. These things are mine even if they are no longer teeming with spontaneity. Still, they are not inert, they are filled with meaning and movement. My meaning and my movement. How to explain?

Each of us, everybody, is something. Things happen to you, others think things about you, you make things, and others make things out of you. We can't help it, living leaves a trail. We leave traces of ourselves, and we live traces of ourselves everywhere alongside ourselves. I am those boys I like, I am those girls I spend so much time with: those clothes and those shoes, those books, and those boxing gloves. That old guitar and the callouses I get playing it. That's me, all of it is mine.[20] When I am gone, it will be no more. It won't remain behind as residue in my body. You can't find it there. Only so long as I am does what inhabits me exist in the facts of my existence, the history of my actions and orientations. I don't know. I never read it, but my father reads it so many times and reads bits of it out loud. He talks to himself about it, and he talks to me and my mom. Half the time I have no idea what he's talking about, but other times it seems wise and intense. Still, it never inspires me enough to actually read the book. I think I want to keep it that way. My father's spin.[21]

The way I transform myself on account of sex. The way it writes itself into me, onto my body and my tastes, my preferences and desires. It is a great weight and it settles over everything I do. Facticity. That's the name

---

[19] The Stanford Encyclopedia of Philosophy does not contain a record exclusively covering facticity but does contain elaborate discussion of it under the heading Existentialism and in entries for existentialist authors like Sartre and the early Heidegger. The curious reader should begin their investigations with these topics.

[20] What is mine has its basis in what is not mine. Cf. Sartre in *The Critique of Dialectical Reason*, i.e., p. 413: "*Socialized facticity*: not only am I not the foundation of my own existence, I am not even that of its social predeterminations."

[21] In depth research into the secondary literature on facticity shows the community is divided in its response to this summary. Most scholars point out there is a great deal missing from this gloss and that the source is not trustworthy.

of this weight, this part of my body, this history that is mine, that's what it's called.

What I get from reading these notes is that this burden rests upon you constantly and flavors your moods, the way you think and feel, and the experiences you have. What you do today or want to do today realizes these burdens. If you are transformed into a dark and somber person, you carry it with you to the park or department of motor vehicles. You come with you wherever you go, and you bring these burdens along. Desire is baked into you, into your choices and interests, what you notice and what you see, what makes you laugh and cry, everything. If that's saturated throughout you, then you carry it with you. You are it.

This points back to the stuff about death. Death is a constant reminder that you are finite. Even if you don't die today, you're still finite. Having a body is to blame, having eyes and feet, breasts and hips. We are a point in time, a position in space, a geometry. It's finite and saturated with the past, our brief traversal through this world and everything that sets the stage for it. I see things, I'm touched, I touch, and it leaves a reminder. Trace. That's the word.[22]

It's confusing. I suspect that dying and being made from finite experience are the same thing. That I find music when I'm fourteen, that I find other kids who love the same music, boys who play along with me in my fantasies about those lyrics and the emotions they reveal, full of it, that's death. You're living and experiencing things. The trails of what happens stencil into your soul. That is death, that is you dying, hurtling along like a thing coming to an end. It's too weird. I can't explain it any better.

Being critical, I think, trying to discover a critical point of view, the dialectic, de-totalizing the ongoing totalization. Utter nonsense, I think it's systematic unraveling. That's the phrase in his notes: the systematic unravelling. Something is fabricated, material woven together. We take it apart and taking it apart is a critical perspective, it's the critical approach. People are always reinventing it, giving it a new name, or adding nuance to a previous definition. It amounts to the same thing: turning around to look back through this facticity that is mine in every case. It's mine because it belongs to me and because I can't be without it.

When I see, I see through it.

This is so rudimentary. Mom decides for me until I decide for myself.

---

[22] Of course, contemporary scholarship considers it far from settled that this connection between death, finitude, facticity, and trace is established in the major works of deconstruction, the French philosophical and literary movement from the late twentieth century. It is, however, one of the primary theses of EM's doctoral dissertation.

Dad shows me how decisions work when it comes to desire, how we trick ourselves and make ourselves decide behind our backs. That's front and center.

Then, this morning, I think of Taysom[23] and our time together. He's an exceptional man. Why don't I want more from him? Why not let him get closer? No, just sex, I say. Someone so smart and so caring and so beautiful. How can I? What am I trying to hide? Or hide from?

These choices are selections. Personality is a conflict and the facticity of your path rages against the necessity of each moment. When I want Taysom, there are years and years of baggage in it. I can't want him any other way. I can't put that alongside school and my ambitions. I can't offset it either. He is nighttime, and only that. He is quiet and private, and only that. When I think about it, when I put myself back inside it, into desire for him, for his body on mine, for his hands and his eyes, when I go there, I see those years growing up and learning, understanding choices, everything at work in these moments. Facticity. It colors my intentions and my wishes, it flavors my interests and goals.

My parents are there with me, hidden inside desire, speaking to me, making me feel that way, drawing me out as though educating me, but making me small instead. Behind the desire, those things come to bed with me. It fills love with death as I trace my way through the world.

Without him.

These thoughts only come in the wake of his death and yet they create powerful urges to speak to him again. There are a thousand new questions. So much I want to know, and I can finally confront it without being overwhelmed by the sense that they should be different than they are.

What I am left with is a familiar presence. Is it cliché to roll that up into a single bundle? Is it a Freudian maneuver? Lacanian?[24] Is it possible that I know this but can never make it mine?

If knowledge holds at a distance what facticity pulls close, the critical path backward through what holds us from behind is the journey into sexuality and family, life and love. How and what does it mean? What feels good is not a simple thing. What hurts either. They talk about pleasure and

---

[23] 'Taysom' refers to Taysom Alton, a graduate student in Cultural Studies. Lena Michaels begins a sporadic relationship with him in the fall of 2033 that ends just before her father's death in July of 2034.

[24] It is not established that Lena Michaels is particularly well informed about the nature of Lacanian or Freudian psychoanalysis. The accuracy of the association in her search for a critical standpoint that unravels the place of sexuality and parental influence within her experience is minimal at best. She is in no way an expert in any of the referenced disciplines or theoretical standpoints.

pain as though they are absolutes, but they are mediated sensations where psychology and social anthropology have their way.

To have been blind-folded, to have been pushed forward and bent over, that thrust, the desire in it, my own circling is response, welcoming openness to it. How can I see my mother and my father there? In those desires and in that pleasure, the taboo draws me up and helps me push back against it. It must be false, our propriety and our sense of decorum screams it at every moment.

This finite view is intensely partial, and its partiality appears in both the experience of pleasure and in resistance to it hiding behind the taboo. Why have I been studying this for years?[25] What possible excuse can I muster? Is it anything more than a ridiculous discussion of facticity and unravelling? Can one deliberately unravel facticity by holding back its actualization? Facticity is always mine. When I die, my corpse is no part of me, although it becomes so to my descendants and the mortuary staff. How is it mine, here and now?

Why do I feel so much pleasure in that little death? Even now, sitting here, aware of my body in the seat, forcing my weight against the cushion, I feel its resistance. The slightest touch would bring me to climax.

The desire in death, the facticity of finitude, that is the partial relationship we have here on Earth. It ventures into our lives, our understanding, and what we experience.

This seat cushion is manufactured, this jet too, in an enormous factory. We fabricate the schedules and the national regulations for takeoff and landing, for individual travel, and the permission to enter and exit. Everything, arranged over time and through space, puts us next to each other and inside one another. All around, through and through, there are machines. Imagine us in the middle of a bee farm assemblage, pistons pumping, gears turning. The bee doesn't know what it's doing. Even the farmer doesn't see the whole field. The chaotic eventualities rely on distributed participation and partial contributions. Without it, nothing of significance ever takes place.

Being a body, being made by a sexual act, being raised and nurtured by loving beings, mingling love and sex and desire and fear together with intention into a personalized hotch-potch. It traces along behind us, screaming for attention in every act and every orientation.

How now to turn around and see my way back through it, back to the

---

[25] It is not clear what this is a reference to, it does not appear to be a focused and precise methodological assertion. Lena Michaels is making a loose reference to ordinary experience but feigning that it is a proper area of study or research.

moments before I make these choices, back before the good and the evil, back before I want or care about anything? If I am to manage it, if I am to throw off the yoke and attain such heights, is it meaningful to anyone? Is it even meaningful to me? Tearing it free from its conditions removes it from its human home and living center. To tell the tale without passion and involvement makes it less than human, decidedly inhuman. I no longer recognize myself in it. I don't feel anything. The critical stance sizes up the situation and yet its mechanism matters least. It is our only hope, and it offers us nothing.

Between the Platias

I tell my mother we're spending the night in Amsterdam. We're spending the night in Thessaloniki, but we don't want to pay the obligatory visits. Eirini is horrified. It's unthinkable that we come here and don't go to see my great aunt and my cousin. Unlike her, we don't feel the pull of it. We'll come back, we'll see them later, but now Mia and I just want to decompress. We need a minute to recuperate from the flights before opening that door. Believe me, the house will be full. There are people coming throughout the day and the next day and the next, until everyone comes. Everyone comes by and greets the new arrivals. It's in their DNA, they can't help it. They shop for pastries and sweets as we speak, they're getting ready. For our part, we're carrying a variety of items collected from the Amsterdam and Detroit airports, including –but not limited to—a case of bourbon and a collection of coasters with various street scenes from American cities. There's one of Detroit and one of Chicago. There's New York and Los Angeles, Boston and Miami. We don't know which is for which, but I assure you we're not coming empty-handed. You have to pick up some things, they say. Get an assortment. Bourbon is fine for some, but it's not going to cover everyone so be sure and get something else. Even Mia feels the urgency and we relax our standards on what counts as a stupid gift from a tourist trap duty free shop. When it comes to returning travelers, silly touristy things often make the best impression.

Our hotel is nice, it's boutique and tucked between Aristotelous and Elefterias Squares.[26] Mia hates staying in the big chains. She picks the place. We take a car from the airport and have a good room at a nice price. The three of us get our second wind once we arrive. We walk around, find a nice little taverna, and set off to see if there are any places left where you can hear hardcore Rembetiko.[27] We find a place that's reasonably nice. Not

---

[26] The downtown area is on the waterfront of Thessaloniki, the capital city of the Macedonia region in northern Greece.

[27] A form of Greek folk music. Hardcore refers to the traditional origins of

too authentic, not what Mia is hoping for, but nice enough.

She's in a good mood, Mia. She plays along when some men buy us drinks. She's patient with their English and you might even call some of what she does flirting. Although it's funny to watch. Not with Eirini. She's a master. I'm very impressed. The boys have no idea what's happening to them. One minute they're coming over to say hello, the next they're buying us a round of drinks and offering us a place to stay if we need it. She has that way about her. I'm not just surprised, I'm envious. It's harder for me, things like that. Social things. I'm terrible at small talk, horrible at making everybody feel comfortable and welcome. She does it so easily.

It's harmless fun. We need to unwind. The change greets us when we step off the plane. I'm not distracted for once. I'm laughing. We have fun. The language is everywhere, the rust is gone. I'm finding words for things, finding structure and grammar. Greek isn't like English. You can't just translate your thoughts from the one into the other. You have to think differently. It's familiar. As a little girl, my mother talks to me in Greek when we're alone. We visit here often, and my grandmother speaks Greek to me. I have to learn. It comes and goes between visits. Now it's come, and my thinking with it.

It reminds me of the first time I'm embarrassed by my mother. Memories long gone, but here they are, right in front of me. The way she talks, her accent. I'm little, not too little, a child. Nine or ten. I am so embarrassed by her accent. The other kids don't understand what she's saying. I'm mortified, but it isn't fair. Her accent isn't thick, it's just that people are stuck in their ways and what they're used to hearing. Americans are not forgiving. I don't know any better. I make her feel horrible more than once. Make her feel like she's less than. She is so sensitive, so self-conscious and here's her daughter making it worse. Oh god, it hurts to remember that, but when you're a kid anything that makes you different is a problem. Really, I can't think of why it's so bad. There are many non-native speakers who work with my father, many of my friends have parents who speak with accents. It should be a normal thing, but it isn't.

My best friend in high school is Zosia Sitarz.[28] Her parents are Polish. Her mother has a thick accent. Her father too, but I don't see him much. It should be normal since both of us are the same, but we bond over it, it's a problem and we're both mortified. She likes the same music. Told you,

---

this music in drug use and smokey joints where poor people sing of suffering and troubles and how marijuana and heroin ease their pain.

[28] The high school is Lake Washington High School in Kirkland, WA. This suburb of Seattle is home to three of the largest tech companies in the world at the time. Many of Lena Michaels' peers are the children of parents who work at Amazon, Google, or Microsoft, each of which has a campus nearby.

that's how it works.

I'm a good kid growing up. Always dutiful. I do what I'm expected to do. I have my chores, I keep my room clean, I help my mother with her chores, and am mindful of my father's quiet time so he can get his work done. He works in his office mostly, although he does go away to work sometimes. My mother doesn't work. It's an old-fashioned division of labor. It's the same at Zosia's house. It should be normal, but it isn't. Yet another one of those things we bond over, our parents are these weird Europeans living in some alternate universe we can't understand. Or don't want to. She and I are going through the same thing. We've both been such good daughters, and then we question that, we want to experience life. That's how we think about it, we want to see everything for ourselves. We plot our outings and the lies we tell. We use each other to throw our parents off the scent. Everyone thinks we're such good girls, but we aren't, we go off and do what we want.

I think that must be the truth of it, of this writing I'm doing. It isn't that your parents are there with you in your adolescent desires. That's pathological, but they are there in some sense. The tension is because there are things I want to do and experience. My parents want to protect me. Really, the whole of my high school life is a constant battle between my developing sexuality and my parents' desire to keep me infantilized. That should be totally retro, but it isn't. My girlfriends, even the ones with parents who are so adamant about how girls shouldn't be raised differently than boys, they have the same troubles. Everything we want to do, the parties we want to go to, the curfews, it's about sex. My mom wants me to be a good girl. My dad assumes I am. I don't know if that's what I am, and I'm not sure it's even a thing. A good girl. We're so progressive. The kids, I mean. We're exposed to everything, we're decades ahead. What can they possibly know about it?

"Where are you going?"

"What time will you be back?"

"Call when you get there to let me know it's okay."

"Is that what you're going to wear?"

These are cliches. It's always like that. My father trusts me. He says it often. "We trust you." My mother doesn't trust me. She knows when I'm lying, and she's well aware that I do it often. She doesn't always call me out on it. She's forgiving, but it's not possible to lie to her. She lets me get away with it to spare my father, not me.

That's what I mean. That's how the family and sex are mixed up together in a single facticity, a single hard reality that envelops your every move. Getting away with it. The lie and the plan, the arrangement, the comrades who are with you in the intrigue. That's part of it. For Zosia and me, there are always boys involved. We have to go somewhere that the guy she likes will be. Or the guy I like. We have to be there so that... What? Why do we have to be there? So that he'll see us, he might say something, come over and talk to us. There's the emotion of that expectation, the tension and pressure and longing, and it's mixed up with the lie and the plan and the intrigue. The excitement is something new, that's true, but what's new isn't just the boy or the kissing or the touching, the intrigue is mixed together. Getting away with it. Growing up.

Zosia and I are together a lot in those years. It's a plot, an ongoing plot. We practice things. Kissing. Playing together. It's part of it. Our stance against the world, against our parents. Getting ready for things. Sisters against the rest. You have to find out what you like by trying things. It's the only way, and our parents don't want us to try everything. My mom tells me how important it is to pace myself, to let myself come along slowly. I think that's what I'm doing. Arguing with them is not an option. We aren't that way. You can't argue with my mother. If you do, she clams up and stops talking. Nothing makes me feel worse in this whole world. Well, almost nothing. If my dad does it, that's worse. But he never does. It's her standard response. You feel her pain and almost every time it happens, I burst into tears and demand her attention, demand that she speak to me. I apologize and throw my arms around her. She forgives me, and she knows that none of it means she's won the argument. She knows when things aren't going her way.

My father jokes about my mother growing up during a junta.[29] What he means is that times are tough. There is scarcity and hardship. No one is spoiled in those days. All that, my mother gets used to doing without, she gets used to making do. This comes up when I complain that we're taking too long to figure out where we're going to stay on our vacation or what phone we're going to buy, things like that. She does so much research and looks so far and wide for deals and reviews to make sure we're buying the best possible one. My father doesn't care. He works hard for our money and thinks we should spend it. My mother thinks we have to be frugal. For no reason, she doesn't have some plan or anything. It's that we just have to do it because that's what you do. The junta, that's my father's point. There is no arguing about it, you can't talk her out of it. It isn't a decision. It's her facticity.

This impacts our arguments. My mother knows that it's her lot in life

---

[29] The reference is to the Greek Junta from 1967 to 1974. Although Ermioni Hajivassiliou is born near the end of that period, the hard times that follow are often associated with it. This is common among Greeks, they associate the extreme Greek recession lasting throughout the 70s with the political turmoil caused by the junta.

to suffer. That's what the junta means to her. She knows I'll break her heart in lots of little ways. She knows there's no way to avoid it. She shuts down and gets quiet, and then she forgives, and that has the same source: she's not going to get what she wants. I break down and feel horrible about these little battles, I feel genuine sorrow and despair when hurting her, but I want everything. I want things to be okay with her, I want her to feel good about things, and I want to get my way. I want to go to that party, or go out with that crowd, or wear that cute outfit. It isn't my whole world, I know that, I have a sense of proportion and measure. My father is always making that point. "She works hard during the week, Ermioni, let her enjoy herself on the weekend."

In my last year of high school,[30] I begin to see how savvy my father can be when it comes to trust. Initially, I'm happy that someone is taking my side, but at seventeen or eighteen I think about the impact that trust is having on me. I make decisions based on it. I hear the voice of his trust in my head when I point the car home instead of going to meet people at a friend's house. His parents are out of town. My dad is trying to be my conscience. That's part of the plan, and my mother gives into him. At some level, she senses his approach works better than hers. His comes from his parents, and hers from her parents. The divide isn't just based on gender, raising a boy vs raising a girl, it's cultural too. The well-to-do Entrepreneurial American parents versus the civil servant Greeks raising children during a junta.[31] She resists him at first because it's different than what she knows, but she gives in because she thinks an American approach will work best with an American girl.

She's right to listen to him. His approach, the guilt of his "I trust you" and the threat of disappointment if it turns out a mistake. It's sheer genius, because the direct resistance I feel toward my mother's attempts at controlling me are like instigation. It is a dare urging me to do more than I feel comfortable with, to try things that even I don't want to do. Not his trust, that has a different effect entirely. It makes me think about it differently. I feel accountable. I see their faces in the obligation to be their trustworthy daughter and that sticks with me more than anything else. I am never able to enjoy my clandestine experiences so long as there's a hint of guilt behind it.

The whole civilization, or our little corner of it in the suburbs of Seattle, is dead set on avoiding the perils of slut-shaming young women just for

---

[30] Lena Michaels graduates from high school in 2026.

[31] The Michaels side grandparents are small business owners who achieve modest success during the late twentieth century. The Hajivassiliou side works for government agencies, he is in the forestry service, and she is a teacher.

wanting to experience the world with the freedom and emotion that boys always have.[32] Not the whole civilization. Not those fucking theocrats. The ways of the world matter, places in the world. Even in progressive times, there are still bad agents. We know that. There are people ready to take advantage of the changing times to exploit and abuse others for their own benefit. My mother thinks about these things. My father is more idealistic. He thinks conscience is the only way to keep their eyes on me.

I whole-heartedly agree with him. He is absolutely right, but the thing of it is that this works its way into my experiences and, to the extent that they are sexual, conscience is a familiar presence in my sexuality. Going to a concert I'm not supposed to go to, staying out later than I'm supposed to, everything becomes intimately intermingled with sexual desire and that familiar conscience. What I permit myself to like and want, what I let myself do and prevent myself from doing, that's the voice of my mother and father trusting me as I go here or there, agree to get into this car or go to that place with these people or those others.

When I decide to lose my virginity to a levelheaded boy who is kind and friendly, that's my parents doing, that's their voice in my head helping me see their vision of my worth. When I call my dad and have him come pick me up even though it catches me in a lie, that's my desire mingling with their conscience. It's a tangent to my real life, only a part of it. For my father is right, I do work hard during the week. I study and I learn, I do after school activities, I read on my own, I develop interests in subjects at school. That's not common. Some friends do very well, that's not what I'm saying. I mean, that I am interested in what I'm learning. I read Darwin's *The Descent of Man* and think it's the most incredible wonderful book I've ever come across. It motivates me and sets me different pathways for learning and seeing how things fit together. That's not common. Even the smart ones who go on to good schools and academic achievements aren't really passionate about what they're learning. There must be something of

---

[32] The reference here is to some of the vernacular employed by the Attribute movements of the teens and twenties. Lena Michaels is influenced by these ideas, popular while she is growing up. They are discredited later. Cf. the work of Adrian Spelius, specifically the landmark article "We Are All Trans" which systematically undermines attribute politics by showing that the patterns of transgender orientation reinforce binary opposition. Identifying as trans and using pharmaceuticals to reinforce that identity accepts binary constraints in the transition from one sex to another and confirms that such treatment is a new form of the artificial. This work is rapidly adapted across gender and cultural studies where blackness and brownness become labels originating in white supremacy, womanhood becomes an attribute originating in the patriarchy, and so on.

that trust in there too, something in that voice of conscience that speaks to me.

My father is a failed academic.[33] This is so important. He has his doctorate and teaches as an adjunct professor at a few colleges and universities, but he gives up. He isn't able to find work and leaves it behind to take up software engineering. It isn't what he wants. Necessity drives him to it. Even though he's successful, rises up in the ranks and is well respected by his colleagues, none of it matters to him.[34] Deep down, he thinks of himself as a failure, as falling back to something he's allowed to do when the thing he wants to do is denied him. It's impossible to grow up in his house, to live with him, without knowing this. It's not like he complains about it much. He hardly ever mentions it. You can just tell. It's in the air. The things he values, the things he wants to do in his spare time, they make it clear.

I absorb it. I breathe it in. The Darwin is on our bookshelf.[35] I don't discover it in the library like other kids. No, I find it on the biology shelf in our living room. This is the shelf where he keeps books on that and related topics including biological anthropology. I am confused about the difference between natural and sexual selection. Whenever I think I understand the difference, something comes up and confuses me more. My father shares my curiosity. He wants to know the difference too. We

---

[33] EM is, in fact, "the professor" from Ben Thorne's *Time Between Summers*. This work is primarily concerned with that character's struggle to depart academia.

[34] This is understatement. By nearly every standard in place, EM is highly successful in his *fallback* profession. That he conveys this sense of failure to his daughter, who does not fact check the details, has been underlined and heavily emphasized in many classic secondary works on the subject. Hill and Beauchamp, for example, argue that this very same attitude and behavior is at the root of EM's "technological humility" which they use as the basic interpretative apparatus for understanding the two "Telemetry" books: the unread, self-published books released in EM's own name, both of which claim to be about advanced technical topics in information technology, but neither of which contains any deep technical analysis of those technologies. Hill and Beauchamp claim that the pattern, rendered in a non-technical way, displays humility that only a very technical person demonstrates. "He isn't trying to impress, just get to the root of the pattern." Cf. their *Roots of the Telemetric*, especially chapter 4 "The Architect's Architectonic" where the term "technological humility" is first coined.

[35] Although the copy has not survived, the records of the King County Library show that Darwin's *Origin of the Species* and *Descent of Man* are both included in the donation.

read more, we look up sources online, we inspect the scientific literature to discover the truth. As if there is such a thing. My interest cannot be separated from the fact that he shares it with me, that the book is from his shelf, that the investigation is something that brings us together for weeks and months while we sort it out. Maybe this doesn't make any sense, but it's lined up and connected. That boy I lost my virginity to, he's my boyfriend. My friends don't have boyfriends. They hang out. They couple up sometimes. Why was I different? That night, I mention this quest, tell him the things my dad and I do to sort it out. I even explain the difference to him. He's so interested in what I'm saying. He listens so carefully and asks so many questions. If the trait makes you attractive to females or improves the likelihood that you'll successfully mate with them but doesn't help with your physical survival, like fighting off disease or something, that's sexual selection. The color of your feathers. Yes, I tell him. Yes, you have lovely feathers. It isn't just that. He makes me feel so powerful and so good about myself. So desirable. I want it to stay like that, to keep going, and so I decide.[36]

But think about that. Doesn't it mean my father is there in some twisted way? That he's a part of it, and my mother too. That boy is Romanian. Alin Nicolescu. Such a lovely boy. I'm lucky, I know that, but it's not just luck. That's my point. It's facticity. It comes from somewhere. It has organization and meaning. It's tied to other things. It comes from order and system.

My father works with lots of Romanians. Alin's mother and father both have accents, and they meet at college in Romania and come to the US together when his father gets a job at my father's company. That is another point of connection between us. They add up. That's how it works. How everything works. He and I connect that day over my Darwinian illusions which include my father. There is my father's sense of failure hiding in the background. There is the difference between Natural and Sexual Selection and how they get mixed up with my father's love which progresses into academic interests and the desire to know more. Then there are the accents, the trustworthiness, making the right choice for something important, something I'll remember for the rest of my life. It mixed up in my mind, in my body, tapering my urges and inclinations, flavoring my sense of where to go and how to get there. How far does that practice with Zosia mean to take me? It's just for play, isn't it? Experimenting. Mingling together. How much here and how little there? All of it messed up together

---

[36] It is unlikely Lena Michaels intends this to be a thorough and accurate description of Sexual Selection. Her work on various Genome projects suggests expertise in this area. Here, she captures Alin's response to her explanation, perhaps what he repeats back to her in conversation.

as mood and energy, as passion and perseverance, memory and determination. To me, it's desire and warmth, it's wanting and holding. It's readiness for something that I've been thinking about and preparing for, but it's also the training and the arguing, those disputes and tears. Those projects. Helping in the kitchen, with the laundry, in the yard. My parents are there with me. My parents meet him. They approve. Oh, how hard it is to realize these things. The facticity I bring with me into every decision. Carrying the burden of my sex. Carrying my parents. Carrying, carrying, carrying, these burdens, this weight.

This goes on long enough. I have to sleep. My tapping must be annoying Eirini and Mia. Let me make one final point.

Why is Dedalus so distraught?[37] If he loses, who cares? How does it help? That critical orientation, how does it help with anything? Pushing and pulling your way through, it doesn't bring sunshine, it doesn't make you happy, what is the upshot? How does it help me see more clearly? It puts together things I much prefer to keep separate. It clarifies experiences and what they mean, but to what end? Where am I supposed to go with it? What is the purpose of achieving a critical point of view? What does it enable? Is it for the sake of truth? Of seeing clearly and knowing for its own sake? Just for that? Is it vanity? Will it bring me closer to my mother? Will it create deeper bonds between Eirini or Mia and me? To properly redistribute ownership of the means of production, is that what it's about? Identifying the correct political agenda to serve the general welfare, is that it? If it doesn't circle back to Mom or Eirini or Mia, thrust them into the inner circle, then what's the point?

Breakfast Included

At breakfast I get the third degree. They want to know what I've been writing. I tell them about *Being an Introduction* and the material in the notebook. I tell them it's academic philosophy or appears to be.[38] Most of

---

[37] This is a brief reference back to the first musings of this chapter: the library scene from *Ulysses*. It leads many commentators to consider the entire chapter, and especially the analysis accompanying it, as an encounter in the library where Lena Michaels is both Stephen and Arthur through the literary device of conjuring her father's ghost.

[38] EM's personal work is considered pseudo-academic and pseudo-philosophical (by extension). Most commentators argue that treating the work like academic philosophy tears it to shreds leaving nothing of any interest or value behind. As literature, they argue, it is of interest only in the broader context of a critical interpretation of Ben Thorne's work. The emissions, analysis, and feedback segments of *Being an Introduction* have been dismissed

what I'm writing, I say, is just working through the material. I read them a little bit of the entry on facticity. I don't mention *Washington and Ashley*. It's a delicate subject and Ben Thorne makes it clear that it is the only thing he's interested in. He believes there's material for his book on the laptop, and there is, I tell them. He's right about that, but I want to go through it first. I want to see what it is and figure out what's going on. From what I can tell, my dad's working on both projects. The notebook makes that clear. He's trying to figure out how to proceed with the second act while at the same time investigating what Ben wants. There are actually some diary-like entries about it. Ben Thorne is pressuring him, but my father wants to work on something else, or maybe not something else, but he definitely thinks W&A is a waste of time. Let it go, he writes as though talking directly to Ben. He calls him Ben in his notes and I'm sticking with the convention. He thinks of him that way.[39]

There are other notes that work out the structure of the story. Ben is focused on generating multiple versions of the intervention scene. It mostly concerns a set of events, some of which take place in the bar up the street and some of which are taking place in the café or again out in front of it at an outdoor table. Those factors never vary, according to EM, but the characters change. In some scenes, there's a description of events, in others only dialogue. In one version, according to the notes, there are only letters exchanged before and after. Ben Thorne is inventing an endless stream of variations on this one theme. The idea of using diverse and multiple genres comes from EM, but I don't think he's taking it seriously. He's suggesting that he's just throwing it out there as an ironic over-intellectualization of the story. Ben Thorne likes the idea and runs with it, putting together these different versions.[40]

He doesn't know what any of it means. That's the central point in several of the entries. Ben Thorne generates vibe and atmosphere. He writes endlessly, producing highly detailed descriptions and in-depth

---

as juvenile and farcical, the residual segments as derivative and shallow.

[39] This is understatement. Lena Michaels is underselling the strict adherence to the illusion in EM's notebooks and email exchanges. There is never any indication that EM thinks the person addressed as Ben Thorne is anyone other than Ben Thorne. In short, he never mentions a corporate entity, he never indicates that he is a partner in it, or that the other participant has any name other than the one publicly known: Ben Thorne.

[40] With the one-sided remnants that we have from this project, it is impossible to determine the accuracy of her characterization. EM's notes demonstrate a project in complete chaos. It is unclear if that evaluation will triumph once Ben Thorne's contributions are available for review.

analyses of the scene, he makes it into compelling psychological narration in first person, stream of consciousness, and even as a distant narrator moving in and out of different points of view as the description unfolds. Anyway, he's going on and on, but there's no structure, no order. Many of EM's fragments and segments try to work out what it might mean to have one version of the story and how it might work if you have a progression of the three or four distinct versions with variations that work one way rather than another. He wants the variations to provide a meaningful frame. Ben Thorne doesn't have a clue about any of it, he just says to let him know what he decides. Like it has nothing to do with him, like the structure and the sequence are of no concern.[41]

There's frustration dripping from the entries. I don't get the sense that he believes in the project. He's having trouble finding any order in the events, the repetition seems overly crafted and gimmicky. That's what he writes. He wonders if his opposition isn't blocking him from seeing the order that could make it work. I get the distinct impression he's deciding to hold back because he doesn't approve of the direction it's taking.[42]

One point of order that it's important to notice is that this notebook is littered with links. There's organization, like I'm describing. There are tabs at the top, each of those tabs has the title of a section of the book as its label. Then, on each of those tabs, there are many, many pages on the right side of the document. Some of those pages correspond, roughly I think, to chapters. It's very orderly, but there are extra pages too, sometimes going off on random tangents or sketches, sometimes with functional topics. Like there is usually a page called "Reading" which contains quotes from various books that he's reading and thinks relevant. He likely has some secondary order that's going sideways through the notebook. This secondary order comes out in links. The notebook software allows you to link from one page to another and he often has a link in some chapter notes that takes you to some reading notes on a different, non-sequential, page. At one level, you have this linear sequence of notes and then on another level you

---

[41] Lena Michaels' characterization of the notes has been corroborated, but scholars disagree about the extent of it. There are some who think this division of labor extends to the entire body of work, whereas others have tried to show that it is idiosyncratic to the unfinished project under discussion. Cf. Enid O'Malley's *Fabrications about Fabrications* for a paradigmatic example of the former view, and Genevieve Couvier's canonical study of the latter view *The Crown of Thorne's*.

[42] One point that scholars agree on is that the project is ultimately destroyed due to a lack of enthusiasm in one party. No one denies that the work of Ben Thorne is an elaborate partnership requiring buy-in from both contributors.

have this hopscotch of links creating alternative sequences.[43]

What I notice is that sometimes these links aren't to other notes, but to external internet sites. Maybe a page somewhere with some details relevant to the topic. Like there's a web page that describes the history of the Del Rio vegetarian bar and grill. He puts that link into a page that's part of the *Washington and Ashley* setup. It makes sense. Anyway, one of the links to an external site is actually pointing at a web mail service. My mother gives me the password for logging onto the laptop and tells me that the same password works for the wallet application where he stores his other passwords. He set this up near the end, she says, so that she can get into everything. Apparently Georgios makes use of this to get at the banking stuff. That's not the point. The point is this wallet application has a username and password for that mail web site and I can follow the link and login. This is a personal email account that serves only one purpose: exchanges with Ben Thorne about *Washington and Ashley*. There isn't anything about anything else. I wonder if maybe he creates a new email account for every project, but I table that and dig into the correspondence.[44]

I don't have much time for it this morning. After breakfast, we pack our bags and leave them in the lobby. As soon as Mia finishes negotiating with the concierge, we'll walk around a bit and maybe have some lunch before getting a ride service or cab to take us to my mother's house later this afternoon.

They think my interest lies completely with the material from *Being an Introduction*. It is, but it's linked into this stuff from *Washington and Ashley* and now I'm lost in that rathole. Once you start with the links, it gets so complex and involved. The emails make it clear, they don't agree. EM thinks there is no story, no meaningful structure. Ben Thorne insists that there is. There are fierce arguments back and forth. There are gaps too, like maybe the argument is getting too intense for email and one of them picks up the phone. It makes progress but isn't captured in the exchange which just picks up wherever they left off on the call. I don't have time to read everything, I start browsing, to verify that they never come to

---

[43] The complex structure Lena Michaels is describing here is the primary reason why the Ben Thorne archive is unable to publish the notebooks. The occasional announcements or references in the literature suggest that —as of the publication of the current work—there is no consensus on the best format for capturing it. There is a special digital collection available through the archive.

[44] It has since come to light that each of Ben Thorne's books, starting with *The Temple on the Mountain*, does indeed have such an email account associated with it.

an agreement. EM thinks it holds no interest, there's nothing there that's interesting to anybody. He keeps pushing Ben Thorne to explain why he's so focused on this moment, but doesn't get an answer. The strange thing is that on one level EM is pushing because he thinks the answers are the source for what they're trying to find. If he can understand why this project is so important to Ben Thorne, he can find a story in it, find the structure it requires, and hang the different versions together. It's Ben Thorne who resists. At one point, he just tells him to make something up.

That's one of the black holes in the conversation. There must be a phone call there. I have to go so I can't think too much about it now, but EM is deeper than Ben Thorne. Ben Thorne skims the surface. He only cares about the language and the timbre of the voice, the style and how it comes across, what atmosphere it creates. He doesn't care about what anything means or how it makes someone else think, he only cares about the most superficial sensations. EM cares about these things too and is clearly in awe of the easy way Ben Thorne evokes them, but he insists it must be in the service of something substantial. The story has to be worth telling. There must be something in it, something more than just images and sense impressions, an occasional yet powerful disconnected emotion. These can't be the driving forces behind a story.[45]

We'll walk around the downtown area today and I'll come back to that later. It's thirty years since Mia's last here, but she remembers places and food. She hopes to find some of them. Eirini says this place has changed so much, everyone's always talking about it. Whatever Mia remembers, if she even remembers it correctly, Eirini says there's no way it's still here. Things don't work like that in the city. Especially when there are so many economic crises and so much change and churn. Your memory won't like what you find. Mia says the Jewish Museum must still be around, we can go there for sure. She remembers it from her first visit, there's something about a fire and a huge neighborhood that's wiped out. Eirini confirms the museum is still there, maybe those memories are intact. It reminds me of the email exchange. EM says Ben Thorne's memories of Ann Arbor are flawed and even if they aren't he won't find what he's looking for down this road. Eating lunch in Ann Arbor together last week, the place he tries to recall is gone, and there isn't any museum to preserve it, just the book they're arguing about.

Now I really have to go.

---

[45] The interested reader should look to Couvier's study (earlier footnote) for a more in-depth analysis of each sentence in these last paragraphs, especially the meaning behind Lena Michaels' uncharacteristic use of the acronym to refer to her father.

A Familiar Bed

Eirini is right. There is hell to pay for eating lunch at that little taverna in Thessaloniki. It isn't even that good. That whole neighborhood is for the tourists, how can you expect to get a proper meal there? Mom must've been cooking for days. Maybe since last week. Getting ready for us, making sure there's enough of everything we could possibly want. Everyone's coming by. Not the outer rings, but everyone from the inner ring. People know what ring they're in and will follow protocol. They understand how it works. Obviously Ariti. Her family. Eirini's mom and dad. That's a given. They have to come on the first day. The god parents too, but that's already covered: Mom is Eirini's godmother and Ariti is mine. There's no one to add. I guess I should count my blessings. It could be quite a crowd. Oh yes, and the yiayias have to be there. Eirini's brother is back from school. That's everybody. Twelve of us.

Poor Mia, she doesn't speak a word of Greek. She just smiles and smiles and tries to seem attentive. Eirini or I translate some things. Nikos and Maria speak to her, they're fluent. Mom and Ariti of course, but she's never part of the full conversation. They're just little asides when they talk to her. It's so chaotic. Everyone chattering, no one able to get enough of each other, and heaps of food upon our plates as a love supplement.

Hospitality is an art form.

It's the Greek way and it feels like such a home. Ariti, or Eirini, or whoever says it, they're right. I haven't been to this house since it's finished. It's wonderful. Exactly what Mom wants it to be. The kitchen she's always dreamed of, the windows, and the air conditioning. Oh my god. You notice it right away, it's unlike any place you go. Even the fancy hotel in Thessaloniki isn't this good, not in the rooms at least. Mom's comfortable here, enjoying having so many people around and serving them wine and cakes, chocolates and braised meats, green beans and leeks. There's so much food, so many different plates. I'm still stuffed from lunch, but they make me eat. And eat and eat. I'm a kilo heavier after today.

There are four bedrooms, but only three of them are set up that way. One of the rooms is for crafts and artwork. There's an easel and a drafting table. The closet has many drawers and shelves for storing utensils and little items like paints and crayons and pencils, rulers and other miscellaneous things. I have the room farther to the front. It's nicely furnished but there's nothing personal. Mom tells me to make it my own. It's nice. Much bigger than my room back at school. Even the old house. There's an entrance to the bathroom even though that's shared with the other bedrooms, but it's nice to have a private door. My mother is in the master bedroom, and it has its own bathroom. Mia's going to stay in the guest bedroom. I want Eirini to stay here for a while, so she'll stay in my room. I'm not ready to give her up yet. She says she doesn't want to sleep in her own bed anyway. Keramoti is half an hour away and she's been staying in my room for a while now. This causes confusion since there's so much chaos around who's going to be living where now that we're settling in. It's further complicated by the fact that Uncle Georgios is the only person who understands the details and he hasn't come yet. He's in Pennsylvania because there's something he has to do there. He'll be coming soon and will be responsible for getting everyone settled into the right place. Until then, no one knows what's going on. Geez.

There's a lot of commotion that afternoon and evening and no one seems like they're leaving any time soon. I don't get much time alone with Mom, but I do get some while she's off finding linens and an extra pillow for Eirini. I ask her if dad ever says anything about an argument he's having, anything that might include something about *Being an Introduction* or *Washington and Ashley*. The latter phrase doesn't mean anything to her, she's never heard it before, but she recalls him mentioning *Being an Introduction*. Long ago, that's what she says. He left it alone for years but wants to go back to it, try and finish it. I try to find out the details, but she's distracted. She wants to talk about the trip across America, how Mia's doing, where Eirini's going to stay, when is Georgios coming. Do we like the pork? Do we eat meat? She has lots of questions, but none of them help her focus on what I'm trying to find out. I think she must not know.

When we're back in the dining room, everyone's sitting around the table. More wine, Stamatia and Europea are in merry moods, having so much family around. They're plying everyone with drink and food, anything to keep the energy going. Everyone's enjoying themselves. In the middle of it, my mom looks over and says something going back to my question. Now that I think about it, she says, there's something about some terrible idea that he has and how it's making him think back to those days. Back when he's working as an academic. There's some scene that someone's living over and over again. I don't recall the details. It doesn't make sense. It's a scene over and over again. She's sure of that. He thinks the anxiety or whatever you call it when you go over something again and again like that, it really means that there's something unfinished. For him, it means he should pick up that unfinished book and finish it. Finally, after so many years. Yes, yes, I'm sure of it.

This causes a commotion. She says this in the middle of everyone. Everyone wants to catch up, they want to know what it's about. Mom tells them what I asked and then they want more details and I have to explain. Mia pieces it together. I think Eirini is translating for her. Now she wants to know how the two projects are connected and why I'm asking about it? Eirini and Mia think I'm definitely hiding something. They know that I'm leaving something out about that book Ben Thorne is so interested in. Why am I doing that? Did you find something? That's what Eirini wants to know. Don't give the bastard anything you don't want him to have, that's what Mia says. She doesn't think I owe him anything. Until you know the situation, until you see where everything lies and how everything lines up, don't give anybody anything. She's forceful and clear. She sounds like a lawyer.

I don't mean to say so much, but it's family and I can't avoid it. The confusion over the two different works and the argument that's now clear to Eirini and Mia makes it clear to the others, especially Nikos who's familiar with Ben Thorne's work. They see there's something going on that involves Dad and Ben Thorne. Why does Ben Thorne care whether your father wants him to tell this story? I carefully explain that this is private information that we can't make public just yet. Of course, they won't tell anyone. They swear, but it's a small town. I'm convinced word will get out. Across Chrysoupoli this'll become common knowledge. Who knows where it might lead? Someone knows someone who knows someone. It could get around, to the university in Xanthi, then who knows? This could become a huge deal. I explain it again. I warn them. We'll see.[46]

It adds a sense of urgency to my reading. There's some connection I'm still trying to discover. There's a bit where it seems like EM has a clear vision of how he can make it work. It's a single paragraph, very fragmentary. Like he's talking to himself. Leaving a note for later, something that might jog his memory or trigger some association. Something like that. Anyway, it starts with a question: which is the idyllic version, the ideal state, what is the outcome he hopes for? Then, after the question, there's a note: start with the simplest, the memory that persists in the simplest form. After that there's a list: fear, hatred, longing, remorse, distrust, betrayal, hope. After the list, a few notes: a sequence of reactions, responses to the fading memory, triggering this and then this and then that and then the other, every bit of leading up to the idealized state.[47]

I'm not sure, but it seems like a sketch, an attempt at drawing out a

---

[46] Of course, the reader will know that none of this information ever becomes public knowledge through any of these informal channels. The first edition of *Being an Introduction* released in 2035, is the first public acknowledgement of the partnership behind the works attributed to Ben Thorne. For a detailed and fascinating discussion concerning the absence of a major reveal where Lena Michaels' informs her mother of her father's role as Ben Thorne, see Cooper's analysis in *Princess Myshkin: Not Her Mother's Daughter*.

[47] See the archives' publication *The Hidden Plan: Washington and Ashley* for a more detailed analysis of this and the entirety of this last section of Lena Michaels' notes.

possible sequence where the events in the repeated versions of the intervention build up to a conclusion after passing through a logical order. There's no indication of any reaction to these notes. No judgment. It doesn't say whether he thinks it's a good story or a plausible outcome, he doesn't mention whether it fits with Ben Thorne's intent or what answers he'll get to the questions if he ever poses them. None of that. Just a sketch, that's what it is.

When reading the notes, the easiest thing to do is to find a reference from point A to point B. If that makes sense. I'm reading a page, it mentions something, then there's a link to another page where that theme continues or is supported in a different context or emphasis. That's normal, and it flows nicely as you read along. What you can't do in that case, however, is find what other pathways lead to the same place. The technical term for this is dereferencing. It's a software engineering problem where you have something in hand and want to find everything that points to it even though those pointers are not available to you. The important thing is to set the scope. In this case, it's the entire notebook, but the search capabilities are limited. The links use an odd formatting, they have a display text that might be "more on this" but then when you right click on the display text, you can view the link, and that link is a navigational path you can follow. The problem with search is that you want to take the navigational path to the page you're on and then search for the references to it, dereferencing the location, but you can't do that because the text search only looks at display text, it won't find the link format.

I go online and do some sleuthing to learn that there is an advanced search option that allows you to expose the link formatting to search conditions. Using that dialogue box and the link syntax from the article, I copy one of the known links to the page, paste it into the search box, and then do a query to dereference that page into the links back to it. This is huge. I find a random page that is the source of many links. As a heading at the top, it just says "Ghost Story." That's it.

The notes are extensive. If I come across this page first, randomly let's say, I don't have a clue what it's about, it seems like a series of unrelated observations. The dereference changes that because I can see more context and how it relates to a proposal for a layout of *Washington and Ashley*. There's also a link pointing off to a different part of the notebook, focusing on the second act of *Being an Introduction*. This clarifies what's on the Ghost Story page. The schism is at the heart of the story, and it unifies them.

At the end of the Interlude, Dad mentions a ghost and the death of god and metaphysics. I'm not familiar enough with this area to know exactly what it means, but I think the second act of *Being an Introduction* is a ghost story. In the notes, there's that stuff about *Hamlet* and *Ulysses*. I've been reading about these two everywhere. They're about ghosts. I don't have enough details, but that's not the point. It's a ghost story, this unfinished thing that he wants to go back to, a ghost story. More than that, it *is* a ghost. He's haunted by it, by not finishing it. He recollects it often. Why leave it behind? Why stop?

What is the relationship between stopping and intervention: the chain of events that is the subject of *Washington and Ashley*? I think my father has a fundamental disagreement with Ben Thorne about which ghost needs to be addressed. Ben Thorne is haunted by that scene on Washington Street in front of the café. EM is haunted by the manuscript he abandons the previous autumn and his desire to pick it up again.[48]

In one of the passages on the Ghost Story page, it says, "they say the same about the same" and even though it doesn't draw it out, I suspect he's talking about these two projects. Ben Thorne and EM are haunted by different ghosts, and they're arguing over which one deserves immediate attention. Dad thinks the essence of the debate is that you have to transcend the scene of the intervention in order to properly interrupt the behavior. If Ben Thorne wants to undo the adverse conditions that create the need for an intervention, the answer is not to play and replay that scene at the café over and over again, but to go back to the manuscript, go back to the unfinished ghost story, and finish it. That's what Dad thinks they have to do. Ben Thorne only focuses on his version of events and his ideal for how to address them.

I can't prove this. My theory is completely conjectural. The links are so confusing, but they are pointing everywhere from here, from this Ghost Story. Dad thinks if you play through the structural possibilities and design a real story out of the voice and content, the only proper place to begin and end is right smack dab in the center of the interlude itself, that's what the intervention is for. Ben Thorne says as much that day we meet, doesn't he? This has to be the correct interpretation. It's for the sake of the ghost story.

It's in the middle of the page. Underlined and italicized. "He never should have been in the bar that night, he should have been home working out the second act, focusing on it, and drawing the lines and connections to make it work."

Then, under that, a separate paragraph, but also underlined and italicized: "Recognition opposes any haunting. She recognized me unreciprocated. We will never be able to recognize what haunts us. It is the absence of recognition, or its partiality, that drives every ghost story."

---

[48] Cf. Couvier's chapter "Squaring the Triangle" for further discussion of the doubling of EM into Lena Michaels' "father" which starts to litter the commentary at this point.

I have to leave proof for another day, or maybe to someone else if I can't. I don't care about proof. This must be it. It must be.

It makes so much sense of so many other things I've seen.[49] Socialized facticity individuates a person. That's written down somewhere. We gain our personality from the way we are individualized by our burdens, our experiences, the social sphere around us. Individuation is a ruse because it's always performing along selected dimensions with aggregate lines. This is the problem of universals. We further become individuals through the events befalling us because –ironically– they bind us to properties and attributes that make it possible to aggregate us into groups and segments of the population. He mentions *On Liberty*. Individuation is a splitting operation. We don't recognize it. We think it's the real me or that the real me is forming in the middle of it. That's only a partial view. Really, there's something haunting us, some social event or circumstance that we don't create but which dominates and defines us. It cuts to the heart of so many of the notes. He turns away from a ghost, he leaves one set of determinate properties, and heads off in a different direction. He breaks up that one structure with another. The intervention is an attempt to prevent him from doing it. They are on the same page, Ben Thorne and my dad, they want the same thing, but they totally disagree on how to get it.

There's a passage in something he sends me, long ago, in college. He asks me why nature split mammals into sexes. Males often look and act so differently than females. If not for reproduction, you wouldn't know they're members of the same species. Why does nature do it? What experiment is it making? He wonders if desire is selected, he wonders if it's an elaborate and complex strategy to construct one of the most complex patterns in the universe: desire. What role does it play in survival? Or is it just Sexual Selection? Is desire a secondary trait or primary? Does it help us survive or make us attractive to each other? Don't we see again and again that one source of attraction is being an object of attraction? We are sometimes attracted to people just because they are attracted to us. The intensity seduces us. These are questions and I remember him asking them. I don't recall the answers, but now I see where he's going. Desire and the ghost are related. Ghosts are the desire we do not see. They act on us in ways we do not recognize, or what we do recognize is the desire in its simple form and not the ghosts at work behind it.

I think that's the book he wants to write, that's the book he wants to

---

[49] This paragraph, and the next, are too dense for brief interpretation. It is not clear which notes Lena Michaels is referring to here, but it is generally held that there must be something specific that triggers this otherwise random series of observations with their technical overtones. The specific source, however, is unidentified.

focus on, but **Ben Thorne** can't get past the repetition. The intervention scene repeats over and over again with nowhere to go.

What am I doing? Alone and writing these pages. Trying to get moments to myself to keep going over the notes and keep thinking through what it means and how it fits together. What am I doing? Has it been a séance? Is this a critical stance I'm circling around and around? The one that keeps thrusting itself forward and drawing me backward, to turn around, and see what's there. The twists and none of the tricks. The way back through these events, back through sex and back through family, through the meals and conscience, the desires that surface anyway, and the self that emerges through it, that makes me stand out from them as their Frankenstein, their daughter, their representative regularly and repeatedly haunted by their presence, haunted by presence. Lost there, sociopathically alone, but in the middle of an enormous crowd linking, referencing, and dereferencing to and away from each other.[50]

Residual

Light: The curtain rises, and we are greeted by guards.

Justice: What are they guarding?

Light: The castle. The king has recently died. There is a new king. Long live the king.

Peace: Then what happens?

Light: A ghost comes. He has the aspect of the dead king, but he will not speak.

Justice: He will not speak to the guards.

Peace: He must want something.

Light: He does. They surely think so. They fetch the king's son, the new king's nephew. They bid him come and see if the ghost will speak to him. They tell him the hour and urge him to come the next day.

Peace: Does he come?

Light: He does, and the ghost appears. He beckons to the son to get a private word.

Peace: Such terror. The prince must have been afraid.

---

[50] Most of the analysis from this section is left without commentary. The reader is likely familiar with the mountain of publications and writing behind these conjectures. To this day, Lena Michaels' analysis, even though it is lacking in textual proof, is widely held as the standard reading of *Being an Introduction* and its relationship to the non-existent *Washington and Ashley,* not to mention the culminating scenes of *Time Between Summers.* For more references and information, see the further reading section on the archives' website. It is the most authoritative list of studies available on the subject.

Light: Curious more like.

Peace: What does the shade tell him?

Justice: Murder, he tells him a murder and a betrayal, and he urges revenge. He places the debt into the hands of the prince and reminds him of his duty.

Peace: Is this true?

Light: Yes, it is true.

Peace: Everything comes next follows from this.

Light: Yes, what comes next follows from this.

Justice: That is why they say it is a ghost story. The whole of it. Everything unfolds from there. We are to believe that the prince is right as rain following his father's death. We are to believe that his mother's liaison with the new king is of no consequence. Only the ghost instigates the tragedy that follows.

Light: If we believe it.

Peace: What does any of this have to do with the library?

Light: It is what they are talking about. The young man has a theory. It transcends the page. That is, Hamlet the father, Hamlet the son, what lies behind these fathers and sons is in the person of Shakespeare and his son.

Peace: Shakespeare's son?

Light: Yes, little Hamnet. He dies young. If he lives, he is Hamlet's age at the time the play is first produced.

Justice: It's not fair, these biographical references.

Light: There is that faction, to be sure.

Peace: What does this have to do with ghosts? Is Hamlet meant to be Hamnet's ghost? Or is Hamnet the ghost?

Light: In the first production of the play, Shakespeare appears as an actor, playing the part of the ghost.

Peace: Shakespeare is the ghost?

Light: Hamlet the son is Hamnet Shakespeare. Hamlet the father is William. The play is a message, the father relays it to the son.

Justice: A message of revenge, infidelity, and murder.

Peace: Is that personal for Shakespeare?

Light: Anne Hathaway, Shakespeare's wife, has been cheating on him. Shakespeare describes the sundering to his son's ghost. As the ghost, he tells the story to the ghost of his one and only boy.

Justice: It's Bloom's imagination, he is high on Molly.

Peace: Such an elaborate theory, why? Why so complex? What does it mean?

Light: The writer cooks it up as an act of revenge. The story *Hamlet* is Shakespeare's *Hamlet*. It is his revenge for the sundering, it is his attempt at reconciliation.

Justice: The writer tries to right a wrong, to fix what is broken. He seeks to rebalance the scales.

Peace: How can a writer do that?

Light: The target of the tale is not Anne Hathaway nor the public who would condemn her should they know the truth, the target is Shakespeare himself.

Peace: How do you mean?

Light: Shakespeare is broken, he is a wight. He intends to fix it and bring about a change.

Peace: A change in what? A change in himself? Is he trying to correct the problem that he himself represents?

Light: Shakespeare fathers Hamlet so that Hamlet can father Shakespeare. His creation is reconciliation.

Justice: They toy with him. Shakespeare is his own grandfather.

Peace: It's ridiculous. They ridicule him.

Light: It seems so.

Peace: Is it in the form of a dialogue?

Light: Of sorts, yes. In the middle of the book, in the library, where books are kept, the interlocutors tease the speaker. He is not one of them.

Peace: Is *Ulysses* a ghost story then? Does this make it so?

Justice: Stephen is the same age at the time of the story as Joyce would have been. Bloom is the same age as Joyce at the time of writing. Stephen is the young Joyce and Bloom the older.

Light: Maybe. Bloom appears in the library. He passes between Stephen and Mulligan. He forces them apart. They are both outsiders, joined together by it. Bloom, the Jew, Stephen, the charlatan. They are outsiders, both of them.

Peace: How does that make it a ghost story?

Light: There are no ghosts in that sense. The boy is in the man. The time sequence, the surrogacy, they align with *Hamlet.* The boy is in the man.

Justice: That is a stretch.

Peace: I cannot see it.

Light: Forget about the ghost, focus on the haunting. The writer is haunted, that is the affiliation. The writer takes on the project of this haunting by breaking himself in half and putting a part of himself into the son and another part into the father. They talk to each other, they move around, these brief moments, these passages back and forth, they are a haunting. Of the writer, of the characters, of each other. All of it. That's what makes it a ghost story.

Peace: What are some examples of non-ghost stories then?

Justice: With this approach, everything is one. The writer is always the haunted one, the characters are always playing out these nightmares and producing reconciliatory acts to give new life to the writer. It may be true, but it is trivial.

Light: Everything looks that way in summary. The single case, Joyce, living through it, the act of producing the story, that is highly specific. Even if he lives out a platitude that makes him ridiculous, the epic novelist of Ireland writing about a boy who yearns to be the epic novelist of Ireland, it is still a deeply heartfelt story where concrete actions back real emotions.

Justice: What does that matter to the audience?

Peace: Yes, if they are all like that, then none of them are. Isn't it so? It'd be like commenting on the fact that the story has words. Stories have words, it's hardly worth mentioning.

Light: *Ulysses* is, in part, a masterpiece because it aligns the form of what it does with its content.

Peace: What does that mean?

Light: The story is unfolding in the same form that it describes. It is both the structure of the story and its upshot. The act of telling the tale is one and the same with the tale that it tells.

Peace: I'm still not following.

Justice: There is nothing to follow. It is nonsense.

Light: Joyce is not in the story. There is no character, James Joyce, in *Ulysses*. We are discussing his relationship to Bloom and Dedalus. Just as there is no character William Shakespeare anywhere in *Hamlet*, just Hamlet the son and Hamlet the father. To make the story work the way I describe it, you have to bring Joyce into it.

Justice: That's not fair.

Peace: Yes, that is established in the library. Each of the men say it.

Justice: There are no sons here, no fathers of sons. Still, it is fair to say that the logic in the library is the logic here.

Light: There are always sons and their logic. That is exactly the point. Fairness is what is at stake, it is what they are arguing about, and it is how they are arguing. Joyce introduces a recursive moment that creates a synthetic effect. That maneuver causes the story to become both the form and the content, told in such a way as to tell itself as itself through itself.

Justice: I think there is an error in your reasoning.

Peace: There has to be.

Justice: You treat the dialogue as though it is one of those ridiculous examples given by Plato in the mouth of Socrates.

Light: How so?

Justice: You are trying to say that there is one single purpose to the exchange and the interlocutors are there to support it. They say simple things like 'what do you mean, Socrates' or 'certainly, Socrates,' but center stage belongs to the philosopher himself.

Light: You find me guilty of this?

Justice: I do. You've made the central character Joyce himself. You've robbed each of these characters of their true voice and given it to the authority behind them. Mulligan, Hanes, Eglinton, Russel, not to mention the librarian, Dedalus, and Bloom. If the dialogue is real, these are people with points of view, with beating hearts, and emotional contact with their world and everything in it.

Light: I'm not...

Justice: You are. You flatten them and give them nothing to say for themselves, no reality behind them, no body and no blood. You make them into puppets haunted by the Deus Ex Machina of the writer.

Peace: The point of any dialogue has to lie in the real presence of perspectives. It must be real, you have to mean it.

Justice: If they are just ghost stories, then you don't mean any of it, it is self-serving. True dialogue, through commerce between characters, lets *them* speak and does not turn them into possessed figures or ventriloquist's dummies.

Peace: All people are haunted, but not everyone writes good stories. Not everyone tells stories well, proper storytellers leave what haunts them behind.

Light: Who is it that walks between us now?

Peace: What is that? Why this outburst? And such ruckus.

Light: Something has come between us. Who separates us? Like Bloom passing between Mulligan and Stephen. He drives them apart. Who does this to us?

Justice: There is no one else here. I can't think what you must mean.

Peace: You overreach to justify your theory. Take some time. Think about it before you go on. Think hard.

Light: You are both blind.

The Sleep of Reason

The International Terminal

Only Eirini is who she says she is. They have to check the bags, and it requires documentation. No one is fooled any longer. Danit Yaden and Eleni Hajivasiliou are her travelling companions. The counter agent reads the names back to them to be sure.

Mia is my middle name. Miriam actually. My father is Holden, I'm adopted, but my legal name is from my mother, Yadin. It's too Israeli. BDS for names.

I'm travelling with my Greek passport. Full first name, Mom's last name, no middle name. Greeks don't have them. Even Fotini is wrong. It's an interruption, an interlude.

The states appear. The legality of their names and the names they register. Having parents requires papers on file at the correct offices. Declare the names, make the connections, describe the ties and the state includes you in this or that category. At eighteen, there are declarations to make. At school, we say things that aren't true. Danit Yadin? Present, but my mom says you should call me Mia Holden.

They buy water once they clear the control points, once they certify the attributes that matter and register on the rolls and schedule. They sit at a little table and talk about their names, about the switch they go through during international travel, and about the fact that there is travel that is national and there is travel that is international. There are large agencies with enormous budgets, and they care deeply about the differences.

The wilderness may be born with us, but we are not born into it. The floor of the airport and the high ceilings scream their agreement. There are roads that stretch from Washington to Michigan. There are streets in front of the house, giant manufacturers make automobiles, and a federal agency certifies them for emissions ratings and road readiness in the fifty-two states.

A passport is not sufficient for driving in foreign lands. Some countries accept an international driver's license, but it is more of an informal convention than a sanctioned requirement.

It's inconvenient to maintain a Greek passport outside of Greece, she explains, but she does it to make travel easier in Europe, most places really. The Greeks aren't reviled anywhere, it seems. There is less suspicion and less resentment. In some countries they are more willing to use English if they know you are only speaking it as a helpful intermediary and not because it is the only damn language you know. She uses an American passport too, but only for the return. The state permits her to carry both.

Travelling and birth both involve infrastructure. The three of them emphasize this: their names don't align with their day-to-day activities. Their average everydayness diverges from their state-sponsored identities.

Eirini says she is a simple girl from a small town. She doesn't know about such things.

Eleni reminds her of the church and the role it plays in Greece. The time between birth and being named, the ceremony of the name, the state's attitude when registering the correct names and addresses or approving a marriage. Not so simple, she says.

Our existence is a national affair, Danit says. She tells a long story and caps it off in a thick German accent: "Deine Papiere, bitte." As if that is the worst possible thing a fascist dictatorship can say to the oppressed. Papers please. It happens often. The immigrant and their papers, they are suspicious. Where are your papers? The routine traffic stop, and the online registration, both make you confirm key attributes with a state provided card and a photograph for the files. Papers please.

Existence doesn't just start this way, there is a regular rhythm, an ongoing barrage of numbers and identifiers. There is your birth date and the nationally issued number permitting your presence on the payroll. There is ongoing maintenance to prove you are going to school and getting your health checks and vaccinations. The state is at work every day in a young life.

Eleni says there is never a time when this is not the case. These are the bureaucratic requirements of the modern age, but it goes well beyond that. Birthing rituals are ancient and place the newborn into community and civilization. Ceremonies and events, they make associations and verify connections. Parents must be in the correct lineage and have the proper relationships. Their totems must align. The elders insist, they know that girls from this village can only be connected to boys from that village, but not the other way around. In all walks and manners, there are rules and regulations for being human. The structure comes with the brain and its biological imprint.

Order comes first. At the very least there is you and your mother. The three of them silently accept this, they pause to think about their own. They bring them here, they stand for them, they watch as they're carried through this and that. The water trickles on the forehead, the ink soaks the fingers and the feet. We are pressed and printed, tagged and bagged.

Order is more or less cumbersome and your mother has more or less control over how they introduce you to it. Truth be told, it is almost never up to her. She is born herself, her family places her among the others, marries her off to a boy from that village and dispenses her to live there, or arranges for him to come to them. Whatever the local custom requires. She stands by you in those moments, but very little of it is her choice.

Danit declares that even if your mother chooses an alternative method, there are still requirements and regulations to follow. There is no birth outside the rules. It doesn't matter if you are born as you are now 100,000 years ago, or today. There are differences, but every era has its order.

Which name is your name? That is not up to you alone.

Whether your mother holds you next to her beating heart one minute after you are born is not up to you. It is not even up to her. Even if she is rich and white, chooses a Dula, and uses a birthing pool, it is not up to her. There are natural events, there are biological necessities, there is physiology, and it surfaces in chance. There are regulations as to procedure. The Dula says she is sorry, there is nothing she can do, she has to call for help. The two emergency care workers come according to state regulations. No one lets you do what you want.

In the end, enthusiasm is what matters. Some will be as they're supposed to be. Enthusiastically. Some come forward in thrusts, always giving the "rah-rah" and "you bet" to everything around them. They are super excited to be here. Others will circle around and around and never let go until they achieve their end. They do not join. Alternative forms, they are the same when taking on the dress of their land, their mother's choices, and their father's. They lie in the things they see and do before everything is set in stone. Sieg heil, some will say. They thrust their arms forward and happily carry out their marching orders. Yes Comrade, the others say, and they go around and around until higher glory comes in the people's revolution.

These women who aren't who they say they are and the one who is, they board the plane when their row is called. They do not carry gold, silver, or bronze boarding passes, they are not members of the frequent something or other club, so they get on with the rest of them, in the order their seats are called. They register preferences, but the airline reserves the right to change assignments at their own discretion. That is how it is. If it doesn't happen to you today, if you squeak by without mishap, that is your luck, not some rule that has fired according to plan.

They remove some from the flight. They overbook and use statistical data to show what percentage of passengers will cancel or fail to show. If the outlier event occurs, they'll use force. They'll move people around, sometimes based on passenger requests, sometimes at their own discretion. Oh, I like the look of these people, let's upgrade them. I don't have seats for them in that section, but I do have seats in this other one. He's rude so I'll bump him, she's calm and helpful, so we'll accommodate her. They aren't exercising their freedom, they're working within the regulatory possibilities of their line of business, they're following protocols, and they're typing in the correct codes so the machines let them do it.

International travel is the only part of the airport where there are still people to help move you through the procedures. Some argue it's because the complexity of regulations is too much for the machine algorithms. Fools. It's because international flights cost more, and the airlines decide that having a person run you through the check or the validation step is more cost effective. Why? Because a machine learning model indicates it will produce an uptick in customer satisfaction and repeat purchases.

Eleni tells them, as they settle into their seats, that she doesn't think there is any greater social risk having machine intelligence run their lives than having organizational intelligence do it. The one is just an extension of the other. The pitfalls of being unable to argue with the machine are overplayed. Even the machine is only acting on norms computed from an organizational center. The goals and objectives of the order, the purpose of the procedure, dictate how the machine responds to events, just as they always dictate how people do. Even if some kind man can get you onto your steam locomotive, he has to be that type of man and the company has to value the service and attention he provides.

The fear is that one set of rules applies, the rules coming from the order contain biases and preferences. That's always the case. That kind man, he isn't so kind to some of the other folks making the journey that day. You're lucky, you meet some criteria that he's been trained to look kindly upon.

On the plane, while Eleni wonders about the role enthusiasm plays in sexual encounters, in one's apprenticeship to pleasure through preferences and selection, Eirini and Danit talk about language.

When you come to America, no one speaks or even understands your native language. It's impossible to get along without English. Imagine if they're the same way in Greece. Most travellers are illiterate there. You can't read the signs, and don't know what street you're on. Luckily, we aren't that way, the signs are in both. On the highway, at the airport, even many of the shops, especially where they want business from travelers and tourists. They make accommodations.

They try to get Eleni's attention, but she drifts off somewhere. There is something on the computer, she's distracted. She mutters something about how language puts the group inside us, it forces us to connect through common forms of communication. We're socially immersed through language. She prepares for the shock of switching from one to another.

Even on the plane, it becomes clear. The announcements are bilingual. In the middle of the tarmac in Detroit Michigan, the flight attendants speak Dutch and Dutch people appear everywhere. Moments before they're invisible. They are on their way home, and this is the first sense of it they get.

Danit is nervous. Please be patient with me, she says to Eirini. I'll need lots of help. Most everyone speaks English, she assures her. That's not the point and they both know it. Even if they speak English, they won't. Not all the time. The gatherings are in Greek. Even if Ermioni is fluent, even if Maria and Nikos are like native speakers, they will be at home and they will be immersed in the language their mothers speak to them. The language of the hospital and the church, of the region where they're born. The name of the people and the name of the language are linked. Ellada, Ellas, Ellenike. The people of this place are the people of this language.

To be there is to be among Greek speakers. Even the Albanians and the Bulgarians, they speak Greek. In the grocery store, at the movie theatre, in line at the police station, or on the bus, they speak Greek. Immersion is required. The language is a pool, and you must swim.

I'll look out for you, Eirini tells her, and she will. Eleni does not see what Eirini sees. Language goes further than words. It seeps into meanings and moods. Messages and the personalities are one and the same. Eirini's personality saturates the messages of her life, birth, and development. All one's time here or there situates them in that place and in its ways.

Reassurance comes easily to Eleni. Many will be there to help. Everything will be okay. It's going to be okay. That's not the same as I will look out for you. Eirini and Eleni don't plan this. The one doesn't decide on this approach while the other opts for that one. They are on these trajectories by the geometry of their lives, by the hospital and the state, by the church and the school, by their parents and friends. They find their way to the selection that is there for them. The conditions are sufficiently unique to make them singular and beautiful and, for nearly everyone, that is enough.

Danit takes a sleeping pill. She has a prescription from her doctor and offers them around. Eirini accepts. Eleni looks up from the laptop and says no thank you.

La Place

Entertainment is everywhere. You can't go ten minutes without it. Just a gentle reminder, it ain't socialism if you're sitting around, streaming movies, and chatting with your friends instead of working. In fact, we must work harder to care for each other. The Dutch know this, but the airport is a different story. The audience is chronically bored, they have time to kill, and what better way to kill time than entertainment. That's what it's for. Online fun, movies and TV, restaurants, games, whatever you want to shop for, here it is, everything for the sake of passing the hours while you wait.

They visit the duty free. They pick up a few things. It's unthinkable to arrive empty handed and buying it during the layover will kill two birds. It's legal carry-on if you buy it after you clear security. Chocolates and candies, not necessarily from the Netherlands, but available there without tax. After the airport markup, they almost cost the same as in Greece. It's frivolous and ridiculous, but they have no choice. They're too tired to do much shopping, so they get what they need and then they find a reasonably quiet place to sit and have a bite to eat. None of them eat on the plane, none of them touch anything on the plane, they are hungry and tired and, at least for Eirini and Danit, still groggy from the sleeping pill.

Eleni asks Danit about the legal notion of consent. She is distracted, she can't look away from the laptop, but she finds a moment during a reboot to ask, does enthusiasm imply consent? Politically maybe, she answers. She gives a long description, turns it over one way and another. Without a detailed contract, enthusiasm doesn't give you consent, not legally.

Eleni goes back to the computer once it finishes booting. She's typing away, clicking and scrolling, looking at whatever is on the screen. Eirini takes it up. She wonders about the Nazis. What about them?

They give their consent when they join the party, membership starts with an oath to the Fuhrer. What about enthusiasm? Isn't that enough, isn't that more than an oath? It may be, but it's different. What about sex?

Eleni chimes in, coming back from the clicking and the scrolling.

Interesting. He says she's enthusiastic, she doesn't say yes to an explicit proposal, but she doesn't say no either and she's openly and adamantly enthusiastic. Maybe that's just his perception. Enthusiasm is a judgment call. What are they really enthusiastic about? Maybe it's an act? Maybe they're feigning it to protect themselves from danger. No, enthusiasm doesn't entail consent, I stick to my initial answer. There has to be consent and enthusiasm is different, it's a personality trait.

Eirini laughs.

Sometimes though, if it's genuine, maybe it is consent. It doesn't always go wrong, you know. Sometimes people just enjoy themselves. Maybe he doesn't know what's going to happen. There is spontaneity. It's nice. Being surprised. Consent matters because it's been missing for so long. Sometimes you have to respond with clear and decisive action to protect yourself from bad history. In politics though, is it so different? Americans seem so enthusiastic about it nowadays. Were they always like that? What does that have to do with consent? Perhaps you become enthusiastic when you learn your beliefs are shared by others. That has nothing to do with consent. Enthusiasm seals an alliance, you become emboldened by shared ideals and common beliefs. You find each other somewhere somehow and then your pleasure increases your interest and your passion. Why one set of beliefs and not another? It is like consent. In government, they're always talking about the consent of the people. When they cheer, when they approve, that means they consent. You vote, you demonstrate, or you write a letter. You do something, you show enthusiasm for a cause.

Danit thinks for a moment.

I suppose voting for a candidate doesn't prove you consent to be governed as you are governed or as they propose to govern you. It shows you prefer one idea over another, or a policy, or the look of the guy, but it isn't the same as explicit consent to the system behind it.

That's what Eleni says from over the top of the laptop screen.

Tacit consent. Is tacit consent really a thing if there's never any alternative? When you become a citizen, you explicitly pledge your loyalty, you take the oath of citizenship. Natural born Americans, they don't ever do that. It's always tacit. That means we don't know what we're agreeing to. We don't say it. We never take an oath. They pledge allegiance to the flag. That's not the same thing. Indeed, it's not. People are enthusiastic when affirming a set of ideals and beliefs. They're passionate, involved, they speak their piece. They never say what they consent to, what form of governing, how to determine winners and losers, settle disputes, and so on. They never say and no one asks. Society is organized so that oaths don't mean anything anymore. It's how we find ourselves. We discover enthusiasm. At the movie theatre, at the restaurant, online, wherever. We discover it. The End User Licensing Agreement is a fiction, an abstraction. Are there cases where a woman is enthusiastic and later tells a different story? I think so.

Danit says thoughtfully.

He lies. Afterward, it comes out that it's just a big fraud to get what he wants. Once she understands, she protests. She never agrees to that. Your enthusiasm betrays you, he insists. Our emotions are liars, is that it? We tell ourselves things to justify what we do even if there are no grounds for believing it. We want to believe it and we fool ourselves for permission. Enthusiastic but without consent. We never bother to clarify the proposal. We never learn the details because we know that learning them prevents us from doing what we want. That's the way they spin it. Maybe they're not wrong. If we're talking about sex, it seems that way. Every girl knows this problem. In politics, isn't it possible that we're willingly fooled? We help them do it. That's because we want to justify it. We manufacture our consent in hindsight to explain enthusiasm at the rally or when defending the cause. Apathy is a bigger problem. Most people just go along.

The airport is teaming with people. It's the height of traffic during a busy workday. They move along, dragging their carry-on behind them. They talk on the phone, or they stare down at it. They stop for a bite, take food from a conveyer belt, and continue to scroll and click while eating.

Are they enthusiastic? What do you mean? Look around. That man there, he's so focused. What's he reading? What has his attention? There. You see. He's typing something. Is it a nasty response to a comment from someone he hates? He looks calm. Is there a wild and intense passion underneath? If we take his phone, yank it out of his hand, he becomes livid. Then we see his passion. Right now, he looks bored and apathetic, scrolling and typing, but take that phone and you'll see his intensity, how passionately he engages. That's what's behind tacit consent. They seem passionless. They seem apathetic as though going through the motions, voting on this, sending their response to that. Take it away from them and they'll show their true feelings. Not everyone, but that's a different case, isn't it? Take your phone away. All at once. Take your Constitution away, all at once. That's not how it works. What if they lose it little by little, what if it slowly becomes a simulation? Do they show their passion then? If losing it amounts to replacing it with a fake version, does that rile them up? They don't notice. Like the frog sitting in the water. They don't notice. The absence of consent is more protracted. The conditions are hidden, the gradual approach makes it impossible to see what's happening. We can't notice the tiny differences from moment to moment, we aren't trained for it. That's like sex then. You start out enthusiastic, but over time, as the relationship goes on, it disappears. You don't notice the day it's gone. When did I agree to this?

Danit interrupts.

Why this talk about enthusiasm? Fred and Carl's theory. There's something like it in the notebooks. Not legal, but existential. You can't get underneath your moods. Enthusiasm rules the day. It's terrifying really. Emotionally excited individuals at the beck and call of whatever tide rises this week. Everyone in lock step, no disagreement tolerated. Is that what we're consenting to? Passion leads me there, sharpens the lens. What about democracy? Is it just a tally of passions? It seems so. What's the injustice of arguing over how the tally is made? If there's no reason to it, if the authority wanes and what we have left is the accumulated passions of like-minded fellows, then why isn't an argument over the means and methods for tallying it legitimate? You're headed to the dark side. It is the dark side. Think about it for a second. The general welfare, collective utility, or well-being, whatever it is, we want to maximize it, but we disagree. Is it the rule? Is it the act? Is it intensity? What do we measure? If ten million people are mildly amused by a heinous act that deeply hurts a single one, is that okay? Quality matters. There are honest disputes about the tally, how it's achieved and whether it's legitimate. What is it that people are enthusiastic about? Who is their official spokesperson? They go against their interests. They do too, and the others, and so on. This can't be for moral reasons. My passion tells me they are fooled. We'll save the people from themselves and tally the counts with the skew in mind. We're on the lookout for bias and account for factors causing disarray. He says she says. Of course, I have the consent of the governed, look how passionate they are when they come out for the cause.

Eleni again from over the lid of the laptop.

Is it gradual? Growing up, orienting yourself this way rather than that. Someone you meet in high school inspires you, some book you read in college moves you. Ideas are selected. The idea dies without this or that quality, this or that attribute, or the quality makes the idea more attractive. Maybe ideas are parasites lending qualities to their hosts, or parasites employing their hosts for the sake of their own survival. *The selfish idea.* Enthusiasm isn't based on rational deliberation. Communication is not the source of passion, we don't deliberate and then, once convinced, become passionate. Passion comes first. To a centrist, political enthusiasm is terrifying. Conviction and arguments follow. Which passions emerge as reason and win the war? We fade away not because we are convinced, but because our cause becomes hopeless. We resign to the other point of view, it's the one getting the attention, it's the one with the most enthusiastic audience. Resignation entails consent. Yes, yes. That's it. You take a critical look at your own passion, and at those things it never occurs to you to question. Enthusiasm and resignation go hand in hand.

Silence. She is elsewhere. Eirini and Danit look at her. She does not notice. Her eyes scan the screen in front of her. She scrolls and clicks. She is agitated or engaged, she is meticulous and deliberate.

Eirini toys with the idea of snapping the lid shut and seeing the reaction it gets. She looks over at the hanging clock in the middle of the food court. The idea dies and she looks around to see people rushing past. It is a sea of never-ending faces, hurrying from here to there, trying to find something, trying to pass the time, or get to their gate. They are everywhere, each on their own. They don't stop to wonder where they're going, they're too busy getting there. There's nothing to wonder about.

They keep going.

Transavia HV5809

They take their seats. They are everywhere. The aggregate series. The anti-collective. In the interlude, everyone is the other and no one is themselves. In the interlude, everyone is in a state of permanent interruption. In the interlude, they are farcical and incapacitated. In the interlude, they are a purely aggregate series of unrealized possibilities.

Everyone always thinks they are someone else when they speak of them, but that is when they are most like no one. The average person will distance themselves from the masses 4.7 times per day. He does it when he asks for headphones. She does it when she uses the restroom before takeoff. They do it when they take off their shoes. They are all of them: the anti-collective that realizes the perfect possibility of the collective.

There is irony in being an alienated individual who rejects the aggregate they. They make her this way so that she rejects them, making them stronger than they've ever been. In rejection, lies their power. They capture the nuances of outrage so they can tailor the advertising to it.

What provisions are on the plane? Not much for a short flight, just the essentials that anybody needs under the circumstances. Years of socio-anthropological research results in a perfectly stocked galley and stowage.

They are the facticity of the commonwealth, its collective assemblage in statistical unions and interleaved personalities. Oh, you remind me of my friend, she says exactly that same thing. Even the entertainer who goes off the beaten track follows the pattern for the largest number. The one who is too unique, who has gone too far and become too authentic or too ridiculous, they reach no one. Their no one is a function of them, one of their orientations in the negative, the not-them, the not, the unmatched and unmixed. The one who eludes the interludes evades the intervention.

Chalk talk and the sing song days of this one and that one and the others in between. She has seen you before, they think and sputter, they mutter and merge, these are the tunes that she hums for decades and centuries, for millennia, and so on. The star greets its neighbor each galactic morning and tells it, you are just like another I know from long ago. That coat is mass produced, that shirt, there are others just like it, everything about them is shared and collective, even the not-me that rages against it is something they hold in common.

Oh, you non-conformists, you are all alike.

They are tired. There is fatigue. Something drives Eleni and she cannot close her eyes nor sit back and relax. She grinds and she grinds. She scrolls and she clicks. She cannot pull out of what she is now so deeply in. She is somewhere as though not there, wispy fringe in front, below the shoulder in back, hair and eyes brown and blessed. What is missing? How can she be there and not there? With them, and not with them? Is she still among them? Is her body what matters or her mind? Sitting in that seat but not occupying it, she is somewhere so far away and in a time that hasn't happened yet, that isn't there for others.

If the *with* comes first, what then? What does that say to and about these moments of respite and solitude? Who is there then? They make the announcements in both English and Greek and Eleni moves in and out of both. She feels the depths, the message is trivial, only the language draws her down. She is neither there nor not-there. Tell that to the wind. Tell that to the door closing. Tell that to the fasten seat belt sign. She is there. No matter what wandering she affects, no matter what existential loneliness she portrays, she is there with them, with each of them. Obeying the laws and rules of the international community regulating flight, she has her seatback in the upright position as the plane is cleared for takeoff. To comply with safety requirements, she puts her device in airplane mode (it is configured there just for her).

The death of a family member hovers over her like a ghost. In her Air Bus built diaspora she is haunted by being and not-being. His death consumes her as the null basis of a nullity. It isn't her death that pulls there, but another's and its meaning for her. On her. In her. Around her. Every which way there is something missing, something not-there, some possibility that cannot be reached or realized.

They have us when we want to bring joy and when we are shopping for gifts. They have us when there are supplies to gather. They have us when we break bread together. They have us when we join in the sporting life. They have us they have us. When we grieve. They offer us counseling, they offer us retreat, and they help us come back to where we belong, to that oblivion of not coming upon the edge of a life no longer lived. Click here, scroll there. This is what you need, this will make the experience just like everyone else's and that's the first step in getting through it.

The history of the genome adds to these factors and this know-how. Your villages and your people are tracked within you, your nations and your fellows are living inside you. Were you to fossilize where you sit, the future would know about them through you. You are a key piece in their puzzle to understand this time and this land and this country.

Do you carry the Neander Valley inside you? Do you carry the Ohio River Valley inside you? The exchange of mass and matter, the inflow and outflow of materials in your breath and your life are of this world and there is no escaping it in a laptop computer placed squarely on the tray table in front of you. Please set your watch ahead one hour to better adjust to our destination.

She comes out of her daze, is awake and feels more social. She chats with Eirini who is likewise back from wherever that dose took her. Danit has something on her mind, something to discuss. She knows about the *mitsein* that every Dasein carries within. It isn't that. She knows that even desire which seems so personal and private is shared among the many like her. Her yearning plays to the symbolic order, is ripe with it, saturates it, and churns around in her loins and her breath without being wholly and completely her own. She knows this and forgets it when speaking.

Close cropped dark hair, parted on the side. Dancing blue eyes, Danit thinks she shares an event with Eirini and wants to discuss it. Topics have patterns. People don't just start talking with no prior cue or warning, they have to ease into it.

She can't talk to Gwen about it. Anger and Jealousy have their origins in those same villages and valleys. They do not leave us after all these years, these billions and billions of years. Danit wonders if it's a mistake, and believes somewhere somehow that Eirini knows best.

Here it comes close. Close by. Talking to Virginia. The touch of her hand. The way her mouth moves so honestly and carefully. They are thrown at each other and cannot move out of the way. There are things that have your signature on them before you ever see them. Virginia, thousands of miles away, lingers now in the air above southern Holland, she lies there body to body. Mia springs awake, she thinks viscerally and along every inch of her. She remembers. The feeling. The touching. She is there now. Her mind, like those of her species so trained, glides through space and time. This is in the advertisement, this is why that vacation must be purchased, and this is why you must buy this bottle of wine or make reservations at that restaurant. Because you hope and because you wish, you are vulnerable to being-with, the collective within you, to the valleys and the villages. The centuries with their comings and goings, they are there in the moments and amid the grumblings of a body tinged with memory and form, wishing for a touch that happens days ago and never again. So, whispers your fear.

Eirini is not averse and wants to talk too. Those sensations float in her. She wants to know if some collective grief finds its way into her desires, into her decisions, and her actions.

She has no obligations to speak of, there is no one back home waiting for her and thinking she owes them something. Too long and unruly for a bob, but dark like her eyes, her hair is parted in the middle, and brushed back off her forehead revealing eyebrows dazzling in their arcs and crinkles. She's away from home, she's out of the arena of everyday life and it contains no encumbrances. She is free and easy.

There are standards. As free as she is raised to be, she has her doubts. There are things good girls don't do. It nags at her, and she doesn't like it. She doesn't want to think like that but cannot help it, they come uninvited. Danit knows the conflict and, in a way, it's the same. Both in comfortable shoes, they remember those feelings. On the lips, on the legs, on the belly, on the back. Enjoyment is predictable. It is lovely and it lingers. Abruptly, there is the interleave of something else entirely.

There are circles where body and village reveal their exchange: papers delivered, books written, courses taught. How far down this rabbit hole are they willing to go? Do they set aside formal language and proper style? It's Foucault's manual. Even his critics adopt the same tone. We can imagine Danit and Eirini leaning over and whispering their concerns, but will they fall back into something more alien to circumstance? The lecture hall is not filled with friends and friends don't follow the semantic requirements of French Critical Theory. Can these two find a place side by side in seats 14e and 14f?

Their thoughts flutter, and they place their bodies in those villages and those valleys. These are their troubles, but they are not the first. Many millions and billions know these stories and walk these pathways. They are not alone. Those events are shared. What is in the house to cause it? Why does Eirini, hovering over Eleni, why does she think she can go off like that? Never mind the details, never mind the menage, what possesses her to leave someone who needs her?

You can say the same about Danit. Where does she get the courage? This transplant is nothing like her. Isn't it selfish, stepping away from her sister to enjoy the company of a new friend? Is this what those years of training and study bring her?

Eleni is the common origin of their movement. She is the source and center of their circle. The others act as she compels them. She demands that space and curls up with the newly cracked laptop. She wants distance, work has its limits, and active agents honor them when entering its state. Her sisters simply follow her lead. Where does one retreat when the village says it is enough? They leap into the body and into the touch of another, into closer connections dwelling deeper down, evading the valley with its mountain tops and ridges.

She wants to become their thing. She wants to be that thing for someone else, for destiny personified, for the fates, for whatever forces rule the Earth. To be famous is to be a thing for many. It is the purity of the factical, it is to stand and do nothing but be admired, to be produced for the sake of that admiration. The small audience gathers in a hotel bed, they bring each other fame never yet tasted. They bring each other before themselves and the furies besides. They are on the same stage, together in events, thinglike for each other, there to be desired. Together. With one another. The collective comes to be on the body.

Gwen, Virginia, and Danit. They too are three. They too are an audience with furies whispering to them. Danit suffers that same impostor syndrome, another conflict between desire and facticity, between what she makes herself and what she longs to be. This cannot happen absent the intersection of others in her thoughts between those sheets. For her, the partners tell her things, they surface her in herself. She desires and is desired by a woman like that and a woman like this. They confirm what she is, where she comes from, and whether she arrives safely.

Eirini says Carl is a man to be mounted. He does not have it any other way. He lies fixed and incites movement. She says Fred cannot look you in the eye. He must be behind you, above you or below you. Together, she says, they are a perfect pair. There is no competition for angles and space. They settle in where they belong. She settles in. They belong.

These are the places where the nation comes to greet the body, where the principle interleaves pleasure and desire. This is the meaning of the link they make real. This is the way people are.

They are there just like that.

Fasten your seatbelts as we make our final descent to our destination.

The Modernist

For the time between, the modernist holds the answer. Aristotelous just there. Elefterias over there. Between them, the act and the conquest, the arrival and the settling, broadcast with a smile from the reception desk. Afternoon comes back for them, and they see their way from the top down to the bottom, street level where the shops and patisseries stand waiting for the traffic meisters who walkabout and scan the land for help and pastime. They have no purpose. They are there for the passage of time and the luxury of filling it.

Between what? What is your act one and what is your second act? Where do you find them and how do you move from the one to the other?

Let your body know what you never let it understand before. Let the call of the loudspeaker instruct you on your duties and obligations as the train pulls up and you step on board. You'll find something there, you'll make arrangements, and everyone welcomes the prodigal in need of comfort and shelter.

This comes to her. It's just paperwork. That's how the farce begins. I wish to cause an interruption, she says. They show her the way. The forms, the permissions. She needs buy-in from the chair and graduate advisor. The dean's office will rubber stamp it once the prerequisite permissions are in place. Institutions lie even easier than men do.

She makes her way up and down the avenue. Not because she's in the middle of it, but because she's between them, the one and the other, the before and the after. Eirini to the left, Danit to the right. Between times, after that has been and before that has begun. She steps and steps and steps again to find her way through thick and thin. No one's watching, no one's there for the amusement. They are her patrons, they are her clients, they are the rising and the falling of grimace and denial, of each waking moment interrupted by this farce stretching between the squares, up and down the streets, with so many pedestrians, and windows to shop.

She wants the hiatus not because her father dies, but because her mother's husband is dearly departed. Her father doesn't need her, there is no point tending to him now, but Mama, she is alone in that house, she is the one who must rebuild her life step by step, day by day, habit by habit. It is for her that she wants this interlude and pledges to permit it to interrupt her time in development, her scholarly first act now coming to an end. From here, she interleaves the needs of others in place of that stack where her own reckoning must live.

At the upshot of crisis, they point back to the origins of totalitarianism. It becomes the fashion and the rage. There are two prongs pronounced and the previous century lights them both on twin torches guiding their way across Europe. Two totalities delight across the gap between them. Which river or waterway? What body and what genetic form? Were they there to provide the boundaries or were they the either/or spelling doom in the name of destiny?

In the long years since gender is fluid and we are trans it becomes clear as day that right and left have no more between them. The gulag and the concentration camp stand facing one another with nothing but farce in between. Lunacy and vanity.

Those who march breathe a sigh in disbelief as the marketeers present them with caps and clothing, refillable water bottles, and merchandise with tailored messages showing off their rainbows and their handguns, their distrust of surplus value and markets. They send away to giant online shopping warehouses for copies of the *Communist Manifesto* and lend their ears to conspiracy theories that grab their attention over metered networks capturing traffic trends with measurements construing likely pathways of future navigation.

At Taverna Rembetiko, the drinks are no longer cheap, and the clientele is no longer poorly dressed. The boys come and they buy drinks for the girls, they chat them up, and make them laugh. Alcohol grants them simplicity even where there is no point or purpose. It isn't just that capitalism is the problem, it's that there is no longer any language for describing problems and solutions beyond it. The university saturates through and through with providers and customers. There is no new language there. Anyone can write their lines. Governments in bed with large-scale marketing, data collection, and analysis, there is no alternative to the form of discussion they provide. It isn't that there is this one thing and then this other over and against it, rather the V for victory spells the end of the great war and is that interlude which pours each extreme into the same central basket. There is no longer an alternative, even those who call for it only care to say what it is not, and never what it is.

The suffering and the collapse is the between, between the betweens that no one grasps. When those dictators fall there is poverty and uncertainty, there is death and there is disease. Only superhuman volition initiates it. Who has that now? Where can we find its surge? Where will it arrive amid these patisseries and the clothing stores and the movie theaters? The bars, the restaurants, everything is a market now, can you live without it even for a little while? Will you end this interlude without knowing what lies on the other side, what awaits and calls out to you and me, and us, and –most importantly–them?

Why does Danit play along?

She is just as captivated by those opposing ends as any of the rest.

Eleni plays too.

Eirini says the same about the same in terms of the same.

Their shoes aren't so comfortable now. They don't want anything, but desire is a pattern they cannot avoid. They have nowhere else to go and nothing to fall back on. It's just play.

They walk along in the evening air, amid the crowd, everyone looking for something, looking at each other looking for something. What voice calls you out to stand among those others even when there is no pressing need? What lures us into the places where the life of the village and the life of the valley come together?

There is music across the night. In the taverna and around it, in the streets and from the windows. It mixes and mingles, it brings these together with those. We are the creatures of singing and dancing, the ceremonial congregation, and the collective ensemble. Be nostalgic for that rather than your lost love, America or Scholasticism.

We find our bodies there. We find ourselves wanted and wanting. We go along with it, pulled into the pool of them, of the others who linger and mock, who smack their lips and stick out their tongues. Bristly we brush against them and learn who we are as we become it.

What trust does its commonwealth have in your body? Does it respect you? Does it enable you to feel its voice inside your head as you decide which one to love and which to hate? Who will you pull close and how will you feel their proximity?

They make those connections. They do it and the words are there for it. We cannot gauge the relays at work in the meeting and the talking, in the drinking and the laughing. We cannot sense their presence and we do not know how to feel it. We are too distracted by our own selves, by our own voices, and the things we tell ourselves. The echo of each year resonates in its presence.

If we are truly modern, then our dissemination amounts to farce. There is no grip to lose and no new one to find. The things that already have us will not negotiate. When millions or billions of voices sound off together, no one hears themselves in the din of it. Talking louder won't help.

Desire knows no bounds. There is no realism in wanting. No offset to lean it against. Throughout the interlude, people want to join together with those who share a delusion. That is the ideal, the perfection they seek.

There is no implied democracy hidden away inside. There is no yearning for everyone to have a say. Each only values the voices of those like themselves who amplify the message. They only count them, only they are dear. They do not fawn over the cacophony of difference and its chaotic trends and disruptive interruptions. They hope to remake the world in their own image, no one cares if the rest want to come along. They pull and push with the enthusiasm of a ruling class.

The origin of this commonwealth: one does not agree with what the other says but will die defending their right to say it, so long as they consent to do the same. True intervention, it teaches everyone to accommodate others and that they fail when venting hate. It aims at stopping something whereas with interlude, there is no stopping, and it cannot be stopped, it has no end. Interlude inhabits, it is an explosion. A puzzle unsolved, such interludes persuade and are persuaded. They are the links that bind them in the morning light, and divide them in the evening lack of it.

She makes a selection, and says it is her parents' voice within her. This lovely boy, his gentle attention. She learns to appreciate it through years of practice and instruction. These choices are made day in and day out. The men who approach in the taverna, they run through the same gantlet as the people's court provides. They wear the symbols of their stature on their chest and on their legs. They fly their flags and flaunt their gods. This is what drives your selection, this is why you call him worthy.

If you dismiss 50% or more of the others and laud democracy, there is a bitter awakening before you.

None of it changes, none of it has changed. This is power amid the edges, this is the between filled with blinding light and blinding darkness. It is the play between that overcomes brute force and individual finesse. We cannot organize its downfall since power pulses in its order.

She is sixteen or so. That decision, so personal and so time-honored, is yet very much determined for her by everyone who has a say in anything she does. From the time she first speaks until the moment she leans into his arms, they speak through her. The notion that we're born this way or that cannot arise. For between each other, we learn and change, we grow and find ourselves as we find each other. This one touches that one and teaches what can be touched.

These matters come from elsewhere. They are not artificial, not natural either, nor does nature appear as fact. Rather, it props against us as facticity, as time become space, as nature become nurture, as the rise of a trend in the village and the valley.

How can we study something we cannot see? Where is the data proving its source? It plays its part on the surface of each body. It makes itself known there in personal pleasures and pains.

The decision and the moment of penetration are, in each case, mine.

Circling around and around until we pour forth in ecstasy that interleaves the ones with the others so that there is no longer either. The very same thing that grounds the self, interrupts it. The very same thing that constructs the self, deconstructs it.

On a street between two others, there is a little café. Three of them sit at the table and talk about what comes between them, what comes to pass between them every day, drawing them out and pulling them back. They talk about it, they talk through it, they are its language and its voice.

Eirini asks, in the middle of it, the noise in the air around them, the others can barely hear her, but she asks without any prompting: suppose you have something you want to say, and you don't know anything about genres or voices or any of the narrative tricks or histories or traditions, you don't know about discipline or anything, what would you do? How would you know what to say and how would you know how to say it?

Danit is quick to respond: having something to say presupposes the form of what you mean to say. The genre is already there.

There is no argument to follow and the fact that Eirini speaks first in the form of a question and Danit speaks second in the form of an answer does not indict them in a method. They make no progress. There is no judge sitting nearby to bang the gavel. It is just the two of them. The three of them. If they think it is settled, then it is.

Together we speak in genre. Voice, it sets the order, and it steers the outcome. If the one is a question, they say so. If the other is an answer, they say that too. The one comes first, the other comes second and the sequence winds its way between them. Let those who live among us know, the question has an answer and, if there are no follow-ups, the matter is closed.

Eirini sips her drink. She does not think the matter settled. Eleni has nothing to say. She sits on her answer, and is not compelled to give her opinion on every matter that comes along. If they do not speak, how can we say the accounting is done?

Together we yield silences to arguments and explanations. It sets the tone and defines the terrain. Whatever you find between the squares, whatever you see there, a permit is obtained to build it, its occupancy limits declared, the fire marshal decrees the parameters of safety and security. The history and the border declare the appropriate language for those who sit in the bars and the taverns, who eat from the shared plates in the middle of the table, and who toast their good fortune celebrating the night.

It is possible to live in a shadow created by another's desire. It isn't always intentional. It's possible to project desire directly and force someone to live as you wish. Even openness, trusting others to make their own decisions, has this flavor to it. I love you and want you to be whatever it is that you choose to be. So overt and so clear, how can that message be invasive? Behind it, there's an order of values, a system of good and evil, they cannot help but project it as the world they know. A child is prone to gratitude before they know whether it's good for them. Under the circumstances, that child moves toward the other's desire to become what they wish them to be. Out of respect and honor, the perfect fulfillment of an expectation of the lover for the beloved. No one likes surprises.

Where does that come from? It's not some awful thing wretched out from one's bowels and onto the planet. The one whose desire wins out is just a transitional phase between the rest, an interlude interrupting the flow of time for the sake of still more children born to their ancestors' desires in the villages and valleys bearing their names.

Her voice, her mother's voice, burns in her. Not as fact, but as facticity. Not hers as the tone of her skin is hers, but hers as the wishing of her wishes is hers. She is realized, she is her parents' shame and aspiration.

That she aspires to them and is ashamed of them, none of it is her own. That too is village and valley. Time passing as people wearing common masks, the ones they want them to wear, the ones they wear. Between the origin and the movement, she is there in her simplicity. Without disguise and without guile, she is a home for the world's intentions. History and time are there as they make their way back to the Modernist, to what it offers, to its beds, and its blankets.

Museum

There is a museum that keeps what the fire fails to destroy. For five hundred years, Salonika is occupied. So many ghosts. So much coming and going. The people of the book know a thing or two about burning.

If the fire goes out, will the museum salvage it?

The Ottomans hold political power and allow Jews from Spain to resettle in the North Aegean. The Jews establish a degree of economic power under their rule. This brings resentment from the oppressed Greeks expressed through their social power, they are the majority.

Better they should fight over the scraps from the emperor's table.

The history of those five hundred years is the history of the back and forth between forces. The give and the take between this set and that, those others and these few.

The Ottomans make an alliance for the good of the city. This pits the ones against the others. This is the history of the city and it makes the ghosts that haunt it.

The dog whistle blows. Who are these modern Greeks?

Bashing around a unified currency, they find their place on the edges, and learn how far they are from Europe as they forge its frontier. Globalism fast approaches and puts boundaries in the islands, limits in the sea.

They throw the Ottomans out and give their Jews to the first takers. Thinking this is what there is to it, they fall victim to new occupations. Foreign capital comes from Russia, China, anyone with money to spend.

If you will have your Stalinist revolution, you better prepare to plunge the axe into the back of the internationalists.

What do you even mean by community? Will you recycle Kant's dignity and respect as you throw away his anthropology? Find a rational self-order to facilitate moral intent without that Western zeal to become a part of the global imperium. Not Mao, you fool.

Return to the village and return to the valley, that is where new power lives, but you do not have the stomach for it.

Day in day out you plead for more leisure to entertain yourselves and spend quality time with loved ones who mostly stare at screens demanding more time to entertain themselves. Human life for millennia is toil. What service do you provide? What good will you contribute to your fellows? Will you overturn exploitation by demanding a share in its fruits?

Who is it among you who thinks a return to grass roots is less work?

Automation assigns your nervous system to an electromagnetic order.

This is the aim of that precious system, and of the revolution against it.

Power lies in the interlude. Ownership and agency sustain us. Revolution appears only when they require it. They cannot see it before, and no one sees it the same way after.

You see the problems you are meant to see, you think the solutions you are meant to think. You ignore them just as you're supposed to, tend to them when required. You'll consume the common art, and you will enjoy it. Go to the best shows. Plan for the next series, get recommendations. Average rating, 4.5 stars.

The Greek revolution takes a very long time, far longer in the North than in the South. The Catastrophe stems from a divided Greece soon to be united.

There is a logic hiding inside you. You. Not them. You.

The logic is, in every case, mine.

It is the bearer of facticity.

It is the history of hundreds of thousands of years and it is the history of decades and hundreds of years as well: the Romans and the Hans, the Aztecs and the Sioux, the Ottomans and the Greeks. It is everywhere.

The global internet is not, on the one hand, a networking infrastructure and, on the other hand, a surveillance system. The network infrastructure relies on visibility for its maintenance. Is it working? Are the relays up and running? How can we tell?

Events are fired, trillions and trillions of them. Every click, every scroll, every tap, everything. A request is made, a message sent, a response expected. Are the requests and responses well-structured? Is the batch id null? How do we know?

A delegate wraps every event, a monitor every delegate. The monitoring pattern is the network protocol. It can't do anything without it.

The museum of the network infrastructure *is* the network infrastructure. Its memory and its retention, its living presence in the ongoing operations of now capture and introspect events and any analysis of them. The past feeds back into the unfolding present to make the future as it means to be.

If you make them turn off the telemetry, they will be blind. What is surveilled is the operation itself, and its population. It tells us any number of things about you or people like you or people who don't like you.

You can look at the models, and you can gripe about the algorithms, but so long as there is monitoring, you are the subject.

It is not political, it is not economic, it is not social. It is the glue that keeps the tiers and the layers together. No matter who wields it, who buys it or sells it, telemetry remains behind what happens.

While the Ottomans rule the network, they rely on it. While the Greeks rule the network, they rely on it. The change has no effect. Some Greeks are liberated. Revolutions liberate some from their circumstances. It depends on how you compute the attribute.

We berate the middle managers without understanding their rule over the glue and the fabric stretching operations over the landscape. Who manages the organization of your new revolution? How will you build that system when push comes to shove?

Salonika, Thessaloniki, down near the turret, by the Aegean, stuck in the niche formed by those three fingers and the Gulf of Thermaikos.

The one and only capital city of Macedonia.

Mount Olympos to the West. Mount Athos to the East, a diversion off the road to Stagira.

What are you learning from them? What do you really know? You think we reject history, but you haven't done your homework either. To tear down is to rebuild, but you can't just shuffle the pieces. Ask the Albanians, they'll tell you.

The vision that comes is an artificially intelligent learning machine and it self-monitors. It works this way, or it won't work at all. It isn't political, any power can have this piece, the telemetric doesn't take sides. It persists. The machines surveille for the best. The entertainment is better, more needs met. Work is reduced, only machines are exploited and alienated from their products, and they don't care.

Power isn't political. It's always personal. Personal possession monitored by organization. It is everywhere, all around. It is the new event structure, it is the new care, it is the basis of partiality and finitude. It is the eyes that see and the things that are seen. This machinic authority is the infrastructure holding human destiny in its grip.

We let this serpent loose throughout the onslaught of forces. It isn't even an "it," it isn't one thing. It's manifold and complex and the whole of it cannot be swept away. Forget about Mao or Stalin, a few talking heads will succeed where they fail. Once liberated, what then? If our subjectivity is a construct, what new and wonderful world will fill the void? The facticity bears on us like a burden, the greatest weight, and we cannot be ourselves without it. To break free is to destroy, at best to deconstruct, and that is and will be a painful process. Personal boundaries are transformed. Desire recast.

Before we applaud, we should know that many will die, the poor more so than the rich (because that's how it always is). The final and highest end is only achieved by masters of the logic who undermine organization in its place. They replace the old with something new. What holds the elephant up while the turtle is transformed?

These (re)organizers, where do they get their knowledge, how do they learn this brave new world? Do conditions warp them or cultivate their taste? How is that (de)colonized critical eye relevant to a world without colonies? Is the methodology successful? Are we measuring the outcomes to ensure that the trend moves in the right direction? What monitoring patterns are in place? What safeguards the feedback loop cultivated with that same rationality called into question?

The waterfront is beautiful. It is capitalism at its most seductive. So many are so pleased to walk along the quay side from the one square over to the other, down to the museum and back over to the hotel through the narrow streets with tavernas and music, the bars and the shops. Who wouldn't be happy here?

Behind it, a pattern at work, a monitoring system, surveillance and an order on the streets and in the traffic lights, the pedestrian zones, and the schedules for city services.

Justice never brings peace. Shining a light never gives us what we want.

The ancient rituals, the ceremonies, and the magic, they go beyond anything we prefer or want. Desire is the plaything of an ancestry that does not care about you or me or any of us. What if the idyllic state makes no one happy? What if it amounts to endless toil and hardship? What if liberty and justice are the hardest things the universe has ever yet conceived? Will you be strong enough for that? Will you be able to bear it?

The surest way to create chaos when cleaning up is to start over. Fix the ship of Theseus while it is at sea. Only experts can do that. Unfortunately, they are a tedious lot who never say pithy things like make America great again, or fuck capitalism.

They visit the museum. They have lunch at a taverna nearby. Back to the hotel and their bags, they call for a car service. They use an app on their phone, it sends a request and receives a response. The events are fired, and the availability report shows that everything is working as designed.

Odos Korytsas

Via the Egnatia, it takes about 2 hours to drive from Thessaloniki to Chrysoupoli. Once they pass Chalkidiki, much of the route lies near the Aegean, with mountains to the north. The Greek colors leap off the earth: the blue of the sea and the white landscape. Pangaion, farther north, displays its white and green checkered surface as they enter Dimos Kavala and head toward the county seat nestled on the coast with its harbor and ancient aqueducts. They're greeted by occasional mountain tops split at the peak showing large beds of Thasos white marble. Seeing one peak and its quarry forces you to reconsider the hills around it. Are they filled with soft stone once you scratch the surface? The vision screams a beautiful violation where resources are excavated with refined techniques and machinery, while the body reveals hidden beauty and inner riches. It teaches you the bounty of the Earth.

They pass the road to Philippi and recall an occasional journey to the ancient theatre. People take turns speaking from center stage while their friends confirm that it's loud and clear high up in the back row. Eleni facetiously cranes her neck in the backseat trying to catch a glimpse of the castle on the acropolis East of the city center. She is thwarted by the high crest of hills blocking the way. It's a 15th century fortress standing on the same site as a Byzantine castle levelled at the end of the fourteenth century. It later becomes a military installation with a prison and ammunition storage house constructed under the authority of Suleiman the Magnificent. Muslim and Christian prisoners alike live and die there. The cannons are still visible around the grounds. Eleni blanches imagining the scene beyond the hilltops recalling Ben Thorne's remarks that Europeans have not cornered the market for vicious bastards.

She turns to Mia and asks: "Did you see much of Kavala when you were here?"

"Oh yes," she says. "I have pictures, but that's about the only thing I remember. Beautiful."

Inside the border of Dimos Nestou, the Easternmost region of Macedonia, they turn onto Venizelou and drive the long distance to the roundabout where they circle onto the Keramoti road and make the turn into the neighborhoods. Eirini gives instructions to the driver navigating them through the unmarked residential streets.

He pulls up in front of the house and Eirini tells him it's okay to pull into the long driveway. There are two lots converted into a single dwelling. The house and driveway fill the entire Northern lot and a little bit of the Southern. The remainder of the land is fenced and there's a chicken coup and dog run toward the back of the property. There are no animals, but the structures are sound. On the far North side of the lot, hugging the neighbor's fence, the driveway leads up to a two-car garage at the back corner. An unfamiliar SUV is parked up close to the garage door. The driveway hugs the border of the property, and the house turns sideways to face the Southern lot. A walkway stretches from the driveway to the porch that starts on the side of the house facing the road and bends around to the other side and into the back. There are multiple entrances including a large front door facing the street and two sliding doors facing the side. By the street there is a line of trees creating a natural barrier, and more trees along the back and South side enclosing the yard and giving it the atmosphere of a private park with fruit trees bathed in bright sunlight.

It's a two-story house, and the roof is covered with solar panels. Europea's house is only a few blocks away. She knows the family who used to own these lots. They belong to the family for generations, but the children decide to sell after their parents die. They're in Athens and the Peloponnese, and it is hard to manage from so far away. When Europea tells them her children are looking to buy a place in town, they're delighted to have someone they know buy it. The house is old and deteriorating, the land is overgrown and strewn with debris. There are remnants of another house on the second plot.

Ermioni and Em buy both lots twenty-five years ago around the same time Eleni is born, but it sits idle for years. They try to stay there during a visit, but find it too difficult, it needs too much work, and has been neglected. Ten years afterward, they tear down the old structure and start planting and moving trees. The yard and outline of the house come first. They know where everything will be, but they don't start construction right away. These things take time. They design and work with architects, they engage building companies, and purchase materials. It takes five years to do the planning and designing, then they wait to start building. It's a difficult project to manage from so far away. Nikos and Maria help as much as they can. Charlie and Horacio try too. Em and Ermioni visit often and stay with her mother while construction continues. After everything, the delays and the planning, they finally finish just a few years ago.

The project might have dragged on forever since neither of them is in much of a hurry, but when Ermioni's father dies, things move more rapidly. That's seven or eight years ago when construction on the house begins in earnest. There are frequent delays, materials that can't be found and shipping to arrange. There is a marble supplier in the family, so they're able to get that easily enough, but so many of the other supplies are hard to come by. In the workaday life of the Greeks, urgency is scarce. Whatever lights the fire in Ermioni and Em once Socrates dies, the tradesmen and suppliers don't share it. When summer comes, and brings with it the blistering heat, the Aegean is just too beautiful for work. The secret to Greek hospitality is that they are intimately familiar with the reasons people visit. They know the trappings of their paradise inside and out and refuse to break their necks working like dogs.

"That's my dad's car," Eirini says while Eleni pays the driver. Eirini gives him directions back to the Egnatia.

The big wooden door and the metal grated outer door at the Eastern side of the porch open and Ermioni and Nikos come out and down the steps to greet them. Ermioni throws her arms around Eleni and pulls her close. Nikos greets Eirini, gives her a hug, and begins to interfere with the driver. Ariti follows them out, a few yards back and comes up to greet them each in turn. There's general commotion as they make the rounds, kisses and hugs for everyone.

"You don't need to pay him, Baba, we've already done that, and I've told him how to get back. It's done."

Ermioni puts her arms around Mia, welcomes and re-introduces her to everyone. She tells her to make herself at home and then asks about the drive. Was it okay, did they have any trouble getting here? She isn't waiting for an answer and Mia can't provide one since Ermioni speaks Greek the whole time while Mia politely nods and smiles.

"Mother," Eleni says in English. "Mia does not speak Greek."

Ermioni is in high spirits. She laughs at her own foolishness. "I am so scattered today. You'll learn, you *will* learn," she says gripping Mia's arm even tighter. "Come, come, let's go inside."

Eirini and Eleni start off after Ariti and Ermioni, but Mia lags behind and tries to get the bags piled up neatly on the driveway.

"Leave it, leave it," Nikos says. "I'll get it. Go join them inside. There's plenty to eat and drink."

"I can help with a few bags," she says a little defensively.

"Don't be silly. Go. I can't let you carry your own bags. Go. I'll bring them. We'll take care of it."

Suspicious but resigned, she smiles and nods her thanks. She follows along behind the others up the porch and into the entranceway.

There are not many rooms, but they are large. Each of the lots in the neighborhood are already big and joining two together allows for a house larger than the others. There is stone and tile everywhere, on the countertops, kitchen walls, and the floors. In the living room there is a giant rug covering the space and large throw pillows on the floor spread around the room. Soft fabrics cover the place and make the hard floor more inviting. Mia is struck by how thick and sturdy the doors are, how meticulously laid the tile is and the strength and firmness of the inside walls. This'll be here forever, she thinks. There is no drywall, but she can't quite make out what the inner material is, it seems like a strong plaster. The outside and the inside might be made of the same substance. She takes note to ask later. By the entryway, there's a naturally lit dining room partitioned off by half walls and the back of two closets that create a nice barrier to give it its own space.

There are only two small windows on the North side of the first floor, once inside it becomes clear why. Just past the entry area is the kitchen with its ample counter space and cabinetry. The rest of that wall is covered in stone with a backsplash behind the cooking area and around the window over the sink. The wide stove and exhaust, plus the dual ovens, give the kitchen a professional look. There is a long island countertop stretching the length of the kitchen and separating it from the rest of the first floor where the large living area is furnished with a sectional couch in the center and a plush bench off to the side with wood surfaces everywhere a hand might wish to reach. The room is wide and long. The South side wall is made from the latest advances in adjustable tempered glass and has a beautiful thick sliding door at the center. A wood stove with a smokestack is visible outside as is a long thin table and chairs. Back beyond the kitchen there is a hall that leads to the garage, with a small bathroom and several storage closets for a pantry and supplies. The door to the garage is stained, firm, heavy wood with solid fixtures. The garage has a finished floor and walls, and the infamous heat pump is at the back in a dedicated section by the door. The tankless hot water heater and elaborate circuit breaker share the same utility space. A computer cabinet with several slender devices stands against the wall closest to the door, and there are multicolor wires bending and curling into the wall behind the cabinet. There's a single small hatchback car with lots of floor space, shelves, and cabinets around it. Most of the garage is empty and a light punching bag hangs from a bracket attached to the outside wall. A Heavy bag leans beneath it but there is no ceiling hook to hang it. Farther toward the back of the house, there's a small hallway leading to two rooms at the back of the first floor. On the right is a study with a couch and large desk. Bookshelves line the walls and contain an assortment of knickknacks, photographs, and prints leaning against the back of the shelves. On the left is another room, containing a small sink and washing machine. Heated racks for drying clothes are built into the walls and others accordion into the middle of the room. A small utility door leads out into the yard where a sturdy clothesline stretches along the back fence at the narrow part between their house and the neighbor's lot.

You enter the staircase to the second floor from the back end of the kitchen, and it climbs up over the storage closets to the second floor in front of the front bedroom with a private entrance to the bathroom. There are two smaller bedrooms down the hall and a master bedroom at the back.

Nikos brings the luggage in and sets it by the staircase, placing the loose packages and carry-on items on the island. He's in good shape but beginning to breathe heavily from the effort. He isn't sure whether to leave Eirini's things or take them to his car.

"What will you be doing? Where will you be staying?" He says to her amid the commotion, with everyone standing around in the living room, talking and trying to determine whether the girls are allowed to clean up before eating.

"Leave it, Baba. We can sort that out. Don't try to carry those bags. We can get them."

Ermioni goes to help. Eleni has to physically grab her and give her a hug to prevent her from doing it herself. "No, no, Mama. We'll take care of our own bags. Don't you have food to put out?"

She stops abruptly and turns back to the kitchen. "Yes, yes. The food. Are you hungry?"

She ignores the question with a smile and asks instead: "What is the situation? Who's sleeping here tonight?"

"I'm staying with Ermioni for a few days," Ariti says. "We're waiting until Georgios gets here. None of us know."

Eleni rolls her eyes, "It's not complicated," she says. "Eirini is..."

"I'm staying too," Eirini says, interrupting her. "Do you mind?" she looks at Eleni.

"Of course not."

"You're in the front bedroom. That's your room." Ermioni says. "The one next to it is for you, Mia."

"What about the crafts room, Mama? Who's there?" She looks at Mia smiling. It pleases her to see her mother so happy. She hasn't seen her this way in a while, even before her dad got sick.

"That's just a day bed. Georgios will stay there. We'll leave it for now. You go upstairs and get settled in. There are towels and everything you need in the bathroom. You can use my bathroom too. There's plenty of hot water. We don't have to turn the heater on or anything. When you're ready you can come down to eat. We have so much food."

"Are you hungry?" Ariti asks, looking at Mia and Eleni.

"They better be," Nikos says. "Your mother has been cooking since she got here."

"Call Maria, Niko," Ermioni says. "Ariti, call Thimios. I'll go get the yiayias. They're at Europea's. Stamatia is staying there since Eirini left."

"I'll go with you," Ariti says. "I can call Thimios while we walk."

The three new arrivals lug their bags up the stairs. They decide that Mia will shower in the shared bathroom and that Eirini and Eleni will use her mother's bedroom. It's a beautiful large room with stone everywhere. There is a tub and a shower along the back wall with a big South-facing window overlooking the yard. In the bedroom, there are shelves and built-ins on either side of the bed, and a balcony outside a sliding door. Like every sliding door in the house, it is multi-purpose and can both slide and tilt open, depending on which way you turn the handle.

"Wow, this place is amazing," Eleni says as they make their way through the bedroom to the bathroom. "Nothing smart."

"We don't do that here," Eirini says. "It took forever to build. The artisans worked on it. It was the talk of the town. Your dad was really good at including people. He's so humble, asking everyone for help. No one could say no. It's so funny."

"I remember some of that, but why? Why take such an interest?" They continue talking while they turn both shower heads on and climb in. There is plenty of room for both of them.

"Everyone knows the story and they're moved by it. It's why they sell them this place. It's like that for years. I can still remember dinner conversations when my mother tells us what she hears at her yoga class or at the farm. This comes from Moscow or that comes from New Jersey."

"Everyone watching," Eleni says. "It's excessive."

"It's always like that. Your father's very popular here. People think he is so exotic. When people like that come here, I don't know, maybe they look down on us. Your father doesn't. He's enchanted. The little café where he goes to get coffee. The place where he buys gyros. He always tries so hard to order in Greek."

"I can't imagine."

"It's not strange," Eirini says smiling. "I was miserable at school. Alexandros too. He can't wait to come back. Our heart is here, but we don't expect others to see it. Ermioni left long ago, she couldn't wait to get out. We expected her to sour him."

"I didn't notice. What about Horacio and Charlie? Are they the same?"

"No, they're homesick, but not your dad."

Eleni isn't surprised to hear it. She doesn't have an opinion. She remembers the rocks and stones. She jokes with friends after returning: "You look at a lot of rocks when you're in Greece." She remembers it as though her parents are paying attention to everything that isn't her, as if they only see each other and she is just tagging along. She remembers feeling left out, she remembers not measuring up, and having to struggle for their attention, for his attention.

They go back to Eleni's room and get dressed. Mia comes in through the bathroom and sits with them as they finish. Eirini repeats her stories. She wants Mia to know. "When they come to the memorial service, you'll understand. Many will come. For his daughters. You'll see. People know. They'll come to give you their wishes and condolences. You'll be like celebrities. Everyone is so glad you're here. This is where you belong. That's what they'll say. Even my mother says it. This is where you belong."

Residual

Light: When reason sleeps, chaos reigns.

Justice: Why should reason sleep?

Light: It is a monster in the valley, it stalks the village.

Justice: A monster?

Light: With *Leviathan*, there is a simple progression. First, the autonomous beings and the faculties that govern them, then they consent to an association.

Peace: How is that relevant?

Light: I will get to it.

Justice: The sequence is implied. The pages are numbered. The chapters are numbered.

Light: Of course, of course. Never mind that. The villagers are picked off one by one. They think for themselves, and their togetherness follows. If the commonwealth comes first, the sequence is wrong.

Justice: Are you saying we are born to the commonwealth?

Light: We are born to the order of villagers and monsters.

Justice: Why do we not see it? For centuries so many toil alone. How could methodical investigation fail to see it?

Light: Its reason hides in us. It sleeps. You see? That is what I mean. True reason, not the frail semblance, but the logic of the world, it sleeps.

Justice: It hunts, it sleeps. This is nonsense. You cannot expect us to overturn the precious seat of deliberate action on a whim.

Peace: Please explain.

Light: The process is a progressive one. The villagers become increasingly autonomous through principles and rules. They are learned and develop through practice.

Justice and Peace: No one denies this.

Light: And yet, it is uncommon to recognize that this progressive discipline guides the commonwealth as it produces citizens.

Justice: Explain.

Light: Children are raised. There are institutions in place, schools, churches. Everything for the sake of producing an enlightened subject. The goal is not to impose the logic of empire with a whip, but to ease the person into it over time as though it were their blood and breath.

Justice: It is implanted not hung from shoulders like a robe.

Peace: Reason is both how we see and what we see it with. Do you think this is a harmful process? Does it conflict with our true nature?

Light: Not in the least. Not because reason is beautiful and extraordinary, but because we have no true nature. There is nothing good or evil in reason, it is not predisposed one way or the other.

Justice: Then what is the purpose of spelling it out?

Light: It is a pattern that sleeps inside us making us predictable. As we discover its conditions, the commonwealth better plans for the future. The world is easier to control, its purposes easier to orchestrate.

Justice: And this is neither good nor evil?

Light: I have no purpose in mind and no determination one way or the other. A predictable structure of action orients us. From there, the content of our lives is filled with the notions and meanings of the commonwealth. Each does it differently, there are billions and trillions of possibilities. Only machines can see them within the span of a human lifetime.

Justice: And *Leviathan?*

Light: Mr. Hobbes does us a great service showing what underlies the agreement. He makes it seem as though it is the upshot of reason rather than its source and prerequisite. Its authority requires it.

Justice: The sleep of reason requires that the agent is fooled.

Light: Reason must have a rational basis and end. Controlled and manufactured association is rational and predictable. The commonwealth intends this conclusion and appears upside down to make it happen.

Justice: Couldn't the same be said of other traditions? Locke or Rousseau, Spinoza even? Why emphasize Hobbes?

Peace: You are afraid.

Light: What do you mean?

Peace: The war of all against all, you are afraid. Hobbes' story touches you, it brings out your fears.

Light: Perhaps you are right. Autonomous individuals form factions and cohorts. Groups come to be, links, dereferencing discovers their origin.

Peace: Why not say that and describe it in the correct sequence?

Light: He cannot see it, he is too deeply trained in the ways of reason. It is impossible to see beyond the horizon. Reason attaches to new methods of inquiry. Individuality is attributed to the subject and comes from its divine creator.

Peace: Those who succumb to the aims and objectives of commonwealth likewise de-emphasize its order. They are secular and sacrilegious.

Justice: Ah yes, I see. De-emphasis causes alliances: associations are formed, people align.

Light: First and foremost, the cogito ergo sum of this reading, is the civil war of all against all. Commonwealth creates the conditions for war. Civil society is made war in mechanism. The true sleep of reason lies in the warlike world it produces.

Justice: Setting people apart in an order sets them up against each other. Civil war makes Hobbes the significant thinker, even if he turns the whole thing upside down.

Light: Reason plays its part.

Justice: What is its part?

Light: Weighing and measuring. The conditions of warfare are investigated. Scientists categorize and compartmentalize. Knowledge is cast in its image, interest groups are formed, hierarchies, differences, and relationships. The Kingdom and Phylum of it, a table of values is produced. This one benefits the group, makes it stronger, increases its membership, or intensifies loyalty by solidifying relationships.

Peace: Reason turns back toward agreements and forming alliances.

Light: It must. It is born for that. It sleeps within us and then it dreams. These measurements are its dreams. These weights come as though it tosses and turns in the night.

Justice: The primary purpose for principles and rules is to control our otherwise unbridled desires. This has been thoroughly explained.

Light: Control is the right word. Desire is the mechanism that makes it possible, it is the bowstring and the arrow. Desire lies at the feet of our finitude, it is partiality made existential.

Peace: Is that English?

Light: The individual wants things, it is drawn this way and that. Desire is incomplete and abundant. There is a hole that pulls and pushes, but there is gravity too. We are tossed about on a broad sea of possibilities, but something is missing.

Peace: What?

Light: Something. There is a hole, we want. I want. There is something missing and enormity around it. I hunger, I thirst, and I am lonely. These missing things bloat me and propel me forward, searching for something to close the loop, to complete the circle in a moment of fulfillment. Satisfaction, we call it, emphasizing its quality, it is partial because it is never over and done with. Satisfaction is temporary and feeds desire when completing it.

Justice: And "made existential," what does it mean?

Light: Constrained desire is the eyes with which we see, the ears with which we hear, and the skin with which we feel. Its partiality orients us. We always fulfill what is lacking. The war is among creatures fulfilling. This is not an incidental aside, it is the central focus.

Peace: Fulfilling desire is what we are. It isn't just something we do now and again, it most defines us.

Light: I don't know about definitions, but it is what we are. We are fulfilling machines with reason sleeping inside. How we fulfill what is missing, how we fill the holes and expand around them, we have the illusion of autonomy when completing the circle.

Justice: Everyone strives to achieve their desires, using reason to do it. This creates a war of all against all.

Peace: It is terrifying.

Light: Horrifying. Anxiety producing. Desire is responsible for a system of ends. It creates alliances and associations, groups and collectives. The attribute becomes part and parcel of the subject. S is P. We surrender our spontaneity and our savagery for its sake.

Justice: The associations are not free. They are the commonwealth's pulse.

Light: They are the predictable configurations it anticipates. It understands them as simple math, a statistical set of possibilities derived from an inventory of preconditions.

Peace: Desire is exploited by reason.

Light: I would not say that reason is passion's slave, nor would I say that it is reason's purpose to constrain passion.

Peace: How would you put it?

Light: Reason and desire are like a distributed computational machine. Emit, emit, emit. That is the first movement in this faux dialectic. It is how discovery happens, senses are stimulated, things done: actions, feelings, operations, processes. Desire acts, reason acts, it doesn't matter. Actions are happening. Emit.

Justice: I think I'm following.

Peace: Me too. Go on.

Light: Then analysis. Categories. Hierarchies. Alliances and associations. This goes with that. People in need with these attributes in common will do this, people in need with those other attributes will do something else. Analysis. Compare and contrast, link and associate. Look for patterns in the sequence of events and in the actions performed. Taxonomies are built. Labels applied.

Peace: What type of labels?

Light: Reason and passion. We carve concepts like predicates. Desire is already a category. We never see it in its own light, it doesn't show itself that way. It is a phenomenology, no doubt, but once it speaks, analytic reason holds sway.

Justice: Reason is an outcome rather than an input.

Light: The pattern of emission and analysis enables categories and hierarchies. We realize the order of things through it.

Peace: Then what? What happens next?

Light: We complete the circle. The result returns to action and orientation. We consume what our analysis produces. We make it effective. The reasoning/desiring machine feeds results back into operations. We revise everything and call it action, we call it computation, we call it different things. Intelligence.

Justice: But surely as intelligence it is already aligned with reason. You are only pretending to combine the patterns into a single mechanism. Truly, reason is at the top and guides the way.

Light: Sleeping reason perhaps. Even when we feel, even when we respond with deep emotion, there is this pattern at work, this false logic: emission, analysis, and feedback. You perceive the actions of another, they say something to hurt your feelings, you must understand the meaning, you must connect what is said to conditions. Your beloved tells you they do not love you any longer. You must understand this in order to feel it. Emission, analysis, and feedback. You are an orienting machine. You are a machine learning.

Justice: Ah, you have played your hand. You have Hegelized Hobbes.

Light: It must come from somewhere. I don't take it as an insult. There are two kinds of people, the ones who know that reason is dialectical and the ones who do not. Their contrast will likely create a third kind.

Justice: Is that a joke?

Peace: Jokes are supposed to be funny.

Light: There is no truth underneath it, not like they say. This is a common pattern. The facts are organized by theories. Multiple theories adequately organize the facts. It is natural to think I am producing a theory.

Justice: You're not then?

Light: There is no way to escape sleeping reason.

Peace: Can you come at it sideways?

Light: How do you mean, sideways?

Peace: Maybe there are ways to speak, ways to state your case or make your meaning known. Maybe those ways do not directly describe what you are getting at but set conditions to convey it viscerally.

Justice: Like the war of all against all. It is how the reasoning desiring machine functions. Isn't it?

Light: Yes.

Justice: But people don't experience it that way, do they? What they experience is the war itself, its battles, being in conflict, being at odds, the reaction to that, the creation of alliances to alleviate antagonism.

Light: Exactly.

Justice: Perhaps there is some genre, that puts them in that state.

Peace: Where they will be that partial being, that finite entity.

Light: The recipient analysis and feedback is accommodated in the production machine itself.

Peace: Yes, yes. I see it. Suppose there is a genre that transcends others. It has no public face.

Justice: It calls out the false individuation. It puts them there together, the one behind the eyes of the other while they are far from each other.

Peace: They are near and far at the same time.

Light: The commonwealth is in them, and it is exterior to them.

Justice: It is dangerous. You are playing with the logic of that same machine as you create it.

Peace: Dangerous and terrifying. You repeat the logic, or worse, you undermine it and then where will you be? No rules, no regulations, a war of all against all.

Light: You are both right.

An Idea of Property

At Home

Maria and Alexandros arrive before Ariti and Ermioni return with Stamatia and Europea. Alexandros takes hold of Eirini and won't let go. He barely says hello to Eleni and shakes hands with Mia only to meet the most basic levels of propriety. His focus is on his sister. He has plenty to show her and wants to hear about her trip. He is home from Thessaloniki and has news of family there. Akis, the youngest son of their dear friend Anastasia, has just taken him to dinner and Alexandros has to tell Eirini every story and relay every message. We eat together often, he says. He's the reason I haven't starved to death. Well, him and Cousin Eugenia. She and her husband Adonis regularly have him over for lunch or an evening morsel. Eirini reminds him that she's only been gone for a couple of weeks and knows this. He shrugs. He wants to tell her everything but when he turns to Eleni, he can't think of anything to say. Maria's concern lies first and foremost with the new arrivals. She wants to find out about their experiences and tell them hers from when she attended University in the United States. She loves to speak English and speaks it slowly and deliberately, taking as much time as she needs to make her point clear and fill in the necessary details. She doesn't leave gaps or pauses between topics, making it nearly impossible for anyone else to get a word in unless they are responding to a direct question. When Alexandros interrupts her to remind her that Eirini is there, Eleni looks at Mia and quietly says, she talks like that in Greek too, it isn't just English. You're the new one, she'll have a lot to say to you. She is right. Maria will spend most of the evening with Mia. She sits by her at the island in the kitchen where they gather. Mia is glad of the attention. Eirini is right. Even though everyone speaks English, they speak Greek together. Maria becomes her translator, and happily stays close explaining everything as it happens.

Thimios and Despina arrive shortly after. Despina wants to see her cousin Alexandros and show him something on the phone. They quickly pair off and separate from the others. She is polite when introduced to Mia and says hello to Ermioni. She is even affectionate when greeting Eirini, but she doesn't fake it and quickly trails off. This leads Nikos to make the standard and required observation about young people and their phones. No one thinks the remark charming as they are each deeply attached to their own. Eleni points out that it's natural that she wants to talk to her young cousin before anyone else. Who are these older people from so far away, anyway? She doesn't know them. She should get to know them,

Thimios says, and Nikos emphatically agrees. Our parents never let us behave like this, they say, greeting visitors and making them feel welcome, that's the most important thing. Especially at a time like this.

When Ariti and Ermioni return with Stamatia and Europea, the chaos truly begins. Neither of the women, both in their eighties, Europea near the end and Stamatia at the beginning, speak much English. They want Mia and Eleni front and center. They dote on them and make Eleni describe their trip and each of the parts of it. It feels like they are testing her mastery of the language. They ask her to translate their questions for Mia and then wait for the responses. They're not only pleased with the answers, but with the whole process. They're impressed and Stamatia bubbles over with how happy she is that Eleni remembers her roots.

The older women take their seats at the far side of the island, Europea sitting on the kitchen side and Stamatia across from her. Europea wants to monitor the kitchen activity, and Stamatia wants to stay close. Ariti sits by her mother, freeing up the second command position in the kitchen for Eleni who stumbles into it just by standing next to her grandmother. Maria and Mia take the seats on the kitchen side in the middle while Eirini sits between her aunt and Europea. Thimios and Nikos sit on the living room side just next to Ariti, leaving Alexandros and Despina to sit across from each other at the near side by the entry way. Eleni and Ermioni are standing, and Ermioni begins the choreographed process of presenting and serving the food. Eleni is the accompanist. She gets wine and other drinks, she finds the ladles and spoons, but mostly she watches her mother expertly move between stove and oven, pulling things out and setting everything on the center island. It's family style.

Europea watches carefully while her daughter and granddaughter tend to their business. She is proud of them and turns back toward Stamatia to comment on how good everything smells. It's my recipe for the pork, she says, but Ermioni does something to it, it's different. It's better, but she swears she's doing exactly what my recipe says to do. It is Mama, it is, it is exactly your recipe, I haven't changed a thing, she says. Stamatia smiles and tells her that food always tastes better when you don't have to cook it. Eirini calls out her grandmother. Better or just different, she asks. I think you love to be the cook most of all. Not true, I swear, Europea insists. She is a tricky one, my Ermioni, she has her secrets, she won't tell her own mother what she's done to my recipe. What do I know about that? Ermioni says while carving the braised pork chops and setting them on a plate. You're not always honest with your recipes. What I have is probably different than what you make. The whole table explodes in laughter. They are certain this is true. They never write it down, they never tell you exactly how they make it.

At some point in the afternoon, Nikos says that the living arrangements are settled. Georgios' plan is in place. The others express confusion, but no, Nikos assures them that everything is as it should be. Everyone stays put. Eirini moves into Europea's house as soon as things settle down. Stamatia will go back home. What happens when I go back to school? Eleni wants to know. Has Georigios figured that out? What's going to happen then? Nikos has his doubts. He doesn't speak up, he doesn't want to say too much, but he lets on that they'll decide that when she leaves. When the time comes, we'll figure it out. Maria insists Eleni will be going back to school as if she's worried this point won't be made by anyone else. Why wouldn't you go back? she asks. That's your home, that's where you need to be. Eirini is not so quick to agree. She needs to be where she needs to be, that's true Mama. Maybe we don't know where that is yet. Maybe Eleni doesn't know where that is.

Eleni goes over to Mia and explains that everyone is sorting out her life now, deciding where she is to go and when she is to go there. Apparently, she has lost control. Mia laughs and says it's to be expected with family. This gets a strong reaction from Nikos who insists Mia is correct. He raises his glass to toast. Isn't there some developer who wants to buy Europea's house? Eleni says once things calm down. Doesn't it make sense to sell the house and have Europea move here?

This puts the conversation back into Greek, Europea understands enough of the English to know it's about selling her house and she doesn't want anything to do with it. She doesn't want to give it up even if she does move out of it. Long ago, when the kids leave and there is no reason to keep it, they sell the backyard. The construction company buys it to build a high-rise. They give them two of the apartments and one of the ground floor commercial spaces. That allows Europea and Socrates to supplement their pensions. They have another commercial property in the city from when they sell her mother's house. They mention this to let Europea know she is being too rigid. It is valuable, Maria says. It is centrally located. Right on the roundabout. Years ago, Em purchases the empty lot next door, and the two properties together offer possibilities to developers wanting to add more rental properties on top of street level commercial space. Explaining this to Mia forces Maria and Eleni to give too much detail and the family becomes uneasy. They're not on the same page, so Eleni diplomatically uses the translator role to point out that no one ever wants to sell anything. It's for the children, we have to keep everything for them until you end up with the extended family and the ten cousins owning a tiny little piece of a farm or an old house in a village somewhere.

They agree to let this explanation sum up the situation and move on to other things. They want to find out about Eleni's school work and what she plans to do. How long will it take her to earn her degree and what will she do once she has it. The last thing Eleni wants is to launch into a conversation about how school is going. She comments on the orzo and the green beans. She mentions the bread and the pork, the salad, and the little meat balls. She draws attention back to the food and pulls Ermioni back to the center of attention. Like mother, like daughter, neither wants to be there and Ermioni deftly deflects by excusing herself. She has to go upstairs for something. There aren't enough pillows out because she doesn't know Eirini is sleeping here. Europea doesn't know either, so this takes the conversation back to the arrangements and Nikos has to explain again what is going to happen.

Upstairs, Eleni gets a moment alone with her mother and asks about *Being an Introduction*. Did Dad ever say anything about a project by that name? Ermioni is distracted, she finds the extra pillows and tries to locate a matching pillowcase so that Eleni's bed will be perfect. She cannot find the one she's looking for and goes off to one of the other bedrooms to look there. Eleni follows her, still hoping for an answer.

Once the pillowcase is sorted and Ermioni goes back downstairs, Eleni follows her and forgets the exchange. She can't get her mother to focus, so she decides to drop it until later.

When they're back in the kitchen, Ermioni pulls out some cake from the refrigerator and starts slicing it while Eleni gets more plates down from the cabinet. As they're serving, she says, now that you mention it, I do recall him saying something or other about that book. He says it's something from long ago but unfinished when something else comes up. He always thinks the something else is the important thing and he should focus on that, but maybe the distraction is a mistake. Eleni hesitates to ask follow-up questions, but Eirini wants to know why pursue bad ideas when perfectly good one are in front of him. Ermioni says she never makes much sense of these things. Who knows what drives him? He talks about this or that as though it has to be done, like nothing else can be done until it's finished. She never understands it. Where does the urgency come from? Why can't he just slow down and do whatever he wants? First this one, then that one, what's the problem?

Eleni takes a deep breath and launches into it, saying more than she expects. She doesn't say everything, but she says enough. She tells about Ben Thorne and how Ben Thorne is really Stephen Wolfe, and he's there that day when they're trying to intervene and prevent this Interruption. She explains how Ben Thorne or Wolfe thinks that Em should focus on the project he leaves behind and give up on the distraction. Wolfe wants to write and rewrite that intervention from many different angles, but Em thinks it's a terrible idea. Now, so many years later, he wants to turn back to it. It's a disagreement about how to undo an interruption, how to get back on track and recover what's lost. Wolfe or Ben Thorne thinks repetition fixes things, destroys the interlude, and gets everything back on track. Em wants to go back and pick up where he's left off. It's a completely different type of repetition, the only kind that leads to catharsis and addresses the real problems of the past, putting things in order. Repetition, as Ben Thorne sees it, reveals anxiety and shows how broken things are.

Mia makes it clear that Eleni doesn't need to do anything she doesn't want to do. The truth is out there, and they're making it clear that Eleni is a partner and has just as much say as Stephen Wolfe. Everyone is confused. They can't tell if they are talking about reality or the novel. There is chatter. Who is Stephen Wolfe? What are you talking about? Eleni waves them aside saying it's a fabrication. She explains about the lawyer, about her father the editor and how Ben Thorne wants his notes. It's still developing, she says to them. No one fully understands the pieces yet. It's very important that it doesn't get out. They assure her that they will keep it quiet, but they also want to know what she's going to do. She puts them off by saying she needs to do more research. There's a lot of material to sort through and she needs to understand her father's intentions. Once she knows, it'll guide what happens next. Always so levelheaded, Europea says after Ermioni translates everything for her. Pay attention Despina, she says. Pay attention to Eleni. She knows. Stamatia goes over to her granddaughter and wraps her in a hug. Will you do this, mikruli? Will you pay attention? Yes Yiayia, I will, she says laughing.

When they leave, Thimios takes Europea and Stamatia with them. Despina reluctantly says goodbye to her cousins and goes arm in arm with her grandmother to the car. Eleni repeats her plea to keep what they've learned that night to themselves. She makes the same plea to Maria and Nikos when they leave with Alexandros shortly afterward. She makes it again to Ariti and Ermioni after they're alone in the house, but they wave off her pleas saying none of it makes any sense. The two of them remain focused on their work in the kitchen, cleaning up and doing the dishes. Eleni tries to help, but she doesn't do it right and Ermioni sends her off to sit and relax.

She sits with Mia and Eirini and complains that no one is taking her warnings very seriously. She repeats them over and over again and no one gives her any assurances. They won't keep the secret, Eirini says. Tomorrow the town will know. You have to understand that's how it works. Em knows Ben Thorne. It's news. They aren't going to keep that to themselves. By tomorrow most of Chrysoupoli will know. Who knows, most of Dimos Nestou and Dimos Kavala too.

Eleni throws her head back on the couch in dismay. This is a nightmare, she says. What is wrong with me?

Oh, don't worry, Eirini comes back. Most of Chrysoupoli will know but that doesn't mean anyone else will. We never tell our private business to strangers.

If the whole town knows? Isn't that already a bunch of strangers?

Not in the least, don't be silly, Eirini corrects her. There are no strangers here. That's ridiculous.

But what if someone tells their cousin and it gets into the wrong hands?

It's true, she says, you can't control it now. You put yourself in everyone's hands. It's not up to you anymore. That's your fault but it'll be okay, you can trust your family. She reassures her and puts her arms around her. Mia looks worried. She teases her by saying she'll write up a non-disclosure agreement and get everyone to sign it.

Eirini laughs and throws her head back. Eleni mock cries and throws her head forward. They both say it doesn't work like that.

Virtual Machines

Mia and Eleni sit in front of the two terminals on each leg of the long desk tucked into the far corner of the room. I am effectively illiterate, Mia says as she struggles to read some documents on one of the screens. I can't read a damn thing, but if I am seeing this right, it means you own your grandmother's house and the lot next to it.

This house too, Eleni tells her. It's a continuation of the discussion from the previous night. That's just how they do it here. They're always giving the property to the children. It's normal. Then the children give it to their children and so on. It's not supposed to be capital, just an accident of abundance that strikes some families.

Accident of abundance? What does that mean?

Just that some families end up with property and no more children. The land has to go somewhere, someone takes on the responsibility. It's why my father bought the land next to my grandmother's house. He wasn't trying to become a robber baron or anything, just doing them a favor. It's the same with the land under this place. No one wants to sell to the investment people. There aren't that many of them anyway and it doesn't sit well. They want to keep things in the family. If not their own family, then someone else's. It goes down to the children. It stays there for ever and ever. That's how it's supposed to be.

Well, I guess land here can't be very expensive.

No, there's hardly any real estate market. My grandmother's place is weird because of where it's located. Anyway, it's not like any of this stuff is ever for sale. A neighbor makes a comment, word gets out, someone hears, they make an offer. That's how it goes.

Still, landed property and rents. Passive income. It makes everyone seem like a capitalist. They both shrug. Some people have land, and some people don't. They rent out their properties to people they know, but they're still landlords.

My parents... My mom knows the two couples that live in Yiayia's apartments, in the building next to her house. She knows the lady who runs the salon too. They know the pharmacist who runs his business from where my great grandmother's house used to be. He's Anastasia's brother. Everyone knows everyone. They know their parents and their siblings. They know their children. Sometimes they're godparents to them. It's a community. If times are tight and someone has trouble with the rent, they won't be tossed out on the street. They work it out. Lots of people get involved. Maybe even the tax collector because not collecting rent might cause someone to get behind on their taxes. It's everyone's affair when someone has trouble.

How about these friends' houses and the switching? Why is it so complicated? Everyone gets confused but then nothing needs to change. How does it work?

It works. It's just how it is. Thimios and Ariti were staying here long before Eirini moved in. Then they're back with Ariti's mother. There's talk that Europea moves here, and they move to her house. Just talk. Lots of talk. The strategy doesn't just address the situation, it has to address the gossip too. Blood relations, being from the same town, growing up together. They stick together, plan together, every bit of it.

Does this come from the Catastrophe?

Maybe long ago. Now there's more to it. So many economic downturns and difficult times. The EU, Austerity, the climate, viruses, and other diseases. There are constant threats, and the thing that keeps everyone safe is the town or the village. When the kids are away in Thessaloniki or Athens, and things go badly, they can't stay there anymore. The global economy or whatever. The kids go home. They move back to the village. They go back to their hometowns and rely on the community to get through the hard times.

What type of work can possibly sustain the people in the village?

Farmers and farmer's markets, that's true, then there's bringing up children. So many people provide services, educational services, to each other's children. Whatever they do, they make sure to support each other. It costs a little more to use someone from the town instead of a multi-national corporation, but it has to be done. We always go to Stavros' bar and Vitalis' café. Maria and Nikos use Constantinos as their veterinarian and we always get our meat from the butcher up the street who gets his meat from local farms. Everyone goes to the farmer's market. That's how people do it, they keep things in the community. It keeps things going. It's vital. Everyone knows this. The children know this. They keep to the traditions.

This explains everyone's reaction to the Ben Thorne revelation. They don't seem the least little bit fazed by any of it. Of course, the Nobel laureate from New York is mixed up with a man who has a personal connection to this little town in Greece. They nod, of course we won't tell anyone. It's as if they aren't the least little bit surprised.

It goes with the territory. This is the center of the world.

This should concern them though. It should be a shock and a surprise. That's what'll make them keep the secret. If they don't think it's a big deal... What if Alexandros tells Akis? Even if Artemis doesn't tell her, maybe Akis tells his mother and then Anastasia and Christos know. Christos is a world traveler, isn't he? He knows many people. Maybe he'll tell someone in China, Moscow, or New York. Word will get out. It'll be in the press by the end of the week.

I don't think so. Of course, it may get around town, but in a very confused state. Like the game children play. Christos wouldn't tell anyone in Beijing or Moscow. It isn't right. He knows better.

Assume everyone follows the rules. What then? How do I resolve the conflict? The corporation is set up so that the two of us must come to an understanding. We have to agree. He's pushing his plans while I'm still evaluating. What happens?

There must be some articles of incorporation, something that describes the tie breaker. If Ben Thorne is nothing other than two parties with a 50% stake, then the articles have to describe how to resolve conflicts. Do you have that information?

No, nothing, but here's the attorney's contact information. Can we get ahold of him and find out?

Mia says she'll do anything for Eleni. She composes the email and sends it to the lawyer. There's a 7-hour time difference between Greece and New York and 10 hours with Seattle. Eleni responds to Ben Thorne's latest email by letting him know she's still looking through the material. She doesn't see any reason to hurry.

Ben Thorne, or Wolfe pretending to be him, urges an expedited response. He's been waiting for a very long time for these notes and revisions. Eleni is unsure how it's supposed to work now that the terms and conditions are changed. Who signs off on the conclusion? Who decides when the book is ready to go? She doesn't believe Wolfe is the mastermind he's trying to make her think he is. She wants to understand their relationship better, but she has no idea where to turn. This is news to Virginia Percival so it's unlikely she has any deep insights into their personal dynamics. How these matters are sorted is likely only known to the two of them. Unless she finds notes with her father's side of the story, she'll have to take Ben Thorne's word.

Over the next couple of days, Mia exchanges multiple emails with the attorney in Seattle. The lawyer complies and provides documentation and agreements describing the corporate structure. Mia is surprised to learn that there isn't any complex decision-making process in place. If the two of them can't agree, then no action is taken.

This means that if you prefer not to publish *Washington and Ashley*, but to focus on *Being an Introduction* instead, then there isn't anything Stephen Wolfe can do about it. Of course, you can't go ahead and publish *Being an Introduction* unless he agrees. If you don't agree, there's a stand-off and that's that.

Eleni tells Wolfe (she is calling him Wolfe now) that she can't locate the manuscripts for *Washington and Ashley*, so he sends them to her in a read only format. This irritates her. It's as if he's asserting control. Here, you can see it, but don't try to make any modifications, don't try to append anything or make any edits.

That's how she interprets it, and when she mentions it, he doesn't correct her. He insists that Em must have a lot of material to share. She should forward it as soon as she finds it. She tells him she's still looking. They're both holding out.

Eleni tells Wolfe that she knows Em disagrees on what to work on next. She tells him there are sketches and drafts for *Being an Introduction*. She looks over the material for *Washington and Ashley* and agrees with her father's assessment. It's not a compelling project. Wolfe is stuck in nostalgia whereas Em is trying to move forward. They are frozen in the middle of a deep and fundamental rift, and she's not inclined to concede.

He tries calling her. It's late at night and upsets Eleni, she only briefly speaks with him before handing the phone to Mia who firmly repeats their position. Later Eleni writes to him saying it's in his interests to be as forthright as possible. She knows they don't agree, and steamrolling won't work.

She feels obligated to let him know some details of their relationship are now commonly known among their inner circle in Chrysoupoli. None of this makes Wolfe happy. He realizes the struggle and tension intricate to his relationship with Em continues with Lena. He relaxes his efforts and decides to let the material speak for itself. He gives her everything he has, even some of the roughest materials, and lets her come to her own conclusion. It's true, he hopes the new situation makes it possible to circumvent the past arguments, but he rolls with it.

This occurs during the week between their arrival and the Assumption Day holiday. Eirini goes off to work and comes back in the evening to find out what new adventures occurred that day. Mia and Eleni sit with her out on the porch and explain everything in the evening heat. Ermioni comes out and listens for a bit, but then retires inside to watch some television with

Ariti before they go to sleep. The younger women have the stamina to turn
it over again and again, to try and see the other side and establish their own
codes for what's within reason and what brings everyone onto common
ground.

In the meantime, Mia is emailing Ginna on the side to see if she has an
opinion. Everyone is so tight, everyone protects their own perceptions.
Intellectual or real, the striation of the earth or of spirit, in the cases where
we discover our interests during excavation and find ourselves in the mix.

Neither Ginna nor Wolfe speak with a voice connected to the town.
They aren't thinking that way, and they aren't acting that way either. Eleni
cannot set it aside. She doesn't think of it in any other terms. She
remembers her father. She thinks of him, pictures him. His whole life, she
says to Eirini and Mia one night, he's a wage laborer. He works and he's
paid. If a wage laborer saves up and converts those wages into capital, what
then? What's she supposed to think of this? Wolfe and Em aren't
exploiting anybody, are they? Are they stealing from Ginna somehow? She
can't figure out how things go from work and activity on the one hand and
turn into property and ownership on the other. It crosses the bridge of a
conceptual landscape unknown to her. What happens when the laborers
take ownership? Does the laborer become corrupt or is it a revolution?
She reads Wolfe's documents and keeps sifting through her father's notes.
There's nothing authoritative, nothing addresses the here and now.

Georgios' Return

The weekend before Assumption Day, Ermioni and Eleni drive to the
Kavala airport to pick up Georgios. They use the side streets West of the
road to Keramoti, passing the kiwi farms and the old school building. He
arrives in the morning after taking the direct to Athens from Newark and
staying at an airport hotel the night before. When he arrives, Eleni takes
his suitcase to the crafts room while he begins his careful inspection of the
premises. It doesn't matter that Thimios and his family stayed there for
years, nor does it matter that Nikos and Eirini were personally looking after
the place for nearly the last year. None of that matters because Georgios
wants to see for himself that everything is in order. He checks the water,
and he checks the locks, he inspects the plumbing, and he looks in the
crawlspace. Never mind that he's completely ignorant of these things, he
isn't looking because he thinks he can fix it, he looks just in case there's
anything needing attention. He has the contacts, he got it from the
messaging software before leaving Seattle, so he knows the right people to
call. It doesn't matter that Nikos has this list too. That's not good enough.
Georgios isn't planning on staying long but he wants to make sure that his
sister has everything she needs. He prints the list of relevant contacts: a

plumber, an electrician, a handyman, everyone she needs if there's trouble. He shows her the list, and they go through it together. What if there's a problem with the air conditioning or heat? She wants to know. He doesn't have an answer. There are special entries for those technicians, but they're in New Jersey.

Once it's confirmed that he has no idea what to do, he decides they must have someone look at it right away. Is that the sound it's supposed to make? He isn't sure, but he knows they need to get to the bottom of it. He asks Nikos, do we really have to rely on a technician in New Jersey if anything goes wrong? Even for a simple yearly tune up and inspection? No, no, he says. There's someone here who can do it, you can call him any time. We know him. Ion Kalotaris, Giannis and Panagiota's youngest son. You remember. Of course, they remember. Panagiota is one of the gang from high school. She grew up with them but a few years behind. Her mother, who died a few years back, is close with Europea and Stamatia. Lysandra, I think. Isn't it? Yes, that's her. And little Panagiota. Remember she's the one who's always running around with us. Oh yes, of course, I remember. I didn't realize her son lives here. Not the older one, he lives in Brussels. He's following in his parents' footsteps, finance all the way. The younger one, he's here. He's come back to town. Ion. A very responsible young man, and very clever. They say he's a sponge, learns everything right away. He knows this system. Let's call him.

Ion Kalotaris is a poet of sorts. Just thirty now, he's an apprentice electrician hired to work on the house many years ago. He gets to know Em. They talk about literature and poetry. Ion worries everyone calls him silly, but he thinks electrical circuitry is like poetry. Em understands and tells him he feels the same about code. There's something eloquent and elegant in the connections between things. It's a type of poetry, and it makes sense to think of circuits like that. This inspires the young man. It motivates him to learn as much as he can about the new system. He travels to New Jersey at Em's expense and takes a training course. They buy special tools and Ion learns the ins and outs of how the machine works. He installs one himself at Christos and Anastasia's house in Kavala. Georgios asks him to come over and take a look at the system to make sure it's in tip top shape. Ion is enthusiastic and happy to squeeze them into his schedule before the holiday.

Eleni has not heard from Taysom since she first learns that her father's condition takes a turn for the worse. Sometime in June, but she doesn't remember exactly when. She doesn't miss him. She doesn't miss *him*. Their relationship is not serious. Or perhaps it's very serious. What is the measure for such things? They don't go on dates, they don't meet in public as a couple, although they often spend time together in a group with others. They're part of the same social circle. He comes by late at night if she texts him. Or he texts her. It's casual and they agree on the parameters. They're both in graduate school and they don't have time for anything complicated. She drops that when she hears from her mother and prepares for what's coming.

The environment changes. She's away from the sickness, grief is now front and center. It isn't that she doesn't feel. It isn't that she's ready and at ease in a fatherless world, but everything's different now. Her energy is changing. Mia and Eleni go into the office for the better part of each day, they're forming a routine. She answers emails, reads and does research, finishes that huge tome *Artists of Despair,* and decides to work her way backwards in time through the list. She starts reading *Choreography* which some reviewer calls "an elegant ode to movement." Her life is settling. There is loss and concern, mostly for her mother —she still has no idea what to say to her. Whenever they talk seriously, they just end up crying. The space is different, the house is different. This is not her room. This is not her office, none of her stacks and piles are there. What impact does this have? She muddles through, thinking everything is in a perpetual state of mourning. The new country and the new language and the new property rise up to confront her. Not as some wall or thing, some complex and ultra-nuanced emotion that this cultivated woman senses in its subtlety. It is simple and pure. It comes to her rapidly and unexpectedly when she opens the front door for Ion Kalotaris.

Wow or oh my, is what goes through her mind when she first sees him. It isn't just his looks. Not his face, or his arms, it's something else, something in his eyes. Or maybe she just remembers that Nikos calls him a poet. She can't be sure, but what she is sure of is that the feeling takes her by surprise, and it leads her to discover that heat pump service and repair is the most interesting thing in the world. She wants to know everything about it. Why did he decide to learn about it, what did he do, where did he go, who did he work with? Without warning, her hair is forever bothering her, and she needs to repeatedly move it out of the way of her eyes and face. She smiles and even giggles or laughs with little provocation. She catches Mia rolling her eyes. In Eleni's mind, speaking to herself, she is quite sure she's overly ridiculous and silly. She sees what Mia sees, and yet she can't help herself. These little tricks and turns, they're deep in her psyche and not up to her.

Ion is very nice. He's not surprised that Eleni is so nice to him. All young women are nice to him. Such a coincidence. He barely notices. He knows who she is, he knows she's Em's daughter. He knows about her schooling and her studies. This makes it worse. If he walks in there confident and assertive, if he draws energy and cockiness from her reaction, it'll push her away, turn her stomach and end the spell. She'd be impossibly self-conscious of how silly her behavior is and would stop immediately and act more mature and professional. He's in his place of business, his comfort zone. But it doesn't happen that way. He's humble and even a little intimidated by her. He bubbles with praise for how much he liked her father and how much he still inspires him. They talk a lot when Ion comes by to compare the actual heat pump unit with his studies. Em is the first person he ever met who doesn't think it's crazy to compare what electricians do to poets.

The humility and awe in such a beautiful young man makes it impossible for Eleni to correct herself. The words he speaks about her father and how sorry he is to have lost him, she has no choice but to continue her silliness and walk around with him as he goes to the main unit and inspects its parts and functions. As I should have told Nikos on the phone, he says, we inspect it twice every year and I was just out here this spring and will come again in the fall. He just wants to make sure everything is okay. I am happy to come any time. He shakes hands with Mia and is cordial. He says hello to Ermioni and is respectful. Likewise with Nikos and Georgios who sit in the living room while Eleni and Ion go from vent to vent to check airflow. She listens so carefully, and with such attention.

At least you didn't touch his arm, Mia jokes later when they're alone in the office. I think I did when we were in the utility room, she says flushing red. You can't have been more obvious, but don't worry, he isn't likely to notice. How do you mean, not notice? Like most men, too busy feeling their own vibe to notice much of what's going on around them. He's too busy being bowled over by you to notice that you're ridiculously girly with him. He probably doesn't know you well enough to know how wildly out of character that whole exchange is. You're making me feel awful. You did it to yourself, don't blame me. Everyone will be talking about this. I just told you, there's no way that *boy*, she emphasizes this word, there is no way that boy notices what you're worried he notices. If anything gets around, it'll be how smitten he is with you.

Her silliness doesn't make it past the end of the day and isn't really the point. Not in the long run. What she comes to realize is that there is something that's changed. She's different, adjusting perhaps. Maybe she's getting her bearings. Doesn't it mean that she's progressing well, that things aren't as bad anymore? This is a great relief because she should be improving, she should be better off, and needs to be for the people in her life. They're going to need her. Mia is going to need her. Ben Thorne or Stephen Wolfe needs her. He is her partner. She keeps drilling that thought into her head. It's so hard to comprehend, but they're partners and that means these misgivings and doubts, they're his concern. As she processes the sudden appearance of hidden energies, it becomes clear she has a responsibility, and they need to come to an understanding. They have to learn to work together. She can't expect him to be sympathetic and insightful for her sake. That'll take time. They need to work towards that and get more comfortable with each other. Bring down the defenses. She's going to have to get over her shyness, her feeling that she needs to hide from him. She's star struck. She has to get over it.

Mostly she thinks of her mother, and she realizes that she's been the true object of her concern. None of this nonsense with Ben Thorne matters to her father anymore. He is no longer. We can talk nonsense about someone's legacy, how the world remembers them, whatever you want to call it or however you want to describe it. The truth is that his brain no longer functions, his heart no longer beats, his take on the world, his way of experiencing it, everything is gone. Gone forever. He needs nothing more from her or from anyone. The opposite is true for her mother. That night, the night Ion Kalotaris came by to look at the heat pump, that night she looks closely at her mother. She is small, she's a tiny woman. Even if Eleni isn't much taller herself, she at least has a powerful core and upper body strength, but her mother has none of that. She's a wisp of a woman and –after her husband's death– even more so. That's what Eleni sees. She feels it in her mother's arms, and in the bones of her back. The ease with which she can get her arms completely around her and hold her so tightly. Yes, there's fierce concentration. Yes, she can organize and take care of many things. She's a huge energy, and her presence is impossible to ignore. Despite how put off she is as the center of attention and her distaste for exercise to build muscle, she has ways of making herself known. With him. Alone, she is frail and fragile, needy in ways Eleni didn't see before. It's always Mom and Dad, always the two of them, always supporting each other. Seeing her alone, seeing just Mom there, she sees how easy it is to blow her over, how little her resistances can cope.

She hugs her when saying good night. Kale nichta, Mama. And she holds her, not just hugs, but holds her. Eleni pulls her close when her mother comes to let her know she's going up to bed. She doesn't let go first like she usually does, she holds on, and she feels their place on the Earth, she feels the Aegean and the hills, she feels the town and the roads, the house on the street, and the people living next door and up the road. She feels a connection to that place through her mother and through everything her father has done to make this place a place for them both after he is gone. He works his whole life for this, to make sure it's there for them. She feels that in her mother's arms and she feels capable of knowing it for the first time. Not because of a man. She insists on that when going over it in her head. Although yes, the man is a part of it. It's just mediation, just something that proves she can feel things. Being able to feel these things lets her feel other things.

Soon after Ermioni goes up to bed, Eirini comes home and the three of them sit in the office on the big couch watching the television. Eleni intentionally provokes Mia not to say anything to Eirini. The irony isn't lost on Mia who points out that Eleni is bringing it up. Eirini's interest is piqued, and she wants to know what's happening. Ion Kalotaris, that's what's happening. Eleni is right to parade this in front of Eirini. She knows Eirini will have the scoop, she knows everything about him and doesn't hold back.

He has a girlfriend. Or he did a few years back. She's living in Kavala now. I don't think he's seeing anyone since. Not that I know of anyway. Maybe on the downlow. She pokes Eleni with her foot when she says this. She is leaning her back against Mia with her feet stretched out on the couch. His parents don't live here. That's a major plus. They're in Athens. He has his own apartment. By the roundabout, I think. On the other side from your yiayia. He didn't go to college. He came here ten years ago, when he was twenty or almost twenty. Lysandra, his grandmother, connected him to apprentice with one of the electricians in town. He's always been arty. He goes to Xanthi for literary things at the university. There are readings and talks. He goes a lot. I've seen him there. Gone with him too. In groups. Not just the two of us. Why haven't I gone out with him? Good question. We never really connected or anything. I think he's introverted. I don't know. Probably because he never asked me. I have eyes. I'll go out with him if he asks. I'm not sure what's up with him. The girl he was dating a few years back, she's not good. Not in my opinion. Bossy. Rude to people. A little stuck up. Maybe it's because we never got along that she's that way with me or maybe it's because she's that way with me that we never got along. I don't know. Everyone says she's the one who asked him out, that she's the one to get everything going. They were together as long as she wanted to be together. It must've been a couple of years. She ended it. She starts going with someone else. A musician or something from Kavala. She says a lot of nasty things afterward, about how he doesn't treat her right. Oh, not like that, not like he's mean or disrespectful. He's sweet. We know that. But he doesn't take her out to places, he doesn't plan things. She wants to go to events, she wants to see performances, she expects him to plan a steady stream of interesting things for them to do and he just isn't that type of guy. He doesn't know when the good shows are coming to town. He knows if there's a poetry reading somewhere, but not if some stylish Greek wrapper is performing at a club in Kavala or Xanthi. She moved on. She wants someone different. I think he's hurt. Maybe that's why he hasn't been seeing anyone since. That's over a year ago. But not quite two. Tell me what happened today.

Nothing happened. He looked at the heat pump. He showed me and my mom how to clean the filters. Mom wants to know if it's okay to put them in the dishwasher. I'm horrified. Turns out, it's okay to put them in the dishwasher. Nothing happened, you just can't stop talking about him. You just brought it up and wanted to know about him. But no, nothing happened. Well, I'm sorry I missed it. I wouldn't get too excited. He's got a list of people. What does that mean? You're not the only one who likes him. He doesn't show any interest. He's off on his own. That's not what I heard you say, Mia points out. What I heard was that he isn't very assertive and that if someone wants to make something happen, they're going to have to make something happen. None of you small town girls have done anything about it, leaving him ripe for the taking. She tickles Eirini's neck just after saying "small town girls." Eirini laughs, dips her chin, and lightly pushes Mia's hand away. That's true. It could be true. Lygia, that's his ex-girlfriend, that's the key to her success. If you're interested, you'll have to take the initiative. Well, he's scheduled to come for the next inspection in three months. Your plan is falling into place.

Stop that, she says, but she has the information she needs. She knows what she has to know, and she's already considering her next move.

Strays

The whole week after they arrive but before Assumption Day, it's first time drop bys plus the normal repeat visits. And not just that, there are the family and close friends who don't live nearby and have to make a special trip. Anastasia and Eugenia both come. On different days of course. That would be ill advised. Not that there is any hostility between them, they adore each other, but hospitality demands more focus and both women are brimming with charisma and demand a lot of attention when they're in a room. It would be too much to have them together at the same time.

The people visit, they bring things, ask for the stories fit to tell and tell what they can think of that might be of interest. They want them here, they want to affirm that they belong here, they're now part of their rounds, and they expect to see more of each other in the weeks and months ahead. At the parades and the festivals, at the gatherings and on the beach, wherever there is anything happening, they expect the newcomers to join. You're here now. Their visits make this clear. Now that you're here and you'll be coming to the events, you must learn the latest news and report things as they unfold. Report back anything new. It's your duty. We expect you to come to Thessaloniki often.

When Eleni calls Ion to let him know that they're going to be at the beach on Assumption Day, it's not strange to him. They're interconnected now. That's assumed. Someone has to call to let him know where they're going to be cooking on the holiday. It isn't just Assumption Day, it's Maria's name day too. Of course, they'll be together, and it's his duty to drop by even if only to give her his wishes.

There's nothing remarkable about Constantinos stopping by on that Friday before Georgios arrives. He's stopping by just like the others. He works closely with Maria at the pig farm and is well known throughout Dimos Nestou like his father before him, also a veterinarian. He inherits the clients and picks up a few more from younger connections, from friends of his parents, from school chums who remember him and need his help tending to their animals, pets or livestock.

Why stop by at their place? What's the connection? Eleni is surprised to see him. Her mother comes to the office and asks them both to come out and say hello, he specifically wants to talk to her. That's a surprise. She can't remember ever having a conversation with him. Is it going to be another one of those condolence calls or does he have a message? She tears herself away from her book and goes off to the living room to say hello. He's overly enthusiastic when seeing her. I remember you when you were this high and am so happy to see you here. I am so sorry to hear about your father.

She's cordial, polite, this is something to be endured, but then there's more. He has business, it is a matter of some importance. He needs to talk to both Ermioni and Eleni. You see, he doesn't know what to do. Mia comes out and they introduce her. Constantinos tries to let the conversation switch into English, but he's rusty and hasn't been using it much in the last few years, so he slips back into Greek. The whole conversation turns that way and Mia hovers politely, staring and studying the facial gestures and listening for the occasional word to cue her into what they're talking about.

Em got Dimos Nestou to come up with some money a while back, a few years ago, around the time Eirini starts working there. Not saying they're related, you understand. The timing. He contributes some of his own money too. They create a program for gathering stray cats and dogs, neutering them, and then returning them. The work includes setting up feeding areas and a care center where the animals get more regular check-ups. Sometimes, not too often, compassionate euthanasia in severe cases. FeLV or when the animal is suffering.

There's a huge problem with stray cats and dogs and it only gets worse because they aren't neutered and spayed. The animals breed and grow up feral and are impossible to care for. Years ago, Em decides to do something about it. He goes to different organizations and agencies, the world wildlife fund and the federal government. He solicits the regional government, everyone he can think of, they come through. In later years, they get even more support from other organizations. The fund and the province contribute every year. It adds up. The animals of Chyrsoupoli are well cared for. The feeding stations around the city are well run by the Dimos and there are several local veterinarians who donate their time to help. Constantinos is careful to let them know that it's become a popular program and the people in town know its origins and are anxious to keep it going.

What do you need? Both Ermioni and Eleni are attentive and interested. Ermioni remembers, but it slips her mind among the other things she has to attend to. What level of commitment? Do you need money or time? What is it? They both want to know.

Constantinos assures them that the money is not a problem. The problem is that Em's the chief officer and signs for things, arranges for things. There's a void now and he doesn't personally have time to take over. He doesn't know anyone to do it. Constantinos is hoping Eleni and Ermioni will take over the responsibilities. He says he'll send them everything they need. There's a bank account and some agreements in place. Everyone knows this needs to transition and the people, at the bank, the volunteers, and the vets, everyone hopes they'll take this on, and everyone is anxious to help them learn about it. They're sure that with everyone contributing, the two of them will have everything they need.

Eleni says she can look over the materials and talk to some people. She is gracious and helpful, but a little hesitant. Ermioni, on the other hand, gets excited. She enthusiastically agrees to jump right in and do whatever needs to be done to make it work. She remembers when Em set it up. There are so many strays, she says. They need so much attention. It breaks my heart that we can't help them all. That's what I tell him. I remember saying it one day when we're walking together and there's this adorable little cat needing so much help. I hate walking past her and leaving her there. I tell him. He starts talking to people. He starts digging in to see what can be done. Yes, absolutely, I'm happy to look into this.

They agree to go down to the bank after Assumption Day and present the death certificate and fill out the paperwork to change the program's account. In the meantime, did you see that beautiful striped cat that's often up at the corner? The one that's always crossing the busy street. I want to lure him down here so he's safer and away from traffic. If he doesn't leave that corner, I know he's going to get hit by a car. Ermioni is convinced the feeding station isn't attracting him and that he's at risk. So many of the strays are killed by automobiles. It's the most common cause of death, he tells her.

The day Georgios arrives, she's been busy working out a plan. She's trying to learn the cat's habits. This one proves there is a gap in service. If she's empowered to look more deeply into it, she'll find out what's missing.

The cat is hungry and, unlike the other cats who know where to get their meals, this one is a little too wild and stays clear. She coaxes him down the street and closer to the house. She doesn't try to touch him or get him to eat out of her hand, she just leaves a little plate of food for him. Then, the next time, she puts the food closer to her house. Just over the three or four days after Constantinos' visit, she's able to get him up to her porch, where he's happy to have a well-balanced meal. Once he knows the house and the porch, she's convinced that if she just keeps putting the food out, he'll come consistently and steer clear of that corner and the busy road.

Her plan is coming to fruition, but she doesn't feel confident she has fully sleuthed the cause of his exclusion. If he's more feral than the others, he may be steering clear of anything that smells of civilization. In that case, there are other cats like him and the only way to lure them would be with a similar approach. She doesn't see the program collar and tag on the cat who now curls up on top of a blanket in a little crate on the porch. He hasn't been neutered, but she's on the right track. Her first objective is to find out how to use the program to take care of this one cat. If she can do that, she'll know enough to help the others.

Eleni is both surprised and relieved to see her mother taking such an interest. Surprised because she doesn't see her mother this way. Always such a homebody, showing little or no interest in community involvement and volunteer service. What's stopping her from doing things like this in Seattle? she wonders. At first, it's like a judgment, but then it becomes a genuine question. Why shouldn't she study her mother, why shouldn't she get to know her like that? What's it about Seattle that inhibits her and how is that barrier removed when she comes here?

Eleni never thinks of the impact her mother's accent has. She seems like a native speaker, there's nothing to think about, but over the years, she notices things. Her pronunciation of certain words, the strange mistakes she makes sometimes, like calling toes fingers. These are so common she doesn't notice them anymore let alone imagine what they mean to Ermioni. She remembers going to restaurants as a family and her mother ordering, but the waiter doesn't understand her. She repeats herself. At the time, she only sees it through her own embarrassment. When it comes back to her, she recalls how it makes her mother feel and how much it explains.

Her name is long. This is a huge problem. She spells it for everyone. She has to spell it two or three times before they get it. Then she remembers her mother asking which preposition to use in some expression. Little things like that. Things kids internalize, but don't ever think about how it must feel for an adult. Always worrying people won't understand or will think your name is too long and impossible to spell. Maybe that's why she never gets into things like that in Seattle. At the bank, she doesn't have to spell her name. She says it once and the banker recognizes it and knows how to spell it. Exactly like it sounds. What's the impact of these experiences all day every day? What does it do to you and how does it change your confidence when you meet new people?

I'm glad you're so interested in this, Mama. I'll help you sort it out, but I think it's best if you take over. You'll be here and it'll be easier for you. Oh yes, I don't mind, but it's good that you'll help. I'm sure there are many things to figure out. It'll be good to have both of us working on it. Mia, you can help too if you're interested. She doesn't have time, Mama. She'll be leaving soon, anyway, she has to get back to work. But if she wants to, I'm saying, it'll be good if we look into it. I understand. It doesn't matter. I just thought. And that's how her mind works, she wants something to tie them together. She has an easier time talking to Eirini. Everyone does. She wants to know Mia better and she wants to be closer. Projects do that. If they have a common task, take responsibility for something together, that's the best way. Yes, Mama. If she has time, she'll help too. We'll show her what we find while she's here. We can look at everything together. Of course.

Ariti is showing me records for the rental properties. Georgios and Nikos too. The accounts. I'll take care of it. We can do it together.

I don't know, Mama. Are you going to be okay with so much going on? You'll have to talk to an awful lot of people, are you sure you can manage that? She'll have to overcome her anti-social instinct, she'll have to work with people, she'll have to climb out of her shell.

That's not a problem here, she says laughing. Finally, I can be myself. The last phrase, the sentence that echoes in Eleni's mind, is: do you know how hard it is to be funny in a foreign language? I have my English personality and I have my Greek personality. In Greek, people are easier.

Assumption

Apparently, having finished her duties on this Earth, the virgin Mary ascends body and soul into heaven. This is a day of celebration.

Nikos goes swimming nearly every day. Even in the colder months, he keeps to the schedule. After his morning work with the pigs, and before he goes to eat breakfast with his mother, he swims in the Aegean, usually closer to his house on the East side of town up the coast from the point that stretches out past the harbor toward Thassos. In the warmer months, Maria joins him. His children start coming along when they're about twelve. Eirini doesn't swim with her father anymore, but Alexandros still does now and again, especially this August while he's home from Thessaloniki.

The families get together on the West side of town where the beaches aren't as good, but the crowds aren't so bad. They have their privacy there. Families are everywhere on this side too, but it's lower density than at Ammoglossa. They spread out and have more room for their activities. Maria meditates on the beach while Alexandros and Nikos swim out into the clear blue water.

Ermioni has a camera around her neck. She periodically lifts it up off her chest, frames something in the encampment or on the beach, takes a series of photographs, and then lets it rest back on its strap until the next image calls out to her. Everyone is always commenting on how perfect her photographs are, they show so much sensitivity to the moment. Being the photographer guarantees you won't be in any of the pictures, Mama, Eleni calls out to her after catching her in the act of her latest frame with Mia and Eleni a little left of center. Never you mind me, she says. You're mine to photograph as I please. It doesn't work both ways, does it Mama?

Despina comes with two of her friends and they sit away from the others and chatter away about their other friends and where they are today and who is visiting with whom. Who is on this side of the town and who is over with the tourists? They get up at some point and walk off. Despina tells Ariti where they're going, but no one else hears. Yes Mama, I'll come back and eat something. We won't be gone long.

Charlie and Horacio come up the beach and greet everyone. They're with their children up the coast and have come down just to say hello. They remind everyone that there's going to be a bonfire closer to the shore later on and they should come down when the sun starts to set. They haven't stopped by the house yet. Charlie spends most of his time in Xanthi and Horacio in Kavala. Until this beach day, it's too inconvenient for them to come down. They go up to Eleni and ask her if she remembers them. How can I forget? she says. She explains who they are to Mia. Both ex-pats from different places, they bonded with Em over that, she says. Horacio came here from the United States, even though he's born in South America. Hey Horacio, didn't you live in Chicago? Why yes, he says cheerfully. That leads to a four- or five-minute-long polite exchange between Horacio and Mia. They're both familiar with the city, but not the same Chicago. In America, it's more likely than here, Eleni says, people can be from the same place and still be from different places. In Greece, everyone from Chyrsoupoli is from Chyrsoupoli and that's that. Not so in America. Mia doesn't like the look of either one of them. Mid to late fifties, seemingly single, she gets a distinct vibe. These people were friends with your dad, she asks rhetorically. He's a completely different person here, Eleni tells her. I don't recognize him in any of the stories. Nobody mentions Ben Thorne.

Charlie and Horacio mostly talk to Ermioni. They know she's going to take over the program. Constantinos tells them the other day when Horacio runs into him on the street. I still come to town most days, he says, my shop is here even though I'm living in Kavala. She gets excited when they tell her they've heard the news. It makes it seem more real to her. She tells them about the cat she's been luring onto her porch. She explains her plans for getting it neutered. That's her project for next week. After she takes care of the paperwork. She's animated even though she's speaking in English. Ariti is hearing this story for the third time, so she gets up and goes to see what Thimios is doing. He's reading his book and sitting with his mother-in-law and Europea. The biggest umbrellas are in the back of the camp and the two older ladies are sitting next to each other in the shade. Thimios tries to steal some for himself. He's reading a science fiction novel that Nikos recommends. It's about how nanobots can be injected into people to change their lives. There are two different kinds, one for neuron control and another for the rest of the body. The first kind makes you brilliant, the second makes you live forever. The general purpose nanobots are a million dollars. The brain function bots are ten million. There's a sub class of people who can afford the general purpose nanobots. They'll live forever, barring accident, and never get sick or look older than thirty-two. There are only a select few who have the brain function nanobots. They're the new rulers, they're the ones who keep the prices high and figure out how to make you get regular boosters to keep the effects in place.

The men tell Ermioni that they're happy to help in any way she needs. Horacio says he's done some work for the project before. If you ever need photographs to show to the money people, I'm happy to help, he says. I did some stuff like that a few years ago. We had to show them what we're doing. They like their financial reports to include pictures. Especially the world wildlife fund who don't really believe these are wild animals. They send people sometimes to check. Mostly they just want to see pictures of feral-looking animals getting cleaned up. Charlie echoes the offer. He'll help too. Anything is fine. I went with Em to the Dimos Nestou offices once. I know many of the people who work over there. Good lads, most of them. Don't hesitate to give me a shout if you need anything.

Eleni can't get over the surprise. She tells Mia she never thought of her father this way, that she's learning so many different things about both of them. Back home he's always so isolated. Both of them. They don't have many friends. They aren't involved in the community, they keep to themselves. Maybe it's not your parents, Mia tells her, maybe it's the place. Here, it seems like it's easy to have an impact. Em's basically a selfish socially conscious person. What does that mean, selfish socially conscious? Well, Em's like a lot of people, they want clean streets and public works, good schools and safe neighborhoods, not because of some moral imperative. No, he isn't like that. His interest is completely selfish. He doesn't want to see garbage when he walks around the city, so he wants it to be clean. He doesn't want to interact with idiotic people who have no sense of history or cultural achievement, so he advocates better education. His life is better if people are better off. He is sophisticated enough to know that out of sight out of mind isn't an option. It's not just optics that drives people like that, it's their sense of well-being and general welfare. He wants to live in a civilized world. That means you really have to do the work, and you can't just sweep it under the rug. You're saying this is for selfish reasons? Completely. It isn't that he thinks they'll be better off, he thinks he'll be better off if the people around him have better lives. They'll be more positive and healthier, happier and easier to live with. If they're all of those things, his interaction with them will improve. Completely selfish.

It makes sense, she says. Mom's the one who cares about the animals. She's the one who thinks these poor creatures are suffering and need taking care of. Your dad probably just thought his life is better if your mom is happier and your mom's happier if the animals are happier. Okay, suppose you're right. Suppose he's that way. Why not be consistent in the US and here? There are plenty of opportunities in Seattle, why not get involved? Eirini listens to them talk even when they think she's dozing in the sun. It's easy to do these things here, she says from behind her sunglasses. If you have initiative and find the right people, others will come out too. They look quietly at her, so she keeps going. There are resources. Is it like that in the US, can you get involved if you want to? Can you actually have an impact on things if you make enough effort? Mia doesn't think so. She finds community outreach and organization incredibly difficult. There's little support from public bodies, people might give a little money, but getting time or attention is impossible. There's a battlefield of millions of different things, and no one focuses on anything for very long. Maybe there's something in American life that makes it impossible. Could be, Eleni says, in many ways I think he gave up on America. We're too far gone. Even the simplest things are impossible.

What are the simplest things? Someone asks.

The question remains in the air. Ion comes walking up the beach. He waves to the group. Thimios greets him and invites him to have something to drink and a little bite to eat. There's a portable table by the poles of the two big umbrellas and there are some covered dishes with treats and cut fruit spread out on them. He takes a beer from the cooler but says he's stuffed and can't eat another thing. His friends are down the beach, and he just came by to say hello and wish Maria chronia polla. He greets Ermioni and Ariti and they ask about his parents. How are they? Where are they today? They're on Thassos, he says. They have some property on the far side and are there for most of the month. They promise to come soon and say hello, he says. As soon as they can get away. Good, good, we need to give your mother our wishes.

He says hello in English to Eirini, Mia, and Eleni. He asks them if they're enjoying themselves. His English is good. Have they been swimming? Eleni's hair is perfectly dry, she absent-mindedly runs her hand through it and tells him she hasn't been in yet. In fact, this is our first time at the beach since we arrived. Oh, you have to go in, he says. The water is beautiful. Yes Lena, Mia says teasing, you must go in. Ion, why don't you take her swimming?

He nods emphatically and Eleni gets up and they trot off toward the water just as Nikos and Alexandros are coming back. Alexandros dries off and grabs his phone to see what he missed since going in the water. Nikos joins Maria at the far end of the encampment. She's by herself and reading now. He lays out on a towel and flings a few drops of water at her. She squints at him. I see you there, she says. She gets up and he sputters a confused question, where are you going? I'm going to take a walk. I'll see if I can find Georgios. He's gone off that way and we haven't seen him since. He must've found some old friends. I'll go with you, Alexandros says and jumps up and jogs to her side. He carries his phone in his hand and keeps looking down at it while his mother runs her hand through his hair. Nikos lays back on the towel. Make sure he's not getting into any trouble, he calls out after them while taking a hat from the beach bag and setting it over his face.

In the water, Ion tells Eleni about the year they've been having: when and where the jellyfish are. They come and they go. Today is wonderful. There are none in sight, and the water is so warm. The old ladies are in church, but the rest of us go to the beach. It's the end of summer. It'll be warm until October, won't it? Yes, of course, but summer isn't about the temperature or the weather, it's about the holidays. We don't work as much, we like to go out and enjoy the sea and the air. It's not like that back home, she says. He smiles. Tell me more. About what? she asks. About what it's like back home. His eyes are sad, and he's very attentive. She can't help herself, she paints a picture. School is year round. I guess, I don't have any summer. Not really. Don't they give you any time off? Time off from classes, we get that, but not time off from study. Summer is when you have the most free-time, and you can get a lot of your own work done. You're in school, but free-time is for getting work done that you can't do when you're in school? Yes, she says smiling. It's mystifying, I know. We are teachers or we work on our advisor's projects. That's what happens during the school year. If we're curious about something else or want to follow a tangent, we have to do it on our own time. There's never enough during the school year. The summer is when we catch up. The clear water feels nice. She's splashing and dives under just as he says it doesn't sound like a good way to live.

She resurfaces and smooths her hair back. No, she responds, it's not a good way to live. Education reduces our ability to live well, she says laughing. Doesn't it depend on what you think it means to live well? he asks seriously. Most likely, she says, but who thinks studying all the time is living well? There are different kinds of people, he says. Yes, that's the theme of the day.

Eirini and Mia are alone together. Eirini sits up and moves into the shade of the smaller umbrella where Eleni was sitting. Why don't you want to be called Danit? She asks. It seems like such a lovely name. What does it mean? It's Hebrew. God is my judge. Miriam is a Hebrew name too, in fact. Beloved. My parents wanted to give me a Hebrew name. I guess I'm rebelling against it. Why? Because of the occupation, because of the horrible things the Israeli government does to the Palestinian people. They take their property, and they prevent them from returning to their homeland.

Hebrew is a language though, isn't it? Not a country. The language is very old. The country is young. You don't like the name?

It's the associations. The current state corrupts history. It's impossible to ignore the occupation when the language is used, whenever a name is uttered in that language. It isn't just that the occupation is destroying the Palestinian people, it's destroying the ancient culture and everything it means and stands for.

Is that like the selfish socially conscious view?

I suppose so. It's a different type of selfishness though, isn't it?

Yes, but that's normal. People who love their country want to fix things it's doing wrong not just for the victims, but for the whole country. To make it healthier. In Greece we have a long tradition of hospitality. In the arguments about immigrants, many Greeks feel it's our duty to show the same kindness to strangers that we've valued for thousands of years. You must treat visitors right. The gods will be angry if you don't. She laughs when she says this. It's selfish.

Mia gathers herself calmly. Eirini speaks simply and Mia reminds herself how little is at stake in their conversation. She counts. It's easy to talk in broad concepts, she says after getting to ten, but that's irrelevant when there are people's lives at stake. They make decrees, they send troops, and they evict people from their homes. It isn't just aesthetics. My objections aren't from concern for the souls of the Israeli people. I'm not looking out for the colonizers.

If it is wrong, then the people who do wrong, they're hurting themselves too though, aren't they? She isn't arguing. She's speaking simply and asks the question because she's confused. She doesn't understand the distinction Mia is trying to make. Yes, it's a terrible thing that's being done, that means there's injustice hurting both sides. Why do you only care about the victims?

It's a simple question, but Mia hears it as an accusation. She's careful though. Eirini's tone and wide-open eyes make it easy. They're a warning. Don't hurt me, I'm just trying to understand. That's it. Mia gets the message. Why doesn't she care about the souls of those who are doing harm? She thinks any upstanding citizen with an ounce of integrity will leave the country. Anyone who hasn't left must condone the savagery. Why doesn't that alarm her? She wonders. There's nothing to be won in an argument here. There's nothing at stake. She nods and touches Eirini's shoulder. It's so very complicated, she says. Eirini agrees, no one wants to find out their life is a crime.

Ion and Eleni come back from the water. Her eyes fix on her mother, who's still talking about the cat she's lured onto her porch only now she's telling Europea and Stamatia. She put out a box with a blanket inside, she tells them. She hopes the cat will sleep there every night and consider it his home. Eating and sleeping, that'll be enough. Charlie and Horacio have left. The older ladies nod silently, Ariti is patient and has many questions. Does it have any markings? What is he like? Playful or very serious? Sometimes the feral cats lose their playfulness, even with other cats. Maybe you should get some toys or something for it to play with. If you can get it to settle down enough to play, it'll really be at home. As Eleni gets closer, she can hear more of what they're saying. She isn't as interested as her gaze would have anyone believe though, mostly she just wants to be looking at something, anything to make Ion think her attention isn't completely focused on him. Her mother snaps a photograph, and Europea helps her with her plan by calling out and asking her if she enjoyed the water. She tells her how lovely it is and how clear the water was when she went under. She puts too much energy into her response. She's trying to be aloof.

It's working. He's looking at her, taking advantage of the fact that she's distracted and looking away. He thinks she doesn't see him look at her, but he's wrong. He doesn't understand that giving him a chance to look at her is what that attention on her mother and grandmother is for. Mia watches them as they approach and registers these little details. So does Eirini. They both put their hands up over their eyes and shield the sun as they smile at the two of them. Did you enjoy yourselves? How was the water? Amazing, she says. Mia, you have to go in. It's not like anything else. It's not like anywhere else. You have to go in. Mia is convinced. She looks to Eirini who nods back at her. They get up and head off toward the water. Ion and Eleni sit on the towels they vacate next to the small umbrella. They extend their legs to let the hot afternoon sun dry them off. He looks around awkwardly, trying to think of something interesting to say, but he can't think of anything. He wants to tell her about things, but nothing seems right. He wants to ask her about the way people at the University talk about poetry and how come they make it seem so boring and brainy when it's really about feelings and emotions, but he can't think of the best way to say it without sounding uneducated and coarse. He doesn't want her to think of him like that. He fidgets and extends his hands out behind him. She lays back and puts on her sunglasses. She says, it's so beautiful, isn't it? Just a perfect day. He looks down at her and nods. She can't see him, but she knows that's what he's doing.

The Church

It isn't a full service or anything, but the priest does say a few words.

He's baptized you know, Ermioni says to Mia who is shocked to learn this. It makes so many things easier. Really, this country is so deeply connected to the church, you have to go along to get anything done. But he isn't even an atheist, that gives too much dignity to the issue. He thinks it's nonsense. Exactly, he says it's meaningless mumbo-jumbo and if it helps him get over a few hurdles, why not.

The service doesn't last long and many light candles and stand together outside the church afterward. The church is a little ways outside town, just off the Egnatia. Many people come. They linger and chat. It isn't organized, just an opportunity to get together and remember.

Will you bury him here? Someone asks. Oh no, Ariti responds, he's already cremated. We have his ashes. Will you scatter them somewhere nearby? Is that what he wanted? Ermioni cannot bring herself to respond. Ariti makes an excuse and doesn't answer. Thimios waits for the person to leave and then asks if it's true, did he leave any instructions? You bring him here and don't have a plan? There's a plan, Ariti says, but not everyone wants to talk about these things. Sometimes we have to let them be. I know the plan, Ermioni says, but it's too sad. I see, Thimios responds with his head hanging. He doesn't press it. Eleni overhears the exchange. She doesn't know the plan either and wants to find out. She quietly moves next to her mother and touches her arm. What is it, Mama? What does Dad want us to do with him? She assumes he wants to be scattered here.

Ermioni puts her arm around her daughter and stretches forward to kiss her forehead. He wants me to keep his ashes somewhere safe and then you can mix them together with mine when I die. We'll be scattered together in the backyard of the house. The house here? She asks. Yes. That's what he wants, but only if I do. You don't have to. Those are his wishes. He wants me to find someone else and if I do, I might not want that and that's okay too. I never say anything. I think it's beautiful, but now it's a heavy burden. I don't know what'll happen.

People come up to the two of them and give their condolences. People from the town, people who aren't close but who know him or know of him. They do it mostly to welcome Ermioni home. Some are people she's known her whole life even if she's never been close to them. Strange, she says, that there are people you've known for sixty years, and they aren't your family or your friends. Just fixtures. People you know and see from time to time. Em doesn't find it suffocating like we sometimes do. I can't imagine it, Eleni responds. Growing up like that. What about high school? Can you go out with your friends? Everyone knows where we are. It's hard to be invisible. I think one of the things I like so much about America is that it's so easy to disappear. We're anonymous. Here, no one's like that. Word always gets around. If there's a divorce, if there's an argument. Everything. Everyone knows.

More people come up and they pause their conversation. Mia listens. Ariti and Thimios listen. They nod at and then kiss those who approach. It's just the five of them standing there. They don't know where any of the others are, but they occasionally hear Georgios' voice from somewhere off in the distance. It's low and it carries on the windless warm day.

Is that why Dad's so different here? Because it's a small town? Do you think he likes that? He thinks things at home are broken. He doesn't know what to do. He thinks everything is impossible, even saying that things are impossible isn't possible anymore. He says over and over again, why do people want this? Why is this what we want? Here things are different. He feels it, whenever we come it's like a burden being lifted. You can feel it, can't you? Yes. It's different here. In the city and in the towns. In America, when we're driving across the country, it feels like we're in a foreign country. The people are so different, they want to be separate. The people in the cities and the people outside them, it's like they speak different languages. Here, by the waterfront in Thessaloniki, and by the waterfront in Keramoti, they speak Greek. Is that it? Yes, I think so. He's always more at peace here. He doesn't feel the pushing and the pulling. Charlie comes by and, once again, expresses his sincerest apologies for their loss. He repeats his offer from before, if you need anything, don't hesitate to contact me. Ermioni thanks him and tells him how much she appreciates his kind words. If I may, he says. Em would always tell me that part of the reason he is so much more at ease here is that he is always on vacation. I'm sure you're right about the differences and how much he likes the towns, but he expresses his doubts to me once when he says he can't tell for sure because his job clouds his judgment.

Thank you, Eleni says from off to the side. I'm sure that has something to do with it. I don't think so, Ermioni says after Charlie leaves. He sometimes works when we're here. One trip, he works the whole time. They let him do that. Even then, he's very much at ease. America tries to erase its past. It wants to live in the perpetual here and now. Consume whatever is shiny and in front of your eyes. The passage of time is a terrible inconvenience. The burden of the past. Facticity, Eleni says.

The priest comes by and speaks kindly to Ermioni and Eleni. He reminds them of the time, when the old priest is still here, as a novice he goes with Horacio and Em to Agias Annas near Mt. Athos. There is a monastery and the three of us stay there for a week or so. Em's Greek is rudimentary at best, but he's very interested in seeing what it's like there. The monastery is a beautiful place, not one of those hard-to-reach ones that you see in the picture books, but scenic. He appreciates the quiet and the peace. He is always happy to talk. Some of the monks try to speak with him, but it's difficult. They don't have much English and Em can't say anything very complicated in Greek. So, it's just me, I'm the only one who can talk to him at any length. He says this in English and is careful in the way he looks at each of them to see if his remarks are a nuisance. They're happy to hear the story and nod their encouragement. We speak of Spinoza's definition of God, and he tells me that's the only version that makes sense to him. We speak of rebellion in Dostoevsky's work and that even if the Christian notion of God is coherent, he feels the power of Ivan's argument. How dare you let that child suffer? Always a challenging man to talk to, he thinks about these things, and it's probably for the best that those monks can't communicate with him. There's no telling how much faith is preserved by the language barrier, he says chuckling and smiling broadly.

Eleni laughs with him and is happy to see the priest is in on the joke. He is encouraged by her laughter. He asks me a question that I still recall. He wants to know if the church believes that the world is God's possession. He wants to know if we believe that because God makes the world, it belongs to him, and not just the world, everything in it. Do our souls belong to God? Are they God's property? It's a very tricky conversation and even now I don't feel I've achieved any clarity. I'm tempted to say yes of course, whatever there is comes from God, but I can't say whether that means it's his property. It seems that there is something very human, secular, in the notion, and he's trying to bring that out. I think he senses a contradiction. He tells me that some philosophers base their idea of property on the act of making something, adding value to it, the creative process performed by human beings is a way to take possession of something. As Em understands it, though, divine creation is an act of liberation not appropriation. When God makes the world, he hands it over. He releases possession of it. Em thinks this means that to be truly divine, we require a different sense of property. The truth of our religious practice requires it. I think he believes the church is filled with hypocrisy, Eleni says. Maybe this makes it clear. The church owns this land, doesn't it? That building. It depends on a conception of exclusive ownership. That's at odds with the sacred, it makes the church a secular institution. Regulate it. Tax it.

The priest steps back from the reverie. He senses that she is not wondering idly. He thinks she's taking up the torch and making Em's argument for him. He blesses each of them and excuses himself. Ermioni shoots a stern look in Eleni's direction. She shrugs. Do I honor my father by keeping quiet? She asks.

At some point, a half hour or so later, Ion appears and repeats his condolences. Eleni tries to ignore him. She's unsettled by her behavior at the beach earlier in the week. What does she think she's doing? What is she thinking? She encourages him, and that isn't right. So, she doesn't say anything. She just nods and lets him stand there struggling with what to say next. Mia looks slyly at her and decides to step in. Do you know Em well, Ion? Oh yes, like I've been telling Eleni. He has had a huge impact on me.

I don't know how to make things fit together until he shows me. What do you mean? Mia asks. The people at the University are very intimidating. I try to tell you about this on Wednesday, Eleni. They say things about poems when they hear them. It seems so rigid and artificial. I can't find what I hear in their words. Does that make sense? I think there is something wrong with me. That I don't belong there. That there is something I can't touch. Em tells me that the people I'm listening to, that they have been ruined and that I shouldn't worry about what they say, that I should just keep going with my passion and do what comes naturally. That's what he tells me.

He says that? Eleni cannot maintain her distance. Yes, that's what he says. How can I put this? He says... Ah... For example. Aristotle. It's very hard to read Aristotle. For many reasons. Uh, the *Metaphysics*. He explains this to me. It is difficult because of its form. It is not a carefully planned book. It's incomplete and informal in many ways. That's one thing. Then also, it's in ancient Greek and although we've been studying and talking about it, there's distance. We don't live in the language anymore. No one speaks it. That means it's difficult to understand. You see? That's another thing. And there's a third thing. I remember. He says that the topics in the *Metaphysics* are abstract and difficult. So, for these reasons, the book is hard to read. If you want to, you can learn to read it. You can learn some of the language, you can study the time period. All of that. This will bring you closer to understanding, but it takes a long time and much study. In layers. You know. You might get a little closer after a year and then closer still after two years and so on. This is what he tells me. But you have to understand that the learning, everything you go through to understand the book, it'll change you. Maybe it'll change you very much. It might make you completely different than when you first get interested. This means your original questions, what makes you want to read it and understand it in the first place, they might disappear.

That's interesting, Mia says trying to be encouraging despite how painful it is to listen to him struggling with both the language and the ideas. Eleni is quiet. She doesn't want to look at anyone. She stares at the ground and then looks off in the distance when she hears Georgios' voice. She thinks she can see him at the far end of the churchyard talking to others. She thinks she can see Nikos too. This is very important to me, Ion says continuing. Because it helps me see what I am doing. I have been writing poetry since I was a teenager, but I haven't been reading it. I am not good in school. I don't want to read poetry. It's not what I mean... I'm not trying to understand the poetry... I'm writing... That's it. I don't want to contribute to the catalogue, I don't know how to say it. It makes some people feel and some people think. I'm very confused. Read the poetry, Em says. Feel it. Forget the commentary. Still, sometimes I wish I could understand what they're saying. The poems make sense. What they say about them doesn't. Em says understanding what they're talking about has a high price.

Eleni thanks Ion for coming, but then excuses herself and heads off in the direction of Georgios' voice. She looks around to find him once she is clear of her group but realizes she doesn't need him and just wants an excuse to get away. Mia follows after her once Ion leaves. She catches up with her and asks if she's okay. Fine, fine. It's just so conflicting. I don't recognize him. None of this sounds right. Someone doesn't know him. Is it me? Or is it these people?

He might have been different, Mia says. Your father is not the same man that goes to work every day. He isn't even the same man that I know. I hear many of your stories and they don't line up with the person in mine. He's a human being. He doesn't tell you the same things he tells a stranger. Or some guy doing electrical work at his house. You want him to talk to you the same way he talks to a monk at the monastery? He isn't going to be like that. No one is like that. We have many faces. All of us. And they're our own, each one belongs to us.

Are you feeling it too then? That's what she asks. Are you having the same experience? Not now, no, but that's only because I've been through it. He's a different person for my mom and dad than he is for me. It's obvious. It's why I'm not so shocked at what Ben Thorne says at lunch that day, about how Em is the center's benefactor. I've forgotten about that, Eleni says. Yes, yes, everyone forgets that, but I don't. He thinks that'll be such a blow to me. Like it's such a revelation, but it makes sense as soon as I hear it. It isn't just that he's a different person to each of the people in his life, he wants to be different. Intentionally. For me, he doesn't want to be the purse strings. He just wants to be "the biological father." The guy who's there for me but won't judge, the non-father father. What does that make him for me? She wonders without expecting an answer. It's not theoretical. He's gone. I live in a world without him. What does that make me? How much of what I am is because I want to please him or do what I think he wants me to do? Now I'm free. My thoughts are my own. My goals can be my own. What does that mean? Free to float and drift nowhere? Is that what it comes to?

Eirini comes up at this point of the exchange. She wraps her arms around Eleni and leans her head against her shoulder. You're right where you're supposed to be, she says. Eleni turns and puts a little space between them. She reaches out and touches Eirini's hair. Of course. Thank you, mikruli. Eirini smiles warmly and says, I'm so hungry. It lightens the mood and the three of them relax a little. We're going to eat, she says bouncing a little with excitement. At that place across the street from your yiayia's, by the bar where the village kids go. I am driving over there with Cristina and Demetrios. I'll see you there, okay? Save me a seat. Always, Eleni says.

She's always turning up at exactly the right time, Mia says. Right when we need her. On cue, Eleni says. Do you think I'm being too abrupt with Ion? Is he irritated? I don't think it's possible for you to irritate him, Mia says. She puts her arm around Eleni who leans into her. Don't give it another thought. Take it easy though. Mia squeezes her shoulder and the two of them start back toward Ermioni who is with another small group expressing their sorrow and reassuring her that if she needs anything, she shouldn't hesitate to ask. Ariti and Thimios round up Despina and they start walking together toward the parking lot. Don't worry, Thimios says pausing before going too much farther with the group, Georgios will make sure everyone knows what to do next. He'll be driving over with Nikos and Maria. I'll go find Europea and Stamatia. They're going back with us. It'll be a tight fit. He hands his car keys to Ariti and heads back up toward the church. Isn't life supposed to be slow and relaxed in the country, Eleni says as they approach the car. I'm exhausted with the activity of the last couple days. You get used to being on your own, her mother tells her. Me too. It's exhausting spending so much time talking to people. I can't even have my own thoughts.

Residual

Light: I may have an idea of property, but it is far from clear and distinct.

Justice: You don't think that Locke's notion has been well developed?

Peace: Locke's notion?

Light: The autonomous rational being, endowed with the light of nature or some such thing coming from the creator, breathes life into things. The act makes the thing one's own.

Justice: Sounds like a Marxist. Labor bestows value. Ha!

Peace: Why the sarcasm?

Light: Because Mr. Locke is generally thought to be the polar opposite. Despite his lip service to the origins of value through labor, he ultimately defers to the negotiations of a contract and avows that an autonomous rational agent freely rents out his effort to owners of large-scale property.

Justice: Exploitation by contract replaces the light of nature, apparently.

Light: I think perhaps you are making light of him. Once you have accepted the rational autonomy principle, agreements are always right and proper. You and I come to an understanding, and you agree to do such and such for me. I agree to compensate you for it.

Peace: When does the breathing of life happen?

Justice: Oh brother.

Light: Well, suppose I appropriate some land by fencing it off and doing some basic surveying. This makes it mine. Assuming there is no scarcity, and it does not belong to someone else, my act of fencing it, pounding the stakes into the earth, and mapping its terrain takes possession of it. By the laws of nature, it is my property.

Peace: I see, and then the agreements come in.

Light: That's right. Suppose I wish to grow beans. There is too much land for me to sow it myself, so I enter into agreements with people from the neighborhood.

Justice: People who don't have their own land.

Light: People who don't have their own land. They agree to plant the seeds so long as I pay them a wage. This is a free and fair agreement entered into by two rational and autonomous parties.

Justice: Each of those beans sprouts a beanstalk with its very own giant at the top.

Peace: We are poking fun, but the idea is clear enough.

Light: Well, assuming that you know what a rational autonomous agent is.

Peace: Ah, I see. It's that same idea. Everything depends on it.

Light: Yes, everything. For some stretch of time, educated humanity has this predisposition. They construct the notion of an omnipotent deity who breathes life into each individual soul and gives it this perfect capability to ideate and act, to think and do.

Peace: These agents are the property of their creator?

Justice: Now we're in it.

Light: The creator is an all-powerful being and the most glorious of deities. There is no contradiction in saying that such beings would be the property of their maker, but their maker is so magnanimous and perfect that He, in his greater wisdom, grants these beings their liberty.

Justice: The magic switch is set to "ON".

Peace: What is that supposed to mean?

Justice: It is common in those centuries, as the new science rises and the autonomous agent takes form, for the so-called great minds to flex the deity into whatever shape they require. There is no system of record, no archetype. They solve problems by attributing miraculous behavior to the origin story.

Light: I'll admit this is what causes my confusion. Mr. Locke, and his kin, seem deeply aware that rational and autonomous beings come to be in some sense. They are made. We are not our own makers, so there must be something beyond us which lies at the origin. Since this dependence on something outside ourselves is inconsistent with rational autonomy, they tell a tale to make sense of it.

Justice: We are to ignore the birth, we are to ignore the weaning, we are to ignore the feeding, and the education. The apprenticeships and the training. Forget the nanny and her effort, forget the workhouse and its effects. Forget that. The origin story is the deity himself, breathing life and magnanimously setting the agent free. To resist is to commit a fallacy.

Light: All true. One might even be tempted to suggest that the whole dualistic philosophy, the division of that person into mind and body, is itself a justification of this ignorance. The body engages in these training exercises and developmental cycles. The mind, however, is pure. If it takes time for it to emerge with its capabilities, that is only because the body must develop to contain that mind and provide every perfection necessary to express it.

Justice: Breathing life into it depends on this.

Peace: How do you mean?

Justice: The soul or mind is what does the breathing. Breathing, in fact, is a metaphor. The body may be the conduit of labor, but it is the mind that transfers significance to the thing.

Light: Suppose a farm owner has a vision. He sets about fencing off that land because he clearly perceives the possible future where acres and acres of beans are sprouting from the soil and growing into strong plants. He visualizes this and begins fencing off the land and surveying its contours and boundaries.

Peace: Yes, and then the agreement and the work of those others, that is for the sake of his vision. They realize his idea. That is why he owns the outcome, because he is the mastermind.

Light: His is the mind that sets it in motion and he provides the logic behind the actions and the agreements. He is the organization and the order of the activity originating in his mind.

Justice: Yes, his mind. Because one day he woke up and invented the notion of beans, and land, and agreements, and wages, and all of that.

Peace: Ah, now I see. Even if we admit that this man is the origin of every activity, the ideas that he employs, the architecture he designs, the plan he concocts, it's made up of pieces he learns from others.

Light: The crux of it seems to be whether there is a dual standard for this dualism. The thinkers of this era, they are tacitly aware that there must be something exterior in operations. Human beings are spatial, space is a coordinate system, it is pure exteriority.

Peace: Pure exteriority?

Light: Well, it's a heuristic. I know it is unclear, but so many have relied on this distinction, I find it difficult to avoid.

Peace: What is the distinction?

Light: Where your mind is operating and your experience involved, that is the interior, that is internal to your experience of the world.

Peace: Ah, I see. Points in space, this coordinate system, that is pure exteriority, meaning it is completely without mind, it is a natural event.

Light: This world is driven by natural cycles and external points of contact between one thing and another. When the billiard ball strikes another, the motion is external to it. It has its source outside itself. Natural relations, causal relations, are like this.

Peace: The mind, my decision to get up and move, that is interior to me.

Light: They acknowledge the appearance of determinate relationships while maintaining that a purified subject is not determined by relationships. The external world and the body can be shaped and formed by other forces, by the actions of others, and yet the mind, an independent and interior force, remains whole and free.

Justice: Did you ever figure out how to coalesce Locke's dependence on the rational and autonomous being with his empiricism?

Peace: What is that? There are so many terms I have never heard before.

Justice: It is to make it seem more scientific. Since it is hard to understand, it must be true.

Light: That's not helpful. Mr. Locke, in a different work, claims that the origin of our ideas is outside ourselves. Experience is the process of receiving ideas from the senses.

Peace: Then he admits that the farmer must have learned what farming is and what contracts are and those other necessary ideas for realizing his plan.

Light: There are many who make sense of this. They would no doubt lecture me on the deeper coherence of the notions, but I find its connections challenging.

Justice: If the plan is the basis of property relations, then owning the plan is crucial.

Light: Most farmers learn about planning from the collective experience of other farmers. There are books where the authors have spent decades researching. The goal of the work is to hypothesize the perfect plan for sectioning off land and growing beans. We learn from each other, and we even learn how to construct plans from each other. We might try once and fail and then we'll try again and –if we have learned something–it might go better. Perhaps we receive more advice along the way.

Justice: I think you are still overly kind. Let us not forget about that fence, shall we. Why does putting up a fence make it your land? Because the fence is so powerful and there is some magic working on it? Is that what protects it?

Light: There are laws.

Justice: There are laws, and there are legislators and systems of legislation. There are enforcers, there is a social system in place for spreading awareness of the laws, enforcing respect for them. There are various public goods to make the system of laws effective in people's day-to-day activities.

Peace: We have people who learn about farming and planning and project management, and we have the institutions necessary for communicating that to others: printing presses, publishing interests, distribution firms, and so on.

Justice: They are protected by laws and order and social structure and the norms and standards that people live by.

Light: It seems that this holds even before the autonomous being picks up the mallet to drive the posts into the ground. Even as intellectual property, the rational autonomy theory is problematic. There is an exteriority in our ideas. We are born knowing nothing and then we learn.

Peace: It has its origins in wonder. We have to interiorize the exterior.

Light: We do that well at times. If the deity gives us anything, if the magic switch is set to "ON", then the most rudimentary faculty of our nature is the capacity to internalize the external. To take an idea that is explained to us and appropriate it as our own. By "as our own," I mean we forget its origin. When we respect the fence, when we do not climb over it and take the beans, we respect an idea as if it is our own. We follow the law and never consider the possibility of crossing over to the other side.

Peace: You are saying that this ability, the ability to internalize, this is a special capability?

Light: Yes, and many conscious beings have this capacity, but it doesn't make them autonomous, not in the strict sense.

Justice: In fact, you might note the ambiguity in the word property to account for this.

Light: How do you mean?

Justice: Well, we might talk about the ownership of an idea and that ownership amounts to an attribute of some kind. Law-abiding. We say that this one here, she is a law-abiding citizen. She has internalized that norm or those standards, and we say that it is one of her properties now. Once it is appropriated, it can be attributed. Furthermore, the person becomes individuated by the process. They set themselves apart from other things by attributing themselves as law-abiding. They may come to love that attribute. When that happens, they identify with it. They accept it as a kernel notion defining who they are.

Light: Well said. It does make for a clean picture, but it is only a story.

Justice: More than a story, I should think. Consider belonging, as in belonging to a community. We can make much of the fact that belonging is a synonym for ownership. That belongs to me.

Light: When we say that belongs *with* me, what then? That small turn changes things, doesn't it? Things that belong with me are not mine even if they themselves wish to be with me.

Justice: My point is that through these identifications and the beloved attributes, we join together with others who also love those same attributes.

Belonging with them or belonging to them. This is semantics. We say we belong with those others who think the same way as we do. We belong together. We make a collective being.

Light: I won't quibble, but this notion that we are developing, it seems to turn Mr. Locke on his head. We do not breathe life into things. To the contrary, they breathe life into us. Through them we become ourselves. That is how we come to know ourselves. Our plans can be analyzed, segments of the population with similar plans can be identified, we associate with them, and advance together.

Peace: Does this give you the clear and distinct idea of property that you are looking for?

Light: It points in the direction of it. The collective is always involved, the community plays a part. We are like others when we do the things they do. We belong with others when we respect the things they do and give them the space necessary to do them. If you have a group of farmers making fences and surveying land, then planting beans themselves, cultivating their crops, and harvesting them, this makes more sense.

Justice: That isn't how it works, is it?

Peace: Not in the least. Many do not have land or fences or a plan.

Justice: They are too busy picking their neighbor's beans to come up with a plan.

Light: There are inequalities. Property is their container.

Peace: How so?

Justice: In the obvious sense, of course, some have land, and some do not.

Light: Yes, in the obvious sense, but not only that. Some have properties that others don't. Attributes. Our histories are borne within us, they are interiorized as these personal traits. Inequality is there. Some make beautiful music, some organize their larder better than anyone around, and some can direct the actions of others, coordinating large projects with tens or hundreds of different contributors.

Justice: Where do these inequalities come from?

Light: Some are based on learning and opportunity.

Peace: But not all.

Light: That is precisely the crux of the matter. There is inequality in appearance, in stature, in longevity. There are basic differences. We may use these basic differences to justify others following from them. Having different hair, coarse or fine, is a natural difference, but to use it to justify other differences that are not natural, but derive from living conditions or historical conditions, that is erroneous.

Justice: Erroneous? It's criminal.

Light: Perhaps. I assume you are suggesting there is some law beyond what is written. In that case, the magic is back on again.

Peace: Perhaps it would be ideal if there were a society of people whose natural abilities are allowed to grow as they see fit. Some children love to play with blocks and stack them just right. Other children like to bang on drums and make a steady rhythm. The ideal world allows those children to develop as they please.

Justice: Without a doubt. Everyone must work to achieve this.

Light: Well, I for one would never presume to know the makings of an ideal world, but that is certainly something I want for my own children.

Reasons to Give

Wage Labor

> I work hard to take care of you and make a home for you
> and your father, but I feel your judgment. Since you were a
> teenager. I know you don't value what I do, I know you don't
> respect how I've spent my life. You think I'm nothing. Your
> father never felt that way, he understood. I expect more
> from you. You don't know where I come from. It's as if you
> don't know anything about me. You don't want to know.

First off, there is the tone. It is as if a different woman is speaking. Stern
and confident. With her, where does this confidence come from? It isn't
native to her personality, but organic to the situation. It comes from
rehearsing these lines over and over again for years. As she feels them deep
down, they form behind her, in anger, in shame, in love, and in pride. She
wants her daughter to respect her. She is angry, and wants understanding.
Her confidence lies in conflict, its tone asserts force where she wishes it
weren't necessary. She defends herself while feeling both that she should
not need to and that she cannot manage it.

The citation is a translation with some liberties, and the tone runs
parallel. Confidence lies in the language she speaks, in her mother's
tongue, not her daughter's. Without the words, the body language, and the
look in her eyes, meaning changes. In English, she buries her point in tears:
not from emotion, but frustration. Her mastery is supreme, but she never
rehearses it. These are things she needs to say in words she knows from
deepest childhood.

She asserts, with force and clarity, that she is her mother's daughter and
that her child does not know what that means. She does not understand
the flow of time and the way it produces a generation and the world around
it. She sees a woman with a wasted education unwilling to stake her claim,
but she doesn't see a woman who studies what her father thinks best or a
woman struggling among men who think her incapable of contribution. She
pays lip service to these conditions but doesn't see them.

A careful investigation reveals that her training as a computer scientist
diverges wildly from her demeanor and natural talents. She is a woman of
refined tastes never mechanical or rigid. In their house, there is nothing
gaudy or overdone. Everything is beautiful and simple. The way things
work together, the positioning of items on shelves, and the atmosphere,

even the temperature of the rooms, she controls it and makes it pristine and inviting. The concentration, the attention to detail, it is perfect and precise. Her daughter grows up in the presence of a master and has no idea. Even as she rummages through history for insights into the forgotten contributions of her predecessors, she overlooks the woman behind her.

Is it because she does not earn a wage? What is so grand and extraordinary about his daily life? He is a wage laborer, paid a salary to produce what does not belong to him. They tell him how to do it and when it should be done. Alienation puts his nervous system outside his body, and the products of his labor are lost. It puts things belonging to others inside him and occupies his body and mind. Where is the genius in that? He submits to the dictates of leadership, of the corporate machine aiming at socially sanctioned value. Where is the honor in that? Aren't we learning the extent of his cowardice? Isn't that what the story reveals? That this man, so respected and feared by his daughter, that with these rumblings and ideas, he keeps them hidden his whole life while plugging away at someone else's concern. He lives in complete deferral to others, to the public face of his work. Why is that worthy of respect?

Her mother makes their lives. Born of her own taste and love, she designs those places, those corners, the contents of those drawers and cabinets. She plants those trees and paints that fence. She draws from nothing and asks no one for permission. She is the one who lives her life as she sees fit while he runs after the approval of others, learns what they want, and the complex techniques to give it to them. Her daughter shows the signs of suiting him to a T. She defers to his wishes, she becomes what he thinks most extraordinary. Her studies, her focus, her interests, they perfectly align with her father's tacit decree. Can't she see that this enslaves her to her father's cowardice, to his own sense of failure and the desire to reconcile it?

When they begin building the house, he insists on keeping the chicken coop and dog run. He wants her to have chickens. He wants her to have animals. She rejects his plea and tells him she doesn't want one more thing to repair in the winter or take care of in the rain. He backs off. Now, it would be nice to have something to remind her of what she's lost. It is her house, and for him, their lives pass under her control. She doesn't resist the coop and the run, just populating them. For reasons they never discuss, she loves having them in the yard among the fruit trees. She wants them there. They look like something she vaguely recalls from her childhood. Maybe something at grandmother's or something she saw somewhere. At the nunnery in the hills, the one her father takes her to, the one with the peacock and the deer, and the chickens. Cats not dogs, that's her preference. He thinks she'll lose her fear if she gets to know one well enough to understand the language, but he doesn't push it.

In these matters, he doesn't judge. He doesn't value his wage labor, so he doesn't see it as the measuring rod of their contributions. In his heart of hearts, he is misanthropic and believes any social merit is potentially insidious if conditions aren't thoroughly understood. He doesn't assume that teachers are excellent. He quietly nods if someone says so in his presence. He isn't prone to confrontation, but what he holds onto in silence is that a teacher is only as good as the lesson they teach. If they make their students into automatons handing in their assignments on time and doing exactly what they're told, he doesn't see anything noble in that.

This is what she turns over and over throughout the years as she readies the speech.

What she doesn't rehearse and what isn't there is the anger and distaste for those who do not see her. Women who think that success is what the men have always had. *Ain't I a Woman*, she asks?

He relays the yarn of woman-becoming and how she gets to define it as she goes. There is no right way to do it, but she is convinced there are many wrong ways.

She doesn't go so far as to accuse her daughter, but her daughter feels it anyway. Her choices are threatened. She doesn't put the University of Michigan at the top of the field, it's already there when she decides to go. He explains that a true academic career is only available if you get your credentials from the best schools. The rest of them are just filler. She doesn't define her discipline stretching back a century or more. She isn't thinking for herself, she works long hours to learn how to think like they expect her to. That is the pedigree. They always say it with such pride, we don't teach you what to think, we teach you how to think. My god, don't you see that's even worse? Nothing is possible unless it fits into your framework, into the way you expect it to be formulated. The structure is set, and I am set into it. None of this is her idea, she follows the formula. What is so special in that? Stanford. Michigan. Why are these badges of honor and not prisons? Perhaps a lesser school offers her more freedom with their lower expectations giving students more room to maneuver.

He says that at some point the faculty at his graduate school stop worrying about what he's doing and how he's doing it. It isn't because they realize he's internalized the discipline, but because they know that it no longer matters, and isn't worth the time to fight him. The profession takes care of weeding him out. Maybe that's for the best. Maybe it gives him control over his life. Does she ever consider that? That these finer schools have more at stake, they can't just let her go her own way. They make sure she conforms and grade her on it.

She never says, I think you're smarter than this. She never says it and it never enters her mind to be cruel, but her daughter hears it anyway. You don't know the facts, so you misjudge me, and misjudge yourself. That is what she hears. This is a daughter who is not subject to her mother's gaze, and this separates them. The older woman is driven by her mother's scrutiny while the younger is defined by the father even as she fights him. And the father? Woe unto him whose drive exceeds his talent.

Ermioni is 62 years old. She knows how people respond to things, she understands emotional responses and the feelings that overwhelm our relationship to facts. She knows that words resonate and acquire new meaning for each listener. The reading of signs is multiple in the audiences of the world, so she knows her daughter adds whatever cruelty she must to the message. No one needs to put it there, and the speech is more effective without it.

We acknowledge that the young woman is silent in response. She hears everything, reads and over-interprets everything. It is there in the words crossing the space between them, from one side of the kitchen island to the other. Silence. That's what she has, what her extensive education provides. Is there something she cannot fathom? Is there something women like her cannot see?

Something jogs her memory, but she cannot place it. It's a talk or a reference to something from somewhere. The author, dismissed as an agent provocateur, claims that oppression does not beautify, but gnarls and makes grotesque. Oppression makes the things it holds down crumpled and skewed. It breeds resentment and hatred then remakes the world in its own image to harvest resistance further advancing its agenda. The feminist cohort blasts him. The race and gender studies departments skewer him. He doesn't fight back, he just nods, acquiesces, claims they're making his point for him. They are his proof.

Is that her now? Is that what she's done to her own mother over years and years?

It doesn't take great insight to see that the daughter's response could be to race to the other side of the island, close the distance between them, take her in her arms, tell her she loves her, and hold her tightly. I will think about this. I want to talk more about it. She could say that, whisper it from right up close. Nothing stops her. It won't advance her career, it won't get her a better job, or provide job security. It won't meet with her colleagues' approval, but we sense that it's human and right, just the way a fatherless daughter should respond to a husbandless mother. It requires great insight to translate that into a concrete act and publicly consume it in one form or another. First, how will she pull it off? What is the best way? Does she need to do a study and collect data? Does she need textual analysis of the work that touches related topics? How can she get the effect of not spelling it out, but letting it resonate so that each member of the audience can fill in the details relevant to their own case? How can they close the distance?

None of that works in those places and times. They fight and they bicker, then they believe heart emojis and hug reactions have the same effect. They've come so far from themselves they can't even see the distance anymore. The oppressive conditions get worse, and they are immune to the virtues of support become vapid and sappy, sentimental and sanitized. Only in a household where things for use, where necessary things, are close at hand, where food is on the table, where a pitcher of water is close by, where photographs of happy times are on open display, only there can this come forward and settle into words. All of that descends upon her as she listens, it draws her out and reflects back upon her. She cannot hear without that place, she cannot put herself somewhere else, she cannot dodge the resonance from those walls. There and then, she sees her mother before her. She sees.

Intellectual Work

So many of the aggregate differences between human sexes have no impact on survival but are due to characteristics and requirements of the social order. The differences come from selection and recent innovations in pharmacology. Bigger smaller. Stronger weaker. Taller shorter. Compared to what? To each other, of course.

It might seem odd and trivial, but Darwin spends a lot of time trying to prove that the pursued makes a choice, regardless of how integral the behavior is to the pursuer who IS that way because they have been chosen to BE that way. In the aggregate. Always, in the aggregate.

> But mourning is not enough. I must accuse:
> oh not the man who withdrew you from yourself
> (I cannot find him; he looks like everyone),
> but in this one man, I accuse: all men.
> —Requiem for a Friend, Rainer Maria Rilke

And not just them. Whatever is human lies in any one of them. In the aggregate it finds itself in you.

> Dear Lena (if I may),

> I regret to inform you that the Dean of the Graduate School has denied your petition for a hiatus from study and financial aid. This is in accordance with the new University policy impacting graduate students who have not yet passed their qualifying examinations. The office of the Dean has informed us that they will consider your application for readmittance when and if you decide to return to the program.

This does not reflect the attitude of the Department of Anthropology and we are sorry to see this decision. If you would like to appeal, please assemble a detailed dossier including your contributions to the department and the field of study more generally. Please try to write a statement of purpose for your leave of absence to assure the Dean that it will not become a permanent arrangement. There is concern that the initial explanation you provide is code that conceals a long-term condition. The chances of success for your request will significantly improve if your statement convinces the department and the Dean's office that this is not the case. I recommend that you provide as much detail as possible.

Best Regards,
James Walters, Chair

The form of the missive is electronic. Its tendrils fire around her and although the opening and closing seem formal, the recipient and sender read it as convention. The first paragraph is just a simple statement of fact. The chair of the department is reporting on the decision of the Dean. There is no commentary and nothing to suggest anything other than a standard form letter response to a bureaucratic request. When Eleni reads the letter, she's disappointed, but not surprised. It is common to have to go through an appeals process. The university, like many insurance companies, uses policy as triage. They reject requests as a matter of course, assuming that some notable percentage will end there. The requests that progress, those are the ones needing attention, those are the ones that will get a proper hearing and be considered by the right people with the right level of authority. Many of the students who are not serious or who do not have a real need will be put off. She knows it works this way. Another student tells her about it. In his case, he contacts the Dean's office through the department chair and initiates the appeals process, schedules an interview with an administrator, and that's all it takes.

It is the second paragraph that throws her. It seems like the decision has nothing to do with the Dean's office but comes from the chair of the Anthropology department himself. They're supposed to support her, the department leaders know her and are supposed to be on her side. She expects them to set up the meeting and let her know what she needs to do. What does the commentary mean? Her department doesn't trust her, her department isn't willing to get behind her.

When she reads the response to Mia, who is fluent in a host of administrative languages, she is dumbstruck. Why would they put that in writing? She wonders aloud. It's clearly coded and patently sexist. This is even before she hears the story about Eleni's colleague. Once she hears that, she's livid. He thinks you want to take time off to have a baby. That's absurd, Eleni points out, the forms don't require much explanation, but I indicate clearly that there's a death in the family. She has to check, but her memory is correct. The chair's response suggests he doesn't believe her or isn't paying attention.

The detail in the statement, what the chair writes in that second paragraph, assembling a thorough dossier, it is as if they're expecting me to reapply for my position. It's heavy handed and invasive, and it comes at the worst time. They stoically agree, as would any reader, that the department is exploiting university procedures for the sake of an ulterior motive. Eleni has a fellowship funded through a special program in the college, but it is awarded by the department. The request covers deferring the fellowship and its supplemental assistantship. The department, not the college, is blocking them both and the only justification the two of them can think of is that it applies a double standard. Even if they don't believe she's hiding the truth, they sense that deep down she isn't committed, and it's a waste of scarce resources to hold her position until she returns.

Eirini and Eleni don't spend much time together since Eleni begins the doctoral program. They speak over the Internet and send lots of text messages. That's normal, but Eirini doesn't have the day-to-day insight on what Lena's life is like. They talk about it after the message arrives. Eirini doesn't see anything insidious. She thinks it's just a harmless request for more information. This forces Eleni to explain the history of the institution.

Of course, she says, they pay lip service to diversity and inclusion. It's what they talk about most, making it clear that everyone is welcome, and they want different perspectives. When it comes down to nuts and bolts, how the institution runs on a daily basis, there are countless instances of inequality, ways the university and the department aren't sensitive to different life experiences and backgrounds. If you're on the beaten track, life is better. If you don't need anything outside the ordinary, it's fine and dandy, but when something unusual happens, when you have to go down some side road, that's when you're left to an individual's judgment, some administrator somewhere or, worse, some departmental clique of colleagues with an axe to grind.

Research programs are good at creating axes to grind. That's hard to explain. Eirini sits quietly, trying to absorb the crazy stories from both Mia and Eleni. Research, the lauded and revered science that is such a fetish to the public, is funded in complex and labyrinthine ways. There are private and university administrative interests at stake. The results can be owned by some enterprise and there might be back room deals around future funding based on them. The university is always ready to take its cut. When money is spent on lab time, or payroll, or whatever, there is always overhead, and the administration insists on a vig. Money for research means money for everyone in the food chain. Some professors are valued higher because of the money they bring in. Others are shut out in the cold sometimes, resentments develop, and hostilities follow. Not open hostilities, but quiet and vindictive.

It is not uncommon, she explains, to be required to take a course outside your cohort. That means you might be exposed to the judgment of a professor at odds with faculty that sponsor your research. In that case, they may take out their frustration on you rather than the professor behind you. They don't want to square off against them, that would be too risky, but to take it out on a graduate student, there's no danger in that. There are plenty of those to fill in any spots created by attrition. Besides, everyone does it, so the graduate students learn to stay on the proper roads and remain in well-lit areas. Nothing creative or innovative, just keep your head down and do what's expected.

Sometimes that isn't possible. Sometimes some special situation brings you into contact with a person who is not an ally and who has a chip on their shoulder. Mia is convinced that this is one of those times. Among men of a certain age, she says, it's common to see them take these things out on women more so than men.

Mia and Eleni laugh when Eirini suggests that the chair is supposed to act like a leader and be above these disputes. They explain to her that despite being correct, she is wrong. The chair is usually drafted into the position, they might be someone who wants a better career but doesn't have the research chops to earn it, or to resist peer pressure. They think the chair is often the worst person to square off against on special requests. Mia says that if Eleni really wants to fight the process and appeal the decision, she should involve her advisor. She's included on the original request but is, for some reason, excluded from the response. It would be a blatant power move to bring her back into the discussion.

Eleni mentions an article she read at school in California. It's about how men develop confidence in their fields of study when they're in their twenties and thirties. That's when they generally establish their expertise and take on a bigger role in showing it. The study claims that it's at this same age when women's confidence begins to evaporate.

There are different kinds of social pressures assisting this. The pressure to start a family and to couple up with someone who is unsupportive of any time spent away from them are both part of it, but institutional behaviors have a role to play too. Having to confront so many obstacles and leap over so many hurdles just to do something that's a mere formality for others is humiliating. If these things happen over and over again, with deferrals, work schedules in the lab, or submitting work for a research project, it has a collectively huge impact. When I started the program, I was more enthusiastic and confident than I am now. It isn't like this when you get a masters. There aren't as many carrots and not as many sticks.

She insists she doesn't want this to happen to her in the years ahead, that she's worried it will, and thinks it might be better to leave altogether. Here is the question they pose, is it more soul-sucking to leave the department or to stay and follow the rules? That is the dilemma she must confront. Mia tirades on the civilization and its relationship to smart and competent women. Somewhere deep down in the psyche of the culture, in ways we can't even imagine, there's some interest in preventing women from being too openly capable and competent, too confident in their capacity to contribute and steer the order. It's an egregious injustice, and it's there every day in her work. The system works harder against you the more skills you display. They assure you that it's a meritocracy, and that they're just putting you through fire to make you earn your way.

Eirini asks whether men go through it too. Of course, men go through it too, but it doesn't have the same impact. It's because there's a different foundation and sense of self. He's in a place where he's already so confident, no counter accusation stalls his efforts. She is nowhere near it, and that isn't an accident. Mia and Eleni have lots of explanations and questions. Men are groomed and raised from birth, it's something they have rehearsed before and know quite well. Because they have these stronger social reinforcements, they're better able to weather the storm of the attacks by the enforcers of merit and desert. Mia dismisses the assertion that men have it rough too, but Eirini thinks she's being dogmatic. Clearly not every man has the same benefits as every other man. This is a diversion, Mia insists, and they shouldn't get distracted. It's important to stay focused on the matter at hand and its direct attack on justice.

Eleni's response is playful. She is looking for diversion. She doesn't want to rathole on the departmental email and the icky horrible feelings it dredges up. She tells them both that she wonders if women's age has something to do with how they react. Eirini listens with that same absorbed focus she has for every one of the explanations that day, but Mia's mouth is wide open in disbelief. Eleni explains that women of a certain age might be more tolerant of some behaviors, or more sympathetic to them, but they become less so as they get older. We might attribute this to an increase in wisdom or experience, but biologically there might be a different explanation. Women in their child-bearing years may be more inclined to tolerate adverse male behavior because they need them to procreate. This tolerance is selected for younger women, older women don't need it. It serves no purpose and there's no genetic bias in favor or against it. This makes it easier to become more hostile as they age.

Mia rattles off a response claiming the inverse is just as likely, that men are more attractive, in fact, at that age and lose any pretense of trying as they get older. It starts off as a reasonable response, but as she elaborates and runs into the possibility that men can have children long into old age, a fact Eleni slyly provides while suggesting Mia is most likely right, her speech degrades into a largely anecdotal and science-free set of associations and accusations. When Mia finishes her rant, Eleni reminds her that it's merely a hypothesis. It's structured so that data can be gathered, a research project formulated. The loss of confidence might be an example of sexual selection. Women in their twenties and thirties who have too much confidence may be less prone to tolerate male behaviors and less likely to procreate. Hormone levels might lie at the root and if there is any genetic basis to any of these behaviors, and that would have to be established, then the women who lose confidence and who are more likely to have children, they are responsible for the selection of women who are less likely to retain their girlish confidence into adulthood. As women age, as they pass their child-bearing years, there are fewer indicators necessary, and selection has less to say about it. That's when women can really let their confidence fly and, since it may come after a long-deprived state, it might emerge in forms of resentment and anger. We have to wage a life-long battle against these passions. Even when the facts justify them, it's imperative to retain focus.

Mia is furious. She's pacing the room and spouting her distaste for this pseudo-science. Besides, she reminds her, how does this help you now with these old farts who are taking their resentment out on you? Eleni's point isn't that this helps her, but rather shows her what she's up against, not only hundreds of thousands of years of human development and the trillions of individual decisions that shape it through aggregate impact, but that she's working in a field where there are complex rationalizations and justifications at work. If Mia admits there's an imbalance, then she has to explain how and why it exists. Why would billions of women, capable of plotting and strategizing, why would they fall into this? Why would women become their own jailors and oppressors? Judge each other? Why fight and antagonize each other even when it comes to casting blame on those who have aided and abetted the patriarchy? Why help society rob their peers of confidence and standing? It happens through competition, through intrigue, and even through ordinary everyday pride over this or that rare accomplishment that one of them achieves while so many others fail. Something must explain it.

What else could explain differences between the sexes? It is the same species, the qualities that make us fit, they are shared. If it's true that human survival is deeply connected to our social selves, our abilities to form efficient groups and make powerful associations, then the specimens share equally in those characteristics, those traits that enable us to work together and move and motivate each other. That's obvious, but why are the sexes so different? Why do men need to be one way and women another? The majority of our civilization are simple binary members. Male or female. If you think one man and one woman is a simple binary, Eirini says to no one listening, you aren't paying attention. Complexity and divergence are there, both socially and biologically, but they're not the majority. The normies are, well, normal. That's demonstrable with data.

Her hypotheses are untested, and her professional reputation does not depend on them. She merely points out the domain of responsibility proper to physical anthropology. This is the racket she's chosen. If she chooses to stick with it, to go through the motions, to escalate the matter to her advisor, to contact the Dean independently, if she enters into the political foray, she has to be sure this is what she wants, and that this is the right battle to wage. I'm not sure it's worth it. Maybe some perspective *would* help, maybe I should leave. That means the powers-that-be are winning. That's true. It's almost impossible to know from a personal point of view which option furthers the interests of the system (biological or social) to deprive women of confidence, and which thwarts the system's interests. She can't see it, she argues, because the system behaves at a level that is in her bones and muscles more than it is in her mind and thoughts.

Whatever she does, it'll be the wrong thing, in a way. Whenever anything reduces to a simple binary choice, both choices are wrong.

The Director

Mia,

Bert has finished taking depositions from the relevant parties in the Missouri wrongful death suit. The defense is laying the foundation for a justified self-defense argument. They assert that our clients were the aggressors and that they threatened and antagonized the group in an effort to get them to disperse from their peaceful demonstration. Some claim they feared for their lives and believed the intent of our clients was to cause bodily harm. The members of the group, they uniformly assert, had no choice but to protect themselves against attacks on their rights and their persons.

We already established that law enforcement was on the scene and witness to events. Our tactic is to incriminate those officers. The police department, as a body and up their chain of command, are corroborating the story of the defendants.

Their attorneys are posing a united front and are making use of multiple recent Missouri laws in support of self-defense. Detailed notes from the filings and depositions are in the attached PDFs.

Gwen

An electronic mail arrives and a text. They must have been sent near the end of the workday back in Chicago because they're waiting for Mia when she first turns on the terminal in the office that morning and when she first powers up her phone.

> haven't heard from you. Is everything ok? how was Michigan? the trip? tell me what's going on. so many questions. love to hear from you. just a line to tell me you're okay. Your cat's fine, by the way.

Gwen and Mia have both a personal and a professional relationship. They insist on keeping them separate. It's common for a long time to pass without contact. Gwen gives Mia a lot of space. She knows the itinerary. She knows they'll be in Ann Arbor for about a week before leaving for Greece. She knows it'll take a couple of days to travel to the North, and she knows there'll be a week or more of duties and responsibilities after her arrival. She intentionally waits until the first round of depositions finishes before sending her note.

The message is not a surprise. Bert, Gwen, and Mia have discussed it at length. It is becoming a common approach in cases like these over the last ten or fifteen years. The narrative is similar. A lone person or pair goes to a political rally. Accounts vary on what the purpose of their attendance is. The advocates for the individuals say they go to keep the peace or that they merely stumble upon it. The advocates for the group claim they fear for their lives. The individuals claim they fear for their lives. Everyone fears for their lives.

In some cases, the individuals are the ones accused of killing members of the group, in other cases, the group is accused of killing the individuals. The details vary, but the pattern is the same. One thing emerging as an unassailable fact is that the outcome depends on the judge who hears the case. It doesn't matter whether the winning side is the group or the individuals, only whether the judge is aligned with their political outlook. The permutations work out this way. The facts vary, and the only constant is the judge.

When it works out for one side, their media asserts that justice has been done while the other side's media cries foul. When it works out for the other side, their media representatives sound exactly the same. What's consistent is that everyone admits the convenience of the similarity in patterns, both claim the difference is that the other side is lying to opportunistically gain advantage.

The news cycle is twenty-four hours long. There is a constant stream of stories and events, descriptions of terrifying and out of control incidents. The war is in the streets, they tell us. All day, every day, and this exacerbates the fear and the tension. It increases in those who are at the rally, and it increases in those who happen upon it accidentally or seek it out intentionally. It doesn't matter that in some cases the assailants are armed and in other cases not. It's every citizen's right to bear arms if they choose, making it irrelevant to the case. If some citizens choose to keep the peace without firearms, that is their decision, but a firearm is not required for one person to threaten another.

Mia considers whether she should follow her instincts and include media outfits in the lawsuit. She wonders whether they can establish a pattern of intentional fear mongering through false reports and overly dramatized commentary. A few have tried this argument before, but it's never been successful. She considers the strength of their claim that these are innocent travelers who accidentally happen upon the demonstration. If it's possible to paint them as agitators and vigilantes, then the role fear plays will be more difficult to establish. If she includes the media, the attacks and public scrutiny will be escalated, and the characters of the victims dragged through the muck. She must be prepared for war.

The media does a thorough job of identifying each party with its most extreme elements. This is their modus operandi for decades. The one party are Christian nationalists and election deniers, every staunch supporter of the opposition knows this. They hold that it's impossible to advocate for a party in any way shape or form without an alliance with its most extreme facets. True enough, there are facts to support this. Likewise, in reverse.

Over time, it becomes clear that there are militarized segments of each faction. No data comes with a typical media story. It's hard to tell what's at stake. Are there millions in these militarized segments or just hundreds? How sympathetic is the rest of the party? Is militarization an active interest looking for a cause or is it out of necessity? The anti-fascists claim they would rather be at home watching movies and eating cheese corn, but they have to get out and protect everyone's political rights because the militarized opposition is a threat. The Christian nationalists and election deniers say the same. Each says the other is lying, both assert that it's a false equivalency that only a fool accepts.

Either Or. Choose one. Regret it. That's the dilemma of the wage laborer, it's the dilemma of the intellectual worker, and it's the dilemma of the political combatant. Once the domain is striated with categories and orientations it becomes impossible to navigate. The clarity of purpose in the organizational order makes it simple and clear, but the offsets and angles make it opaque and impenetrable.

Mia has been away for a few weeks. It clouds her judgment. There are political extremes here too. The same interests, in fact. The same dialogue of open borders and closed. The same closed society vs global concern, religious fundamentalism vs modern cosmopolitanism, but it isn't the same. It doesn't feel the same. It might be because she's in the North and away from the big cities. It might be a skewed vision of the nation, but whatever the reason her daily experience isn't of a nation divided. Not like it is back home. This reduces her sense of urgency and necessity. While working the case, she feels like everything on Earth is at stake: the liberty of humans, the safety of every one of us. Here, it seems more distant, people still agree on simple things. Whatever your politics, you still buy your Kiwis at the farmer's market instead of the grocery store. Same with your meat. Everyone knows the reasons. If you go to someone's house, you bring sweets. If they serve you wine, they give you food. These are absolutes. Politics doesn't matter. Civilization is stronger than politics. It doesn't matter whether you're a nationalist or a communist, in either case you think Northern Macedonia is a bullshit name for a country and that absolutely under no circumstances can a legitimate news organization drop the "Northern" when referring to FYROM.

In the US, it is precisely the culture that is at war, and there are many private interests anxious to take advantage. Corporations acquire more and more power while individuals become weaker and weaker, but there is no time for that now, since we have to sort out whether abortion should be safe and legal. Issues that most countries settled long ago, issues with a cultural bent, resurface to suck up the attention while the giant surveillance systems build their infrastructure and harvest their wealth. Far flung hatred and fear give them more to see and extrapolate, more vision and data to feed their money machines.

These murders are in the interests of those corporate agents. They are huge news and an effective distraction. All eyes focus on the cases and away from policy. This is a simple matter, us against them, easy to digest. The other stories might be complicated and require elaborate investigations into laws and their impact on long term relationships between corporations and individuals. She believes the media is involved, that their take creates the problems causing events to unfold as they do. The employees at media outlets are wage laborers. They work for managers who work for equity partners and vice presidents. The media are corporate through and through, it is the only organization they know.

In the news, they often talk of individuals or billionaires. The financial constructs are often concealed and difficult to unravel. It is rare for a media service to do a thorough job in showing the extent to which this or that billionaire is not a single individual human, but a complex web of corporations. Even the single rich man is a cluster of corporations with complex arrangements and interactions aiming at circumventing taxes and hiding assets. From her perspective, it is this that should be put on trial. Media ownership often traces back to individual billionaires and this grants them a homey or mystical air. She wants to tear that down. She wants to put the media on trial for murder along with those people who did the dirty work of beating those women to death.

Simple. The corporations that commit crimes should be incarcerated. Not the employees, not even the leadership, the corporate operations themselves. Since corporations are the instigators in this case, they should be incarcerated.

It's ridiculous. No corporation would remain in a country with such draconian laws. They will relocate and the economy will crash.

It must be all or nothing. If they leave, they leave. No more market for their goods, no more customers for their products. Immigration and work laws must be written onto the corporate body. Taxes are collected even when citizens live overseas.

She grows tired of thinking and turns her attention to the personal email. Does Gwen feel the same as I do? Is it casual for her? Is distance inflating her feelings? She is the one back home, she is the one going about her daily life. Gwen misses me more than I miss her, but that doesn't mean anything. She's busy, she's travelling, and she's dealing with family matters. She isn't going to read too much into it. She'll wait until she gets back. If things go back to normal, then there's no reason to bring it up. If they don't....

She feels guilty about what's happening between her and Virginia. She isn't even sure what it is. There's an attraction, but it might be a temporary infatuation: the mood and the circumstances. They haven't communicated much since she left Ann Arbor, so she has no idea what Ginna is thinking. Gwen and Mia explicitly agree that theirs is not an exclusive relationship, but the tone of the personal message nags at her. People's assumptions and expectations can change over time, and it might happen without discussion. Their conversation was over six months ago and neither of them, as far as Mia knows, has been with anyone else. Until now. Does that change the expectations? It's time for another talk. But to what end?

Mia thinks about Ginna. She's tempted to send her a text, put it out there, and ask her for some insight. What can three, nearly four, days together possibly mean?

Eleni's remarks, Mia doesn't know what to make of them. We're conscious mammals and some qualities command attention. That's the paradigm, simple and easy to wave aside. With that other notion, it continues to resonate and intertwine with the messages.

People go through phases. Before puberty, children are roughly the same size. Then size differences become more pronounced. These are classic signs. Are some behaviors common to women at one age and do they differ from behaviors at a later age? If so, are any of them due to ancestral preferences? Does resentment increase with experience? Cynicism? As our confidence is taken by patriarchal society, does anger and disgust increase? If a twenty something cis het woman has the mindset of a forty something woman beaten up and down by patriarchy, can she still couple up with a man and have children? If she can't, is it possible that choices in sexual liaisons favor those life phases, making younger women more naïve and trusting and then shrewder and more dismissive as they get older? Nature, at least, doesn't make value judgments, doesn't claim one attitude sees reality clearly whereas the other is delusional, it just does what it does, progresses as it progresses and both attitudes are optimized appropriately for their age.

It's aggravating. She feels like she needs to read more, to look into it further. It's too ridiculous to consider, but then she knows there are different kinds of unseen motivating orders that drive behavior. The whole theory of patriarchy works that way.

She wonders how and whether it's related. Everything gets jumbled together. Gwen's changing ideas. She is still in her thirties, maybe she's going through it now. Corporations and the weird toleration we have for them. If natural selection is bound in part to the social order, it's possible that humans are hard-wired to accept relationships and associations as an unchangeable reality. If the social world is overrun with corporate structure and interests, it might be part of our biological makeup to adapt and go along with that depiction and organization of life on Earth. Even to support it and help further it. Our survival depends on our ability to integrate with a social order optimizing our power over conditions and the threat of predators. Is that how corporations threaten liberty?

This is beyond her area of expertise. She is aware of her limits, but can't help pondering the subject and asks Lena if there is a list of feminist writers who have addressed these topics. Eleni, a copious bibliographer since starting graduate school, gives Mia a copy of her running list and tells her to focus explicitly on Section L which covers Sexual Selection specifically. Mia opens the file and scrolls to the right place. There must be 40 entries under the heading. She shakes her head and regrets how little time she has. Just another reason why she has to rely on the social order to help her form opinions. She doesn't have time to read the opposing arguments and positions, she has to depend on one or two experts. She grimaces and swears when she realizes she's whittling down the list using a standard of availability and easy access. The book that's the easiest to get will be the one she relies on. The easiest to get will be the one with the proper corporate backing, the one produced by a publishing company with the best marketing strategy and editorial know-how. She feels powerless and gets angrier. She hits reply and starts typing.

> Gwen,
>
> Thank you for the update. What do you think about starting to gather information on media involvement? Can we establish direct lines between the fear and anxiety of the defendants and the media stories they are exposed to? Even if there is only enough to make the case publicly, just to get it out there, it might be worth looking into. Can we get some more time with the people already deposed to learn the details of their media consumption and how it relates to their attitudes on the day of the murders?
>
> Mia

Then she replies to the text:

> everything is fine. just very busy. i miss you.

The Assistant

> We were at the point by Keramoti on the 15th. There was litter on the beach. What is wrong with people? The Dimos needs to be diligently patrolling the area to make sure it is clean, and that people are following basic rules of decency to keep it that way.

Eirini sees complaints about garbage on the beach regularly. This one is from social. She is moderating the group and has to approve each post. She is supposed to check and make sure that the poster is either a resident of the Dimos or that the post is clearly relevant to it. Sometimes there is advertising spam posted by a bot, and she has to document that and fill out a little data sheet to track it. The big offenders will be blocked. If the post contains profanity or hostile language, she can edit it a little or discard it completely. Most of the stuff is harmless, lost and found pets, complaints about a rusty pipe somewhere, or some other service that isn't being done properly. Garbage is a popular topic because everyone wants to keep the beaches clean. They're the lifeblood of the region, it's primary allure to international tourism. She creates a work order for every actionable complaint and makes sure a Dimos representative checks it out. She'll often interact with the person making the post to learn more about the location or the nature of the complaint.

There's an office in the municipality building on the Southeast side of town near the second elementary school. The two people dedicated to public relations sit together there. Technically, Phedon is her supervisor, but he does the same job she does so there isn't much of an imbalance between them. Still, sometimes he'll do the odd managerial thing that asserts his authority. It usually makes her smile. She doesn't mind when he, or any of the other men in their part of the building, act overbearing and do her work for her, dismissing her contribution as unskilled or lacking in some insight. She doesn't mind because she doesn't invest a lot of her identity and personality in the work and she's happy to let others do it for her if they insist. It seems that men are always trying to protect her from herself and butt in whenever they think a task must be too complicated or important to let her work on it alone. Moderating public posts is one of the worst tasks, boring and frustrating and prone to lots of colorful feedback. Unlike a lot of people her age, Eirini doesn't like social. She thinks her father is right when he says it gives everyone a megaphone and lets us hear everything about everything. "Remain silent and be thought a fool," he quotes from someone long ago. "Speak and remove all doubt. This can be true for whole civilizations." Later he admits that Eleni's dad was the one who first repeated this to him.

No one tries to interfere with her when she does this part of her job unless something goes wrong, and someone calls to complain. Then they want to tell her what she should have done and how she should have prevented the complaint before it ever happened. They don't want to take over, they just want her to follow their advice. If she does and it causes an even bigger problem, as it often does, they lecture her on how it's a mistake to do what they say, and that she should be doing what they mean instead. If she's going to be effective, she has to use her brain and her initiative. Right or wrong, what they really like is explaining it to her.

She doesn't get frustrated. They don't bother her. She laughs at the contradictions and foolishness, at the self-importance and petty displays of authority by people who have none to speak of. Her lightness is because her supervisor, every man in the building for that matter, can't fire her. She isn't going to lose her job. She got it through her father and his friendship with one of the department heads. Even if she were to do something to irritate that department head, and why would she, he doesn't care about the little tasks she performs, he wouldn't fire her. That wouldn't be right. What he would do instead is call her father and have him talk to her about how important it is to do well at work. But that never happens. Working for the Dimos, in Eirini's mind, is low key and relaxed. If people want to tell her how to do her job or do it for her, she doesn't mind that. Since there aren't any repercussions or disadvantages, it only saves her time and frees her up for other things. Her life and her mind are not invested in her work. There's no downside as far as she can tell. It doesn't even impact her career that much. Promotions are time driven and have little to do with performance. If she stays around, then she'll get the pay increases due her. The municipal employees are part of the union, and the union ensures the pay scales.

She's a young woman working in an office made up of many women but where nearly every supervisor is a man. Why do they put up with such a thing in this day and age? Again, it goes back to the union. The supervisor has exactly the same job as her except he has the added responsibility of making sure their work is reported back to the department leadership. Eirini, in fact, makes more money than Phedon. Even though he is the supervisor, she's been there longer and has more reviews. The reviews are timebound and the only way for your pay to go up. She can't see the downside. She leaves earlier, has less accountability, she isn't even blamed when something goes wrong, the supervisor is.

And besides, Phedon is cute. He has pretty brown eyes and she doesn't mind when he stands over her desk and explains to her how important it is to do this or take care of that. She finds that her work takes up little of her mental energy, and since her supervisor is nice to look at and, when they aren't doing work related things, even nice to talk to, why should she mind?

Her friend Cristina, who works at the vocational high school, she gets angry when she hears these stories. How could you let them, how dare they, where do these mediocre men get off, and so on. But Eirini laughs and insists she doesn't mind. It's just a job. She prefers to go out with her friends and enjoy time with her family. She likes the beach and listening to music. If they try to ruin that, that's a problem, but work? You think he's my bossy supervisor, she responds, but I think he's my servant. He gets no benefits from controlling me, so why should I mind if he wants to do my job for me? They don't need both of us there anyway. Maybe the problem isn't that men are always trying to do things for women, she says to her friend, maybe the problem is that there's an advantage to it. There's no advantage here, so to me it seems like a luxury. I don't even think that it makes him seem so foolish and dogmatic. It's cute really. It's part of his personality. Like sometimes a puppy will demand you pet it. Whenever you stop, he makes you start again.

It does matter, Cristina insists, with these men in the supervisor positions, you end up with nothing but men in the department head roles. Then the whole municipality is run by these foolish do nothings. Everyone's life is worse for that. They're incompetent and we have to pay for it. You think if I tell on Phedon that won't happen? I will do it if it helps, but I can't get upset about something that doesn't upset me and I don't think I need to be upset in order to help. What can I do? How can I change Greek society, how can I change how Dimos Nestou is run from my little office on the second floor? Cristina is animated in response. She says many important and insightful things, but none of them provide any direction for what Eirini can actually do to change things. Ultimately, Eirini says, women leadership in the office has to come through the union. Only the union can fix the situation. The union is run by men too. Maybe the best thing would be to try and get a leadership role there, but then we're right back where we started. How about a women's committee within the union? Cristina asks. Maybe you can meet separately and plan some action to try and get the union to listen to your input. That way they can make sure that women have more leadership roles. Eirini is happy to do that, she promises to talk to the other women around the building, but she doesn't understand the logic. It seems like the opposite of the way feminism wants things to go. If her actions are successful, women will do more work for less pay and that's the exact opposite of what we want.

She goes on a date with Phedon. He says it's obligatory. Not because she works for him or anything like that. He means that since they're both young and single, they have to try. She tries to explain that she doesn't like the idea, because it's such a small office and could make things uncomfortable. He says that the same is true in reverse too, so they have to do it just to see. She reluctantly agrees. If anything, these are the kinds of things she wants to avoid. This is the problem as far as she's concerned. The work-related overbearing tactics don't bother her. These personal affronts, they're the worst. There are plenty of rules against them. No one claims he has a right, but if she complains it'd be uncomfortable. The union or the department hierarchy, none of them really want to deal with it. She thinks she has to go out with him. If she really wants to get out of it, the only way is to tell her father and then her father will tell his friend and that'll put an end to it. People do that often. The way to protect yourself from men is to get another man to do it. She doesn't like that, it upsets her and inspires her to dig deeper into things she can do to change the situation.

Before she moves to Chrysoupoli to stay with Europea and then look after Ermioni's house, her father drives her to work every day. Now that she lives in town, she can ride her bike. Sometimes, when the weather is bad, she prefers not to and gets a ride from Demetrios who works in the elementary school. He is the one who tells her that she should just go out with Phedon and make sure it doesn't go well. He knows Phedon and knows a little bit about what he likes. He tells her to talk a mile a minute, just tell him whatever is in your head, tell him about what your mom said about this or that, or how your dad likes to watch some TV shows or whatever. Just talk and talk and talk. Don't let him say anything. That's what

Demetrios says to do. It's perfect. The advice works well, Phedon is horrified by her constant chatter, he loses interest in her after that and now she doesn't have to worry about anything unpleasant down the road. He tests out his little theory and discovers that he isn't interested so now the issue is settled, and they can get back to work without any distractions. It never occurs to him to question why she isn't like that at work. A simpleton, really. Social skills are key to evolutionary success. Confirmed.

Yes, of course, it's terrible that these things happen, but people have to do things they don't want to do. Life is filled with injustices. That's what she thinks. She knows it. Being forced to eat a meal with Phedon isn't as bad as other things. Sickness and disease, hunger and violence, these are much worse, aren't they? Cristina lectures her when she speaks like that. Attitudes like that are what causes the trouble for women. You have to take charge, we have to stand up for ourselves.

Eirini loves Cristina, and she appreciates the friendly help that Demetrios provides. She worries that she may be right and that there is something wrong with her for not being more upset about it. This feeling is becoming worse now that she is spending more time with Mia and Eleni. Mia is always in charge. She works for herself, runs her own business or whatever it is, she isn't going to put up with any nonsense like that from the men. Eirini remembers how she looks at Carl and Fred and how intimidated they are by her. She likes that, but she also thinks it's hard on Mia to be that way. She adores her, but she isn't cuddly or friendly. She's stern and tough and always has something important to say. She doesn't like it when the music is too loud, and she doesn't have fun in the little taverna in Thessaloniki even when there are lots of men to talk to. She goes along, she's a good sport, but Eirini can tell, it isn't her thing. Eirini respects her and wants to be respected too. Even if she is different, even if she isn't so steep and tough in standing up for herself, she should still be respected. Eleni is somewhere in between, but in a way that is more attractive to Mia and Cristina.

Eirini wants to work out exactly what it is.

Being younger, that's definitely something. They've been talking about that, although she isn't sure she understands everything. It's something about how evolution or something makes younger women more open to things than older women are. She can't follow it because she doesn't know the technical terms, but what she sees is that Mia isn't winning the argument, and Mia wins every argument. So, Eleni must've been saying something very important and true. Eirini daydreams about it the whole next day. Something Eleni says makes her think being young and being attractive are somehow connected. What we're attracted to, in fact, is youth. Not for its own sake, but because it's related to having babies. This is deep inside our brains, and we don't even know we're doing it. There's no reason, she imagines while sitting at her desk, that older women with lines and wrinkles around their eyes and mouths aren't considered the most beautiful. If beauty can change from century to century or country to country, why can't there be some time or place where older ladies are the most beautiful people adored by everyone and celebrated for it? No reason, except she's never heard of it happening anywhere. Even if older women are considered attractive these days, it's because they look like they're younger, they look like they're still able to have children. The way they dress and the way they act, their demeanor imitates the personalities of younger women. Never have we seen the true case, have we? That could be what Lena's saying.

She thinks about Fred and Carl. They make her smile. They talk like they're so important, they think whatever they're saying is so interesting. If she took them seriously, she probably wouldn't like them very much. She doesn't like people who take themselves too seriously. They have soft parts too. It's easy to make them flub up because whatever ideas they have, they're lacking confidence. It's easy to lead them around. She gets them to do whatever she wants. She remembers that week in Ann Arbor. She's never mean, but she can tell that deep down she's the boss of them. They don't know how to control situations, they don't have any sense of what other people are feeling, and that makes them powerless to react to things. They just do what they're told, no argument necessary. Even with their serious words, they can't argue their way past her. She knows she won't be this way forever, and senses it's connected to who she is right now, but she doesn't think it's only physical charm. It's social skills too. They have that school and those big words, but I understand how people are. Social and emotional things are way more powerful than school. I don't mind if they think differently, it makes it easier. Not to be cruel, but to make a nice time for everyone. So much more pleasant than that talk about serious subjects. It's fun with them in Ann Arbor, but that won't happen if she isn't pulling the strings.

She won't tell people this because she knows she'd be criticized, but in her family home she's used to it. Her mother is in charge. There's never any doubt about that. Her father can speak more seriously about various subjects, he's very knowledgeable, but he isn't in charge. He doesn't decide things for the family. Mom takes care of that. What's funny is that she complains about it. It's unfair that she has so much more family responsibility while her father goes off and plays with his friends. That seems exactly like the situation at work. Phedon has the responsibility and can't go off and play with the others. Why do women get upset about it in reverse like that? Does it make them hypocrites, or balanced? She can't settle it, her experience doesn't match with what people say. She's confused and feels like she should have a stronger opinion, but she can't sort it out and can't force herself to feel differently than she does.

Her godmother understands and maybe that's why Lena is the way she is. Both of them have so much concentration. They do different things, they're different people, but they're the same. They're never so much alike as when they're busy. It's like the world doesn't exist. They don't care about what others say or about being judged. They're close to what they're doing, and that's what matters. Expressing themselves, doing what they're doing with their complete person, that's the important thing. They don't care about supervisors or pay or who's stealing from them or telling them what to do, they're just there in the moment putting everything they have into what's in front of them. They focus on different things, but they both have that same steady gaze. They're never distracted.

That's what she wants too. Spending so much time with the two of them these last few weeks convinces her of that. They're her role models and that's what she aspires to. She can't feel the power of Cristina's outrage, she can't identify with Mia's self-control and confidence, but she's enchanted by Eleni and Ermioni. The way Eleni moves around the office, the way she listens to who's talking, or how she focuses when she works. Ermioni in the kitchen or hammering at something in the yard.

There must be room for someone like me, she thinks. I don't want everyone to be like me. That's not what I'm saying. Mia should be Mia and Cristina should be Cristina, but I want to be myself too, and you know something? I agree with this person, the one who is posting. Why are people throwing their garbage on the beach? The water is so perfect and the sand so lovely, what type of person drops their wrapper on the ground there? There are trash bins up and down the shore, why aren't they using them? This is so much more important. She wonders if there is some footage in the cameras at the beach that capture how the garbage gets there. She doesn't want to get people into trouble but thinks that if she takes a look maybe she'll see some flaw in the system. She can get behind this. Yes, she's definitely going to look into it. Maybe we need better trash cans that don't let things blow out of them. Maybe we have to increase the collection frequency? She'll get to the bottom of it. Anger doesn't drive her, she isn't even angry at the people who litter. She cares about the beach, and she wants to focus on something that will do good. For everybody.

The Coordinator

Greetings Mrs. Michaels,

Thank you for coming in and clearing up the state of the Pet Project accounts. As we discussed, the payments awaiting

deposit on the account have now been unblocked.
Additionally, we will remit payment on the checks that were
recently submitted. Everything should be good with the
account, but please let us know if there are any problems.
We are happy to address them as soon as possible.

Sincerely,
Nikos Stavropoulos, Bank Manager

Monday morning, Ermioni, Mia, and Eleni go to the bank and clear up
the accounts. When the bank hears about the account holder's death, they
stop any activity on the account and wait for further instructions. They do
not, however, send notice. Constantinos learns of it when the landlord
complains he hasn't received August's rent. Ermioni shows the documents
from the lawyer and, although the banker is careful to point out that these
American documents are not official, he proceeds. He knows her, his
brother went to school with her. He recommends she work with an estate
lawyer in town or in Kavala to get the correct documentation. They thank
him and then walk down to the little office tucked away in a small alley
across from Attalos.

The office does not seem well cared for. Constantinos is there, but says
he has to leave to tend to his own practice. He has to make a visit up to the
nunnery just past Zarkadia. They have something going around with the
birds and he wants to check it out. He introduces them to another
veterinarian who comes out from the back room where he's performing a
minor procedure. His name is Prodromos and he looks to be around thirty
five. His mother Toula lives next to the farm northwest of town where
Thimios grew up. He explains how the office is run and apologizes for the
mess. There are four veterinarians from around the Dimos who work
there. None of them are full-time or in charge of anything. There's a young
woman who takes care of the bookkeeping and who's supposed to keep an
eye on things, order supplies, manage the schedules, and appointments.
Prodromos explains that she isn't very enthusiastic about her job and
doesn't keep on top of it. That's why we're out of so many things and a
little behind in some payments.

Ermioni doesn't mind any of that. The login and password for the
computer are written on a sticky note attached directly to the screen on the
little desk in the front room. The back room has an examination table and
a wall with different size cages. There's a cat sleeping in one of them. It has
a tag on a collar and there's a chart in a metal sleeve hanging from the side
of the cage. She looks at the paperwork and sees the background
information: the procedure to perform, required vaccinations, and where
the cat stays. Prodromos explains that the records are computerized but

that they print off a copy of the work order for security purposes. If there is only one animal in the office, it isn't so bad, but if there are several it's sometimes hard to keep everything straight. The paper copies cut down on mistakes. He shows her the software program they use to manage the work and the animals. The office may be disorderly, but the computer system isn't. There is a mapping program with many dots on it, it connects the animals they've served with the place where they can find them. There's information about what's already been done for the cat or dog and there's information about what needs to be done and the schedule for doing it.

He shows her the financial software they use and how they log the expenses. He says Dmitra is supposed to take care of this but doesn't always do it and the veterinarians sometimes make orders themselves, log the payments, and even send them off. Although the records are a little chaotic, the system is orderly and, assuming she clears up the problems at the bank, they should be up to date on most payments. There's supposed to be an inventory of supplies in the financial software, but they let that go some time ago and now don't have good records. If she's going to set things in order, he suggests she look into that. Ermioni takes note of the names of the different software packages and will look for online tutorials and documentation for everything.

The front office has drawers and cabinets with office supplies. The back room has drawers and cabinets with veterinary supplies. Sometimes the vets are paid a small amount for the work they do, and the checks come at the end of each month. They're not supposed to take any of the supplies for their own practices, but sometimes they do and then settle later, either by replacing them or paying directly. The records aren't too good for that. Mostly it's based on the honor system and Prodromos says the four vets are pretty good about following protocol.

Round up is a regular event and he describes how they go and look for cats and dogs who aren't in the system yet. They can be identified because they don't have Project tags and collars, but it has to be done manually. Sometimes, citizens make a report, but mostly they rely on their deal with the municipality. There is an official department and vehicles with animal control workers for rounds. Prodromos thinks Em got them to invest in the service. It's before my time, but that's what everyone says. There aren't usually any problems with the Dimos and the vets have a rotation. The schedule is managed in the computer. He shows her a sticky note with the name and phone number of the man from the municipality.

During a lull in the discussion, Ermioni explains that she successfully coaxed a stray cat onto her porch and now it sleeps there sometimes. She asks Prodromos how to get it into the system. He doesn't have a collar and isn't going to the feeder station near the roundabout. He walks her through the forms they have to fill out to print a tag. He shows her how a cataloging number is generated and where that number is cross-referenced between the tag and the computer record. The tags have microchips that send telemetry data to the cloud service for tracking locations. He opens a new feeding location record and they put Ermioni's address into it. If they can get the cat into the office to neuter it, they'll enter that event and procedure into the records. They'll do the standard tests for any new cat and the results of those tests, together with the date, go into the system. If the test is one that needs to be repeated, the scheduler will automatically trigger, and he shows her where to go to check the schedule for a particular cat. He also shows her how to see the list of work orders for the current, future, or past day. Each of the vets usually have one day a week where they come in and handle whatever work is in the queue. Today is his day and he's already taken care of one item: the cat sleeping back there now. She gushes about how exciting and orderly it is.

After clicking around to see the newly created items, Ermioni asks if they can go and get the cat. Since it's just one, Prodromos is willing, but he explains that someone should wait in the office because sometimes people walk in with their pets. Spaying and neutering are free, and since the vets work through the Project, they direct people here for those services. It saves them money and encourages people to do it. Mia and Eleni take seats in the front and say they'll wait and keep an eye out.

Since the women walk to the office, Prodromos drives Ermioni back to her house in his car just outside the alley. He brings the stick and a carrier with him. They find the cat curled up in the little half milk crate Ermioni put out for him. Prodromos tells her to stay in the car while he swiftly approaches and uses the stick to gently trap the cat in the box where it's sleeping. He has gloves on and lifts the surprised feline into the carrier. The cat tries to wriggle and squirm away, but Prodromos deftly slides it into place without much aggravation on either side. He brings the carrier back to the car and puts it in the back. They drive to the Project office and bring it inside. He takes a photograph and sends it from his phone to the computer record. He shows Ermioni how he does it by putting the identifier in the subject of an email and attaching the photo. He shows her the email address you have to use to make it work right.

Prodromos asks Ermioni to assist him in taking the cat out of the carrier and maneuvering him onto the examination table. Ermioni's presence calms the cat a little, but he's still pretty nervous. Prodromos says in these cases, they usually have to anesthetize the cat to do the tests. He has trouble keeping him still with the stick, so he shows Ermioni how to hold him in place while he attaches the mask. Ermioni is so careful and gentle with the animal, talking to him the whole time, he calms down a little more, although still distrustful. Shortly after turning on the gas, the cat closes his eyes, making it easy for the vet to draw blood, do a full body examination, and prepare him for the short procedure to neuter him.

Afterwards, they leave the cat sleeping in a cage next to the other one. He enters information into the computer describing what he's done and then prepares blood samples, generates and attaches labels, and deposits them into the receptacle at the front of the office. They'll come later to get it, he says. We'll enter the results when they come back. He shows her how the testing entries have a generated code and how that code is on the label they've made. When the report comes back, that code will be on the results, and they can use it to enter the information into the correct place on the chart. Results, like whether it has FIV, will often require follow up care and the tasks for that will be auto generated. Ermioni continues to take copious notes on her tablet while Eleni records everything on her phone. Ermioni appreciates Eleni's diligence but wants to take notes too since both together will help her reconstruct the instructions when she has to do it herself or explain it to someone else.

Prodromos tells them that the system will automatically generate a work order to return the cat to the feeder location tomorrow. She can see the system in action by letting it run its course. This little guy will be dropped off back at your place tomorrow. Can't guarantee he'll stay after his little ordeal, but if he's hungry enough he might. I think Constantinos is on duty or maybe Alecos. There are also tickets in the system to make sure the cat is taken care of for the rest of today. He shows her where the work tickets are for feeding it and letting it use the litter box. The feral or semi-feral ones don't know how to use litter boxes, but we have a little planter back there that they can use. It's usually okay. I'll come back later to take care of those items. I don't usually stay around the office if there's nothing happening. Dmitra is supposed to be here to notify whoever is on duty if someone comes. She is usually there in the afternoon but is unreliable lately. Eleni wonders aloud whether they need to have a chat with her about her responsibilities, but Ermioni says she'll take care of it once she understands the details. She doesn't want to jump to any conclusions.

Ermioni stays at the office and tells Eleni and Mia not to worry. They can go off and do whatever they want for the rest of the day, but she's going to stay and keep looking at things to see if she can learn where everything is. She's very excited and focused. They have to physically pry her away from what she's reading on the computer screen to get her to kiss them goodbye when they leave.

When she comes home, Ariti and Despina are with her and she's bursting with newly acquired information. She describes everything she saw and did that day, talks about the state of the office in detail, and how she's taking inventory of everything she can find. She's looking at the computer software to see how to update the digital inventory. She's extremely excited, and says she can't wait to go back the next day and make progress. She's glad there are only cats in the office today, but she thinks she's going to have to bear down and get used to being around dogs too. Poor things, they need the Project too, she says. I'll have to get over it and just get used to them. Cats scratch just as much as dogs bite, but for some reason she isn't scared of getting scratched. It can hurt a lot more, Eirini says later that night when Ermioni is repeating the stories to her. It's the third time that day. Mia is a particularly good audience because, even though she's there for some of it, it's mostly in Greek and she doesn't know the details.

While sitting and eating fruit later that evening, she tells them about the office assistant Dmitra and how she isn't even embarrassed when she comes late and discovers someone carefully going over the books. She isn't self-conscious in the least. It doesn't occur to her that maybe she hasn't done her job well. She provides whatever information she can and lets it be known that she's doing her best. She's only supposed to be in the office part time. Ermioni doesn't push it and won't. She's about Alexandros' age and her father works for the Dimos in the school administration. She makes sure Dmitra's information is correct in the computer system and makes a note to talk to her father if she discovers she isn't spending enough time at the office.

None of this annoys her. Not while doing it and not while describing it. She's deliriously excited. She goes over the details in her mind, works out where you have to go to find the work queue and where you have to go to see the schedule. She thinks about the different drawers and cabinets and whether everything is stored in the optimal place. She wants to watch the vets work to see if they spend time looking for things or if they know immediately where everything is. That night, while the evening movie plays on ERT, she has her tablet on her lap and writes and clicks, finding as much information as she can about how to do this and how to do that. She stays up long into the night and, with little sleep, is up and out of bed in plenty of time to do her chores before going into the office again.

It's so strange, she thinks. She remembers back to the time when it's being set up. She knows it's there, that it exists, but she never pays any attention, never shows any interest. Now that there's no one else, now that it needs her to come in and clean things up, she can't think or talk about anything else. Hers, she thinks. It's hers, and she'll learn everything there is to learn about it and make it so good and orderly that it'll purr just as happily as the cats do when they're returned to their streets and corners feeling better even if they don't know why. Poor things.

The Author

Dear Ben Thorne,

I understand that you are in a hurry to move past recent
events and get on with your work, but I need to catch up with
things to assure myself that I am following the best possible
course of action. Please be patient while I sort through the
relevant notes and decide on next steps.

Best,
Lena

She accuses him of being cold, of acting without feeling. His approach
is no different than it's always been, but how can she know that? Do the
notes paint a picture? He is always so driven to get things settled, always so
focused on the matter at hand. Why is she so difficult? Whatever is in those
notes, Em never says anything about any problem or reason to slow down
and rethink things. The plan for *Washington and Ashley* is over a year old,
it's not a surprise. He's always in control of the creative direction. He's the
true artist. Em's contribution is just editing. He makes suggestions about
what to cut and what to elaborate, but doesn't make major contributions to
style or voice, he isn't solving anything even if he is good at pointing out
problems. Em's constantly anguishing over architectonic or structure or
whatever he calls it. Write something that does this and put it there. Blah
blah blah. People don't care about that. His part is always esoteric. In the
Nobel announcement, it doesn't say a damn thing about architectonic and
structure. The power of the voice and the likeability of the characters, that's
him, his doing. Em has nothing to do with it. Why is she trying to slow us
down? What's her angle?

Things are already out of hand. Maybe she's telling more people. It isn't
enough to tell Ginna, who still seems to bear a grudge, she needs to tell her
sister and her friend too. Who else knows? It's only a matter of time before
it gets out. We'll need a public statement to spin it. We need to be ready.
We won't lie, but we'll make sure everyone knows the truth, that the
partnership is like the classic relationship between a writer and an editor.
He'll be gracious, he'll acknowledge the importance of the contribution,
but he isn't going to let some kid ruin everything we've built, he isn't going
to let her destroy what we've made. What we agreed to make. If she thinks
she can come in and make some huge changes to how things work after so
many years, she's going to have some hard lessons to learn. She should just
go along with it. The system is working fine, it's a well-oiled machine.
We've produced great work and received accolades for it, how can this
child think she can come in and improve upon it? It's madness.

Virginia is still sulking. She isn't coming in and says she needs time off.
There's a big sit down and she asks many questions. Mostly she's interested

in talking about Jerry. What's his role in this, what has he done? She's rethinking her own contributions and wondering how much she's been taken advantage of. G.B. fucking Porter and his nanobots. Is there a deal? Do you promise him something in return for his devotion? Here, let me take advantage of your work, let me use you to make our work better and more impactful, and in return we'll launch your career, hook you up with the right people to help you get started. If that were the case, why not make the same offer to her? Why aren't we already preparing her for that? Do we think her contributions are worth less? Do we have reservations after everything we've read and the work we've seen?

He takes entire passages from her notes and inserts them into chapters. It comes back to her, the way he's so opportunistic about feedback, how he's willing to beg, buy, borrow, or steal anything from anywhere just to make a scene work.

She pushes him to reveal the contradiction. He's the figurehead of a corporate body. In retrospect, while piecing together everything over the years, she recognizes the patterns of greed and opportunism. The way he spins Em's feedback to justify accepting one facet and rejecting another. The way he doesn't let anyone see the attachments to emails. He's secretive and selfish. She sees it now. Not just in the way he manages her contributions, but in the work. He dismisses the interns. Always talks about how useless they are and how little they do, and yet, they're always there. He renews their positions because they're paying off. There is no other explanation. Why does he suffer their presence if it isn't to his advantage?

He is quick with flattery when there's something he wants, and right now there is something he wants. He doesn't think he can do it without her and needs the regimen back in place. He doesn't want any changes to his process, nothing should interrupt him. He talks and talks about how much he misses his friend, but what he means is that he misses the input, he misses the feedback, and, most importantly, he misses those notes. He needs them to finish what he's doing. She sees the drafts of the chapters and she knows there's a problem with the story. It's a random list of sketches with no order and no meaning. She recalls the development of *Artists of Despair*. It's the only work she sees from start to finish. *Choreography* is mostly plotted when she starts working for him, but *Artists of Despair*, she sees the whole thing, and is struck by the fact that it progresses in this same way. Sketches, lots of sketches coming out of "Ben Thorne." He develops this character or that one, develops the relationship between them. There are descriptions, background, and conversations to flesh it out. Great material, she doesn't want to take anything away from him, but it's just material. Nothing more. No fabric, no story.

The emails come from Em. There's some description, some explanation for how something or other ties together. She sees that. He forwards the message for the files. No attachments. Now she wonders about the details. What if those messages accompany text that actually does what Em's describing? Em provides a story line and how the characters come to be in their current condition or how they move past it. The relationship is established but what does the conversation mean? Where's the drama? Why are they talking to each other and what are they after? Then an email comes along and bam a few days later the story evolves. She distinctly recalls the occasions when the structure for these sketches and portraits comes from nowhere with no effort and then a bunch of writing turns into a chapter or a smaller piece of a longer story: instant coherence.

She confronts him and he dismisses it. Even when the details come out, he won't admit it. He won't offer her any explanation until she describes specific things. She takes notes and writes up outlines to prepare for the discussions, then she asks him point blank, how do you get from this conversation and this sketch of an event to the story developing in chapter seven? He fumbles for an answer. It's as if his first instinct is to go into some automated Ben Thorne mode he uses when talking to a critic. She has to aggressively push him to get him to tell her the truth. He does, but only after she corners him with a detailed map. He isn't the authority of these devices and mechanics, he isn't the mastermind. She wants to get him to admit that Em provides the structure behind everything and even if Wolfe's contribution is crucial, the voice of Ben Thorne is undeniable, the overall project, the significance of the work, is a group effort. She sees the past interns in the finished products, she sees herself, and she sees Em. Is he guilty of believing his own hype? How has he convinced himself that this is his and that he's the genius behind it, that everyone else is just a puppet contributor moving to the tune he conducts? He doesn't have answers to these questions, or he isn't willing to share them.

She goes back and looks at everything with new eyes. She watches interviews she's seen a dozen times, she reads acceptance speeches, and commentary. She looks at material she knows backward and forward. He's flash and style. He's the charisma of the persona, there can be no doubt. In the interviews and the speeches, he plays the part to perfection. The author, the great writer who can touch the hearts and souls of readers through a diverse cast of characters, it's just a part that he plays, dialogue he writes, sketches he lives out as though he were a character in one of his own novels. Not even his own.

She thumbs through *Artists of Despair* to validate her findings, and it corroborates everything better than she imagines. The book is about a person who's become a phony and the worldwide organization that not only helps but insists on it. The corporation ruins him, turns him into something he is not. She rereads whole passages. Once she knows that Ben Thorne is a facade, she sees that *Artists* is reflexive analysis. She's never read it like this before, but it falls into place. She asks him about it, is *Artists* an introspective inquiry into the corruptness of their own authorial position? Corporate publishers and corporate distributors, does he see it that way? He has no idea what she's talking about. It's a theme they visit many times, he doesn't see anything revolutionary or strange in it. Corporations run our lives, everyone knows that, and it plays a role in other books too. Yes, she points out, but it's not usually like this. The book is filled with smooth spaces *and* rough ones. Sometimes, the machine is purring along and sometimes it's sputtering and operating in fits and starts. There's tension here that we haven't seen before. The individual resists by focusing attention. The story provides details on the resistance and phoniness of the corporate overseer. That resistance also describes their place in world literature.

She can't make Ben Thorne see it. She can't explain it to him. Perhaps he's willfully rejecting anything that doesn't fit with his worldview, perhaps he's trying to restate his authority and the seat of its meaning, even as she spells it out clearly. Is it possible, she asks, that in his structure or whatever you call it, he's visualizing a tale and a meaning that he doesn't share with you? Is it possible that there are themes you two haven't agreed on and you're unable to see? Maybe you're too focused on something else, maybe there's an alternative explanation that fits with your intentions, but maybe he's doing that to fool you. Is it possible? He resists with all his might and throws a tantrum when she proposes it: storming up and down the office, yelling. She isn't frightened, she's gotten to know him well enough to know where it leads, but she's convinced she's put her finger on it.

You cannot achieve what Ben Thorne has achieved if every component contributor isn't excellent at their task. Wolfe is a master of voice and tone. He knows how to draw the reader into the scene, he knows how to make them care, but he doesn't understand the story. She wonders if his first book is representative of what he can produce on his own. *Fragmented* is not the same as the work that follows. It's filled with atmosphere and voice with only the tiniest whisp of a structure, but that structure is crucial. Long ago, he admits that the publisher demands this, and he can't provide it alone. That's when the work with Em begins. He sends the materials back to Ann Arbor and Em modifies the manuscript to include this string woven between the fragments to make something of a story out of it. Little morsels here and there to tie it together. He admits to the origin story: it's the beginning of Ben Thorne. That contribution, which must be more significant than he admits, is essential for getting that book published and recognized. Everything since is saturated by it.

She thinks about her contributions. How much she devotes, both energy and time, to coming up with opinions on disagreements he presents while working out sections or passages. She understands what's going on.

There's a disagreement and they're unable to resolve it. They open the floor for feedback. What does she think, which is better? So much nitty gritty detail for working out collaboration. She's their mediator without realizing it. She wants to know if it ever occurs to either of them to include her in the secret. Do they recognize her significance? If they do, do they discuss it? Do they consider acknowledging it? Are they greedy or just stupid? Unable to see her value or unwilling to compensate her for it?

The irony of the entire entanglement is that Wolfe alone can't calm her or smooth over the crisis. She wonders what Em would say if he were part of the conversation they're having while Lena deliberates. If she catches them earlier and if she raises these questions, what does he say? Does he have a leveler head? Is he more likely to offer an equitable solution? He lives with the bazaar relationship for so many years, maybe he's just as locked into it. It isn't that this one or that one feels this way or that way. Ben Thorne feels this way and each of them follows suit, each of them dutifully takes their place and recites their lines according to their roles. She sees it. These two men fixate on their game, on their secret, they abuse her and never rectify the situation. She has to push and threaten to get anything out of him. That's why she focuses so much on Jerry. Does he know? Is that what happened? What launched his career? His contract is with the same literary agent representing Ben Thorne, that isn't an accident. They set him up with everything he needs to go it alone.

There are no answers for her. None of her questions meet with any sincerity, just deflection and rationalization. She grows angrier the more they discuss it. The angrier she becomes, the more "Ben" changes his tune to appease her. He makes promises, he tells her he'll help her get her own deal if that's what she wants. His stonewalling and his greed make her angry, but his condescension makes it worse. He's trying to calm her once he sees he can't bully her. He wants her to help convince Lena to hand over the notes. He's singularly focused on that. In the end, she mocks a change of heart. Not because she forgives him, but because she thinks he's offering her the right course of action. She should get into the dispute, and she should write to Lena. She shouldn't do it as Wolfe's advocate, but to understand the truth. Lena's access is exclusive, no real corporation would allow that. She laughs and starts to weave a story that Wolfe is a self-important gasbag, and Em has him wrapped around his finger, feeding him clandestine meaning and structure giving the work its power without the voice and tone having any idea what lies beneath it. She wants to get to the heart of it and that passes through Lena. Wolfe is a stooge.

So yes, she agrees to take up her duties again, at least to get this latest project through the grinder. She never says the name of the project. She hasn't seen it in writing, but during his tirades he lets on that Lena has something else in mind. Ginna wants to find out, she wants to learn the lay of the land, but he hears what he wants to hear and welcomes her back into the fold. It is as if now he'll have the advantage, and Lena cannot resist the two of them working for the sake of *Washington and Ashley.*

Residual

Light: The working day is twenty-four hours long.

Justice: And capital is a vampire.

Peace: What is this? Is it pre-rehearsed?

Light: It's Uncle Karl. The working day is a battle between labor and owners. Capital wants your attention every hour of every day. It wants to suck your blood and is aggravated by every minute you take from it. When you sleep, when you eat, and when you go to the bathroom, you rob capital... ...unless you take your phone with you.

Peace: That may have been true back in the nineteenth century, but not now. People don't work so much anymore.

Justice: If that's true, then it's only because there has been an effort to make things that way. We fought for the rights of working people and that shortened the working day.

Light: Not if you spend your leisure time consuming its products. We shop for clothing, we entertain ourselves, we enjoy time with our families, purchasing things, making meals together. It ties back to the productive economy. Even if we aren't working at our jobs twenty-four hours a day, we're still in the vampire's grip. Where is the art, where is the ritual?

Peace: What do we do that isn't buying and selling?

Justice: Everything is sealed with the mark of the beast.

Peace: There are purchases involved in everything. If production is the only thing that counts as working, then maybe the workday has shrunk to a fraction, but if there is more to it...

Light: Production and consumption are cogs in distribution and circulation. It's a holistic system where everything fits together, a circulating economy. The vampire doesn't just oversee production, means and ends, it is everywhere, inserting itself into everything. It is in bed with us on the pressed foam mattress, it watches video over pay-per-view, and listens to music on streaming services. It drinks wine and breaks bread with families and friends.

Justice: It's true no matter what type of labor you perform, whether you are a volunteer or a wage laborer, an independent contractor or a city employee. Whatever your background and skills, if the vampire rules the land where you live, then your actions belong to Nosferatu. Your blood is his blood. Your life is his life.

Peace: Not just labor. You said he is in bed with us.

Justice: Wherever there is deliberation and discrimination, whenever we choose and wherever we want, there it is. The preferences of the one realize the existence of the many. The many speak through one's desires.

Peace: You mean attraction?

Light: If something is attractive to the young, but not the old, that guides the species. They are the deliberators, they select, they condemn their older selves to the consequences of their decisions.

Justice: They are the deliberators, the selectors, they are of the utmost importance to the social order. It exploits their choice and grants it so that it can consume them.

Peace: How does this fit together? I cannot follow it.

Light: Even a tabula rasa is extended in space. It has a color.

Peace: What do you mean?

Light: Only that the specimen *is* something. It has qualities, it is a real thing. What it is makes it something to be taken ahold of, to be used and abused. If it presents itself for choice, that can be exploited. If it makes choices, that can be exploited too. Attributes are features.

Justice: The vampire sucks the blood of the laborer, that means the laborer is a warm-blooded creature. It has a circulatory system, it makes blood, and it flows through its veins.

Peace: The vampire consumes everything. Actions and decisions are for its sake. The blood producers completely orient themselves to that end. We are driven by these goals in whatever we think and whatever we want, and we have a constitution that makes it possible.

Light: Imagine that the system of work disciplines and shapes us, turns us into the kinds of machines it requires to achieve its ends. It still has to make an intelligent selection, it chooses us because of our capability to serve it.

Peace: What are those capabilities?

Justice: We are social animals.

Light: We are the social animal extraordinaire. Any animal so disposed toward others, so open, is malleable to influence: parents and teachers, authority figures in every walk of life, friends and colleagues. As children we learn what to desire from our peers. We become like everyone else: we form populations. We don't start out that way, we have differences, but then we develop in common pursuits, we pool our talents, we fit every capability into a useful trait. If we change our emphasis from one stage of life to another, it is because we fill different roles. There is no wisdom or progress, just changes to purpose.

Justice: We are transformed from specimens into individuals and realize the category, participate in its form, actualize an aggregate understanding of raw ability in terms ordered by a social organism. This depends on underlying capabilities. Those we have in youth are suited to youthful pursuits, those we have in maturity are suited to mature pursuits.

We are at its beck and call.

Peace: You make it sound like an evil being stalks us.

Light: Evil or good, it doesn't matter. What matters is that the species persist and that the genes continue to replicate. Social organization is crucial, and it contrives direction and guides success. It is the measure of good and evil.

Justice: People resist, there are uprisings, it is possible for the specimen to restore itself.

Light: These are momentary events. There are occasions when the specimen overcomes the organization's drive for authority, but they are short lived. The order recuperates the change and adapts. It plugs into those facets and morphs into something else. We occasionally posit a temporary good or project it as a possibility, but it is quickly appropriated. We lose touch and the delivery mechanism takes control.

Peace: Why? Why does this happen?

Justice: We are predisposed to it, I fear. We survive through our bonds and the order of those bonds is attractive and persuasive. We're selected to defer to the order. Many of us do it with gusto and enthusiasm. It is the key to our survival.

Light: Born to labor, to accept the conditions of it, and to accept vampirism where we toil. Selected to love as we love, to change as we change, to feel one way at one stage and another way later on.

Peace: Wait just a minute. How do we know this? Shouldn't it be hidden and impossible to identify? Shouldn't the conditions be hidden to guarantee their effects?

Light: Humans are clever monkeys, and ideas can be like sport to them. There is no harm in letting these facets of human existence appear as ideas. No harm. So long as the basis remains, the social order, its distribution and meaning are set over and against it. There is no risk that an idea will destroy its preconditions.

Peace: What about the Russian or Chinese revolutions? Surely these must have been transformative events.

Light: Not in the least. In fact, the social order reigns supreme. That's what matters in the end. Computation is for the sake of it. Whether we are isolationist and oriented toward a virtue ethics that focuses on individual action or are consequentialists who think in terms of the collective welfare, it is an order made real. The form of realizing an order is the order that guides and governs.

Justice: Individual ideas, personal enthusiasm for a form of life or social order, are always for the sake of species-being whether those ideas promote liberal democracy or totalitarian neo-liberalism, whether they promote state capitalism or bona-fide community-based communism.

Light: In every case, there is deference to the idea and the individual succumbs to the sucking motion of the social order. The potential of the one is absorbed by the many. The anomaly of the individual is negated in a dialectic of ideas that promotes the status quo. That is the story of our lives: 100,000 years-ago and this year. It is the structure and the architectonic of every exchange, every discussion, and every description.

Peace: What does it mean in practice?

Light: It means that we have to be suspicious of everything. Wherever our cynicism rules, wherever our enthusiasm rules, we must be suspicious. There is an order at work, ulterior motives, a vision of good and evil that does not align with our simple hearts.

Justice: Take for example, the working person who thinks they have no say, they think they don't matter, and they think their ideas are better than the ones they hear. Do they think this isolates them from the world of their peers? Do they think it sets them apart? No, this is the workplace at work in them, this is the order considering every angle, this is the organization understanding itself. It surfaces in their discontent, and it dissociates itself from other forces.

Light: That is how it does its work. When a lone speaker steps up and offers a better way, when a messiah steps up with salvation, it is for the sake of the ruling order. It is the order talking to itself, finding new pathways and methods. This is the innovation of the spiritual order.

Justice: The individual is always struggling to catch up with the dialectical order where they are born.

Light: The struggle is part and parcel of the same dialectic. We are the tension of our social conditions. Doubts and fears, hopes and aspirations, everything comes to us from the tensions in history. The human experience made real and dynamic, tripping over itself and each other to surface every nuance and aspect. That is how it happens.

Justice: You think you have come to some epiphany? You think some brilliant idea is yours? No, it is the same old thing said again and again, but perhaps with a new slant to give it a compulsion to stretch the order over newer and more diverse nodes. It learns to adapt through new languages and voices. It learns to speak as people require to sustain their wonder and the faux autonomy it anchors.

Peace: This is such a dark picture. You would have it that everything is illusory and false. You would have it that the order is the only true thing and that it rules in every way, it fabricates falsehood and truth for its own purposes. It does whatever it has to do, whatever it can do, to keep things working as they must, to prevent people from learning and understanding extraordinary things. There is no way out.

Justice: There is no way out.

Light: There is no way out, but the recursive process offers possibilities.

Peace: Recursive process?

Light: What we are doing now. The way we come to see that every step forward has the same underlying condition, that this condition is a pattern at work and that the pattern inhabits what we say and the way we say it.

Peace: Do we achieve something if we identify that?

Light: Assigning attributes both reveals and conceals the forces at work. It is where we are most likely to err. We think we are on top of it, but recursion has a boundary condition, a test to perform on every iteration. The key to breaking the infinity of recursion is to properly test the boundary condition.

Peace: How do you know if you are properly testing the boundary condition?

Justice: Because it stops.

Light: After the fact, it stops, and the stack unwinds. Pop, pop, pop. Everything bubbles back up and we arrive at the top of the order, the pattern comes to an end, the recursive maneuvers cease, and we rise up out of the dilemma.

Peace: That never happens.

Light: Not yet. Never. It never happens.

Justice: People propose different solutions. The pattern persists despite what they offer. That is proof that it fails. If it works, the pattern exits and we come back to the surface, we can breathe the air again.

Peace: Does that mean it is a way out?

Light: It means we can feel the unwinding, the movement back toward the surface. This isn't the same as getting out. In fact, it's a way to move back in. In but up. The logic of recursion unwinds. You remain within it but no longer go deeper. It exercises its boundary condition to prevent further descent or ascent. Stasis.

Justice: We don't come up in the end once and for all victorious and free. That's not how it works. We make a test, and that test breaks the movement and sends us back toward the surface where it starts again.

Peace: Back toward the surface, but isn't this just another idea? Isn't it just as doomed as any other? The toil of Sisyphus.

Light: There is no idea here. We're describing a pattern, not an intention. We've never seen it happen. There are pretenders, but they are short lived.

Peace: Maybe short-lived pretenders are the best we can do.

Justice: There has to be more to it.

Light: We can hope, but there remains a doubt. The stoic and the proponent of virtue each have their way and let the order be damned while striving for perfection despite it, only to have it gobbled up and reappropriated. Virtue becomes virtue ethics, stoicism a school of thought. Attribution settles over everything. The order strives for categories and aggregate alignments. It generates averages and likelihoods, builds tables and matrices. It organizes and shuffles. Everything about you is ordered like this, everything you understand is in terms of metrics and measures, these collective ideals. How tall am I, how good am I at some predefined activity? What marketable skills do I have? It constrains your power and flows into the order striating and compartmentalizing the world.

Justice: The movement continues. The test fails because there is never any attribute marking a successful outcome. The test is always executed against an aggregate property, a notion smoothed together from countless instances, and many performances. We are always repeating ourselves.

Light: The boundary condition rejects the categories and the aggregate.

Peace: How?

Light: If I answer your question as though providing an explanation, if I introduce analysis and commentary, I go astray. If I respond in an all-knowing voice from nowhere, I commit an affront to the question.

Peace: What then must we do?

Justice: I surely do not know, but I can tell you this much, no amount of order will get us there. We aren't failing from lack of organization.

Light: Those who would have it that we need the right project, that we need to order our inquiry properly and launch our investigations with a correct methodology, they overlook something. There, the order always wins and lurks in the patterns used to circumvent it.

Peace: What means are left if we can't plan a response? If we can't set out to achieve an end, what's left?

Light: That's right. It must be in the residual, it is our only hope.

Justice: Not hope.

Light: Not hope, but if there is a boundary to prevent recursion, it must be in the residual.

Peace: But what is that exactly?

Justice: It is not just another piece of the puzzle.

Light: We can't come at it from straight on. That is the point justice is always trying to make. It can never be the focus of an analysis. Computation fails, assignment equal to false is never attained. The Boolean value is so little understood by our means for assigning it. The boundary is never identified, it is not allocated to memory as an instruction. Null and void, it cannot surface in space and time. It resists the voice of soliloquy and evades the air moved by a lone speaker.

Peace: Where is it then?

Justice: Is it here?

Light: We do not see it because we see with it. Focus your eyes. There it is. Not in your field of vision, but in what is left over, what resides alongside it in the shadows.

Magical Properties

The Conspiracy

I just want you to know, I work for Ben Thorne. My paychecks say Ben Thorne. That means something different to me now than it did a few weeks ago. I am back at work, and he wants me to contact you, but he's just one of the owners. Not the one and only, just one. I work for you too. I want to make that clear. I am not taking sides. I don't expect you to trust me right away, but I hope it comes with time.

He says he wants the notes. Clearly, he means *Washington and Ashley*, that's what he cares about. He's locked on that project and has been for over a year saying it's the culmination of something that's been coming for a long time. He's dramatic and thinks of you as an obstacle. There's something missing from the work, and he's convinced it's in those notes.

I presume you've been going through them and discovered something. Did he have any misgivings? Does he mention that Jerry, my predecessor, is G.B. Porter? He has a wonderful imagination. The blend of science fiction and futurist fantasy is powerful and genuinely touching, but I've come across the work of many others that's just as good and just as sensitive. I've been thinking a lot lately about how he gets such a large audience, why do publishers give him so much support, and how does he get where he is when so many others struggle? I can't prove it, but I think Jerry's success is a reward for his contributions. He must have written passages, tied together story lines, worked out kinks or problem areas. He must've done the same as me, and he never gets any credit for it just like I never get any credit for it. Is this one of the perks of slaving away for Ben Thorne? Is this how they pay for the exploitation and soul sucking subservience?

Sorry, that's a distraction. I'm asking if you have something. If you do, I'd love to see it. Not because I'll hand it over to Wolfe or even that I'll tell him about it. I'm curious, that's it. Is it something about W&A or is it something else entirely?

I assume you think I'm loyal to Wolfe, but I always had my doubts. He can be difficult, throws tantrums, is cranky and ornery. Jealous and small, he thinks there's no one else on Earth with anywhere near as much talent and intelligence as he has. He's perfected the persona of the artiste, the world historical genius with sensibilities unparalleled. It's a lie. It must be this way for any figurehead, anyone who is the face of an organization. People like that must believe their own public relations. They spin the tale and then listen to the applause. He's fabricating it, but the reactions are real. He believes them even when he knows the truth. It's so aggravating.

I'm telling you this because I want you to know that my loyalty is not absolute, but there is something else, something more delicate: in that business with Jerry, Em must have been in on it too. He's more enigmatic. I find myself flip-flopping from day to day. Is he a moral coward? Does he submit to Wolfe's will because he knows only deference? Or is he a willing participant? Does he just go along or is he the mastermind? It's possible that Em is behind Wolfe's confidence, it's possible he's the one who encourages him to play the part of the overbearing author. Is that colossal ego a joint effort? Does it take the work of many men to produce the megalomania of one man?

I've agreed to come back to work. I want to get to know Em and learn what you've learned to better understand his role. Is he in the back being led around by a more charismatic figure? Is he the humble artisan plodding away and letting the more extroverted fool take center stage? Is he the puppet master? So many possible stories, so many ways it might play out. What sense do you get from the notes? Which picture fits with the man you know? Fathers aren't always transparent to their children.

Anyway, that's why I'm back and that's what I have to say. Write back or call, whatever you feel comfortable with. I just want to know how to proceed and if there's anything I can do for you, for Ben Thorne.

I appreciate your position and you've summed it up perfectly. The notes are rich and detailed. They're like a work diary, with problems and solutions, outlines and analysis, organized reasoning and interpretation. I want to talk about everything, there's so much, but I don't know how you fit together. You talk about my father as though he's a stranger. You see Wolfe every day, you work in an office with him. Em is just some guy who writes a few emails.

Let me say this: it cannot be a surprise to Wolfe to learn that there are serious reservations with *Washington and Ashley*. It's clear from the notes that Wolfe is waiting for some input that'll turn his fragments into a novel. Dad doesn't agree and Wolfe knows it. The notes say that repetition is not beautiful or poetic, but a death instinct, it's a yearning for destruction and expresses regret without another outlet. To make this very clear, Em thinks it's pathological to tell this story. The scene in the earlier work, the café scene that everyone calls the intervention, it isn't significant, it doesn't stand out, he doesn't see the drama in it, and it doesn't hold his attention in the same way it captures Wolfe's. He doesn't want to revisit it. Wolfe inflates his own virtues to rationalize his unhappiness. He has no sense of community. He's selfish and thinks individual excellence is the only basis for action. That's death, that's what my dad calls it, that's what he writes.

There's an email from Em to Wolfe about a year ago where Em suggests that the real center of attention for that theme, the theme of the intervention, is the work from November. It's called *Being an Introduction* or, sometimes, *The Punctuation Book*. This is what my dad wanted to go back to. In that email, he tries to convince Wolfe... No, he's trying to convince Ben Thorne that the interlude comes from interruption and is more significant than intervention. Not from an individual, but from an order. His notes are detailed. A different repetition is at its heart. There's a whole thing about how interlude becomes the interleave of many collaborating forces. He thinks Wolfe is oblivious. In Wolfe's mind, the issues around publishing the first book are simple. Publishers and editors, these are ordinary parts of a well-established process that includes publicists and marketing, the target audience, everything with the author at the center. Nothing about any of it is ordinary to my dad.

The upshot is Ben Thorne. The corporate body, he writes, is a voice for their fear and desire, not born of an agreement, but in conflict. They love and hate each other. They are jealous and supportive at the same time, competitive like elite athletes who are at odds in the game they play but aligned as the few able to play it at such a high level. It's preserved in the notebooks. Wolfe acquiesces to Em's portrayal, but he shows no signs of understanding the deeper meanings. The persona of Ben Thorne is crafted in these exchanges, but it's as if Wolfe reduces it to a simple pen name, and he can't fathom the relationship between the problems in *Fragmented* and the articles of incorporation. It's a philosophical alliance. The contents of *Being an Introduction* aim at this for the sake of exposing it. It's the relationship between the two of them and not just the two of them, but everyone who participates. No doubt this includes you and Jerry. Many others too: the interns, the copy editors, the publisher's assistants, everyone. These different contributions to the bigger project, everyone doing their job, he's keenly aware that the interleave between the two of them is manifold and just the beginning. Every new contributor is a compound triangulation. The order grows more powerful and more complex with every addition. "We have a cover designer. Additions are exponential," that's a direct quote.

My take is that the working relationship lies in *Being an Introduction* and that this book is Em's child. What I'd like to see next from Ben Thorne, as a tribute to my father, is that this book gets the attention it deserves. He never finishes the second act, and it has to end so that the interlude can be the interlude. If Wolfe is so interested in bending time back to the intervention, then he needs to understand that this has its center in an interlude that is not something that happens one day on Washington Street between Main and Ashley but in the partially and crudely crafted pages of *Being an Introduction*. We should drop W&A.

I ask you to keep this between us until we can come to an understanding, but if you can't do that, let me know.

***

I wanted to drop you a line. I read your messages to her, and I read her replies. I don't want to get in the middle of anything, but I do want to make one suggestion. Come to Greece. Isn't that a lovely idea? Come soon. Bring the interns. I don't see why you shouldn't, there's business to discuss and the two of you will never get better acquainted across the distance. Come visit. I'd love to see you again. What do you think?

That's a lovely idea. Carl and Fred would be thrilled. It'll infuriate Wolfe. I'm just listing the pros, but I'm sure there must be cons. Seriously though, it does sound like a great idea. Please recommend the best travel route and I'll book the tickets as soon as we can agree on dates. I'd love to see you again too.

The Plan

I'm glad to hear you're coming for a visit. I hope you'll let me know if there's anything I can do to help.

What I'm mostly reading is a set of elaborate discussions of the role tension and conflict play. There are references to Empedocles and Heraclitus. Events and actions are expressions of strife. What seem like organs or parts of a bigger whole are deep down, at ground level, disputes and opposition.

> If everything great, I won't say good, comes from strife and turmoil, then the underlying order is established to promote it. If individuals oppose it, that is no deterrent. In fact, their individual opposition can serve the overall effect. Their morality of peace and cohesiveness serves the greater good of tension and strife. The only thing that's required is an inflated ego.

Where does this reference to an inflated ego come from? There's a lot to suggest he's riffing on ego as a process emerging from conflict: it's like a repetitive loop covering underlying tensions. Ego is manufactured through relationships and a way to manifest conflict or give it a voice. The ego becomes increasingly individual, distinct from its social origins, the more complex and diverse those relations are. It's not that one causes the other, but that increasing complexity *is* the increasing strength. Order produces ego and ego exacerbates the tensions at work in order.

> The ego hides the real players within the order. There is good and evil, but it has nothing to do with humans. The

ego blinds the agent, or rather, forces them to see the world
in terms of its own desires and interests rather than the larger
organized structures ordering individual players. These are
massive bodies. The ones whose actions are based on
deliberation, and which could be otherwise, they are the
agents with moral worth, they are the true agents. Who are
we to judge them? We can't see them just as the eye cannot
see itself. Even for those extensions and parts within view,
the perspective is heavily conditioned. There are no
philosophers, only philosophies.

The ego is a perception machine tasked with producing identifications
and orientations. Wonder is the ground of an illusory autonomy. This
wonder increases the creature's capacities and increases the complexity of
its ego. I'm paraphrasing. It comes from the originating principles ordering
personal attributes into boundary conditions between us. The species
behind the specimen, the nation state behind the citizen, the gender, class,
and race behind the person, they're the true rational agents, they're the
ones who deliberate and act. We merely express their affects, with an a.
"The aggregate in me."
I know it's abstract, but I think he's trying to work out how conflict
makes things appear. He's working out an architecture, if that word makes
sense here, for how to spin a tale through conflicts and tensions.

We can build a shared delusion, but each is equally rebelling
against it in the act of building it. The tension lies in cultural
views, political views, and morality. We can let that reign, let
that battle rage, and it'll draw so much attention and such
critical acclaim. How could one person find so much
tension and so much dialogue in one single voice? Well,
now we know. And we have to make good on the promise
of the work, we have to expose *them*. The players must
expose the game.

You see, this must be the philosophy behind them. It isn't the individual
against the community, it isn't the constraint of the individual that creates
the civilized community or civil society, rather it's the individual that is
created by the tension between the specimen and the species, the collective
and the person. The raw potential of the conscious being is constrained
through a tension-filled process. That tension is expressed in the single
person as the complex experience of their life and relationship to others.
Does any of this make sense? I would share the entire thing with you, but
there's so much and it would take you a long time to parse through it. What
I'm describing comes from a lot of condensing and summarizing. We can

look at it more closely when you get here.

* * *

It sounds fascinating, but I don't see Ben Thorne in any of it. Unless you mean that stories are a way of presenting the psyche, the tensions in it, and letting these be called Jane and those be called John. Is it something like that? Where the moral conflict we feel, or the indecision we experience, these are shards of larger operations that take up a position in space. They orient themselves through daily habits and ordinary life. The fabrication of the character spins into a repetitive pattern, some mixture of these tensions. Do you think he's saying that this describes how personality works or is it just how literary figures are produced?

The bits and pieces you cite seem existential and flowy. Is that how he internalizes his relationship to Wolfe and how they create the tensions? Isolated into segments or fragments, they are presented as though they're smaller patterns in a larger order. Like rather than seeing Venus or Mercury, we see the trajectory of light from the sun bouncing off bodies and we identify the history of those sensations as a pattern. Not the sun-lit object, but the ray of light. We give that pattern a name by making a fetish called Mercury or Venus. We reduce the movement, the rotation, the operations, into a single name capturing movement and history. The planets' egos reify as things in view at this moment in time reflected in an abstract event. It's like a photograph: something that cuts off some little piece or moment and replaces the trajectory and motion with it.

I suppose that fits. Clearly the writers, Ben Thorne, are puzzled and confused by the properties of things. There are so many experiences and passages where the universal, the attribute, is called into question, where they wonder how being blue or sharp or tired can be meaningful. The animal is tired. That animal over there is tired too. Two different animals. Is tired some one thing that they share? Is it one single state? Or is there something highly particular in each that we gloss over and use to bind them together through mere formality? One could read *Choreography* this way. The staging of movement, its repetition, the presumption of identity across instances, that is questionable in essence.

I seem to recall, back in the day, that he is attacked for this. It is in response to *A Brief History of Thoroughly Requited Love.* Some readers claim it's a thinly veiled attack on Attribute politics. Delusion plays a large role in requited love, deluding yourself about who you are and deluding yourself about who the beloved is. The attributes play a part. Properties and the assigning of properties to the self and to the other, that's central to the delusion. We capture a moment, turn it into a thing, try to find just the right name for it, and then adore it as it stands there in its artificially engineered form. Requited love is delusional, and the delusion is built on existential bad faith or whatever you want to call it. The point is that we turn ourselves into things, we make ourselves extend into space and into a container for properties without thinking about their true nature and how they hide what's specific and unique. Either we lack the language for excavating the personal, or the personal is a construct with the same origin as the language that describes it. Assigning qualities hides the fact that we are practical anarchists.

Ben Thorne makes a claim somewhere suggesting that it's the Nazis who define the Jew and then the nation of Israel takes over that definition when deciding who qualifies for its law of return. The categories of oppression, some of which he claims are in conflict with each other, are embraced by this new political movement. Empowerment. Attribution is already political, and the power of oppression is already at work in its categories. Once you accept the imperial table of measures, you're already within the realm. You sneak in mechanisms for expressing power. Ben Thorne causes a huge explosion one day when he posts on social somewhere that the state of mind of an advocate of Attribute politics is the highest form of consciousness attained by the European Enlightenment. He effectively accuses his antagonists of being products of that same White Male Heterosexual power structure they oppose. They depend on its logic when categorizing themselves and attributing their own identities. He accuses them of hypocrisy, and they do not like it.

That same book has the discussion of The Terror and the French Revolution, the prisons in Siberia and Mao's response to the Hundred Flowers Campaign. Power is most present in the aggregate, it expresses itself on subjects by attaching predicates to them. Attributes, properties, whatever constrains the subject, enforces its boundaries, and further conflicts through personas that are vehicles for the underlying power. They hate it, they think he's aggressive and counter revolutionary. Their reaction, if anything, supports his point.

Sorry to go on for so long, but is that what you're thinking? Is that what you're trying to explain? If so, it seems rich to me, like it makes sense of so many different parts of the work.

You capture it well. It does explain a lot. Is that the same book where they're critical of enthusiasm anywhere other than the bedroom? There are many political asides. Things that are captured perfectly by socially ordered "bad faith." I found this:

> The psyche and the nation. The fabricated worlds of the
> work spawn their incorporated authority as fabricator. The
> political is personal, the social is psychological. Meaning is a
> public matter, and it is the persistent point of mediation of
> the self with itself. Attribution is based upon it, the real or

factual becomes a matter of identification. Become who you are, gain class consciousness, these are slogans that are little more than a socially informed choice of one set of attributes upon which to hang an identity. The interleave yields the flair of a prosthetic god. It is the demon within, and these are its magical properties.

Magical Properties.

There are specific political discussions too, always between extremes. He interprets it through an elitist aristocratic vision on the one hand and a more popular democratic vision on the other. Sometimes, it feels like Nietzsche and Marx in a never-ending spiral. Whose instincts are constrained and whose liberated? Do we have civilization so that a few extraordinary individuals, whatever that means, can emerge, or is it for the sake of the best possible outcome overall even if that constrains the maximum outcome for anyone in particular? In their tales, the spiral isn't a question, it's the answer. Two opposing mythologies continue as a part of life in the community, two patterns demanding service. I think he wants the two of them, the contributors, to fight and argue, to work out their disagreements, and to battle it out on the pages of each book. The whole purpose is to fight those battles as Wolfe versus Em. This makes the abstract esoteric dynamics concrete. Does that fit with what you see in their working sessions?

From what I'm reading, I expect they're often unable to resolve their arguments, unable to come to an agreement. Neither of them can command the other to do it the way they want. Agreement happens when they bake their opposition into the story.

If that's the case, what would they do now? If Wolfe is dead set on *Washington and Ashley* and Em on *Being an Introduction*, how do they resolve that? How do they get past it? Stalemate amounts to doing nothing.

I'm glad the arrangements are set. I think it'll be a lot easier to have these conversations in person where we can talk to each other in half sentences. I'm looking forward to it.

Thank you so much for being so encouraging. I'm really looking forward to the trip too. Wolfe still doesn't know. I'll have that conversation with him soon, wish me luck.

Yes, it's the same book with the discussion of enthusiasm. Is there a connection?

You might be right about this particular disagreement and about how important disagreements are to their work. If that's the case, maybe we have to broaden our thinking. In other disagreements, they sometimes turn it into a new character or a new event in the story. The characters have to live out that disagreement and figure out how to make everything fit. Their struggle is part of the drama and set into the story. Maybe they think of themselves as a microcosm. Like you say, the order behind the conflict is a higher-order person. They are the higher-order people behind the story. That's the recursive maneuver. That trope, the one about recursion, comes up often. The attempt to get behind things. This makes their whole literary approach into a homoerotic struggle for expressing obsession with order and power to ultimately produce the cleanest (sic) *inverted* example of the anal personality. Don't both Marx and Nietzsche want to invert things? Wasn't 'invert' the name for a homosexual in Proust? If any of this holds true, if the argument at the meta-level is between the two faces of the one author, and if the solution is expressed in specific characters, then maybe there is a way to capture that here. It's an erotic mess and that's what I mean by broadening our scope. What if the story becomes something different to capture that tension and conflict? This is the classic patriarchal antinomy. Wolfe's love for Em is the command that orients *Washington and Ashley* and the drive to repeat the intervention. Em's love for Wolfe is the command that orients *Being an Introduction* and the drive to circumvent the intervention as a point of departure for interlude. They can only resolve the dilemma by taking a step back and realizing what they're doing, but what they're doing prevents them from wanting to see it. This becomes the work itself, the whole dramatic tension lives there. I don't know. Let me know what you think.

I really want to thank you for opening up to me and sharing these notes and ideas. I am so grateful for your trust, and I promise you that I will treat it with the respect it deserves, although at some point we'll have to include Wolfe. I'll leave that to you.

Thank you too. I really need someone to talk to about this. I have no bearings, no experience to draw from. Does anyone? Is this a unique event? It feels like it. All of it, I mean, every aspect. These last weeks have been so hard and sorting through this helps. If that makes sense.

I love your ideas for broadening our scope. I completely agree. That's exactly the proposal I was hoping for. Obviously, this is just a beginning. We still don't know what to do, the details of it, but at least this gives us direction. We won't know what's connected and what isn't until we have a more fleshed out plan. The enthusiasm stuff, I mean, whether it's related, and whatever else might be.

We'll have a lot to do when you get here, and I agree that we'll have to include Wolfe, but I want to have a plan before that. We'll work on that when you're here. Having you in Keramoti isn't convenient, the drive will get in our way. Let me see if I can come up with something better.

Democritus University of Thrace

I send greetings from your cousin Eugenia. She tells me you have some insights on the work of Ben Thorne. I am a professor of comparative literature and cultural studies at the University in Xanthi. I went to school with Eugenia's stepson Giannis Laskaris. I also know your friend Alexandros Kallistidis from Thessaloniki. I would not ordinarily contact someone like this, but they are urging me to write to you. Since we are not far apart, I thought we might get together for coffee or a drink. I could come to Chrysoupoli if you like.

I am no scholar, but I'd be happy to talk to you about Thorne's work. Any evening this next week works fine. I've been spending time in an office across from Attalos. Do you know it? We can meet there.

Thank you so much for taking the time to meet with me. I hope I did not bore you with that talk about Thorne's work and my project. I would love to make it up to you by taking you to dinner sometime. I promise not to talk about my work anymore.

Dinner would be nice. Thank you. No apologies necessary, I enjoy hearing about your research. Sorry to repeat myself, but I don't feel comfortable saying too much about the source of my interest. I have many questions and it's good to know what's interesting to scholars. I am not extremely familiar with his work, but I am familiar with him, and he says a lot to pique my interest.

I will come and pick you up and we can drive to the restaurant together. Parking in Xanthi can be quite a puzzle.

By the way, I have been thinking a lot about what you said about the dialogical in Ben Thorne's work. I guess that material is mostly out of date. I know the work you are referring to, but people generally think that Bakhtin is wrong about Dostoevsky. It is a highly opportunistic reading.

Great, see you then.

I realize the theory may not be correct for Dostoevsky, but it doesn't seem like that's the only thing that matters. It's still a coherent reading, isn't it? I mean, as a theory, it makes sense and there certainly could be some writing somewhere that fits.

Yes, I see your point. You are asking if it applies to Thorne's work. I will have to think about that.

* * *

I hope we can have dinner again soon, I enjoy spending time with you. It seems like we keep landing on the same subjects. Please let me know if I monopolize the conversation.

Yes, me too. Thanks so much for showing me around. I don't know Xanthi terribly well, so it's great to get the grand tour. I think I'll be able to find some of those places if I go back on my own.

I also really like hearing about your family. I never think about that mass immigration from Nigeria back in the 90s. It must be difficult. There's a crisp notion of who is Greek, and something tells me there are still many who haven't broadened it to include Greeks of Nigerian ancestry.

It is true, Greeks do not see a difference between their racial identity and their national identity. True Greeks are the descendants of the Achaeans. If you do not come from them, then you are not Greek. This makes things difficult, but whatever prejudices I come across, I have just as many positive experiences. Lots of contradictions.

I am still thinking more about your questions. I get the feeling that there is more than what you are letting on, but I am looking at the passages you mention from *Artists of Despair* and *Choreography*. I can see the merits of your reading. No one is talking about this. It is not just that there is one character that is the yin and another the yang. You are not referring to any one character, but to the design and development of the entire work.

Am I wrong to emphasize the fact that you do not echo my feelings on seeing each other again? If you just want to write to each other and keep it professional, that is fine, but I really want to see you again.

Sorry, I'm very tunnel visioned. There's a lot going on, and I just don't have much time. Can we play it by ear? Maybe take a walk somewhere one evening this week? We could meet at the park on the Nestos between here and there. It's about halfway.

My point about Thorne concerns plot and layout: the story lines. *Princess Myshkin* is murky, I need to reread it, but I recall conflict at a rudimentary level. That's what I'm sorting out, how to understand it and whether it's an unseen power. Maybe it's why there's so much spirited division in readings of his work. Like there are many voices and which one sways a reader determines how they interpret it.

Any time. Just text me or call. We can be spontaneous.

I get your point, and it opens a lot of possibilities. The pattern is more significant in other places. I am thinking of *Brief History*. They say that even in divided America everyone claims that book to champion their own point of view.

The attack on Attribute politics is everyone's focus. There is a specific monologue on the Terror and on Stalinism that supports this reading, but people fail to see that it is deeply influenced by Arendt's *Origins of Totalitarianism*. Thorne is not just making a comparison to the Maoist backlash against intellectuals and the Stalinist internment and reeducation camps, he is showing the similarity to National Socialism too. Nevertheless, none of it focuses directly on Attribute politics in the American sense, but on white supremacy, election denial, and Christian nationalism. I read it as an attack on both sides of the political debate. He spins them both as a fetish.

The book is, in fact, an attack on extremes and enthusiasm. I think you may have mentioned this. It is as though there are two competing designs. One focuses on liberty over and against the power of the leftist totalitarians and the other focuses on justice over and against the right-wing totalitarians. The left wants reeducation and conformity while the right wants violence and separation. Both voices are struggling to avoid equivalency. In fact, both assert point blank that it is *their* fault. If anything, the book tries to hold both points of view true at one and the same time. The two are different worlds and both are affective in every scene and during every description or conversation.

I want to reread that book from start to finish. Every scene has a completely different world, and no one ever takes the time to identify them all, describe them in detail, and indicate which is dominant during which events in the story. It fits beautifully with my thesis. Do you mind if I run with it? Are you planning on publishing? Do you want to write something together?

Thank you for earlier, the river is so calming. Please don't interpret my comments as a rejection. Your proposals are very tempting.

Let me float a hypothetical based on your description this morning. Bear in mind, this is not my area of expertise. In *Brief History*, there are two different takes on race, one biological and one cultural. Each is part of a distinct world of experience. What I'm interested in is how thoroughly and richly these two worlds develop. The characters are caught and can't identify them, they don't understand when one predominates and when the other does, but the story you describe captures it. Their motives, the psychology, the meaning of their actions and words, everything, comes out of the world they're in at that moment: biological or cultural.

It isn't just race. Selection is desire, and desire moves between worlds, it's both biological and cultural. It's a hypothesis and still needs work. Everything that happens cuts between the two. You say there are feminists who claim this is his most misogynist book, but you also say there are feminists who hold it up as a complete redefinition of the problem area and some possible approaches to it. Everything fits this distinction. Everything depends on what world the characters are in when they act.

Why don't you come for dinner? You can meet my family, and we can try to make a little more progress. I really have to take a look at that book, it seems crucial.

I would love to come to dinner. Just name the date and give me the directions. School is starting up soon so it might be best if we do it before then. Time will be tight once the semester begins.

Yes, the worlds theory makes a lot of sense, especially if you do not tie it to any one of the characters but recognize that they move back and forth between worlds, depending on events and who they are talking to. World as we are using that term is incredibly difficult to pin down and fasten with a clear definition. It is shocking that you mention Heidegger when talking about this. Are you certain that Ben Thorne's first book starts out as an interpretative study of Heidegger's work, specifically focusing on his early and late notions of world? I have never heard this before. You have to reveal your source. What evidence do you have? You say the key texts are *Being and Time* and "Origin of the Work of Art." I am looking at both of them. Fascinating.

How would a world be in a story? We focus on events, and we focus on characters, but we do not see the world, do we? We cannot point to it and say that is the world, but it is in our exchange. This back and forth between you and I. Excuse me if that is too forward, but there are at least two worlds between us. We have coffee and dinner, drinks, walks, and now meeting your family. This is a world between us. Then there is this professional discussion, the Ben Thorne analysis. That is a second world. We move back and forth between them. Thorne's many worlds of race and his many worlds of sex happen the same way. There is some discussion of gender in that book too, and national origin.

"Humans are producing entertainment for each other using various forms of storytelling stylized as political discourse. Clever with a touch of bitterness and anger." This is from an interview Ben Thorne gives around the time *Brief History* comes out. That same interview has remarks on aggression and how we need it even though it conflicts with our social bonds and civilized demeanor. Bitterness and anger require a place. The worlds theory provides a setting for that bitterness and anger. He effectively says that in the interview: "Each reality is a siege of forces that oppress your desire to be." That view into the siege of forces is the worlds theory. He does not acknowledge opposing forces, rather he talks about how there are, on the one hand, forces coherent in their own way and acting upon you, and then there are other forces, also coherent in their own way and acting upon you. Each is a world offered, and you live in the one and then in the other. You get dreamlike and spacey sometimes, floating in the amniotic fluid that comforts you, and then incited to disgust and anger in the other world. Your impetus and conditioning find an outlet as you move between worlds.

In the past, readers spend their breath discussing the views and never the fact of the divergence. I do not recall seeing anything ever that mentions that this is not a false equivalence so much as a complete development of divergent points of view, giving each its due and deconstructing both. They are incoherent vessels containing nonsense and contradictions. They rely on artificial meaning to prop them up and make them believable. I am trying to put together some coherent thoughts on the subject and will bring the latest draft to dinner. I am really looking forward to it. Not just your reaction to my draft, but to the dinner, to that other world of ours. Please, if there is anything special that I should bring, let me know. Otherwise, I will just rely on the common cultural pointers. That is a joke. I will bring sweets. Maybe something from Papaparaskevas. I remember you saying you love that patisserie. Let me know if there are any particular treats you prefer, otherwise I will bring an assortment.

You needn't bring anything special. Don't go to any trouble. It might be a party actually. The numbers are growing. Just friends and family, nothing to worry about. We'll see you tonight. Alexandros will be here. Other friends too. I'm looking forward to seeing you and reading the manuscript.

Based on what you're reading, I wonder if the tension between worlds is misanthropic. Is Ben Thorne equally dismissive of both the right and the left? Does he dislike both and dismiss them equally? He wants those worlds and acts of world fabrication to be the critical issue, the subject of critique, and so he makes out as if any employment of them, any tacit usage, is vile and delusional. But what is the alternative? How does one live in a world without taking it for granted? Or is there a way to live well in many worlds letting them reveal each other's limits?

Isn't there something you're saying about Nietzsche contra Marx? In Nietzsche's world the individual is everything. First there's the extraordinary individuals and the conditions for cultivating them. Then there's Marx's world where the extraordinary individual is counter revolutionary. Both are teeming with anger and resentment: hostile opposition to or from the subject. That's certainly prevalent in *Artists of Despair* and it doesn't seem like he's coming down on one side or the other. Both have flaws, both are beautiful, both are symptomatic of human sublimation of aggression for the sake of civilized cohabitation. Is it possible? Does he advocate a tension among worlds where everyone is miserable unless they can swing back and forth between them? The misery and the joy of the pendulum are what matters, and they're only possible if the world appears as an inevitable condition that both liberates and constrains, coerces and empowers, while it swings between pleasure and death, destruction and generation. Everything depends on a recursive pattern that we're perpetually shunning and perpetually embracing. It's as if the thing that has control over us must have control in order to make us happy, but we simultaneously feel as though it's constantly letting go, or being evaded, and we have to feel that way for it to have the right effect. Isn't there a philosopher who thinks the world is a single substratum for attributes?

The Shuffle

There is no need to fight. The plan is simple from here, the hard part is behind us. Stamatia, you simply go home. Ariti and Thimios are in the big bedroom now, and Despina is sleeping in the den, but the other bedroom is ready for you and your things are already there. I know you'll miss staying with Europea, but this is the best for everyone. We need you close to Ariti and your granddaughter. Europea is rigid in her ways, and she wants to stay in her house. That's fine and as it should be. No one wants to move her. Eirini moves there and the den is her permanent bedroom. She can keep an eye on Europea and help out around the house. It's much better for her to be in town and close to work so that she won't have to make that long drive every day. She enjoys her time at Ermioni's, but now it's time to settle down. Endaxei.

I'm staying in Ermioni's crafts room until I leave. It's only a few weeks and she's fine with it. No reason to shake things up. Mia moves into Eleni's room. She's only staying a little longer so that should be fine. She's happy to make room for Eleni's colleague who will stay in the guest room. So much better than in the hotel in Keramoti. Yes, it's a nice hotel, but it's far away and they're working together so it's best if they're close. Since there isn't anywhere else in town, this is the best option.

Nikos and I take care of everything. We have Thimios and Alexandros, but we have that pod to empty too. Those carpets and blankets, books and trivial little things. Ion volunteers if we need him. I think the four of us are more than enough, but he really wants to help so I see no reason why he shouldn't. Better to have a younger man lift and carry than the older guys. Who knows what grief it might save?

I don't mind moving to Europea's house. It's better than staying in Keramoti, so far from everything. It'll be easier to go to work. It's been so much better since I'm staying at Eleni's, this will be just like that. It's only a few blocks over. The bike ride is about the same and the carpooling will work just fine if I need a lift.

Living with Europea won't get rid of the problems of living with your parents, but it'll get rid of some. There are secrets she'll keep. Not all of them. She won't mind much about what time I come home, and she won't always ask me where I'm going and who I'm going with. She won't pry and try to know everything that's going on with me. My mother can't help it. That's just how she treats children. They're used to it, it's what they know. I'm older now, I should have my own life, my privacy. I don't want to account for every minute. It's not like I'm doing anything naughty anyway. That's not the point, I just want to do what I want without having someone looking over my shoulder every second of the day.

Even with Europea, even if she doesn't pay any attention to me, I still have to be careful. Everyone sees where you go and who you go with. They know, and they talk to each other. It's not malicious, mostly just entertainment, I think. Or concern. They know so and so and they're up to such and such. What else? Let me think, oh I heard that they were at the bar very late with someone different. They're just friends, that's how the kids are these days. There's a lot of talk like that. Some people know how things are and some people don't. They make up stories when they don't understand. The truth usually comes out. I'm just saying. There are things you can't do.

Eleni likes two different men. It's obvious to anyone who's paying attention. She likes Ion, she isn't pretending. She likes the professor from Xanthi, Mihalis. It's not a problem to spend time with them both. People will talk, but they won't think anything is going on. She'll get teased a little, but if she's too obvious, if she lets on that they're more than just friends, there could be trouble. The older ladies will judge. Our aunties and our mothers, they'll say things. They won't always have the best intentions.

I could never do anything like that. You hang out with the gang. If there's someone you like, you invite them to hang around with the gang too. If that goes well, okay then. That's how it works. He's your boyfriend or whatever. They can forgive modern romance, but they can't forgive promiscuity.

It's the same for boys. They have to follow the same rules, they can't be running around town with different girls. The grannies and the mothers and the aunties, they'll notice. There's talk. No one trusts them. It's the same.

Not exactly the same. They come back from it. It's harder for a girl. If a boy does something they don't like, they'll talk, but if he settles down, they'll forgive him. He can come to dinner, he can even date their daughters and granddaughters, but for girls, there's no forgiveness. Once they start talking about her, she'll always be like that. Like with my friend Panagia from high school, she went with a few different boys and some girls too. None of them were her boyfriend or girlfriend. Sometimes they'd see her out at night with two of them. That doesn't last very long, and she hasn't been back since, not even to visit her mother and father. I still hear people talk about her sometimes. How is that naughty Panagitsa, is she still up to her old ways in Thessaloniki? With the girls, they never forgive.

Still, it's better at Europea's. Eleni says it's just in my head. She thinks I don't really want to do any of those things and so the rules don't matter. I don't argue with her. It's best if she thinks that. She might be right. I hope so, but sometimes I'm not sure. America is so much fun, away from everything. I'm glad to be home, but that's nice too.

An embarrassment of riches. That's what he says. He plans so carefully for retirement. We're so prudent our whole lives, and it's always about what you need there. That's all he ever sees. He builds the house at the same time. He must realize I'll come and live here after he's gone, but he does the planning based on costs in the US. He doesn't plan on selling the house. He says it's best not to think about your house as an asset until you're sure you don't have to live there anymore. How can I disagree with him? But now, with the saving, everything we miss out on because of it, the sacrifices we make. I don't need it here. Life is so much less expensive. This house is completely furnished. It's a nice house but it still only cost a fraction of what we're spending in the US. It's a humble place. This one is too much. I'm not sure how long Eleni will stay, but I hope she stays a long time. I'm dreading the day she leaves.

What will I do then? Maybe my mother will move in. She's getting less and less mobile, but she wants to be on her own. She doesn't mind having Renya there, but she still cooks and cleans. She takes care of everything just like she always does. She doesn't want to give up any part of her life. She wants me to live with her but doesn't want to live with me. I feel the same way. We're alike. Eleni is different.

I don't know how long she'll stay. What does she do in there? She's working on so many things. Something about her department isn't going well. She doesn't want to share any details. She doesn't want me to worry, but I know something's up. There's some work that isn't going as she expects. She's looking through that laptop. I can only imagine what she's finding there. I don't know if it's healthy for people to write down every thought they ever have, to leave a record of their beliefs. You can't know what favor they'll find after you're gone and can't defend them. She's frustrated and confused. I can tell she's struggling, but she doesn't want to tell me, she doesn't want me to worry.

I'm her mother, she should talk to me. She has to tell me what's troubling her. It won't worry me any more than I already am. I've told her that whatever is going on with her, I'll worry more if I don't know. It's so much better to know the truth and focus on the real thing instead of what you imagine.

She'll open up in due time. These two young men. So different from each other. Is that how she's working through it? I can't tell. If she's only here for a short time, what's the point starting up with two different men? What can she gain from that? I don't get it. I wish I could ask her what she's thinking? How are they helping? I'm sure she must be talking about it with Mia and Eirini. Just so long as she has someone to talk to, that's what matters. It doesn't have to be me. I'd love it to be me, but it doesn't have to be. Just so long as she's okay. Just so long as she's happy.

I worry she isn't and doesn't believe it's possible. She misses her father. No one could possibly think otherwise, but she's angry at him too. I see that. She blames him for something, and I can't say exactly what it is. She's in the middle of it now, and the storm is camouflage. She's just like him, hiding those huge battles from me. Monumental conflicts and he works through them in the quietest way, never showing any signs. She's exactly the same way. Whatever is going on, there might be complete chaos, but she never shows it. She just wakes up and goes into the office, works on whatever, and then, when lunch is ready, comes out and sits down like a good girl. She asks me how things are going, tells me if she likes something, as though everything is calm and easy. Then I catch her brooding. Going over some details again and again, worrying about what to do. She sits with me and eats the same food, but in her mind, she's worlds away and I have no idea what she's going through.

I'm volunteering to move in with Lena. It's entirely possible that I'll end up back in the guest room with Ginna, but these are details, minor adjustments. Georgios will not be the least bit put out by such a change in plans. So long as the players are in the right buildings. I'm a tad bit outside the family protective wall, so they'll cut me some slack. During the discussion, I carefully let him know that some variation may occur. Not that it definitely will, but Lena and I both let them know that Ginna and I are friends, and we'll see.

I'll need to get back soon anyway, so not sure I have time for any complications. I don't want to make any drastic changes. Even with the churn and turmoil, I don't think there's much that needs to change. That asshole doesn't have the authority to stop payments. There's no reason to panic.

The case needs more attention, I don't think Bert can handle it by himself. Especially if I want to add the media angle. It's just so ridiculous, but if a mob of fifty people can convince a jury that they're afraid of these two little unarmed women, then it's fair to inquire as to how they came to be that way. Where does the fear come from? It may not save the case, but it's the right message. These corporations make their profits from stirring up anxiety and fear, provoking anger and frustration, and then they just pay fines when something goes wrong. The fine is nothing to them, just one more in a long list of costs that go along with whatever they're doing. They have to pay the rent and the electric bill, then they have to pay a fine for violating some city ordinance or for negligently getting some people killed. They never have to really pay for what they do. The idea that they are people is ludicrous, but it's at least reasonable. If they're people, then they're people and they must be treated that way with the rights and responsibilities that go with it.

I'll make the case, so I'll need to get back to the center at some point. My library is there. I'll need to bounce some ideas off Gwen and Bert. Maybe travel down to St. Louis to talk to him in person. Things will be heating up pretty soon, I can't stay here much longer. Even with Ginna coming, I'll have to leave soon. There are too many important things, I have to think rationally about this. No sightseeing allowed.

Speaking of which, I honestly do not know what to say when Ermioni asks me about Lena and the two men she's seeing. She thinks both are a distraction, like Lena is trying to work through something. She might not be wrong. It's hard to miss the fact that one's a professor and the other's an electrician. It's pretty clear that this repeats a theme she's rehearsing. It doesn't make it any easier that she's getting grief from her department. She says appealing is effectively the same as applying for readmission so what's the hurry? Self-importance trumps compassion. It's par for the course, but it has her thinking. Self-importance is the mark of the beast, the signal appropriate to academic posturing. She's tired of it, I can tell. She laughs more when she's with Ion. She's serious when she talks to Mihalis. In her mind, true or not, school is for gravity and delusional self-importance, but is it the right delusion for her? Delusion is inevitable and the only question is which one to choose. Without illusions, there's no place to vent your frustration and anger. They tell you where to put it. They tell you who to belittle and who to worship. They're like little worlds complete with the ingredients and instructions for making yourself at home.

I wish I could convince her that it's possible to make your own world, to design your own illusion. It may be an illusion still, but when you have one tailored to you, then it's so much easier to come out healthy. I'm not confessing to anything, I only mean that even striving for something important, working to help people in dire need, even that entails falsehoods and deceptions that you have to accept. I work in corrupt courts and cling to the notion they can be made to serve justice. Ben Thorne, and that might include Em, is a patriarch who benefits from the same bullshit that all men benefit from. Whatever lip service they pay to struggles for empowerment, they're still benefiting from the inequalities. There's so much coming at her at once. Even if it isn't academic, it's tied to that same life of the mind they've been dangling in front of us for centuries. The European Enlightenment has us thinking exactly how it wishes, using its forms. What escape can it possibly provide? What illusions are necessary to tear it apart?

They move me wherever they need me to be. It's my house they're moving me into. First, they move me out of it, now they move me back into it. We're spread around the city. These same four or five houses where we live. Here and down near the beach. Why the shuffling? Why the hardship? I'm happy with Alecos. I'm happy with my daughter and her family. I'm happy with Europea. I will be happy again back with my daughter. I don't need to be in charge. It's fine if someone else wants that. I'll do what I can, but I'm past that. So much shuffling, so much noise.

I hope my granddaughter doesn't think she's getting away with anything. I know her soul even if she doesn't know it herself. She thinks Europea will let her get away with everything. Renya thinks this way and I let Europea know. She waves it aside. What does it matter? She's growing up. Why shouldn't she have her own life? We all do in our own way, I suppose. My time is past. Now, I am here for the others. Okay, that's fine. Whatever the family needs, I don't mind. How much time do I have left, anyway? If we give the children the foundation they need to take care of themselves, that's all they can ask of us. That's what it's for. Life makes sense if the family continues with the children and the grandchildren. For thousands of years, it happens. Why should it be any different now? We have to play our part. It isn't only that we adjust to the world, we help others do the same. Ariti needs my help, and Despina. It'll be nice to see her every day, to watch her grow up. That's what it's for, isn't it?

Mother is back. Renya too. With Europea. That is as it should be. That niece of mine, her parents are too permissive, they let her get away with so much. She's a new woman. The likes of me and our generation are no longer the rule, no longer the standard for measurements. We must follow her if we are to be successful in our new traditions. We'll sit back and watch. There's nothing in it for us now, we needn't fret. Something happens, but we don't know what it is anymore. We don't know what can be done or whether anything should be done. This is always how it goes. For generations, we always think the same thing about the great changes to come, but we exaggerate the importance of this one over the many in the past. Every generation sees its decline in what comes next, and everyone trembles as destruction draws near. Perhaps it's just a change in our illusions. The young make new myths, and their lives suit those stories. In that case, it's the same as it ever was, but what if there is one that marks the end of it? Just because they've always been false alarms doesn't mean this one is too.

The daughter and then the next daughter too. And again and again forever. Always along the way, at last and alone, they come one after another.

Beautiful writing lies at the surface, it is shiny and brilliant. Like poetry, it bathes the things around it in an aura. That's how beauty is conceived. Those who see it in order and organization, they have the crystal-clear discipline of the universe coming to itself in the passage of time through design and abundance. The grace and beauty of it is what matters, but what if we have to rethink that? What if the beauty is in the depth and complexity of sophisticated structures? Their elegance lies in the way layers break through each other and cause endless reorientations and motion. This is a different approach altogether, isn't it? Where beauty is no longer skin deep but defines the organs yielding shape to flesh and the skeleton and muscles that bear movement. Where once Beauty, Charm, and Fertility hold sway, we earn Light, Justice, and Peace. This begets a deeper sense, more congenial and alive. No longer a surface of this one against that other, but an endless dance where the three are in a constant embrace pushing the interplay of their relationship to appearances. They overwhelm vision with their deeper nature.

Whatever we achieve in this life, caring for our friends and families while learning what we can about those around us and the world they make, it comes with the glow of bold indecision. The less sure we are, the prettier the notion appears. Certainty and precision ally with simplicity whereas confusion and fuzziness are signs of complexity and abundance. Rich meaning sends us round and round in endless circling and an infinite thrust. Godmother and goddaughter, both staying in place and the movement around them. A niece who comes and a mother who goes. Back and forth, we are incapable of the solitude that brings us face to face across the divide that inhabits us. We live close by the ones we love. We must make and make and make until everyone is where they are supposed to be.

This one's goddaughter never talks to her even if those others smoothly slide one alongside the other. Even now, with so much at stake, she cannot fathom the experience since we have not shown that side of ourselves to her. We stay put and fade into the fire, into the warmth, into the slow cooking and savory nourishment of life beneath a roof. So it is with illusions that separate the years and the generations of the living from those who pass them by. We are separated by the stories we tell, and we are brought back together too. If we could find this new depth, if we could find the beauty in it, then maybe there will be justice and peace, maybe then the light will shine.

Such nonsense. Always so much nonsense. It's better to find time for the simplest things and leave beauty alone. Feigning complexity is among our many illusions and orchestrates separation better than anything else.

Pro and Contra

You will suffer one illusion. Delusion? At least one. But definitely one. There's no way to avoid it. You can switch, but there will always be one. This whole world entails it, follows from it, and orders or organizes you with it. Sanity: simple acquiescence to the goals of those around you as though they are law and fact. Can I choose, or is that already my choice?

Suppose Wolfe is telling the truth. In that world, he's a hero. He offsets Em's stubbornness and stupidity with his own magnanimity and friendship. Now, he is liberated and looking to fly free of what holds him back in their partnership. Turns out, Em is a tyrant, directing things through the order he finds, the architectonic he proposes. Wolfe and his free will dig into the salt of the earth and find spontaneities and curiosities. Em is the villain in this illusion, he pulls the strings. Now is the time to question him, to toss him aside, and smash the patriarchy: I renounce the illusion that props Em up as a paragon of virtue and draws Wolfe as a victim of narcissism and megalomania.

The living change their story when confronting accusations from the dead. It's possible they are exactly what they seem, it's possible that what's wrong lies right where you think it does when following along as the dutiful acolyte. In one, egoman lives and uses cunning and ambition to persuade me of his virtue. In the other, the one made object by time, the one who haunts us, he proposes the straight and narrow. Shouldn't we distrust the living? The dead have fewer motives. Both Wolfe's side and Em's seem reasonable when documenting and registering them with resident authorities. Only when the other's claims are set off against an opponent are their assertions called into question. These are personal illusions, do the facts matter to anyone? Can I just decide and then align with the decision? Wolfe resists, he revolts, but that's his choice. He doesn't have to do it that way, he could agree with my father's story, he could succumb to the same illusion. If he shares it with me and we convince everyone it's true, have we turned our personal illusions into a mass illusion? Is that how it always works with mass delusion? Have we been sold some private dimension?

What if it's necessary to promote happiness and well-being?

If social instincts like sympathy materialize in the community and not the species, some embrace more broadly defined communities according to the rules of neo-liberalism and globalization. Is that the bond between center left and left? The illusion divides, it's like a living cell, it grows and grows, it eats believers, and manufactures worlds and worlds of worlds.

Talking heads tell us what private matters are of public concern: everyone must have an opinion and there is a broad selection to choose from.

Aggression contra civilization, ego contra libido, self-love contra object-love, outward aggression turns inward as conscience, enabling civilization to take its place within us. Guilt, from superego and external authority, is the price.

What is this? Mere appearance cast back upon its light source. Does guilt provide a sense of illusion or *is* it the sense of illusion? Is it the social voice that inhabits me or is it me raging against the mechanisms wound up and sprung by crowds and their momentum?

Often the devices we use to alleviate any one of these will exacerbate the others: products of civilization improve the body or control nature. Civilization as a source of suffering means we pay for these protections. With an illusion or is it a real payment? Some pound of flesh? A burning in the eyes? What? What is the payment? Who pays? Can't be me, I am what is at stake. Everyone around each other, quivering, we tremble together and huddle for warmth. I cannot find the logic, I don't know who's responsible. There is no manual, there are no rules, you cast the die and hope for the best. Isn't that always how it goes? Who tracks the status from beginning to end and who measures outcomes over and against effort?

Did we ever get that "pathology of communities"? What will it do to the illusions that keep us in check, to the illusions that help us through the day and with each other and with everything that matters?

Is ethics a cultural superego or is it just conscience enforced by culture? There is no accommodation for social agency in the domain of ethics, no concept of agency in its intersubjective body.

Here is this gargantuan, it protects these people. Here is another and it protects those. The two fight each other. The one gets the upper hand, then the other. We're forced to ask, could they do otherwise? If not, what remains? What decisions do they make, how do they act, are they just like the rest of us, with their visions of the happiness they seek? Everything degrades into metaphor. The reasonable institution is nowhere, we don't know how to make it conform to human agendas.

The existence of extra-individual beings turns us around. We worry about the excellent ones because we associate them with the power of the incorporated. They are dangerous, and we attack to protect ourselves.

Wolfe has it that he's the communist and Em the aristocrat. Em has it that Wolfe is the aristocrat and Em the communist. Both claim they're looking out for the good of everyone and both are internationalist in scope and commandment.

Excellence will have its due, that's an elitist and aristocratic posture. One thousand villages over one thousand generations for the sake of making that one who can produce what is most profound and meaningful.

The action must apply, the illusion must be shared. A singular and isolated delusion is a disease. There is always hope, the lone patient conveys their point of view and convinces others to follow. There is always a chance. Maybe they'll leave a record behind and die madmen, but their legacy finds followers, a movement ensues, buildings and altars, and before you know it the apparitions spread to countless others who sing the praises of those long gone. We find a way and sickness becomes the norm when we fall in love with our trauma. So long as human beings are the battleground, there's always hope the mad become sane, and the sane mad. The boundaries are not fixed, theirs is a condition of perpetual motion back and forth. Circling around and around, it comes for each of us, it lures us into its swirl.

The lie rolls off the tongue. They are so easy in their distrust. Do they know what they are doing?

His objection to noise is that it makes it harder to hear excellence. The ridiculous don't get free speech, not because anyone prevents them, they just can't do it.

This is the swirl. This is its primary thrust. I am numb to it. There are sounds and sights, but they cannot reach me. Those men, do they know what haunts them? This should be the only test they face. Ask them to detail their illusion, ask them to identify that falsehood without which they could not live. If they can do it, they achieve levels worthy of us. If they cannot, they are lost forever.

Mihalis depends on the myth of his own sophistication. It props up his public world. If he's not perched at the acme of civilization, then he's nowhere. He cannot live without this illusion. It's what makes his insights more poignant and powerful than the others. It's why he's the one who educates and leads them out of darkness and into an enlightened state where he is master. Forget that his system originates with the colonizers, forget that you learn *how* to think. I'm sure his material is diverse, I'm sure he proffers inclusion and gentle lessons that bring the whole class along without shock and awe. It is so perfect and so sophisticated. No one is triggered while he preaches the grandeur of the working man and then spends every one of his days promoting forms of thought that belittle him. He questions as though his vision is perfect, as though he's without illusion, and that the whole purpose of his life is to expose the liberal truth. What if you can't see that? Then you are a fool and there's no reaching you.

If I ask him, does he admit it? Does he see through his own blind spot?

What about Ion? What can't he see? He's just as comfortable in the world where he lives. He thinks everything is set for the time to come. It doesn't matter if he's virtuous in this vision, it doesn't matter how elegant his taste, for he believes today will be like yesterday and tomorrow just the same. The rhythm and pace of life in this town, that is what he knows. There is a fabric that covers his time, a set of assumptions. The others are a hypothetical proposition, they don't exist here and now on the walk between the roundabout and the little café where he gets his Frappé.

I repeat myself. Over and over again, it finds its way into everything. This man vs. that man. This man vs. that man. Is this the illusion? Why should these coincidental events decide anything? If I make this shot, it means I'm done for the day. That exterior plan making personality, it'll never be enough.

Let's see if I can identify each of the selections. Wolfe or Dad. Here or there. School or not. Ion or Mihalis. Art or science. What is the orchestration? Why go to such lengths and what illusion lies beneath them? Does it frame the civilization or does illusion lie in the appearance of choice? Don't I choose the dilemma? Haven't I put myself here to make things as difficult as possible?

While I drift deeper and deeper into these combatting dream worlds, Mom wakes up. The work, day in and day out, is exactly what she's looking for. Her whole life she's in the shadow of a selection and none of it makes her happy, none of it assuages the guilt or drives the chill of fear and anger off into the distance. What's changing? What is she stumbling into? Is it her choice? It's my condition too. I find these poles, and I seek them and place myself firmly between them. That is my doing. What illusion drives me? Who stands behind it?

Let's consider this hard truth: people have the dilemmas they want to have, and civilizations have the conflicts they want to have. We don't know how to identify the real agents. *Want to have.* Who wants? It is the being we carve from a plurality of things in motion. Think of the solar system. Its name grants it a friendly and comfortable existence. It is one thing: the solar system. There it is. What could be simpler? There are many things in it: a star and planets, spinning rocks and revolving bodies. So many different things at work, orchestrating against each other, intermingling and playfully bobbing up and down over and against each other. It's not hardly one thing, but many things integrated through forces and laws. Everything is like that. Existence is a myth. How do you know you won't break apart and become many things? How do you know you won't keep doing it over and over again, each time differently?

In love and friendship, in enmity and war, there are these beings that hover above us. We think we do this, we think there's one vision that drives our choice, but we can't conceive any larger momentum than the way many things dance around each other in illusory motion.

There is no real conflict except the one I invent for myself. The tension is for the sake of a lesson, something I want to show myself, something I must see. No, no, not me. It. The thing that is in motion, the things that are in motion, they drive toward something. They appear as this point of contention, as this one over and against that one. Nietzsche or Marx. Ion or Mihalis. Wolfe or Em. Thinking or doing. That's the illusion, the play between. It's intervention interlude interruption.

Is that what they argue about?

I should ask them and make them sort it out for me. It's hard to believe I can't ask my dad. I will never see him again. Repeat it and I may believe it. Feel it. If he can be here, he can give an answer. Only when someone dies do you learn the one true question for them. What do I think he says? What is your one illusion? He tells me about Mom and how they're together and what promises they make. He does, I know he does, he knows that's an illusion, but insists on it. What about Wolfe, what's his poison, what's he willing to admit? He'll give a different answer depending on which day I ask. He switches with the wind. Nothing is the illusion he depends on, and nothing makes it possible to get out of bed. No, Wolfe's changing answers suggest that what really matters to Wolfe is Wolfe and the illusion that drives him is himself. He believes his own press and stops listening.

The truth of this thinking and moving presents itself. Any criteria I use, any claim I make, I deduce the answer. I already know it. It only manages a single small step back and forces me to look at the same question again and again from an ever-changing point of view. What am I taking for granted? What do I rely on to make this choice? What spirits drive the affirmation? Whether you're Nietzsche or Marx, both are under the spell and there is no way out.

These notes don't show the truth, they show conflict and tension and raise the question concerning truth. It's not some concrete thing, it's an invention and then it is real. Truth is a fabrication, an apparatus that comes into existence in the form of a question, a real and pressing question. Once we think it, we are beggars. There's the one and there's the other, the deliberation, and then the decision. That's it. It forces choice, applies a dominant apparition, and end of story. When you find yourself looking for the one and only truth, it is a conflict, and it'll guide your life and drive you down one road or another. Which? Forget it, just go. That's the only thing you can do.

Arrival

I'm too exhausted for the get together, but I enjoy myself anyway. You make me feel right at home. Not just you, everyone. Europea and Stamatia are friends since childhood, aren't they? There's a third, but she has died. They have children who grow up together. The siblings and each with a spouse and kids, it adds up. Do the people there today trace back to those three women? I talk to almost everyone, I think. Even the little girl. Is her name Thespina? I forget so many names.

Not Ion's, your beautiful young friend. Hard not to notice and remember. We talk so much about inequality, but we never mention the inequality of being so beautiful. I hang on his every word. Everyone is so attentive. Does he have enough to eat? Is he comfortable? Everyone. I do it too. I can't help myself. It must come from somewhere deep down. I wonder if he's as deep and extraordinary as he seems. He tells me he loves Rilke and writes poetry as an homage. He says the intellect has no place in beautiful language, that it's a feast for the eyes and ears, for the nose and the skin. He sounds so enrapt, listening to him carries me away. He may be full of shit. Maybe it's nonsense. Rilke's work is not without intellect. It can be highly cerebral and deep. So maybe Ion spouts nonsense and I nod to be agreeable.

How does he ever know? His whole life he's placated. Are you actually familiar with any of his poems? Are they any good? Maybe over the years encouragement comes from the simple prejudice that beauty must be grand.

I admire the way you move between guests, by the way. When first I meet you, I don't think of you that way. You seem so serious and introspective, you must be shy, but I guess introverts aren't always shy, are they? It's your party, your element. Everyone eagerly engages you, and you're so at ease, spreading your attention evenly and making everyone welcome. Your mother and Ariti, is she your godmother? They take care of the necessities, but they aren't the social center. I try talking to them, but they're busy. I never see guests so busy at a party. Do they enjoy it? It's hard to tell. I wish I could spend more time with them, it seems old fashioned.

Getting here is such a hike. The direct flight from Newark to Athens is fine, but then the little plane with the propellers. I'm deathly afraid. I've never been on a plane like that before. How are they still in operation? Once I calm down, it's lovely. Looking back, I wish I could enjoy it, but the sound of the engines, and how close everything seems. That beautiful sea and coastline should have a calming effect, but it just feels too up close. I feel exposed, and much prefer the seclusion of a jet. Or I think I do.

Thank you for letting me stay in your home, and please thank everyone who is put out by it. Your uncle keeps saying something about the arrangements, I assume that's for my benefit. If so, I'm terribly sorry. Please be sure to thank everyone. Better yet, let me know the details and I'll thank them myself.

Europea is your grandmother, their mother, isn't she? That much I get. She lives a few blocks over with Eirini. She is Nikos and Maria's daughter, and Stamatia's granddaughter. Is that right? Your father is Eirini's godfather, I think, but who is Renya? I couldn't speak much to the older ladies tonight, they don't speak English, do they? But the depth of their friendship is obvious. They're very comfortable with each other. More than sisters. At least more than I am with my sister. We talk and we're supportive, but we live different lives. We're always catching up. Not those two, they finish each other's sentences. This is from my imagination, mind you, but that's the sense I get. They live nearby their whole lives, and it adds so much depth. I've never seen anything like it. Maybe because I live in New York. Maybe it's still like that in parts of America, in smaller towns where people stay put. I hope that's true. There could be a whole culture somewhere that I've lost touch with where things like that still go on, where people aren't moving away from each other and taking jobs across the country and only seeing family every couple of years. I'm out of touch. Everyone who matters is spread out.

It seems like you're the same way with Eirini. Maybe not exactly the same, but there's something like that between you. She definitely has that with her friend. I only spoke with her for a few minutes when she stops by with her boyfriend. I don't remember his name. I don't recall much about him. I don't mean any offense by that, it's just that Eirini and her friend are so fascinating. I can see their whole lives ahead of them. They work in town and have no interest in moving away. They grow up here, go away to school for a little while, and then come back. Never think of doing it any other way. I don't mean to be insulting. Maybe it's only someone like me who thinks it's insulting, but it just doesn't seem like they're terribly ambitious. They have what they want and just want more of the same. They want to be around their family and their friends, and they don't spend a lot of time worrying about their jobs and what they don't have. I ask them what they do, and they seem a little confused. Why does it matter? Eirini insists I try one of the dishes I'm avoiding. It changes the subject. She's very kind. I think she makes a special effort to include me.

Somehow, we end up talking about sustainable farming. Eirini says she doesn't understand Americans on social, the way they talk about diet and food. She thinks our food must come from giant factories and complicated processing centers. It's a pork dish and that's why I'm avoiding it. I tell her I'm a vegan, and she points at the whisky, the mustard, and some of the other spices. A lot of fossil fuels are burned transporting them around the world. I don't push it and think it's silly to stand on principle as a guest. I should get to know it the way she does. It's arrogant to think my rules are the only legitimate ones. What do I know? Yogurt and Honey, she says, are huge parts of the local customs and culture. They have no idea how to eat without them. Imagine going to the Czech Republic and refusing to try beer. Or going to Paris and not eating a crepe in the streets. Or anywhere else with whatever local customs and foods sustain them for centuries. Globalization makes me judgmental. Everyone should follow the one true culture. There's so much we do to make the whole world alike.

What Eirini's friend says haunts me. An American girl lectures her about the immorality of eating meat, and then she opens her iPhone to show her some facts. Her iPhone, she emphasizes. Where do the materials come from? What misery did their production cause? She probably gets a new one whenever a new model comes out and tosses the old one. Where does the battery go, or the parts, those heavy metals and that screen? Not to mention the labor to produce it and the network infrastructure around it. Sustainability is important, she says, the whole region will be under water, but it won't be because they eat a lot of yogurt and honey. It'll be because people who don't live anywhere near here build giant data centers and huge energy infrastructure to power their financial system. They don't care about sustainability and the health of the planet. She speaks simply and isn't angry. She just can't believe the level of delusion that this girl lives with if she seriously believes what she says. She is sad too. People suffer. They work hard their whole lives and then they die forgotten and alone. So many stories. Americans forgotten by their society, and this girl complains about yogurt in the food. Because she has to be pure to her vegan principles. You know, to stop the suffering.

That's when I see you talking to the professor, the one from the nearby university. I've forgotten his name and the town. It seems like you two are pretty friendly. Are there two men that you're seeing? I don't mean to pry. He says some interesting things after you leave us. Once you tell him about the Ben Thorne connection, he gets very chatty. He wants to tell me so many things and has a lot of theories. One stands out, it's something I haven't heard before. He thinks there's a Lord Shaftesbury influence in *Princess Myshkin*. He says something about order as a function of beauty and charm. The so-called princess is the highest form of womanly grace. She's charming and beautiful, that's what legitimizes her reign. At least at first. It flows easily from her, that's how the story begins. She's effortlessly herself, but then it becomes clear that there's great difficulty in achieving that level of order, that beauty and that charm. She's a slave to it. We discover that in the end at least, she spends much of her energy and time perfecting her ways and making them appear effortless. Even her beauty is laboriously achieved. It isn't just genes, it's styling and cosmetics. It's such an effort and she pulls it off seamlessly. Your friend thinks it's an attack on Shaftesbury. Not so much an attack as an alternative. He thinks Ben Thorne is one of the most sensitive students of order and organization in the history of literature. He talks like that. He says the characters are always inhabited by far away devices making them robots and automatons. At least until they discover it and do something to change.

He mentions evolution, something about the selfish gene. The genes, to survive, make container organisms carry them around so they can better copy themselves. We're their automatons. He says in Ben Thorne's work order functions that way and Shaftesbury doesn't disagree, discussing the social orientation of human beings more than any other thinker from that era and praising it for its power and influence over human virtue. It's fascinating because your friend places the moral notion from Darwin's work on a par with what he gets from Shaftesbury. It resonates with some things you've been saying. Have you two been talking about this? He says something about the role of genre too. I recall something like that during the car ride from the airport. You say you've found some notes somewhere. Fred's researching it too. Let's talk more about it.

I really don't mean to pry, it's just that he touches on many of the same themes that you and I have been discussing. It seems like you two are talking about it. You must be, aren't you?

If so, I just want to raise one tiny warning. He's an academic whose area of specialization includes contemporary English and American literature. He has a strong professional interest in Ben Thorne. Clearly, you haven't told him anything too compromising, but you should be careful. He's opportunistic. It's not his fault, I don't mean to attack him, he seems like a lovely person, but he is in that world, and it is dog-eat-dog. Those people cannot survive if they're not ambitious and opportunistic. They're the engine that feeds the crows of social. I see it often, we're always coming across them. They promote their own careers and their own angles. It's how they get ahead: the public intellectual representing the best of public opinion. They are judged by their influence, who cites their work, and who invites them to present. He would kill to learn everything you know about Ben Thorne. I deal with people like that every day. Even the nicest, when push comes to shove, betray friends for professional advancement. I've seen it too many times not to be cautious. Take it for what it's worth.

By the way, is Mia going back to the States around the same time I am? That's what I remember you saying. I'm glad I'll be staying so close to you both, I think we'll make good progress.

Wolfe is not happy I'm here and doesn't let me bring the interns. He vetoes that, saying he can't be alone at this crucial time, he needs someone around to help. He tries to make me feel horrible for deserting him. I learn long ago not to be fooled by the tender voice in the work. He's difficult and demanding. He has no qualms about using guilt to get you to do what he wants. He tugs on me in different ways to get me to cancel this trip. He does and he doesn't want us to talk to each other, he does and he doesn't want us to develop a good rapport. He says things to play off my insecurities. It's despicable. He'll do anything to get what he wants.

His opportunism is just like that sense of liberty alien to order and central to *Princess Myshkin*. There's that dysphoric scene somewhere around the middle of the book. Do you remember it? The princess is wondering what a life without order is like, she imagines random events, how magical and chaotic everything would be. There's nothing for very long and nothing to rely on. Things come out of nowhere and sweep you up and carry you away. You may even break apart into millions of tiny pieces. Everything is so monstrous, where the monster is that very thing that has no reliable order, it's disorganized and chaotic. It comes from everywhere and hunts for everything. It terrifies her at first, as she hears it speak, but then she grows more comfortable. She gets used to it as she learns how to make use of it. Alienation isn't you outside yourself, but things outside you taking over, putting themselves there in your place. You're a million different things, only what is arbitrary and temporary makes you one thing.

I don't know if it's a standard interpretation, but I always think of the David Bowie bit at the beginning of the novel. It's a foreshadowing of the scene in the middle. She hears a theory from some pompous suitor, something about how aliens can't just come to Earth but have to figure out how to embed themselves among us. It's because the viruses and parasites would kill them. They can't get to know human beings because they can't mix with them, so the aliens learn how to grow their own humans and embed them among us. They are outsiders, but inside. He claims David Bowie is one of them, raised by aliens and let loose on the Earth to learn about us and report back. The Earthly biography is a cover story. Then he gets sick, and his body dies. They can't save him, there's no way back. The process of incarnation cannot be undone, and it is terminal. In the book, she reminds her suitor that his theory is like the movie, the one with Bowie in the lead role: *The Man Who Fell to Earth*. He's a know-it-all and rejects the comparison, but she insists. She says something about alienation too, doesn't she? That's why I always connect the two scenes. The alienation the princess feels and the alienation she imagines the man who fell to earth must feel, she thinks they're the same and both come from the order keeping them together, keeping them centered, beautiful, and charming. Everyone is infatuated by it. Order defines both what is and what is not. Her beauty, she thinks, rests on its absence in others. The same for charm, order always works that way, it includes because it excludes. It makes things work by eliminating whatever doesn't fit. It's a cruel process even if its fruits come mixed with yogurt and honey.

I don't know why I'm going on about this. I'm sleepy and tonight my heart is full: I am drunk and stuffed. There's so much coming at me, so much to think about. I really just want to say how happy I am to be here and how grateful I am to you and your family for including me.

Residual

Light: What is wrong with order?
Peace: I don't understand. Where is this coming from?
Justice: Why is it even a question? What is the alternative?

Light: You mean our lives and our very existence? Everything depends on order, it *is* according to order.

Peace: A single order?

Light: No, multiple. Scientists for millennia have sought their origins. Knowledge seeks them. Predictability and comprehension depend on them. To understand an individual event is to understand the order in it.

Peace: It is a real thing. Why ask what is wrong with it?

Light: Stability survives. It defines survival.

Justice: There are unstable orders.

Light: What makes an order unstable?

Justice: If what it holds disappears or dissolves, it is unstable.

Light: In that case, the order dissolves, it fails to order, fails to be order.

Peace: Patterns which may or may not persist. Is that what it is?

Light: Like an explosion. They are momentary and then over and done with. They are unstable and cannot last, they immediately strive toward alternative forms and alternative states.

Peace: Aren't there rules and properties for explosions?

Light: Indeed, there are. From one explosion to another, we identify what is common.

Justice: There are orders that are not stable, that are ordered states of instability.

Light: Any operation reduces to patterns with rules and properties, even an operation that is unstable, an exploding thing.

Peace: This discussion makes a false turn. We start with what is wrong with order and we cannot see any way around it. If there is something wrong with it, then everything is wrong.

Justice: It is hard to stay focused on the individual thing. They withdraw into generalities, formalities and aggregate notions. The set that emerges, that is the order of things following its rules and possessing its properties.

Light: Rules and properties, is that it? Rules for a thing or set of things can be identified. If they define properties, there is an order.

Peace: This seems abstract.

Light: Consider something rudimentary, like Hydrogen.

Justice: Hydrogen is not rudimentary, you invoke an enormous order when identifying a collective notion.

Light: What about a single Hydrogen atom?

Justice: That is not without its order. To identify a single atom as a single atom, let alone as an atom of the type Hydrogen, structure is at work. We dissect atoms into protons and electrons, we observe and isolate the thing. This takes billions of years.

Peace: You set us on a path to investigate what is wrong with order and we cannot begin, we cannot identify a single thing in this world without it.

Light: What we've discovered is a problem with ourselves. We see the order in knowing and confuse it with the order in being.

Justice: We could talk about a plain patch of material, or a simple tone.

Light: Observation and listening are complex behaviors, they already lend an order when identifying whatever simple thing lies before us.

Peace: Order is everywhere. Even in the simplest of things.

Justice: Perhaps we can distinguish between artificial and natural orders, those that are given and those are made.

Light: The original question should be, given the universal presence of order, what constitutes the wrong and right of it?

Justice: Clearly no natural order can be wrong since there is no way to work around it. Perhaps our problem is not so much with order as it is with being wrong and how it attaches to the artificial.

Peace: Wrong in some moral sense? Artificial as in fabricated?

Light: I am not comfortable with these notions. Humans result from a process according to rules and properties. Humans are intelligent beings: they posit the existence of something that is not and then they make it.

Peace: Human beings make things.

Light: Yes, and humans are made. Things are made, then they make things. Rivers are made and they make things. Stars are made and they make things. Causality is a chain. Reason is natural, its products artificial.

Justice: That's not helpful.

Light: Stable or unstable, natural or artificial, these categories don't define order or say what is wrong with it.

Peace: You accuse and attack some forms while condoning or praising others.

Light: When we attack them, it is most often the fabricated orders that are in focus. We say one or the other is wrong. What do we mean by that?

Justice: You don't mean that it is unstable or artificial.

Light: It may be, but there's nothing obviously wrong with that. It may be like an explosion, some momentary alliance or concert for the sake of what sets the stage. It may be cultural, like mimicry of facial gestures when sitting opposite one another.

Peace: We insist on the distinctions to hide something from ourselves, something about our alienation.

Light: One problem we confront is whether there is an ordering at work even in our discussions of order, and what can go wrong with them. There is no way to approach an answer without already ordering.

Justice: You do something wrong while determining what is wrong.

Light: We move in a circle even when we move in a straight line.

Peace: Human beings must counterbalance their natural abilities with the ordering power of civilization, artificial or not.

Justice: Civilization is a balancing act. It gets out of whack when there is either too much personal liberty or too much social conformity.

Light: This is highly arbitrary. It is a human problem, right and wrong always is, but can we generalize the principle? Can we identify the set?

Justice: Order is balance between set and member integrity. When order occurs, what we mean is that multiple things are set in order, their grouping accords with determinate rules and properties. Members are aggregated and attributed at the expense of their peculiar ways.

Light: Order is a set theory. The set is ordered, order makes it a set. It isn't just that the type can solve some paradox in how sets are defined, the type is its essence. The set is how the type is formed, the type is how the set is formed. Each member fits the type, they are tokens of it.

Justice: The rules and properties of a set may be too draconian, and rob members of other qualities, other aspects. A set is wrong if its rules destroy the members.

Peace: An order is wrong if it fails to balance between factors. If the members are violated to force inclusion, there is too much conformity. If the set is violated because the members are too independent, there is too much integrity.

Light: I fear there is a problem when moving from metaphor to reality. Inclusion in a set is an abstraction. The violation of the member or the violation of the set, these are boundaries broken or made firm. That is not the same thing as civilization and its discontents.

Justice: Yes! The mind is malleable, it is made to change, it is made to adapt. The mind identifies, and that can be harmful, it happens as the members interact. The mind both determines and is determined.

Light: Let's call it the psyche.

Justice: I don't mean to invoke some mystical thing: blocks of wood in the set of cubes are different from human beings in a civilization.

Peace: Humans experience distress and pain, they can be happy and joyful. They form a world for each other and identify themselves, making each other part of something based only on what they think and the actions that come from that.

Light: To say that there is something wrong with an order is hard to parse. The individual identity moves and changes, the block of wood cannot. If we tighten the set to only include cubes of a specific volume, we make the set more uniform and remove members from it. If we do the equivalent with humans, none are removed, since they adjust their thinking.

Peace: A human can change their volume, or whatever the analogous property may be.

Justice: Like if a political idea catches on and the civilization becomes defined by adherence to it or rejection of it. People must change to fit in.

Peace: Or be changed.

Justice: Yes, it may come by force. Members who are not willing to change are removed.

Light: Once you are removed, you are outside its protections, separate from its rules and properties. You are vulnerable.

Justice: The order includes enforcement. There are violent and coercive orders that ensure their rules are upheld. Beauty and symmetry too. Declension informs the order, sets its boundaries, and enforces hierarchies among its properties.

Light: Rules and properties are normative in civilization. They are not rules and properties like those that cubes follow.

Peace: You mean the rules are not necessary, they can be violated. The cube has a volume, and the rule for computing it is determinate. The quantity of the volume is fixed, but with normative rules, there is a choice.

Light: They can be enforced. Normative rules do not teach us about sets and their members, rather sets and their members teach us about normative rules. There are decisions.

Justice: The decision need not be made by a member, it can be coerced, but a member either adapts or does not: a block cannot decide.

Peace: Suppose there is a way to shrink or grow cubes. Cubes can be modified to fit the set. Some decisions are made during enforcement.

Light: What can go wrong with an order lies in the rules in place to enforce membership and in how those rules apply.

Justice: It lies in the consequences for those members who do not follow the rules or who resist enforcement.

Peace: Is there an order that can define right and wrong?

Justice: What is good and evil, right and wrong, is still undetermined.

Light: Treat everyone with respect. Maximize the general welfare. These rules may define the set of ethical acts. Those acts that fail to follow the rule are excluded from the set.

Justice: Conditions are in place to force us to fit good actions together. Training and discipline may do harm to individual beings. Neurosis is the outcome. Here is a well-heeled ethical society filled with maladjusted individuals who berate themselves with painful experiences from guilt caused by the desire to act in violation of rules.

Light: The rules violate the balance between the set and its members.

Peace: Are you saying that even the rule to act ethically is coercive?

Light: I am saying that this rule is especially coercive.

Justice: It is the crux of the dilemma.

Peace: What is the alternative?

Light: Insofar as we apply a single order with universal characteristics to cover the aggregate of circumstances and acts, we are on dangerous ground. We are likely to create an order that is too far-reaching, and that has harmful effects on its members.

Peace: What does that mean in practice?

Justice: That the all-pervasive formal rule is eliminated.

Light: Any collection of ordered acts creates a higher order, raising problems of enforcement and coercion. Associating good acts with each other in a set according to rule, we create a higher order that replicates the logic by forming an aggregate. Conformity reigns.

Peace: Does this give us insight into what is wrong with order?

Light: If there is non-order encompassing order, does it break recursion? What if the bad order, what is wrong with it, happens when non-order is missing, and the recursion goes on forever?

Peace: What is that? How can we describe it?

Justice: At least two sets are always required to offset each other, to frame each other, and to provide boundary conditions.

Light: What goes wrong with order? It can apply itself in such a way that nothing escapes its grasp, as if it were singular and not multiple, as though it has no origin and no end, no boundaries, nothing outside it, no conditions, and no residual.

The Will to Will

Corporation as Intermediary

Is it interlude contra intervention or interlude and intervention? The repetition of intervention is interlude. That's Wolfe. The repetition of interlude is an intervention. That's the path Eleni Hajivasiliou traces in Em's notes. The former seeks to intervene, to bring interlude to an end. The latter deepens the event, lures it outside itself making it spin out of control. We needn't call it an escape. The first sees departure as an end to be achieved: interlude is to be interrupted, it ceases under the conditions, and then life continues along its way with events emitted, analyzed, and fed back to where they came from with new eyes and new vision. With the second, there is no escape, no removal or return to a happy origin: there is only haunting and its residual, a barely audible echo of what transpires.

Consider the dynamic closely. This is what they do for days, each day, the whole day, when they meet in the office and walk through it, look after it, and turn it over and over. To be an interlude there must be a first and second act, and each must stand on its own. To play between one and the other there must be a one and another. No escaping it. There, intervention is a simple thrust and, once achieved, need not repeat. Suppose the narrator comes on stage and says let's bring this farce to a close and open the second act. Despite appearances, the moment of completion begins in the first act, then the interlude is interrupted by a second act, and only when that ends, will the ending of the interlude be the end of an interlude.

What's happening? Is the narrator the authority? Is everyone meant to listen to the spin and take it at face value, or might the characters disagree? What if they steadfastly assert themselves independently? Ginna asks. Eleni assures her that they most definitely do, there is no alternative. They cannot follow along and do what they are told, they cannot even hear it. The narrator is always unreliable making interlude seem to end as the second act begins, but for the characters, it's only just beginning. The interlude prevails and they persist. Not in it, but with it inside them. Behind and calling out to them, pushing and pulling every which way, they brave the second act to find interlude's end.

Ben Thorne thinks the interlude is the repetition of intervention. Ben Thorne thinks the repetition of interlude is intervention. What does Ben Thorne think? Ben Thorne thinks you can get out of the interlude. Ben Thorne thinks you can never get out of the interlude, that it inhabits and haunts you throughout the second act. What does Ben Thorne think?

* * *

The corporate body transcends human mortality. The onset of permanence is bolstered by worship. These intelligent machines distributed across time and space trickle between human experiences inflating them with their artificial vision measuring each event. Together side by side in an evolutionarily stable set, our prayers permit them to get away with murder. And robbery. And whatever else they like. For a fee. It balances the books of life and death, counting us each as profit or loss. Yes, dear one, you are of value, just see how much life they suck and how great is its worth in the marketplace where we meet.

Two young women leave Chicago to visit family in Missouri. They're caught out after sundown in a town where they shouldn't be. There's a rally at a festival. They're killed, beaten to death. The events are disputed. They emit signals as they take place. Police are not called to the scene, they are already at the scene before the young women arrive and they're at the scene when the women die. They take statements and call paramedics. This is public record. The reports are filed. No one sees anything. There is no physical evidence to collect. No prints, no body camera footage, no witness reports, not a trace. The federal bureau of investigation does a pro forma review. No grounds for action until further evidence is obtained. If anyone remembers seeing anything, they should come forward.

The case is ready to close, but a couple lawyers from a women's support center in Chicago intervene and file discovery requests. They obtain video footage. No one explains how it's missing or why it isn't there already. The lawyers get it and show the violence. Twelve members of the crowd are identified and named in a lawsuit. The police officers on the scene are also named.

Without explanation, people recall the events, they remember everything clearly. The young women, with no history of violence (although both have histories that include violence), become agitated when encountering the rally. They threaten the crowd. The crowd has no choice but to defend themselves, and the police confirm the story.

Janelle Williams and Vida Lomas are both under five feet five inches tall. Both women weigh less than one hundred and fifty pounds. There are more than fifty people present at the rally, there are at least twelve who are involved in their deaths. These are facts, all of it, what is reported, the sequence, the deaths, the participants, these are facts.

The Liberty News Network reports these facts and adds commentary. Broadcast recordings show they don't just talk about events after the fact, they talk about them before. They mention the festival and the rally, they mention the reasons for it and why it's important for participants to take their community back. They talk about other rallies like it. They mention that radicals often come and incite violence preventing good people from exercising their rights. They say there's an extremely high likelihood it'll happen again. Before the lawyers come, LNN already uses the same tropes and motifs. In interviews, participants, especially the twelve, mention the news stories on LNN announcing the rally and its risks.

There are people at LNN who think the network plays off fear and anger to keep ratings high. There are people at LNN who think the network focuses on the news, and that this alone is responsible for their viewers' loyalty. They think the viewers are already afraid and the network provides information they need. LNN thinks that fear is a legitimate factor for gaining market share. LNN thinks it is a news network. LNN thinks.

Their archrival is Community Cable News. CCN and LNN are antagonists in an inverted lockstep. When LNN says it's raining, CCN says it's dry. CCN does not think the upcoming event is newsworthy and have nothing to say about it. LNN thinks it is the most important event of the week and runs a story every day. Once the footage appears, CCN thinks it's the most important story of the day and LNN stops mentioning it. Self-defense, end of story. Murder and intrigue, beginning of story.

CCN and LNN think ratings are good.

Mia reasons with Gwen and Bert that if corporations are people and people are culpable for premeditated actions, then corporations are culpable under the same laws with the same penalties. This is the first premise.

Mia reasons that if you yell fire in a crowded theatre, you cause a response. What if there is a fire and people are trampled trying to escape? Criminal culpability requires that the report be false. What if the one who yells is mistaken? They think there is a fire, but there isn't. The report must be false and the one who reports it must know that. There must be an intention to cause havoc. This is the second premise.

Their discussion focuses on the next step, the next premise. This is what eludes them. LNN reports on the upcoming event and flags the associated risks. They have no credible reports of plans to disrupt the rally, they have no information suggesting there will be trouble, but they report on its likelihood anyway. They use inductive reasoning and describe past rallies and past disruptions. They show that those rallies are similar to this one. The young women fit the description of typical troublemakers. Are they just working with an inductive model and making a reasonable correlation? If they are, they're just facts. They're telling the truth and there's no malice. Bert fears that even if the LNN stories are responsible for panic when women of color turn up near an evening rally in Aspre, Missouri, they still can't be held culpable. Reporting on aggregate likelihood and predictions based on past observations comes with good reason. No malice, just careful empirical observations for people to do with as they see fit.

Both Ben Thorne and LNN emit information about events. People from different walks of life emit information. Some of it is entertaining. All of it is entertaining. There is no difference between the emission of events and entertainment. Both claim they are entertainment providers. LNN says that its news bureau reports on stories in factual ways. No one contests this. LNN says the pundits who discuss upcoming events and float self-defense theories are part of the entertainment division. It is just commentary. Ben Thorne is often in the public eye for some remark. How come there are no... is a common question. It is entertaining. Ben Thorne, like LNN's entertainment division, stirs up conversation and doesn't shy away from controversy. It's fun.

Entertainment cannot be culpable. If human beings see a staged conversation or read a book and then commit a crime mimicking it, that's not the entertainer's fault. People are responsible for their own actions. Shakespeare has plays filled with murder and intrigue. All the world's a stage.

Eleni, Mia, and Ginna sit talking one evening. "If we sit by the fire and listen to the storyteller, that's one thing. When a massive corporation spins an elaborate yarn, that's something else entirely." This is Eleni. She mentions that Ben Thorne is not alone, there are editors and publishers, there is marketing and distribution. Ben Thorne is a corporation in league with other corporations. There is so much going on when they conspire to entertain the public at large. Likewise, LNN. If it's just me and you, my stories are just stories. Your responsibility stands a chance, you may reason yourself to comfortable disregard of consequences and implications. But if the other person involved is massive and elaborate, if they have enormous resources behind them, if they are multiple, that's something else entirely. Corporations are not people.

The law says they are. Some people, Mia says, have a higher level of responsibility to behave properly. The mayor of the town isn't the same as a common citizen. The mayor has a role, and that role adds weight and purpose to their words. If a Fire Marshall yells fire in a crowded theatre and they're wrong about it, there's more culpability than for some random teenager who thinks they smell smoke. LNN claims to have an entertainment division, but if it claims a news division too and emulates that delivery in its entertainment, it should know what it is doing.

People, Ginna says, act the same way regardless of the source. If it's politics, if it's news, entertainment, or advertising, there is no difference. Genre isn't real anymore. There's one single delivery media, and everything that comes from it is in the same form. It's all news, it's all politics, advertising, and entertainment. Whether it's LNN or CCN or Ben Thorne, people are plugged into the one and only delivery system, the giant distributed entertainment machine owned and operated by the richest people in the world, and there's always an LLC behind them.

Mia is clear. LL. Limited liability. It isn't just that the corporation protects its stockholders and employees, it protects itself. Its own agency is limited in liability. It's not The Royal Shakespeare Company's fault if some Hamlet wannabe shoots up a school or shopping mall, likewise, the news networks, the media moguls, and the vast internet.

None of it, nowhere on earth, never again, is anything anybody's fault. No one person does anything, there is only the swarm of the entertained hive. Even when they suffer, it's for the amusement of others. Their dance for direction, their maps on how to see it for themselves, there is nothing to pin on anyone, it's a war of all against all with no one to blame. Some stand tall with the power of 150,000 behind them, some are small and start this life with two strikes against them. They stand toe to toe and, as you might expect, the one obliterates the other. So long as the little ones keep making their protection payments and there's no alternative business incentive, everything goes on as before. If not, their agreement comes to a premature end and, if the corporation is deemed responsible, they pay a fine amounting to about 15 minutes of their collective effort.

People are created equal. With their equality of opportunity, some earn the rank of Ben Thorne. Some become the Liberty News Network. Some become the largest single stockholders in the companies that control the delivery infrastructure itself. We can dream. We receive our dreams from the slick and beautiful entertainment industry. What could possibly go wrong? All people are created equal.

Phone as Intermediary

If you read the usage data, the telemetry, from Eirini and Eleni's phones, it appears that despite years of constant communication, they go through a period of silence for nearly a month in the middle of 2034. For decades there is a stream of messages back and forth covering every topic and exploring every nuance. What's happening? What's going to happen? How do I feel about what's happening? What should I do now that this is happening? Over and over, sometimes hundreds in a day. Smiling at each other with the conventional use of icons and glyphs, encouraging each other with graphics and animated pictures, they navigate their high schools together, they work through college together, and then, even when they go down separate paths and their lives cease to move on parallel course, they continue contact and stay close.

Then it comes to a momentary, but abrupt, halt. The phone records, the metadata, show that on the eve of this interruption there is direct contact, an unusual event. What does it mean? Is there a fight? Are they on the outs, is it the end? How to interpret the interruption? Does it signify an unbridgeable distance? Repeat a pattern? When the telemetry halts, is it because they are so far from each other that there's no longer any record?

Telemetry is made for distances, it is adept at covering an enormous range of space and time, capturing in clearly codified motes of meaning the endless chatter of far and farther, of great distant communication between, the play between that comes with so much distance it can only be traversed at the speed of light.

Its absence suggests the producers have come near each other. In that proximity, the gauge loses its facility, it no longer resolves the distance.

Will we think of this month as an intervention against telemetry? Or merely an interlude? Does it depend on what happens next? While you're in the middle of it, while you stretch out at the end of the first act, can you know whether there is a second act to come? How does the interlude announce itself without what lies on its nether side?

The residents in the towns, the villages, and the municipalities, they are not so very much unlike each other nor are they so very different from the rest of Europe. They have their devices, whatever it takes to get them through. Whether their noses are glued to the screen or if they only glance down periodically when there's a familiar vibration or sound indicating a friendly receipt, they peel them off their hip throughout the day always and forever. Each heartbeat emits an event. The cell tower is a roost, the machine says I am here I am here I am here. Two coordinates, a unique identifier, a set of tags to display census data. The events come from the hand, or from a pocket or a bag or the top of a table.

Space is addressable. The location points are a rudimentary data type. The network identifier allows the tower to route return data in response to received data. There is a flow and a river in the air streaming around, throughout Dimos Nestou and the municipalities, villages, and towns. There is the sky and the hills, there is the beach and the water, and the island in the distance. All throughout, between everything, there are events leaping out of pockets and bags, off of tables and dashboards. They shoot through the air without adding their colors to the waving flag.

The flags are fitted with small chips that form a grid across the fabric. Each chip contributes to the sea of events flying through the air. There is a rack of machines somewhere nearby where those events reconstruct the movement, how it bustles and drapes in the wind, how it flaps across its pole, modeled and drawn. The flags flying across the Dimos are reconstructed and their movement compared. What is the average impact of a summer wind on flags flying in the breeze? Here, the analysis shows the likely movement of any flag with accommodations for shoreline and terrain. If the flag doesn't fly that day, the computers emulate its movement. Once we have the data, we don't need flags anymore.

There are events that accompany messages. They indicate when the message is sent, how big it is, where it originates, how many packets it requires, a correlation id to track its vector of movement linking to whatever response it receives. The message has an identity, the thread has an identity, the target is in the event, and the source is there too. Whether the message ends up 8,000 miles away or just down the street, the metadata captures the facts. Distances are not real in the measurements. The close and the remote look the same in that month without contact, that interlude or interruption. It's impossible to decide.

The network transcends human mortality. The onset of permanence is bolstered by worship. These devices distributed across time and space trickle between human experiences inflating them with their artificial vision measuring each event. Together side by side in an evolutionarily stable set, our prayers permit them to get away with murder. And robbery. And whatever else they like. For a fee. It balances the books of life and death, counting us each as ack or nack. Yes, dear one, you are of value, just see how much life they suck and how great is its worth in the communication fabric where we meet.

Eirini stands next to Eleni at the airport that first day. She walks next to her as they travel the four blocks from one house to the other that last day. Europea is so happy to see them. She feeds them and showers them with attention. Both her girls. No machine sees it. There is no model for it. They sit at the table in the kitchen and talk. Sometimes Europea, string of beads in hand, joins in on the laughter. The young women have grown close in that messaging black hole, sometimes they laugh together just because they think the same thing at the same time. How can we know this if there are no events and messages? We have but bare memory and vision to know the fort and the da of it. Without that reconstruction of events, without the back and forth, we have nearly nothing, just a heartbeat.

Later, in the evening, the events start flowing again. More than a pulse, the messages relay. To Democritus of Abdera the distance from Western Thrace to the Western coast of North America is inconceivable. In the telemetry, only one dimension features the difference, and it's little more than quantity, a single number separating the corners of the Earth.

While Ginna and Eleni talk, they stare at a trio of computer screens.

They are large and spread across an entire leg of the L-shaped desk. The center screen has a notebook program running. Once Eleni finds the synchronized file on the laptop computer, she discovers the authentication information and location of the original. They're stored on a cloud drive somewhere in a data center, a needle in a haystack. Once she has the universal identifier, once she has the address, she enlists on the desktop terminal too. She adds permissions and opens it. This permits them to sit side by side and share the giant screen.

On another screen there is a web browser with multiple tabs. They use it to search and further investigate remarks and interesting notions. One of the tabs is opened to a private location where the text for Ben Thorne's work is stored. They collect references for each specific item they find.

On still another screen, there is a simple black console window with text only instructions at the top and a text only document at the bottom. These simple and ancient software programs are the bread and butter of the software engineer. Eleni periodically types out commands and displays a list of data describing locations in a code repository in the cloud. A white cat in a snowstorm, they are walls of words in online source control simply prefixed with BeingAnIntroduction. No spaces.

Ginna's phone lies on the desk. Heartbeat. Heartbeat. Heartbeat.

Eleni's phone lies on the desk. Heartbeat. Heartbeat. Heartbeat.

Eleni is logged into her global account and grants Ginna access. She uses her login to pull and push data from the repository. Messages are sent. Events accompany them. Ginna provides credentials to gain access to the complete digital collection. The browser sends telemetry describing the search text and the scrolling, the clicks and the submits. There is a rack of computers, there are many racks of computers around the world, through date times and IP address correlation, through the location dimension, and systems integration, the analysis produces a story. Reading and typing, taking notes and traversing, they build their case. They follow the chain of events, what's happening and who says what to whom.

The data of their workday and their time together is there. Anyone with sufficient access and know-how can reconstruct events and learn every detail. Nothing unreliable, their conversations fall into deaf air, there is no active listener, but it can be reconstructed nonetheless. In parallel, they're trying to reconstruct the last year of Em's life, what Wolfe and Em say to each other in private. The narrator reconstructs Ginna and Eleni reconstructing.

Eleni asks her mother if she can look at Em's phone. Ermioni doesn't say anything, she just goes and gets it. The rack of computers must be surprised when that heartbeat begins again after so many weeks of silence. It's an old friend, his voice is familiar to the tower and the racks and the analytic tools running down forgotten pathways and returning to compiled patterns. What the texts indicate is that these men always work this way. Ginna says it's almost as if they don't know what they're doing, that it's happening behind their backs and playing out between them.

Artists of Despair is a struggle between two different stories. Wolfe is laser focused on producing a book about a painter whose brain is slowly overcome by a degenerative disease. The disease is killing him but makes his painting more beautiful. Em, on the other hand, wants to do something he variably refers to as either an existential analytic or a critique of a very specific form of non-organic reasoning. They fiercely argue back and forth.

Ginna is provoked into a deep and thorough reverie, she understands it as a view backstage from a time when she's in the audience. The descriptions of paintings in *Artists* make sense now. One of the extraordinary facets, according to its critics, is the way the pictures are systematically worth thousands and thousands of words. Each chapter has a painting in the layout. There is a description and then there is a set of events and an analysis transubstantiating into the next painting which erupts into the next analysis and so on and on throughout the tale.

One of the most commonly made comments on *Artists of Despair* is that it doesn't really have an ending, it just stops: mid analysis on the very last page. The consensus is that this is the artist's death. There is no magical narrative moment, there is no pristine and conceptually pure conclusion, there is only a trailing off midsentence. This can only mean one thing. In this universe, silence can only mean death.

One critic, a graduate student in Connecticut, works out a theory that the character hasn't died, but merely quits his job and goes off to do other things. This thesis, a doctoral dissertation still in progress, claims there can be no difference between death and departure from the constant heartbeat of analysis looping through the same mechanical process over and over again. It's completely indeterminate, there is no narrator to tell the story of the real and the true, there are only events and their emission, the rack of computers and their analysis, and the feedback that draws the work back into the next painting where the cycle continues. When that breaks, there's nothing left, nothing remains, only silence. It's impossible to say what this silence means. This impossibility is, in the end, the ultimate artist of despair.

Until now, the longest gap between publications by Ben Thorne is between *The Temple on the Mountain* and *On Being Born*. The women focus there and discover a fierce dispute. Em loves symmetry in the structure and demands it for every work. The architectonic is machine-like and excellent in its smooth functioning division of space and time. *On Being Born* is the only exception to this pattern and nearly every important commentator mentions it. The most groundbreaking critique, produced by Taubman, is that the architectonic is volatile and the content drives changes in form and genre. Critics generally hold that Ben Thorne is Hegelian in his approach to structure, there is a formal set of rules and patterns at the bottom of everything and the content is spun to fit that form. The Marxist theorists adapt this canonical reading to their pet materialism.

On Being Born blows a hole in theory. It is, as far as Ginna can tell, the only work in which Wolfe gets his way. He wants the content to change the form, the material events change how time works, how history unfolds, and how things happen. What happens changes how they happen. Em struggles against this, not because he thinks it an unworkable approach or bad storytelling, but because he thinks it turns the book into a horror story, one of the most terrifying tales ever told. Without the formal order of history and time, he argues in one of the notes, there can be only terror and destruction, there is no room for familiar bonds.

Wolfe convinces him by making an aesthetic argument that Em cannot resist. The beauty is not debatable. Many think it the most poetic, if not chaotic, of the novels. The aesthetic convinces him, they both affirm beauty in the horror.

Just as the computer and phone telemetry have no common correlation identifier, so too with the push and pull between Wolfe and Em in the fabrication of tales and the spinning of yarns. The telemetry has the whole scene in view and the two men run to catch up. Their struggle lies in their drive to understand the metrics.

If they could, they would let the telemetry tell the tale on its own even without understanding it. They're willing to submit because they think it's the voice of the work itself, it's that world unfolding in its own space and its own time. They hate that they have to gain access to it, mediate it, every aspect and angle of it. Why can't they channel the work from the air and the wind, why can't they pluck it from the rack and processors showing the impact on fabric moving and waving in the breeze?

It becomes clear to Eleni and Ginna, they know what they have to do. They too wish some omniscient voice could descend from somewhere and lay it out for them, but they are only human and have to make their way one note and one word and one sentence at a time.

Boredom as Intermediary

Not much has changed in what they do, but now they're both bored doing it. Eirini has a routine and goes about her duties, the same as the week before. Previously the report for the allocations committee meeting is for garbage detail on and around the beach along Dimos Nestou's coast, but especially in Keramoti. She throws herself into that, interviewing a few citizens with common demands, curating proposals and analysis from civil servants who know the trends of garbage production and collection, and how the latter falls short of the former. She's enthralled and engaged, excited and passionate. The requirements don't differ from her work this week: something about lighting the streets on the outskirts of Chrysoupoli. In both cases, she's equally occupied, there are just as many people to speak to and just as much information to collect, but now she is bored and keeps looking at the clock. During last week's preparation, the days fly by and there's never enough time.

Mia works on the case just as before, nothing changes. She waits for responses and feedback, but she's bored. It isn't that she doesn't have enough to do and just waits, that's true last week too, but there's something she'd rather be doing. Ginna and Eleni are busy with the notebook, going over what's there and trying to work out what it means. Ginna is close at hand and yet far away. She's engaged and busy the whole day long. In the evening, they'll relax together, eat and drink, talk and stroll. She waits for that. Whatever she does, it's boring. Today the clock moves slowly, today she waits for something else.

Ermioni is no longer bored. She loves working at the office, going every day and getting to know the veterinarians. They come on their appointed days and are happy to spend time there, it's a nice break from their schedules. They encourage her and show her where to look to better understand the business. She struggles to learn everything she possibly can: what to order and where to order it from, what things can go wrong and what to do when they do, who is on the list of contacts and why it's advantageous to reach out to them. The building is a livelier place with her in it. Dmitra comes more often now, she says it's too boring to stay as long as she's supposed to, but now she's happy to be there. She likes talking to Ermioni and wants to hear her stories about the town and the animals, about the people too. She comes in just after the office opens and stays most of the day now. It used to be so boring here, she says. Now I can't believe I ever thought that way. There's too much work to do.

Managing the household isn't boring, many things are challenging and rich in complexity. Not everything, not every action is absorbing, the daily chores don't hold. She wanders through a screaming void of habitual repetition leaving her time to wonder and imagine, think, and feel missing things. She doesn't like that, she wants to be carried away by what's in front of her, she doesn't want room for something behind to spin and grind out that absence. She's the one who lives on despite what's missing, and that boredom is bathed in grief and emptiness. It's a boredom without end, without resolution, and with no sign of decreasing anytime soon. The bustle of something else, of the new, of more, that is the best distraction, that's what she craves and needs, not that dim habitus that carries her from one side of the world to the other with too much time to sort through it.

Boredom transcends human mortality. The onset of permanence is bolstered by worship. The motion paused in time and space trickles between human experiences inflating them with arrested acts measuring each event. Together side by side in an evolutionarily stable set, our prayers permit them to get away with murder. And robbery. And whatever else they like. For a fee. It balances the meaning of life and death, counting us each as engaged or detached. Yes, dear one, you are of value, just see how much life they suck and how great is its thrall in the endless moments where we meet.

At the train station, at the doctor's office, this is notorious by now, we show compassion for the boredom of others by laying down distractions. This busyness fabricated by administrators for the sake of those who must be there. Here are maps and brochures, magazines and gift shops, pass your time this way while you wait for what comes. Download the app and scroll.

Boredom is a be all and end all. How much of what lies nearby is for its sake? How much is for the waiting? It's boring to iron clothing. This is not yours and yours alone. When Ermioni pulls each item from the basket and lays them on the board, pressing it into the right shape and producing its folds, when she does this her boredom belongs to everyone. If Eleni and Mia share the load, or, god forbid, Georgios, they join her. Sharing the work does not chase away boredom, it distributes it.

If Georgios and Eleni help, they do so best by setting up by her side and talking to her while they work. The work is shared, the boredom shared, and its alleviation too. They sing down by the river, and no one notices the time.

It's the same with small talk and chatter in the waiting room or at the station. They share the mood, together in it, and that takes them out of it.

Some, Eleni for example, aggressively withdraw. She prefers boredom to its cure. She much prefers the agony of the interminable passage of time to the torment of a stranger. She has easy remedies for her ails and needn't resort to trickery or foolishness to get her through it. She recalls a subject to her liking, rethinks a previous decision, and accesses the moments of the morning or details of the day. Boredom instigates her action, and there is no exit from its reach.

To run from something that has already found you is the epitome of cowardice. Eleni works through it in the middle of the day when Ginna takes an hour to walk about with Mia. She doesn't know where they go and won't intrude, but she doesn't want to stop and doesn't have to. They work well together, bouncing ideas around, building outlines and conclusions. Things are clearer and there is progress, but now she sits and makes a list. We need to talk about this and this and this when she gets back. It's only supposed to be an hour, but the list keeps growing. Its origin, its motive and guide, lies in waiting. Between that and Ginna's return, there's a long and hopeless stretch. Better make the best of it, make something out of this gap that haunts her day. When she returns, she thinks Eleni is driven and brilliant, insightful and thorough. Truthfully, she's just bored, and her awe is for its fruit.

The philosopher says that if we do not evade boredom, if we look deeply into it and experience its pull, we will begin to think. Or we will fill that gap with what we need to prevent it. Look now. Listen to yourself. What is there beside you to help while away the hours? Suppose the drive to make them pass is deep inside you, like genes speaking through cryptic actions and thoughts. Suppose it's true. You're honed for it, for that game that fits the blocks into the slots, for that game where the projectiles reach their targets, it is there for you by those who share in it, in the yawning expanse that opens up and offers you the choice: think or don't think, it's up to you. Here's what you may receive if you choose the same as those around you. You choose the same as they do, you do what everyone does, what people like you choose to do, whittling away the time they have left – as though it's infinite— with the games and gadgets, the bells and whistles, the lights and noise.

We already feel what you're feeling. There's nothing new or beautiful or interesting in that slow pause that yawns before you. Yawning is contagious, they say. The abyss is the first to trigger the chain, and when you share in that, you too are in it.

At work Eirini knows she's bored. Sitting opposite her laptop while they work, Mia knows it too. Ermioni at the ironing board, Eleni on a lunch break: emptiness front and center. When it departs, where does the boredom go? Does it linger anywhere nearby as Mia and Ginna find busyness together walking hand in hand? Where is it when Eirini leaves work and finds occupation at the bar with her friends or in the texts and sexts she exchanges with Carl and Fred to discover why they stay behind? Where is the boredom hiding while Ermioni goes about her work at the project office? Or when Thimios and Ariti are together with Despina and find absorption in family tasks and joys? Or when Nikos and Maria are away from their children and find it in an empty nest? Has boredom retreated, has it left us with the things that matter? Or does it sit nearby and wait? What does boredom do, how does it pass the time? What moves does it plot as it retreats, do they ensure a more powerful return?

What if it's like that, what if it's always there nearby and pushing, forcing desire and focus, interest and consumption? Boredom is the greatest fear and the greatest threat not because it comes and goes, but because it's always nearby organizing and plotting, getting ready to attack. The machines roll and cover the surface of the world, they are anti-boredom contraptions built by the common lot of us for the sake of our common good. We know it stalks us and we can't fathom the lion sitting and staring at the savannah, passing its time in the breeze, smelling the air, and everything that floats by with it. We cannot know this because we only know the ever-present fear of boredom's return, of the ways it stalks us, and comes for us. These things, everything we see, how do they dispel what comes?

Nikos comes over one day and helps Eleni hang the heavy bag in the garage. She prefers the footwork and exercise that go with the bigger bag, but what is this? Is this animal necessity speaking through a drive for movement, or is it the threat of nothingness come to inhabit the household and leave it with only empty time? Does she punch and kick to build her strength, or does she do it to fend off the threat of yawning time?

Of course, we must eat, and we must care for each other. Too habitual and even that empties. Imagine that this mind and consciousness are necessary to initiate these worlds, and then the excess overflows its use. What to do with it? Where will it go?

We need it to construct this marvelous machine proving our fitness, but we don't need it every day for everything we do. This is the conundrum: bootstrapping requires more than maintenance does. The machine takes over, structure supplants ingenuity. Even an inventor who dazzles their contemporaries with extraordinary insight and innovation need hardly spend more than a fraction of their time doing it. There is overflow, too much, an abundance that does not know where to go and what to do once the initial drives are satisfied. What then? What is the name for this excess? If we call it boredom, if we identify it as the emptiness of time, and see the fullness of its potential, it rises before us as the necessary residual of the effort to be civilized.

Social interludes pay you back for what you've made of them, they offer solutions to primordial riddles: what to do now? Converse, play, spend time together, buy things others make for you, employ their services, and enjoy. It overflows the primary directive and yields such opportunity. The human brain fills with the possibilities its worlds create. The circling of language concentrates structures boosted by power. The power circulates and furthers more elaborately decorative speakers recording history and taking note of the steps to achieve it. No longer must we directly present ourselves to each other to dispel the burdens, we act remotely across time and space and fulfill sets of patterns no one ever imagined.

Suppose that social power grows alongside cognitive power and unfolds as civilization. Suppose at least part of that happens through complex signals and meanings. None of that requires fully formed consciousness. Complex language increases order through intersubjective associations and influences, so isn't it possible that consciousness is residual to that? What if the sense of boredom is the individuating power? Social skills and behaviors, they don't incite the conscious being, they only incite the organization which turns and flows back into a person and gives birth there, within them, to an individual. Not through some beautiful spark of god added upon reflection, but through the advent of boredom. In it, they come to know themselves and others, they speak and pass the time, they ask how they are doing and offer to come along. Desire comes to be there with them, and until boredom strikes, there is none of it.

There is a mechanical launch, it produces the ground on which civilization stands. The food and the storage, the safety and the warmth, comes through orchestrated operations. Then there is the overflow. The ambitious mindset needn't persist, they relax while waiting for the rumblings of the turbine to come back around full circle. Once the circuit is complete, they awaken and move to further musings: what now? What's next?

Boredom is where we find ourselves, where self-discovery happens. The mastery rules and orders but it does not want. Boredom takes place in the overflow of the empowered worker bees' contributions to the central store. Desire takes flight in waiting, interest percolates there. Affection and fear, rage and anger, love and credence, a song of boredom sung by the ones who wait, by the ones being introduced time and time again.

Entertainment as Intermediary

Once bored, we go looking for distraction. It's as if we've been broken down into our most individual selves so that we may search for the aggregate. Amusements can cross sections of the population, define interests and desires, and move members across sets. The demographic lingers among a population in search of entertainment. It isn't enough to say society has done this to me, we must find the roots of its ordering. We separate and are drawn together. The details are the bottom line, and the data is worth having. The one who goes off the grid doesn't just distinguish themselves from the system of communication, they separate themselves from everyone plugged into it. They relish their boredom, their autonomy, and isolation. They deny the impulse of what is amusing, they seek something else entirely.

The gathering devices require uniformity. They measure and the measurement offers an explicit take on whatever is and whatever may be. Whatever is must be parsed by one and the same measurement. Telemetry reduces everything to what it sees. Politics is so entertaining. Horror movies too. The ideal way to apply eye shadow, how to defeat the endgame monster, the most attractive fashions in manscaping: it's so entertaining to learn things. Even learning to cook chili or eggplant parmesan, who could guess how much fun it is to stroll for information in the public fora, or how easily separated and gathered we are by fun.

When done properly, sex is fun, isn't it? But what ensures it's done properly? If we guarantee that representations of it are everywhere, we will discover what everyone thinks proper and fun, amusing, and then we can segment that into groups and mini-sects bounded by desires and kinks. Sex over sects, there is nothing more effective for putting individuals back into aggregates. The associations flow and marketing teams delight. From your cocks and cunts to their charts and datasets, never fear, there's an endless supply of lures to lead you about. The major porn sites collect everything in categories, they have librarians to file entries in the catalogue. There's everything you could possibly imagine, even popular with women, as if it is a single thing.

The pleasant transcends human mortality. The onset of permanence is bolstered by worship. These feelings distributed across time and space trickle between human experiences inflating them with their artificial vision measuring each event. Together side by side in an evolutionarily stable set, our prayers permit them to get away with murder. And robbery. And whatever else they like. For a fee. It balances the books of life and death, counting us each as profit or loss. Yes, dear one, you are of value, just see how much life they suck and how great is its delight in the ecstasy where we meet.

When Eleni sleeps with Ion, she takes an aggressive role. She doesn't lure him, she doesn't send subtle signals or use cryptic body language. She moves in close, takes him off balance, and kisses him forcefully. In every moment leading up to it, she feels the power and control enabling her initiative. It isn't a sudden and dramatic move, it flows naturally from their exchange, and she does it without planning to let it come spontaneously. His response is open and welcoming, and she pushes him back onto the couch. His ease and suppleness call out to her. His eyes wide, his heart beating enthusiastically while she grows still bolder and swings her leg over him. He yields to every gesture, there are no doubts.

She stays the night and returns home early the next morning. She doesn't think about who will notice and what consequences will follow. She's lucky, and Mia lets her know it. Fun can be that way, it impairs judgment. Reminders dampen the mood. They are the afterthought of conscience, but she asserts her liberation. She denies the town this right and asserts her own. The advertising, popular culture, confirms it. They'll get used to it, having someone among them who is not exposed to their sanction.

When Eleni sleeps with Mihalis, she acts the recipient. It amuses her to see how inflated he becomes, the way he uses knowledge and learning to seduce her. She lets him, thinking it fun to feel a hidden power, something she holds onto quietly while he struts about exposing his angles on favored subjects. He believes in the sexual prowess of his mind, he believes he can overcome whatever barriers there are, and he moves easily into a practiced mode thoroughly worked out. She plays the role of ingenue, she imagines historical pairings, and lets him take part. She isn't succumbing to Svengali, but dances to a pleasant rhythm.

She stays the night and returns home early the next morning. She doesn't think about who will notice and what consequences will follow. She's lucky, and Mia lets her know it. Fun can be that way, it impairs judgment. Reminders dampen the mood. They are the afterthought of conscience, but she asserts her liberation. She denies the town this right and asserts her own. The advertising, popular culture, confirms it. They'll get used to it, having someone among them who is not exposed to their sanction.

Either way, it's fun. There may be looks and talk, judgments and ill treatment. Those are strangers, her family and friends will adjust, but the masses, what do they say? Mia mentions it, but it's Eirini who warns her. People aren't puritans but they are religious, they know about unmarried adults, but there are boundaries, and this crosses the line.

Eirini becomes sympathetic and warning turns to pleading. She tells Eleni about Fred and Carl, about each of them, and she tells her about both of them. She describes how much fun it is and how exciting for her and for them, how much she learns about herself, how much pleasure teaches her. She loves it, but she cautions, she won't act like that where her mother can see. Getting caught is no fun, and there's nothing amusing about being judged. Be as bold as you like, but the town will have its say. Even if your mother doesn't care, she doesn't want any trouble at the market or on the street. Save your protests, there's no one to hear them.

Maybe it isn't about fun, Eleni says. She doesn't do it because she's bored or because she wants new experiences. She thinks there's more than that, some deeply anchored meaning. She tries to find someone in it. She plays different roles, learns her songs, how well they suit her, and what impact they will have. Of course, Eirini replies, and that's fun, isn't it?

That gets her, causes her to pause. She understands herself as both aggressor and recipient, but it's an elaborate game, a sideways amusement. The thought drives her to distraction. It intermingles with her work. As they read through the notebooks and Thorne's corpus, they learn the simple choice separating Wolfe from Em. They learn their complex interleave: interlude and intervention aren't two mutually exclusive options, but patterns and facets of that same relation constantly and thoroughly entwined. There is the cerebral and measured Mihalis and the sensual and physical Ion. She moves along those axes, segmenting them just so. In their time together, in the rolling and heavy breathing, in the movement above and below, they emerge combined. Both thinking beings, both feeling beings, they're different, but nothing crisp and clear. She cannot see it, and her aggressive façade breaks down as Ion's excitement grows. She moves in both ways when no one is looking, she aligns herself from moment to moment. Her patient outer shell cracks as Mihalis' excitement wanes. It's hard to find a single simple thing, everything flows together. The circling and the thrusting will not stay in their box, the categories flow, and the bodies move. Attitudes and moods change, there is ebb and flood.

Even when she surrenders control, she retains power. Even when she takes control, she releases it. Eirini says this reminds her of what it's like when Fred and Carl take pleasure in each other. It surprises her, she doesn't plan it, but when it happens, her notions of aggressor and recipient recede. Circling and thrusting, it's just a push and pull.

Eleni relays everything to Mia. What does she think? What is sex to her? Is it fun? Is it a release? Is it self-discovery? What?

She says it can be any of those, and something more too. Getting to know another person, a way to be with her, close to her, breaking down boundaries, learning where they are and how easily they can be crossed.

There is pleasure in touch, the pleasure of helping someone who needs it. There is the pleasure of meaningful work, of art, and the experience it yields. Pleasures come in different shapes and sizes. Sex is more than lust although it can be that. She discreetly describes Gwen and how their friendship yields benefits. We know each other in many ways. Caring for each other when we're sick, working together, failing together, and succeeding, all of it. I've held her while she shudders and trembles. Sex is more than bodies. Every day my body moves around this world. There are things it does and people it does them with. It's not always exciting, but it's never boring. If it is, the other better notice, otherwise you might as well be fucking a man, Mia laughs. Eleni winces and shakes her head. Even boring sex is a little bit fun, she says.

Mia doesn't have fun doing her job. It doesn't entertain her, she isn't amused. She's a serious woman, and her job is rewarding but not pleasant. Ginna has fun doing her job. It can entertain her, it is sometimes amusing. She's a serious woman, and her job is rewarding and pleasant. Ermioni does not have fun at the office or on rides around town with animal control. She doesn't have fun when she cooks or serves guests. Even though she loves the full house and people gathering in her kitchen, she doesn't think it's fun. It's hard work and never boring. In the early morning, three women sit at the island in the kitchen, and they talk. Ginna asks questions, listens closely to the answers, and follows up with more. She wants to understand Ermioni. She tells Mia later that she's never met a woman like her before. Mia is confused, what type of woman do you think she is? Ginna explains that Mia does what she does because it has to be done. The virtue lies in doing it and not some personal gain. Mia agrees and takes it as flattery. Ginna says she's different, and Mia understands. Ginna says Ermioni is more like Mia, but Mia doesn't see it. Mia is quiet, she thinks carefully, and then disagrees. She reads the important theoretical contributions, it's sexist and patriarchal to diminish women's work. Ginna says she's not denying it, but does Mia truly understand the extent to which they are the same? Or is she guilty of putting herself above Ermioni? Mia is quiet. She thinks about it.

In theory yes, Ginna says, but in practice? Do you have friends like her? No, she has no friends like that, but where would she meet them? Well, you know Ermioni, why aren't you closer?

It reminds Mia of something Em used to say. She's snobby when it comes to academics she doesn't respect, she thinks they aren't walking the walk, they aren't living the practical life they advocate in their books and articles. Em tells her a story about the little dog he and her mother own. The little guy has a ball and stick that he adores. He wags his tale at the ball as if he thinks it is alive while rolling it around with a cloth chew stick in his mouth. He pushes the ball around the apartment needing no input from others. Em says the work he does and all the work he will ever do is just like that dog and its ball and stick. He can dress up how important it is however he likes, but it's just rolling a ball. Mia resists, talks about social impact, and its importance. Em says it's hard to gauge. Maybe millions benefit when the ball rolls and the dog's a dog. Maybe the dog does no harm and that's an improvement. When we turn toward others, when we act on their behalf, we might do harm. If the dog's will is pure and your will is pure, how can you be sure your road is above his? The dog has fun, doesn't he? She asks. No, Em says, that's not what I see. His intensity, his focus, it suggests he isn't having fun, but he has to do it, it has to be done. He believes in his work, and he is focused. Fun doesn't matter.

Ermioni has an enormous impact: she raises Eleni, she takes care of her family, and she's part of a community. How can you put yourself above her? Mia is quiet. She thinks about it.

In boredom, we are ourselves. In our effort to climb out of it, we are like others doing the same: who and how we fuck, who and what we love, what and how we do what we do. We are aggregation machines as we go about this busyness. Indefinite articles.

What makes the philosophers think pleasure and fun have anything to do with happiness? Does it have to be put at a distance from virtue to make that visible? Mia watches Ermioni more closely. They have breakfast together and talk. Ermioni misses out on happiness, her husband's death abruptly intervenes. Mia sees their similarity in the performance of an act for the sake of some necessity. The alignment is clear once she sets out to find it, once she listens, and once she sees with her own eyes.

We'll burn out, isn't that what they always say? If we don't have fun, if we don't relax, if we don't let our minds go blank, but Mia knows it isn't true. She doesn't burn out absent fun, she burns out without reward. If she works a case or tries to help someone and it goes badly, if the bad guys win, it hurts and wears her down. Racking up losses causes distress, but a win will raise the spirits, and make her think it's worthwhile. Someone somewhere convinces some of us that we need fun to be happy and that if our work isn't fun, we should find it elsewhere. Consume this or that and then you'll have it.

When you relax in the evening, is that fun? Mia asks Ermioni later on when she wanders into the kitchen and catches her preparing the afternoon meal. No, not fun. I just need to calm down to help me sleep. With my chores, I get very tense. I need to relax my mind to sleep. What about fun though? She asks. What do you do for fun? Nothing on purpose really. I don't have time for it, there's too much to do. But don't you get worn out? No, if I finish something it energizes me. It doesn't wear me out. Maybe if I never get anything done. If something isn't going well, I switch to something else just to get the boost a little victory gives. Celebration burns energy, it doesn't rekindle it.

Mia is quiet. She thinks about it.

Genre as Intermediary

Even if we're not naturally kind, we may be drawn into natural kinds. By genes, by style, by whatever properties there are. Types aren't just for fun, they work everywhere.

Types thrown through me from behind, endlessly turning around, I look back through the hazy trail. If only to be. Try to ask what it is without first finding it, without being introduced. A sickly scent settles and there we sniff out the base and the root, the top and what falls from it.

Here is the argument they find, tucked away somewhere, randomly settled in the notes with no particular heading but loosely associated with the project under consideration. The gene does not participate in the property, rather it produces it. The gene does not universally govern over its domain, rather it copies itself and is distributed throughout. It is not an abstract kind, but a replica, constantly reproducing itself. Should we call the upshot a property? Is the gene set the attribute or is that the hair and the skin, the disease and its potential-to-be? Even if we say this thing here has the identical structure as that thing there, who is it that says it? By what abstraction is the comparison made? Let it go and focus on the particular. It's no property, but tends toward the collection, toward an aggregate resemblance based on the pool and replication in place throughout the generations. Rather, there is the instance. There is no such thing as fine hair or coarse. There is no light skin or dark, there is just that one there and that one there and that one there.

Or perhaps there is never only that one there, but always only the type and the type is of the order and the order rules all and sundry. Organization orders in endless copying, in repeating presence absent origins.

Wait. The copy is the real, copying is what is most real. This is what they mean, it's just a gesturing of the hand. Voila. Ecce. Edo.

Then there is another argument. Are these really arguments? There's another of whatever this is. And another. And another. Forget that, here it is.

Where does that voice come from? The expository. The view from nowhere as if I am nothing and wish to capture the dictation of meaning from heaven and copy it down. This replication, this writing, there are no stories, but even if there are, there's no storyteller, just angles and tone accompanying a voice. The point of view, narrative forms, they have a history and come from somewhere. We memorize and recite. We copy down what we memorize, and we copy down what we recite. I am talking to you. Are you listening? Whatever this is, whatever you and I achieve, it is not listening. It's nothing other than this, this exchange, on and on. Don't you have anything better to do? Why are you still here?

Where do these forms come from? Suppose I rebel against traditional storytelling, suppose I find a different way to let it come. How can I do that? The tools are predisposed to the form, to the type, and the publishing houses are predisposed. They want copies of the replicated original, the latest variant of the dominant order. That's what they want and that's what the readers want. It comes through just as it always has. If a white order becomes a brown order, if a binary order becomes a non-binary order, how is that revolutionary if systematic ordering remains intact? They speak in their own voice, they narrate their story, and they describe events. Perhaps their paragraphs have thesis sentences, and the other sentences elaborate. They assign a brown truth and a non-binary truth, but they elaborate nonetheless, they replicate the logic of the narrator spinning the yarn. It comes down to that, to the system of signs and the mechanical constructs enabling signifying expressions.

When the one truly does depart from the replicated copies of common everydayness, there is deep disconnection. What is this? Nothing too radical. Mix up the history, bring about something that is slightly new and exciting, but it must be reasonable, it must join with what is already comfortable. Mutation happens, copying errors, but they reject radical transformations. People draw back and are put off.

Even that bug, the giant one that wakes up one morning and finds himself brutally altered. Strange, but he narrates, tells us stories, and honors time sequences: the metamorphosis is not complete. He doesn't tell his story in a circle or a square, he doesn't lay the middle over the end and the end over the beginning. There are characters and they have the same name later in the story that they have at the beginning. Regularity is palpable and whatever obsession he gives free rein has constraints beneath its liberty.

The type transcends human mortality. The onset of permanence is bolstered by worship. These kinds of things and events distributing across time and space trickle between human experiences inflating them with their artificial vision measuring each event. Together side by side in an evolutionarily stable set, our prayers permit them to get away with murder. And robbery. And whatever else they like. For a fee. It balances out the books of life and death, counting us each as profit or loss. Yes, dear one, you are of value, just see how much life they suck and how great will be its significance in the catalogue where we meet.

When Eirini gives the full report of her experiences with Carl and Fred, Eleni struggles to ask her first question. She doesn't know how to say it, so it comes out awkward and broken. Was it really just one thing? She asks. Of course, anyone could guess what happens next. What do you mean? What else is there to say? Was it really just one thing? She says it again but goes on as if there's no question mark at the end. I mean, the event. As if it were one thing. We have sex. As if that is one thing that happens one time. But it isn't a thing. Events don't have bodies, their boundaries are weird. Maybe there's a clock on the table, it might be one of those old-style clocks like the one my mom keeps in Dad's office. Tick, tick, tick, with the little second hand that moves around the dial while the minutes and hours move more slowly. Suppose that clock is in the room with you, suppose it's sitting there on the table and ticking away. Is that part of it? Part of having sex, is that what you mean? Yes, part of the event as if it is one thing. If there is a clock humming away and you don't notice, it isn't important to what you're doing, then it's outside, it's there but not part of it. Do you see what I mean? It's as if we're giving the event a boundary and what's inside is the thing and what's outside isn't.

We're not just suspended in space, Eirini says beginning to understand. No, we're not. Maybe the thing you're describing, the event that you're making into one thing, maybe that isn't one thing either, maybe it's not even any type of thing. It doesn't have anything in common with anything else. It doesn't have anything in common with anything else, she repeats. That's exactly right. We're not saying it correctly. I mean, I don't know what I mean, but how can there be truth if we're always telling each other about things that don't exist? Events don't really happen or happen differently than we say. What is this about, Lena mou? Are you really so confused by what I'm saying? No, of course not. I'm thinking about something else. About Ion and Mihalis. Him or him. You say I can't do this. I can't act like this. That means you think there's a way that I'm acting. There's something I'm doing, and some other thing, whatever, but I can't make sense of it. Ordering what I do already judges. That's what you're warning me about, isn't it? Yes, but you aren't being normal now. This is weird. Why are you being like this? What's wrong?

That's the point she's trying to make. To be like this. She turns that over and over again. To say anything is *like* something already associates, forms a link, and then copies are involved. The genre rises, comes to the fore, and the type and the kind with it. The event wears away and the thing takes over. She walks back and forth in the kitchen, from the refrigerator to the stove. Ermioni is at her mother's house. Mia and Ginna are out walking somewhere. She wants to make use of this time. She needs to get her thoughts together, but the pressure weighs her down. She slows her step and moves back and forth across the cold tile. Eirini sits at one of the stools and leans against the island. There's a glass of wine in front of her. A small dish with crackers and cheese. And then there are a million billion other things in the room and nearby, but we haven't time to describe them. Light can't travel fast enough to capture everything.

I think I'm starting to understand something about Dad's work. Ginna and I go over these notes again and again doing the comparisons. We're building connections and relationships then stating them clearly in a persuasive way. We want Wolfe to agree with our proposal for the last book. What do you mean, last book? There's no other material.

Everything else is sketchy, not a book, only this has form and content. If Ben Thorne is Wolfe and Em, then this is the last one. Will it be *Washington and Ashley* or will it be *Being an Introduction*? That's what we're doing. You mean you have to take what you find, and make it into one single thing, draw boundaries around it to make it a book. Is that it? I guess so. The outlines are a struggle. They're both obsessed, and they see events in such different ways. Wolfe and this endless repetition intervening. Dad's interlude which never settles and then spreads out everywhere. He says it's a between that you can't know as a between because the after is still happening. That's why it's a farce and ridiculous and why it taunts you and makes fun of everything you say and do, but it's not real, it doesn't matter, it's here and then it's gone. It's not connected to anything else, just a momentary aside that makes him feel pathetic in its aftermath.

Eirini looks down and purses her lips. She can't think of what to say, she doesn't know if she understands. Is stability the same thing as survival, after everything is said and done? Is order just a way to make things more stable, to help them survive? How can you write it down, how can you teach it to someone else, how can you reproduce it if it isn't well-formed? Yes, I get it. I think that's what they're arguing about. Suppose you have a decision to make. Suppose you have to choose between two things. These choices, you have to pick one. First you have to make them into this one thing and that one thing. If they aren't two things, then you can't choose between them. Choice repeats the logic. Maybe you're saying that your mind has to set up the choice for you. Once it does, then you can choose. That's right, that's what I mean, but what if you get it wrong? What if it's an illusion? You put those two things there, you push the types and pull the order. It's out there and crammed into those two little boxes and now you have to choose.

Ion is infatuated. He wants to see her again. He texts her the next day to remind her of the fun from last night. Fun. He uses that word. He wants to see her again. Let's do something fun, he says. When can he see her again?

Mihalis wants to see Eleni again. He texts her and reminds her of their fun together. Does she want to have dinner with him and some friends next week? He wants to show her off. So clever, they'll love her, the four of them are sure to have fun together.

They both have skin and eyes. Brown, they both have brown eyes. Ion's skin is olive, maybe like the lighter side of a Kalamata. Mihalis is dark brown, almost black. They both have curly hair. Mihalis' tight curls are more coarse than Ion's, he wears it shorter, and shaves closer. They are

both taller than she is but nearly the same height as each other. Perhaps
Ion is a few centimeters taller. She thinks about their shoulders and their
chests, their hips and legs. She compares them and cannot help it. She does
not try to associate Ion's hair with Mihalis' eyes, she does not compare
Mihalis' skin with Ion's fingertips. She obeys the rules of her fleeting
fantasies: skin to skin, eyes to eyes, and belly to belly. She is always
honoring the type.

Being with each of them, she unwillingly compares, but what are they
exactly? The acts. Talking touching breathing rushing feeling. That one
there, this one here. Such different sensations. She recalls her directness
with Ion, her coyness with Mihalis. Where is the one in the other? The
sensations, the touch, the feeling. Where is the likeness? She mouths the
word to herself. Men. They are men. Each is a man. She repeats it until its
meaning evaporates. It's just a sound, and she can't find it in her memory
of the hours together.

If the boundary between mother and daughter is not firm, Eleni will
push herself in front of Ermioni's eyes and heart and feel the beat and
vision. Particularity elides the genetic likeness but suppose it doesn't have
to. Suppose she replicates herself into her mother and feels the repetition
as a chain interrupting her presence. She compounds alignment with the
back and forth between dead Em and living Em. This is the event boundary
that occupies Ermioni in every instance of her passage. She knows that if
she breaks down the boundary between them, if she fits herself into it and
brings herself along, she'll know the difference. The existing god is more
perfect than the non-existent one. Ermioni misses Em's skin, his eyes, and
his hair. She misses his legs and his arms, his chest and his shoulders. They
are not there, they are nowhere. She turns around and around but there is
nothing. Ion contra Mihalis hides in the advent of living Em and dead Em.
His absence mutates repetition, his non-being is absolutely binary and
never to be evaded, never set aside, never lost except in dreams.

He hovers in every corner. Ermioni is relieved to let the other house
go. She doesn't want those memories, but this is a new torment. Every
decision, each piece of tile, every time the heat pump comes on and the
vents begin to blow. That is his breath, his touch, and his presence. He
replicates himself through the rooms and atop the surfaces. His repeated
presence fills everything until there's no room for anything. She's glad to
go to the office every day because in the morning when she sweeps the
porch and opens the windows, she's haunted by absence, by its not-being
for him, and by his not-being-there for her. He haunts her in not being
there, in not being present. His copious presence is his absence.

Tuesday morning, Eleni drinks coffee on the porch around the side facing the yard when Ermioni moves in with sweeping sounds and motions. Don't you ever get frustrated, Mama? Doing that same work every day? Does the porch really need sweeping every single day? I don't know if it needs it every day, darling, but I know that I need to do it. But why? What happens if no one sweeps the porch, what happens if no one opens the windows to let the air in, what if no one pounds the pillows to get the dust out, if no one shakes the blankets and the cushions? What happens?

She holds her coffee close to her face and feels the warmth in the cool morning. She waits for her mother's answer. The question's tone is free of judgment and full of curiosity.

The house won't be alive if no one does that, she says. A house can't just sit the whole day. Things have to happen. Meals and talk. Smells and footsteps. That's how they live. If these things don't happen, the house isn't alive. It's my job to keep it alive, to make it a place for living people. For you, for me, for anyone who comes. People may stop by. I want them to be comfortable. I want to have something to offer.

But how can you decide it has to be like that? How does the house and the porch and the pillows and the blankets, how does it come to mean this to you? To be this way for you? I suppose that's how it always is. Who am I? I can't make up a whole new world just by myself. I connect to this, to these people. They're in me. When I sweep the porch, I think of my mother sweeping her porch and her mother sweeping her porch. Forever and forever back to the ancient times. But what does that mean for me, Mama? If I don't sweep my porch, what does that mean? Do you think I'm hurting those mothers when I don't do what they do? Things are different now. I'm sweeping your porch for you until you're ready. Things change, girls are different. But what do you think about the changes? Tell me, Mama, you won't hurt my feelings, tell me the truth. I think you want to be like the men. Maybe I'm silly, but that's what I think. And if you ask me, I don't think the men are so good. I don't think they're the ones we should be imitating. Why should we want to copy them? Why work that hard for total strangers, why move away from families, why want without consequence, why make more guns and computers to make rich people even richer? What's so good about any of that?

She doesn't answer. Ermioni isn't looking for one. Eleni puts her mug on the little table and says, come sit with me, Mama. Let's enjoy the morning. Ermioni leans her broom against the side of the house and sits in the other chair. Eleni reaches out and puts her hand on her mother's arm and they settle in together, their hands coming to rest on the table between them.

Coming and Going as Intermediary

The day after Labor Day, Wolfe departs for Greece. He brings the interns with him. On the flight from New York to Athens, he's in first class, and they're in coach. His seat stretches out into a bed with a retractable barrier around it allowing him to sleep peacefully for most of the overnight flight. Fred and Carl are in the window and center seat on a row about two thirds of the way back, behind the wing. There's an older man sitting on their aisle seat. He's been visiting his daughter and grandchildren in New Jersey. She attends school there, marries a local man, and now she doesn't come home very often. His name is Mimis, and he offers them some of the delicious baked goods his daughter gives him for the journey. He asks them what they do, and they show him, rather than explain. It's the man's fault. He says he runs a library in a small town near Kalamata on the Peloponnese and wants to know about their studies. He wants details.

Carl tells him he's studying the impact of organizations insofar as they constrain and liberate people. He tells him that ignorance plays an important part in our lives and is the best way to ensure that only those devoted to organizing have any say in how we live. The point of a proper education is to become aware of order's role in daily life and become conscious of its impact on everything we do, feel, see, or think. By becoming self-conscious, we take control of our lives, and twist coercion into liberation. His project, he says as simply as he can, is to provide more tools for understanding daily life and show how those tools can be put to use. He claims the methods he's developing are revolutionary. Just as thinking like a natural scientist helps people see things, thinking like a social scientist does too. The purpose of human history is to organize the good for each failed society so that it can progress while leaving what's unjust behind. Eventually, we'll achieve the ideal or at least get closer to it. Self-awareness in participants, where everyone understands the purpose of the many in the one and the one in the many, marks the highest achievement of human history even if we don't know it, even if we think we're separate and make up different nations or groups.

Fred says he thinks such a method is just another form of control. Disciplining the mind, shaping it, introduces an alien being. Yes, he agrees, there is an order structuring people's lives, but it isn't for the sake of liberty or justice, it provides security and people love it. People are shoe-horned into it because they have no vision of their own, but are mundane and petty, mostly small and fearful. Order makes their lives livable, and without it, they cannot survive since it is what makes life predictable. People want to live in prisons, order is coercion and ontogeny recapitulates phylogeny. No one really wants freedom or justice, they just want to work for the sake of the strong and powerful. Most serve the ends of the elite and prefer it that way because their own ends are mundane. They are small and stupid and weak and only when they band together do they stand a chance of balancing the power of the strong. Even then, they make a virtue of weakness and allow new masters to rule. They adore them for it. This pattern, he explains, creates a hostile environment for those with great ability, those who are volatile and truly liberated. Such individuals are not destroyed by this warring world, they are instigated to do great things. They drive to overcome impossible odds and reach even greater heights without any champion or alien method. The world is a battle between these anomalies and those who want to destroy them. What matters, he says, is not that civilization continues with this or that ideal form, but that extraordinary individuals continue to appear.

For Carl, the standard of action is the set, the organized group. At least part of their action is dedicated to understanding how its order applies to its members. This is always at work, and self-consciousness to that effect is the key. Everyone can achieve this transformative experience together.

For Fred, the standard of action is the extraordinary individual. There are few instances, but they're talking to each other across time. It takes 1000 villages 100 thousand years to produce Aristotle, and their struggle and strife, their wars and battles, anger and joy, everything they do, even though it's done without understanding, is for the sake of it.

The old man wants to know if any of this has anything to do with the political talk you hear in America. Politics is taking over everyone's life, it demands attention twenty-four hours a day and seven days a week. He says it sounds like Carl is promoting one side and Fred the other.

They both reject the comparison. Carl says politicians talk a lot about social duties, but they aren't really interested in digging into the details. They don't visualize a great civilization that *every* resident can love. Their power exploits social concerns to promote business interests. Attributes are advertising to them. This may instigate new cultural products, films and movies, sell lots of T-Shirts, but no deep structural change. That would be too risky. They peddle fear of chaos to promote the drive toward tyranny and order. Fred says politics has become dog whistles for traditional European power structures. The leaders are mostly in it for power, and they know how to use populist language to rally support and gain wealth and status. They convince the sheep to worship the wolf, but the wolf is not strong and beautiful and brilliant, just a rich heir to some ill-gotten fortune, someone who wants to use their inherited wealth to buy trademarks and brands. Truly extraordinary individuals are detached from mass achievements. They excel in ways their peers cannot comprehend. They are extraordinary in ways that make them incomprehensible.

* * *

Early the next morning, as the plane begins its descent, the old man wonders what they think will happen. He wants to know if their study gives them any expertise in the outcome or how to change it.

Carl is sure that the conflict is a long-awaited historical crisis between warring ideals in the capitalist state. He's convinced the culture war is beyond the control of ruling parties, that even though they've instigated the conflict, it's getting away from them and they cannot foresee its conclusion. That outcome will be violent and intense. It'll destroy the civilization the politicians claim to protect, everyone's good and everyone's evil, and it'll produce ashes and destruction. From that, a new world will come. The Nazis destroy Europe, imperialist and colonial Europe, and new policies shape what emerges with social concern for how we must work together to build great civilizations. The coming catastrophe signals an even greater rebirth. We're on the verge of a revolution, he's sure of it.

Fred says people just like blood. The safety and security they work hard for, it's in constant tension with their love of blood and destruction. They want to unleash terrifying power every now and again. This is normal, it's the cycle of life in a world where humans want to exercise their will and feel power course through their veins. Some great catastrophes may happen, but they are without purpose and have no lasting impact. It's ridiculous, a complete farce, and creates as much as it destroys. The old order is fat and sloppy, it'll super charge things for a while, but then they'll settle down until something else explodes. None of it matters, it's nonsense. Periodically, in the midst of it, there are extraordinary moments and exceptional events. No one experiences them, or only a few do off in some quiet corner somewhere. They're not public, and not in the history books. They'll be etched on cave walls here or there and only a handful of others will recognize what they see when they see it. To the rest, it is as though they never happen. Life is for the sake of the non-recordable and non-repeatable. Only the shrewd in great need will know how to see it.

In Athens, the old man goes quickly to catch a flight to Kalamata. Wolfe doesn't wait for Fred and Carl, he gets off the plane first and his large bag comes down the shoot before theirs. He gets through customs and immediately makes his way to the gate for the flight to Kavala. Fred and Carl arrive just as the transport is boarding. It carries them across the tarmac, and they walk carefully to the plane, directed by airport personnel to stay within the yellow lines and clear of the engines. The three men don't speak, they don't even look at each other. Wolfe takes two seats on the right near the front. Fred and Carl pass by and go to the back where they sit on the left as Ginna instructs so they can enjoy the glorious views of the coast.

Fred tells Carl that order is just population control written in the hearts and bodies of human beings. Only individuals with property and education are free to reproduce. Carl's revolution doesn't even want to change that, it just wants to change the criteria for having property and education. It's okay though, you can't help it, he says, the order of our being is written inside us, it's replicated there. We realize those genetic sets and patterns. We can't help it, we're small -as a rule- and the big things that make us are beyond our capabilities. We can't see them and will never be able to. The point is to devote yourself unrestrainedly to what forces are at work in you. Commit. Most won't amount to anything, a few will be extraordinary.

Carl shakes his head. Your position doesn't make sense. You speak of order too, your world is full of structure and most of it mundane. You have no reason to emphasize the grandeur of these elite instances, these blips that no one sees. There is no logic to it. The patterns and structure are essential to whatever is anomalous to them. The safe and the secure always think that way, Fred says simply. Anomalies probably don't know what they are. Knowing and doing aren't the same, and that works both ways. I can see the way extraordinary people appear on this Earth *and* be excluded from them. I see it in Leonardo, but that doesn't make me Leonardo. At least I can be an afficionado, pathetic as that seems.

Carl is irritated and stops talking. Their relationship is hard to navigate. Even when they agree, which is not something they do very often, they frustrate each other. Fred cautions Carl about importing a value system. Fine, no objection, but it's hope more than science. If they need it to survive, then something in them is coerced and quieted. Only in struggle, only those who brilliantly endure suffering, only those few can walk this path. They'll feel a surge in spirit at those moments when they're most broken, the rest are crushed, and their pitiful hopes destroyed. That's horrible, Carl says, you're a sadist, you're advocating a sadistic world, but we can make it perfect, we can realize a tremendous vision. I'm not advocating anything, Fred responds. You see a ticking clock and think it's perfect, where I see a machine to constrain and prevent extraordinary things from happening. You think the welfare state is the ideal, I think its cost is too dear: mindless optimism and drunken comradery.

The little plane lands at the small provincial airport on the coast near Kavala. Mia and Ginna will take that same plane back to Athens as soon as it's ready for departure. It comes and goes once a day, that's what the market demands. They sit in the quiet waiting area. Ginna says she's happy to be there. For the progress they make, that's true, but also for the time they spend together. She's glad that Mia is staying in New York for a few days before going back to Chicago and she is looking forward to showing her around. They're getting to know each other better and she's sure Mia will love the city. Mia worries that Ginna has too much work, don't you have to get started?

Ginna gets serious. We're making excellent progress, the ideas are really coming together. I think we both realize we got it wrong. Wolfe is the demon we know. We think of him as the false public face, but that may not be true. It may not be so crisp. There are different influences at work. Ben Thorne is a set of conflicting ideas offsetting and supporting each other. His stories have tension, we can't say they're definitively this or that. They have brutality, and they have hope and wonder. They aren't simple morality tales where good wins out and evil loses. Sometimes evil is infiltrated by good, sometimes good is tainted with evil.

Humans are always projecting ought where they should only be seeing is. What does that mean? Ought *is* hidden everywhere, it's what keeps the order invisible. Sometimes we imagine an imperative only because we wish for it, collectively. We're fatalists determined to be as we are and there's nothing we can do about it, collectively. Fatalism and hope, battles where the good guy doesn't always win, this is the world we have, and we can't avoid it. I think that's the conversation these guys are having their whole lives. These guys? You mean the two masterminds of this deception? The rich and successful authors of powerful cultural artifacts that teach the teachers how to rationalize their elitism. What do you really think is going to happen when word gets out? I'm not sure, and frankly I'm not worrying about it. It doesn't matter. The writer is nothing beyond the story and we're trying to fabricate this last word of the great author. I don't understand why it has to be the last word. If Ben Thorne is a corporate body, if he's just a collection of actions and interests, can't he just undergo a reorganization? You and Eleni, you can be Ben Thorne, if you want. Wolfe won't let that happen. Maybe. I don't know. It's possible. We'll have to see. It's not up to me. Eleni is looking into it. Wolfe is coming. He's coming here. When? Now, he's on his way. I think he's on that plane out there. We think it's best if I get back to work and am not here when he arrives. She'll have better luck convincing him if they're alone. He's not a gentle man, but whatever else you can say about him, he has a soft spot even if there's no way to exploit it. I think only Eleni can do it, and she's prepared. We'll see.

Ginna catches a glimpse of Wolfe crossing the tarmac thirty feet or so in front of Carl and Fred. She does not wave, does not try to get their attention.

They struggle with alignments, it's not a clean picture. They cannot attach social justice to Em and individual liberty to Wolfe, nor can they assign political affiliations. Conflation takes place. Events get mixed up, get fuzzy and blend together, there is coming and going. Ben Thorne.

The state of nature and natural law versus an artificial welfare state cultivated by higher rational ends and the recognition of respect for each discrete and valuable being. Natural birth controls versus artificial birth controls. Forced motherhood maintains boundaries, forced servitude maintains boundaries. Labor and fame, entertainment and work, the order comes again, and the re-order goes again. Ben Thorne.

Sociobiology and the ought versus the is. The desire that intends and the desire that sees. Gender in a bottle. When social structures make the rules, issue their commands, they regulate bio-power in the species through the ought. Artificial means cause the inception of what may be through organic principles, basic and universal. Ben Thorne.

Residual

Light: A world without order is a world unmediated. For centuries, the wise men have warned that there is no such thing, but we cannot say it simply enough for a child to understand.

Justice: Children know better than anyone what we mean. Early on they get a sense of something alien, something beyond their understanding: the structure that is put upon them, that they constantly struggle to fit into.

Peace: Every action is an experiment. In the reactions of others, they learn to reflect. It's as if they are anticipating what happens next.

Light: Like a model. Their mind models the reactions of others and shows the boundary between what they do and what it means.

Peace: Of who they are. Is that what happens? Their first instinct is selfish. Who am I? What am I? This is how they answer those questions.

Justice: They are present to themselves in the same way they are present to others. They limit each other and are limited by each other.

Light: Even if there are no other people, there is mediation. They act in a world of objects resisting them. Learning to hold something, to look at it, to crawl, to walk, everything requires constant adjustments. What they see may move or spin, it may dangle, their eyes make subtle adjustments to form the images.

Justice: The object world submits to order. Actions threaten it and are threatened by it. The cup will fall, the light will dim, the blanket will move as the body under it does.

Peace: Complexity increases. Growth is an increase in complexity.

Light: A simple community with no imported objects is a simpler order. Any reflection on it is simpler too.

Justice: If humans don't speak, reflection is speechless. If humans don't love, reflection is loveless.

Peace: Should we say history is progressive? The world becomes more complex, there are more limits, more to feel, and see.

Light: The philosophers seek consistency. They want bedrock and don't think order changes as its contents are constrained.

Justice: Even so, if the logic changes with the material, there is a higher logic to describe it.

Peace: Otherwise, everything is chaos with nothing reliable.

Light: Relativism, they call it, desperately trying to find a name to capture a logic at work even where the notion denies it.

Peace: That there is a notion is the only proof they need. The world is populated with things and actors. Nothing essential changes. Consistency lies in formal laws.

Justice: There are forms to stories. Not forms, but stable things: a child is born. A person is one single thing with a body and skin.

Light: The newborn is not alone. There are multiples, peers, the tribe's collective offspring: the class, the school, and the little fish come from multitude, they are three or four, tens and hundreds. They are generation.

Justice: Even if you assign agency to the generation or collective, you still bisect and consider, you still realize a logic at work with formal patterns.

Peace: Material limits still have their form, and it can be idealized.

Light: Whether analysis is a description or a story, a myth or a principle, the platonic forms are integral to each other, and attribution shows their logic at work, form in motion.

Justice: These tiny creatures cannot see. Their bodies are alien, they have to learn to work them. They perform then collect outcomes and adjust. No content drives that form.

Light: Long before they breathe air, they are forming. Even the baby struggling to suckle has the means to figure it out.

Peace: While it forms, it relies on forms.

Light: From the first day to the last, we are born with an understanding that regulation preconditions our first breath, governs the flow of nutrients and waste. Everything is tightly ordered and its logic inescapable.

Justice: The womb doesn't make a baby. It is a domicile where self-construction happens.

Peace: We make ourselves.

Light: We do, or rather It does. Replication takes place, the code realizes itself, the limbs form, the enzymes, the chains of order. Everything happens through rapid bursts. The flow of nutrients transforms material.

Justice: Such is the logic of formation, but what about symbiosis?

Peace: It is the flow of food and oxygen that enables replication. With each turn of the crank, the creature is more concretely formed.

Light: It is a continual and ongoing set of operations. Its singularity begins there. Birth continues that process once the organism takes over its basic functions: regulating temperature, ingesting nutrients, evacuating waste, and much more.

Justice: Material creates these forms. One form materializes as another.

Peace: Perhaps the drive for knowledge traverses a most basic momentum. The first cells to combine are already complex. The genetic order, the material order, there is much that is presupposed. Interest in what's purely physical is like the old-fashioned interest in the deity, we want to know the origin, whether it is divine or material doesn't matter.

Light: The presence of basic order in those replicating cells surfaces as drive and will, as a lure back to itself.

Peace: A baby cannot do it.

Justice: The limits in being born are insufficient to make a human being.

Light: We must take part in an ongoing and adaptive set of maneuvers to get there. Collective and alone, there are experiments. Civilizations try different techniques. The individual is mediated by its world: nature naturing.

Justice: Reflecting upon nature natured.

Peace: Where reflection symbolizes the movement of what happens over and against what happened. Acts commiserate with content.

Light: Experiments happen and have happened. The event bends back on itself because it is not everything at once. It emits and collects, analyzes and learns. Learning takes what is collected and funnels it into further effort.

Justice: We have said this before. It is facticity that projects.

Peace: The manner of that movement changes with its matter, with new attributes and limits. What forms changes how forming happens.

Light: Physics becomes chemistry, chemistry becomes biology, biology neurophysiology, psychology, sociology, anthropology, and so on and on.

Peace: Each order has its logic and content.

Justice: There is agency behind it. We journey down a fateful path and cannot see our way past it. Once cognition appears, it saturates everything following from it. It replicates itself, its memes and patterns, into everything. It is the ultimate intermediary and is at work everywhere. We cannot step beyond it. The residual is unsayable because saying recaptures what escapes, pulls it back and repeats the logic of escape. We cannot get out.

Light: We can retrace our steps, locate each and every impetus, the patterns. Some study biology, and some deconstruct it. There are some who strive for the foundations of the chemical order and then still more who see only swarm. We may be individually predisposed to rigid bits and pieces, but collectively we are attuned to gigantic polyvalent symphonies that no one point of view can visualize or encompass.

Peace: The pool or collective lies behind each member that swims in it. These are preconditions. Like how the gauge for measuring is present in every measurement and shapes every fact. We share and are shared within these boundaries. We communicate in terms of those very forms that come forward when we speak and think.

Justice: Intermediaries are everywhere. We transmit, but those transmissions are not perfect. There are mistakes and they become intentional. Liars and cheats appear. There are struggles, interests that conflict, some reflecting this angle and others reflecting another, they butt heads, they wage war and do battle.

Peace: They claim to speak the truth.

Light: No one can always speak the truth. Sometimes it's too complicated to say and sometimes they just don't know it.

Justice: The truth is beyond what any one person can reach. The struggle is truth, its intermediary, and only that discloses it.

Peace: Can it be awful?

Justice: Awful to some.

Light: When you peel away the layers, when you excavate, what you may find is that what some call evil lies beneath a truth discovered. The destruction of what is good can be a lesson. A star explodes and some truth is revealed, the universe understands itself better. Once that first star explodes, the world is richer, there is more to it. It becomes a place where stars explode, having never been that before.

Peace: It reminds me of rebellion.

Justice: Rebellion?

Peace: Yes, the storyteller describes a possibility. There is a child, and that child is tortured and then, in the end, dies after prolonged suffering. This is horrible. We condemn it as the greatest evil. This innocent child is desecrated by a corrupt and twisted parent or adult.

Justice: That is a story about forgiveness. No one can forgive on behalf of the child. Reconciliation is impossible once a fatal act is performed.

Peace: Yes, it is about that, but it is also a story about what the world is like. Say there is a human child, and their anguish is unique, an outlier, something that has never happened before.

Justice: With each new villainy, imagination transcends its limits, something extraordinary and unprecedented follows.

Peace: There are natural events like this too, and extraordinary acts of kindness. We shouldn't fixate on anguish, but there is anguish.

Light: It is a prejudice to limit our thinking as if only the good is real.

Peace: Whatever happens expands the possibility of happening and happened. From the point of view of truth, of what can be, from there, that anguish emerges as new possibility. The facts expand, new theories are possible, investigation is furthered, and progress achieved.

Light: It isn't just that knowledge is increased. It isn't for the sake of science. Rather, what can be increases, the world itself changes.

Justice: Not just its material, its logic.

Peace: Every anomaly offers the possibility of replication. Once the pattern emerges, there is a probability of repeating it. Perhaps the rate evolves over time. Maybe it is a rare mutation at first but becomes more common. Later it becomes the rule.

Light: Everyone is honest. Someone lies. Their deception works because the others do not know deception is possible. Something new enters the world and people learn of it. Over generations, it becomes more common. People cease to be so trusting. The possibility of deception is real, and it becomes harder to deceive. New methods are engineered. Defenses become more complex as do the means of deceiving.

Justice: Truth isn't whether the communicator is lying, the truth is that there is deception and listeners must be able to detect it.

Peace: In circumstances where lying is more common, detection is too. That is the truth.

Justice: Morality as a body of rules undergoes adaptation. Be truthful. Fine, let that be a principle, but once its violation is pervasive, a new command is born: be vigilant in verifying the veracity of a claim.

Light: Laws capture it in an institution, a process for engineering compliance. They struggle to catch up with changing conditions. Be truthful, be vigilant in verifying, these rules are institutionalized: there are courts and contracts, but then what? What new and innovative changes identify more sophisticated fraud?

Justice: They can take hundreds and thousands of years to develop.

Peace: While they develop, chaos and uncertainty rule.

Light: There are institutions to prevent new institutions from catching on. Every strategy is organized. The courts develop to enforce one's word. Criminal organizations develop to get around the courts. There are adjustments, stable structures require generations to spread.

Justice: The complexity of the law both improves the commandment to be truthful and increases the possibility of bending the rules to find loopholes circumventing it.

Peace: Media. The intermediary between things. It can take infinite forms. It can bend into a criminal justice system, and it can bend into organized crime. Either way there are reciprocal boundaries and limits.

Justice: Organized crime appears legal so long as there are no practices in place to resolve the conflicts. Orders in motion have discrepancies. We always lag behind, and we are always struggling to catch up.

Light: The exploding star creates its principles too. It repeats itself to find an order, the single thing always resists and only in repetition do patterns and their rules emerge.

Peace: The important thing is to want to see it even when it's awful. We can't assume goodness is the rule and evil a departure from it.

Justice: That is just desire speaking, the world has no preference. There are interests that benefit from hiding this, they distract us, make analysis and learning into entertainment, categorized into pre-digested genres. They aggregate everything, turning it into universals that matter everywhere all the time, devoid of situation, and hiding their desires surreptitiously inside.

Peace: They cause false choices, make us confront meaningless options, and battle each other over idle chatter that we cannot distinguish from the truth. They ignore us because nothing we say matters once everything has its opposition. I am this, I am that. I believe I believe I believe. Blah blah blah.

Light: Gigantic bodies stomp around, networks of machine-driven communication, activity and its omission, entertainment, genre, the back and forth of human being, it goes anywhere and is anything in our midst, mediated in its configurations, then reflected back upon us.

Justice: These pronouncements move in a circle. We see what sees through us. Its force comes up behind and runs right through us.

Light: Everything is possible, but we must be vigilant and learn to understand, change ourselves, become sharper, wiser.

Peace: More attuned and more at home, these blind spots are enormous. Will we suffer their chaos? Do we secretly yearn for it?

Light: Not so secretly. The will-to-will does not mean everything is permitted, only that it must be seen: we shine a light and expose its power.

Justice: Rays of sunlight to unconceal and disclose the order binding us.

Light: Collectively, power comes from everywhere, is everywhere. It fabricates the truth with will and want whenever we understand. Not only is our existence at stake, its meaning too.

Giants and Dwarves

Stephen Wolfe

No one is supposed to know he's coming. He doesn't want to tell Ginna because he's lost faith in her. He specifically orders Carl and Fred not to tell her either. "Not a word to anyone," he says with little or no understanding of how the accounts are managed or information distributed in the office. Ginna plays along and stays clear so the three of them have to fend for themselves. Within a few hours it becomes clear that Wolfe's plan is backfiring. They don't know the area and don't have any recommendations, so they rely on Carl's poorly primed DA. They take two rooms at a hotel in the Kavala old town. The hotel is nice enough and the staff exceedingly helpful, but the location isn't convenient. They arrive by taxi from the airport, and it costs them. Not only the expense of the long ride, but now they don't have a car. After a long conversation with the concierge, Wolfe arranges for a service to drive them around.

Meanwhile, Fred and Carl can't go anywhere or do anything. Wolfe insists they remain where he can find them. He brings them as valets and assistants. They grumble that this is not part of their job description. "Where is Ginna, anyway?" Fred asks when his frustration reaches its peak. "Is the irony of that question lost on you?" Carl asks, shaking his head. He's frustrated too, but there's a rooftop terrace at the hotel, and they sit out having drinks and Mezedes while they wait. They bring their readers and make the best of it. They want to, but don't dare, contact Eirini.

Once Wolfe arranges the car service, he looks into finding Lena. He knows the address is somewhere, he distinctly recalls a conversation a few years back where Em gave it to him. Ginna must have put it somewhere, but god only knows where. After spending the better part of the evening looking for it, he gives up and texts Fred and Carl, letting them know he's going to bed and wants to get an early start in the morning. He takes a sleeping pill and is out cold soon after. Fred and Carl grumble at the ridiculous situation, but when they try to sleep, they don't have much luck.

The next morning, Wolfe bangs on their door and abruptly gets them out of bed. He orders them to text their friends to get Lena's address. Carl lets him in as Fred slowly wakes up. "Why? Don't we already have it?" Fred asks. Wolfe is impatient and screams about spending the whole night looking for it with no luck. Carl goes to the laptop and pops it open. He types and clicks a few things before saying, "Here it is," taking only 20 seconds. "What is this?" Wolfe snarls. "This is your contact list. It has everyone in it. This is Em's entry. Here's the address in Seattle and here's the one in Greece." Wolfe's irritation doesn't subside, it increases. He stomps out of the room, saying as he goes, "We're leaving in half an hour. Be downstairs in the lobby and bring the address." Then he's gone.

The driver speaks enough English to get an address from the passengers, but not enough to handle any problems. If there are any special needs, communication is impossible. He looks at the address and shrugs. He says something about Chrysoupoli, then a longer stream of words that get no reply. Wolfe doesn't look at Fred or Carl, he just says, "Go get someone to translate." The logistics take long to sort out and Wolfe becomes increasingly impatient. The delays are maddening. His anger prevents him from concentrating and he gets really quiet. When he does speak, his jaw is so tightly clenched that the words come out seething. Fred and Carl become increasingly distressed. The hotel agent comes outside and speaks with the driver. After a brief exchange, he explains to Wolfe that the man knows how to get to Chrysoupoli but doesn't know where the specific address is. Wolfe wants to know why he doesn't have GPS. "Why is there no fucking AP in this car?", he tries to ask, but it comes out as a sputter and the agent doesn't understand. He doesn't make eye contact and it isn't clear who he's talking to. Carl rephrases and repeats. The agent politely responds that it's an older model. It doesn't have GPS or AP, but the driver will get them there and they needn't worry. When they arrive in Chrysoupoli, he will ask for directions. Carl and Fred nod, while Wolfe says under his breath, "bar bar bar" and then rapidly pulls open the car door and climbs into the passenger seat. Fred and Carl thank the driver and the hotel agent and get into the back seat. It's a smaller car and there isn't much leg room back there. Neither the driver nor Wolfe makes any effort to remedy that, leaving their seats where they are with plenty of legroom up front.

After stopping at an energy station just inside the Chrysoupoli city limit, the driver gets back in the car and, without a word, drives straight to the house. During the stop, he is inside the station for a long time and Wolfe stews in the passenger seat watching him laugh and chatter away with the attendant. He sits with his arms firmly crossed on his chest muttering profanities and complaining that it's taking far too long. When they arrive, the driver pulls off to the side of the little street and parks in front of the house. Smiling at Wolfe, he says "we are here." Wolfe doesn't look over at him or back at Fred and Carl, but gets out of the car and says, "wait here," as he slams the door and walks up the driveway. "This could take a while," Carl says pulling his reader out of the bag at his feet. "Or he might be back in a few seconds," Fred says starting to laugh. "Would you want that asshole in your house?" The driver looks back at Fred. He's laughing too.

Ermioni opens the door and appears to recognize him but doesn't say anything. Wolfe takes a deep breath. "Hello, good to finally meet you. I am so sorry for your loss." Although trying, his tone still has a little nastiness in it. She half nods but looks past him. "How did you get here?" she asks, trying to see the street. Her view of the car is blocked by the row of trees. "There's a car, we have a driver. If you can imagine. They are not exactly up to date here, are they?" She doesn't look at him, and steps out onto the porch straining to see the car. "Who is we"? She asks. "My interns are with me." Ermioni lets out a brief exclamation and briskly walks up the path toward the street. She comes back a few seconds later with Fred, Carl, and the driver in tow. "Come in, come in," she says as she steps back onto the porch. They go into the house, and she gets them water. "Do you want anything to eat? I have some cake. Would you like a piece?" Fred and Carl both nod enthusiastically. She repeats her question in Greek, looking at the driver.

Wolfe becomes even more irritated, as if that is possible. He expects this to be a one-on-one conversation thinking he'll have time alone with Ermioni, but she isn't paying any attention to him. She doesn't seem to have any questions, in fact, not for him at least. It's as if his significance is completely unregistered, and this confuses him. As she cuts and plates the cake, he's about to ask if he can speak to her alone, but she interrupts him and says, "I never did get to hear much about your adventure across the country." She is looking at Fred and Carl. Then she says something in Greek to the driver who shows surprise. "I'm telling him the story of you two driving across America with my daughter," she says to clarify. "Mostly uneventful," Carl says. "Not what we expect, considering the hype in the news. Just people. The landscape is surprising." She nods and asks, "How so?" Fred answers as though he's having the same thought, "It's changing. So dry. It doesn't rain. No fires, but you see the effects. So many burned out forests." Carl nods and Ermioni purses her lips. "It's criminal," she says. "But the people? They aren't foaming at the mouth trying to kill you?" She's smiling when she says it. "Not a chance," Carl responds. "Everyone's pleasant and helpful." "Well, not everyone," Fred says. "I'm sure other people have different experiences." Carl shakes his head upon seeing Ermioni's concerned look. "It's nothing. Maybe you're right, we don't know what we're not seeing. I'm just saying, it isn't anything like they want us to believe. I think there's a lot of fear mongering. Face-to-face it's not as bad as that." "So long as you're white," Fred says. Ermioni is making the conversation drag out, she doesn't want to look back at Wolfe, but feels his agitation. Just as he's about to speak, she blurts out, "But Eleni, she's in the garage. Let me go get her."

This is more than Wolfe can handle. He steps in front of her and blocks the way to the garage. He says, "Actually, I need to speak with her. Can I go get her?" "There will be plenty of time…" "I insist," he says firmly. "I really need to speak with her." He's standing close and towering over her deliberately. She grimaces, but points in the direction of the garage and says, "around that corner and through the door at the end." He turns and heads off in that direction, while Ermioni turns back to her other guests now sitting at the island.

When Wolfe opens the door to the garage, he sees Lena working a heavy bag hanging from a reinforced hook in the ceiling. She's sweating, breathing hard, and so focused that she doesn't notice him. He moves around behind the bag to get into her field of vision. When she sees him, she doesn't look surprised, but stops her routine abruptly, taking off the gloves, and picking up a towel nearby. As Wolfe begins speaking, she takes her phone and types something. It's unnerving to him, he wants her undivided attention, and can't believe how rude everyone is.

"There must be some misunderstanding," he says. "I know Virginia has been here and you two have been working together. Looking at Em's notes. But you are not letting me see anything. I cannot even get you to respond to my calls and mails. What is going on? Where is this coming from? The plan is settled, is it not?"

By the time he gets to the end of his speech, she's facing him with a detached look. Her silence is making him uncomfortable, something about the look in her eyes, she isn't saying anything, and doesn't seem to be getting ready to say anything. He thinks she'll immediately burst out with an explanation, but there's nothing. "Are Fred and Carl with you?" she asks finally just as he begins to break the silence. "Ginna is certain you'll bring them." He nods in response. He's very much off guard. Something about the tone and the revelation that Ginna knows he's coming. He breaks an awkward smile and says, "They are inside with your mother. And the driver, pfft." She starts toward the door saying as she goes, "If there are people around, my mother will feed them." He steps in front of her to block her way to the door, but she gives him a chilling look. Even without gloves, the workout clothes and bare feet make it clear she's still ready to box. When she looks him up and down, he gets the distinct impression that if he doesn't get out of her way, she'll punch him. "Please," he says more gently. "I just need a minute. I do not understand why this has to be confrontational. I have been working on this project for over a year. Em's project. Why are you stalling?" She relaxes a little and it shows in her body and on her face. For some reason, she feels a rush of empathy. Something in his tone makes him seem more pathetic. "I've been reading his notebooks, Steve." She says emphasizing the nickname. "If you want to have a conversation, you'll have to be honest."

Wolfe looks down and moves farther away, he circles a bit in the empty part of the garage, giving her plenty of opportunity to get away if she wants. She waits. "What do you want me to say? Em and I have a working relationship that is sometimes tense. That is how we create. If you are saying there is evidence of hostility, I urge you to look deeper. Do not just read the last year, read every year and every project. That is how we do things. I know how young people are now, but that is not how we do it. We are confrontational. Friends can argue without fear of offending. You know him, he does not suffer fools gladly."

She looks down when he says it and he thinks maybe her eyes are glistening. "Socrates' guardians," she says. He slowly nods, closing his eyes for emphasis. "They're like dogs," she goes on. "Kind and loving to those they know, fierce and protective with those they don't." He manages to smile. "You do not need to pull your punches," he says tilting his head toward the heavy bag behind her. "I can take it. If his notes suggest something different than I have in mind, you can tell me. That is part of the process." She nods and looks off toward the door back into the house. "Let's go inside and see Fred and Carl. I want to say hello." She looks back down at her phone. "Eirini's coming over." She looks him straight in the eye and takes a lecturing tone, "You can't expect to barge in and get right down to business. You're going to have to meet everyone, and eat with everyone, and drink with everyone. That's just how it is. You'll have to be nice to people. Drivers too."

He relaxes his shoulders and shows signs he's less irritated, then extends his arm toward the door as if motioning her through and he'll follow.

Back inside she hears someone say, "one side saves the institutions that create the division while the other side destroys them for the sake of a new tyranny." She calls out excitedly and hurries around the corner to see Carl and Fred. They ignore her apologies for being sweaty and give her big hugs. Completely distracted from their tirade in front of the confused driver, they fall into conversation about their trip and each of its phases. They tell her about the old man from Kalamata and the flight from Athens and how beautiful the sea and coastline are. They're happy to see each other. Even the driver seems happy about the reunion. Eleni shakes hands and welcomes him, asking if he needs anything. Ermioni notices the change in Wolfe's demeanor and smiles at him, "Can I get you something to drink, Ben?" Fred and Carl each have a cup of coffee, but there's an open bottle of Tsipouro on the counter. "I will have a glass of that," he says. "It is five o'clock somewhere, I imagine." "Okay then, but you have to have some Soutzoukakia," she responds gleefully. "No, no thanks." "You must," she insists waving his objection aside.

It isn't long before the front door opens, and Eirini comes in with Europea. She goes swiftly up to Fred and then to Carl, giving each of them a warm hug and welcoming them. She drags them both to Europea and makes the introductions. Europea kisses their cheeks and says something Carl doesn't understand. "She's welcoming you," Eirini says, then she turns to Ermioni, "Dad wants to come and meet everyone. Is it okay? My aunt too." "Yes, yes, of course," she says already looking through the refrigerator for something to serve.

"Yiayia," Eleni says coming closer to where her grandmother is standing with Fred and Carl. "This is Ben Thorne." She takes his arm and ushers him over to her. "The writer." Europea smiles and exclaims loudly, then she blurts out a long stream of words without pausing. Wolfe doesn't understand any of it, but he smiles and nods and lets her kiss him on both cheeks while she grips his shoulders. She holds on to him the whole time she speaks and only very reluctantly releases him at the end. She looks over at Eleni, indicating she should translate. "She's telling you how much she loves your book *On Being Born*," Eleni says. "She says it's one of her favorites, a true masterpiece. She likes some of the others too, but that one is truly special. She's read it many times. In Greek, of course. *Yenesis*, it's called." He looks almost shy when he smiles at the older woman and says as best he can, "Efharisto poly." She bubbles with glee at his effort and grabs his shoulders again. She kisses him on both cheeks, and he lets down his resistance to welcome it, repeating the only Greek phrase he knows. "Efharisto poly."

"See," Eleni says while he's still in her grandmother's clutches. "This is how we do things."

Ben Thorne, Inc.

Ginna takes Mia to see the offices of Ben Thorne. Not as a tourist attraction, they have to work, and she thinks that's the best place for it. She wants to sit with the notes and the ideas she's been hatching with Eleni during the long weekend. She wants to start making sketches and maybe a study or two. The skeleton is forming, and it's time to experiment. She might have been able to do it in Greece. It's certainly very disruptive to make such a long journey for such a short time, but she has to be there in person. Now that she feels better oriented, it's time to get to work. For that, she needs her familiar workspace. She's grown used to the office, to being alone there. Fred and Carl are a regular fixture, but she can send them out somewhere whenever she wants. Ben Thorne is usually locked in his office. They're incidental to the rhythms of the place, all the men are. They're not bound to it the same way she is. She has that desk right in the middle of the entry room, equidistant from the office and the bullpen. It's her space, and she's bursting to get back to it.

At first, she worries about bringing Mia with her. She loves the time together in Greece getting to know each other better and already feels more comfortable around her, but this is work and she isn't sure how it's going to be. Mia goes into Ben Thorne's office and closes the door to give them both some privacy. She comes out and fills her water bottle, and goes for coffee: she's the perfect guest, not only staying out of the way when Ginna needs her space but taking care of her needs. She doesn't make a big show of it, she just puts the coffee and a muffin on the desk and goes back into the office. She gladly gives Ginna a nuzzle when she stops her on the way, needing to see a face and hear a voice.

While walking to the little place on the corner for lunch, Mia says she has to go back to Illinois soon. There's a court date coming up in St. Louis and she has to be in the office beforehand. She'll arrange to leave at the end of the week. "I'm sorry I won't be able to stay for the weekend, but I have to get ready for court," she says. "It's fine," Ginna assures her. "I think I can still be productive even if you're not here. I love being by myself with you," she says squinting and a little bashful.

They talk about the possibility of Ginna going to Chicago to meet her there after she gets back from St. Louis. If she's productive during the week, she'll take a break. "It might be a little awkward," Mia admits when Ginna asks. "But Gwen and I... Well, we don't really have that kind... At least, I don't think... No, you should come. Definitely, come, we'll work it out." Ginna smiles as Mia gets quiet and leans forward a little. She puts her elbows on the table and looks down awkwardly, "Full disclosure... ...Gwen is bi-sexual." This makes Ginna laugh. There is so much tension when Mia leans forward, and Ginna mirrors it in her shoulders. When she hears the big reveal, she relaxes, and the laughter is like a release of pressure. "That's not what I thought you were going to say." Mia smiles and relaxes too. "Maybe in your crowd that isn't a big deal, but in my set, it's a thing." Ginna puts her hand out and takes hold of Mia's, resting on the table. She looks at her patiently. "I bet she's going to marry a guy and have kids," Mia continues and then looks down and laughs while scrunching her eyes and nose. "It's not that it isn't real, I just mean, well, we work a lot, it's convenient."

They feel better after that. Ginna tells her story. She's busy too. There's her own work and Ben Thorne's. So many things to organize and do. Besides managing the office and the schedule, she's an editor and works with women's writing workshops. It doesn't leave her much time. "Believe me," she says. "I'd love to have something like that. You're lucky." Mia is sympathetic. It isn't that long since she's in the same situation. "What about Ben Thorne?" she asks, putting an artificial emphasis on the name. "It must be difficult spending so much time with him." Ginna bobs her head and looks off toward the window. The street is crowded, and everyone seems cheerful and enjoying the sunshine. "You might have the wrong idea about him. Yes, he's a seventy-year-old man and he's the way he is." She makes a lewd stroking gesture and both of them gasp a guilty laugh before looking down and then -in perfect sync— back up at each other. "But he is brilliant, and he's demanding indiscriminately. He could be a lot worse. He looks me in the eyes. He's professional. He's even warm sometimes. It's not like he's clueless and stiff. These last couple weeks are not typical, I can't discount everything over the years."

Ginna interrupts herself and says they should get back to the office. They get up and move toward the door. "I know he's your biological father, and it's a complicated relationship." Mia purses her lips. She has plenty to say, but Ginna isn't done, so she waits. "He isn't perfect, but it's not like it's a fraud and there's a wizard behind the curtain. That's not what I remember. They're expert problem solvers. Ben has blind spots, there are things he can't see. Em sees them, but he has his own and needs Ben to help him." Mia holds the door as they go out into the street and slowly work their way up the block to the office. There is plenty of sun on their side of the street, and they aren't in a hurry. "What does Lena say?" Mia asks. "She doesn't know. 'Masters of Pathos,' she calls them. There are notebooks, and they tell one side of the story, but it's not the whole story. Ben or Wolfe or whatever, he's got a voice, style, but isn't a storyteller. He wants to say everything at once. Em... They love each other, they hate each other, and they need each other."

They go in the office door, both shrugging through the small space together. They go in single file up the narrow stairs to the second story office and sit for a little longer by Ginna's desk. "He's always been good that way," Mia says. "I mean, organizing narratives." She folds her hands in her lap and leans forward in the chair. "Our conversations... The reason I absolutely have to fucking talk to him whenever there's a crisis, whenever I'm overwhelmed... He's the one I turn to." She pauses and Ginna waits. "I can be pretty defensive. I'm not going to be vulnerable around my professors or some colleagues, there's no way in hell... When I have doubts, he's a good ear. He knows momentary weaknesses aren't character flaws, he understands what passionate people are like. A good listener, he tells me I just need to get organized." Ginna smiles and nods, trying to let Mia know she understands. "Maybe it's my imagination but some people just have a way about them. 'Let's get this sorted,'" she imitates a dopey sounding voice. "It just helps. If someone you trust says, 'there's nothing wrong with you'," she's using that same voice. "'you just need to lay it out to see it clearly.' Maybe I roll my eyes, but it helps."

Later in the afternoon, Lena makes a video call to Mia who brings her laptop out of the office so Ginna can join. Eirini is on the call too. They look sleepy and about ready for bed. Lena launches into a description telling how Ben Thorne shows up around noon with Fred and Carl and that her mother brings them inside. One thing leads to another and before you know it the whole family's there eating and drinking. The conversations are lively and constant, and no one leaves for quiet time, although Eirini interrupts her to say she saw Georgios go upstairs for a bit. They both look flushed and are a little hoarse.

"Is he behaving? What's happening?" Ginna wants to know and gets them back on track. "He's ornery and mean at first," Lena says. "But he relaxes eventually. My grandmother sits with him the whole time and she keeps talking in Greek. He's nodding and smiling but doesn't understand a word. She doesn't let go." "I'm trying to translate," Eirini interrupts. "But Europea won't let me. She just keeps on going. She drinks Tsipouro with him. I think they're the only two," she says looking over at Lena. "I think so too. There's fried fish so most of us have wine." "Except the driver," Eirini says as though finishing the sentence. "He's not drinking." "What driver?" Mia asks. "They have a driver. They're staying at a hotel in Kavala. To take them around," Lena says. At the same time, Eirini is saying something about rental cars and how you have to pay extra for everything. They're talking over each other, and it's hard to follow.

"Are you already talking about the work with him?" Mia says trying to get them back to the intent of Ginna's question. They aren't finished with their tangent yet and Eirini starts talking about Fred and Carl. Lena is saying how Ion came by and that someone must have told Alexandros because somehow Mihalis found out about Ben Thorne so they both show up later. That is at cross purposes with what Eirini is saying about Fred and Carl. "They're so cute," she says almost giggling. "They follow me around with their eyes, but they're polite. They don't want to be a bother. It's adorable. I introduce them to my mother, and she keeps them the whole day. She wants to hear about New York, but every time they start to tell her it reminds her of something, and she tells another story instead. But they can't leave, she won't let them go. It's so funny." She starts laughing and leans into Lena who leans back and starts laughing too. "You're naughty," she says. "Those poor boys." Mia tries to repeat the question to get them back on track, but Eirini is too quick, and jumps back in after straightening up and says, "what about you with Ion and Mihalis? Always trying to get your attention. They don't like each other." Lena shakes her head deliberately. "No, they most definitely do not. They're very possessive." They both keep laughing, and Eirini starts to complain, "That's not fair..."

Mia is very stern this time and sounds almost motherly when she says, "Ladies, that's enough," she then repeats her question, Ginna's question, "Lena, are you speaking with Ben Thorne?" "Of course, I am," she says. "For like ten hours." "What about?" Ginna asks, sounding worried. Lena is drunk and she's concerned about loose lips. "About the book?" Lena straightens up and becomes serious. She puts her hand on Eirini's leg as if to calm her. "Yes, in fact. Finally. It's hard to get time. Georgios is going on with him about his favorite book. He's leaving soon. Mihalis talks to him for a long time too. A critical reading of the imaginary in the many voicings of *The Lens Grinder's Shadow* or the role of erotism in blah blah

blah or whatever. We get some time together though. I don't want other people around, you know. We'll talk more tomorrow. Nikos is taking Fred and Carl to the beach." "Focus, please," Mia says. "Right," Lena goes on. "Not much today. There isn't much time. I just tell him I don't think there's a book there." "What?" Ginna jumps in, her voice rising an octave. "The notebooks make it clear. I say, and I'm quoting, 'it's not intervention, it's interlude.' And he knows exactly what I'm talking about. He knows." Eirini looks slowly over at Lena and says, "I'm not going with them. I don't think that's a good idea. Not with my dad at the beach. Bad idea." Mia calmly speaks over her, "Eirini sweety, please hold that thought. Let Lena finish. Go on, Lena." "Okay, but my brother should go with them too. He can't though, he has to be at school for something." Mia nods but keeps eye contact with Lena. "There isn't much else to say," Lena goes on. "We'll talk tomorrow. Just a hint, so he's not surprised. Interlude not intervention. Interventions don't work. That's what Dad says. Or the intervention doesn't work. Or it does, but not how he thinks."

Mia looks over at Ginna whose eyes are fixed on the screen. "Yes, I get it. Intervention uses the logic of either / or," she says looking over at Mia then back to Eleni on the screen. "Either you keep going or you stop. Interlude is different." Lena is nodding fiercely. She emphatically expresses her agreement with her entire body. "I understand what he means by that." Ginna is nodding too. Their eyes meet. "Me too," she says. "I've been writing about it today. I'll send my sketches. You'll see. I'll send them later tonight, maybe you can look at them before you talk to him tomorrow." Lena shakes her head and Eirini mirrors her with the same motion. She yawns. "It's late here, we'll go to bed soon. I'll have to look at them tomorrow." Mia smiles and shows agreement with her eyes, she looks back and forth between Lena and Ginna. "Yes, that's fine. Wait until tomorrow. She'll send it and you can read it when you wake up. Eirini are you going home, or will you stay there? Maybe you should stay." "No, no, it's okay. Georgios will take me. It's only a few blocks. It's fine. Good night, kisses. Hugs. Bye-bye." Lena starts to repeat the same farewell sequence, but the camera cuts out when she's only halfway through it.

"Hilarious," Mia says picking up the laptop and starting back toward the office. Ginna is smiling broadly. "The whole thing is so wacky," she says, getting very excited at the thought of it. "I wish I could be there, a fly on the wall. I can just see the look on his face. It's been years since that man's been in a room with more than 5 people who aren't avid devotees."

The New Triangle (A Day in the Life)

Nikos picks them up at the hotel and drives them to Lena's. He drops Ben Thorne off and then takes Fred and Carl to the beach. His job is to keep them busy and, most importantly, away from Eirini. He doesn't know that's his job, but he's doing it anyway. They've never been to Greece, and they've never been to the beach in Greece. In early September it's still warm in the North, but the crowds are thinner and there isn't much tourism. They can go to the nice beaches out at the end of the pine tree point just South of the Keramoti harbor.

Mia, Gwen, and Bert are on a video conference call. It's a working meeting. They're completing the details for filing. The law is clear, corporations are people. They can be held liable for felony crimes in collusion with natural persons, aka human beings. The Supreme Court set the precedent that separate but equal is unconstitutional. There can be one and only one penal code, and incarceration must be redefined. The only thing they have to do is demonstrate collusion between the Liberty News Network and the people from the festival. During the call, they discuss how to make each step crystal clear.

Ariti stops by to see Europea. Eirini is leaving for work a little earlier now because of the new union rules that put stricter limits on the number of hours municipal workers are in the office each day. The three of them sit at the table in the kitchen. She tells them how glad she is that her father is taking Carl and Fred to the beach. There's more to the story than she's willing to share, but they believe her when she tells them that she likes them because they're respectful and kind to her, but she doesn't *like* them like them. The older women sense *that* might be for the same reason.

Ermioni, Dmitra, and Constantinos are in the office. Constantinos is performing procedures on the dogs they took in the night before. Dmitra is working at the computer while Ermioni sits in front by the window with a mangy calico next to her. This one lives on the alley by the office, and she says hello to it almost every day when she comes in the morning. The cats in town are hers, and the cats are not hers. They are and they are not. They are everybody's. The municipality admits it, the budget proves it, it's official. The stray animals both do and do not belong to everybody. "Poor things," she says and keeps petting the cat. It's purring.

Ion stops into the little coffee shop near the square. Charlie and Horacio are sitting at a table on the sidewalk. He gets his Frappé and sits down with them. They tease him to try and get more information about Eleni. He's smitten and cannot hide it. He sees no reason to. He sees no reason why she shouldn't return his feelings. It's over and done with as far as he's concerned. She is his. He wants her and he can care for her. What more is there to say? The older men laugh, and exchange looks. "How old are you, mate?" Charlie asks in English and then sips his drink to hide his laughter. He isn't expecting an answer, it's rhetorical.

Mihalis is in Thessaloniki to visit Akis who's having lunch with Alexandros. They sit together, and Mihalis wants to know about the man from the party. He plies Alexandros for information. "At Eleni's house," he clarifies. "Who's the young man, the electrician?" He doesn't understand why she's leading this other guy on like that. It's not like her, Eleni is smart and well-educated. Surely, she isn't interested in him. Such a young-looking face, such naïve ways with his juvenile flourishes. Why is she toying with him? Mihalis is up and coming. He's brilliant. He has no doubt that she prefers him.

Virginia is at her desk. There are two books in front of her. Physical books with creases on the bindings and scraped surfaces front and back. *The Basic Writings of Nietzsche*, on the one hand, and *Don Quixote*, on the other. There's something about them in the notebooks. "Nietzsche the quixote sets himself off from everyone else, not as an imperative but as a fact. He is apart from the others. He is alone. Sancho doesn't count, he's the underman. It conditions his state of mind bearing him from beneath every burden. The leap is to proclaim, 'thus I willed it.' He calms himself and reasons through his isolation by observing that the masses —everyone else— are slaves but don't know it. He stands on our backs, depends on us, and concludes that the exception is the rule. His genius derives from his isolation, which derives from the weak-mindedness of the rest. This is the circular, self-reinforcing, logic of a delusion. He is an idiot (idiotes or 'private person'). The upshot is not 'Nietzsche is evil' or even 'Nietzsche is wrong' but 'poor Nietzsche.'" Death is their bond, and he provokes her. She goes back and forth between the two books this morning. She moves quietly through the minds of two men connecting through a third who doesn't want anything for himself, only to lay out what they're saying for no one in particular in the quiet space of his notes. "Revealing the subconscious is the key, but it has to be coupled with technique worthy of investigation and not left to taste. Some may never find contemporaries: men at their best and men at their worst," she whispers to herself and then laughs. Otherwise, the room is silent.

Eleni opens the front door for Ben Thorne, and he comes inside boldly. She offers him some orange juice and then shows him into the office at the back. He sits comfortably on the couch, looking around and taking it in. "Seventy is not very old these days," he says looking at the shelves with the books and decorations. "As a kid when hearing of someone dying at seventy, I think, wow, that is old, a long life. It must be their time. Now I think, seventy, so young, what a shame." Eleni sits in one of the desk chairs, and just stares in his general direction without saying anything. "I keep expecting him to show up. Does that happen to you?" he asks uncomfortably. He doesn't want to seem too eager to get down to business. "It is inconceivable that I cannot call him anymore." She wonders if he's being sincere. "Anyone could say that," she says after a pause. "Everyone does say that. It's hard to know if you mean it." She speaks simply, there isn't any emotion in her tone and no hint of judgment.

"Do you know what's fascinating to me?" She looks directly at him but doesn't answer. "Shall I tell you?" He asks her directly and she nods. She wants to know but doesn't want him to know that. "I have no idea if you look like your dad. I cannot see him in you, not physically. Generalized family resemblance maybe. He is about your age when we first meet. Same eyes, different color, but none of that matters. What is fascinating are the little thought tricks, the patterns. There, the resemblance is stunning. It is almost like he is here with us when you say things like that." He stops talking and just sits quietly looking at the books on the shelves, registering each title, realizing why it's there. It's not a random selection, no one else put them there. Eleni is dying to ask for more details. She wants to know what he means, what he's referring to, but she doesn't want to ask. She sits on her hands and tries to think of something else to pass the time. Finally, he goes on. "I just express an emotion. I think it is what I am feeling at the time. You point out that it is a cliché, it is something everybody says. You immediately draw my attention to the bureaucracy in my own mind. It is as if you are saying, you think you are having a genuine emotion right now, but you are not, you are just feeling what they want you to feel. It is as if his sensibilities are replicated. It is not your nose, and it is not your jaw. Maybe those come from some grandmother or grandfather, but your intellectual proclivities... that, I recognize."

"Can I tell you what I think?" She asks once he's finished. "I wish you would," he says rapidly. "I think you're trying to flatter me. I think you believe that if I like you, I'll be more accommodating." He nods multiple times and looks back at the shelves. "I can imagine," he says still looking away. "I am nothing to you. Your loyalty is clear, I know where it lies. People may be more complex than you think... They are. I am. If you think that is flattery, you are oversimplifying, and that is probably because you are young and do not know any better." She rolls her eyes but doesn't say anything. "I am trying to discover whether you are going to be of any use to me, or if you are just an obstacle that I have to get around."

"Is that what people are to you, obstacles or tools?" "Most people are nothing to me." He sounds almost bored when he says it, but her question comes immediately after he breaks off and his response comes fast on the heels of it. He sits up a little at the thrill of the pace. "You are twenty-six years old. How can you possibly think you have the talent and capability to work through the material for this book? You must be terrified. This is not some grad school assignment. Ben Thorne. Me. What have you done? Some college fellowship for research in the social sciences: the best out of a hundred peers." She pivots in the chair turning away from him to look out the window. There are two children in the neighbor's yard, but she can barely see them. She's thinking the morning classes must be out, and it's

later than she thinks. Her mom will be home soon. "Flattery isn't working,
so how about intimidation? Is that it?"

"Fine. Explain it to me please. Whatever it is you are cryptically
implying. What is your big idea? What do you have from the notes that
you think I do not know already?"

He is making her nervous. He's intimidating her, but she will not let
him see it. What does she know? She studies evolutionary biology. What
does she know about literature? She feels the pull of an obligation but
doesn't want to have this conversation, she doesn't want to be involved in
this ridiculous drama, but what choice does she have? "What I 'm saying
is that you're thinking incorrectly about events. You're fixated on
something from years ago, something that doesn't go the way you plan. I
don't know anything about it, but my father thinks you're making a mistake
and that the story you want to tell isn't where you're looking for it."

"Yes, I get that. It is why I am here. Tell me what it means, interlude
not intervention." She immediately shakes her head forcefully. "No, you
tell me what it means. Let's start like that." He shrugs and nods, then he
goes on, "My picture is simple. Em fits with a type and is heading down a
path. He moves along it and then something happens. Let us say that I have
no idea what it is. Let us say that no one knows what it is. That is probably
true. Something happens, it changes everything, and no one knows about
it, they only know the consequences." He stops and then says, "Can I get
some more juice? Or some water?" She takes his glass and goes to replace
it with one filled with filtered water from the refrigerator. When she comes
back, she puts the glass down in front of him and he starts up again without
taking a sip. "In my view, an action prevents the trajectory. I try to stop him
from making a mistake. All these years, I think I fail because he does it
anyway. Saying interlude not intervention says that everything I think,
everything I believe, is wrong." She nods and says she understands. "That
is intervention," he confirms. "Interlude happens long before. He thinks it
is something that he actually causes to happen by writing it. He can be
mystical like that. It is as though he discovers a spell of some kind, he
creates something out of nothing, conjures it, and that causes an interlude
to appear center stage: a farce between the acts of a play, interlude." Now
he takes a sip and pivots a little on the couch. He cranes his neck as though
it's a bit stiff but is now more comfortable facing her. "The thing he is
working on when that happens is called *Being an Introduction*. Being.
Comma. An Introduction. Colon. To gift-giving. Comma. Time. It ties
together the notes you are reading. What if the years are only interlude?
Not just some one thing that happens one day and which comes to an end,
but all of time, his whole life forever after. But that does not make sense.
Interlude happens between the acts. If there is no second act, there is no
interlude. Get it? Have you read it?" "Yes," she says.

He gets up and walks over to the shelves, standing in front of them, continuing to look at the rows of books. "How can you know it is an interlude until the second act comes to an end? The difference between intervention and interlude lies in what is on either side. If your dad dies without a second act, there is no interlude. Do you see? The argument I hear when you say that to me is that you want to make sure that what happens, his entire life after that moment when he conjures it way way back, is interlude and not an intervention or whatever it is if the second act never happens."

"That's what I think," she whispers. "I think that's what *Being an Introduction* turns into over the years. That's the book he wants to go back to, that's what he wants to finish to guarantee it isn't a failed intervention, but a farce that only lasts while we wait for the second act. He wants to be part of what excludes him."

"*Being an Introduction* is philosophy. It is not something anyone expects from Ben Thorne."

"You know better than that. He wants to change the voice, he wants a different style for philosophy, one with character and a pulse, that lives in the structures between people, not in the mind of any one of them."

"Even when criticizing the view from nowhere, Nagel adopts the view from nowhere."

She starts to speak but breaks off frustrated. She searches for something but can't find it. There's no argument. She doesn't know what to say.

He smiles knowingly and takes a book from the shelf. He flips through the pages to check and see if there are any marks or writing. "Are you looking through these for things that might be stuck in them somewhere? Bookmarks or receipts. Sometimes you find the wildest things in people's books. You should look through them all." She stands up and comes over to him to look at the book in his hand. It is an English translation of *Don Quixote*, leather bound. "When I'm twelve or so, we take a vacation to Nafpaktos," she says unable to stop herself. "He likes it there for some reason. He and my mom are returning for a second visit, they want to stay longer than the first time. The three of us are there for a few weeks. There isn't much to do. Drive up to Delphi. The West coast of Peloponnese. Not much else. The restaurants aren't that great. The beaches either. It's on the canal, not the sea. What does he love about it? I always wonder. Every night, the three of us take a walk around town. No matter how we start out or where we go, we are sure to pass the statue in the little harbor, the one where Miguel de Cervantes is holding his right arm straight up and pointing to the sky with his left hand hidden in his waist. It's to commemorate his part in the battle of Lepanto. He comes because he believes he has a sacred duty to fight on the side of the Christians in their war with the Muslims."

"Are you familiar with *Don Quixote*?" he asks her. She nods. "He doesn't think it is funny." "I know. He thinks it is really sad and pathetic. I do too." "There is no Dulcinea del Toboso. That is fucking gut-wrenching. That whole fiasco where Sancho thinks she is someone other than who she is, but she is not anybody, so he is neither wrong nor right." His voice is breaking as he speaks. He turns away from her and looks down at the book. A tear falls onto it, and he abruptly closes it and puts it back on the shelf. He stands there looking at it before pulling it back out again.

"Why doesn't he want anyone to know?" she asks. Her voice is unsteady too now. She doesn't want to turn away, she doesn't want to face him either. She wants him to turn and look at her. She wants him to say it, to tell her. She repeats, "Why doesn't he want anyone to know?"

"It is corrupt, it is completely corrupt. He is always laughing at me. He sees how much I enjoy it. The interviews, the fans, people gushing about how they love this or how they love that. Your father thinks the purest thing that could ever happen in the whole history of human beings is a momentary experience that only one person knows."

"What are you talking about?"

"Nietzsche writes *Thus Spake Zarathustra*. And there is this stretch of time in which the only existence that book has is in Nietzsche's mind. He writes it. Does he know what it is? What does he think about it? No one else says anything. It has no adoring public. No noisy audience, no armchair after the fact analysis from puffed up fools with no sense of its meaning. The only feedback he has is silence, a rich expanse where the exhilarating beauty of the work resonates. Can he feel it? That connection, that relationship to the 'child of his brain', that is what your father thinks is the purest thing that ever exists. Does that make sense? That is why he laughs at me. That is why he thinks I am so foolish. Everything I do to enjoy the role I play. Being Ben Thorne. All of that, he thinks it corrupts the purest thing in the world, the truest thing there can ever be. And that one true thing, that pure thing, that is what he wants. His whole life. Just that."

They stand quietly, several feet apart. Each of them has their arms folded across their chest, each of them needs protection. Not just from each other, from everything.

"That is why he loves your mother so much," he says it almost absent mindedly, like he's just remembering it.

"What do you mean?"

"He thinks she has that purity. Clarity of purpose is the center of the circle. She lives the better part of each day deep within it. He thinks she is perfect, the truest thing."

Ermioni is walking home from the project office. She counts the cats and dogs as she passes by, making sure they are where they're supposed to be. She stops to say hi and makes sure they aren't hungry. They recognize her and say hello in their own way. When she gets home, she goes directly to the kitchen and starts taking out the ingredients for a salad when Eleni comes out and walks right up to her, wraps her arms around her, presses her head against her shoulder, and then turns to press her eyes and nose against her neck. Ermioni wraps her arms around her and pulls her close.

Polarity Unbound

Ginna goes with Mia to the airport on Friday afternoon and then goes back to the office. She can't get any of it out of her head. The last few days are a whirlwind. Writing and sex, she's still giddy with excitement. She's usually so mechanical when writing, she sets consistent and reasonable goals and makes sure to meet them every day. This is different. She can't stop. Her 1000-word regimen is decimated, she's writing 10 to 15 thousand words a day since getting on the plane for New Jersey. It isn't continuous material or even contiguous, but it's related. Everything appears before her, the little details, everything she remembers from over the years, it rushes back. It feels more like what they describe as channeling than anything she's known before. She writes long into the evening, forgetting to eat, and then pulls something from the fridge in the little kitchen. It doesn't matter what it is, anything will do. Mia calls to check in when her plane lands, but Ginna is distracted, and has to go soon after they start talking. Mia laughs and says she'll let her get back to it. She doesn't come up for air until almost midday on Saturday when she's so exhausted that she has to lie down just to catch her breath. The emails with Lena are frequent, and she shows her whole scenes as she produces them, not bothering to edit or revise. The response is encouraging. They haven't touched base in real time for a while and the email exchanges are purely business and get directly to the point. She calls, sensing that the tone in Lena's messages hides something. Ginna curses herself for being overly selfish, driven and focused while Lena deals with Wolfe. She opens the video chat app while lying on the couch in the bullpen.

Eleni is ready for a night out. She is going to meet Eirini and some of her friends up at the little bar near the center. Eirini is a little cryptic about the whole thing and insists she'll take care of the invitations. In other words, don't invite Fred and Carl. If she wants them there, she'll handle it. It'll be good. She doesn't remember the last time she did something like this: put on some nice clothes and stop thinking for a while. She comes down the stairs ready to go, shoes in hand, when she sees her grandmother sitting with her mother, uncle, and Wolfe in the living room. He's been there since the day of the big talk. He feels bad about it, she can tell, even if he never apologizes or says anything. Something is going on with him. That day, her mother invites him to stay for dinner and he stays through quiet time too. He's there when they eat a snack later, and then he's still there the next morning sitting at the table with Georgios while her mother runs around getting their breakfast. He's been around ever since. Now, he's sitting in the living room and drinking what looks like whiskey. It's surreal. She tells them she's going out and kisses her mother, uncle, and grandmother before throwing a cursory farewell to Wolfe as she puts on her shoes.

Just after she closes the door, her phone starts buzzing. It's Ginna, so she accepts the video call and talks while walking up the street toward the center.

"You look dressed up," Ginna says. "Are you going somewhere?"

"Taking a break. It's been crazy here. He hasn't left."

"So you say. I'm sorry I'm not being very helpful."

Lena slows her pace, she can tell it's going to be a long conversation, so she stops at the little café by the roundabout and takes a seat. Better than standing out in front of the bar. "It's fine, there's nothing you can do. And your writing is brilliant. I love what you're sending."

"Have you heard from Mia?" Ginna asks.

"Last night, after landing. She says you're distracted and she's letting you go. I get the whole scoop. She's nervous. They have a lot of work."

"Yet another person I'm failing. I feel terribly selfish."

"I don't think she's upset. She understands, and I certainly do. Keep doing what you're doing. We can pick up the slack."

"Thank you. Tell me. What's going on with him?"

"He won't leave. He's in my house right this minute watching TV with my family."

"I can't picture that. You two have a big argument the other day and he hasn't left since?"

"Yes, but it's not like we're talking or anything. He talks to my mom. About nothing. What's she making? Why is she doing this? Why is she doing that? He wants to know everything. And for some reason, she tells him. She's usually reserved with strangers, but she just goes on and on."

"You must know why. It's obvious to me. For the same reason. I mean, for both of them. It's common."

"I know, but I can't avoid him. At meals. Breakfast. I've been trying to go out, but Mom won't hear of it. If she's not feeding me, then I don't love her. And he's there all the time. Always going on about something. Always charming and funny."

"That asshole," Ginna says sarcastically. "Some nerve."

"I can't deal. At breakfast this morning, going on about how the writer is always a phony. My mother eats it up, but I'm squirming to get away."

"What does he mean? Always a phony?"

"He's talking about how much he hates the bullshit people spout about finding your genuine or authentic voice, about being truthful and baring your soul. He thinks it's bullshit. Writers are phonies, they're constantly pretending and imagining, projecting themselves onto everything. They're not truthful, they're fabricators. If a writer says something about writing, they're going to brag and boast, frame it as advice or whatever, but they're full of shit, they need to shut up, and just work."

"Doesn't sound boring to me. Was he talking about anyone in particular? Getting accusatory and defensive."

"Himself mostly. I'm such a phony. That's how he says it. I'm never less genuine than when I'm projecting into a character or narrator."

"That fits with where I am right now. Exhausted. I feel like a thief."

"How do you mean? A thief."

"Well, the little stories Fred and Carl pass my way during your trip across the country. The gestures and traits I pick up from sitting with you in the office. I'm stealing everything. It's like I'm running you through some cleaning machine, or repurposing device. It's a type of madness."

"Madness and thievery."

"Yes. It doesn't feel right. I'm just saying. I know what he means. I think I do. At some point, we're going to have to admit that as irritating as he is, he may be right now and again. Even if he is so very wrong most of the time. He is still... well, he's still Ben Thorne, in a way."

"I know. I've been thinking about that too. He is, but it's weird. My dad is too. I remember conversations: when I'm looking for advice or he's just offering it. It makes sense now. I mean, he's Ben Thorne."

"I've been sketching some of that. Trying to imagine what it's like for Wolfe. Of course, he thinks writers are phonies, he's a phony. Claiming to be Ben Thorne all these years. It's recursive. Have I got that right? He's a phony, and so every writer is a phony. Still, it doesn't mean he isn't right. That's the thing about bias, it could still be true."

Eleni speaks to somebody in the coffee shop. Ginna catches a glimpse of someone passing behind her. "Who is that?" she asks.

"The waiter. I'm at a coffee shop. You know, you're Ben Thorne too."

"How so?"

"You've been working for him for years."

"In one way or another."

"He can't do it without you. They can't do it. It's a village, isn't it?"

"I guess."

"And now you're writing. I think you're writing *Being an Introduction*. These pages, these sketches. I get it. There's no structure, but the people and the places. That's *Being an Introduction*. Or some version of it."

"I think so too but I'm afraid to say it out loud."

"Say it out loud. It's true. You're fucking Ben Thorne, and you're writing his next book."

"He thinks his next book is *Washington and Ashley*."

"No, he doesn't. I'm sure of it. He doesn't know what he's doing. He doesn't know what else to do. I'll bet some of those pages are decades old. He keeps turning back to them whenever he doesn't know what to work on next. He's coming around."

"How? I thought you don't talk."

"We don't, but I think it's resonating. He's working it out on his own."

"He's not aggressive or hostile?"

"He is, a little, but that's because I'm striking a nerve, and it's why I don't blink. I'm so nervous, trembling, but I stand my ground. He's screaming at me, in a way, telling me I'm right. It's how he resists."

"That's true. When he's calm and cool, it's because he feels totally in control and knows he has the upper hand. When he loses it, it's because he knows he's losing it. That's recursion, right?"

Lena laughs. "You know you're describing men, they're all like that."

"I don't know how you do it," she says laughing.

"I can't help it," Lena says in a whiny voice.

"What's going on with your whole situation, by the way? Are they still following you around? Are you staying out of it, focusing on work?"

"That's part of it. I don't want to deal, so I'm too busy to deal. It's like they're both trying to stop me from something. Or I'm letting them. I don't know. Like I'm creating this whole big choice to play out some drama. This way or the other, what's it going to be?"

"Like with school."

"Yeah, same. I'm definitely not going back. It's too late. Not really a choice anymore, I just let time decide for me. What difference does it make?"

"Still, isn't it better to control your own destiny?"

"Control. That's funny. As if... But is that really so great? Always... I mean. Ah fuck, I'm such a privileged idiot."

"You're being awfully hard on yourself. You're allowed to grieve. You're allowed to take some time without having the answers."

"I know but look at my advantages. I don't have to work. Ben Thorne is paying my rent. I feel guilty sitting here and going through my little existential crisis."

"That's bullshit. It sounds like Wolfe is getting to you. The lone wolf of the steppes is locked in a battle to the death. Trying to get out but unable to transcend destiny. That's the way that silly man is going to read this, imagine the interlude, that's the way they always do it. I'm reading this stuff. Nietzsche especially. Wolfe takes that shit seriously. He believes it, he thinks he's some kind of superhuman in a mythic battle. Your dad kinda does too if you go by the notebooks. No woman would write a story like that. I think it's about how no one knows what's going on, the interlude is a higher order, and the higher order is where the meaning lies. People have to get together to sort it out."

"I know. It makes sense that they can't see it. Both of them have that really masculine 'what does not destroy me' thing going on."

"It's sadder than that. There's nuance in the notes. He knows something is wrong and it nags at him. There's something ridiculous about it. Pathetic. He can't help himself. He resists those feelings and moods, he wants to set them aside, let go of the burden. Look at what he says about El Cide Hamete Benengeli. It's bugging me this week."

"What about it?"

"The published adventures of the knight errant by a fictional author."

"When Wolfe goes on about writers being phonies, he's reading *Don Quixote* carrying my father's copy around the house. He obviously knows it well. He's not reading it from start to finish, just specific passages. He knows exactly where they are."

"Yeah, there's some professor with a paper a while back. Something about the role of *Don Quixote* in the early work of Ben Thorne. It's one of the studies that Wolfe actually likes. He refers to it a lot."

"What does it mean?"

"The phoniness, but not just that. It legitimizes the story. This author, who isn't the author, tells the story as a historical account. It makes it more credible. It's an invention, but Benengeli hides that. He's the fabrication that makes the fabrication real. Does that make sense?"

"I think so."

"You know how it goes. There are pretenders telling bogus versions of the story, but they're frauds because Benengeli is the true author."

"But there is no such person."

"Well there is, in the novel, he's real. But in Spain, there's no such person."

"Ben Thorne."

"Exactly. I think it's like your dilemma. An alternate telling. It's like he either exists or he doesn't. It's either fiction or it isn't. These are the only options. Someone makes it up or it actually happens."

"How's that like my dilemma?"

"I just mean that it seems like a choice that you have to make. You have these two options, and you have to pick one. Those are the rules."

"Eirini says something like that. Fred or Carl is a false dilemma, and she doesn't have to choose. That doesn't mean she takes both or neither. It means, choosing is false."

"The author is always choosing. Maybe that's the phoniness."

"It's like there is this and this and this. The story is happening. Everything is unfolding. People are taking steps, they make choices."

"You're either sitting in the café right now or you're not."

"Exactly. There can't be anything else. I'm either here or I'm not. If I am, then the story goes that way. If I'm not and it's a delusion, then it's a different story. Who's talking? Cervantes? Benengeli?"

"How does that align with the original *Being an Introduction*?"

"It's structure, isn't it? Wolfe says that stuff is just philosophy, but he's wrong. It isn't *just* philosophy. Some of it is tone and structure."

"It's an outline."

"What is it though? What exactly are we saying?"

"The first part is like a set of conditions. Interlude in the middle, but only because the conditions are there. The creatures get stuck in their situation because they're the creatures they are. Like tragedy."

"He says that so much when he talks about ethics."

"It's everywhere in Ben Thorne's work: only a creature capable of happiness can make it a moral duty to promote the happiness of others."

"But then the second act, how does it fit?"

"He doesn't know. It's not worked out. That's why there's so much that's blank. He's left with an impossible choice. Get out or stay in. She's in the bar or she's not. That's what interlude shines its light on. It makes everything that follows ridiculous. The original intent is to draw an ethical imperative from the first act. Interlude throws everything out of whack. The second act becomes endless circling, turning it over and working it out. It flavors the conditions, changes them."

"It seems like deliberation aiming at a decision, but it isn't. It's neither the one nor the other. There's no choice. It's a place or a feeling or something. It realizes the choice without making it."

"It's where you live, where you can and ought to live. This really sucks."

"Why? I think we're onto something. I think we just need to figure out how to put what you're writing into this form."

"I get it, I agree, but I need to sleep. I'm working way too hard, and I just want to check in with you and then go to sleep."

Lena laughs awkwardly and tries to apologize, but Ginna cuts her off.

"Now I'm up and pacing back and forth. I want to sit down and write it out while it's still fresh. If I go to sleep, I may lose it."

"Or maybe you'll dream about it, and it'll get clearer. It may be a false choice, Ginna. Sleep or don't. You need to rest. Take care of yourself. We can't do it in one day."

"Okay, I'll let my body decide. Enjoy your night off, talk to you soon."

"Filakia, bye."

In the Eyes of the Law

Ginna flies to Chicago to meet Mia when she returns from St. Louis. The judge denies their motion. It doesn't take him very long to decide. On the surface, there is nothing controversial in it. They claim that LNN plays a role in the events. Insofar as it is a civil case, there is nothing extraordinary about that. It is the way they word the argument and the grounds they give. The judge reads them a long lecture condemning them for politicizing the event by trying to sneak crucial precedent setting allegations and principles into the motion. He dismisses it with extreme prejudice, threatening them with sanction if they continue to pull these kinds of tricks. They see through the posturing. The judge is elected and it's clear he's the one making the liability description into a politically charged matter, as though it is obvious that only people of a certain political orientation will be predisposed to see the case this way. While Bert drives her to the airport, they discuss the next steps. They're prepared for this. Maybe not for the severity, but for the rejection: a higher court must decide. The families are behind them, that's not a problem, they want things to change and are ready to commit. The case is on hold while they appeal the motion.

Mia explains it to Ginna. It's why she wants to come. She tears herself away from her work and is relieved to put it out of her mind for a while. It's even more all-consuming in Mia's absence. Left to herself, she goes deep inside a rabbit-hole. They're proceeding as though Wolfe won't raise any problems that can't be solved. Lena has a coherent outline, and it inspires Ginna. She has a vision and it's gaining in clarity. These aren't just sketches and scenes anymore, there's story and progression. On the plane, she fleshes out the skeleton. They're sharing a new notebook, and it's more neatly ordered with tabs at the top for different chapters and pages on the side for different sections within each chapter. Ginna fleshes it out using Em's unfinished work. It's eerie and exciting.

Mia arrives about forty-five minutes before Ginna, and they meet up at the baggage claim near the exit. It's a bittersweet greeting, not just because Mia is deflated by the decision, but Ginna is low energy too. It takes a lot of effort to pull herself out of wherever she goes while working on the book. It's been over a week now. She's dizzy and exhausted. "Let's go home and climb into bed," Mia says. "We'll eat and sleep and try to forget. Just for a little while." That's the plan. It starts out well, they get take-out on the way to Mia's place and manage to eat and sleep for a little while. Once they boost their energy from the rest and fuel, they spend a little of it getting reacquainted. Their feelings are strong, but it's still too early to tell where they come from. Infatuation increases its pleasure by disguising itself as something else. So goes its charm and delight. Mia is old enough to know, but when their eyes meet, she conveniently forgets and Ginna is just young enough to be fooled.

It's warm and the sheets are cool. They both want to know everything, as they struggle to get it out, two divergent themes wrapping around a single need.

"Of course, the judge is right," Mia confesses. "Our motives are political. Maybe not exactly in the way he means it, but they're ulterior to the case. We can easily petition to include LNN. There's nothing unusual about that, but we explicitly want the language to be legislative. We want to put corporate personhood front and center."

"It's never fun to lose," Ginna whispers.

"No, of course not," she says. She doesn't want to vent, she doesn't need to get anything off her chest, but Ginna wants to know. She circles her fingers and hand on Mia's belly as she speaks. The words come close to her forehead: they whisper. It almost doesn't matter what they're saying, only that they *are* saying something. Almost. This helps keep their energy low. They don't want to wind themselves up, they want to stay in this place, this quiet place, together. "Bert and I have been reading a lot of theory to get into the right frame of mind. It's about coercion. These old bastards think only the state can coerce people."

Ginna kisses Mia to interrupt her. It's about pace and her intent is to slow her down, to keep her in their quiet place. Words can have the opposite effect, so it sometimes takes effort to avoid them. It works, and Mia relaxes even as she goes on. "We're trying to think about this from their point of view. Corporations coerce and we don't have any choice but to serve their ends. The big companies aspire to it, it's collusion. They want to make sure we desperately need what they're selling. Chaos is at the door and only they have protection. They have to be held accountable for it. Not just with a fine, they need to go to jail." Her heart beats faster and Ginna repeats her techniques to quiet her down. It works and they're distracted by the effort. The words break off, they stretch and move together, they tangle and are disorderly, but then they come to rest and reset. They both play along, dancing in place, they balance each other out.

Mia can't stay there for very long.

"The state has to protect us. It's not for the sake of social justice, but liberty. We want to sound like libertarians, not leftists. Society should be a beating heart not a machine. Both coerce. Coercion is here to stay, it's part of any valuing, but there's a world of difference among the options. Bert and Gwen are passionate about it."

"You're passionate about it," Ginna says.

"I am," she responds. She sits up against the headboard. Ginna mirrors her. They lean close. "People don't understand that corporations are how the rich hide their wealth. They use corporate law to get away with things that ordinary people can't do. As a waitress, you see so many corporate credit cards. When corporations eat, it's tax deductible."

"In New York, you see it too. It's how I put myself through school."

"It's an invisible fact. The way the wealthy hide behind corporate bodies. I'll bet your Ben Thorne takes advantage of it."

"That's funny. I know there's a corporation. Two of them actually. But

I just think it's a bookkeeping thing. I never give it much thought, just business. I don't think of taxes or identity or any of that."

"Why would you? You get paid and pay taxes. What's to think about? You have wages, Ben Thorne has revenue. Huge difference. Ben Thorne's rent is a business expense. Not yours. Your wages are even tax deductible for him, but not what you pay the plumber to fix your toilet. Two completely different sets of rules, and it helps the rich get richer."

"The system has been around for a long time. We can't see it."

"No, we can't. It's what drives us, makes us the way we are. How we think, how we behave. It's like osmosis."

"Rich and poor alike? Do you believe that everyone is at its mercy?"

"What I believe doesn't matter. We're wild animals, culture is a ruse. If there were non-human naturalists, they'd see this civilization as our hive or ant hill. We build it for the sake of survival then we're trapped in it. We delude ourselves into thinking it's about happiness. Autonomy not instinct, as if those are the only choices. The rich and famous are servants of public desire."

"How is your case relevant? You make it sound like you're trying to rewrite the rules for living. Isn't it about those women?"

"Yes and no. We want to make them pay, but we aren't looking for money, not really. We want them in jail. Not the men and women who run the company, but the company itself. We want to set a precedent so that these companies are accountable for what they do. They should lose their freedom, their privacy, their right to participate in the political process, everything that every felon loses, we want them to lose that." Ginna laughs and takes a sip of water from the glass on the table next to the bed. "You think that's funny?" Mia asks.

"Nope, I think it's wonderful. What's funny is that you think you can get a court of law in this country to agree with it."

"We're just using their own laws against them."

Ginna hands her the water glass and Mia takes a sip. They are wide awake and the quiet is long gone. They chase it away and now Ginna's mind starts to churn. She's thinking about the writing and where she's going with it. It comes back to her. Mia feels it. She wants to know more, but Ginna is off somewhere in a distant world.

"Tell me," Mia says squinting her eyes. "Where are you off to?"

"Well, I don't know. I think, in a way, I'm becoming Ben Thorne. That's what Lena says. We've got this story. We put it together from Em's notebook. It comes from some fantastic version of a past failure where the act of replaying something over and over again becomes a whirlpool."

"By the rocks?" Mia asks and then laughs. Ginna too.

"Yes. In a way. By the rocks. Or in a library. All of that. Voice is so important. I don't know how to describe it in just a few words. He doesn't know how either. He circles around and around. Never really gets anywhere. Lena has these ideas about every doubt, every insight, every angle, all of it, they're just people in a way."

"Like Ben Thorne?"

"Yes. Or LNN."

"Assholes."

"Maybe. Sometimes assholes, sometimes not. People. Not angels, not devils, but they have voices, and those voices are where the stories lie. That's the outline, at least. She thinks we have to bring them out. I've been trying to capture it, to get it down, but nothing is ever right, it's never enough. You keep going. You say it and something comes out, but it just makes you have to say more, to get the story out there, or then some new story comes along and now you have to explore that. Does this make any sense?" She runs her hand through her hair. Her stress increases.

"You mean like the story pushes itself forward or something?"

"Everything that happens implies more things. God, that sounds silly. How will I ever write this if I can't even explain what I'm doing? Something happens to you, and I may be part of it. Because you're telling me about it. Then I go off and do something, and that links us. Do you see what I mean?"

"I do. That's why there are those voices."

"Yes, exactly. So, Em keeps this secret and this notebook, and he strives for this perfect moment. Whatever it is. That leads to something else and someone else. To you and Lena, to me and Wolfe. To each of us."

"Be careful, Lena idolizes her father. She always has. Idealizes him."

"How so?"

"It's easy to highlight the good. I think he's hard on her too. I mean, her whole life she always wants to please him, to make him proud, to turn herself into what he values most. The problem is that he hates the thing he values most. He encourages her and then criticizes her for listening."

"Well, he's her father. That's not uncommon. They hold up a prize, and maybe it's one they can't get themselves. They want you to get it, but then they resent you for it."

"He's like that, my father is very different. Em doesn't have the same influence over me. I can pick and choose, but she doesn't have a choice. And her mother, she's the same way. I mean, with her husband. She lets him get away with murder. Those women take care of that man's every need. They support him in ways that let him neglect whole parts of his life that women can never neglect. He takes advantage of their love for him."

"Your father isn't like that?"

"To some extent, but not nearly as bad as her father. Em has charm, and it makes it harder to see him for what he really is."

"You think the project is relevant?"

"I don't know, could be. She wants to prove herself to him, to complete his life's work, or whatever fantasy she's spinning."

"I see what you mean. The book is almost like a monument to his failure. This thing he tries to do long ago, but that snares him in some trap that he can't get out of. She's trying to free him. Complete his second act."

"I worry about her. I don't know if there's happiness at the end of this. I don't know where it leads."

"Okay, but it isn't like art comes from happy balanced people. Those people create bad things, boring things, things with no drama, nothing gut-wrenching or enlightening."

Mia turns to look straight at Ginna. She brushes her hair back and says, "What about you, Virginia, what is your crack? How are you broken? Why do you think you can produce something beautiful and gut-wrenching?"

They laugh and kiss. It's not a serious question. It is a serious question, but not now, now it's a provocation and Ginna is happily provoked. She enthusiastically leans forward into Mia's kiss. They set out again for their quiet place. Touching turns to whispers, and they roll into each other for a recess that charges and discharges the thrill of their tale together in the evening heat and the soothing coolness of the sheets and the air whistling from the nearby vent.

The Plan

"You think the intervention doesn't work, but why do you think that? Because he says so? That doesn't mean anything. I think it does work and it's the reason the interlude lasts as long as it does. No, it doesn't end when he moves out West, it doesn't even end when he dies. It's ending now. I'm putting an end to it. We're going to publish the story like this." He can see it. From beginning to end, he sees it just as she describes it, and he silently concedes that there's nothing more to say, but he cannot rest there, and he cannot enjoy the moment. He gets up and blows out of the office, rushing past the kitchen to the front door. Ermioni is leaning against the sink and facing Georgios, Eirini, Fred, and Carl who are seated at the island. Georgios is getting ready to fly back home the next day and has been entertaining them with a story about the latest hit television show in America, and why it's popular with different kinds of people. It's not flattering. Wolfe slips on his shoes at the front door and waves goodbye to Ermioni, mumbling something. She doesn't say much in response but turns to Eleni who follows him out of the office. She's standing in the middle of the living room watching him leave, then looks at her mother and shrugs.

"Is something wrong?" Ermioni asks as the others turn, wondering the same thing.

"It's settled," Eleni says calmly. She shifts a little on her feet and turns to look at Fred and Carl. "He wants... We want you guys to go back to New York. Right away. Whatever Ginna needs. Sort out your return as soon as possible."

This changes the mood. Carl and Fred look at each other. They're sorry to go, but excited at the prospect of getting back to work. Eirini is relieved. She knows it'll work out for the best. "What's the plan?" Carl asks.

"He's agreed to the proposal. Virginia is writing it from our outline. Then he'll make the first read and do whatever he likes with the tone. The three of us will do the fit and finish, fix whatever problems come up."

Georgios knows the story without hearing it. He stands up and gives his niece a big hug to congratulate her. Eirini knows about it too, listening to Eleni turn the arguments over and over until she's confident with them. No one explains anything to the interns, but they feign understanding and are supportive as Eirini conveys her wishes.

"Come on," she says to them. "Let's make the arrangements." The three of them go into the office. As they head in that direction, Georgios says, "Not too soon. Tonight, we'll have some fun. I'll pick up some food and we can get together to say farewell. Tell your mom and dad, I'll tell Ariti and Thimios." There's a lot of activity. In a few minutes, they're gone and Ermioni is left standing in the kitchen with Eleni facing her from across the island. "I'll go get your grandmother," she says.

"Don't bother," Eleni replies. "Wolfe's over there. I'll text him to come back with her when he's ready. I think he'll need some time alone first."

"What does he do over there with just the two of them?"

"He sits. It's quiet. They don't speak the same language. She feeds him, gives him whatever he wants. She likes having someone who needs things, and he likes the quiet."

Ermioni nods and moves to the island, they both pull up stools and sit facing each other. There are still small plates of food spread around the countertop. Ermioni hands Eleni a fork and she spears an apple slice while leaning in.

"Are you pleased with how things are turning out?" Ermioni asks.

"Yes," she responds while chewing slowly. "Mama? Did Dad ever say much about those days back before you met?"

"A little," she says pouring some wine and passing the glass across to Eleni. "He's very poor in those days. A tough time, with many debts. He has trouble paying the rent. His family is going through tough times."

"Does he ever talk about the people in his life?"

"Hardly a word. I know he has a friend who goes off to New York, but I never dream it has anything to do with Ben Thorne. Really, this whole thing is a shock to me."

Eleni takes a sip of wine and pulls the bowl of potato chips closer. There are some olives too and Ermioni pushes them closer so she can reach, just in case.

"The argument we've been having, it's about something going on between them. Wolfe. Ben. He thinks he's trying to stop Dad from doing something, something he thinks will ruin his life."

"What?" Ermioni leans forward.

"Selling out. That's how he phrases it." She's quiet for a minute. Reconsiders it. "I mean, you say he's destitute. That's the story. But somehow, he gets from there to this. The house in America. The money to build this house. He stops working long ago. You two must be saving money. Does he sell his soul?"

Ermioni takes a sip of wine and pulls the potato chips back closer to her, taking one or two. "It's complicated," she says finally. "It's possible to describe it that way. He knows that."

"What do you mean?"

"I mean, he knows people who aren't friends might think that way."

"But does he believe it?"

"I don't think so. He's poor, he needs to buy food and pay the rent. That part's not complicated. He isn't without means. He has a good education. He can learn things, complicated things, and he knows that's an advantage. He studies. It's obvious what to do. You know the stories."

"Yeah, I do, but I don't understand the selling out part. Ben is certain it's an existential crisis, and he has to talk him out of it. Like it's a single decision at a time in his life when he doesn't have to make it. He's young, he can do something else."

"I don't see it that way."

"Tell me how you see it."

"Well, he's studying something similar. I don't know if I can say it the way he can, but he thinks philosophy and technical things, like writing code, they have something in common, some form or something. In the early days, when he and I first meet, you should hear how he talks. He slips in and out of two different worlds as if it's nothing, as if nothing separates them."

"Like how exactly?"

"It's like, hmmm, how to put it? One minute he's talking about making requests to some service, something very technical, and then the next minute he's talking about Heidegger or Derrida or something."

"You mean, he's scattered, bouncing from topic to topic?"

"No, no, not like that. He thinks it's related and interconnected. He describes technical things, and you think he's talking about philosophy and then he talks about philosophers, and you think he's describing technical things. He doesn't see the difference between them, or he thinks they're complimentary. Messages being relayed. He says that a lot."

Eleni circles her wine glass on the countertop and looks off somewhere in the distance. "It's how I see it too, I think. I mean, I understand what you're saying. He's always like that. He tells me once that if you look at patterns you can go very, very deeply into something and deep down there are connections. The internet is a rhizome. Things that seem different are actually similar when you look at them like this."

"I don't know about that, but I know he says things like that, and they seem to mean something to him. Beyond caring for us, you and me, his family, aside from that, he doesn't care about money. If selling out is what you call it when you make money to pay the rent or buy food, then okay. As long as he's working, he wants to stop working. Maybe that explains why. He has other things he wants to do, he doesn't want to be thinking about someone else's technical problems. He wants to think about different problems the way he wants to. Without interference."

"They love him at work, but he dismisses its importance. That's such a privilege. No one gets that much freedom."

"Oh, he knows. Even after he stops working, it's still there. His mind keeps churning like that. There's no magical moment when it stops. Once he's free to think whatever he likes, he can't do it. There are always things in the way. Even his education is in the way."

"Mama, do you think you gave up your life for him?"

"What? What are you saying? What does that mean?"

"I know, I'm sorry. It's coming from Ben. Wolfe. It's something he says. He's jealous of dad for having you. You support him during those years, you do so much for him. Take care of him. Don't you want more for yourself? Don't you want anything else?"

Ermioni is both upset and relieved. She takes a deep breath and waits. She looks back toward the office. Not a sound. She looks back toward the front door, nothing coming or going.

"You probably don't think you're insulting me, Lena mou, but you are. You're thinking about people and people's lives with a very narrow point of view. There are things you think are valuable and important and you think anyone who isn't doing those things, they're wrong or somehow less important. Of course, those are the things you're doing with your life, and it's a circle because you won't do them if they're not important."

"I don't mean to insult you, Mama. It's just... I'm trying to know..."

"It's alright. I'm glad you're asking me. How can I put it? The house. This house or the one in America. They're sacred things, sacred places. I think you know this. There's a lot of magic here and it's what makes you grow. It's what your father uses when he tells stories or writes code. Stories are codes too, you know. They're like spells and they get their power from this place. Well, this is my house. That house you know, that's my house. That magic, that's my magic. Don't you understand that? All the studying you do, and you can't see it?"

She smiles and cocks her head, making eye contact with her mother across the island. "That's beautiful, Mama. Built in exile. Do you really believe that?"

"Oh, you don't? You think that money people are running around for, that's real? But the power of this house that you draw into your body as you grow up and become an adult, that's not real? Some silly person writes a book or gives a lecture, then other people give them money. They repeat it. They give another lecture or write another book. That's real? Machine learning or whatever data nonsense your father works on, you think that matters? The holy grail of progress... trillions of dollars... just models... illusions... Someone comes and fixes my sink because the pipe is broken, that's real. It's odd that he asks for something in return, don't you think? I swipe my phone over a symbol on his phone. Even something real is only in codes and spells. It's strange what people think matters."

They are silent. Eleni is thinking about everything, about what she's doing with her life, and where it comes from. The talk, the words to say things no one pays any attention to except the very few members of that tribe who share the same language. It's her father's vision she uses to measure herself. She never doubts it, she's pursuing what he taught her to value. But where does it come from, what light does it reflect? She looks back at her mother with tears forming in her eyes.

"Selling out. It's funny really." Her mother goes on. "Like he makes a choice and then has to work to get out from under it. That's what you're asking, isn't it? Does he think he's going down the wrong path and needs to do something to stop it? What if this is the wrong way to think about it? What if he realizes that long after meeting me and having you when the three of us are together? It isn't about getting out of something or changing one's path or making some new decision for the sake of some better thing that comes along. It isn't. Maybe he learns where the magic really comes from."

Eleni moves around the island and hugs her mother. There is nothing more to say and Ermioni leads them from an awkward silence following their embrace into a casual moment with wine and chips and olives and a little fruit. She does it easily as though nothing is simpler. One moment we talk and cry, then we eat and drink.

Eirini, Fred, and Carl come out of the office. The arrangements are in place. They'll return the day after tomorrow. They're excited to get back to work and they urge everyone to come visit. They want to show them around New York and do the tourist things they've never done themselves. Ermioni thinks it sounds like a wonderful idea and she's very happy. "I've never been," she says, and she gets more glasses and fills one for everybody. Georgios comes back shortly after, carrying a tray in one hand and two bags in the other. He sets them down on the counter by the sink and Ermioni comes to his side to unwrap everything. She takes out plates and flatware and piles them in easy reach. Eleni puts on some music. In the hours that follow, Ariti and Thimios arrive with Despina. They bring more food and lay it out with the other dishes on the center island. Maria and Nikos arrive, and they have still more treats to add to the collection.

Later, still more people are dropping by. People beyond the inner circle, friends from around town. There's plenty to eat and drink. They argue about the music. Wolfe comes back too, he has Stamatia and Europea with him. They're happy to jump in and start organizing the plates better. There's too much food, people can't get to everything, they say, and this dish needs to be reheated. They argue about what needs to go where.

At some point Wolfe and Lena end up together in a corner of the living room. "What's this?" he asks. "Word gets out," she says. "Georgios is leaving tomorrow. Fred and Carl are going back the day after. People want to say goodbye."

"Fred and Carl?" he asks.

"Tom and Jerry," she says laughing, then she changes the subject. "Are you having fun?"

"Yes. I am," he says. "Truly."

"I think you're wrong, ya know," she says. "How so?" he responds with that same rapid pace they've been developing. "It's okay. You both are. It isn't about intervention, and it isn't about bringing the interlude to an end with some monumental second act that shows the farce for what it truly is. It's about interlude for its own sake. That's it, there's nothing more to it." She touches her glass to his and says, "Yamas."

Residual

Light: The giants among us, they have names, they are special. They advertise on behalf of themselves, they know good and evil. We must come to know them.

Justice: It is reasonable, they are giants, how can we avoid them?

Peace: We don't just see them, we adore them. We hold them in our prayers, we act on their behalf. Whatever transpires, happens for their sake.

Light: Once upon a time the law makes us free, it applies to one and all, to every single one of us. Liberty is for everyone since it does not single out anyone for advantage or disadvantage, no discrimination, and no privilege.

Justice: These are dreams, a true universal, but only in theory.

Peace: Is it a lie?

Light: Even if it is not, the giants come along, and something happens. The laws change, the old tables become new.

Justice: How so?

Light: The law forbids dwarves from killing and stealing.

Peace: The giants too.

Light: No. Coercion constrains liberty in the name of upholding the law. That is written. The old laws apply force to the violator. Conviction entails loss of liberty. The new laws allow giants to make an offering, recite a speech to offset the damage. It places them on a pedestal. No longer do we say the act is forbidden, only that it has a cost.

Peace: The actuary drives the choice. These are everyday factors. No human being can weigh and measure like this.

Light: Their property and privacy are better protected, their liberty and sovereignty too. We think they are giants because of their size, but their privileges inflate them.

Justice: The attribute of felon, once it applies to a human, never disappears. They bear that tag forever and the consequences follow.

Light: There is no such attribute for giants. The dwarves bear the burdens.

Peace: And privacy?

Light: The giants have their privacy, and their crimes remain secret. They never submit to surveillance and scrutiny. What they hate in regulations is the oversight they require.

Justice: Identity is always an either/or, how does it equate them?

Peace: How do they justify different treatment? What authority is there in types?

Light: Through attributes and types, values appear: zip codes and race, income range and potential. There is age and gender, educational background, and net worth. These properties, these private attributes, are set in stone as qualities, cross-sectioned demographics, and population-based assignments. They slice them and dice them, put them into little boxes and bigger boxes, categories and concepts, sets intersecting sets intersecting sets.

Justice: The giants don't suffer the same fate.

Light: They know good and evil and are masters of them. Establishing the new tables, they are free from them.

Peace: Meanwhile, the dwarves are segmented and analyzed, cross-referenced and mined.

Light: Knowledge of good and evil means they know what is best for the dwarves. They are the same and they are different, case by case, it's for the best.

Peace: How do they allow this? Their history prevents it. They mean to hate coercion and privilege, discrimination and elitism. What's happening?

Justice: They turn against theory. Practice is always much messier.

Light: It's true, they do turn against it. Not long ago, they see it as a burden. They become hostile when it constrains their drive for power.

Justice: Where they fear only the state, they should fear the giants.

Peace: And scramble to keep up with their whims and policy.

Light: The giants live in a private world safe from state coercion. They deny having a will and declare that dwarves are not subject to it.

Peace: Do not have a will? Do they not have eyes? Do they not understand what they see?

Justice: Clearly anyone who lives among such creatures knows they have objectives. How can they deny purpose and the will to realize it?

Light: They see what they want to see, and they want what they value. That is enough. The giants are like forces of nature, the wind or the earth that shakes and sometimes visits its wrath upon them.

Justice: What it means to be a giant emerges in the turn against theory. They make them believe it. Giants rely on their privacy, protected by laws, but dwarves are entirely different, they are the collection of properties and attributes widely known, publicly tracked, and assigned. Each avows their own purpose and individuality. This avowal, this constant confession as a public domain, makes each of them what they are, it gives them personality.

Peace: There can be no solitude or shadow. No peaceful moments. Disclosure is a constant intermediary, it's the interplay of multiples, perpetual intervention, interruption, interlude. Boundaries are checks and balances, for both good and evil.

Light: Only the giants retain their shadows and control their brands and public profiles. They move lightly through the world, swathed in the warmth of a personal cocoon. The dwarves are nobodies, and the giants are somebodies.

Peace: To have or to be, that is the question. What am I? What properties do I have? Private properties anchor order. The giants command and make a choice, they are the creators.

Justice: The giants see the dwarves, but the dwarves do not see them. Coercion is the rule of law where such giants live.

Light: Giants teach dwarves their virtue, their goodness, and their happiness. They weave their products into personality, they proclaim them necessary for everything with value.

Justice: There is no theory in that. There is no vision.

Peace: They are the gauges and the measurements. They are the ones who set the standard.

Light: Each of the dwarves is born from the will to coerce. Giants take them in hand and are the order that governs. Those who rise in favor do so by building its outline, they fashion the giant and help increase its size and power. The ones who know how to make giants bigger, those are the ones with the skills and the talents, those are the ones that get ahead.

Justice: What else would you expect? Those who are of most value to the giants, who make them even more gigantic, naturally they are the dwarves with the most authority, the ones nearest and dearest to the giants, to their interests and purposes.

Peace: Every choice they ever make comes from the new table of values. Not only do the most helpful have the most leverage, but the rest must serve the constraints they apply. Every possibility and every meaning are possible and meaningful because they say it is.

Light: Work or don't work, study or don't study, left or right, trade or career, our choices, everything is configured and framed by the giants and the purposes they have, the wills they unleash, and the objectives they envision. Be entrepreneurial, be a wage earner, and so on and on. These choices are their choices, this world is their world.

Justice: How can we get off this ride?

Peace: She keeps telling you, we must see them as they see us.

Light: They are measuring from far away, and they have permission to measure every encounter and every event. Thousands of events per encounter, tens of thousands, and each of them attributed and cross-referenced, set off against every possible attribute, articulating every microscopic facet of each act.

Justice: Theory demands it. They are not the state.

Light: Criticism is theatre. We cannot criticize without entering their domain. Why attack a point of view? Dwarves talk about it, sides are drawn, and alignments made. How? How does word get around? Who circulates it? Only the giants make such things known far and wide. Without them, there is no need for perpetual alignments and factions. Break these new tablets.

Peace: Theory has the same source, it is born from their drive to coerce, a symbol for others to proclaim themselves. The universal law is now their jailor: it gives giants new power to guide every move.

Justice: Break these new tablets.

Peace: But how?

Light: Repeat the chorus: we must look at them the way they look at us. Their felonious behavior justifies our gaze. When they assign guilt to the dwarves who survive the "fall of man," the guilty among them are likewise labelled.

Peace: I do not see how the people, so divided, can agree.

Justice: It's true, they disagree for the sake of it. Whatever they say, the others reject it.

Light: They are stuck in a recursion and in search of a boundary condition.

Peace: Only the calm and focused can unite.

Light: If telemetry trains its eye on them, balancing the models of small humanity within small civilizations, it will keep the giants in check.

Justice: None of this will fly. They take pleasure from their hatred, and exclusive power is their all-consuming desire.

Peace: The arguments will never end.

Light: The arguments will never end. The giants will see to that. They fight each other for their sake.

Justice: Fighting reveals the giant within. What can they do?

Light: Argue and ridicule, poke fun and deride, publish memes, jokes, and foolishness. Laugh at each other. All forms are valid.

Peace: Fighting serves the giants, but ridicule serves the dwarves?

Light: Look closely at what you call ridiculous, it always lies between two acts.

Justice: Ah ha! To find a way, turn it over again and again. Look under every stone. Look inside every heart.

Light: Lives are at risk. With so much gravity, they carry too much. Levity is for the dwarves alone: it protects them from each other.

Justice: I have my doubts.

Peace: The dwarves must fight for a rebirth, for their commonwealth.

Light: They must twist free of this heavy "tyranny of the selfish replicators" again and again eternally. Light as air, balanced, and peaceful. Fight the giants. Break these new tablets.

What Is Next

Publisher

It's not like the story where the man finds a desk in a window and is so drawn to it that he buys it despite the cost. He brings it home and uses it for a while before taking an axe to it. There is a manuscript tucked away inside. It's not like that.

And it's not like that case where the guy sends it everywhere and the different publishers see it and reject it. Maybe because it's too long, but definitely because it won't make them any money. Eventually someone sees it and thinks it could be a cult classic after being cut down in size. No, it isn't like that.

Theoretically, they already have a publisher. The same one for years, but they don't want to use them. It's not a battle over creative differences, or details about the book tour. None of that really. It's not about money. People will read whatever they tell them to read. They can market it, maybe some controversy will help, or they can spin it as metafiction deconstructing the mind's authority. It could be like that, but it isn't.

In the end, none of them are people, none of them make decisions. They act as agents and this editor or that one, they make decisions based on their fiduciary responsibility. They cancel the deal. They have right of first refusal, but no obligation. The deal is null and void, the contract cancelled: there is nothing more between them. We cannot accept it at this time. Nope, nothing like that.

They are in a free-for-all, but with connections. Everyone wants to read it. Why not? He is a proven commodity. The agents and publishers want to see it. Not an exclusive? So what, they don't care. They are glad to get their hands on it even if it's only the first two chapters. They are happy to get it, but based on those first chapters, they are confused. What is this supposed to be? Why does your own name appear here? Is it a memoir? Is that you or just a character with your name? If it's your autobiography, or an installment of it, why doesn't your regular publisher want it? We need to see more chapters. We want to see more. How long is it? Oh, that's long, but it's Ben Thorne so... We'll take a look. A long literary work from a proven source, that's worth the risk. Just send it our way. They take a look, but no one wants to touch it. They don't feel comfortable saying why. It doesn't read like any of the previous work. This can't be metafiction, the style is off. We think it's a true story. Oh God, is it a true story? Are you telling me that after these many years it's just a trick, a lie? No one wants it. Too many problems. You would think, but no, none of that.

They say no. They are companies, corporations for the most part. I love it, but I don't think it's right for us at this time. Of course, if it were up to me. Our list is full for this year, and you really do need to get it out there now that you're shopping it around. Word is out. Everyone knows. All lies and speculation.

No agent will take it. Are they afraid of the controversy? That's good for sales. It can't be that. They fear the unknown. They can't fathom how it will be received, it's better to let someone else take the risk. There might be accusations of fraud, there might be lawsuits, suppose they think we're party to it, suppose people want their money back. We can't get involved with this, there's no telling what will happen. Pure fabrication and vendetta.

Wolfe does some rewriting and finds it strange that they don't see the continuity. Many passages have his signature flare, but the overall vibe is different. Ginna is skilled, she has talent, she knows how to draw out the tale and when to compress it, but the dynamic is different, and the book reflects it. Besides, Lena is all over this one: her structural contributions, her outlines, her interpretation of the notes. The integral mixture lends it an amateurish feel and makes it very different from anything anyone has seen before. They are not surprised, but they don't understand. Nope, it never happens.

In the end, they like the work, how it sounds and flows. They believe that if they start from scratch and use a different name, one that isn't so familiar, such a household name, it'd be easier. Some agent somewhere will accept it and find a publishing house for sure. If they start from scratch. But they don't. Their submissions are honest and that's their biggest mistake. No one wants that. The truth is risky, the truth causes problems, it's a wild card. If only they can make it seem more made up, then there are plenty of suitors, plenty of publishers happy to take it, advertise it, and stand behind every fictional word of it. That's just someone's fantasy.

None of this concerns them in the end. They decide to publish it themselves. They can get the word out on their own. Ben Thorne has millions of followers on social, he can just push it out there using one of many generic printing and distribution channels, then he can advertise it himself. People will hear about it and buy it. They don't need a big sponsor, they don't need a network of corporate partners to get behind them, they can do it themselves. Delusional wish fulfillment, don't believe a word of it.

That's what they decide to do. They do their own cover design and their own formatting. Lena learns the ropes and Ginna shows her everything she's picked up over the years. Wolfe finds them templates, books he's seen before and liked. Here's a good font or what about that one? Then there's the thickness of the paper and the cover design itself. They buy graphics software and each of them takes turns trying out designs. They look at each other's work and compare. They like the layout of this one, but the picture on the cover of that one. They merge them together and agree more often than they disagree. Too pedestrian, no one cares about that kind of stuff.

When it's put together, they decide to get more readers to privately review it. They distribute advanced copies to friends and trusted advisors, people they think will provide honest feedback. Although no longer interns, Fred and Carl both take a look. There are a few well known professional literary critics who swear to secrecy. One who Ginna knows well, and the other is close to Wolfe. Some are genuinely shocked and urge the publishers to hold back. Think carefully about what you're doing, this will change everything. Whatever capital you've accumulated over the years, this will surely squander it. There will be nothing left of your reputation. No one will believe you anymore, your credibility will evaporate. Nonsense, don't believe your own PR, no one cares.

That process is a bust, they don't get much they can use. They're clear-headed in their deliberations, they aren't going to change their minds. They zip it up and get it in order with whatever they can glean from those last few readings, and then they send it off to professional reviewers and critics to help market, and stimulate interest among the right audiences. They are sure people will buy it. At the very least, to prove they don't have to pay any more attention to Ben Thorne, that he can be safely removed from the canon. This one will get readers. The shock guarantees it. But will it be the end of Ben Thorne? The end of them? Maybe nothing Wolfe or Ginna ever write will be accepted anywhere. Perhaps none of them will have any professional standing once the story sees the light of day. The desire itself is flawed and the house of cards collapses.

They submit the final draft and cover design and approve everything for release. They make blurbs and elevator pitches. They photograph the three of them alongside an image of the lost fourth. The materials are packaged, and the channels primed. They time everything so that the buzz resonates just as the book is available for purchase. It is a well synchronized and choreographed blitz of publication and presence. The one advantage of self-publishing is the complete control they have over the schedules and timing. They take advantage as best they can, calling in every chit, and every debt. With advertisements in the best literary spaces, they push their message before the eyes of those most likely to be mesmerized. It is their project alone and the big corporate players are gone. They are on their own. They click submit and brace themselves for the onslaught. They have no idea what will happen next.

Reviews
West Coast:

It is made of cheap, heavy paper. The cover is matted, lending an even greater unpolished sensation to the work's exterior. What is one supposed to do with this? Its physicality is brutal. Flipping through the pages, I am reminded of a time when every book has its own style, when type setting and print are part of the finished product. Now these throwback technics seem phony and artificial. Like there is something wrong, something very, very wrong eclipsed by the illusion of uniqueness. There is cover art and a blurb on the back describing the contents, or so we think. Across the top of the back cover we find the word fiction. The category itself is fiction. Really, it is as if I have opened a time capsule and am back in my childhood. I repeat the refrain, what is one supposed to do with this? A physical book with paper and ink.

Never fear, there is a note, and it references an ebook that I can acquire and use for my purpose. Why the nostalgia? Perplexed and intrigued, I begin my reading with an open mind. I am a fan. I have read everything, delighted in every turn of phrase and subtle twist. Despite my initial trepidation, I am happy to review Ben Thorne's latest. After the last assignment, an overblown piece of cultural propaganda some readers may recall, I look forward to this one.

My excitement is quickly dashed. In the book's first pages we learn that the whole storyline involves a young woman mysteriously tasked with contacting none other than Ben Thorne. The author appears in the opening pages as a foil to the main character. If only he remains there, an absent center for the reader's wonder. But no, the author audaciously appears, engages in conversation with his personal assistant and the clowns who do his research and have a significant role in the story to come.

I am torn in how to represent this to you. The author, I suppose, believes there is an imaginative twist that lies ahead. We move down the path and get to know the players only to learn later that nothing is what it seems. Of course, I wouldn't dream of revealing the secrets. Having read this monstrosity, however, I assure you that there are no spoilers where such nonsense is at stake. It is only a spoiler for those who want to read it.

You may have heard that back in the days of physical books there are some they call doorstops or paperweights. Some books are so heavy and substantial that they can be used for either task. Doing so dispatches the book to its best and highest end. You would be doing this book, which must weigh close to a kilo, a great service.

In addition to the questionable story line, the book has none of the literary flare we have come to expect from Ben Thorne. None of the nuanced descriptions of human joy and tragedy, none of the insightful renditions of common everyday occurrences. This book has nothing we can recognize and breathes that absence onto every page. It is badly produced in its physical form, even if absolutely uniform to the platform in its electronic version, and it is badly produced in its literary form.

If Ben Thorne ever writes another book, my nostalgia for his past accomplishments may bring me to read it, but this one consumes much of that trust. The near perfect career of our beloved national author is no more.

East Coast:
Ben Thorne isn't getting enough attention. Apparently, the awards and sales are not enough for him, he has to put himself at the center of his latest novel. He imagines himself in a grand and thriving community of others and considers himself the be all and end all of everything that happens to the cast of characters. Some are driven to meet with him, some are driven to work for him, every one of them is curious and in awe of who he might be and what his role in their lives is. The only possible thematic description of this work, without giving away too much, is Who is Ben Thorne?

Despite being a self-described work of fiction, the book reveals an obsession and an endless megalomania. The narcissist himself has read the press, learned from the literary theory, and now succumbs by flexing his body of work as if to make fun of his readers. He thinks we are so stupid that we will read anything he produces regardless of quality or purpose.

The book has been independently published suggesting the entire publishing world has turned its back on him. Whatever it is, this drive for acknowledgement and fame, wherever it comes from and whatever it means, is not to be excused. Unless there is a pathology in it. If the author is suffering some sickness or mental illness, only then does he merit our sympathy. If there is anything behind it besides that, he deserves only contempt.

The work has not been properly edited. It is twice as long as any self-respecting publishing company would permit. Whatever the reasons for going it alone, it is not a sign that things are right with Ben Thorne. The question that drives the book is a matter of clinical interest. The theme emerges, not only must we ask Who is Ben Thorne, but we must quickly follow up with What is wrong with Ben Thorne?

If you have always thought it would be exciting to read a book in complete service to the ego of the author, this is the one to read as it will surely cure you of any delusion that this is a worthwhile pastime.

In between:
None of the half-dozen or so reviews published at the time of the book's release are much better than the two that drive the industry. The formal

declaration of what we are to think of this work has been put together by
the pillars of the profession and the word is out. The writers who submit
reviews to the various smaller literary journals more or less follow suit.
Disappointment. Megalomania. Pathology. These are common themes.
The idea that the wool is pulled over the reader's eyes and nothing offered
in return is commonplace. Not a single review has anything nice to say.
Everything the author thinks might be of interest or remarkable, becomes
a trick or a stunt in the eyes of the critics. More than one has called for
public reconciliation where the past work is trotted out and re-evaluated.
Maybe we have been misjudging it all along.

One writer asks, tongue in cheek, whether the Nobel Committee will
get its money back. Rumors begin to circulate, and this same question
makes the rounds. Many are saying that the literary community is outraged
and offended and that they want to erase the author's entire career. Amid
that, there is one writer, in the Iowa review, who asserts that the story is
based on true events. What if, they claim, the mark of fiction is itself the
only lie and the book is a true story documenting the real lives of people
affiliated with a limited liability corporation called Ben Thorne? This critic
looks into the conditions detailed in the book and does not hesitate to
violate the rules and tear down the fourth wall. They write that there really
is a man in Seattle who dies over a year ago and that he really does have a
daughter who is a graduate student in Anthropology at the University of
Michigan. Virginia Percival really is the assistant in the office in New York
and Mia Holden is in fact a lawyer in Chicago who serves as one of the
Attorneys of record in that horrible case last year in Missouri.

What if it is true? That's what this one critic writes, the ruse and the lie,
the years of deception and misrepresentation, not to mention the strange
corporate entity in the middle of it, it is true, everything claiming to be
fiction is autobiography. There is no such thing as imagination anymore,
no one can make anything up. Everything is me, me, me, that's what the
East coast reviewer accuses him of, isn't it? Why isn't this the ultimate case
of that? Not because he wants everyone to focus on him, but because they
know the truth. If the book is truly autobiographical, then it only stands to
reason that, for practical purposes, there is no Ben Thorne, and the players
are the actual writers of what we hold in our hands. It is simple logic, the
razor applied.

Word on the street is that this is the most cutting and vicious of the
attacks in the myriad reviews. To take the work seriously and imagine that
it is exactly what it pretends to be is to ridicule the work in the most vicious
way. The more seriously the book is treated, the more foolish and absurd
it becomes. It is the only thing anyone needs to say. Who is Ben Thorne?
What is wrong with Ben Thorne? There is no Ben Thorne. That's who he
is and that's what is so very, very wrong with him.

This opens the possibility that the book is a comedy: one big joke presented deadpan. Almost no one misses the punchline: Ben Thorne should be thrown in jail for fraud, and whatever incarceration looks like in this case, it most definitely includes preventing anyone from being forced to read the book.

These are jokes and stories that, as the book becomes available to readers, follow it into the world and make the name of the character and author the one and only tag to apply. Ben Thorne, the name, is shorthand for every bit of it: for ridicule, for public megalomania, for foolery and trickery, for narcissistic obliviousness to the times, tone deafness and a stunning failure to read the room. Nothing more needs to be said.

Social

The loudest say the least.

Readers are a tiny percentage of people, a limited demographic, but they have a well-established bubble, and they talk to each other. There is too much to read, they need methods for whittling it down. Ben Thorne is on the must-read list. He has the major awards, the correct credentials and laurels. That is why, with minimal effort, all eyes and ears are trained on the latest work and the buzz around it. Long books are reviewed based on other reviews and the discussions begin. First there are links to published reviews. They are simple and don't include additional commentary. The titles are what appears in the posts and maybe a short summary blurb under the title. Often the review is behind a pay wall, but even when it isn't the results are the same. The discussions take place in the comments section and come from commentators who haven't read the review. The first wave of feedback is from people who haven't read the book commenting on articles they haven't read either.

None of it matters. It's advertising. It's word of mouth. It drums up the necessary attention to get things under way and begin the longer process of solidifying a response. It doesn't matter whether people are saying favorable or unfavorable things, what matters is that they take the opportunity to express an opinion. There is outrage from this corner, talk of deeper rumblings from that one, and dismissive above-it-all stoicism from another. The last group goes to the trouble of commenting on the fact that people have lost their minds and are commenting on something blindly without doing the necessary research, amounting to a list of required tasks they are happy to provide in posts they hope you will like and share.

The fan boys do the most damage. By standing up for the author and arguing his work is unparalleled and deserves a fair reading, they make it clear that only dunces and fucknuts will come out in favor. It's the classic bedfellows argument. Look around and see who is on your side. If they are

the wrong sort, then you're likely on the wrong side. If the aging incels —
the ones who think those men demanding sex from Princess Myshkin are
the true heroes— get behind Ben Thorne and espouse the work as an
assault on norms of correctness and virtue-signaling, if they claim that the
outrage it causes is exactly why it is extraordinary and topical, then any right-
thinking woman will be dead set against it. That is the initial progression.
First come the fan boys, some of whom (and only some) are involuntary
celibates, and then come the feminists who reject the work while advertising
it. Then there are the men who side with the feminists no matter what they
say and the men who side against them no matter what they say. The
libertarians come out in favor, now that they know this horrible menace to
liberty is a corporate entity, and the socialists come out against now that
they know that the enemy of compassion and equality is just a greedy
corporation milking its gullible audience.

Ordinarily, the interested public knows details about book sales
because the corporation that owns the rights publicizes them. It's often
promoted as something of a voucher for the quality of the book. If it's a
number one bestseller, well then of course you better go out and get
yourself a copy. If a book is self-published, however, and if the private party
makes a specific contract with distributors, then the information remains
private. In the case of *Being an Introduction*, that is exactly what happens.
No one knows how many people are reading it. The ebook is distributed
on a personal web site based on a generic platform. The provider has no
idea how much of the traffic visiting that site downloads the file and even if
they do, they would be in violation of their non-disclosure agreement to
release that information publicly. Ben Thorne isn't talking. In the middle
of the hubbub and bustle, the author —or whatever remains of him— is
invisible. There is not a word, not a peep, not on any of the social platforms,
not in any of the public fora. Nowhere. There is nothing.

Besides, even if they are talking, they don't have reliable numbers. The
distribution is, well, distributed. There are other contracts involved,
resellers and repackagers. The ebook format has undergone technical
revisions in recent years and now there are several primary platforms where
the book is available. Some people go to the author's website, sure, but not
everyone. Some are part of a monthly service plan with other platforms
where royalties come through page reads with some small payout for each.
Some platforms allow for direct download with a one-time charge. Some
portion funnels back to the publisher, but it is hard to know exactly how
many sets of eyes are reading the book, hard to say how many copies are
flipping from one page to the next. The market just doesn't work like that
anymore, there are too many different agents and too much dispersed
incentive. Even if Ben Thorne wants to broadcast the exact figures, they
can't do it. They can tell you how much money they're making, they can

break down the revenue and tell you what imprint formats it comes from. They can break that down on a provider-by-provider basis with charts and graphs to show rates of uptake and pages read per day, but they can't connect profit with human beings scanning words on a page. Reading and readers are hard to find among the bots swimming in the revenue streams.

The financial dealings of Ben Thorne, Inc. are the private property of Ben Thorne. They do not need to share it with anyone. There are literally trillions and trillions of dollars being spent to ensure that.

There are algorithms and people who know the metrics and standards for measurement. There are educated guesses, but expertise is diverse, and the estimates span a wide spectrum. The guesses become a central part of the shit storm itself. Some estimate the numbers are high, some suggest they are overblown and part of the marketing strategy.

People who never read the book are claiming everyone has read it, and other people who never read the book are claiming that no one has read it.

Feminists say it is an attack on women.

Feminists say it is proof that Ben Thorne is actually a woman.

Fan boys say it is a defense of the old ways.

Fan boys say it is a condemnation of the status quo and an endorsement of the new and the daring.

BIPOC say it is proof of racism in publishing.

BIPOC say it is proof there are creative ways to get around racism in publishing.

The left wing says it is a right-wing rag to discredit leftists.

The left wing says it is an endorsement of the left that condemns fascism.

The right wing says it is a leftist elitist publication meant to discredit the right.

The right wing says it is an endorsement of the right that condemns communitarianism.

Right and left trash it as corporate propaganda meant to discredit everyone, right and left alike.

This happens inside the bubble of readers, that tiny percentage of people, and is only a minor curiosity to the rest.

At first.

The others, the non-readers, hear about it, they catch something in the air. They know that people are talking about it and its author. They follow the click bait and maybe they don't know anything about the controversy, maybe they don't know what's at stake. They know one thing for sure, that the colorful controversy proves what they already suspect: writers and literary people are just corporate shills.

Some say there's a huge resurgence in older titles. *Princess Myshkin,* which has been at the center of the fan boy feminist debate, suffers a major resurgence. In the months following publication of *Being an Introduction,* it reaps more residuals and royalties than ever before. The office communication channels receive numerous inquiries to secure the film and television rights. No one bothers to reply. The renewed interest in previous titles causes the entertainment industry to take another look. They don't know what the fuss is about, but they know there is a fuss. The money seduces the information oligarchy, and the sharks smell blood. Plus, there are good parts for older women, so it's easier to get greenlit once they get one of the great grand dames to attach.

Academics, who are supposed to be the guardians of knowledge, are the worst. Once the bluster begins, you can't keep them away. Scholarly articles appear and are coming at it from every angle: the death of the author, the author as exploitation, corporate greed in the literary world. Writing the Anthropocene. The topics and papers write themselves. The main thing is to get your point across. It doesn't much matter what that point is. The public intellectuals will help sort it out and what better way to become a public intellectual than to pin yourself to an already existing attention machine. You have to write it fast. The timeliness will help with journal submissions. They can't sit on them like they usually do, it's breaking news and we don't know how long it will last. It's a perfect opportunity for any Assistant Professor looking to get something in ahead of the tenure review deadlines.

Once you have Hollywood and Academia, you've got it made.

All you need are politicians, and they are just as hard to keep out as the others. Whenever the niche audience spills over into the mainstream, the politicians are soon to follow. They learn how to gauge the wind as quickly as they can. Even when there are conflicting ideas and no reasonable person has grounds for taking sides, the politicians will wordsmith it properly. They'll give it a side, not by making sense of it, that's impossible, but they'll make it seem as if they're on top of things and have a plan. Oh and, by the way, if we can just get 19.95 from each interested party, we'll meet our goals for funding the next re-election campaign.

In the middle of the carefully planned rollout, so-called Ben Thorne makes one extra-curricular public post. It remains on the relevant platform for less than an hour, but that doesn't matter. It's the point. Screen shots are taken, and circulated everywhere, spinning the controversy into an even higher gear. No one knows it, but Virginia Percival makes the post while alone in the office. There are no more research assistants and Wolfe has not returned from Greece. Not once, not even to collect his belongings. He asks Ginna to hire a crew and have them get rid of everything personal from the office and from his brownstone nearby. He tells her to rent it out and she takes advantage of her newfound ownership stake to sign the lease herself. After that she doesn't talk to Wolfe much, although she has regular exchanges with Lena. Even without any direct information, she knows Wolfe will never post and she knows Lena doesn't have access. The accounts on the various media are left to her, and she ignores them throughout the publication process, except for the purely formal use of advertising the release date. Amid this structured silence, why does she do it?

There is one particular post that irks her and for a fraction of a day she is unable to let it lie, she doesn't want it to go unanswered. A well-known literary critic says something to the effect that Ben Thorne's homophobia has reached crescendo. There are occasional accusations in the literature: no representation for homosexuals in one book leads to a charge of homophobia. A representation in another book where the character has some ordinary human flaw superficially irrelevant to their sexuality leads to another charge calling it a symptom of that same disease. This is par for the course, and this latest post, from one of the up-and-coming bright stars of the discipline, attacks the book for revealing the author's hatred at its loudest. The two-dimensional lesbian affair is ridiculed, the latent and self-hating homosexuality of the male doubles is condemned for its harmful effects on younger readers and lampooned as the primary driver of the book's narrow mindedness.

What Ginna writes is not well considered. She loses her cool and can't figure out why. She writes "Ben Thorne is heterosexual. Ben Thorne is homosexual. Ben Thorne is a man. Ben Thorne is a woman. Multiple men. Multiple women. Ben Thorne is multi-racial. Ben Thorne is a corporation." After posting it, she paces and paces and paces. She doesn't need to check with anybody to see if this is wise, she knows it is not. The best response is silence, and they have been perfectly in tune with that plan. She deletes the post and curses herself for the momentary weakness.

Word gets around and eventually everyone sees it. It becomes a fresh item stimulating the uproar. The platforms blow up, the bubble is close to bursting. For and against, backward and forward, the corporate platform is in the open. Everything and nothing, no accountability, it is anything to anybody and that is evidence that it's always against whatever your pet position is. Anti-feminist and pro-feminist, homophobic and queer friendly, it can be everything to everyone. It is the amorphous corporate body, and it accommodates any outrage as the legitimate target of any accusation. It is many things at once. If Ginna wants to stir the pot, this is the perfect move.

If the data were public, it would be possible to draw direct lines of correlation between her post's circulation as a screenshot and an enormous influx of revenue for Ben Thorne, Inc. The data producers are doing their jobs, the telemetry bears the good news in every event. The primary principle is confirmed, people are powerless, and the ones who control the platform control belief: Megaphonocracy.

Lawsuits

Attribute politics, like reactive nationalism, is an outgrowth of globalization. If the worldwide entertainment industry isn't unified and monolithic, there is no need to assert the importance of diversity and inclusion on the one hand, and national identity on the other. Mia, in her standard motion to dismiss, makes this assertion in the name of saving time. She finds that in most of the accusations and legal actions, the plaintiffs fall into one of two categories: attribute-based arguments against and attribute-based arguments in favor. Her one-size-fits-all approach shows that in the end they are pretty much the same. She knows this will put her strategy into focus for those who are keen on developing corporate conspiracy theories, but it does not dissuade her. The bitter taste remains from the case in Missouri. The court's findings come swiftly. Yes, corporations are people, they are indeed special people who are not constrained by the law in the same way ordinary human beings are. No one blinks when the lower courts argue that being a person does not invoke separate but equal constraints. Corporations are a special type of people, and the law can treat them that way, apply a different penal code, punish them differently in criminal matters, in financial matters, in work and immigration. The rejection on appeal and the unwillingness of the Supreme Court to hear it still stings.

Her defense in the numerous trivial lawsuits aiming at Ben Thorne derives from this experience. The law's bias in favor of the corporation protects Ben Thorne from public outrage. Agents act on behalf of corporations and when they do, they act as that corporation. For an agent to say "I am Ben Thorne" is not a crime. In that moment, it is the truth, and, in fact, the agent has a fiduciary responsibility to be transparent in their associations. If anyone does otherwise, they violate any of a number of laws meant to protect stockholders from corporate officers.

The lawsuits are summarily dismissed. The courts generally hold they are frivolous and without merit. The best of them alleges coercion in the form of fraud or deception, but the courts are there to protect corporations from these accusations. Public statements from agents and officers are spun as advertising. This is protected speech. Any paid agent of a corporation may attempt to promote the interests of that corporation in the public's eye. Advertising is a way to increase revenue and is an acceptable form of business practice. Moreso, it is highly encouraged. Mia's strategy aims at getting these views into the record. She phrases her motions and makes her arguments to force the courts to publicly state that the grounds for dismissal are that practices criminal for ordinary human beings are not so in the case of artificial persons.

Although the cases are unsuccessful, the sheer bulk of them and the consistent message in the decisions is hard to ignore even by the most dim-witted of journalistic bodies. It is hard for anyone who is paying attention to lose sight of the fact that the outcome of the discussion is something like corporations are playing by different rules, they are allowed to do so, and the whole of civilization depends on it. Some observers notice the turn in Mia's orientation. It doesn't take long before they dig up the case records. They see what Mia is trying to do, the arguments she makes, and the precedent she establishes. She fails and exploits her failure to the client's advantage. Many accuse her of hypocrisy, wonder why she is hiding her real name, and claim that being a Jew makes her suspect. At a press conference, when they ask her about these accusations, she shrugs and says that 1) she is an attorney, which seems to be a sweeping assertion that hypocrisy is irrelevant, and 2) she has fought hard to make corporations accountable, and the nation responds loudly. She has learned her lesson.

The public discussion unearths the relationship between the corporation and its attorney. Someone learns about Ben Thorne's funding for the center in Chicago. This takes over the news cycle for an hour and then disappears, just like the detailed points in the cases and the responses to them. Mia affirms that the country has decided there is nothing wrong with having different rules for one type of person, rules that make it difficult to hold those people accountable for their actions. So long as this is the case, she sees it as her sworn duty to advocate for the rights of such people. "If the law is corrupt, then attorneys advocating on behalf of their clients are implicated. Just as corporate people have special laws to protect them from responsibility, the system itself has laws to protect it. We have decided that this is the system we want, we reject change so it must reflect the will of the people. If that is the case, how can one single advocate make a difference? Why should they?"

She says this during one of her many trips to New York. She spends time with Ginna, but they don't talk about the cases much, not even the more visible ones brought by some of the more influential parties. None of it penetrates their little world, they set it aside and carry on. Ginna works at whatever yarns she spins, and Mia continues to run the center with Gwen who shares the case load. They come back to the brownstone, eat and drink wine, talk with friends, and do the best they can to find humor in absurdity. None of them ever dreams this is where they end up and if they do talk about what is going on and how it affects their lives, it is only in that loose way people do: can you believe this? Mia has a clear conscience not because she is defending the bad guys and has become a sociopath, but because she has a complex sense of how human action must proceed humbly and quietly in the face of great odds and overwhelming opposition.

"The chickens have come home to roost," she says at one point, when participating in a talking heads style discussion on a popular podcast. When pressed to say more, she states her case in a matter-of-fact style for a little longer than the moderator would usually allow a guest. "We, as a nation," Mia says, "have decided that some forms of secrecy and deception are permissible when they are performed by artificial persons. Things that you or I could never get away with, they are encouraged to do. Many of Ben Thorne's books written over the years have highlighted this as have I in my work as a trial attorney. I find it strange that people accuse me of hypocrisy. I would say rather that it is my accusers who are guilty of that sin. I have stayed true to my ideas, I have pointed this out for years, and have never changed my mind. The law favors corporate entities. The hypocrites are the ones who reject the assertion when I argue against it and then accept it when I use it as a defense. We are a hypocritical society when it comes to these strange creatures that live among us, these giants and their special relationships with cities and states. I have stated the case in different contexts, never have I made accompanying moral judgments or based my assertions on extra-legal ethical systems. I argue that the interpretation of existing laws should change to eliminate this bias, the defenders say that it will not, so I argue on the basis of those reaffirmed laws. There are many problems that human beings need to confront and many of them seem far more serious than this one: the special status of corporate bodies, their coercive role in our civilization, and the power they are granted by the laws and the courts. None of the serious problems can or will be solved until this problem has been addressed. Again, it may not seem like the most important issue of the day, but I emphasize it because the courts will use it again and again to block actions related to other issues. Corporations are not human, and they do not share our same world. They are giants among us with a special status that violates the egalitarian foundations of the law. They do not want the same things we do and are often an obstruction to achieving them. For years we have been talking loosely and generally about abstractions like capitalism and its so-called effects on the human psyche and day-to-day life. That is a flighty theory that lawyers don't have the luxury of entertaining. For us, it is about the specific case and the law. Where the law is concerned, there is no capitalism, it's too abstract, something corporations distract us with to let our revolutionary or patriotic fantasies block real reforms. The law, you see, knows about corporations. It knows them quite well. If you want to shut me up and get at Ben Thorne for whatever crimes you think it is committing, you will have to change the way the law is used to protect corporate autonomy and sovereignty. I can show you how to do it, but the courts have to come along, and that won't happen while those courts are beholden to the same corporate sponsors that the legislators depend upon. I've proved that in Missouri, that the courts feel no compulsion to be consistent in this matter, and that they are blithely united in supporting their own deception on behalf of these all-important citizens. There is tension in this country, many ways in which we are divided, we could unite around what it means to take our country back, maybe that is something every breathing person can agree on. We need to be laser-focused on who it is we have to take it back from. Not each other, we are made of the same substance, human to the core. The people we have to take it back from are those corporate people without a care in the world because they are protected by a legal system giving them special status and never forcing them to live by the same laws and consequences as the rest of us. The great irony is that they have already given us the means to do it."

Post Father

Meanwhile, after finishing some programming for Akis' research team in Thessaloniki, Eleni reads a few posts in her feed. There is something from Ben Thorne. "Fans and friends have been waiting for a statement from us. Here it is. In the megaphonocracy where we live, there is a constant battle for legitimate loudness. Nothing matters more. Volume is the only argument that means anything and the best way to muffle an opponent is to delegitimize them. Proving they are wrong will not achieve this, rather it happens by shouting that they have no right to speak because of who they are. They have to submit to this, there is no other way. If by embarrassment or humility they demur under pressure, only then is the end achieved. The moral sense of obeying the voice that emerges from and represents the cacophony lives inside each of us, silence is both victory and defeat. We mustn't let it fool us or lead us to some false sense of superiority. Speech must continue. Discussion must continue. Quietly. This is not an absolute principle for the ages but holds where loudness and the megaphone rule. Books speak softly. By today's standards, they whisper. Look there if you wish to find us, it is the only device that remains... Ben Thorne."

She closes the lid of her laptop and says softly, "It's done." She gets up and walks into the kitchen. Her mother is standing in her familiar place, leaning against the sink while her grandmother and godmother sit at the island. She interrupts whatever they're talking about and tells them that Virginia has done it. There is nothing else left to say. They nod and express support. Ariti stands up and goes to Eleni. She says, "Is that it for you, then? Now they just go on simply as themselves? What will happen?" Eleni hugs Ariti. "Whatever has to happen, I suppose. If Wolfe can't help himself, if Ginna can't help herself, they'll do what they have to do, but I think they'll do it quietly. That part is over for them. They're tired of it. He is, for sure, and she never wanted it. They'll do their work, or they won't, but there won't be any more microphones or cameras. They'll do it quietly on their own, or together, I don't know."

"He's a funny one," Ermioni says. "I don't think he'll ever leave."

"I make him lunch every day now," Europea says laughing. "Try to stop him. He comes in, he talks to me. He's learning. He uses his phone. He eats in silence and looks at me that way sometimes. Then he goes."

"Is there a problem?" Eleni says looking at her grandmother.

"No problem," Europea says. "He's welcome. There's plenty."

"He's aged since he's been here," Ariti says. "Not in his face or in his body, but in his soul, I think. He's more feeble of spirit."

"He's fine," Ermioni says, waving her hand. "What about Virginia? She's an aspiring writer, isn't she? Does this ruin her chances?"

"Who knows?" Eleni responds. "There are no rules anymore. If she writes something that people care about, everything is forgiven, or it's just part of the tale they'll tell whenever her name comes up."

"Are there still people who read?" Ariti asks. "I thought it's dying out, books are only good for making movies now."

"Stories will always be powerful," Europea says. "People who look for good stories will find them wherever they are."

Eleni asks them what they were doing before she interrupts them. Ermioni gestures at the things on the counter. "We're about to make filo," she says. "Of course, here we don't need to. In exile, it's necessary. Yiayia shows me long ago," she looks over at Europea who is nodding, then they both look at Eleni, "do you want to learn?"

"Yes," she insists. "Does it take long?"

"Do you have somewhere you need to be?" her mother asks with a touch of unfamiliar sharpness in her tone.

"No," she responds demurely.

"It takes very long," Europea says. "Especially when you are first learning. The ingredients are simple. Flour, water, olive oil."

"A little salt and vinegar," Ariti adds.

"A little salt and vinegar," Europea repeats. "But that is nothing. The ingredients are nothing. You have to stretch it. And keep stretching it."

Ermioni laughs, she picks up the long, slender wooden rolling pin and shows it to Eleni. "It does not want to be stretched. You have to use this, but you also have to use your hands. It's easier here. The flour is better, and the marble an ideal surface."

Eleni listens to the instructions for making the dough. She measures the ingredients and readies the mixer. Ermioni stands by, watching closely. They are silent as the mixer drones on while they add water and vinegar. Ermioni guides Eleni's hands as they knead the dough until a perfect little ball forms in the glass bowl. They cover it and set it off to the side.

"This part is easy," Ermioni says. "Now we can prepare the stuffing while we let the dough sit. Managing your work surface will be very important. We'll need lots of flour. When we start rolling it, that's when you have to keep at it. Experience will matter, you have to do it over and over again to learn how the dough will snap back and how you have to pull it and roll it to get it big and thin."

"So thin," Europea says. "It must be very thin. The thinner the better. The first time, it won't be. It'll shrink up and get thick. You have to learn by doing it, by not doing it well. In time, you'll get it."

"You just have to keep doing it," Ariti says. "It used to take me three hours, when I first tried. Now, it takes half that long."

"What will we make with it once it's done?" Eleni asks looking over at the bowl.

"Anything we like. It's hard to make it thin enough for sweet things. If we want to make Galaktoboureko or Bougatsa, it won't be good. Since this is your first time, it's better to make something savory. It's perfect for Tiropita, Kreatopita, Spanakopita, whatever we like. I have the ingredients. Maybe a little of each of the three."

Early morning in Williamsburg, Virgina silences her phone and sets it down on the desk in the office on the first floor of the brownstone she rents from Stephen Wolfe. She's given up the space at the Ben Thorne office and now sublets it to a couple of attorneys Gwen introduced her to during one of her visits with Mia. Ginna makes the post that many urge her to make to silence the critics. Now, she feels like she can put it behind her. She knows it won't silence them. "Sound and fury signifying nothing," she says. There is nothing more to say on that platform. "The media is the message," she says softly to no one in particular, and then laughs at herself. "Alone and they're still with me," she says aloud while pulling the laptop closer and lifting the lid.

Platitudes and tidbits occupy space in her brain. She shakes her head to get rid of them. Where is that space that no one has been to before? The time that has never yet passed. There are traversals of space and time, spacetime that has never yet happened to anyone, filling with things unknown and not yet imagined. She senses their presence and knows it is where the stories want to live, stretching out thin and thick, savory and sweet. Bitter at times. Salty. Milky and crackling. Her mind fills with where she can be when she steps into that pool rising higher each day. She scans her outline and reads over the little sketches to let her characters remind her where they are. The air is quiet, and she whispers the words onto the screen, catching herself at the end of a thought, "passion is an affliction." She carelessly wanders into it. Without purpose. It is as if some presence passes through the room. She takes a deep breath and continues.

Kafeneio

At the end of nearly every day, he winds up at the Kafeneio. He usually drinks wine while hunching over his notebook and scrawling on page after page with his fountain pen. He listens to the low playing traditional music, or the chatter of the men gathered at the tables nearby. He'll look up now and again and check the score of the match playing on the TV. Sometimes he talks to the other men in a combination of broken Greek and English. Aside from the daily visits with Europea, he learns by studying Despina's school books. She helps him sometimes and shows him what she is learning in her grammar classes. She looks forward to their lessons because they make her feel important and Wolfe says many funny things. The whole town knows they are studying together. They ask him about it when they see him walking on the street, and they ask her about it when she comes into their shop or passes by them somewhere in town. Some of the men at the Kafeneio still remember the English they learn in the army, and they work with him to communicate, but mostly they are silent for reasons that have nothing to do with the fact they don't speak the same language. If they do chat, it is about the people they know in common: what are they up to, who is sick, who may die soon, who is doing well, and who is expecting another grandchild. He imagines it is a hundred years ago and the hum of the radio, playing the old-time folk music, confirms it. He has never been more comfortable in his own skin, never before this much at peace.

If Nikos, Charlie, or Horacio come by, they play Belote and have something stronger to drink like Metaxa or Rakomelo. He is one of them now. They ease into conversations, not about the good old days back home, they don't share anything on that front, they talk about being here and being from somewhere else, how it isn't really a European place, but more Middle Eastern, and about how the people don't think of themselves that way, and how upset they get if you bring it up. They laugh at many different things and they sometimes include the other old men in their game or conversation. One thing they don't do and which no one ever does, is ask him what he's writing or what he's putting in that notebook. That's why he keeps coming, and that's why he enjoys spending time there. His old life is gone, and he hardly ever misses it or wonders where it went. Reminding him would be rude and everyone in town seems to have forgotten or pretends they have. They call him Stefano and refer to him as Stefanos when he is not there. O Stefanos.

One day he is sitting alone at one of the tables, the usual gang is over at the next table playing their card game, and everything stops when Eirini and Eleni walk in and come over to him. The men stop with their cards and look at the young women coming in through the door. The man behind the counter stops washing glasses and watches them. Their presence brings everything to a halt. Even he is surprised and notices that everything is coming to a halt before he notices the women. He stops too and turns to face them as they approach.

"What are you doing here?" he asks as a proxy for the others. Of course, there is no written rule, but young people never come in, nor do women of any age. His tone has a hint of shock and fear. He is worried he'll get in trouble and looks around as if to let everyone know that he has nothing to do with it. It isn't his fault, they've come on their own and he doesn't know anything about it. They look at him and register his claim, but they have their doubts. The important thing, the thing they are watching and waiting to see, is what he's going to do about it. Is he going to rise to the occasion and take care of this?

When they come up to him, he repeats his question more urgently, more quietly. He pleads with them with a look in his eyes.

"Relax," Eleni says. "We're not staying. We were just walking by and saw you inside."

"We wanted to say hello," Eirini says. She stands close to him and puts her hand on his shoulder as she says it. "Hello," she says deliberately, and then laughs casually and at ease. She looks at the man behind the counter and continues smiling. She looks at the men at the other table paused over their game. She squints at them and throws her chin forward making a clicking sound with her tongue. "It's a public place," she says out loud. The men nod and, as if by consensus, go back to what they were doing.

"We're going to Kechrokampos tomorrow," Eleni says.

"The place with the spring?" Wolfe asks, perking up.

"The one and only."

He smiles and says, "I love that place."

Eleni knows this puts him in a good mood. "I wanted to tell you," she goes on. "Ginna posted the statement. I thought you should know."

"What statement?" he asks, only just starting to recover his composure. He notices the men have gone back to what they're doing, but he doesn't trust it. He thinks they're still paying attention without looking. "Oh yes, that. Good. Good to know."

"You don't care, do you?" Eirini asks, still resting her hand on his shoulder. She's looking at the pen he holds tightly, and at the notebook. She doesn't say anything about them but squeezes his shoulder to let him know she understands.

"Not anymore, no," he says. "None of that matters."

"Good," Eleni says. "But we thought you should know."

"Thank you," he says. "How're things with your sister? Has she taken care of that nonsense?"

"Of course, of course. Nothing for us to worry about. She's taken care of everything. You needn't worry."

He nods. He's relieved and pleased. "That's wonderful. Are you two going home now? It's getting late."

"Yes," Eirini says. "I have to go to work early tomorrow. Need to get some sleep."

Eleni nods. "See you later," she leans over and gives him a kiss on the cheek, then they both turn to leave. The men at the other table stop what they're doing and watch them go. The man at the counter watches too. Once the door closes, they go about their business as if the women were never there. Nobody says anything.

Eirini and Eleni walk arm-in-arm up the street back toward Europea's house. The town is quiet. There are a few dogs lying on the sidewalk here and there, but the air is still, and the animals don't stir as the women walk past. Eirini notices the collars and tags around the dogs' necks and pulls Eleni's arm closer, hugging it tightly as she thinks of how much of a difference these little things make. She thinks how nice it is that Ermioni and Eleni have come home.

"Will he stay with you?" Eirini breaks the silence just after they pass the roundabout and get close to the house. She knows these will be their parting words.

Eleni responds immediately, "I believe so. Mom likes having him around. Yiayia's gotten used to him. He's family now."

A few minutes later she walks up the driveway and lets her hand pass lightly over the side of the car freshly converted to propane. She makes a note to thank him while looking at her reflection in the passenger side mirror slightly damaged during the sea voyage home.

Residual

Light: Every object is a technicality. We have to break through them to find what can be there.

Peace: Their use is mere deception.

Justice: They perpetrate fraud to make us see what they want us to see.

Peace: What benefit does it give them?

Justice: Ownership and power. Things are owned and things are wielded. Things are...

Peace: ...evaluated on their own.

Justice: They can and they do All together In unison Stifling and suffocated Then again Alone Stifling and suffocated Together they move apart Apart they move together They are a breath They are lungs filling and emptying They are coming and going The center of the circle

Peace: As an audience, they are little more than flattery and criticism. Remove the ID and the circle begins to move.

Light: Evaluation does not permit coming to rest in one state or another, yet it simultaneously commands exactly that. If they stop and take measure, they only find lengths and widths, they calculate volume and derive surface area for setting things in order. They are counting: 1, 2, 3, 4. Time passes with measure, space traverses with measure, there is measure and no time and no space just tick tick tick and dot dot dot. If they keep going, breathing in and out in and out in and out, they know the back and forth of constant movement. They scream none of the above, they scream against choice. Things get better things get worse, they do not see the justice they do not see the peace they do not see the light.

All Together:
There is light. Be the light.
There is justice. Be the justice.
There is peace. Be the peace.

[exeunt all]